Praise for Irene Radford's *Dragon* novels:

"Ms Radford's considerable gifts as a mesmerizing story-teller shine with undeniable luster."   —*Romantic Times*

"A rousing adventure of magic and treachery."
                                        —*Library Journal*

"Plenty of popular elements: an intelligent cat, an enchanted wolf, a redheaded witch, a missing prince, the apprentice mage with misunderstood powers, and, of course, dragons."   —*Locus*

"A big, adventurous, satisfying climax to the trilogy by one of the more interesting new voices working with the traditional quest story."   —*Science Fiction Chronicle*

"This action-packed plot makes for engaged and thoughtful reading. The author manages to keep the story clear, and the characters interesting to follow. Several themes interplay successfully, with the reader caring what happens. Not surprisingly, the volume resolves one conflict, but keeps the door open for continuing obstacles. This reader, for one, is eager."   —*KLIATT*

The Dragon Nimbus
Novels Vol. II

Also by
Irene Radford

The Dragon Nimbus
THE GLASS DRAGON
THE PERFECT PRINCESS
THE LONELIEST MAGICIAN

The Dragon Nimbus History
THE DRAGON'S TOUCHSTONE
THE LAST BATTLEMAGE
THE RENEGADE DRAGON
THE WIZARD'S TREASURE

The Star Gods
THE HIDDEN DRAGON
THE DRAGON CIRCLE
THE DRAGON'S REVENGE

Merlin's Descendants
GUARDIAN OF THE BALANCE
GUARDIAN OF THE TRUST
GUARDIAN OF THE VISION
GUARDIAN OF THE PROMISE
GUARDIAN OF THE FREEDOM

THE
DRAGON NIMBUS
NOVELS
VOLUME II

THE DRAGON S TOUCHSTONE

THE LAST BATTLEMAGE

Irene Radford

DAW BOOKS, INC.
DONALD A. WOLLHEIM, FOUNDER
375 Hudson Street, New York, NY 10014

ELIZABETH R. WOLLHEIM
SHEILA E. GILBERT
PUBLISHERS
http://www.dawbooks.com

First Paperback Printing, December 2007
1 2 3 4 5 6 7 8 9

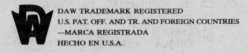

DAW TRADEMARK REGISTERED
U.S. PAT. OFF. AND TR. AND FOREIGN COUNTRIES
—MARCA REGISTRADA
HECHO EN U.S.A.

PRINTED IN THE U.S.A.

Introduction

Welcome to a world where dragons are real and magic works. If you are new to the Dragon Nimbus, pull up a chair and join us as we revel in tales that have touched my heart more than anything else I've written under any pen name. If you are returning after an absence, I am very happy to have you back.

This is a world that began with a Christmas gift of a blown glass dragon. The dragon sat proudly on the knick-knack shelf for several months, loved and admired, reluctantly dusted, and totally inert. Then one night at dinner my son remarked, "You know, Mom, I think dragons are born all dark, like that little pewter dragon, then they get more silvery as they grow up until they are as clear as glass." The dragon came to life for me.

Out of that chance remark came first one book, then three, five, seven, and finally ten. I built a career on these books and loved every minute of the process. These characters still live in my mind many years after they jumped into their stories and dragged me along with them.

Many thanks to DAW Books and my editor Sheila Gilbert for reviving *The Dragon Nimbus* a lucky thirteen years after they first debuted.

With these omnibus volumes, you can read about the dragons with crystal fur that directs your eye elsewhere yet defies you to look anywhere else. Wonderful dragons full of wit and wisdom. Magic abounds. Magicians and mundanes alike learn about their world and special life lessons as they explore dragon lore past and present. The books will be presented in the order in which they were written, and the order that makes the most sense of the entwined tales.

So, sit back and enjoy with me.

And may reading take you soaring with Dragons.

Irene Radford
Welches, OR

THE DRAGON'S TOUCHSTONE

For Benjamin Colin
my little baby boy
who knew all about flywackets
before I did.

Prologue

A lovely rising thermal current caught Shayla's wing as she glided one last time from the mountains to the Great Bay. A hundred dragon lengths below her, whitecaps danced on the gentle spring breeze. Sunlight sparkled on the water, reflecting rainbows from her nearly transparent wing.

Mandelphs darted in and out of the water in a game of catch me if you can. One youngster leaped through a rainbow, laughing.

Join us, crystal-furred dragon. Play with us, the intelligent water-dwellers chirped. *Dragons cast interesting shadows and offer new hurdles to leap over and dive under. More interesting since you are nearly invisible.*

(Thank you, friends. Not today,) Shayla declined. Her lair was a long way away and the twenty babies growing inside her had become too large for her to be confident of her mobility. Tonight she would feast on a fat cow and build her nest. For the next few moons her five mates would feed and pamper her while she could not fly. At any other time, except during mating, she wouldn't tolerate the presence of her consorts within her hunting territory. The male dragons wouldn't tolerate each other except during the cooperative effort to support their gravid mate.

Five fathers for her first litter of twenty dragonets. Pride swelled through her. The more fathers, the larger and stronger the litter.

She widened her circle of flight inland, enjoying the changing air temperatures against her wings. The Great Bay dissolved into a chain of islands then merged into a solid landmass split by a mighty river.

Curiosity sharpened her FarSight to spy on the humans who inhabited this land. A bustle of activity in a wide-open space below drew her attention. She dropped lower to spy on the strangely intelligent, yet sadly immature race who had invaded this planet several millennia ago.

One of the humans below threw a ball of bright magic across a field. The ball arced upward and burst into thousands of glittering shards.

Sharp burning pain snaked from the tip of Shayla's tail up to her haunches, numbing her muscles as it progressed. Without the maneuvering balance of her tail, she fell into a downward spin. Startled, she didn't immediately compensate with stretched wings and extended limbs.

Too late! Another pain spiraled around her left rear leg. Muscles jerked out of control. She lost another dozen dragon lengths in altitude.

Too low. Dangerously low. The humans came into sharper view without the aid of FarSight. A cloud of magic residue hung above them. As this fact registered in her mind, more magic flashed across the field, adding to the residue. She barely escaped a responding flash that hurled upward from the edge of the meadow before it fell toward the opposite side of the open space.

A magic duel! How dare these puny humans battle with forces they couldn't control!

Flame burst from her mouth with a roar of rage. She refocused her FarSight, seeking a victim to atone for this outrage against her body and the forces of nature.

Spells of varying complexity and strength continued blasting back and forth between the men. None looked up to see the source of her flame. They ignored her fair warning.

She dropped heavily through the air as a new pain reminded her sharply of the weight within her womb. No! Her babies weren't ready. No nest awaited them in her distant lair.

A new spell lanced upward. She veered sharply right, barely avoiding it. Fire burst forth as she bellowed her outrage. She folded her wings and plunged into a dive.

Her wing membranes snapped open at the last minute as she shifted and fought to regain height. Her flames drenched the field, turning the entire army, stubble, and nearby trees

to ash. No sense of triumph followed the obliteration of the threat. The pain in her womb enveloped all thought.

Shayla swung upward, slow and unwieldy with the extra weight in her womb. Greedy flames from the burning battlefield singed her belly. The babies twisted and fought for exit.

Not yet. Not until she found safe haven.

Where? Oh, where could she go? If she accessed the void long enough to find her lair, the babies would never survive the birthing. The void between the planes of existence would choke crucial air, light, and warmth from both her and her babies.

Who could shelter her? None of the males. Their lairs were small caves, barely large enough to secrete a single dragon; all of them too far away.

(*I come,*) an ancient dragon voice hailed her.

Iianthe. The oldest dragon of all and the only purple-tip known to have ever existed.

Shayla stretched her wings a little under the guidance of the telepathic voice, and she gained a little more control. But she kept dropping. She had make headway. East. Where the mountains met the sea. Iianthe's lair, huge, designed to house many litters of baby dragons.

Barely skimming the tops of the trees, Shayla forced her wings to keep going. Her belly cramped in time with her downstrokes.

Iianthe appeared beneath her. His right wing supported the dragging leg that threatened her balance and her altitude. With the injured limb tucked back where it belonged, they gained elevation.

Everblue treetops receded from view. One dragon length, then two and three. They caught an updraft and glided east to safety.

The plateau in front of Iianthe's lair appeared before her, almost level with her sagging legs.

A heavy, awkward landing sent her nose into the spring beside the cave opening. Exhausted, she lay there, wishing she could cry as humans did.

Iianthe landed beside her, almost as tired as she. Near the end of his span, he'd lived longer than any living dragon could remember. Without moving, he crooned a *Song* of healing that only she could hear.

She could walk, a little, far enough to get inside the cave where a nest of leaves and soft sheep's wool awaited. Had Iianthe known she would need the nest?

No matter. She collapsed upon the bed as the first baby dragon squeezed from the protection of her womb into the waiting nest—an undersized mass of wiggling limbs the color of dark pewter. The tiniest hint of red touched its wingtips and the nubs of horns. A male. Alive and squalling for food already.

Shayla licked the last of the afterbirth from her son's fur. She paused a moment while she panted in rhythm with her labor. The miracle of new life filled her with awe. She stared at the tiny form in wonder.

Two more mewling dragonets made an abrupt entrance. Twin purple-tips. Purples! Rarest of all dragon colors, assigned only to personalities of great power or wisdom. What strange portent did their birth signify?

The cramping pains did not abate.

(My replacement is born. I must die now. There can only be one purple-tip alive at any given time,) Iianthe said from the cave entrance.

Shayla waited through the birth of two more dragonets before answering the hovering dragon.

(Do not fly into the void just yet, wise one. We need your advice. The humans must be punished!)

(Your mates must not interfere. 'Tis not their destiny. This is a matter to be settled between your babies and the human magicians.) Iianthe heaved a weary sigh. *(My next existence awaits, I must guard the beginning place of magic. The humans will find it within a century. Only those worthy of the power must find it.)*

(The intruders have grown too strong, without the maturity of the centuries to guide them. They weave magic they cannot control,) Shayla reminded him. *(The beginning place needs a powerful guardian until humans can use the magic properly.)*

('Twas foretold long ago by Purple Dragons wiser than I that your children must teach the humans what they need to know.) Iianthe's voice faded as he backed out of the lair entrance.

(But they are twins. Which one takes your place and which must be destroyed?) Shayla panicked. Her babies were too

small, not ready to grasp their destiny. Who would take on the task of dropping the extra purple-tip baby from the void into the Great Bay—to live or die as fate decided.

(Seek answers in the void. Until you know the destinies of both purple-tips, do nothing to either. Perhaps they have been chosen by the fates to solve the problem with the humans.) Iianthe gathered his wings for one last burst of energy and disappeared into the void. *(I can die now, Shayla. The lair is yours.)* Iianthe's voice faded.

Shayla caught a glimpse of winking amethyst crystal in the distant blackness that opened before her but did not touch her.

Shayla's wing folded protectively over all six pewter-colored dragonets that lived. Four males and the asexual twin purple-tips. No females. She pushed aside fourteen dead babies. No more infants awaited birth. A new kind of pain swelled within her. She lifted her muzzle in a mournful wail that pierced the silence and echoed through the mountains of Kardia Hodos. The sound lingered and replayed itself as sorrow overtook all of the dragons. The future seemed bleak indeed.

Too many dragons fell victim to the wild and aggressive humans who hated and feared all they did not understand.

Shayla nuzzled each of her babies, willing them all to live and grow. She had time to make a decision about the redundant purple-tip. Time to find a way to save both. Time to plot and persuade before dragonkind took drastic action.

Chapter 1

Eighteen Years Later

"**D**on't do it, Keegan. Don't try that spell, boy!" Nimbulan yelled across the din of the battle. He projected his words with magic above the noise of death and destruction.

Keegan, Nimbulan's former apprentice, ignored the command, if he heard it at all. On a slight mound, opposite the raging battle from Nimbulan, the young man wove his hands in a stylized, intricate pattern.

"That spell draws its symmetry from stars that disappear at midnight! Dawn is but a few heartbeats away." Nimbulan tried once more to warn his opponent. He climbed onto the stump of a tree that had been blasted by magic gone awry during a battle on this same field nearly twenty years before. No one had survived the fires then. Neither would they survive Keegan's spell.

False dawn shimmered on the horizon, barely discernible beyond the witchlight that illuminated the two armies battling between the mages. If Keegan continued to weave his magic one heartbeat past sunrise, the spell would go rogue with disastrous results.

Keegan's chant became a steady, rhythmic incantation. It slid under and around the noise of seasoned troops slashing and hacking at each other. Nimbulan watched as Lord Hanic's men wielded their weapons in time with the words of the spell chanted by Keegan. The front line of Lord Kammeryl's troops sagged and gave ground in the same rhythm. Nimbulan thought furiously about how to protect Kammeryl's men. He had to stop Keegan's spell before it drew too much power from the sun, rather than a balance of moon and stars.

All day and most of the night the battle had raged. Keegan's spell was a desperate attempt to tip the balance.

Nimbulan ran the words of the spell past his memory. Keegan had said them correctly. The spell would begin as planned. Keegan sought to encase Nimbulan and his army in a stasis field, unable to move or protect themselves. Lord Hanic's smaller army could then slaughter Lord Kammeryl's troops at leisure. If the spell worked.

But the light of the sun was so much stronger than the stars. Keegan's magic would distort and destroy all of them. "No, Keegan. No," Nimbulan moaned.

Perverted by the fading moon and stars, the stasis field would freeze all life within ten leagues, including the grass, air, and river. Nimbulan's belly chilled at a vision of winds from all of Kardia Hodos rushing to fill the vacuum created by the spell. Tornadoes, dry hurricanes, all manner of catastrophic storms would wreak havoc across half the planet.

Keegan was too young and too arrogant about his talent to realize the dangers of his actions. He wanted only to win this battle.

"I can't let you do it, Keegan," Nimbulan mumbled as he rammed his staff into the Kardia to steady his own spell. He raised his left hand, palm outward, fingers slightly curved to weave the energy of the Kardia. Trickles of magic power meandered up the twisted grain of wood into his palm. Not enough. The ley lines that fed his magic were empty. He needed fuel for his inborn magic talent.

Nimbulan snapped his fingers impatiently. A fat green leaf with pink veins appeared in his hands. A leaf of the Tambootie, the tree of magic. He licked the essential oils from the veins and spine as his mind formed words and images of a great wall surrounding Keegan.

Fire burst upon Nimbulan's tongue. He chewed the leaf eagerly. Colors sang through his blood and into his eyes. Ugly sounds of battle faded, and the Tambootie took hold of his talent. His raised palm tingled, ready to weave his magic into a protective spell.

Keegan completed the last hand motions and singsong words. The chant lingered in the air just below hearing level.

Power began to vibrate within Nimbulan. Time slowed.

Keegan wound a spell into a tight wad and drew back his arm to hurl his magic outward with all the might of his youthful body.

Nimbulan's invisible wall rose out of the depths of the Kardia.

Keegan's spell crashed into it. Power erupted. The shield buckled. Sparkling shadows flitted along the wall.

Thunder rolled. Lightning flashed. Sparks flew in all directions. A crack spiderwebbed around the wall of magic from the point of impact with Keegan's spell. Natural green fire, unholy red, magical blue, and blinding yellow followed the crack lines and sprayed backward into Keegan's eyes. A momentary outline of a winged form spewing fire appeared on the damaged shield, then vanished, taking the fire with it.

"A dragon! We've been cursed by a dragon!" men from both armies cried at the fleeting shadow as they threw down their arms and fled.

"Yieee!" Keegan screamed. His own spell backlashed and knocked him flat, drenching him with magic gone awry.

The battle stopped. Both armies froze in awe and fear.

Nimbulan covered his ears. His apprentice's screams reverberated deep in his skull.

The screams echoed a distant time when he'd heard another apprentice scream in pain and desperation.

He'd been thirteen at the time, a new journeyman. Most boys didn't pass Druulin's arduous magical tasks to become journeymen until they were much older and better trained. Ackerly, his best friend and fellow apprentice, had recently failed Druulin's tests for the third time.

And been beaten for it.

Druulin's rages and beatings formed an expected part of the boy's life. The hot-tempered and often irrational Master Magician claimed he taught his apprentices defensive mechanisms by flailing them with various magic tortures.

The day Ackerly failed his journeyman tests for the final time, Druulin took a mundane whip to the boy's back.

Seven apprentices and journeymen stared in horror at the viciousness of Druulin's attack. Only Nimbulan found the courage to wrap Ackerly in defensive armor with one spell and freeze Druulin's right hand mid-stroke with another.

"A few days in the dungeon without food or light will cure you both of insolence!" Druulin said between gritted teeth. His eyes narrowed in speculation, noting the precise moment Nimbulan began to tire. He broke the spell and quickly cast another to compel both Nimbulan and Ackerly into obedience.

He prodded the boys with the whip handle until they marched down the spiraling stairs. Down they marched, from Druulin's private study and bedchamber on the top floor, past the common workroom and dormitory, down another flight to the ground floor past the kitchens with the enticing smell of supper cooking.

Nimbulan's mouth watered at the thought of fresh bread and meat. The two spells, thrown without preparation, had drained him. He needed food and rest to replenish his magic. His knees weakened as they marched down yet another flight of stairs into the storage cellars.

Druulin conjured a small ball of witchlight to keep himself from stumbling on the damp stone steps. The light didn't extend to help Nimbulan and Ackerly.

Nimbulan tried to step carefully and avoid slipping. A fall now could result in nasty broken bones at the bottom of the steep flight.

Ackerly wobbled and clung to the wall for support. His face was gray with pain and his back bled through his torn tunic. A night in the dirty dampness of the dungeons would probably infect the wounds.

Nimbulan ached for his friend. He didn't dare give in to the tears that clogged his throat and made his eyes burn.

At last, they staggered off the last step into total blackness—as black as the void except for Druulin's tiny wisp of witchlight. The old magician shoved the boys forward into a tiny room, then slammed a heavy door closed before releasing the compulsion spell. "Think about your crimes against me, you ambitious little upstarts. When you are hungry enough and sick enough to apologize, I'll think about letting you have some light and food."

The little glow of witchlight vanished. An ominous series of clicks signaled a locking spell on the door. Druulin's retreating footsteps faded quickly.

Ackerly collapsed upon a heap of rags in one corner,

moaning and crying. Nimbulan felt his friend's forehead. No fever yet. "We've got to get out of here, Acker."

"Not yet. Not until Druulin settles down for the night with his liquor." Even in pain and defeat, Ackerly thought ahead better than Nimbulan.

"What then? I don't think I have enough strength left to break his locking spell." Nimbulan snapped his fingers and produced a little witchlight. He looked carefully at the lock but couldn't figure out the spell. Quickly he doused the light as his stomach turned over. He was so hungry he was queasy.

"Rest a little, Lan. Then you can open the door with magic, and we'll sneak out and steal some food. We'll come back and relock the door. Druulin will never know the difference." Ackerly shifted uncomfortably.

"We'll also steal some medicine. We can't let those wounds fester." Nimbulan wiped his running nose and eyes on his sleeve. The dungeon was colder and wetter than he remembered from the last time he'd been punished. He wished he knew some healing spells. Ackerly really needed help.

He'd never known Druulin to lose control of his temper so badly before.

"Maybe we could run away together when we get out?" Nimbulan asked. Hope of escape from Druulin's tyranny filled him with a quivering warmth.

"Where would we go? No other magician will take us on since our parents gave us to Druulin. Even masters of other trades won't take us on until Druulin releases us. And he won't let you go ever, Lan. You're too good a magician. He needs you to correct his mistakes," Ackerly replied between sobs.

"Then I'll have to take care of you. You could settle nearby—but not so close Druulin would find you," Nimbulan offered. The hope in his belly turned into a cold fearful lump. Neither of them would ever get away from Druulin. The old man intimidated all the mundanes for miles around. They'd betray Ackerly's presence.

"What will I do? Magic is the only thing I know and that not very well," Ackerly asked.

"You know lots more, Acker," Nimbulan soothed his friend. "You think ahead and plan much better than any of us."

"But I can't do the great magic. That's what makes a Battlemage," Ackerly protested. "That's why Druulin got so mad when I failed the tests. He needs stronger apprentices to make up for his failings. He's getting too old to do it on his own."

"Apprentices and journeymen helping the Master Magician is what makes a Battlemage. Not one man alone," Nimbulan mused. "When I'm a full Battlemage, I'll make you my chief assistant, Acker. We'll be a team. Just like always. Remember the time Boojlin and Caasser ganged up on us and pelted us with rotten eggs all the way from the kitchen to the cellar? You were the one who thought up the idea of the bucket of water atop the door. When they opened the door, the bucket fell right on top of them. They both nearly drowned . . ." The two boys smothered their giggles at the memory of the two older bullies spluttering and choking as repeated cascades of ice cold water caught them unaware.

Druulin had discovered the mess and made all four of them clean it up, and do without breakfast the next morning for wasting supplies and magic.

"We'd never have escaped Boojlin and Caasser if you hadn't thought of the water bucket," Nimbulan whispered through his giggles.

"But you were the one who had the magic to hold the water up there without a bucket, and keep it coming," Ackerly reminded him.

"See, that's what I mean. We're a team. We'll always be a team. Now help me figure out this locking spell."

Thirty-six years later, Ackerly was still Nimbulan's chief assistant, and they never beat their apprentices or made them go hungry. So why had Keegan run away? Why had the boy felt he had to prove himself a better Battlemage than Nimbulan before he was fully trained?

Guilt piled on top of Nimbulan's grief.

"Why, boy? Why'd you have to push me to kill you?" Nimbulan shuddered in the cold mist that drifted over the now silent battlefield. The first rays of dawn almost pierced the gloom of fading witchlight. Clumps of sparkling moisture shimmered and wavered in the golden light, like the ghosts of the dead men who littered this unlucky wheat field. Would the victims of this battle haunt the site for generations to come?

Nearly twenty years ago, two other armies had fought on this same field. Indiscriminate and uncontrolled magic had killed them all. Troops, lords, magicians, and camp followers, all reduced to ashes in a moment of screaming agony. The stump he stood upon now, an ancient elm tree so large three men holding hands couldn't span its girth, had been toppled and blasted to ash by that same magic. A stroke of luck had sent Nimbulan and Ackerly elsewhere that same day. But not today.

Druulin, Boojlin, and Caasser had been among the thousands who had died that day, eighteen years ago.

Today Nimbulan had been forced to murder his most promising apprentice with magic in order to save the few men who still lived at the end of this most recent battle.

Thousands more dead would haunt this field now.

Nothing stirred within Nimbulan's narrow field of vision. No one cried for help or solace. A peculiar mound of ashes on the rise opposite him silently taunted him with warped magic.

Ashes that had once been Keegan.

"I called you 'son.'" His words dissipated with the mist as a chill wind blew up from the river, half a league away.

The only response was a twisting groan of eternal pain that lay trapped in the ashes.

"I'll never have a son of my body. You could have filled that aching hole in my life, Keegan."

He'd have to liberate the ghost. A father's duty. No one else was left. Trapped, unable to pass on to the void between the planes of existence, the boy's spirit begged him for release.

Nimbulan leaned heavily upon his staff, feeling twice his forty-nine years, as exhaustion drowned him.

Many men had died on both sides of the fray. Many more suffered wounds so severe they shouldn't live. For the first time in almost three decades as a Battlemage, Nimbulan wondered if the victory won by Warlord Kammeryl d'Astrismos was worth the cost.

Keegan was dead. "You should have been my successor, boy. Not my enemy. What lured you to hire on as a Battlemage before your training was complete?"

Placing one foot wearily in front of the other, Nimbulan trudged across the field toward the opposite rise. He had to avert his eyes from the carnage around him. Recognition of a corpse or wounded friend might deter him from his mission. Many of the soldiers had died an honorable death at the hands of an enemy. Many more had died from the volleys of magic lobbed back and forth across the battlefield by the magicians. *He* was as guilty as Keegan for their deaths. The lords may have called the men to battle, but the magicians working behind them determined who won and who lost; who lived and who died.

Nimbulan stumbled and nearly fell over a dead man. Blood and mud obscured a uniform or identifying crest.

"Keegan and I did this to you." He shifted the outflung arms of the corpse into a more natural position. "Go in peace. Find your next existence and happiness," he murmured the death prayer, too numb to do more.

He supported Lord Kammeryl d'Astrismos, the one lord who might unify Coronnan. Time and again the rival lords proved that peace could only be achieved at the tremendous cost of war. He tried wrapping a cloak of justification around his emotions and failed miserably.

He trudged up the hillock to where Keegan had stood. "The Stargods would never forgive me if I made you suffer the hell of your own spell backlashed against you, son," Nimbulan sighed as he planted his tall staff beside the mound of ashes. "I would never forgive myself."

Tongues of unholy red flame licked outward from the still smoldering ashes. Sparks tried to reignite a life from the residue. Each time the essence of Keegan found an anchor, his final spell doused it.

Echoes of torment lingered in the air.

Nimbulan stretched out his hand, palm toward the pile of ashes, fingers curved as if capturing the essence of Keegan as he tried escaping his unholy prison.

He had no strength to summon magic from the depths of Kardia Hodos to work this one last spell. Nimbulan's bond with the four elements, Kardia, Air, Fire, and Water which together with the cardinal directions formed the *gaia*, had shriveled with the death and destruction wrought this day and night.

The spirit in the ashes writhed again. An irritating burn

crawled all over Nimbulan's sensitized nerves. He resisted the urge to douse them both with water.

" 'Twouldn't soothe either of us."

"Come, Lan, sup and rest before you discharge this final duty." A new voice intruded upon the magician's weary thoughts. "Perhaps if I grind a few Tambootie leaves into your meal, you will feel better."

"I've used enough of the weed today, Ackerly," Nimbulan replied to his assistant. "I need food and rest, not drugs. When this spell is finished, I'll be able to rest."

"At least wait a while before you weave this spell. The boy's spirit deserves to linger in torment for a time. Perhaps he will be less impatient for power in his next existence, if he suffers in a hell of his own making."

" 'Tis a hell of my making! I'll not wish that fate on any man." *And I loved you, Keegan.*

"Had he waited 'til his powers were fully grown, you'd not have defeated him. We are both getting old," Ackerly grumbled. "Old and losing our stamina. That ungrateful youngster wouldn't have wasted his strength liberating your soul from a pile of ashes." Ackerly lifted his foot to scatter the residue with a kick.

"No!" Nimbulan pushed him aside to keep him from spreading Keegan's soul too thin to regather and liberate.

"I like to think my apprentice would do me this one last service. I tried to teach him respect for others and for the power we wield."

"He only wanted to learn the spells; not the *right* way to use them," Ackerly spat. "Go back to your pavilion, Nimbulan. Let me perform this chore. I may not be a great magician who can weave the Kardia into my spells, but I can send this ungrateful wretch where he belongs."

" 'Tis my responsibility. I caused his final spell to back-lash." Nimbulan shored up his sagging willpower. Ackerly's manner suggested an animosity toward Keegan that would stand in the way of a proper weaving. Nimbulan could have plucked Ackerly's true intentions and the source of his grievance from his mind. He wouldn't.

"I'll speed the boy on his way to his next existence. Dru-ulin wouldn't have bothered. You know as well as I that *I* must do this."

Chapter 2

Nimbulan rummaged in the pockets of his formal robes for a small wand of the Tambootie tree affixed with a perfect faceted crystal.

Sadly, he looked through the crystal into the pile of ashes and chanted.

> *"Walk with me, son of my learning,*
> *Walk with me one final time.*
> *Walk with me the paths of life,*
> *Walk with me to the place of your yearning."*

"Greedy wretch doesn't deserve this." Ackerly turned aside, grumbling under his breath.

Nimbulan ignored his companion as his mind sought a deeper contact with the essence of his apprentice. Bright green flames and burning pain flashed from the crystal into his weary eyes.

One deep breath, hold three counts, let go three counts. A second breath filled his lungs and released. On the third inhalation he found access to the void between the planes of existence. His spirit lifted free of his weary body and found solace in the black nothingness. A second soul stood beside him, dim and unformed.

Coils of pulsing colors that represented the lives of all the souls Nimbulan had encountered in the nearly fifty years of his current existence sprang into view. A silver umbilical, tinged with blue, symbolized his own life. It wound away from his sight into a tangle of life forces.

Seeing others represented in symbolic colors was easy. Only once had Nimbulan glimpsed the full texture of his own life and aura—during the day and the night of his rite of passage into adulthood. On the eve of his twelfth birthday, his tutors sent him to a windowless stone room, with only a Tambootie wood fire for heat and light. His trance, induced by the mind-altering smoke, had been deep and profound. After thirty-six years as a magician, he still didn't understand the reflections of reality that he had seen. But ever afterward, he knew the true colors of his life-pulse in the void. A rare achievement.

Now, during his saddest trip into the void, he saw life forces of clear crystal, reflecting all colors dancing around him. The crystal dominated the tangle of symbolic lives. He'd never seen them before—didn't know who they represented.

Beside him the dim essence of a fading soul drifted away. The red umbilical dulled toward gray.

Nimbulan had to weave Keegan's life force into the tangle of umbilicals soon, or he'd be lost forever, denied his next existence.

> *"Walk with me, son of my learning,*
> *Eternal pain is not your due.*
> *My silver path to you I lend,*
> *Walk with me a path we are earning.*
>
> *"Walk with me, son of my learning,*
> *Walk with me one final time.*
> *Find with me the paths of life.*
> *Walk with me till seasons cease turning."*

A great shuddering possessed Nimbulan. The red chain beside him regained color and vibrancy. It coiled up through him, encasing Nimbulan's silvery-blue umbilical. All of their knowledge joined, their memories twined, and their secrets unfolded. They were one man, one life force, one mind.

The vast tangle of life forces shifted and collapsed into images of men, generations of men, marching in intricate patterns, sometimes peaceful, sometimes at odds with each other. Magicians ringed the intricate dance patterns, calling directions to the men. He became a part of the vision, manipulating the resisting lords. The patterns swirled into violence, became the battle he had just fought and dozens of other battles, each indistinguishable from the other. Battle after battle, he lobbed spells into the fray at random. Death and destruction sent waves of revulsion through him. And still he sent men to their deaths with his magic.

He watched men step away from the vision of battle, ready to retire and reform the balance of the dance patterns. Nimbulan wanted to join them, but he found himself pulling them back into the asymmetrical violence. . . .

Keegan's essence burst free of his mentor and sped outward into the knot of pulsing lives, leaving Nimbulan alone with access only to his own thoughts and memories. The vision faded. A sour taste lingered.

A vibrant red umbilical wrapped around Nimbulan, urging him to follow deeper into the void.

Symmetrical patterns. Balance. Harmony.

Keegan beckoned to him to walk beside him in intimate friendship, as father and son, till the seasons ceased their turning.

Nimbulan moved with the compelling vision, stretching to unite with other life-pulses as well.

Unity. Peace. If only . . .

An invisible barrier slammed down in front of him, blocking the enticing vision.

(Go back, human. 'Tis not your time!) Unknown voices resounded throughout the eternal blackness. *(Premature joining with the void is forbidden. Go back now, lest your immortal soul be torn from you and cast aside.)*

Nimbulan dropped back into his body with an ungraceful thump. The aches in his joints still hurt, but his soul felt lighter.

"I hope I never have to do that again, Ackerly. Something happened in the void—something important to all of us. But I couldn't quite grasp it. I almost followed Keegan into my next existence."

"Never think that, Master. What would Lord Kammeryl do without you?"

"He'd find another magician. Yes, yes, I know, suicide is forbidden, Ackerly." The Stargods had firmly reminded him of that. "But there is knowledge in the void. A vision slid around me, begging me to learn. I didn't have time to do more than glimpse the edges of the lesson."

"What? What did the Stargods show you?" Ackerly leaned forward eagerly.

"I'm not certain. I need time and solitude to meditate."

"Neither of which are you likely to have soon. Lord Kammeryl comes." Ackerly pointed to a broad man with the reddish lights of his Stargod ancestors in his hair. Their employer marched determinedly across the field toward them.

"Is that Quinnault de Tanos, the Peacemaker, behind him?" Hope brightened inside Nimbulan at sight of the tall figure gliding in the wake of Kammeryl d'Astrismos' powerful form. De Tanos' blond head shone in the dawn light like a golden aura of pure energy. The minor lord, who had studied for the priesthood until he assumed responsibility for his clan, was known for his wisdom and might help Nimbulan understand his vision in the void.

"Meddlesome priest. Why doesn't de Tanos stay in his monastery and count the stars?" Ackerly complained. "We don't need his version of peace to win this war."

"Priest no longer, but an anointed lord," Nimbulan replied.

"Lord of a miserable chain of islands in the river and a farm on the mainland—not even a proper fortress. He commands no armies and leads no men. No one respects his meddling in the name of peace." Ackerly spat on the ground beside his boot. "Compromise and treaties won't find us a new king. Only a warlord who can defeat all rivals will unite Coronnan under one crown."

"I used to believe that, too," Nimbulan whispered. He needed to think and think hard.

"Go back to your pavilion, Lan. Sup and rest while I divert Lord Kammeryl and the failed priest."

"Find Kammeryl a woman." Nimbulan suggested. Their employer's aura roiled like an unbalanced storm cloud— *like the patterns of men dancing in the void when they stepped out of the planned formation into violence.* . . . Splotches of black marred the layers of orange, green, and yellow energy surrounding d'Astrismos. 'Twas always thus before and after a battle. Only the camp followers soothed the violent outpouring energy of his mind and body.

"Make sure it's a willing woman and not a young girl under a compulsion," Nimbulan added.

"He prefers the girls. He'll linger longer with them. They cost less."

"A woman, Ackerly. Find him a camp follower who knows the payment, and the cost, beforehand."

Behind a delusion of thickening mist and smoke from the funeral pyres, Nimbulan withdrew.

"Stargods, help me interpret your vision correctly!"

A cold wet nose touched Myrilandel's cheek. She opened one heavy eye, shrugging her shoulders against the predawn chill. Her dream of flying high over the Great Bay vanished, leaving her curiously empty.

"Good morning, Mistress Badger," she responded to a second prodding from the animal's nose. "Thank you for the use of your burrow. I'll be on my way." She took one extra moment to rub sleep-sand from her eyes and dragged herself from the tight confines of the badger's home.

The joy of greeting a new morning filled the emptiness, and she forgot all but her excitement at facing a new day, a new adventure.

"Grrrr," Mistress Badger said, urging Myri to hurry. Dawn approached, and clearly the bristle-furred creature wanted to sleep.

"One more moment." Myri crouched in the den opening and reached back inside for her familiar and her pack before Mistress Badger could dash to her bed.

"Merawk?" Amaranth protested the abrupt move. The flywacket peered at Myri through the narrowed slits of his eyes and extended his claws for balance. A hint of heaving within his black fur released his feathered wings in automatic response to Myri's awkward grasp.

"You don't need to scratch, Amaranth!" Myri batted at the flywacket's offending claws. Half cat, half falcon, Amaranth usually exhibited the best qualities of both creatures. But for the first few moments after awakening, he was as cranky as Old Magretha, the witchwoman who had raised them both.

Myri dropped Amaranth beyond the badger's reach and stepped aside. He settled into a morning wash, pointedly ignoring her. The badger waddled into the narrow opening without a backward glance.

"Thanks again, Mistress Badger. 'Twas the snuggest nest

I've had since I began this quest." Too long ago, with only
her magic talent tugging her toward some distant place and
anonymous voices in her head to guide her. *(East,)*, they
said. *(You will find a safe home in the east.)*

She stood, brushing dirt and twigs from her leaf-green
overgown. Her fingers provided the only comb for her
silver-blond hair. Out of long habit she braided the length
of hair and coiled it beneath a kerchief. People accepted
her more readily if they didn't notice her strange coloring
right off.

A sense of wrongness buzzed like a bee around her head.
She rotated her shoulders, hands held slightly away from
her to catch the wind in her sleeves. The magic within her
coiled, eager to spring forth in healing. Slowly she walked
in a circle, waiting for her magic to point out the direction.
North by east—not due east as the voices urged her.
Stronger and more compelling than the voices. Something
terrible awaited her. Close.

A chill breeze and her own uneasiness sent lumbird
bumps up her spine. "My cloak!" Healing always left her
weak and unbalanced. She didn't dare approach a spell
without the means to warm herself later. She reached back
into the den for the thick woolen garment. Her hand closed
on the fabric just as Mistress Badger claimed it for her nest.

Myri tugged. The badger sank her claws into her prize.
"I can't afford to let you keep it." She pulled harder. The
sound of rending cloth sent her heart sinking. "I've no way
to replace it, Mistress Badger. And I don't have your thick
fur to keep me warm."

The fabric sprang free of the animal's grasp. Myri dragged
it out into the glow of false dawn. She examined her peat-
brown cloak with sensitive fingertips. Her fingernail caught
on a small rip near the side seam. She found no other
damage.

Eagerly she turned east to face the rising sun at its equinox. The sense of wrongness intensified, disrupting her joy
at greeting the morning.

Just over the next hill, due north, lay a village. The triple
Pylon at the exact center of the community stood ready for
fruit and flower decorations. All of Coronnan would celebrate the change of season today. Dancing. Feasting. Games.
Especially dancing. Men and women weaving intricate pat-

terns around the Equinox Pylon in ancient rituals that thanked the Stargods for the harvest and prayed for an easy winter.

Myri and Amaranth had escaped Magretha's vigilant eye every spring and autumn for as long as she could remember to watch and participate in the dancing.

Did she need to heal someone in the village?

(East. Go east. We will give you safety and rest. Do not turn aside.)

"I want to go to the village," Myri replied to the voices in her head. "They might need me." Why shouldn't she run away from her quest for just a few hours? She'd followed the compulsion to go east for over a moon now. Surely whatever called her could wait a little longer. As long as the first dance at least.

She doubted they'd allow her to dance in this village. The patterns required equal numbers of men and women to balance the forces of nature. Unlike the Spring Equinox Festival, partners of the harvest dance were usually determined long before the celebration date. But she wanted to watch, to tap her foot in rhythm with the music and sing along with the age-old tunes.

Myri ran up the hill to catch a first glimpse of people emerging from their homes as the sun crossed the horizon.

The wind joined her healing talent and circled around her in a fierce howl, pushing her back east by southeast. Lumbird bumps marched up and down her arms. Wordless pleas carried by the moving air begged her to follow without delay.

Her talent threatened to drag her due north faster than she could run.

(Save your strength. Put aside your talent until you have more training. Go east. east and a little south, avoid the north.) The voices took on a pleading tone. *(Do not linger in this area. There is danger to you.)* The voices urged her to alter her route.

She sat down on the damp grass in protest. Her talent and the anonymous voices warred within her every time she encountered people who needed her healing. She was getting tired of the compulsion always choosing her path for her.

"I want to watch the dancing for a few moments."

The wind died. Her talent still reached out, sensing pain and suffering, but no longer dragging her in its wake. The voices silenced for a moment.

She straightened her skirts and draped her cloak over her shoulders, spreading her arms just a little so the cloak billowed behind her like a giant wing.

"Let's go Amaranth. Maybe we can share a cup of cider and a crust of new bread."

Her mouth watered. Dry journey rations and creek water didn't seem enough right now. Her stomach growled in agreement.

A distant drum sounded the rhythm of a pulse—softly at first, but gathering volume and tempo with each beat. Myri hurried over the crest of the hill. She didn't want to miss a moment of the first dance of thanksgiving. For four years now she'd participated in the dancing wherever she and Magretha made their home. This ritual offering of the first and best of the harvest, of all those dedicated to the Stargods, seemed the most important. Spring festivals, with all their emphasis on fertility, tended to be wild, drunken affairs. Autumn rituals brought people into harmony with the Stargods as they displayed their gratitude and reverence for the season's bounty.

She lifted her voice in a song that followed the same cadence as the drum.

The Kardia pulsed beneath her bare feet in unison with her song and the drum. Feminine voices from the village joined hers as people burst from the huts, wearing their brightest and newest clothing.

"Mew?" Amaranth asked in his cat voice. He wove a path of protection around and between her ankles. His sides heaved again and a wingtip protruded from the concealing folds of skin and fur. His preparation for flight revealed the depth of his agitation.

Myri came to an abrupt halt at the edge of the common.

"Yes, Amaranth. I know something is not right here." Myri bent to scratch his ears. His mild protective spell extended to her.

A circle of pounded dirt around the Equinox Pylon bespoke of many generations of ritual dances. Nine men, nine women, nine drummers, and nine children must circle the decorated three-times-three poles of the Pylon. Only healthy people filled with life and joy should participate in the dance. Nine, the sacred number of the Stargods. Always nines and always a balance of male and female.

But only one man joined the women, and he half crippled. Beardless boys, their faces set in dutiful concentration, filled the positions of the other men. A solitary ancient woman, well-past childbearing held a padded stick over the solitary drum. The young women in their prime seemed most out of place. None appeared pregnant from the Vernal Equinox fertility rituals.

None of them.

Because there were no men.

"Where did they all go? 'Tis not yet the season for them to go away hunting. Surely no plague would kill only men." Myri sought an explanation for the out-of-balance dancers.

The rhythm of the single drum faltered. Faces turned toward Myri and her black cat. Silence stretched across the bowl of the village until the hills themselves begged for the return of the drumbeat. Pain poured from the eyes of every dancer. They knew the unbalanced numbers. Then the old woman slammed her padded stick against the skin-covered hoop of the drum. She beat again and a third time. The rhythm returned. A flute joined in. Dancers moved in the ancient pattern.

Step, hop, clap, hop. Stamp three times in a circle. Step together, step, hop. Clap, clap, clap.

The voices joining the festival dance slowed to a dirge. Many of those in the circle of dancers wept openly. Still the dance continued. Step, hop, clap, hop.

"Where is the thanksgiving and the joy?" Myri asked the empty sky. "Where are the men?"

(The plague that took them is called war,) the voices said inside her head. *(Go now, quickly, before the plague catches you, too. You must delay no longer. Come east. We will protect you from war.)*

Myri whirled from the sad sight of the Equinox ritual, choosing a direction at random. The rhythm of the drum continued to beat in her head. *No more men. No more men. No more men.* Up one hill, and another, and yet another, she ran, trying desperately to escape the horror of a village without men. Men to plow and plant, to hunt and sire new babies.

No more men. No more men.

The drum seemed to follow her, louder and louder. Her heart sped with the effort of her running. The drum increased its tempo to match.

(Turn away, turn to the east and south!) the voices pleaded. *(You are going the wrong way!)*

She held her hands over her ears. The throbbing sounds grew louder yet and so did the voices. The farther she ran, the closer she came to the source of the pulse. Amaranth flew circles over her head, mewling his concern for her.

As she crested the third hill, Amaranth dropped awkwardly to the ground, as stunned as she.

She stumbled across the body of a dead man. Blank eyes stared at her, his face twisted in pain. Blood covered his torso from a deep sword slash that split him nearly in two.

'Twasn't the drum that had followed her. She'd run away from a feeble attempt to celebrate life toward death and destruction.

"Pass in peace to your next existence." She closed his eyes with her left hand as she crossed herself with her right.

Below her, in a broad river meadow, lay thousands of men, dead and dying. Hideously wounded and needing her help.

Two generations of men, wasted.

The compulsion to heal pulled her feet toward the horrors.

(Turn away now, before you fall so deeply into a healing spell we can't pull you out. Save yourself. You need more training. More maturity and wisdom.)

"I can't run away from these men. They need me!"

Normally one healing spell dragged her spirit so low she needed a full day of rest and solitude to recover. Below her lay thousands of men needing her.

The drum continued to pound in her ears. *No more men. No more men.*

She had to save some of them. Some of them at least had to return to the villages.

No more men.

Healing drained the very life out of her, pouring it into her patients.

"I have to heal them. I have to try. What good am I if I don't give my talent to those who need me?"

(You will die.)

"Then I will die now rather than later. I have to do this."

Chapter 3

Myri pushed through the mist and the smoke hovering over the battlefield toward the core of pain that called to her. The intense suffering ahead made her talent reach out in healing comfort without conscious thought or preparation. She reeled the tendrils of power back within herself.

Screams pierced her heart. The stench of blood and fear embraced her and drew her deeper into the aura of pain and agony. And yet more pain and horror.

(Resist their call. Conserve your strength. Leave now before their pain swallows you whole. We will protect you, give you a home. You must come east now.)

"I can't leave them. They need me." She moved swiftly through the ranks of dead and dying. Her passing touch would only numb the injuries for a little, not truly cure. She would be drained before she reached those she could save.

Outside the hospital pavilion a young trooper stared at row after row of wounded men awaiting the attention of the healers. Myri grabbed his sleeve, yanking him away from the paralysis of bewilderment. His close-cropped hair that would fit neatly under a helmet identified him as a common soldier, not an officer or noble. He needed something to do.

"Hot water, lots of hot water. And bandages. Set your comrades to tearing up cloth—clean shirts and undergarments," she ordered him.

Desperate to relieve the pain all around her, Myri slapped the young man's face. "Do it. Now!" He shook himself free of whatever trance his mind had settled into.

"Yes, ma'am." His hand moved upward. Almost a salute,

not quite a tug of his forelock. "Lots of hot water and bandages," he repeated.

"And get some of your friends to start washing these men. I can't heal them if I can't find their wounds beneath the mud and the blood." The patients would feel better for the attention until she had time to deal with them.

The young man dashed off.

"Younger than I am," Myri whispered. "But I can't call him a boy. Not after what he's lived through in this battle." She moved into the tent.

Three gray-clad healers, two men and a woman, moved among the moaning men. The woman wore an apron to protect her healer's robe from dried blood and gore. She'd pushed the loose sleeves of her robe to her shoulders and secured them with black ribbons.

Fatigue lined the faces of all three healers. They wore their hair cut short for convenience. Sweat dulled their faces and hair colors to a uniform dark gray. Clearly the healers had worked since the battle began. How long?

Myri began her work in the corner farthest from the healers. What use her defying the guiding voices if she were evicted as an untrained meddler before she began? Magretha had fostered her to an acknowledged magician, she might be one of these healers. But without that formal training she might resign herself to always being a mere witchwoman—maligned and feared by superstitious mundanes, regarded as incompetent by the trained healers.

A head wound on her left needed little more than a touch to remove the pressure and wake the man from deep unconsciousness. She sent him on his way with a fierce headache and orders to remain quiet a day or two.

She treated broken legs, gashes, and other nonmortal wounds. Those patients walked away and freed space for some of those waiting outside. Myri pulled a handful of dried nuts and berries from her pack to restore the energy she'd spent. Her stomach wouldn't tolerate the taste of meat in this bloody environment. She craved the nutrients in meat, though. If only she had some cheese.

Behind her, Amaranth prowled the shadows, seeking those who needed Myri the most.

His plaintive mew called her to the center of the tent.

Already two of the healers and a red-robed magician—
she guessed he was a priest from the color he wore—stood
over an unconscious man with his right arm dangling from
a sliver of bone and tendril of white ligament. Magic hovered in the air around the healers who worked to save a
life. Still the soldier's lifeblood pumped out of him.

Heedless of the censure that might come from the priest,
Myri obeyed the persistent demands of her talent.

A *Song* of sweet healing sprang to her lips as a bundle
of special herbs and moss came to her hand from her pack.
She shouldered aside the older of the gray healers who
stood helplessly at the patient's head.

Breathe in, hold, breathe out, hold. Her head cleared
and magic simmered within her. A second deep breath and
hold. Power tingled in her fingertips, focused and ready to
fulfill its promise of healing.

"Hold his arm in place," she whispered to the female
healer. She nodded, too tired and numb to do anything
but obey.

"Magic isn't enough for a wound this severe," the elder
of the two male healers countermanded. "The only way to
save the arm is to stitch the blood vessels and the layers
of muscle. But 'twill take too much time. We must ampu-
tate and cauterize to stop the bleeding."

"Please, let me try," Myri begged even as she made a
poultice of her herbs in a bucket of clean water at the
patient's feet.

"Ye'll not save him. I sense his spirit passing into the
void already," the priest grabbed her hands in his own.
Gnarled, scarred hands, meticulously clean, even under the
neatly trimmed fingernails. A crescent scar that could have
come from human teeth stood out from the knife-straight
markings at the base of his right thumb.

"I can't allow you to interfere with the man's passing
into his next existence." His voice was soft, caring. An unwary person could fall under the spell of that voice.

But Myri was wary. She noted the patches and threadbare spots where his elbows stuck through the faded red
robe. She looked up into the priest's face, knowing she
would encounter hate and fear in his black eyes. She'd seen
that robe before. *She* had inflicted that scar on his thumb

when he'd tried to interfere with her first serious healing—before she knew enough to fear him.

"Moncriith," she whispered. Not a priest. A Bloodmage who fueled his powers with blood and pain while he preached against demons only he could see. If he were here, then his followers wouldn't be far away. How many hundreds awaited his orders to burn those who interfered with the Bloodmage's wishes?

"Witchwoman Myrilandel." He jerked his hands away from her.

"Let me save this man. Please." She pressed her hands tighter against the severed arm, willing the blood vessels to mend and join before Moncriith could stop her. His campaign against witchwomen as the tools of demons was well known in every village where she and Magretha had sought sanctuary. Hundreds of women wandered Coronnan, homeless and maligned because Moncriith had labeled them witchwomen—whether they had magical talent or not.

"Because of you, a man walks soulless through life," Moncriith intoned. He lifted his hands in an appeal to the Stargods as he raised his voice to carry throughout the hospital tent. "Five years ago, you interfered with a man's destined passage into his next existence with your demon-spawn spells."

Off to the side, a soldier touched head, heart, and both shoulders, the Stargods' ward against evil. Then he crossed his wrists and fluttered his hands in a more ancient sign. Amaranth butted his head into the man's leg and purred reassurance. The soldier jumped away from the cat as if burned.

"Because you refused to use your magic to heal a simple cut, the man nearly lost his life," Myri reminded Moncriith. "Jessup would have died prematurely. His pregnant widow and two tiny children couldn't fell timber to earn a living and keep a roof over their heads and food in their bellies. Because I saved Jessup, the family thrives once more."

Myri continued her binding spell, praying she wouldn't have to go into a deep trance to restore her patient's vitality. Already Moncriith's fervor laid a taint of guilt upon her, weakening her power and control over the healing.

What did he see in her and other women that was so

very evil? He never singled out the wives of powerful men, nor did he accuse men—only women who lived alone, without the protection of husband, father, or son.

"The timberman you cured limps painfully, clear evidence that he left his soul in the void when you dragged him back to this existence. Another soulless demon to aid you in your evil practices." Moncriith's voice took on tremors of righteousness.

Silence spread through the hospital tent. Even the screams of the dying fell off.

Myri ducked her head so the men wouldn't see her tears of doubt. Her talent sprang from deep inside her without her conscious control. Did it come from demons?

She had no arguments against Moncriith's accusations.

The three healers gazed suspiciously at Myri and Amaranth, who now circled the wounded man's pallet. Blue light glowed beneath her hands where the lifeless arm sought to rejoin with the body.

She had to stop Moncriith's interference before the blue light totally engulfed her mind and body.

"This witchwoman is possessed by demons. Burn her before she condemns this brave soldier to a soulless life!" Moncriith implored, reaching eager hands for Myri's shoulders. He jerked back, repelled by the barrier her talent erected even as it dragged her deeper into a trance.

Beneath her fingers, life pulsed into the dangling arm. The soldier moaned and clenched his fist. Then he fell back into unconsciousness.

"Stargods!" Men whispered around the tent. More wards against evil, modern and ancient.

The healers cleared the hovering crowd away to inspect Myri's work. Gently, the quiet woman who held the injured limb in place lifted her fingers from the injury. She saw with her eyes what Myri knew in her mind. Muscles mended and bones knitted. The bleeding had stopped.

" 'Tis a miracle from the Stargods," the healer whispered.

"Or a trick of Simurgh, king of all demons," Moncriith countered.

Myri took a deep breath, trying desperately to stay alert. If she lost consciousness and fell into a full trance, as her magic demanded, Moncriith would have her removed and condemned. He'd done it before. Only Magretha's good reputation in the village had saved her. But Magretha had died nearly two years ago.

Power flowed out of her. Her shaking joints became too heavy to support her body. She sagged to the floor, still holding the wounded arm in place. She tried to remove herself and her talent from the healing. Like a living being the spell enveloped her and fed from her strength.

"Look at the blackness in her aura!" Moncriith beseeched those around her. "Demons possess her. She taints us all with demons. Better to die blessed than live possessed!"

"I know nothing of demons," Myri whispered through numb lips as the void took her.

Nimbulan listened to the wind whipping around his pavilion. Saturated canvas walls bulged inward and sighed slackly with each blow. The candle flames of a dozen lanterns placed around the tent bowed almost flat within mica shields and then wavered upright again in rhythm with the howling of the skies.

Lord Kammeryl d'Astrismos and Lord Quinnault de Tanos argued almost as intensely inside. They paced and sat and shouted at each other while Nimbulan watched and ate his meal in near silence.

Nimbulan hunched his shoulders against the chill wind that crept along the carpeted tent floor. His woolen dressing gown, quilted with layers of silk, wasn't adequate to warm him after the hours of magic battle. The first of the autumn storms had held off just long enough for Kammeryl and his enemy to finish the battle. Now the armies could hole up, rest, and resupply during the winter.

The brazier at Nimbulan's feet helped ward off the chill a little. Four hours of sleep and half a meal had barely restored his strength. But the two lords had awakened him to give them counsel almost as soon as his complaining stomach had roused him from deepest sleep. He left Rollett, Jaanus, and Gilby, his senior apprentices asleep in the back portion of the pavilion. They needed rest more than he did. He didn't know where Maalin and Bessel were. Maybe they slept in Ackerly's tent, adjacent to the large pavilion.

He fished another stringy piece of beef from the salty broth as he watched the warlord and the Peacemaker. The boys needed to eat, too. But they needed sleep more . . .

unlike his years as Druulin's apprentice and journeyman when there was never enough food to fuel growing bodies.

"You must seek peace now, Lord Kammeryl. The weather has turned against you," Quinnault de Tanos said quietly. He sipped lightly at a mug of spiced wine.

Nimbulan looked for clues to Quinnault's mood and thoughts from the shift of his eyes and the bunching of muscles in his shoulders. His aura, his mind, and his face remained carefully schooled. Even the Peacemaker's grip on the cup handle remained steady and relaxed.

"Why should I sue for peace?" Kammeryl roared in his midrange of shouts. The hearty leader had a variety of bellowing tones and no soft ones. His aura showed a balance of colors as he paced the circumference of Nimbulan's tent. "'Tis not me who started this feud with the Baron of Hanic. His grandfather kidnapped and raped my grandmother fifty years ago. I'll not have Hanic bastards set themselves up as rivals to *my* crown, when I am king. I'll be ready to pursue the fight at the first break in the storm."

"Fifty years is a long time. Wounds of honor should heal when the participants die a natural death." De Tanos raised one eyebrow and cocked his head. For a moment, the shadows from the dancing firelight cast a different image on Quinnault's bone structure. Something large and elongated, not quite human.

A whiff of Tambootie lingered in the air. The sweet smell of Tambootie flowers in spring rather than the sharply musky odor of the oily leaves and aromatic bark.

An eerie chill passed over Nimbulan. He resisted the urge to cross himself in the ward against evil—against the unwarranted smell of Tambootie out of season or the bizarre shadows he didn't know. Instead, he turned his left palm upward, opening it to any stray power. An itch, unlike any known magic, irritated his palm. He twisted his wrist, seeking the source. The strange sensation evaporated.

"The bastards my grandmother bore Hanic now rule that clan and claim my lands." Kammeryl's roar rattled the cups on the wobbling camp table as he restated the ancient grievance.

"Bastards? More than one? Perhaps 'twas not a kidnap, but an elopement," de Tanos said quietly. Too quietly. The tug of a grin banished the mask of shadows. Nimbulan returned the grin. 'Twouldn't be the first or last time a noble bride foresook a political marriage for love. Quinnault sucked at his cheeks to control the smile. The mask of shadows returned.

Without the Tambootie in his system Nimbulan couldn't penetrate the secrets behind those shadows. But he'd had too much already. He didn't want to grow dependent upon the weed.

The void stripped away lies and delusions to lay bare a soul in the same manner. Nimbulan reviewed the vision of lords dancing in harmony he had experienced in the void. Had he seen the essence of de Tanos in the patterns and not recognized it? He shook his head clear of the puzzling vision. He had to concentrate on the present.

"You dishonor the memory of my grandmother, a queen descended from the Stargods!" Kammeryl's scream of rage drowned out the wind.

"The land you fought over yesterday was your grandmother's dowry. She bequeathed it to her son by Hanic, a symbol of her need to protect the boy. Her son by d'Astrismos claimed it by right of her lawful first marriage to your grandfather. Isn't it time you and your cousin sat down together and settled the issue?" Quinnault set aside his mug of wine. No grimace of distaste touched his face. Yet Nimbulan sensed the drink had gone sour. The drink or Kammeryl's company?

"The time is ripe, my lord," Nimbulan jumped into the conversation. The bread was gone, as well as the broth and the yampion pie. The sweetness lingered on his tongue. He craved more of the thick tuber baked in cream and eggs, laced liberally with sugar—a favorite treat that Druulin had always reserved for himself.

Nimbulan needed more fuel for his body. The two lords wouldn't give him enough peace to fetch more until they settled the argument or took it elsewhere.

"Consider," Nimbulan continued. He raised his hand, palm outward, as he talked. "Hanic retreated in disarray. His army is broken, at great cost. He has no resources left to defend his stronghold. A blood oath from you not to pursue and destroy him in his moment of weakness would require a concession from him. What has he left to give you but the deed to the disputed land, signed in blood? He might also renounce all claim to the kingship and put you one step closer to ending this war forever." He finished his wine. It had indeed gone sour.

"Another magician already whispers in Hanic's ear of a way to wrest victory from this defeat," Kammeryl protested. "I'll not appear weak by offering peace when I can destroy Hanic and have all of his estates."

"Hanic retreated. Certainly that entitles you to claim victory. But at what cost? Your army is reduced to two battalions." Quinnault kicked his camp stool out from under him and began to pace. "This victory shed more blood than the last three battles combined. The healers are worn to the bone and have called in a local witchwoman to assist them— I shudder to think what her untrained talent will do to our patients. Did the dead and wounded win anything? What about the people who huddle in their ravaged homes wondering if they will have anything left to survive the winter with after two armies foraged through here for supplies? And let us not forget the taxes they owe you for a new pledge of loyalty.

"No one won this battle, Lord Kammeryl. No one truly wins any war," de Tanos ended on a sigh of grief. The sweet smell of Tambootie flowers sharpened into the more usual scent of oily leaves and aromatic bark.

A pang of longing for the taste of the Tambootie sent aches into Nimbulan's joints. He resisted the craving.

"My magician won." Kammeryl glared at the Peacemaker. His aura sprouted black spots, losing its recently restored balance.

Grief replaced Nimbulan's urge to indulge in Tambootie. "I won at the cost of murdering my most promising apprentice in order to end the carnage. That is not victory. If we have to kill each other to win your battles, soon there won't be any magicians left. New magicians are hard to find and we rarely beget children to inherit our talents."

He'd never have a son or daughter to replace Keegan, only more apprentices. He had to hold close the boys who remained with him, love them and nurture them as well as train them.

"Nimbulan lost more than a traitorous pupil," Quinnault added. "Look at your magician, Kammeryl, really look at how gaunt and worn he is. In the last hour he's eaten three meals and still he hungers. His bones nearly poke through his skin. How long since he slept a night through? He cannot rest because the lords will beggar themselves to find a more powerful Battlemage. I beg of you Kammeryl, take this opportunity to treat with Hanic. Give your army, your people, your land, and your magician a respite.''

"Peace is useless. Other lords see peace as weakness. They'll stab me in the back.'' Kammeryl dismissed Quinnault's suggestion with an impatient gesture.

"What is left for you to continue the fight with?'' Quinnault continued to hound the warlord.

"My magician. The best magician in all of Kardia Hodos. He guarantees me victory at any cost. He'll have to conjure me the illusion of troops.''

"If Nimbulan breaks his covenant with the Stargods to perform such an unnatural spell, Hanic will have to find an outland magician to defend himself—perhaps he'll recruit Moncriith, the Bloodmage whose talent demands he fuel his power with the death and pain of others.'' Sadness dragged Quinnault's shoulders down as all three men crossed themselves in the Stargods' ward against evil. "There will never be peace once blood powers are tapped.''

"What if all magicians refused to fight your battles?'' Nimbulan asked. A glimmer of hope beckoned to him like the red crystal in the void. Men moving in harmonious patterns until manipulated to violence by . . .

"You might as well wish for flywackets and dragons,'' Kammeryl snorted. "Magicians will never unite. They guard their secrets too well. Too jealously.''

"That is the case now. But what if all the magicians banded together and refused to make war?'' Nimbulan asked.

Quinnault looked up sharply. Ideas seemed to blossom in his eyes. Nimbulan nodded to him and tried to pass encouragement mind-to-mind. But the Peacemaker's solid mental barriers didn't allow such communication.

"Why I . . . I'd . . .'' Kammeryl stammered, at a loss for words and bluster for the first time since Nimbulan had known him.

"You'd hasten to the treaty table,'' Quinnault prodded him. "You'd run with eagerness because war is too costly.''

" 'Tisn't worth thinking about. Magicians can't prosper during peace. Of what use are they but to fight battles for lords such as me?"

Ackerly had asked the same question years ago when he'd first realized his talent would never match Nimbulan's. Neither of them could think of another magical profession Ackerly could pursue.

Nimbulan watched the canvas door flap behind Kammeryl's jerky exit. The lord's stiff spine and rigid knees helped him pretend that his dignity was intact. But his aura swung wildly from orange to purple with growing black spots in each layer. Nimbulan hoped Ackerly had access to more women for the warlord.

As if summoned by Nimbulan's thoughts, his assistant appeared in the doorway. "Nimbulan, please come. The hospital. Terrible. A stranger leads a virulent dispute in the *hospital.*" Ackerly wrung his hands together, looking over his shoulder toward the source of the disruption.

"The hospital?" Nimbulan pulled muddy boots over his house slippers. "Why would anyone disturb the hospital." His filthy formal robe, not cleaned yet from the battle, would have to do. In his weakened state he dared not trudge across the camp in the rain without protection. He checked the pockets for wand and glass and other arcane tools. A rustle of dry leaves reminded him that he'd stuffed some Tambootie in a pocket some time during the battle. He threw it onto the brazier rather than eat it now. He'd had too much already.

"I think it's the Bloodmage, sir. Moncriith. He's demanding that a witchwoman with the healing talent be brought to justice for dealing with demons."

Neither of them suggested they turn the matter over to Kammeryl. Disputes within the camp fell under the warlord's jurisdiction. But Kammeryl d'Astrismos might very well wade into this brawl, *in the hospital,* with fists flying.

"Please wait for my return, my Lord Quinnault. We'll continue this discussion over a meal. Many issues lie unresolved." Nimbulan plunged into the storm.

"*Stargods!* Hasn't there been enough death today?" Quinnault raised his hands in supplication. "That fanatic Moncriith won't be satisfied until he's the only living soul left in Coronnan."

Chapter 4

Witchlight glowed through the bubble of armor around the huge hospital tent. Nimbulan looked up through the armor. Raindrops sizzled and evaporated when they touched the magical shields. The wind circled, howled, and sought new targets when it couldn't attack the tent itself. He shuddered with a chill as several drops of cold rain penetrated the armor and his blue robe of oiled wool.

Something was weakening the armor.

Outside the tent, rows of wounded men waited beneath the bubble for their turn with a healer. Strangely, their comrades, battle-weary men who should be resting and eating, washed and cared for them. He'd never seen common soldiers tend the wounded before. That activity belonged solely to healer magicians.

Shouts of anger and dismay disturbed the aura of peace that should have surrounded the hospital, along with the armor. Lumbird bumps climbed Nimbulan's spine as the warmth faded and two more drops of rain worked through the magical armor to land on his head.

The brawl within the tent must be disrupting the protective spells.

Armed guards converged upon the tent door at the same time as Nimbulan.

"Let me try to calm them before you use force to end this." He waved the armed men to stand behind him.

A sergeant held the tent flaps open for him. Eerie blue light surrounded a litter at the center of the tent. The blue was paler than Nimbulan's robe which matched the signature color of his magic. Whoever was at the core of the light wasn't one of his magicians.

Wounded men filled row upon row of pallets, cots, and litters around the core of blue light. Three gray-robed healers stood in a sentinel circle around the core of the blue light, their backs to it. They held scalpels, saws, and other surgical implements as weapons. They seemed prepared to use them against the shouting men pressing toward the blue light.

"Burning is the only cure for demon possession. We must take the girl to the funeral pyres and throw her into the purifying flames," Moncriith shouted. The Bloodmage just barely reached medium height, yet he dominated the crowd of taller men. His faded red robe took on the color of old blood—indicative of his perverted style of magic.

A shiver of disquiet snaked down Nimbulan's spine. Moncriith pitched his voice to draw listeners into his aura and meld with his opinions, right or wrong.

"Break her magic!" a wounded soldier called from a nearby pallet. "I saw her during the battle, her and her wicked familiar. They called the dragon what nearly killed me with its flames and talons." He held up a hand burned by magic and raked by long furrows. Probably his own fingers had made those cuts, seeking to shed a ball of magic thrown by Nimbulan or Keegan during the battle.

"I saw it, too," another man agreed. His wounds weren't evident.

"Dragon dung!" Nimbulan pitched his voice to penetrate the verbal fray. No one paid him any heed.

"She saved my life and three others that I know of." A man with a bloody bandage around his head joined the healers in defense of the blue-lit litter.

"Look what she's doing for Sergeant Kennyth! He lost that arm saving me." Another soldier limped to join the man with the head wound. "The witchwoman saved his life and she's givin' him back his arm, too. We owe her. Kennyth's the best sergeant in the whole *s'murghin'* army."

Moncriith advanced on the bubble of light. "Myrilandel wields the power of demons. No healer blessed by the Stargods can do the things she does. 'Tis unholy. 'Tis evil. The demons who possess her body will attack us all. Kennyth's soul has already moved into another plane of existence. Yet his body lives. He will become her undead servant."

"Enough!" Nimbulan shouted. The ridgepole vibrated with the power of his voice.

Silence reigned. All the participants turned to face the Senior Magician. Moncriith turned slowly, almost contemptuously, to confront a recognizable authority.

"So you finally crawled out of your lair, Nimbulan," Moncriith said without inflection.

"You are not welcome here, Moncriith." Nimbulan took two steps closer to the bubble of blue light, trying to see around Moncriith and the healers.

Not a bubble, an aura. He saw two forms within the glowing layers of energy. A kneeling woman lay collapsed over a supine male, her hands locked onto his upper arm at the source of the blue light.

"My mission is to halt the encroachment of demons into the very heart of Coronnan. My followers are prepared to take this witchwoman by force, if necessary. My people are fresh. Yours are battle-weary, Nimbulan. Will you throw them against my people for the sake of one demon-possessed witch?" Moncriith raised his voice again to preaching tones.

The thought of another battle exhausted Nimbulan. When would it stop?

When the harmony of dancing lords is no longer disrupted by self-serving magicians, he thought. Moncriith was the one breaking the harmony this time. Where were the Bloodmage's followers? Surely not in the hospital tent.

"You dare condemn any healer? You who take lives to fuel your magic, dare condemn healers! Do your followers know how you fuel your magic?" Nimbulan aimed his words at the wounded more than at Moncriith.

A wavering in the blue aura diverted Nimbulan's attention. Something important was transpiring and he needed to investigate and study the phenomenon. He needed Ackerly at his back, protecting him, warning him of intruders.

"I don't hide what I am behind platitudes. I draw blood only from myself and my enemies. I never feed upon innocent lives like you do!" An odd light gleamed in Moncriith's eyes as he turned his full attention on Nimbulan.

Fear of Moncriith's fanaticism swelled within him. This one man might charm half of Coronnan to his distorted view of magic.

"Healers serve all who come to them in need. No matter which lord they serve." Nimbulan fought the urge to back away from Moncriith's fervent appeal.

"Every true healer in Coronnan is occupied solely with the armies, Nimbulan. The common people have no one to turn to but demon-possessed witchwomen. Your healers do nothing but patch up and mend enslaved soldiers so that Battlemages, like yourself, can throw the men back into the wars. Endless wars. *Needless* wars."

Nimbulan's vision of magicians manipulating lords flashed before him again.

"Without healers, the death and carnage would be much worse." Nimbulan ignored the idea that soldiers were slaves to the lords who recruited them—sometimes by force. "Men will fight with or without magicians to back them up. You threaten to renew the battle over one witchwoman. You are no different from any other Battlemage, Moncriith," he said, half believing his own words. The other half lingered in the void with the vision of symmetry and peace— magicians standing away from the balanced, political dance of the lords.

"With every true healer employed by the armies, you condemn the innocents of Coronnan to the mercy of demonic powers wielded by witchwomen," Moncriith said. "Dangerous powers that risk the immortal souls of all of us. The witchwoman here, Myrilandel by name, a demon by birth, leads her sisters in this evil work. Only I can protect you, the men of Coronnan, from her."

For the first time, Nimbulan caught a glimpse of the woman at the core of the blue light. The power she wielded reached out to touch his own, begging him to add his strength to her spell.

He coiled all traces of magic deep within him lest she taint it, or learn from it.

Suddenly he realized the truth of Kammeryl's accusation that magicians would never work together.

"There are no such things as demons. They are the product of your overvivid imagination." Nimbulan latched onto Moncriith's latest argument. All his other defenses of his profession and colleagues were shaken to the core by the events of the last few hours.

"You close your eyes to the evidence of demons because you have been bewitched by her. I see how your eyes linger on her false beauty. I see how your aura reaches out to join hers. If you, Nimbulan, and your ilk could do aught but lead innocent men into battle, you would oust the demons and keep them from destroying souls. You, Nimbulan. You are responsible for this carnage and the perversion of magic."

Myri awoke from her trance instantly alert to danger from Moncriith. No fire menaced her, and she lay on a soft mattress, not a pyre. She couldn't relax beneath the warm furs that kept off most of the chill wind leaking through the pavilion walls. She didn't trust the feeling of comfort or the sensation of protection shrouding her. She knew Moncriith would try to trick her into confessing her association with demons.

If only she could remember her childhood, or her parents, she might know if he spoke the truth about her. She rarely managed to keep images of her life for more than a day or two. Already Magretha and the village in the western foothills where she died were fading from her memory. Only Amaranth remained constant. The flywacket, in his purely cat form, purred gently where he rested, a heavy, secure weight on her chest.

Someone moved nearby. She turned toward the sound of footsteps shuffling on carpets. Through closed eyelids she sensed light around her; light that would stab and blind while her head ached with the aftermath of a healing. Yet she had to know who stood by her so protectively.

"Who are you, Myrilandel?" a man asked her gently. Not Moncriith.

If she knew the answer, she would tell him.

"Overworking magic will rob a person of their wits. Your sense of self will return as your talent and your body revive. Perhaps I should ask where do you come from?"

He lifted a cloth from Myri's forehead and replaced it with a cool one. Blessedly cool. The throbbing in her head subsided a little.

"I come from nowhere," she replied. Her voice sounded hoarse.

"I have never heard of a drained talent taking memories with it. Perhaps you are in need of the ritual trial by Tambootie smoke."

Trial! Smoke! Surely this man was one of Moncriith's followers, sent to lull her into trust.

She had lived many places—none of them home. She had no memories of her parents to tell him. Magretha was the only parent she remembered. Her guardian had chosen a solitary life at the fringes of society when someone abandoned Myri in the woods with only Amaranth to care for her. The witchwoman needed a successor to her work and a healthy youngster to care for her in later years. Home had been a long series of shacks or caves. They'd fled to a new one every time local villagers began blaming an ugly old woman and her strange fosterling for every ill that life brought them.

Myri had few memories of her own about those early years, only the stories Magretha told over a winter fire. Indeed, most of her memories began with Magretha's death.

The comforting weight of her familiar disappeared. When? "Where is Amaranth?" He always helped her recover after a healing. He would warn her of danger—of Moncriith.

"Who is Amaranth?" The man sat down upon the bed where she rested. The rocking of the mattress sent her insides sloshing about and upset what little equilibrium she had attained.

"Merawk!" Amaranth growled and hissed at the man. His weight pressed against her side now.

"Yeow! You miserable animal. I'm not going to hurt her." The man jumped off the cot cursing. More movement, and a weight landed upon her chest.

Amaranth stretched his warm, furry body atop Myri. He butted his head into her chin. She found his ears with her fingers and scratched. She gritted her teeth against the pain in her head. Amaranth was back where he belonged; nothing else mattered. His rumbling purr brought peace to her stomach.

With new courage, Myri opened one eye a tiny slit. A tall man, thin almost to gauntness, sucked on his hand where Amaranth had scratched him.

"You are a magician," she stated the obvious. Only the strange cult of men who controlled the forces of nature cut their hair so oddly, straight at the shoulders, with the back tightly braided. This man's dark auburn mane was shot with silver and slightly disheveled. Instead of tunic and trews, he wore formal blue robes, the kind usually reserved for audiences with noble personages. The length of blue cloth draping from his shoulders and loosely belted added to his height and did nothing to hide his slenderness.

"And who are you, Myrilandel? You have a huge talent for healing, nothing short of miraculous. Kennyth's arm will be weak, but you gave it back to him and saved his life. And yet you are so poorly trained, you let the magic control you. We brought you back from the brink of death." He held his hand out, palm raised, fingers gradually curving so that his little finger almost touched his palm. A curious gesture that seemed a part of him.

"Moncriith allowed you to help me? Probably so he could enjoy the spectacle of watching me burn." He had crowed with delight as he watched another witchwoman burn. Myri had used his distraction to escape that village.

"I ordered armed guards to escort Moncriith and his motley cult from the camp. He won't trouble you again. Lord Kammeryl d'Astrismos agreed to my orders." He smiled slightly as his eyes held hers in a gentle gaze.

"You think me safe while I am under your protection. But what happens when I leave?" She broke the eye contact after a moment, uncertain of his intentions. The voices had promised her a home in the east. How much longer must she travel to find it?

She rolled to her side and tried to sit up, eager to be gone. Amaranth protested her movement with a squeak. Her stomach bounced and pain stabbed between her eyes.

"You aren't going anywhere for a while." The magician eased her back onto the mattress. His hand lingered on her shoulder. The strength in his fingers reassured her where his words hadn't. "I estimate at least a week for you to recover enough to get out of bed and move around a little. In a moon or more we will discuss your homeward journey— if the roads are still passable." His green eyes begged her to agree with him.

"No. I must leave before nightfall." She tried to sit up again but couldn't lift her head from the soft pillow. This time she didn't break the eye contact with him.

She'd heard much of this man's argument with Moncriith, though she'd been deep within her trance at the time and couldn't respond. Nimbulan, chief Battlemage for the lord. He and his ilk had directed the battle, determined who lived and who died. Many of the injuries in the hospital came from magic. She'd stayed away from those men, unsure how to help them. She knew only how to heal wounds inflicted by accident.

"I think you will stay, Myrilandel. I will train you to use your talent properly. Coronnan has need of healers." He stepped behind the shielded candle. His face and aura fell into shadow. "I have other duties of some urgency to attend to now. I've left you a little clear broth and a mug of wine. Don't drink too much too fast. I'll be back to check on you and bring you solid food when you have rested. Some yampion pie, perhaps?" He smiled with the charm of a little boy trying to wheedle sweets out of a stern parent.

Myri wanted to smile with him. Stewed yampion roots blended into a sweet custard of goat's milk and eggs was one of her favorite foods.

Dizziness attacked as she lifted her head to watch him leave. The same dizziness she'd felt as she ran from the village toward the battle. The sight of women dancing around the Equinox Pylon with only children as partners and a single drum for accompaniment haunted her.

"Magician," Myri called to him as he backed into the shadows. "You asked not *why* I came here, only where I came from."

"Why did you come to this particular battle scene when we have been at war for three generations?" He stepped into the light once more. He raised his palm again, almost as if he gathered information through it. His aura glowed blue with honest concern for her. She wanted to trust him. Didn't quite dare.

"I was sent." She had to deliver her message and leave. The voices would guide her to a home where she would be safe from Moncriith and others who needed to hurt her.

"Who sent you?" His hand jerked closed into a fist then opened again—as if caught in a spasm.

"I had a vision. I was sent to remind you of the cost of these battles. In the village three ridges south of here, the women must honor the Equinox in unbalanced numbers.

There are no more men to partner them. No more men to father new lives, to plow and plant, to fish or hunt. *No more men*. They have all died in your battles."

"*Stargods!* The Stargods have sent you?" He crossed himself in the accepted manner and closed his eyes as if in prayer.

"I think that you as a magician, a man who needs rituals to perform magic, are the one I must tell of this terrible perversion of nature. You know rituals must be performed properly or not at all. The imbalance of dancers and drummers means the coming year will bring famine to all, including your precious army."

"This news troubles me. I must think on it." The magician turned without another word and faded into the darkness. A puff of wind from the doorway told her that he had left the pavilion.

Relief at his absence relaxed her clenched fists and tight neck muscles. Such a vibrant man. His aura filled the tent, with no room left for her own. And yet his departure left her with a curious sense of emptiness. Loneliness. She wanted to look into those vivid green eyes of his and read his secrets.

"I will sup and rest, but then we must leave, Amaranth." She stroked his fur, making certain his wings remained concealed. "You will have to hunt for me on the journey. I'm not strong enough yet to forage for myself. Moncriith may come back. Nimbulan and his Battlemages cannot tame my talent. They will demand I give up my life to heal the men they order into battle if I stay."

Chapter 5

Nimbulan paused outside his pavilion. The witchwoman's words troubled him. He needed time and privacy to meditate on all that had happened since Keegan's death.

"What will it cost me to retain you as my personal magician and adviser?" Quinnault de Tanos greeted him without preamble.

"I am not like other magicians, for sale to any lord with the right price." Nimbulan pulled his attention away from the problems of a demon-hunting Bloodmage and the mysterious witchwoman who commanded more magic than any three of his assistants combined.

Magic combined. If only . . . No. 'Twas impossible. Or was it? He stared past de Tanos at the water clock. His vision in the void beckoned him once more. The crystal all color/no color umbilicals of life reminded him of Myrilandel's white-blond hair, visible only after he'd removed her kerchief. . . . He'd never encountered those particular umbilicals before. Both the pulsing symbols of life and Myrilandel's hair reminded him of Quinnault's coloring, but the lord's hair was darker and coarser. Impossible to tell for sure in the wavering candlelight.

"I swore loyalty to the clan of Astrismos eighteen years ago. My oath is important to me," Nimbulan replied instead of voicing his speculations. He sank into his comfortably padded folding chair. Someone, probably Ackerly, had placed hot flannels in the backrest. Just what his aching back needed. Now to ease his aching mind with meditation.

"I do not believe that Kammeryl d'Astrismos deserves your loyalty," Quinnault said.

"He's the best choice among many bad ones to lead a

united Coronnan. He is fair to his followers, unyielding to those who betray him. Strong in the face of enemies. People flock to his side . . ."

"For protection because he is strong," de Tanos interrupted. "Not because he is loved. What kind of leader will he be when there are no wars?"

"There are always wars." Nimbulan heaved a weary sigh. War had reigned throughout Coronnan for three generations. He'd never known life without war. "If we do not fight other armies, then we fight the weather, famine, disease."

When the numbers of dancers and drummers are unbalanced famine will follow, the girl had said. *No more men.* A headache pounded behind his eyes to the rhythm of the last phrase. *No more men.*

Would his remaining apprentices have the chance to grow up to be men?

"Speaking of hunger, I must finish my meal and sleep again."

The Peacemaker didn't seem to understand the broad hint. Nimbulan wondered if he'd have to risk rudeness and ask Lord Quinnault to leave. He desperately needed to think on today's events. He also needed to check the boys, make sure they were all safely tucked into bed.

"You proposed that all magicians band together and refuse to go to war." Quinnault de Tanos leaned forward. A jumping pulse in his neck betrayed eagerness to pursue the subject.

"An idea only, not thought through to a conclusion." Nimbulan's headache pounded. *No more men. Unbalanced rituals.*

"Think out loud, Nimbulan. Your reputation for wisdom is almost as legendary as your prowess with magic. Coronnan needs whatever small possibility of peace you can offer."

"I prefer to say no more until the idea has been thought through. Tomorrow I may have something to offer you." He watched the clock again. Involuntarily, his palms turned upward on the chair arms, opening to new thoughts and ideas. His awareness of reality vanished. He saw only the clock's symmetry and motion.

Symmetrical rituals. Lords pulled away from the perfectly balanced dances by magicians enticing them into chaotic

patterns and violence. . . . Equinox dances falling out of
symmetry without enough men to fill the places. . . .

"Twice in the last hour I have been accused of perpetuat-
ing the wars," he whispered. "By Moncriith and by the girl.
Are they right?"

"I leave tonight. We need to talk now," Quinnault interrupted his meditation.

Nimbulan blinked rapidly, trying to grasp the present reality rather than his vision. "In the teeth of this storm?
Your steed will be mired before you travel a league. I don't
need to look into the fire through my glass to foresee a
dangerous chill at the end of such a journey. If you complete it alive."

*If you can leave, so can the lovely witchwoman. Before
she answers all my questions.*

"D'Astrismos won't discuss a treaty. Perhaps Hanic will,
if I catch him before he walls himself into his fortress for
the winter."

Nimbulan peered at his companion. If only he could see
something of the man's aura. . . . But he couldn't. Trust
must build on other information. Reputation and tonight's
brief acquaintance.

After a long moment he gave in to the impulse to confide
in this austere man. The day's events had been too disturbing for him to sort through alone. "When you studied
for the priesthood, before your family died and you assumed the lordship, did you have enough magic to access
the void?"

"Only by clinging to my tutor's aura; never on my own."

A cautious answer. Every priest of the Stargods had to
have a least a little magic talent to qualify for the revered
calling. Few great magicians—those able to draw power
from the ley lines welling up from the core of Kardia
Hodos—stayed in the priesthood. Spiritual vows confined
their power too much to satisfy them. On the other hand,
minor magicians either became assistants to men with major
talent, as Ackerly had to Nimbulan, or they became priests.
Was Quinnault de Tanos a strong magician practicing in
secret, or a very minor talent who had left his studies to
assume lordship of his clan as he claimed?

The girl spoke the truth. We have wasted generations of men on these wars. If there is to be peace, I must grasp this opportunity while I have it. The girl and this lord are connected somehow. Is it their destinies or their pasts that mingle?

"Lord Quinnault, you have seen in the void how past, present, and future become one. You have known your soul stripped of masks so that every thought and plan is revealed, even those you did not realize you possessed."

Quinnault nodded. His mouth turned down, and his eyes took on a hard glint. De Tanos' experience with the symbolic life-path choices apparently had been unpleasant. Shadows played over his angular skull and once more took on the illusion of an otherworldly creature. Was his umbilical an iridescent crystal or some other more natural color?

Nimbulan wished for the strength to whisk Quinnault into the void and see for himself who and what the lord was. Until his body recovered, however, he'd have to rely on words and instinct. He couldn't help Myrilandel either until he replenished his reserves.

"While I liberated Keegan's ghost, I discovered some disturbing symbolism—which is the only way to view life while in the void. I believe Hanic was ready to negotiate a peace." The reluctant figure who was dragged out of the dance but kept trying to regain the symmetrical patterns wore Hanic's colors. The magician who pulled him away from harmony seemed young and overeager. "Keegan instigated this last battle in order to prove his superiority over me, his teacher."

Where had he gone wrong in training Keegan? Grief made the next words difficult. "Most of Hanic's troops were illusions. Very good illusions drawn from blood magic. Moncriith, the Bloodmage, wasn't present until later. Only Keegan could have conjured those troops. I trained my apprentice well in devising spells. But ethics, honor, and discipline meant nothing to him."

" 'Tis not unusual for a lord to listen to the advice of his magician over common sense. We have to make Hanic see sense now." De Tanos frowned again.

"Yes, we must." The civil war had lasted three generations and more. Magicians guided the lords every step of the way—first to find the best among the barons as a new king when the last one died without heirs. Later they man-

aged the battles, tipping the balance of strength and resources unnaturally. The vision in the void became clearer;
symbolism dropping away to reveal the truth beneath it.

"We must end the wars before Coronnan is destroyed
completely and her people overrun by greedy neighbors,"
Lord Quinnault said as he stood to leave. His shoulders
sagged as if his tall body no longer had the strength to
support all of him.

"What if two or more magicians, who shared the same
dream of peace as you, found a way to combine their magic
to overcome another magician?"

"If such a thing could happen, and I know enough about
magic to realize it can't, then the magicians could be controlled, the battles would depend solely on superiority of
men and weapons and tactics. Lords would be more cautious about starting battles. They might even listen to talk
of peace. A few of them have listened to me, but they are
intimidated by stronger lords like Kammeryl and Hanic."
Quinnault sighed heavily, then straightened with new resolve. "But magicians can't combine their powers. As lord
Kammeryl said, we might as well wish for dragons and flywackets. Peace must be found in other ways."

"Some of the men think they saw a dragon on the field.
I might very well find flywackets hiding in the clouds,"
Nimbulan chuckled.

"Have you experimented with combining magic?" Quinnault leaned over Nimbulan's chair. His excitement stripped
years of care and worry from his face. He was younger
than Nimbulan thought.

"The battles must end for the winter. I have five moons
or more to experiment. I need a place of safety to work
and train my apprentices, to recruit other magicians who
are weary of war. . . ."

"Change your allegiance to me, Nimbulan, and I will give
you one of my islands. An ancient monastery, abandoned
before the beginning of these wars, stands fast against time
and the elements. You'll have safety and privacy there."

"Isn't the peace of all of Coronnan worth lending that
island without having me dishonor my previous vow?"

A smile lit Quinnault's eyes and banished the odd shadows. The candles blazed brighter and warmer.

"If you had given any other answer, Master Nimbulan, I

would always doubt your loyalty. The island is yours for as long as you need it. Find your students and begin your experiments."

Moncriith watched Ackerly, the short assistant magician, through narrowed eyes. No aura of great power surrounded the square-built man, and yet he associated freely with the Battlemages.

"Take the provisions, Moncriith. I offer them freely, without obligations." Ackerly held out a bulging saddlebag. "It's not much but it should see all of you to the next stronghold or village."

"Thank you." Moncriith bowed his head. The humble gesture allowed him to watch Ackerly through his lowered eyelashes.

Ackerly squirmed a little. Moncriith bit back a smile at the magician's discomfort.

"I accept your gift of sustenance freely. But I do not understand why you give me aid when you serve Nimbulan, the man who exiled me from the hospital and my righteous quest."

"Harrumf," the guard tugging at Moncriith's elbow cleared his throat. He shuffled his feet, anxious to escort Moncriith and his followers two leagues beyond the camp perimeter. Five more heavily armed men encircled Moncriith's two dozen, very ragged followers.

Moncriith turned a warning gaze upon the impatient guards. They resumed staring into the distance. Watching elsewhere didn't close the men's ears though. In the army, every man must report to his superior officers. Many men stood in the chain of command between one sergeant and the chief Battlemage, Nimbulan. Moncriith wondered what the men would report and how soon.

"No man should be turned out into a storm without provisions. I don't care if the warlord and his mage disagree with your views. You're a magician and should be respected." Ackerly stopped shuffling and stood straight.

Moncriith stiffened in indignation. "The priests have rejected my vision from the Stargods. Demons have invaded even the hallowed temples. The priests and their puppet magicians have cast me out rather than face the demons who pervert their magic. According to them, you owe me nothing." Every time he thought of the humiliation heaped upon his head by the pompous elders of the temple, anger boiled up within him. His spine stretched taller. Blood swelled within his neck and face. His heart raced while his lungs panted and overfilled with air.

Ackerly stared him directly in the eye. "You and I have a lot in common, Moncriith. Neither one of us can weave the magic of the Kardia into our spells. Because of that we are relegated to minor positions serving those who can. No one is willing to give either of us credit for intelligence or other skills simply because we lack that one talent. Well, you've broken out of the mold this world cast for you and found a different way to work magic. I admire that. I'll never have the courage to do anything but what Nimbulan orders."

"In a perfect world, mundanes, who outnumber magicians one thousand to one, would rule. Magicians should be servants not commanders." Moncriith replied. "Our talent is a gift. But demons control Coronnan now, not mundanes. Demons led by Myrilandel." *Only magicians can root them out and turn the chaos that will follow into order. And I am the only magician who can see the problem.*

"Hanging around the army will only get you killed. Now take the food and seek more followers among those who aren't dazzle-blinded by magicians and their tricks."

"Thank you again. And courage, Ackerly. One day our other talents will be appreciated more than our failure to be great magicians."

"Where are you headed? Maybe I can send more provisions later."

"Money will be appreciated. We need winter clothes and shelter, things that are not easily bargained for or given in hospitality."

Ackerly squirmed at the mention of money. Moncriith smiled inwardly. He'd found this man's weakness.

"We head east. The source of evil that corrupts Coronnan lies in that direction. I will root out demons and their minions where they are born. I have heard reports of dragons flying over the eastern edge of the Southern Mountains. When I have seen to their destruction, I will be back."

*   *   *

Nimbulan raised his boots awkwardly out of the dirty water that always seemed to reside in the bottoms of boats. He and Quinnault de Tanos had just dumped the collection of rainwater out of the boat and set off on the final leg of their quick trip to the islands. Traveling downstream from the army camp with a swift current, they had been gone less than an hour. Walking, or riding fleet steeds would have compounded the time by four. Heavy, cloying mud clogged every track.

He rested his feet on the rocking sides of the rowboat, out of the water. At least the rain had eased from last night. They'd only had to empty the boat twice since leaving camp.

But debris from the storm moved down the river at the whim of nature, dark splotches of black-gray against the brownish gray river, beneath the yellow-gray of the misty sunrise. The dull light blurred outlines, magnifying the size of obstacles. Branches and tree trunks looked dangerous, even compensating for the distortions of light.

Quinnault de Tanos stretched his back and arm muscles against the oars. "The current is swift today. We'll reach the island soon, and you'll be back in your tent by sunset." He chuckled and continued to speed the craft toward the Great Bay, much too quickly for Nimbulan's stomach.

"I'll feel safer if you steer away from that bobbing log." Nimbulan pointed at a floating tree with many of its raggedly broken limbs pointing directly at their fragile hull. "We could have waited another day for better weather and calmer water for this visit to your islands," he added.

If they'd waited, Nimbulan would have had a chance to visit with the pretty little witchwoman. His mind lingered on his plans for training the girl rather than on the boat.

"The sooner you start your experiments and gather recruits, the faster we can end the wars." De Tanos grunted and put more effort into his rowing.

"Who are you, Quinnault de Tanos? You are an enigma among your peers."

"I am the youngest son of a lord who never planned to accede to the title or the responsibilities of clan leadership. I had three brothers and two sisters. The wars and the plagues that follow battle took them all much too soon. Now I am the last of my immediate family. I can't go back to the priesthood. My people depend on me as their lord. I want my sons and daughters, when I have the time to marry and beget them, to have the choice I was denied."

"Magicians rarely have children of their own. But I have apprentices. Those boys and girls come to me as children, between the ages of ten and twelve usually. I feel like I am as much a father to them as their blood parents. I want choices for them as well. I want them to be allowed to use magic for peace and prosperity."

"Then we are allies on the same quest." Quinnault smiled at Nimbulan as he neatly fended off a tangle of vines and leaves with one oar.

"How far has this quest taken you, Quinnault de Tanos? You have been called 'the Peacemaker' for at least three years now."

"I have commitments from four other lords to refuse to join Kammeryl, Hanic, or Sauria in battle if—and it's a big if—I can keep those lords from attacking them in retaliation for that refusal."

"What about Baathalzan?" Nimbulan asked about his cousin, the lord of his home province.

"He refuses to talk to anyone. Can you persuade him?"

"Not likely. He fears his relatives will take his title and lands more than the other lords. My cousin is not a decisive leader. But five of thirteen lords is a good start. They command a lot of land and a fair number of troops. Banded together, they could mount a serious defense. Why have you not led them in that direction, Quinnault?"

"They want to make me king."

"And you fear that responsibility?"

"I am barely comfortable as lord of my own clan. I would make a very poor and weak king. Coronnan needs a better man than I. All I really want is to be a priest."

Silence hovered between them, like a living being, begging to be pushed aside. But neither had anything to say.

"Is this abandoned building large enough for a women's quarters? Almost as many girls seek apprenticeships in magic as boys," Nimbulan asked finally. Myrilandel must have a place there. He couldn't let her enormous talent go to waste.

"I think so. I haven't thoroughly inspected the building

in several years. How many people are you planning on housing?"

"About a dozen to start. I'll bring in others as the need arises. At the moment, Ackerly and I are the only trained magicians I can trust." Keegan had run away and betrayed him.

An eddy caught the little craft and swung the bobbing tree dangerously close. De Tanos shifted the oars in a rapid maneuver Nimbulan couldn't interpret. The boat stabilized and nosed away from the entrapping branches.

"You've spent a lot of time on the water," Nimbulan said with a grunt as he pushed the tree farther away from them with his staff.

"I had my first boat almost before I could walk. Boats are necessary to people who live on islands. Boats are our livelihood. We don't have much arable land in the islands. We make our living by fishing and by transporting people and goods up and down this river. That livelihood has been seriously disrupted by these wars. I'm more comfortable with all kinds of watercraft than with steeds." De Tanos looked over his shoulder at the steep riverbank a quarter mile away. Waves lapped the red clay cliff with a ferocity reminiscent of the Great Bay.

"Neither you nor your father maintains an army." Nimbulan changed the subject rather than think about the wind-whipped water all around him and the next log aiming for their hull. "Yet your manors haven't been overrun. Unusual in these troubled times."

"The river provides a natural moat. We withstood a siege last spring, mainly because my people retreated to the islands with every boat within ten leagues. They supplied the mainland manor in secret at night through the river gate. Lord Sauria bombarded us with boulders and nearly breached the walls in several places. He did overrun the stables and steal my best breeding steeds. We almost surrendered before he decided my small holdings couldn't give him the strategic advantage he sought. He threw away access to the Great Bay because he didn't plan ahead and bring his own boats."

"You've had to fortify your estates, then? Sauria is persistent. He'll return in the spring, with boats."

"Yes." De Tanos gritted his teeth and fought the oars once more as a snarl of tree roots and stumps loomed directly ahead of them. "I am making plans for that. Not a chore I like."

"How much farther?" Nimbulan dropped his feet back to the hull for better balance. He didn't like the way the current swept more and more debris up against that stump.

"We'll get around that menace." De Tanos put more effort into the oars.

Nimbulan crossed himself in prayer twice, the second time for the lord whose attention remained riveted on the snag that loomed closer, seeming to fill the entire river.

Wind gusts stirred the current into choppy circles. The boat aimed for the wall of debris.

"I haven't recovered enough magic to help much, but I might be able to send the wind elsewhere and divert the current around that snag." The stump and its collection of flotsam seemed too firmly anchored to budge with his exhausted talent.

"Tampering with the weather is forbidden. We can't upset the balance." Strain showed in Quinnault's neck and shoulders.

Nimbulan ducked as a huge branch bobbed up out of the water, aiming directly for his head. A wall of water followed the branch.

"I can't swim!"

Chapter 6

Myri crept beneath the outer wall of her tent as a sleepy bird chirped a question at the first signs of light in the sky. She stopped to listen for the waking chorus of birds. Notes of a wordless song sprang to her lips. A smile stretched her weary cheek muscles. Every part of her body was tired. But she shouldn't linger, even to greet the rising sun with the birds.

Standing hunted-still, she tried blending into the muddy colored canvas walls. Her cloak should be the same color as the tent, effectively masking her presence.

Not much of a sunrise. The gradual spreading of light only hinted at the presence of a sun behind the clouds. Good. She'd cast no betraying shadow when she moved.

The guards at the front of the tent paced back and forth. She had heard Nimbulan give orders last night that she be kept secure inside the tent. Escaping them would be a merry game.

She had considered crawling beneath the tent around midnight. Muffled voices had betrayed the presence of Nimbulan's assistant and Moncriith. From the secure confines of the tent she had listened to Moncriith's plans. He was headed east. The same direction the voices urged her to flee. Therefore, she would wait until he was well gone. She would rather follow behind him than have to watch her back in constant fear of him catching up with her.

Pickets patrolled the edges of camp. Their shoulders sagged wearily. Men in bedrolls on the wet ground stirred and yawned. Some pulled their blankets higher while others sat and stretched. By the dim glow of false dawn, she scouted her escape route around them, picking out hiding places along the way. The back of a tent to her right, a stack of weapons beyond. She tugged the hood of her cloak lower over her face and moved toward the perimeter of the camp. She'd played this game before. But then she'd had trees to climb and no one ever thought to look *up*. They always looked straight ahead or down.

Amaranth mewed a protest at being carried beneath the folds of her cloak.

"Sorry," she whispered to him. "We have to stay hidden until we're beyond camp. Besides, you don't like wet on your feet."

The black flywacket settled into her supporting arm. His tail twitched, showing his reluctant acceptance of her wishes.

"Food first." Myri followed her nose to the cooking fires, slipping in and out of shadows, making faces at the men who passed her by without seeing her.

A sleepy-eyed cook stirred a gruel in a huge cauldron over a firepit carefully tended by a dozing teenager. They were protected from the rain by a red, green, and white striped awning. No canvas sides or shadows for Myri to hide within. Besides, she couldn't carry hot gruel. She needed jerked meat, journey bread, and dried fruit.

Carefully she scanned the camp for signs of a storage tent or covered sledge. Surely, the cook would need easy access to his supplies.

Ah. There, on the other side of the cooking pavilion—a low, square tent with alert guards front and back. No slackness showed in the fabric walls. Could she creep under the tent without rippling the canvas and signaling unlawful entry to the guards?

She skirted the cooking area with all the stealth she'd learned in the woodlands as a child. The far side of the awning offered a little concealment in the form of a sledge piled high with pots and other utensils. The harness end rested atop double crates for easier hitching to a steed. The triangular space beneath made a nice dark cave to hide in. A gust of wind, laden with fresh rain, diverted the guard's attention long enough for her to slip beneath the vehicle.

"Stay here," Myri whispered to Amaranth as she shoved his muscular cat body into the shadow of the crates. Gently she slit the canvas wall of the tent with her belt knife. A moment later she crawled on her belly through the small opening.

She froze, waiting anxiously for the guards to betray their exact location. They were as loud and obvious as children thrashing through saber ferns. Slowly, very slowly, not making a sound, she stood, allowing her eyes to adjust to the dimness. Sharp-cornered boxes emerged from the shadows to her right. Lumpy sacks to her left. Grain? By feel, she found a corner of one of the sacks. She held her pouch beneath the corner as she slit it. Slowly the cereal siphoned into her container.

"What are you doing in here, soldier?" a male voice challenged Myri from the front of the tent. "There's plenty to eat outside for honest men. You planning on deserting?"

No time to argue. No time to search for more food. Myri dove for the opening. A hand grasped her ankle as she slithered toward the shadows beneath the sledge. She kicked back with her free foot.

"*S'murghit,* you little demon get!" the man grunted and let go.

Come! she commanded Amaranth, not daring spoken words. She crawled from the cover of the sledge and began running. Amaranth burst from his hiding place in a flurry of glistening black wings.

"A dragon. The dragon came back!" a guard cried.

"After them. The magicians will pay plenty for a real dragon."

"That's not a dragon. Too small. Maybe a flywacket."

"They'll pay more for one of those!"

Myri escaped while the men argued. Her heart beat loud and fast. The rolling hills and grasslands promised no concealment. Nothing to climb. Nowhere to hide. This wasn't a game anymore. Myri willed her cloak to blend in with the morning mist. She locked her muscles.

Movement would betray her. She had no choice but to run. If she didn't, Nimbulan would keep her prisoner, make her a slave to the hospital. She had delivered her message and done what she could for the wounded. Now she must continue her own quest for a home—a safe haven.

Help me, please! she pleaded with the mysterious voices. No answer.

She prayed she hadn't offended them by diverting her path to help a few of the wounded.

Amaranth circled above her, mewling his concern.

"Stop! Thief!" Heavy feet pounded the ground behind her.

"Who cares about the thief. Catch the flywacket," one of the guards yelled.

She ran, clutching the precious pouch of grains to her breast. She wished she could spread her arms and fly like Amaranth. But she had to protect the food. Above her, Amaranth flew higher into the clouds and safety.

Please, save me from the magicians who would enslave me, and Moncriith who would burn me. I'm going east now, as you commanded.

No answer.

"Where's the blasted flywacket?"

"Can't see it. But it will follow the thief. Catch him, catch the flywacket." Her pursuers came closer.

She ran faster. Up to the first ridge. Down the steep escarpment on the other side. Her bare feet slipped on the wet grass. The men slipped, too. First one man fell, knocking into another, then a third. Together all three guards tumbled down the long hillside.

Myri collected her wits and balance before the others. She ran. She dodged hummocks that appeared in her path, jumped across a stream, and rolled behind a boulder that spread across the hillside with a tumble of other rocks.

"Hey, where'd she go? No one could just disappear like that," the youngest of the men asked.

"She's a witchwoman. What do you expect?"

"That flying thing was probably just a crow," said the tallest of the men as he stood, brushing himself off.

"Them nasty birds are a nuisance, always snatching at any food left untended," replied another.

"Think we could catch a crow and dress it up to look like a flywacket?" asked the third.

The men wandered around the hillside more slowly, reluctant to move too far from camp. They looked directly at Myri and didn't see her. As soon as they turned their backs to retreat to the protection of their fellows, Myri ran on.

Uphill again, over the second ridge, and onto the third.

A trade road wandered through the next valley. Where there was a road, there would also be villages.

Two armies had marched through here a few days ago. The warlords probably recruited men as they traveled. Any village on this road would have been deprived of all its men. The few people who remained might welcome her where they would shun more soldiers.

She slowed her pace and steadied her breathing.

Amaranth, where are you? A dark shadow within a shadow circled above her head.

"We're safe now, Amaranth. Come. Come to me." She patted her shoulder in invitation.

The shadow dropped lower, took on form and resolved into a flying creature. The sunlight rippled purple lights along his black fur and wing feathers.

Myri held out her arm. Amaranth dropped lower, wings raised, claws extended. Fanning the air with backward sweeps he slowed and landed lightly on his accustomed perch. Quickly he folded his wings beneath their protective flaps and wrapped his tail around Myri's neck for balance.

"Ready?"

(Yes.)

Myri marched around the next bend in the trade road and into a quiet village.

A woman emerged from the first hut carrying a bucket. Another woman stepped from the next home with a basket for gathering eggs. Together they turned and watched Myri's approach.

"Have you shelter for a weary traveler?" Myri asked with ritual humility.

"Ye're out a might early. Or you been traveling all night?" the Bucket Woman asked. " 'Taint right for a woman to be traveling alone at night—or any other time."

"Makes no difference. We owe her hospitality, like any other traveler," Basket Woman replied.

"She could be a spy for the army. They'll steal what little we have left. We won't survive the winter if they claim our harvest."

"If you can call it a harvest," Basket Woman snorted.

"I have a little grain to share." Myri offered her half-full pouch.

"The red-robe told us to beware of spies with gifts."

"One good breakfast will prolong starvation a little. And that preacher doesn't know everything. You're welcome, stranger." Basket Woman gestured with her free hand for Myri to enter her humble home. "The flusterhens are still laying, and there's sausage."

Myri's mouth watered and her stomach rumbled. "What preacher?" She clamped down on her hunger. Amaranth dug his claws deeper into her cloak in warning.

The women looked to each other without answering.

Myri set Amaranth on the ground, ready to run again. "What preacher?" she asked.

"Moncriith," Basket Woman said quietly.

"*Sieur* Moncriith warned us about witchwomen and their demon familiars." Bucket Woman gave the man a priestly title. She backed away from Amaranth. "Sieur says we aren't to give hospitality to any traveler. I respect the words of a priest. Only demons stray from their homes these days." She dropped her bucket and crossed her wrists with a flapping motion. The flapping hands symbolized the ancient demon god Simurgh. The crossing acted as a ward against him.

The sun pushed aside the thinning clouds, sending a shaft of light into the center of the village. The Equinox Pylon, its harvest decorations slightly wilted, glowed as if on fire. Myri backed up at the omen of fire.

"I knew the Stargods would lead you back to me, Myrilandel." Moncriith emerged from the first hut. His patched red robe seemed to glow in the growing light. Red for priestly orders or red for the blood he shed to fuel his magic? " 'Tis time for you to face justice! My people are camped nearby. I will summon them to join the village elders. They will judge you for your demonic crimes."

Amaranth darted into the shelter of a woodpile beside the house. Myri dropped her pouch of grain and ran.

Moncriith grabbed her around the waist before she had gone two steps. "You'll not escape me again, Myrilandel, daughter of demons."

Chapter 7

Myri clawed at Moncriith's restraining hands with her fingernails.

He latched onto both her wrists with one strong, scarred hand.

Desperate to escape the images of fire that leaked from his mind, she kicked at his booted shins with her bare feet. Sharp pain shot through her toes, hot and intense.

She had to break free before his followers joined them and imprisoned her.

Moncriith laughed. His thoughts broadcast into Myri's receptive mind. She cringed away from the images of herself, naked, writhing within a bonfire.

Myri's imagination added details of pain in her own limbs. Green flame boiled around the edges of her vision. Her lungs gasped and labored with suffocating smoke that existed only in Moncriith's mind.

Or her memory?

She remembered dragging Magretha from a burning hut. Flames had licked at her hands and singed her fine hair as she put all of her childish strength into escaping the fire with her unconscious guardian.

The memory cleared the panic from her mind. Her strength pooled into her hands and feet. She focused on Moncriith's posture and muscular tension for clues to his next action. Though she stood nearly as tall as he, he had the advantage of weight and breadth.

With one last jolt of strength she slammed her elbow backward into her captor's well-muscled belly.

"Oomph." Air whooshed from his lungs into her ear. He didn't relax his grasp of her hands or her body.

"Moncriith, let her go," Basket Woman commanded. "I've offered her hospitality, and I'll not have you bringing curses upon this village for abusing her rights as our invited guest."

"She has no rights. This woman isn't human. Not like us. She was born of demons and stole this body from a human child. She's a changeling seeking to steal your souls and claim your bodies for her own vile purposes. Yesterday she worked her evil magic on a brave soldier, leaving his soul trapped in the void between the planes of existence while she cured his body. Perhaps he was one of the men missing from this village. One of the men who will follow her rather than return home."

"How . . . how do you know this, Moncriith?" Basket Woman wavered. Moncriith could have offered no more damning evidence than the threat to deprive this village of yet more men.

"I have been blessed by the Stargods with a vision of this woman in her true form. I wear the red robes of a priest. Dare you doubt me?"

"I am not a demon. I swear to you, I'm not," Myri pleaded with the woman.

"Meerawck!" Amaranth swooped from the sky, claws extended, teeth bared, aiming directly for Moncriith's eyes.

"Ayii!" Moncriith screamed. He thrust Myri away, raising his arms to protect his vulnerable face and neck from the flywacket.

"Stargods preserve us!" Bucket Woman crossed her wrists and flapped them. Then she touched her forehead, chest, and each shoulder in the more accepted blessing. "I renounce this evil with my mind, my heart, and the strength of my shoulders."

"Demons. Demons from the sky!" Basket Woman buried her face in her apron and fled.

Amaranth swooped and tore at Moncriith's hair with his claws. The Bloodmage beat at the winged cat with his hands. He tried to duck his head within his robes. Amaranth reached again to claw at the man's scalp.

Myri dashed behind the woodpile, out of sight of her persecutor. Her bruised toes complained with each step. She ignored them, running along a trail that guided her east and south, toward the mountains. East toward something that called her. The wind swirled up and pushed her in that direction. She spread her arms, letting the air catch her cloak like a sail, speeding her on her way.

But Moncriith was headed east, too, in search of demon lairs. She fought the wind, turning west and north toward the village where Magretha had raised her. The cold bite of circling air thrust her harder toward the east.

(East.) Voices filled her mind, crowding out every other thought. *(East. Home. Safety.)*

Myri gave in to the driving force of the wind. Before she had traveled a league, a grove of oak trees south of the trail beckoned her. Oak with protective mistletoe hanging heavy in the upper branches. A hiding place. She could watch the pathways for Moncriith, let him go ahead of her. Safer to follow unseen than flee ahead.

(Yes. Hide now.)

Silently she stepped off the established path, blurring her passage with magic as she went. Amaranth would find her. Moncriith wouldn't. She prayed to the Stargods and the guiding voices that Moncriith wouldn't find her.

Nimbulan coughed and spluttered through muddy water, crawling up a soggy embankment. He dragged his staff along with his heavy body, as much a part of him as his arms and legs. Each breath took a concentrated effort and ended in another cough. He expelled more water from his laboring lungs and collapsed, face-down in more mud.

Some force he couldn't understand propelled him onto solid ground. Water ran from his hair, his clothes, from the sky. . . . Everything was as wet as the river. Why didn't he just give up and let himself drown?

"The first lesson you give to your apprentices had better be how to swim," Quinnault de Tanos said. "I'll not have my people risking their necks rescuing every landhugger who throws himself into the river. Thank goodness you wore a tunic and trews and not those long robes you magicians favor. I'd never have gotten you out of the river with the weight of all that sodden wool dragging you down."

"I didn't throw myself into the river. The river threw itself all over me," Nimbulan said between hacking coughs.

Quinnault grabbed the back of Nimbulan's shirt and lifted him. Nimbulan scrambled to get his feet under him, balancing on his staff. He needed to regain some semblance of control.

"Breathe, Nimbulan. You've got to get your lungs working again." Quinnault slapped the magician on the back, hard. Almost too hard. Something seemed to snap between Nimbulan's ribs.

Deep coughs racked his body. He spewed more fluid, from his belly this time. When the spasms tapered off, each breath seemed less painful than the one before.

Instantly he was back in his memories of Druulin's tower. Boojlin and Caasser opened their mouths in protest as the cold water from Nimbulan's booby trap hit them from above. Both bullies breathed in too quickly, taking water into their throats and up their noses. They coughed and choked. Caasser's face took on a funny gray-and-pink tinge.

Instantly remorseful, Nimbulan jumped to slap Caasser on the back, forcing him to expel the water.

"Not so hard, Lan. If you break his ribs with your pounding, you'll only make it worse," Ackerly had warned him, only half seriously. He and Nimbulan had suffered much at the hands of the larger bullies. Returning some of the pain and humiliation brought satisfaction to Ackerly's grim smile.

Nimbulan shifted his attention from hitting Caasser's back to forcing the boy's arms over his head with a firm grip on both elbows. The shift in posture seemed to open the taller boy's air passages. His convulsive coughs tapered off. Nimbulan waited for Caasser's gasping to ease into long sobbing breaths. Part of him wanted to pull Caasser's arms back, hard; to prolong the boy's pain in retribution for all the nasty tricks he'd played on Nimbulan and Ackerly.

The part of him that was growing up and assuming more responsibility knew that if he did, he risked making a life-long enemy.

He released Caasser and rubbed his back and shoulders to ease his breathing more. The pranks and tricks might not stop, but Nimbulan had earned Caasser's trust.

They had eventually become friends and battle comrades. Until that fateful day when Nimbulan and Ackerly hadn't joined Druulin and his assistants in their last battle.

An older and more experienced Nimbulan recognized his vulnerability while he gasped and choked. Quinnault's rough handling emphasized his determination to get Nimbulan upright and breathing again. Nimbulan shifted his back and ribs, assessing any damage. Nothing permanent, maybe a bruise or two.

"My thanks," Nimbulan wiped his streaming eyes on his sleeve. Caasser hadn't been so generous.

"Come along now, Nimbulan. We have an entire island to survey." De Tanos marched forward. He strode easily through the high underbrush, long legs stretching over small shrubs and hummocks.

"We need to build a fire and dry out before we catch the lung rot." Nimbulan hastened to catch up. The slight effort started a tickle in his chest again. He swallowed it and kept moving.

"Nothing dry enough to burn, except maybe some old furniture inside the monastery. Did you bring a flint?"

"I'm a magician. I don't need a flint to start a fire. Even exhausted and half-drowned, I can start a fire just by thinking flames into the wood."

"Then we'd best get under cover and dry off. The sun is coming out, but it's too weak and too late in the year to be much help. You need a drink? You sound a little hoarse."

"No I do not need a drink. I've already drunk half of the river."

"There's a well in the monastery. We'll have to test the water to make sure it's still sweet."

"Well, I won't test it by drinking it, that's for sure."

"Stop complaining, old man, this is the start of a truly great adventure that could change the history of Coronnan." Quinnault fairly bounced over the rough ground.

"I'm an aging magician, not an old man. That gives me the right to be as crotchety as I want."

Quinnault stopped short and stared at his companion. "Crotchety, yes. Interfering and stagnant, no. I hope you have something solid to experiment with. Coronnan needs innovation. Soon."

"Hmph," Nimbulan snorted as he passed the lord on the narrow trail. He glimpsed stone buildings within the dense overgrowth. Eagerness replaced his preoccupation with small ailments. He forged ahead faster than his abused lungs could manage.

He paused to catch his breath just as a ray of sunshine

broke through the cloud cover. Brilliant blue beams of magical light reflected off glistening paving stones in front of the old monastery.

"Stargods preserve us! What is that?" Quinnault crossed himself, paused, then crossed himself again.

"Something special. Something very powerful," Nimbulan gasped. "Only ley lines glow that shade of blue." He forged ahead, anxious to discover the source of the strange light.

"Hold on, old man. This could be dangerous. There are rumors of ghosts and demons haunting his island." Quinnault grabbed Nimbulan's sleeve.

"I'll protect us with magic, boy." Power began tingling through Nimbulan's boots into his feet. Eagerness lifted his spirits and urged him to run. Energy coursed upward through his legs, into his belly and chest. The staff vibrated and stood upright on its own. His heart beat strong and true. All lingering coughs faded from his lungs. His eyes focused sharply.

He watched sap draining from leaves into tree trunks; saw individual drops of moisture in the air; knew every different rock that had crumbled to form the dirt at his feet.

New sounds entered his ears. Distant birdsong, the whoosh and sigh of the river lapping its banks, worms crawling beneath the surface of Kardia Hodos. The moon and stars danced through the universe, beckoning him to join their balanced movements.

His vision in the void took shape before his eyes. This time the magicians stepped back and watched rather than distorting the patterns. The lords danced in harmony with the Great Wheel of sun and moon and stars. . . .

"This is better than an overdose of Tambootie," he whispered in awe.

"What do you see?" Quinnault remained behind him looking anxiously right and left.

"I see the source of all magic. Come, boy, let's find out what other miracles this abandoned monastery shelters."

"Slowly, Nimbulan. We don't know what kind of traps lie hidden, nor what drove the last inhabitants away."

Nimbulan shrugged his agreement. "You go left, I'll go right, but stay within sight." He pointed directions with his staff, but the tool jerked back to the pool of blue between each gesture.

"We stay together, or we don't go."

"Oh, all right." Nimbulan stepped onto a fat ley line to his right and followed it toward the pool of glowing blue. With each step, he sensed the power in the ley line increasing. The line itself grew wider until he placed his feet side by side and still saw blue around the edges. "*Stargods!* I've seen smaller parapets in Castle Krej where Kammeryl d'Astrismos holes up every winter. Ley lines are supposed to be as fine as spider silk."

"I've never truly seen a ley line before." Quinnault turned in a circle, gaping at the lovely blue glowing beneath the Kardia's surface.

"Can you draw the power into you, de Tanos?" Nimbulan's skin began to itch with the magic he hadn't unleashed yet. His staff glowed with power. There was so much of it!

"My feet and fingers tingle. Is that the magic?"

"Yes. Yes. Try something, Quinnault. A simple spell. Anything. See if the massive amounts of power fuel your talent where small ley lines can't."

"I can't think of anything to do."

"Something useful. Shift some of these shrubs to the side and make a path."

Quinnault closed his eyes and screwed his face up in concentration.

Nimbulan watched the plants in front of them. None moved. "Open your eyes, de Tanos. Stare at the fibers of each plant and think them in a different place."

"I . . . I've never been able to move anything before. Not even a simple transport."

"Have you always closed your eyes to try the spell?"

"Yes. It's easier to concentrate."

"Then try it with your eyes open!"

The young lord stared at a small tuft of grass. He clenched and opened his fists rhythmically. The blades of greenery wiggled and waved to the right but didn't move.

"Again. You've got the essence of the plant listening to you. Now be more persuasive. Draw the power up through your body and out your hand. Point at the grass."

Quinnault lifted his left hand slowly, index finger extended toward the tuft in question. Again the blades wiggled and straightened.

Nimbulan resisted the urge to help the lord. He needed to know if the vast reserves of power on this island could turn minor talents into major ones. Quite possibly, after having experienced a large ley line, de Tanos would be able to find and use lesser ones in other places.

And once awakened, could he learn to combine his power with another's?

"I don't think I can do this." Quinnault bent over, bracing himself on his knees and panting.

"Maybe you think too much."

"It's like a wall grows between me and the grass."

"I've heard better excuses from first-year apprentices. We'll try again later. After we've seen the source of these ley lines and the monastery. I do hope the roof is sound." But it didn't have to be. With all this power surging through his body, he could repair any damage with a thought.

Together they walked onward. Youthful vigor put a bounce in Nimbulan's steps. He wanted to dance with joy and energy. He felt as young as Quinnault. Younger. As young as Myrilandel.

"I'm suddenly quite hungry. Do you suppose there are any late brambleberries left?" Quinnault stopped to inspect the thorny vines. Two overripe berries fell into his hand. Both splattered against his palm, too swollen with rainwater to hold their shape.

"You are hungry because you spent a great deal of energy while trying to transport that tuft of grass. Walk on the ley line. It will replenish you."

"I can't see it anymore. The blue is gone."

"No, it's not. It's fatter and stronger than ever!"

"I can't see it . . . or sense the power anymore."

A shadow passed over the watery sun. Both men looked up. The clouds parted, revealing a bright rainbow. The arcing prism drifted until it ended directly in the center of the pool of blue ley lines. A shower of sparks rose to greet the colored light.

"I've never seen a rainbow move while I'm standing still." Nimbulan raced forward to inspect the phenomenon. Large boulders and small creeks diverted his path to the east. The low stone building built around three sides of the pool blocked his view.

A path of sorts seemed to lead him to a doorway in the center of the south wall of the building. His next step sent him flying backward into a bed of thistles. The plants stung his hands and neck and poked through his clothes. His staff lay ten feet in front of him.

What kind of force was strong enough to separate him from his staff?

"Nimbulan!" Quinnault helped him up with strong hands beneath Nimbulan's shoulders. He brushed some of the excess mud from Nimbulan's already filthy clothes. "What happened?"

"I don't . . . don't know." Nimbulan clutched his temple to keep the world from spinning away from him. His free hand came up, palm open and receptive to power of any sort. "One minute I was on solid ground, the next I was flying through the air."

(You trespassed where your kind are not welcome.) A shadowy mist rose up between the two men and the monastery.

"Who are you?" Quinnault addressed the air. "I am lord of this island. This is my land, and I may walk where I will! Show yourself to your rightful lord."

(I recognize no lord. I am the guardian of the beginning place.) The mist, crowded with gray and purple shadows, shaped itself into the vague outline of a man, twice the height of a normal man. *(I guard these hallowed grounds against all who would misuse the power that begins and ends here. The Stargods gifted this power to the peoples of Kardia Hodos for the good of all. I guard against misuse—intentional or accidental. Begone!)*

A circling wind wrapped around and around Nimbulan and Quinnault de Tanos, driving them back the way they had come. Back toward the raging river that would drown them.

Nimbulan fought the wind with an image of calm within his mind. The tornado battered his defenses. He dug in his heels. The shadowy spirit threw slates from the roof at him. He enclosed himself and de Tanos in his strongest magical armor.

Gradually the assault lessened. Nimbulan sensed that the guardian of the monastery merely gathered his energy for his next attempt to rid the island of the magician and the lord.

Nimbulan pulled bits of verse together for his plea, as if they were a spell. Since this creature seemed to be made of magic, he'd address him as magic.

> *"Peace we seek,*
> *here and now,*
> *for strong or meek.*
> *Peace we wish,*
> *for all to kiss."*

The spirit paused. The shape shifted enough to suggest a man tilting his head in consideration. Did he recognize the human tradition of a kiss of peace to seal a treaty and forgive past battles?

"We come in peace. I seek a way to bring honor and good back into the use of magic," he shouted to the four cardinal directions and four elements. In his mind he saw them bound in harmony with all humanity, mage and mundane alike. His staff returned to his hand, passing through the guardian.

The wind slackened. *(How can I believe you?)* The spirit drifted and reformed directly in front of Nimbulan. Some of the shadows lightened, no longer carrying the menace of darkness. *(You directed this honorable lord to clear a path by magic when he need only look with his eyes for an existing path.)*

"I sought only to test his powers, as I must test many things before I find a way to end the wars that destroy Coronnan."

(You seek peace when all around you know nothing but war?)

"We seek peace. We mean no harm to you or the power you guard so diligently. We ask only for time to experiment with the power—to find a way for magicians to band together in neutrality. Only then can we make honor, ethics, and education our priority rather than war."

"Mewlppp! Mewlppp!" A winged form circled their heads. "What a strange cry. Too large and bulky to be a bird.

So black it seems to absorb light." Quinnault shaded his eyes with one hand as he looked up. "What creature have you sent to us, Spirit?"

(You will be tested first. Only those found worthy may use the beginning place.)

The beast and the mist collided and burst into a column of fire. The flames spun in place, then sped directly toward Nimbulan.

Chapter 8

The column of flame engulfed Nimbulan in an explosion of magical energy. Blue sparks invaded his eyes. Each one carried a memory of minor misdeeds, lies, and careless words that had wounded another.

He remembered a time when he and Ackerly had ventured into a village marketplace. Druulin had forbidden them to leave the tower until they had finished a long and boring series of chores. But they had slipped away early anyway.

A band of Rovers was reputed to be entertaining the farmers and shepherds. The Rovers had brought their racing steeds as well. Every man with a steed had met the challenge of a series of races. Betting ran heavily on the local steeds, known winners.

"We can make some money, Lan. Then we can buy some real food at the market," Ackerly urged his friend.

"I don't know, Acker. Betting an illusory coin on a race that we fix . . ." Nimbulan hesitated.

"What's the harm in making a plow steed feel heavy and weary so he won't run? I tell you it's a sure thing."

Just then, Nimbulan's stomach had growled, reminding them both that Druulin had forgotten to buy flour for bread. None of the apprentices had had breakfast.

"We might make enough to buy a warm cloak or an extra blanket, too," Ackerly said. "It will be easy, Lan. No one will know."

"If it's so easy, why don't you do it, Acker?" Nimbulan wanted the reassurance of his friend's participation. He was only ten and Ackerly was two years older, two years wiser and more experienced, though they were both new to Druulin's tower. Ackerly should be able to carry out his own plans and take the consequences if anything went awry. "What if we get caught?"

"We won't be caught. Who can tell that you used magic? None of these mundanes have enough imagination to think we'd interfere."

In the middle of the race, the plow steed suddenly lifted his tail and relieved the heaviness in his gut. The smelly addition to the smooth meadow brought laughter and jeers from the onlookers. The farmer beat on his steed with fists and boot heels to no avail. The steed added a long hot stream of urine to the growing pile of manure.

The farmer spotted the two magician apprentices cheering on the Rover steed as it crossed the finish line, barely winded. He also saw the large number of coins the boys collected from disgruntled locals. He grabbed a whip from a drover and ran after the two boys. Men who had lost good money on the bet took up the hue and cry. Ackerly pocketed the coins and dodged into the brothel tent where a series of semi-outraged squeals followed the passage of intruders.

Nimbulan didn't have the courage to peek into the tent let alone lead a parade of angry farmers through it. He ducked behind a huge pile of jacko squash. A little orange tint to a delusion disguised him as just another ball in the display. Until the vendor tried to lift his head off his shoulders and sell him to Druulin. . . .

He cringed inwardly with the remembrance. Other misdeeds flashed through his memory. Guilt brought tears to his eyes. But regret over Keegan's death outweighed all of his other indiscretions combined.

The sparks turned healing green. His onerous self-blame faded. Druulin's inattention and cruelty had driven his apprentices to seek food and warm clothing elsewhere, any way they could. Nimbulan's grief for his lost apprentice remained at the front of his regrets. He was responsible for the boy's upbringing. He should have seen Keegan's unbridled ambition and burning impatience.

The tiny bits of flame swirled around him faster and faster, fed by his guilt. He became the center of a massive vortex of burning flame. The tremendous circular wind threatened to rend him limb from limb.

He cried out in psychic agony.

A wall of power slammed into his jaw and sent him flying backward.

The vortex died as rapidly as it sprang up.

He landed flat on his back. Pain jarred his bones the full length of his spine. His lungs expelled air in a sharp *whoosh,* leaving him stunned and unable to breathe.

The flames dissolved into a pile of ash. No sign of the flying black creature or the shadowed spirit remained. Was it only yesterday he had watched Keegan die in the same manner? He choked back a lump that lodged in his throat.

"What happened?" Quinnault shook his head spasmodically as if clearing his vision. "Are you all right?" He reached a hand down to assist Nimbulan to his feet.

"I don't know. What was that creature?"

"The guardian or the flywacket?"

"Flywacket?" A smile tried to break through Nimbulan's shock and discomfort.

"A flying black cat. What else should I call it? It sounded as if it were crying for help. 'Mwelp.' Help?" Quinnault looked up in the direction the creature had come from.

"Who knows what strange cries such a creature would make." Nimbulan weighed the sounds in his mind. "Mwelp, mwelp." Just sounds.

"I'm certain that the creature was crying for help, Nimbulan. The look in its eyes, just before it crashed into the guardian, was a plea for help."

"Of course it needed help. It had lost control of its flight path. If every joint in my body didn't hurt, I'd laugh. Just yesterday Lord Kammeryl said that magicians cooperating was like wishing for flywackets and dragons. The men on the battlefield said they saw a dragon. You saw a flywacket here. What other miracles await us?"

Probably just a fledgling eagle. Maybe a Khamsin eagle strayed from the desert and its parents, he told himself. Others could indulge in superstitions and omens. He had a kingdom to save and a system of magic to rewrite.

"I don't know if 'twas a miracle or not. I'm still dizzy from the whirlwind the guardian kicked up." Quinnault shook his head again, pressing fingers to temples. Gradually his eyes cleared of disorientation.

"So am I." Nimbulan stretched each muscle, testing for

injury. He prodded a few tender spots and rotated his shoulders seeking more specific information. "Nothing broken. I'm just shaken and sore. How do you fare, boy?"

"I believe I'm unharmed—a little sore in places. But my feet are curiously numb."

"Mine, too, now that I think about it." Nimbulan looked at his boots. A miasma of ash seemed to float a hand's span above the ground in a perfect circle. Two tall men could stretch out in a line across the diameter. He scuffed at the ash. A bitter smell rose around him. He wrinkled his nose against the unnatural scent. None of the ash moved. He lifted his left foot through the ash with some effort. There residue reformed in a thick covering beneath his raised foot, almost the texture of drying clay.

For a brief moment he caught a glimpse of bright silvery blue as his foot cleared the ash. He set his foot down again. It did not penetrate the covering. The blue winked out. He shifted his weight and lifted the other foot. Again that brief hint of many ley lines coming together. The lovely sight withdrew into hiding again as soon as his foot cleared the ash.

As he set his second foot back down, full feeling returned to his extremities.

Nimbulan looked around before darting out of the now gray circle. "Step clear, Quinnault. Quickly." The ash rapidly solidified beneath him. The young lord leaped free just as the residue hardened into a thick mortar.

"How'd we get into the courtyard of the monastery?" Nimbulan watched for any imperfection in the hardening ash. It looked like a giant piece of slate set as a single paving stone over the courtyard.

"I think the explosion threw you here. I followed as soon as the flames let me pass."

Low stone buildings with sharply pitched roofs of slate surrounded them on three sides. The fourth side of the square looked upon a narrow causeway connecting the island to a larger landmass about three hundred paces distant. The River Coronnan churned through the passage, eating away at the natural bridge.

"I must meditate on these events, my lord. But first let's examine the buildings. The guardian seems to have left us passage to them while denying us access to the pool of ley lines." Only then did he realize the power no longer flooded his body. He couldn't see a trace of the spiderweb of ley lines normal to the rest of Coronnan.

(You must find a different source of magic before peace is possible,) the guardian said deep inside Nimbulan's mind. No other trace of the spirit remained.

Ackerly watched a knot of common soldiers moving toward Magician's Square within the army camp. Three uniformed men seemed to lead the growing procession of excited soldiers, officers, and camp followers. Male voices undulated upward from normal bass tones to cracking boyish squeaks. The sound beat at his ears. He pulled his magical armor around him. He might not be able to weave major battle spells, but armor was essential to anyone serving a Battlemage.

Breathing carefully to maintain protection, he sought another spell that honed and defined the words flying around the volatile group of people. While Nimbulan and Lord Quinnault explored the river islands on some private quest, he, Ackerly, must deal with these petitioners.

"I saw it. I swear!" A fair-haired young private raised his voice above the babble. 'Twas his voice that squeaked as it gained in volume. He probably wasn't old enough to have his vocal cords truly settled.

"You three been sneaking extra rations of ale from the cook's supplies again?" a grizzled sergeant bellowed. "Heard there was a break-in at the kitchen tent this morning."

"We investigated the break-in! *We* chased the thief." Fists on hips, a black-haired giant stopped in front of the sergeant, daring the man to doubt his word. Few men would question the man who stood head and shoulders above average soldiers. The breadth of his shoulders and diameter of his upper arms proclaimed his strength. Ackerly wondered if his mind was as muscle-bound as his body.

The crowd flowed around the tall man and the sergeant until they met the boundary of the magicians' enclave. They stopped between the hospital and the supply tent, unwilling to enter the area without invitation.

Ackerly waited to see if they would go any further.

Some of the men, more curious than brave, nudged the squeaky-voiced youngster and his slightly older companion forward. The two privates stumbled across the invisible boundary. They looked anxiously right and left. The giant joined them. All the others remained firmly on their side of the imaginary line of separation.

For a brief moment, pride swelled in Ackerly's chest. The other magicians might look down upon his minor talent, but these people respected him for having any talent at all!

"What did you see that brings so many to the private enclave of magicians?" Ackerly pitched his voice to carry across the compound and into the ears of all those who babbled as well as the few who had spotted him standing beside the large blue pavilion.

Silence descended as the crowd stood shocked by his words. Many crossed themselves as they stared at him with gaping jaws and wide eyes.

I may not be a great magician, but I am far above these mundanes.

"Step forward, my sons." He beckoned to the trio of privates at the front of the group. "Tell me your tale. The truth never hurt anyone."

"We found the witchwoman stealing supplies," the middle soldier said. He lifted his head proudly, almost defiantly.

"Theft is a matter for your sergeant."

"But she's a witch, one of you."

"So she is. What did you do when you found her stealing supplies?"

"We chased her." The middle private continued to speak. Clearly, the boyish one and the giant looked to him for leadership.

"And . . . ?" Ackerly allowed a little kindly pink to tinge his aura. He schooled his posture and expression to radiate trust.

"That black cat, her . . . ah, her familiar was with her. It spread wings and flew."

"I saw it, too," the boy chimed in.

The giant nodded vigorously.

"Cats cannot fly," Ackerly said.

"This one did."

"Flywackets are creatures out of legend." A *flywacket!* A mighty portent of strange events to follow. Ackerly began thinking in terms of the money to be made from a flywacket.

He nearly bounced in his excitement. The old books he studied to help Nimbulan create spells spoke frequently of flywackets and other winged creatures thought to be extinct. A *flywacket!* Three men had a confirmed sighting.

If Moncriith heard about this portent of demons, he'd stir up a lot of unrest. Mundanes always paid well for a magician to settle chaos.

"Dragons are mythical, too, but we saw one on the battlefield yesterday." The crowd shouted unanimous agreement with the boyish private.

"We shall see if you speak the truth. Sighting a magical creature can only be verified by magic." Ackerly fought to maintain his dignified, slightly disapproving demeanor.

Dramatically he spread his arms wide and slightly above shoulder level. With a blink of his eyes and fierce concentration he transported his staff into his right hand. The crowd gasped in awe.

Good. Let them think he had as much magic as Nimbulan and was more than just an errand boy. They'd treat him with respect next time he requested a service or bumped into them in camp.

"Let those who claim this magical sighting step forward, clear of all the others." He swelled his voice and lifted it to reach far beyond normal human limitations. The crowd flowed backward. The three privates each took two hesitant steps forward. Ackerly nodded his acceptance of the increased separation.

He took a deep breath to clear his lungs. A second breath cleansed his brain. The third put him in touch with the void, the deepest trance he could achieve on his own. None of the onlookers needed to know the strain on his back and thigh muscles to remain upright. Trances weren't easy for him.

Nimbulan wouldn't have wasted the magic to perform this task. A few tricks of crossed eyes and decisive questions by the Battlemage would set the three to babbling uncontrollably.

Ackerly wanted the magic to prove the men honest or tricksters. He didn't have enough magic to *not* use it whenever possible.

Within the trance, Ackerly gathered power in his belly until it expanded throughout his chest and flowed down his arm into the staff. The flowing grain of the wood glowed blue with brilliant green sparks all along the length. He pushed more power into the staff until it rose of its own accord and pointed at the three men.

Sweat broke out on his brow. His shoulders trembled with the strain of maintaining the flow of power. He didn't have the ability or skill to tap a ley line to fuel the magic. Only his own stamina produced the energy for this spell. He'd have to finish soon or drain himself of all strength.

He almost wished the Tambootie worked for him. He could use some enhancement right now.

More power into the staff. The wood glowed with heat, burning his hand. More power still and the blue light shot from the end of the magical tool into a cloud of sparkling dust that settled upon the soldiers. Blue truth glowed around their heads in a brilliant aura for all to see.

"Ooo!" a camp follower in a patched green dress cooed. She reached a hesitant hand to capture some of the glowing dust. "So pretty." She sprinkled the dust in her hair and pranced in front of her customers.

Ackerly lowered his staff to the ground and leaned heavily upon it. His arms and legs trembled with fatigue.

"If any of you had lied, the truth spell would have turned red and burned right through you, leaving only a skeleton," he said. An exaggeration to be sure, but such demonstrations kept the crowd honest. None of them would ever dare lie to Ackerly again. They might even pay him to find out if a comrade lied. That was worth the fatigue and hunger that gnawed at his belly and brought stabbing pains behind his eyes.

"What should we do about the flywacket?" The sergeant stepped forward, ready to stand by his men now that they were proved truthful.

"Did you capture it or the girl?" Ackerly asked.

"No. They disappeared without leaving a trail."

"Which direction?"

"East."

Moncriith was headed east. If the girl and her familiar could be found, the Bloodmage would be the one to root them out of their hiding place. How could he make Moncriith pay for this information?

"Send a small patrol with tracking dogs that way. Report

back here if you find anything. Anything at all. If you find nothing, return here at this hour tomorrow. I must discuss this with the other magicians." He bowed deeply and stepped back toward the tent. He wished he could fade into the shadows and disappear like Nimbulan could. Like the witchwoman seemed to have done.

But he couldn't. He could only retreat like an ordinary man.

Chapter 9

"**W**hy don't we wait for torches and assistants?" Quinnault de Tanos remained three steps behind Nimbulan as the magician measured the long corridor with his paces. Pale yellow sunlight pierced the interior gloom in long streaks through the narrow windows.

"I can see fine," Nimbulan replied. "Sixty-seven . . . sixty-eight . . . sixty-nine. I want to find the kitchens. Maybe someone left some food. Seventy . . . seventy-one . . . seventy-two paces," he said.

They'd found a motheaten blanket, probably threadbare before the priests left, upon a stone bed carved into one of the small cells. Nimbulan had stumbled over a broken sandal in the bathing chamber. Nothing else remained. No furniture, no clothing or linens or decorations. Nothing.

"How long has this place been empty?" Nimbulan asked as he tried the door handle in the middle of the long passageway. He couldn't move the latch with brute strength. Briefly he wondered if magic would remove the weight of years and rust on the mechanism.

"My father explored the place as a teenager. My grandfather mentioned once that he might remember someone living here during his childhood. Caretaker, squatter, or priest, I have no idea." De Tanos turned in circles as he walked, surveying the masonry and the view from narrow arched windows. Even the storm shutters had been removed.

"Help me with this door, please." Nimbulan stood straight and rubbed his shoulder where he had shoved against the wooden panels.

Together they leaned their combined weight into the door while Nimbulan wiggled the latch with a releasing spell. The handle lifted, but the door remained firmly closed.

"We can come back later with tools and more men, Nimbulan," Quinnault said. "The kitchens should be in one of the wings, near an end, not in the center. No sense in burning the entire structure if a cooking fire blazed out of control."

"Yes. Logical. But this secured door puzzles me. Every other door is wide open to the wind and the elements. The stone beneath each window is heavily damaged by repeated rain and sunlight. What is so special behind this door that it alone is locked and protected?" He stared at the door one more time, trying to pry its secrets free of the closed panels.

No images stirred his imagination.

He paced to the other end of the corridor. Seventy-two steps. The closed room sat in the exact center of the monastery.

"Did anyone ever offer a reason for the priests leaving this place?" He hastened to catch up with Quinnault who had turned into the eastern wing of the one-story structure. Only the central portion of the U-shaped building rose to a second story. They hadn't discovered access to basements. On these islands, the water table might be too high to allow digging a deep foundation.

"I have heard only rumors of the haunting. Was the guardian spirit a ghost?" Quinnault poked his head into another empty room, this one larger than the individual cells of the residential wing—a refectory perhaps?

"It didn't act like a ghost. Most spirits of the dead are rather lost and bewildered, seeking guidance to the void between the planes of existence."

Keegan would have been a ghost without Nimbulan's help. *Why, Keegan? Why did you make me kill you?* The pain was still too new and raw to dismiss. The guardian had relieved his other annoying little guilts, but not that one. He must have done something wrong in bringing up the boy.

"The kitchen is through here." De Tanos led the way through a low doorway at the end of the corridor.

Nimbulan added up his mental count of the length of the corridor. Forty-eight paces. The east and west wings were the same size. The south-facing central wing was almost twice that length as well as double in height.

Three narrow stairs brought him down into a room that took up half the wing. Two massive fireplaces, one on each outside wall showed sooty stains around and above the hearth. They'd been swept clean of ashes, but no amount of scrubbing would remove the smoky stains. Kindling and firewood lay neatly prepared for the touch of a flame. Long worktables stretched down the center of the room, clean and clear of equipment or debris. The scrub sinks were equally clean and empty.

Someone had taken time to clean and tidy up—as if they didn't want to leave a mess for the next cook.

Quinnault's footsteps echoed eerily across the stone flooring. Nimbulan tried to walk more silently. The extreme emptiness of the entire building suddenly struck him. Noise of any kind seemed out-of-place.

Nimbulan forced himself to speak in normal tones rather than whisper. The vast emptiness made the fine hairs on the back of his neck stand up.

Had the guardian spirit come back?

He looked around. No writhing mist awaited them.

"The last inhabitants weren't attacked and driven out. Not if they took time to clean the kitchen. Perhaps a plague decimated their numbers and they combined with another facility." Quinnault opened cupboards to reveal more emptiness.

"Perhaps. A hot, wet summer could breed any number of diseases in stagnant pools among these islands." Nimbulan drifted toward the pantries and storerooms at the west end of the room.

"My people have never suffered any plagues living on the islands or nearby shoreline. Summers are either hot and dry or cool and wet. But the river is constant. The tides from the Great Bay keep the level fairly regular, regardless of rainfall or snowmelt."

"We must search further for answers. Perhaps another monastery has records. De Tanos, can you light the fire someone so kindly left us? I'm still rather damp and chilled."

"Not without a firestone and tinder. Is there a firebox around? My magic is too minimal to generate flames."

"What can you do? That's the first spell I learned." Nimbulan stomped back to the hearth. An image of flames dancing merrily among the kindling brightened his mind. With a snap of his fingers and two words to trigger the spell, he transferred the image from his mind to the reality of the hearth.

Flames licked eagerly at the dry wood.

"I never wanted to be a magician. I only wanted to be a priest. When I try very hard, I can pick up people's thoughts. It's so much work though, I haven't tried since I passed the preliminary examinations." Quinnault didn't drop his head in shame at his paltry talent.

Ackerly would have.

Nimbulan smiled at the comparison. Successful magic was as much a matter of attitude as talent. De Tanos would have been a very good priest, and his magic—the ability to help people confide their troubles so he could find ways to help them—would have grown. Ackerly's talent, though stronger than the lord's, hadn't improved one bit in thirty years of constant practice, because he wanted to have more rather than work to improve what he had.

Too bad Ackerly had no respect for his wonderful talent as an administrator. Nimbulan and his apprentices depended upon Ackerly every day.

"At least you can build up the fire while I poke around the pantry, Quinnault. There might be more wood in the firebox by the back door."

The pantry door opened as easily as all of the others, except the center room. Again, Nimbulan found shelves and cupboards swept clean. "Do you know what's really missing? Cobwebs and mice droppings. It's almost as if someone cleans this place from top to bottom frequently."

"Maybe the guardian kept the vermin out as well as people." De Tanos leaned against the pantry door, blocking what little light filtered in from the kitchen. The three high windows in the outside wall offered little illumination.

"Possibly, or . . ." Nimbulan sniffed the air and stamped his feet. "I wish that pool of ley lines hadn't been barricaded. I sense magic of some sort, but I can't tell the nature or source. Maybe there's a stasis spell on the monastery. Nothing changes until someone breaks the spell."

"In which case, our coming here, and the guardian's disappearance may have disrupted the magic field enough to erode the spell. Will the walls come tumbling down once the magic dissolves?" Quinnault looked anxiously at the thick stone walls surrounding them.

"I doubt the mortar will crumble so quickly. How's your fire?"

"Fine. Did you find anything in here?"

Nimbulan peered into the pantry. He held his left palm up and brought a hint of magic into his vision. The shadows took on definite lines, still black on gray, but with outlines and texture.

A single journey pack sat in the center of the middle wall of shelves. He approached the bundle with care.

"What do you see?" De Tanos moved into the room, one hand extended into the gloom to find obstacles before he tripped over them.

"A trap perhaps. I don't know. I am suspicious of something so conspicuous in an otherwise empty building." Nimbulan spread his hand above the pack. Tendrils of magic shot from his fingertips into the heavy leather seeking answers.

He shifted his vision to InterSight. Radiant shades of green surrounded the pack, indicating heat. The temperature beneath his fingertips did not change.

Something within the pack quivered in answer to his magic probe. Nimbulan traced the outline of the minute vibrations. A thin "string" of power drifted away from the core. When he touched it, an image of a closed door rose in his mind. A door very like the one in the center of the abandoned monastery.

"A trap or a clue, I'm not sure." He followed the now-glowing, green "string" around the pantry to the door, one finger extended just above it, maintaining the sensation of a long-dormant being rousing from sleep.

Quinnault walked behind him, two paces back. The lord kept one hand on the hilt of his short sword.

The magic led them through the kitchen, up the three steps to the corridor, and along the passageway to the intersection of the main hall. The image of a locked door grew stronger, more vivid.

"Curious. I've never seen a spell constructed so subtly."

"Is the guardian present in the spell?" Quinnault asked, looking around for the column of fire or mist.

"I can't determine the signature in the weaving. Only the presence of something that has waited a long time." Nimbulan paused at the locked door. The magic led through the keyhole. He touched the lock with his questing finger.

Again the pack flashed through his mind. This time the image hovered beside the lock.

The metal latch grew warm under Nimbulan's finger. "If I'm following the clues properly, we need to bring the pack here."

"It could be a trap."

"It could, but I don't think so. There is no hint of malice in this magic."

"But you said it was a subtle spell. The violent intent could be buried beneath layers of innuendo and diverting spells."

"You learned your magic theory well, Quinnault de Tanos," Nimbulan said. "But I am a Battlemage. I am well-versed in all forms of destructive magic. No. This spell has the feel of curiosity, intelligence, and a quest for knowledge."

"Why don't we leave this for another day when you have the backup of your assistants and apprentices?" de Tanos asked. "The day grows late. If we are to get off the island, we should start now."

"How? Our boat sank."

"The causeway is clear at low tide. There are farms and the family keep on the next island. I have other boats to take you back to camp."

"Why didn't you say so? Here I've been thinking we were stranded and would have to signal a fisherman with a fire after dark."

"Like as not, the fisherman would see the signal as evidence of haunting spirits and stay away."

"How long will the causeway be clear? I want to investigate this puzzle while we're here."

"Several hours. When the moon is full in spring and autumn and the tides run high, the passage can be dangerous, but not today."

"Good. Come with me. We need to bring the pack to the door. But it must not stray from the path of the magic I followed here."

Moments later, Nimbulan held the slight bulk of the pack

beside the lock. Slowly, testing for undue warmth or stabs of light, he pressed the old leather to the latch. A faint hum filled the corridor.

"What? Where?" Quinnault spun, belt dagger extended, seeking the source of the increasing noise.

Bouncing balls of green, blue, and unholy red witchfire joined the hum reverberating around the passageway.

Nimbulan dropped the pack, pressing his hands against his ears. He didn't quite dare close his eyes against the bright witchfire. He had the sense that while he watched them dart around, they wouldn't attack him.

Quinnault ducked a buzzing blue ball, slashing at it with the flat of his blade. The noise grew to an intolerable level. He dropped the dagger to press his hands against his ears. The clatter of metal against stone barely registered against the incredible whine of sound.

Suddenly the witchfire flashed and died. The hum ceased.

Nimbulan's ears rang in the silence.

The latch clicked open quietly.

He looked from the latch to the crumpled leather on the floor. Jerked meat and dried fruit spilled from the pack. He bent to touch the journey provisions. They seemed real.

The door opened a tiny crack. He pushed gently against the panels. The hinges didn't creak. No dust met his nose.

He looked closer. Light spilled into a vast room around the edges of many closed shutters. A sense of warmth and welcome surrounded him. He sniffed for magic and found only the special scent of vellum and leather.

"Books? Lots and lots of books!" He raced to the nearest window, throwing open the shutters. These, too, opened without protest or signs of age.

He turned slowly, holding his breath with anticipation. Walls and walls of books awaited him.

Chapter 10

"**Y**ou've returned at last." Ackerly scowled at Nimbulan. He had said he'd return before sunset, and so he had, barely. Ackerly's anxious waiting hadn't made the time pass faster, adding to his irritation.

"You won't believe the adventures I've had today, Ackerly. Lord Quinnault and I found the most amazing treasures." The Battlemage brushed past his assistant in the doorway to the large pavilion. The glowing aura of the setting sun behind Nimbulan's back followed him into the tent.

Ackerly shied away from the energy his friend radiated. That yellow-gold aura effectively barred Ackerly from sharing Nimbulan's thoughts and enthusiasms.

"Lord Kammeryl has been looking for you most of the day. Some amazing things have happened here as well." Annoyance bristled the hair on the back of Ackerly's neck. Nimbulan positively bounced as he walked. "Will you stop for a moment and listen, Lan? Maybe you need some Tambootie to settle you."

"I've never felt better, Acker. Send a page for Lord Kammeryl now. I need to tell him that you and I and the boys will be spending the winter away from his fortress. We leave as soon after dawn as Lord Quinnault can send a barge for our books and equipment. Books—" He trailed off in a kind of dazed reverie. His aura increased in size, if that was possible.

"We can't leave Lord Kammeryl d'Astrismos! He depends upon you for protection. We depend upon him for employment." Ackerly's supper formed a lump in his belly. What would he do for food and shelter away from the lord's stronghold? The thought of weathering the winter storms outside the snug warmth of his room near the kitchen filled him with dread. No more tasty tidbits pressed upon him by the scullery maid. No more stolen kisses and frantic fumblings with the wenches in the armory. No more gold paid out every moon.

"I'm taking a leave of absence from Lord Kammeryl to study and experiment, Ackerly. Lord Quinnault showed me an abandoned monastery today. The most amazing place. Intact. Good roof. No signs of wear or decay. Not even any cobwebs." Nimbulan started throwing books and pieces of arcane equipment into a pack without regard to efficiency or breakability. "Rollett, have you seen my oak wand with the river agate?" he called into the interior of the great pavilion.

"Your attention is needed here. Nimbulan. Three men reported seeing a flywacket. Three *confirmed* sightings. Do you realize the significance of that?"

"Yes, yes. I saw it, too. A wonderful omen that I belong in that monastery. It's perfect for my experiments. We'll need to recruit some new apprentices, and send an open invitation to trained magicians who genuinely desire peace. We're going to find a way to end these wars, Ackerly. I can feel it in my bones." He scratched his left palm, the one he held up to weave his spells, then moved to another collection of paraphernalia, stuffing it into a large sack.

"The men swear the flywacket was also the witchwoman's familiar." Ackerly dropped his voice, curious to see how his comrade reacted to that bit of news.

Nimbulan looked up from his frantic sorting of mirrors and powders and mathematical charts of the stars. "Impossible. Myrilandel keeps a black cat. I saw the beast—she called it Amaranth. It bore no signs of wings or beak or talons. Unlike the creature we saw today. What we saw was truly an omen from the Stargods."

"What if they saw a true flywacket? What if the shadows the men reported yesterday came from a dragon?" Ackerly asked.

"Illusions. The men were exhausted from the battle. Now where did I put that Khamsin eagle quill? It's my favorite pen."

Ackerly dropped his head in disappointment. Usually Nimbulan listened to him. Tonight he was too full of his own plans to heed anything but the direst shocks. Ackerly vowed to use a heavier dose than usual of the Tambootie on Nimbulan's supper. Maybe then the Battlemage would listen.

"Maalin," Ackerly called to the dark-haired young man loitering near a small two-man tent beside the large pavilion. "Maalin, inform my lord Kammeryl that Nimbulan and I will attend him shortly." The apprentice nodded as he hastened to the other side of the camp.

"We haven't time to waste discussing Kammeryl's latest female companion. And you know he won't hear anything else we say until he gives us a blow-by-blow description of his latest bedding." Nimbulan shuddered slightly with distaste.

Ackerly refused to flinch. They both knew the lord's tastes. Distastes was a more accurate word. But feeding the man's addiction to pretty virgins gave Kammeryl d'Astrismos a feeling of godlike power and thus blinded him to manipulation by the magicians. Ackerly needed Kammeryl in a fog of sexual satiation to keep his treasury open.

"Just send a message to Lord Kammeryl. Compose it for me, will you? Are all of the books on history and moon phases in the trunk?" Nimbulan turned back to his sorting without waiting for an answer.

"What am I supposed to tell *our* lord?" Ackerly gritted his teeth. Nimbulan wasn't listening to him at all—wasn't paying attention to anything but his own thoughts spinning in a mad whirl.

"Tell him anything. You're better at diplomatic notes than I am. Oh, and tell Myrilandel to be ready to travel with us. I'm looking forward to training her. She has the most amazing talent."

"The witchwoman escaped."

"What do you mean, escaped? She couldn't escape. She wasn't a prisoner."

"She left, then. Secretly. Without notice. And she tried to steal supplies. That's when the guards saw her flywacket. That's when she ran westward in the same direction as Moncriith." He smiled to himself at the misdirection. Nimbulan wouldn't find either Moncriith or Myrilandel if he sought them. Moncriith would be free to act upon any information Ackerly chose to feed him, and Nimbulan wouldn't lose himself in his infatuation with the girl.

"I've got to stop her. She needs my help." Nimbulan dashed toward the door.

Ackerly stood firmly in his path. "No. We need to speak to Lord Kammeryl about his plans to follow Lord Hanic's army. We need to help spread the rumor that the flywacket was a message from the Stargods that the House d'Astrismos is their favorite to rule all of Coronnan."

"Get out of my way, Ackerly. I've much more important things to do than cater to Kammeryl's delusions of godhood."

"What is more important than catering to the whims of the man who provides you with food and clothing and a place to work as well as a generous salary? What is more important than his plans for Coronnan?"

"Peace." Nimbulan pushed past Ackerly.

"Peace will be the end of our kind," Ackerly whispered to himself. "And the end of our money." Nimbulan hadn't heard a word he said. No one ever did. No one had listened to him since he was thirteen and had failed his journeyman trials for the second time. . . .

"Fumble fingers!" Boojlin taunted Ackerly as they emerged from Master Druulin's private study. Boojlin had passed the first test set for them. He'd successfully lobbed a ball of witchfire out the window to ignite the scarecrow in a nearby field.

Druulin and Boojlin had laughed at the farmer's frantic attempts to extinguish the fire before it burned the entire field of corn.

Ackerly had failed the test. He couldn't "throw" anything with magic. He could retrieve personal items that he knew well, like his staff. But throwing eluded him.

"How can you expect to be a Battlemage if you can't throw something as simple as witchfire?" Boojlin continued his teasing. "You're a clumsy half-mundane and you'll never be anything more."

"You didn't do much better, Boojlin. You failed the second half of the test," Ackerly retorted. Boojlin hadn't been able to extinguish the witchfire he'd set. The farmer had lost almost half an acre to witchfire before Druulin stepped in and doused the flames with a counterspell.

"I'll be a better Battlemage than you will. When I master

the spell, I'll master the *whole* spell, not just the fun part," Ackerly retorted, not knowing what else to say.

"Will not!" Boojlin launched a torch at Ackerly. He ducked that missile and the books that followed him as he ran away.

Boojlin continued to pelt him with whatever objects came handy to his magic. Ackerly didn't stop running until he reached the kitchen in the ground level of the tall tower. His tormentor pelted down the spiral stairs, laughing at Ackerly's cowardice.

Until he ran into a yampion pie hovering at face level just inside the door to the kitchen.

"I might not be able to throw, but I can think ahead, Boojie." Ackerly wiped a pile of sweet pie filling from Boojlin's face with his index finger. He smiled as he licked his hand clean of the sweet treat. "Looks like no dessert for you tonight, Boojie. You ruined it for all of us. I'll have to tell Druulin precisely why he won't get his favorite pie tonight."

Caasser and Lan had laughed at the trick as Ackerly was forced by Druulin to clean the entire kitchen for wasting the pie. But Ackerly never forgot that he'd had to hold the pie in place with his hands until the last moment before Boojlin slammed into it because he didn't have enough magic to levitate it for long. He never forgot how all the others had passed their tests eventually, leaving Ackerly to clean up the messes they made.

"You don't appreciate me anymore than Druulin did, Nimbulan. I'm still cleaning up your messes."

"Excuse me." A short, wizened man of indeterminate years blocked Nimbulan's exit from his pavilion. "I understand you are looking for colleagues to join you in a new venture." The man bowed from the waist. A sign of respect for an equal.

He wore ordinary black trews and tunic and carried a black cloak or robe over his arm. His skin had yellowed with age, was seamed by a million wrinkles, some of them smile lines around his mouth and laugh lines near his eyes. Even now a mischievous twinkle glistened in his pale blue eyes, so pale they seemed almost colorless.

Like Myrilandel's eyes and hair.

The witchwoman was gone, fled of her own will. Nimbulan needed to go after her. . . .

He didn't have time to waste worrying about her.

Or regretting her absence.

"How did you know about this venture?" Nimbulan asked the old man warily.

"News travels fast among magicians." His smile quirked up enigmatically.

"Excuse me, Master Nimbulan, I have errands to run and chores to perform." Ackerly shouldered his way past the intruder. "I'll meet you in Lord Kammeryl's pavilion in a few moments."

"Yes, I'll join you there, Ackerly." Nimbulan didn't take his eyes off the stranger. "News must travel very fast among some magicians. I didn't decide to pursue this venture until a few hours ago and only announced it to my assistant now."

"Ah, but your delight in the project broadcast a psychic shout of glee across the heavens. I heard and sought you out." The old man bowed again.

"You must have been very close."

"Closer than you think."

"Do you have a name?"

"Yes. I am called Lyman in this existence."

"A strange way of giving your name. Do you, perchance, possess the unique ability to remember your previous existences or know the future ones?" Suspicion crawled over Nimbulan's skin. His need to scratch and worry at the itch was like his need for the Tambootie.

"Anything can be found in the void if only you know where and how to look, Nimbulan. Would you take me there to see if I am what I seem?"

"And what do you seem to be?" Maybe he should have asked what the old man pretended to be.

"I am merely an old magician, tired of war, as you are. I would use my remaining years in this life to seek peace. I choose to join you in the same quest, for I believe you have the answers, though you do not know it yet."

Nimbulan's suspicions dissolved, as if he'd poured water laced with oatmeal over his itchy skin. "Why do I trust you, Lyman?"

"Because I tell the truth. Finish your errands. I will join you on your island tomorrow morning." Lyman bowed again.

Nimbulan felt compelled to give the same gesture of respect.

Then Old Lyman backed up and dissolved into the mist.

"That's my trick, old man! Where'd you learn it?"

A soft chuckle in the distance was his only answer.

Dust motes drifting on a soft beam of sunlight penetrated Myri's awareness. She blinked rapidly several times, trying to remember.

"Where am I?" she asked the sunbeam. "Why did I come here?" She remembered running. Running from . . . something terrible but important. Why couldn't she remember what had happened to her? She wasn't home. That she knew. A vague image of Old Magretha crossed her mind. Home was a shack in the woods or the vague promise of the voices on the wind. This shelter . . . what was this shelter?

Behind the ray of light, she saw rock walls. Not the dressed stone of a man-made fortress, but the undulating flow of natural stone patterns. Yellow and gray layered upon each other in irregular widths. Light to the left. Dark to the right. A glow in the center.

She looked down to discover a neat fire ring and a fresh fish spitted over the coals. Her stomach growled, reminding her that she had caught the fish earlier. She had settled into this cave above a sheltered cove for the winter. The cave was nearly invisible from the sandy beach below, nestled into the shadow of the curving headland. She had run from something to this coastal refuge.

The sound of waves shushing against a sandy shore added itself to her growing picture of her campsite.

Campfires? Dozens of fires serving hundreds of men. An army. The face of a Battlemage who tried to be gentle with her. His green eyes promised protection.

She had run away from the camp. Run to . . . danger.

Danger that was past now.

"How long have I been here?" The sound of her voice echoing slightly within the cave reassured her that she still lived and wasn't lost in some void-induced dream.

No memory responded to her question. Only a sense of

fear and running. Quickly she checked the cave for others. She seemed to be alone.

Someone was missing. An emptiness yawned in her chest behind her heart.

"Who?"

She stretched her arms to her side, expecting to feel wings catch on the slight breeze coming in from the opening. The lift and surge of flight did not follow.

"Not me. I am Kardia-bound. Amaranth. Amaranth flies. Where is he?"

Shadows danced across the sunlight. Myri scrambled to her feet and looked out the mouth of the ancient sea cave. Gulls swooped and soared. A large bird dove into the waves and sprang free of the water with a fish in its beak.

The flying shapes were all too small and white. Myri searched the fluffy clouds and pale autumnal sky for signs of a bulkier black form. Nothing. She stretched her listening senses for Amaranth's mewling cry.

"Merwack." In the far distance. Faint and excited. *(We have tested him and found him worthy!)*

"Who? Who did you test and find worthy of what?" Myri almost laughed at Amaranth's excitement. His mental pictures of towering columns of mist and blue sparks didn't make sense. "Where have you been, Amaranth?"

She dug her toes into the flaking sandstone, stretched her arms as if for flight, and sent her mind on a straight line to Amaranth. Her mind blended with his and she found the freedom of flight she dreamed of so often. Up through the clouds. Up toward the blessed sun. The wind buffeted her. It smelled of salt and cold dampness. A storm gathered beneath her, preparing to assault the Great Bay. She rose above it. Seeking. Always seeking.

She reached out for him with her mind and her love. *We are together now. Come to me, Amaranth. I miss you. I need you, Amaranth.* Awareness of her Kardia-bound body layered on top of her illusion of flight. Finally a black spot appeared to her physical eyes far to the north and west.

Come, my precious Amaranth. Come and tell me all about your adventures, the test, and who you found worthy.

Gradually the black spot grew and took on the distinctive shape of a falcon. The bird broadened. Its tail lengthened and fluffed. Instead of a wickedly curved beak, she sensed a flatter cat's muzzle and whiskers.

"Amaranth." Myri sighed with relief. The one constant in her life. No matter what she forgot, how many days she lost in the void, Amaranth always returned to her.

"Meereek!" The flywacket faltered and lost elevation. Through his eyes, Myri saw a fish glittering in the waves below. Extreme hunger overcame them both. Together they dove to catch the enticing meal.

The vision of the fish vanished, replaced by the symmetrical grid of a fisherman's net. "Pull up, Amaranth." Fear lanced through her. She sent him strength along the line of her mind. "Release your wings, Amaranth. Catch the wind and fly upward, quickly." Her arms stiffened and rose in sympathy with the attitude he needed to assume.

Amaranth reached with his back claws to grasp the fish that wasn't there. His wings stretched and he rose with his prize. The dark strands of netting tangled around his hind legs, trailing backward into the waves. The weight of the saturated strands dragged him back.

"Drop it, Amaranth! Drop it before it pulls you beneath the water and drowns you."

As Myri watched, the net moved in the air currents to ensnare his front paws as well.

He fought the net, beating at it with his teeth and wing-tips as he strove for elevation.

"Come ashore, quickly." Myri caught her breath again, praying he had enough strength to fly the last little bit.

"Merwack," he chirped in a more normal tone. He stretched his neck forward, toward the sandy beach, still fighting the net.

Myri scrambled down the cliff face below the cave entrance.

Amaranth extended his talons and backwinged for landing. The net flew upward catching a wingtip and dragging it down.

Myri caught her breath, praying that Amaranth could land safely under his own strength.

The flywacket's left wing collapsed under the weight of the net. He plummeted to the beach below him.

Chapter 11

"**A**maranth!" Myri ran toward the tide line where salt-water lapped at the flywacket flailing about in the sand. The net tangled tighter with each flap of wing and thrash of foot.

He whimpered in growing frustration. The pain from the net tightening around his legs like a noose lashed her mind as well as his body.

"Stay still, Amaranth. I'm coming." She skidded the last few feet, landing on her knees.

At last she reached out with a single finger to touch his wing.

"Hisscht!" He warned her how much he hurt. His claws extended into full talons.

"Why did you go after that fish, my precious? You could have waited and shared mine," she said softly.

(*I had to. The hunger would not wait.*) The flywacket relaxed a little at the sound of her voice, retracting his claws. His eyes remained fearful and glazed with pain.

Memory of the hunger that had assaulted her at the moment of his dive puzzled her. She hadn't sensed the need for food in him a moment before that, only his excitement.

"You know I won't hurt you Amaranth." She spread her palm over his injury. Blue light glowed beneath her palm. Her talent pulled her toward the source of pain and repelled her at the same time. Energy drained from her arm into the flywacket with no apparent healing.

With a strong effort of will, Myri reined in her talent before she drained herself. The blue light dimmed. "That has never happened before. Why won't you accept the healing?"

(Your healing is grounded in the Kardia. I am a creature of the air. The power of the healing must come from those who fly.)

Myri untangled the net. It relaxed at her touch where a moment before it had seemed almost alive as it wound around and around Amaranth in ever tightening loops.

"You're only bruised and tired." She smiled at Amaranth. "Time and rest will do more for you than I can. But you must not use that wing until it is completely healed. I think your pride is damaged more than you are."

Amaranth sniffed with indignity. He gathered his feet beneath him and sat with his back to her, tail twitching. Keeping his damaged wing half-furled, he began his bath, carefully ignoring her.

"When in doubt, wash," Myri chuckled. "You'll feel better after a bath." She would, too. She couldn't remember when she'd last had the opportunity. "I wonder if the bay is warm enough to swim in."

"Not at this time of year," a deep male voice replied.

"Who are you?" Myri stood hastily. She searched the crescent beach for potential enemies, wishing she was higher to get a better view.

A solitary man stood about ten arm-lengths away. His smooth skin beneath a black, scraggly beard made him look to be about her own age. The squint lines around his dark eyes and weathered skin suggested a decade more in years.

"You're a Rover," she stated the obvious. Only the nomadic traders wore the garish color combinations of black trews and embroidered vest, red shirt, green neckerchief, and a purple head scarf beneath a broad-brimmed, black felt hat that shadowed his eyes. No man native to Coronnan would be caught dead with a large hoop earring piercing his left ear and a belt full of dangling coins from many countries.

"You don't know me. Surely every beautiful woman in these parts knows Televarn, by reputation if not in fact." He swept his hat off and held it across his heart. Every movement he made showed an enticing ripple of muscle beneath his shirt and trews. His limbs perfectly balanced the proportions of his torso. He moved with an easy grace. Even when standing still, he seemed about to step into a beautiful dance.

She wanted simply to stare at him.

Her fingers felt incomplete. She needed to reach out and caress his marvelous face, feel the smooth movement of his muscles beneath his flawless skin in order to become whole.

(He knows not how to tell the truth if a lie is more interesting.) Amaranth's voice broke through her mental fog.

No memory of this man stirred in her. Not unusual. Most of her memories of recent months had fled. An ache of loneliness formed in the center of her chest. If she had ever known this beautiful man, she didn't remember.

Distrust replaced the lonely ache. Only Amaranth remained a constant in her life and her memory. She trusted only Amaranth.

"Where did you come from, Master Televarn?" Myri stepped forward to stand between Amaranth and the stranger.

"The cove beyond that headland." He pointed over his shoulder, never taking his sight away from her. Every movement he made compelled her to watch him. "We always winter there."

"We?" she squeaked. "How many?" Her heart pounded loudly in her ears. Thoughts of spending the winter in her own snug cave halfway up the cliff vanished. A tribe of Rovers so close. . . . Her lungs labored at the thought of so many people invading her privacy. They would demand cures for endless small ailments. Her talent would compel her to help them time and time again until one of them met with a fatal accident or died of old age, or a disease she couldn't cure. Then they'd accuse her of murder and threaten her until she was forced to flee for her own life.

The pattern of life for witchwomen was always the same. Over the years, she and Magretha had met many such women, always on the move. "The next village will be kinder," they said. "If not that village, then the next one beyond that." Rarely did any of them spend more than a few seasons in each village.

She and Magretha had lingered in their last village for nearly two years. Two years of goodwill and mutual dependence before the villagers turned on her.

"Only my family winters in a cave in the next cove. A dozen or so." Televarn flicked his fingers in dismissal of the paltry number. "May I see your pet's injuries, witchwoman?" He stepped closer. His legs were long enough and strong enough to bring him dangerously close in three strides. His aura glowed with warm charm.

"Why do you call me that?" Suspicion flared within her. He was *too* beautiful. She remained where she stood, protecting Amaranth. She fluffed her skirts nervously, hoping the inquisitive flywacket would remain out of sight until he hid his wing.

"Who else keeps a flywacket *familiar*. Both of you seem to be faded from view, or blending with the morning shadows. Is something wrong, witchwoman?"

"I think you are mistaken. My cat is just a cat. He was curious and became entangled in a fishnet. Your net, perhaps?" A quick glance confirmed that Amaranth had his bruised wing safely folded beneath its protective fold of skin.

"Only old women and untried boys use nets. I have skills that charm fish onto my hooks and I reel them in by the dozen. Is he truly only a cat?" He stepped closer again.

"Stay where you are." She erected a little armor around herself and Amaranth.

"A witchwoman's duties include providing relief from all sorts of ills. I have an itch that needs to be scratched." He touched his crotch suggestively.

"Only a witchwoman of little power buys the loyalty of men with her body." She fought her instinct to run. Amaranth was still too tired and sore to follow.

"But I love all women. How could I betray any one of them?" Televarn held his hands out away from his body as if reassuring her he carried no snares or hidden weapons.

"Your women will always be jealous of your whores. They will poison the minds of other men against one they fear or dislike. Their whispers will make her a witch even though she isn't one. The men have the authority to order a burning of a witch in order to please their women." Myri nearly spat on his shiny black boot to keep him away.

Another man wished her death by burning. She knew that. Vague memories of a man in a faded red robe with a compelling gaze and charming voice flitted through her mind in ragged wisps. If that man happened to enter the district, the Rovers would sell him information. Rovers would sell anything. They'd also steal anything.

She strengthened the magic protection around Amaranth

and herself. A flywacket would fetch a high price in the right circles.

Which circles? She had encountered someone who would pay a fortune for her flywacket. They had tried to capture Amaranth. Who? Fruitlessly she searched her faulty memory. No other images sprang to mind. Her feet and arms ached to run and climb as far and as fast as she could.

She couldn't run. Amaranth needed her protection. He couldn't fly yet. Not with the bone-deep bruises he'd earned in his struggle with the net.

"Rovers value witchwomen for all of their talents. You needn't be jealous because you've heard I fathered a bastard or two in my wanderings. That just proves I could give you children as well. You look ripe for motherhood, witchwoman." Televarn continued to assess her attributes with knowing eyes. He reached out a hand, palm upward in entreaty. His slightly curved fingers silently begged her to join him.

She'd seen another man use a similar gesture to weave magic. A man in blue.

"I do not value the company of people, especially Rovers. I claim this cove. Go back to your own camp at once and do not return." She scooped up Amaranth and placed him on her shoulder. The need to stay in a place she knew would provide her with food and shelter for the winter vied with her need to keep people away from her.

She was so tired of running.

"The tide has turned, my exit around the headland is cut off." Televarn stepped closer yet. His eyelids drooped in sultry speculation. "You've fascinated me and kept me talking beyond the time of safe return."

"Then climb the hill." Myri strengthened her magical armor to repel him if he dared touch her.

"A steep cliff. 'Twill be a dirty and treacherous climb. I will stay with you until the tide turns again. You really want me to stay. Only your jealousy wants to send me away." He looked up, then flashed his dark eyes at her, delight and mischief glowing in their depths as if this were a familiar game with him.

She longed to reach out and touch his beckoning fingers. What would the crisp curls peeking out from beneath his head scarf feel like as she ran her fingers through them?

His eyes continued to hold her in place when she knew she should run. A curious numbness spread to her feet.

A woman could get lost in his eyes, with their thick fringe of black lashes. His voice slid over her senses like warm honey. Why had he wished him gone? He was so beautiful.

She'd been alone so long.

She'd known a man's touch. Four years now she'd danced the ritual around the Equinox Pylon at the beginning of spring. Each year she'd mated with a different man, three clumsy and hasty youths. One older, gentler widower seeking a new mate. But never had she conceived, so her Equinox partners hadn't invited her to share their lives or their beds again.

She might never know a man again if she sent Televarn away.

Magretha scorned her for enjoying the Vernal Equinox festival and the men. The old witchwoman claimed a man's loyalty was firmly rooted in scratching his itch, not in remaining faithful to any one woman. Magretha had been betrayed by a man before her face and back became scarred by a fire.

Filling a few hours with this man's company while exploring his beautiful body would result in no harm. She wouldn't conceive. Witchwomen never did. Televarn wouldn't own her despite his desire.

There had been another man who desired to own her. Tall, slender, older, wearing a blue magician's robe. He'd wanted her talent, not her body.

The man in the red robe wanted to possess her soul while he cast her body in the fire. She shuddered away from that memory.

This Rover wanted to possess her flywacket, and enjoy her body at the same time.

Who wanted her or valued her for herself?

She recognized the compulsion to love him for what it was, magic imposed by him rather than desire from within herself. Once she recognized it, she broke the spell by closing her eyes and turning her back on him.

"You should have considered your retreat before you ventured this far. Leave my beach any way you can. I care not if you fall or ruin your clothing. I care only to be alone." She started walking toward the cliff and her high cave as fast as the soft sand clutching her feet allowed.

With Amaranth still draped limply over her left shoulder, she reached for tiny finger and toeholds. Stretch, brace, cling. She mounted the sheer wall of sandstone smoothly. She forced her concentration away from the Rover's pretty eyes and into her climb. She forced her thoughts onto the fish that cooked slowly over the coals. She dared not lose herself in contemplation of weak sunlight glinting off layers of yellow and gray rock. Watching how her blood rose close to the skin beneath her fingernails, turning them lavender, wouldn't gain her the protection and solitude of the small cave she had claimed.

The sound of small stones tumbling in the far curve of the cliff made her pause. Balancing on tiny knobs of rock, she risked a look down and to the far right. Televarn mounted the cliff near where a volcanic headland jutted into the bay. The jagged rocks and slopes offered an easier climb than straight up the smooth sandstone where Myri sought the shelter of her cave.

The Rover glanced her way. A big grin split his face. His white teeth showed clearly against his tanned face and dark clothing. His hat lay against his back at a rakish angle, slung in place by a thong around his neck.

S'murghit, he was beautiful.

"I'll be back, pretty witchwoman. When you need a man, call my name into the wind." He raised a hand in salute.

The unstable rock beneath his other hand crumbled in his grip. He lost his precarious balance, windmilling his arms as he fell into mixed sand and gravel.

The incoming tide rushed at his unmoving head.

"Now I have to go rescue him." Myri sighed. "I'll never be rid of him." She knew she couldn't leave him. Her talent wouldn't allow her to ignore anyone who needed healing.

Chapter 12

"**W**hy do I have to sweep a clean floor?" Powwell, the newest apprentice, pouted at Nimbulan.

"Because we can't afford servants," Nimbulan replied. No need to tell the twelve-year-old boy that sweeping their new home was a test. He needed to know how long before the three recruits figured out how to manipulate the brooms with magic. They could all light fires with a concentrated effort. That ability had proved their inborn talent and gained them places as apprentices. None of them could yet move an object with his mind.

Their minds seemed equally closed to the concept of reading and ciphering. Only magicians were allowed, by law and by tradition, to use the arcane knowledge contained within letters and numbers. The newest boys refused to believe themselves worthy of this secret skill.

Nimbulan spent nearly all of his time coaxing the boys into learning. Not for the first time in the last few weeks, Nimbulan regretted his haste in seeking new apprentices and withdrawing to the monastery. He needed more help than Ackerly, Lyman, and his older apprentices offered. If he had other teachers to work with the boys, he could spend more time experimenting and cataloging the massive library.

"But why does the floor need to be swept at all? It's clean." The boy stared up at Nimbulan. A need to know poured forth from his gray eyes. Determination rode firmly on his shoulders.

Sunlight streaming in through the narrow windows added a glint of auburn to his muddy brown hair. More often than not, any trace of red hair accompanied magical talent.

Buried deep inside the boy's stubborn brain there must be intelligence, or he'd not have figured out how to start fires upon command rather than at random. Nimbulan had to draw it forth by devising ways to stimulate Powwell's curiosity rather than answering every question.

Powwell assumed Ackerly's posture when demanding an answer from Nimbulan when Nimbulan was lost in thought or distracted. He almost chuckled at the one thing the boy had learned as an apprentice.

Nimbulan bit his lower lip, resisting the urge to say, "Because I said so." Too often that had happened during his own training, and he'd wasted valuable lessons because he defied the statement and his tutor. He'd never given up defying Druulin in the all the years he had served the irascible old magician. Right up until the day he had died on the field of battle along with Boojlin and Caasser and two full armies. All of them reduced to ashes by magic gone awry. Nimbulan and Ackerly had fled the impending battle the night before in order to seek employment elsewhere. They'd finally managed to break Druulin's binding spells upon Ackerly and had slipped away from the old man's tyranny.

"The floors must be swept every day, Powwell. We need to make certain they stay clean so that the dust from our shoes and clothes does not mar delicate instruments or interfere with our experiments," he explained patiently.

Experiments that couldn't begin until the three new apprentices had enough training to guard magicians in deep trance and reawaken them if necessary. Sometimes the Tambootie drugs used to heighten magic awareness tempted a magician to remain in the void. Only a trained magician who had achieved at least the second level of apprenticeship could bring a lost master back from the void, body and soul intact. Jaanus and Rollett could almost do it. They were the most advanced and needed to be involved in the experiments. Gilby, Bessel, and Herremann weren't far behind them in skill and control.

The new boys had a long way to go before Nimbulan could begin to work on his grand scheme of combining magic for peace.

Nimbulan sorely wished he could spend more time in the library, searching for magic clues with Lyman and his older boys instead of supervising the youngsters. Just last night he'd scanned a text on Rover culture with a tantalizing hint about rituals and joining magic. But he didn't have time to read further. Libraries and Rover legends had to wait.

"Water works better at keeping down dust," Powwell said with careful thought. "We should douse the stones and then sweep. Everyone should brush their clothing each morning too. That way we'd only have to sweep every few days instead of every afternoon after lessons. If dust is your only concern." He lifted his eyes to challenge his master.

Nimbulan suppressed a chuckle. The boy was quick, if only to find ways to avoid working. Hopefully, his talent would catch up with his brain shortly. In his experience, the best magicians were also the most intelligent.

"Then do it, Powwell. And inform your classmates." Three boys. They'd only been able to recruit three boys on the short notice of the move to this island. No women. No pretty witchwoman with moonlight woven into her hair.

Nimbulan wondered if Myrilandel's eyes always wore deep violet shadows beneath the skin or if that lovely shading was a result of fatigue and an improperly worked talent.

He gave himself a mental slap. He didn't have time to dwell on Myrilandel and why she ran away from the opportunity to train with a senior Battlemage.

"They'll beat me up if I tell them to do more menial chores, sir!" Powwell sulked. His mouth turned down prettily. Too prettily for a boy verging on manhood.

I'll have to keep this one out of Kammeryl's sight, he thought. Not that the lord had set foot on the island since Nimbulan had informed him of his winter plans. Kammeryl d'Astrismos had raged for two days when he heard the news. He'd dismissed the entire enclave of magicians, including healers, from his army, vowing to replace them all.

Nimbulan wondered how soon Kammeryl would need to send emissaries requesting his return. Seasoned Battlemages were few and far between these days. Especially since Keegan's death.

Never again! he vowed. He clenched his fist in rage and grief.

Powwell backed away from him, eyes wide with distrust.

"I'll not thrash you, Powwell. Nor will Zane and Haakkon if you figure out what the lesson is in your chores.

Remember that every task I assign, no matter how trivial or distasteful, will teach you something. Now run along and finish sweeping." He shooed the boy back to the dormitory wing, keeping his temper carefully under control. No need to frighten the boy with the master's private demons.

Briefly he peeked along the kitchen wing to check on Zane. The oldest of the new recruits, a few days shy of his fourteenth birthday, sat with his back against the outside wall, legs thrust out before him. A fierce scowl marred his freckled face. His broom stood propped against the wall.

Nimbulan guessed Zane was trying to make the broom work for him. He quickly noted that the apprentice had instinctively placed himself against the wall closest to the pool of ley lines in the central courtyard. How much power could he feel?

The guardian had effectively masked the massive well of magical energy so that even masters like Nimbulan could draw only normal amounts of power from the radiating ley lines.

He watched the boy for a few moments, praying that he was one of the few magicians who could learn to weave the Kardia into his spells.

The broom wobbled. Zane leaped to his feet with a whoop of triumph. He scowled at the broom again. He closed his eyes. His fists clenched at his sides. His shoulders rose nearly to his ears as he fought the inertia of the broom.

With a small smacking sound, the broom dropped to the floor, refusing to move.

Zane rubbed his temples, clear evidence of the headache beginning to form. He'd be craving sweets, too. Nimbulan's mouth watered at the thought of the candied coneroot Quinnault's cook had sent them this morning. When the boys took a break before the evening meal, he'd make sure he shared the treats with them.

One day soon, the boys would learn that magic took more effort than sweeping. But most adolescents, with their bodies growing and maturing so rapidly their minds and emotions couldn't keep up, exhibited a weird mixture of curiosity and laziness. The two made Zane ripe to discover many things about magic. Powwell was not far behind him in age and discovery.

Nimbulan turned back to the library wing to watch Haakkon perform his chores. The dark-haired lad leaned against the library doors, his ear pressed close to the wood panels. His broom lay forgotten on the floor beside him.

A faint murmur of voices drifted down the corridor. From the library. Nimbulan drew a little power from beneath his feet up into his ears to catch the words.

"You're supposed to list and sort the books by author and title, not stop and read every *s'murghing* one of them!" Ackerly's affronted tones rose almost loud enough to hear through normal senses.

Why was Ackerly in the library and not at the market searching for a permanent cook?

"This text distinctly contradicts accepted magic theory. It claims that Rover rituals give a single magician the combined powers of all those involved in the ceremony," Quinnault de Tanos replied. "I think it's important we set it aside for closer study."

Ah, so the lord had discovered the same text Nimbulan scanned last night.

Quinnault de Tanos had taken to spending part of each day helping about Nimbulan's school however he could. He couldn't perform the smallest of spells, so he couldn't demonstrate magic lessons for the boys. He knew nothing of cooking or cleaning. But he knew ancient languages and magic theory flowed from him in precise detail, even if he couldn't work a spell.

Nimbulan wished he could spend his afternoon hours poring over the books and discussing ancient and modern practices with de Tanos. In a few moons perhaps, when everything was set up and other magicians taught and observed the apprentices, he'd have the time to indulge in long afternoons in the library.

Lyman and the five older boys were qualified to tackle the monstrous job of sorting and cataloging the books. Only Nimbulan knew how to watch the new boys for signs of major talent. The ability to weave the Kardia into their spells wouldn't settle in the boys until they passed through puberty and the trial by Tambootie smoke. Until then, their magic would be erratic.

"Hear anything interesting?" Nimbulan whispered to Haakkon.

The boy squeaked and jumped away from the door in surprise.

"You won't have to be so obvious in your eavesdropping, Haakkon, once you learn to do it with magic. However, magic takes more effort and the normal way works just as well . . . as long as the door remains closed." Nimbulan pressed his own ear to the door panels.

The voices came through muffled, but he could still discern Ackerly's words. "Time enough for study *after* we know what is here and we've sorted the junk from true work." The sound of a book being slapped against a table echoed through the door panel.

Nimbulan could almost see his assistant's tight-lipped control of his face. Ackerly would never lose his temper in the presence of an anointed lord, but Nimbulan heard his vexation. Time to intervene.

"Ackerly, I need you a moment." Nimbulan opened the door just enough to poke his head through.

Behind him, he felt Haakkon withdrawing. If the apprentice could melt into the shadows, he would. Nimbulan risked a quick glance over his shoulder. A concealing shadow crept up from the floor, wrapping itself around Haakkon.

Good. He'd found a way to use magic for a simple thing. Later, the magic would obey his will as easily as his instincts. Nimbulan turned his attention back to separating clashing personalities in the library.

"Ackerly, I am almost ready to begin experiments. But I am concerned about our Tambootie supplies."

"Can't gather the leaves this time of year. But now is the time to collect and dry the wood for burning."

"My personal supply of dried leaves is dangerously low and the time has come to begin lacing the boys' cider with small bits. Breathing Tambootie smoke is too intense until they've learned to handle smaller amounts first. We have to find a new supply soon." An edge of anxiety crept into Nimbulan's voice. He tried to hide it with a judicious cough.

"You had five pounds of dried leaves, Nimbulan. The foliage of nearly a whole tree, sun-dried to perfection. You can't have used it all up so soon."

"I . . . I don't know." But he did know. He'd used it all,

in ever larger doses that worked with less effectiveness in inducing the proper sensitivity to magic. He wondered why. He didn't remember using so much Tambootie since settling on the islands. Maybe Lyman had been dipping into the supply. Ackerly never used it.

"We'll have to find more. Soon." Ackerly pulled at his lower lip in thought. "Lord Kammeryl d'Astrismos has a stand of Tambootie two leagues from his fortress in a sheltered glen. Perhaps we can salvage some of the leaves still clinging to the trees and the recently fallen ones."

"But Kammeryl has forbidden us to return to his lands. He calls us deserters. He does not forgive disloyalty easily."

"You have to have the Tambootie, Nimbulan. I'll make sure you get some."

Myri ran her sensitive fingertips over the Rover's skull. His thick dark hair tangled in her fingertips. The temptation to linger with a caress kept her from trailing her hand down his throat to his nape to check his spine for injury. In repose, he was even more beautiful than when animated.

She settled her eyes on the long fringe of eyelashes brushing against his cheek. Beneath a dark tan, his skin showed an unnatural pallor.

A cold wave rushed around her feet and Televarn's head. He groaned as the shock of the chill water brought him to partial consciousness.

Quickly, Myri scanned his neck with all of her healing talent. The soft sand had cushioned his fall. No broken bones. She could drag him safely away from the encroaching tide. With a hand around each of his ankles she tugged his body back toward dry sand.

Another wave sucked at his weight. She pulled harder, digging in her heels. The quagmire of drenched sand released him. Myri pulled him clear of the next wave.

"I . . . can . . . walk." Televarn's words came out slurred and slow.

Myri released his ankles and moved behind him to help him up. "You won't drown in the next two minutes. But you will get wet and cold." She placed one hand under each arm and heaved while he flailed his feet to gain some leverage.

His legs seemed unconnected to his body, sliding in all directions. He had no balance.

Myri heaved him upward, using the strong muscles of her thighs for leverage.

At last he stood with his arm draped around her shoulders. He was only slightly taller than she and the bend of his arm must have been awkward. His knees visibly trembled. He placed his free hand to his right temple. "Wh . . . what happened?" He swayed, not moving forward.

Another wave slapped against Myri's ankles.

"You fell. Now walk."

"Fell? When? Why?"

"Move your feet, Televarn. You can flap your mouth later, when I know you won't drown."

"Who's Televarn?"

"You must have hit your head harder than I thought." What would she do with him? He couldn't climb to her cave in his present condition. "I'll settle you in the curve of the cliff, away from the wind, and build a fire. Once you've rested and supped, your thoughts will straighten out."

She hoped. He'd never manage to climb to her cave for shelter. Until then, she'd keep him close to this headland and away from the other where her cave nestled.

"I think I know you." Televarn paused in his shuffle toward the cliff. Gently he traced the curve of her cheek with his fingertip. He hesitated as he caressed the outline of her lips. "I sense that we belong together. Are we mates?"

Myri gasped, more from the sensuous appeal of his touch than the audacity of his question. "No, we are not mates."

"Then we are meant to be. Soon." He lifted her chin with his caressing finger. Slowly, he bent his head to touch her mouth with his own.

Heat exploded in Myri's breast. Her lips grew soft and moist under his kiss. She parted them, eager for his questing tongue as she longed to open her thighs for a more intimate thrust.

Televarn enclosed her in his strong arms, pressing her tightly against his body. She rose on tiptoe and tangled her fingers in the springy curls of his dark hair. He'd lost his kerchief in the fall. She didn't remember when hers had blown away. His hands reached down to cup her bottom, caress her back, pull her closer yet to his wonderful body.

Her dreams of a home and family took firmer shape in her mind as she molded her body to his.

(You must come east to find a home and safety.)

Her knees melted with the fire of his kiss. *I'll stay with him for a while. Until he's healed.*

A cold wave shocked them both back to reality.

"You will be my mate as soon as I can arrange it, *cherbein*," Televarn whispered, nuzzling her ear. "We are meant to be together forever."

The foreign endearment grated harshly in Myri's ear. "I never met you until today. We cannot wed until next Vernal Equinox. After we have been paired at the Festival Dance. 'Tis custom so old it has become law."

"I cannot wait that long, *cherbein*. Tonight you will be mine. Tonight and forever." He kissed her again, claiming her mouth harshly, as if to brand her his possession.

The fierceness of his desire awakened new sensations in Myri's womb. Her instincts clamored for her to join him in a ritual far older than law, right here on the sand. Right now, with the cold tide creeping up on them.

(Forget him. He lies. Come east. Now.)

He is injured. I must build him a shelter and light a fire. I cannot leave him.

Chapter 13

M oncriith shivered within the meager shelter of his lean-to. The first autumnal storm had given way to clear skies and chilling frosts. He dared not light a fire to ease the ache in his bones. The witchwoman would flee at the first hint of his presence.

She had escaped him at the village. He couldn't let her go free again. Her kind were poison to Coronnan. Only when she and all her demon-possessed magicians had been purged from Coronnan would he be safe.

She must come here. Demons and their magicians fed upon the Tambootie. This sprawling grove of the toxic trees was the only stand left between the River Coronnan and the foothills of the Southern Mountains. Moncriith and his followers purged the land of the evil trees as they progressed across Coronnan each spring and summer. If they eprived demons of the food, they would be weaker, more vulnerable.

Myrilandel had to come here to feed her demonic powers.

He stared at his small ritual knife. Cleansed by fire and guarded by a silk sheath, the instrument offered the means to draw Myrilandel and her demon consorts to this exact spot. Briefly, he contemplated his choices. If he used the knife to slit the throat of a small animal, the death of the creature would attract Myrilandel more quickly. If he drew blood from himself, the spell of attraction would be stronger and more focused.

Before he could change his mind, he slashed the sharp blade across his cheek. He welcomed the familiar burning pain. The initial flush of power that always followed the pain tingled through his body. His eyes lost focus, then abruptly cleared to sharper, narrower vision. He squeezed the wound with his fingertips until he felt the warm flow of blood dripping from his jaw. Cautiously he caught the drops on a fresh Tambootie leaf he had ready. Then he leaned over a nest of specially prepared herbs and magical powders.

His blood mingled with the ingredients for the spell. Pungent fumes rose to fill his head with clear images of what he needed the spell to accomplish.

"Bring Myrilandel, obedient and docile, to stand before me for judgment."

When cold sweat dotted his brow and the pain swelled into his left eye and ear, he staunched the flow of blood with a square of white linen dipped in a special powder. Then he dropped the bloodied Tambootie leaf and the cloth on top of the nest.

With a stick cut from a Tambootie tree he drew circles around the mixture, each one smaller and closer to the center than the previous one. As he completed each circle, he drew a special rune of enticement. He knew the spell would only work after she started her journey toward the grove. But she had to come here to feed.

Energy streamed up the vibrating stick into his hand and arm. Each of his senses came into sharper focus. He saw the distinct outline of every tree, branch, and leaf within the grove. The scent of wet dirt and decaying leaves permeated his nose. He heard the small rustlings of nocturnal animals below the louder stirring of the wind in the high branches.

A spark of witchfire ignited his mixture into one brilliant flash. The circles came to life with writhing flames running around and around the perimeter, working ever closer to the core of his spell. The runes glowed into fire-green sigils.

As suddenly as the flames sprang from his fingers, they died. All was still. He looked up, expecting to see Myrilandel standing inside the outermost circle.

"*S'murghit!* Where is she?" he cursed. His eyesight still hummed with super-sharp vision. No one but himself waited inside this grove.

He'd wait another hour, then light a fire and curl up in his blankets for the night. Perhaps tomorrow she would come. Tomorrow, when the moon was dark, his spell would be stronger. She wouldn't be able to resist him tomorrow night.

Mist and shadows drifted through the wild trees. He shivered again. Ghosts ran icy fingers up his spine. He dismissed them. The lost spirits of the dead couldn't hurt him.

He concentrated on his vision of Coronnan free of the witchwoman and magicians who provided host bodies for demons. The fire of his resolve replaced the blaze he longed to light at his rapidly chilling feet. As the power drained out of him, the cold night air attacked him anew.

None of his followers had ventured away from the barns and village pubs where they sought shelter for the winter to join in his ritual. Glumly, he realized their zeal for a demon-free Coronnan, united under one priest-king wasn't as strong as his own.

The thin slice of the moon rose higher in the night sky. He waited until chills numbed the burning pain of the cut on his cheek and set his teeth chattering. When he could stand the discomfort no longer, he stood to prepare his bed and a small fire.

The faint slurping sound of people walking among the fallen leaves sent his attention off to his left. He stilled every muscle in his body.

The spell had worked after all!

Patiently, he calmed his wandering mind and erratic heartbeat as he reached for his larger knife. He must kill the witchwoman quickly, before she could summon her demons to shred his soul and take over his body. No one else was near enough to distract the demons. He'd have gladly sacrificed one of his people for the opportunity to end Myrilandel's tyranny once and for all.

"S'murghit," a man cursed.

A man? Which man had Myrilandel seduced into following her blindly to feed from the poisonous trees? He had no doubt that she corrupted innocent men. Magretha had betrayed lover after lover until she eventually died for her crimes against men.

Something heavy plopped onto the ground, followed by a squirt of moisture hitting a tree trunk.

Thick, oily Tambootie leaves rotted into a sludgy mess that inhibited undergrowth and made for treacherous foot-

ing. Only Tambootie seeds could grow beneath a Tambootie tree, unlike honest trees whose leaves decayed into
fertile dirt.

The footsteps came closer and amid muffled profanities.
Several people wearing heavy boots, not a solitary witchwoman who ran barefoot until deep winter. He enhanced
his TrueSight, looking for traces of Myrilandel. He sensed
only males in the grove. Two men. Lord Kammeryl's men?

No. They would carry torches or shielded lanterns. These
intruders must be magicians who needed no light to steal
the Tambootie. Magicians Lord Kammeryl did not control,
or they wouldn't need to steal.

Moncriith shifted position, ready to attack. The death of
one of Myrilandel's consorts would bring her in a hurry.

A smile crept into one corner of his mouth. Perhaps he
should hurry to the nearest village and send messengers to
Lord Kammeryl. The warlord would want to know who
invaded his land in the dead of night. Kammeryl d'Astrismos
guarded closely all that was his. The captured magicians
would die, but only after confessing all under torture. Moncriith would derive much power from the men's pain and
blood.

Lord Kammeryl might even be grateful for the information and grant Moncriith the right to winter in the fortress
or one of the villages.

"There are a few late leaves here, sir. And some Timboor. The berries have almost as much of the essential oils
as the leaves." A quiet, authoritative voice broke the silence of the night.

"Only the leaves carry enough untainted power for my
experiments. We must fill the baskets with leaves and come
back for the Timboor." That voice took on an edge of
impatience. Or was it desperation?

Glee lightened Moncriith's heart. He recognized the two
men now. Nimbulan and Ackerly. Nimbulan, who had had
him exiled from the army camp in order to protect Myrilandel. Ackerly, who had defied orders and given him provisions.

Where was Myrilandel now? Why was Nimbulan stealing
from his own lord?

He'd get answers later. This opportunity to rid Coronnan
of one more of Myrilandel's consorts was too good to waste.

Nimbulan's death would decrease her power and make her vulnerable when she finally came to this grove of the Tambootie to feed.

Moncriith rose to his full height. His knife fit his hand perfectly. He reversed his grip to strike with the heavy hilt.

Blood would attract a horde of demons. He could draw power from Nimbulan's pain and death, but he wasn't certain it would be enough to overcome more than one demon at a time until Myrilandel was dead.

He wouldn't have to kill Nimbulan here and now, merely rob him of his senses with a single mighty blow to his head, then deliver him to Lord Kammeryl.

"Run, Ackerly. It's that crazed Bloodmage again. He has a knife!" Nimbulan screamed.

Moncriith followed the sounds of running feet. Nimbulan's fear fed Moncriith's magic and trued his aim.

Ackerly dodged right, off the narrow path. He crouched beside a massive trunk, hoping his dark cloak would shield him from view.

"You can't escape me, Nimbulan!" Moncriith dashed past him, knife raised high, hilt forward.

Surprise destroyed Ackerly's caution. With the knife reversed, Moncriith must intend to merely stun his victim. Would he then consign Nimbulan's partially conscious body to the flames? The hideous, painful death made Ackerly shudder.

"I know the demon that leads you. I know all of her tricks," Moncriith bellowed. His rage burned sparks at the end of his fingers where they were clenched around the knife, and on the heels of his feet when they struck the ground.

Ackerly examined the details of his glimpse of Moncriith, committing them to memory. The Bloodmage let his temper cloud his judgment. He was also too fond of announcing his intentions and motives to the entire world before acting. Over the years Ackerly had stored a great deal of information within his capacious memory. The right information was as good as gold. Who would pay to know Moncriith's weakness?

He never had enough gold.

The sound of the knife shattering against a tree trunk reverberated through the grove of Tambootie. Ackerly looked toward the source of the sound, bringing as much magic as he could to his vision.

Moncriith stood trembling a dozen paces away. His knife had indeed shattered and lay in pieces around his feet. He crossed and massaged his arms with kneading fingers, probably from the shock of his blow. He shook his head as if clearing it of the rage that gripped him. Reason returned to his eyes and posture. Quickly he picked up a fallen branch and tested the weight in his hand.

Where was Nimbulan? Ackerly hunted the night with anxious eyes. Another crouched figure shifted in the gloom three trees to the left and slightly behind Moncriith.

Ackerly adjusted his magic vision to survey his oldest friend. No visible signs of injury, merely the trembling of fear and Tambootie deprivation. Nimbulan needed a fresh dose of the drug soon. His magic grew more dependent on the artificial enhancement every day. Ackerly made sure he had ever increasing daily doses to feed that addiction. Even when Nimbulan forgot to ask for it.

Thank the Stargods, he, Ackerly, had never succumbed to the temptations of the Tambootie. After his trial by smoke at the age of thirteen, he'd known he couldn't weave the Kardia into his spells and Tambootie did nothing to increase his powers.

Nimbulan had grown to depend upon the drug for more than just magic. In the desperation of battles that taxed his endurance beyond safe limits, the Tambootie was the only thing that kept his magic alive, and therefore ensured his own safety during and after the battle.

The drug also kept Nimbulan oblivious to mundane matters like the cost of provisions. If he didn't count his coins carefully, Ackerly wasn't about to tell the Battlemage how many coins he skimmed from the budget.

Ackerly could tell by the way Nimbulan cowered beside the tree rather than facing his enemy with spells and guile that a lack of the Tambootie in his system left him vulnerable, defenseless.

"Sir, are you all right? Where are you, sir? I can't find you." Ackerly shuffled his feet and threw his voice ten paces ahead of Moncriith. A trick that looked like magic but wasn't.

Moncriith followed the diversion away from Nimbulan's

crouched form. Ackerly crept silently over to Nimbulan's side.

Nimbulan stood and stepped toward Moncriith. He raised his left palm in preparation for a spell. Ackerly grasped the Senior Magician's shoulders. Nimbulan stared at him with wide, questioning eyes. Ackerly pressed a finger to his lips, signaling silence. Keeping one hand on Nimbulan's shoulder, he guided the taller man away from Moncriith and his heavy club.

Nimbulan stumbled on some unseen obstacle. Ackerly smiled to himself as he slipped his arm around Nimbulan's waist in support. Better to make the Senior Magician think himself weaker than he was. Together they slipped back into the forest darkness, toward their waiting steeds.

The sound of running feet brought them up short.

"Come back here, you cowardly magician! I must cleanse you of demon possession!" Moncriith yelled. "Face the wrath of the Stargods and know the truth. Demons lead you into battle. Demons guide your every step. Demons rule Coronnan." His words echoed against the trunks of the Tambootie trees.

Firelight glimmered in the near distance as men ran toward Moncriith.

"What's this? Who are you?" Men wearing half armor in the dark green and maroon of Lord Kammeryl d'Astrismos' colors moved into view. They held their torches high, seeking the source of the disturbance.

"Come back here, Nimbulan. We haven't finished this!" Moncriith's cry broke off. "Let go of me, you imbecile. He's getting away. He's stealing Tambootie from your lord."

"There's no one there, you crazy preacher. You're chasing shadows. Come with us to report to Lord Kammeryl."

"We haven't time. Demons are shielding Nimbulan. They're helping him get away."

"You're crazier than I thought. Now will you come quiet or do we tie you up and drag you to Lord Kammeryl's dungeons?"

The sound of a struggle, grunts and moans, slaps, and a heavy body hitting the ground urged Ackerly to move faster toward the steeds.

He counted an officer and ten men. Enough men and

weapons to contain Moncriith. Unless Moncriith had become so crazed he ignored his own safety.

"We'll be safe now, Nimbulan," Ackerly said when they had silently led their steeds nearly a league away before mounting.

No reply. Nimbulan stood beside his mount, swaying—with indecision, fatigue, or reaction?

"I'll find you Tambootie, sir. We can buy it at the market in Sambol. Then you can finish your experiments." He offered his friend cupped hands to help him mount.

"Buy it? I used most of my gold to buy furniture and supplies for the school." Nimbulan stared at Ackerly's offered hands as if uncertain what to do with the gift.

"I'll find a way to get some. Just leave everything to me."

"I thought you condemned conventional magic, Moncriith. And yet you trespassed into my Tambootie grove—the trees that feed magicians," Lord Kammeryl d'Astrismos said in weary tones that barely reached the seven people standing around his chair of office. "My men found your camp. You have been there for some time. Since you condemn the Tambootie as demon food, I thought you would try to fell the trees, not live amongst them."

The guards who had arrested Moncriith had roused the lord from his bed to deal with the crime of trespass and resisting arrest.

Moncriith stood before the lord, unbowed by the heavy, and totally unnecessary, chains on his wrists, ankles, and neck. He had no intention of leaving Castle Krej, the ancestral fortress of Kammeryl d'Astrismos, until spring.

The lord glared at him from beneath heavy eyelids. Clad only in an ornate dressing gown of red-gold brocade that matched his hair to perfection—too perfectly—Kammeryl lounged against his chair of office, one ankle crossed over the opposite knee. His bare leg was revealed to his upper thigh. He wore no undergarments.

A pretty boy of about twelve stood to Kammeryl's right, his arm resting casually on the arm of the chair. His blond curls dangled delicately around his shoulders. He appeared to wear only an oversized shirt that hung below his knees and well past his wrists, as if he'd grabbed Kammeryl's garment instead of his own. The lord caressed the smooth skin of the boy's hand and arm as he waited for an explanation.

Moncriith didn't feel like explaining himself. Let the guards who had arrested him speak if they must. He needed all his energy to contain his shivers and the fiery ache on his left cheek that now spread from the top of his head to his collarbone. The first sharp intensity was gone. He couldn't use this aching aftermath to fuel a spell of compulsion.

"There were others in the grove, my lord," the eldest of the guards, a man of no more than seventeen summers, said. "I believe they were demons in search of the Tambootie. They disappeared in a puff of smoke, as if they'd never been there." The guard crossed and flapped his wrists. His smooth cheeks flared with heightened color.

Moncriith hid a smile. The guard didn't know the truth. No one, demon or magician, could transport a living being safely. Only inanimate objects survived the trauma of such a spell. Let the guard's fears and superstitious awe work for Moncriith. He could feed their imaginations with horror stories of what demons really did to a man's soul. Given a winter in their company, he'd have them organizing his followers for him next spring.

Moncriith stared at Kammeryl until the lord's gaze locked with his own. "I find it strange that your own Battlemage must steal Tambootie from you, sire." He added the royal title as a bonus to the lord's ambitions. "If you are not giving the weed to Nimbulan and his assistant, perhaps you, too, recognize the evil inherent in the tree that feeds only demons and their ilk."

Lord Kammeryl threw back his head and laughed long and loud. "So Nimbulan is reduced to theft of the Tambootie to feed his powers. I seem to have gotten rid of him at the right time. He is getting old. His abilities as a mage are declining. If the Tambootie kills him, I won't have to have his replacement assassinate him."

"If I replace him as your chief mage, I can purge your army and your household of the same demons who infest Nimbulan. You cannot rule a united Coronnan until all the demons are removed." Moncriith pitched his voice to soothe and calm. Given enough time, he'd have the lord believing a witchhunt for Myrilandel and her demon consorts was his own idea and had not come from Moncriith.

"You may stay the winter and throw the few spells I need for communication and preventing plagues. Time enough to find a better magician in the spring. I intend to rule a united Coronnan with or without demons." Kammeryl yawned and rose from his chair. He placed an affectionate hand on his companion's feminine locks, then let it fall to the boy's shoulder and hip, caressing at each stage of exploration. Kammeryl wandered out the back door of the audience room, preoccupied with the boy.

"A meal and a bed would be welcome, brothers." Moncriith slouched as the guards unlocked his chains. He allowed his fatigue and hunger to show in his face as he looked at the threadbare patches on his red robe—the same cut and color as a priest's.

His followers didn't need to know that he had been exiled from the temple because he would only fuel his magic with blood. The respect people gave him upon first glance of his vestments opened their ears to his persuasions. His followers turned away from the temple as soon as they learned how the priests and magicians harbored demons like Myrilandel.

"There's always a pot of soup and bread in the kitchen." The young soldier gestured toward the low doorway that led to the stone kitchen addition attached to the keep.

These guards were no different from the peasants Moncriith usually dealt with. Tomorrow he'd ingratiate himself into the good graces of the steward who supervised the servants. Tonight he would meditate on how Nimbulan might be killed without casting blame on anyone Moncriith found valuable.

Chapter 14

Timboor sang through Nimbulan's blood. The fruit of the Tambootie tree gave a crystalline sparkle to the auras of each piece of wooden furniture in his room. The simple lines of cot, chest, and table glowed with new elegance.

The nerve endings in his fingers and toes burned with new sensitivity. He drew power from the energy of wood, fabric, and stone. Different power from what the Tambootie leaves allowed him to tap, but power all the same.

He reached out to caress the aura above his worktable. The yellow-white energy fed him in ways food neglected.

He needed nothing more. Thank the Stargods Ackerly had thought to collect some timboor in his pockets the other night. Perhaps this kind of magic energy that allowed him to see everything so clearly was the key to combining magic. If he could see the individual components of an aura or, better yet, mesh his thoughts precisely with another man's, they could join and magnify their powers.

Carefully, Nimbulan folded the power around him in a spell of listening. The thoughts of Haakkon, Powwell, and Zane whipped through his mind with the lightning speed of their youth. Thoughts of lessons and chores, of the mysteries of women, and mixed resentment and awe of their masters. They asked themselves questions about magic and about life.

Too unformed and unskilled. The boys couldn't help him now.

Nimbulan sent his spell deeper into the old monastery, seeking Maalin and Jaanus, the two apprentices in the library. Their thoughts lingered on the smell of baking bread and the stacks of books yet to be cataloged.

For once, Quinnault de Tanos had not joined them.

Nimbulan found himself missing the lord's enthusiasm and his company. He reached out with his spell, seeking the brightly colored thoughts of the man whose patronage made the school possible.

He'd never managed to penetrate de Tanos' thoughts in his presence. If he could break through the lord's natural armor with the help of timboor, then he could read any man. That reading—rather a blending of thoughts and auras—now seemed essential to joining magic. Quinnault's thoughts remained elusive.

He needed familiarity. Ackerly. His oldest friend. They'd studied and worked together since Nimbulan was ten and Ackerly was twelve. Ackerly's mind and actions were almost as familiar to Nimbulan as his own.

Out of the stone buildings, across the wide courtyard to the beaten path and the causeway between two islands. The tide was full and the chain of boulders and land covered with water. The physical obstacles did not stop Nimbulan's questing magic. He flew across to the big island with its farmhouse and fields and the squat stone keep where de Tanos made his home now.

From the big island he wandered up the River Coronnan, seeing every twist and cove with his mind as if his body truly floated above the surging river. Past the battlefield where he'd had to kill Keegan to save two armies. That wound still pained him, more so than his guilt for deserting Druulin, Boojlin, and Caasser the night before they died in battle on the same field eighteen years ago. If he and Ackerly had stayed, would they have found a way to control the awful spell that destroyed everything in its path? Or would they, too, have died in screaming, burning agony?

No answers came to him from generations of ghosts that haunted the battlefield. He traveled on, upriver.

Many leagues distant, Nimbulan paused his seeking magic at the river gate of Sambol. Perched at the head of navigable waters on the river, at the base of a mountain pass and juncture of several trade roads, Sambol played host to merchants from throughout the known world. Anything could be purchased in the market stalls of the city, be it legal, moral, or not.

This was where Ackerly had come to purchase a new supply of Tambootie for Nimbulan and his students.

From his distant listening post, Nimbulan scanned the myriad minds of the city for a familiar syntax, inflection, and accent. He heard jewelers from Jehab, lace traders from SeLenicca, captains of mercenaries from Rossemeyer, and spice brokers from Varnicia. At last he picked up the educated tones of a magician haggling with a pottery maker in a small booth next to a shadowy alley. Any number of substances could be secreted in one of those utilitarian pots. Including the precious Tambootie.

Ackerly finished his bargaining. He withdrew five gold coins from the pouch Nimbulan had given him, one at a time as if counting and regretting every coin. The last of Nimbulan's savings.

Nimbulan watched as his assistant brushed his hand across the side of his face as if swatting a fly between placing each coin into the merchant's hand. As the last coin exchanged hands, Ackerly slapped his pockets as if searching for something. An expression of alarm spread across his features.

Nimbulan chuckled inwardly. Ackerly was probably presenting some ploy to recover one or more of the coins. Money and bargaining had always been a mystery to Nimbulan. Ackerly, however, excelled, keeping the two of them and their apprentices fed and sheltered on the meager allowance Nimbulan paid. The coins Ackerly had earned when he and Nimbulan fixed the horse race so many years ago had lasted them both for several years. They'd used the money for extra food and warmer clothes in the markets Druulin passed through once the boys started traveling with him.

Confident of Ackerly's miserly instincts to cut the best bargain possible, Nimbulan returned to the river and a lazy mind trip back to the islands at the mouth of the River Coronnan.

Briefly he circled the buildings on the big island. If he could find Ackerly in so distant a place, surely he could sense Quinnault. The lord's mental armor might be unconscious, but it also had a pattern of light and dark that swirled in a confusing whirlpool.

Only people with the placid concerns of farm chores and housekeeping met his soaring mind. Into the keep and up

the single stairwell his otherself flew. At the top of the
stairs, he hesitated. Would the lord be in the public reception room to the right or in his private chambers to the left?

Mentally shrugging his shoulders, Nimbulan listened to
the left. Quinnault's quiet breathing betrayed his presence.
Quickly, the magician slid into the mind of his patron. A
thin barrier blocked his entry. He pushed gently. A little
harder.

A worn parchment scrawled with numbers swam before
his vision. Smudged and worn spots that had been scraped
free of ink blurred the new ink. Column after column of
entries tangled and straightened to make some sense. Nimbulan saw the ledger through Quinnault's eyes!

He felt the lord's quill pen in *their* hand. Heard the sound
of the pen scratching across the parchment. Knew the
rhythmic intake and expulsion of air through lungs younger
and stronger than his own.

Black swirling numbness rose up before him, blocking
the sight of the ledger. Physical sensation ceased.

Where was he? Who was he? Endless darkness stretched
before him. No light. No sound. No body to feel with.

Ackerly swatted in annoyance at the soft buzzing beside
his head. *S'murghin'* flies. The city was full of the filthy
pests today. He'd never been bothered by them like this
on his previous visits to Sambol.

The soft flutter near his right temple brushed past him
again. He tried to ignore it. His business in Sambol was
more important than the annoyance of an insect.

He fished the fifth gold coin out of his purse reluctantly
and placed it in the outstretched palm of the pottery vendor
before swatting at the persistent fly.

Silently he gloated at the number of coins left in the
purse. Nimbulan had given him twenty pieces of gold with
instructions to use it all if necessary to purchase the necessary Tambootie. Overuse of the drug had rotted the Battlemage's mind. Tambootie rarely cost over three coins and
never more than eight. Even when the wars and trade em-
bargo inflated prices, and the only sources were in the black
market, he could always bargain to a reasonable level. Who
else would want it but the decreasing number of great
mages?

Nimbulan didn't think logically anymore because of the drug. What he didn't know about prices helped Ackerly. His employer would never miss the remaining fifteen coins.

Well, he might miss fifteen coins, but not another five or eight. Maybe ten.

If Nimbulan had wanted to save money, he should have given him copper and lead. Base metals were for spending. Gold was for saving. Gold was for hoarding. Gold was for polishing and counting.

Ackerly always collected stipend from Kammeryl d'Astrismos in gold and he never spent it. He spent Nimbulan's money, adding a few of those coins to his hoard as a commission for making good bargains. He never spent his own money.

A wave of resentment washed over him at returning any of the leftover coins. He argued with himself that some, at least, had to be returned to avoid suspicion and keep Nimbulan believing in his bargaining ability.

The fly buzzed again. Only this time, Ackerly recognized the pattern of the sound as a summons spell, not a disease-ridden insect. He touched his glass in his pocket. It remained quiet. Then he touched each of his other pockets to make sure he hadn't tucked a crystal or other arcane equipment there that could attract a stray spell. Nothing.

The wizened old pottery seller lifted a medium-sized, handleless jug from the back of his stall and placed it carefully into Ackerly's hands. The old man acted as if the jug weighed more than he did, so Ackerly was surprised at the lightness of his purchase.

Cautiously he lifted the lid. The crisp-sweet fragrance of dried Tambootie leaves caressed his senses. The old man hadn't cheated him. These were prime leaves kiln-dried while still fresh and full of the essential oils. This jug with its contents was worth much more than five coins to a magician who was addicted to the drug. He chuckled to himself as he felt the heavy purse safely resting in the pocket inside his tunic.

His senses tingled once more, as if a summons had gone astray and brushed against every magician, seeking a recipient. But the buzzing ceased. Had Nimbulan's magic decayed to the point he couldn't send a simple summons?

With one arm wrapped tightly around the expensive jug of Tambootie, Ackerly fished in his trews pocket for his glass. The smooth edges of a journeyman's oval mirror fit neatly into his palm. He hesitated to bring it out in public. Clear glass was so rare and hard to come by, only magicians owned it. The appearance of the piece in his hands would mark him—either as a target for abuse from war-weary citizens or as a magician to be kidnapped by mercenaries for sale to the highest bidder. Not that the buyer would gain much from Ackerly. He was only an assistant, destined never to throw battle spells, only to hold them together and assist a true master like Nimbulan.

He almost showed the glass openly in perverse defiance of his fate. Anyone who kidnapped him was in for a big disappointment.

Reality reasserted itself, and he sought the closest open flame to receive and channel the summons through his glass. The young woman selling chestnuts roasted her wares over a small brazier. He smiled up at her. Her mouth curved up in invitation as she offered him a peeled nut from her gloved hand. Maybe when he finished the summons, he could persuade the young woman to roast his nuts in bed.

He liked provincial women better than the jaded camp followers in an army camp. Provincial women brought an innocent delight to bed. Ackerly grew warm in anticipation of unlacing the girl's bodice. She laced it from top to bottom with the ties at her waist, as did any properly modest woman. He licked his lips in anticipation of coaxing her out of the bodice. Only whores placed the ties at top for easy access.

He had to answer the summons first. Crouching down as if warming his hands at her brazier, he held the glass before him. The glass magnified one tiny flame licking the hot coals.

He emptied his mind to receive the message from the sender, expecting Nimbulan's face to flash into the clear surface. The precious piece of glass remained empty. No vibration thrummed through his fingertips.

Had the summoning magician given up? Nimbulan knew he was engaged in business and might not be able to answer immediately. Who else would call him?

He looked around furtively. What if Kammeryl d'Astrismos had hired a new Battlemage who sought to neutralize

Nimbulan? More likely the new mage would try to lure his predecessor's assistants and apprentices away, with the hope of learning some of Nimbulan's tricks and spells.

Abandoning his plans to seduce the chestnut seller, Ackerly scuttled back through the winding streets of Sambol to his inn. Someone watched him with magic. He had to hide his gold before the watcher spied on him again.

Myri paused a moment in her dash through the rain to the lean-to she and Televarn had built against the cliff. Thoughts of the meal she would make vanished. She forgot the three fish tucked into her basket.

Instead, she watched a dark squall line dance across the roaring surf. Iron gray clouds played shadow games with the green-gray of the water. Highlights of creamy surf swirled in an intricate mosaic over the top. Waves rose, crested, and crashed in rounded undefinable shapes and sent a bubble of poetic magic through her soul. She wanted to *Sing* the images into an indelible memory.

(Come up to the dry cave before you catch a chill,) Amaranth said from the lip of the high opening in the cliff. *(Autumn is full upon us. The rain is cold.)*

She danced in a circle for the sheer joy of being alive, of bonding with a precious flywacket, of knowing Televarn's love.

Maybe she should climb up to the cave and spend some time with Amaranth before returning to Televarn in the lean-to. Amaranth couldn't fly yet. His wing was still bruised bone deep. One of the fish in her basket was for him.

I must return to Televarn. The thought inserted itself into her mind, blocking the idea of climbing up to the cave where Amaranth waited for her.

(He lies to you. He is not worthy of you,) Amaranth reminded her.

"Come to me, Amaranth. We'll dance in the rain together. I'll take you to Televarn." She held out her arm to the flywacket, not certain why it suddenly seemed important that Amaranth be in Televarn's arms.

(I do not trust him.) The flywacket turned his back on her, retreating deeper into the cave.

Myri held out one of the fish as an enticement, suddenly anxious for her familiar to come to her. *Come to Televarn.*

Amaranth ignored her and the fish.

A blast of cold air against her face told Myri of the rapidly advancing squall. She resumed her run for the shelter of the lean-to before the rain drenched her.

Amaranth's continued rejection of her lover darkened her mood. Televarn promised her a home and family. The voices that had sent her east promised only a home. Couldn't Amaranth see how important the beautiful man was to her? To them both.

I have to love Televarn. She couldn't question the need deep inside her to love him without hesitation.

Her stomach growled, and she laughed at the ridiculous noise.

"Come in out of the rain, *cherbein.*" Televarn tugged at her arm from beneath the driftwood angled against the cliff where it curved into the headland. Amaranth's cave was well above them and closer to the opposite headland, commanding a full view of the curved beach.

Their bed of moss and grass sprawled across the center of the shelter, inviting her to stretch out there with Televarn at her side. A small fire burned brightly against the cliff at the back of the lean-to.

She laughed again at the pleasure his touch gave her. As his arms folded around her, she traced the shiny embroidery on his vest, delighting in the symmetrical design. She continued laughing in delight at the beautiful contrast of the silver and gold against stark black.

"I don't understand you, Myri. You laugh at everything. I thought witchwomen were supposed to be solemn, predicting doom and gloom." He dropped her hand and retreated to the warmth of the fire.

Some of Myri's joy deflated with the separation he put between them. If she had climbed up to the cave, Amaranth would have warmed her and showed his contentment with his purr.

Don't think about leaving Televarn, ever.

"Witchwomen are women first. We laugh. We cry. And we love like any other woman." She placed her basket of fish beside the entrance and knelt on the bed next to him.

"Mostly we love life and the men who give it meaning."
She kissed the side of his neck.

He enfolded her in his arms. The fierceness of his grip
startled her. Usually he was more gentle and teasing in
his passion.

"What would I do without you, Myrilandel? My life
began the moment I opened my eyes and saw you bending
over me, your black cat cradled against your shoulder." He
continued to hold her close. "All my life before that, my
family, my travels, my other lovers, are all meaningless
without you."

Myri's muscles twitched with the unaccustomed stillness
of remaining in one position so long. Gently she wedged
her hands between them.

"I need to cook the fish. Did you find any of the wavebulbs to go with them?" She squirmed for release.

Televarn dropped his arms from her body slowly as if he
were reluctant to let go.

"I'm getting tired of fish and wavebulbs. We've eaten
nothing else for weeks." He sighed heavily as he reached
for his own rush basket. "My mouth waters for bread and
meat and yampion roots."

Myri examined the five wavebulbs inside the basket,
looking for soft spots where rot would make them inedible.
The green globes were all fresh and ripe. They had dense
skins that would roast to a delicious tenderness. The thick
liquid inside, bitingly bitter when raw, became sweeter with
cooking. Dried or fresh, the long flat leaves of the seabed
plant prevented many ills and gave an interesting, salty fla-
vor to their food. She longed for heartier fare also but
dissmissed the notion. Her life was here, on this beach
with Televarn.

"We've nothing else to eat, but what the sea gives us,
love. The tides have been so high, we can't go around the
headland in search of paths inland," she reminded him. Not
that she wanted to meet his tribe of Rovers camped in the
next cove. She could climb the steep cliff near the cave
where Amaranth sulked, but she didn't want to without
Televarn. He hadn't the sense of balance or extra length
in his toes and fingers to climb with her.

"You'll feel better after we've eaten." She busied herself

spitting the gutted fish and wrapping the bulbs in wet leaves before placing them in the coals.

"As much as I love you, Myrilandel, I'm lonely. Even your cat won't come out of his cave to break the monotony. I have always been around other people. I need to know my people are safe." He slammed his fist into a support beam. A shower of aromatic bark drifted into the fire.

Myri watched the small pieces flare and coil into smoking tendrils. Her mind drifted with the smoke.

"Are you listening to me, Myrilandel? Why doesn't your cat like me? He won't let me touch him. It's almost as if he's afraid of me."

"Amaranth became tangled in a fishnet and hurt himself just before we met. He doesn't want anyone touching his back and side until he's fully healed." Her three attempts at healing had slid right over Amaranth without penetrating to the core of his pain. He needed a different kind of healing that she couldn't offer. Otherwise the bruise might take all winter to fade.

The dangerous fishnet must have come from one of the Rovers. But why had it tangled so insistently?

Televarn had never mentioned that first meeting. He claimed his memory of it had been knocked out of his brain when he fell from the cliff. He remembered only climbing over the headland into her cove and nothing more until he awoke after the fall. If so, he didn't know that Amaranth flew.

"The cat's healing seems to be taking a very long time." He looked at the knife slashes in the beam he had just slapped. One for each day they'd been together. Myri's ten fingers filled a slot three times over plus an additional three. "You may be a witchwoman, but I'd like another healer to look at him. We need to find a better shelter before winter settles in."

"Amaranth doesn't need another healer. All he needs is time and me." Something close to panic clutched at her throat.

Trust Televarn. Myri looked sharply to her lover, wondering if he inserted that idea in her head or if her own instincts did.

"You can't see that Amaranth needs someone else because you love him so much you won't let yourself believe he might be damaged. The moon will be dark tonight. Tomorrow's morning tide should be low enough to get around the headland. We might not have another chance to find another healer for him. To find my family in the next cove. Don't you see, Myrilandel, we have to go now. We have to take Amaranth to my family."

You have to love me, now and forever. Trust me without question, Myrilandel.

Chapter 15

"**M**aster!"

Nimbulan heard the voice in the distance. The directionless, sense-robbing blackness jerked and righted. A feeling of up and down blasted him into the realization that he lay prone upon a hard surface.

"Master, what happened?" The voice—voices?—echoed around him, still defying specific direction.

Pain assaulted him next. More an ache than pain. Above him. That must be his back and neck. Longer. His knees and feet where he made contact with . . . with stone.

"Master, wake up."

Rough movement irritated the discomfort in his back. The ache throbbed and spread outward to his arms and hands.

"Arrrrgh." Was that his voice?

"Thank the Stargods he's alive. Help me turn him over."

Several hands lifted and supported him. More than one person. As many as three. A sensation of floating robbed him of his precious sense of up and down.

"Uughhh." This time he knew the inarticulate sound came from his own throat. The throbbing in his head increased.

"Open your eyes, Master. Please."

So that was why he couldn't see. He willed his eyes open a tiny slit. The effort almost sent him reeling back into the void.

"Light the lantern. It's too dark in here to see if he's injured."

Light filtered around the edges of his perception.

The voice sounded familiar. He didn't dare open his eyes

again. He should know the speaker. Youthful, peasant tones. Ah. Haakkon.

A giggle followed the onslaught of light. Two more young people. Powwell and Zane. None of the new apprentices' voices had changed yet.

"Whisst your nonsense," Haakkon ordered his classmates!

What was so funny about the master passed out cold on the floor of his room? Why were they laughing at all of the aches and pains left over from his astral flight with the aid of Timboor?

Ah, the flight! He'd found a way to merge his thoughts and aura with another's. But at a terrible cost. No magician would willingly endure this aftermath for the sake of joining magic with another.

All the aches centered in his groin. He needed to empty his bladder. Desperately. A bigger itch plagued him. He needed a woman. Any woman. Camp follower, noblewoman, or peasant. He didn't care. Just so the pressure in his groin found an outlet.

No women resided on the island. The only women on the island were Quinnault's servants, most of them married. Even in this anxious state he wouldn't stoop to forcing another man's mate.

An image of Myrilandel's fair skin and pale hair flashed before him. He longed to reach out and caress the lavender shadows around her eyes, to feel her gentle, healing touch on the most intimate part of his body.

Myrilandel had run away. She'd never be his mistress or his apprentice.

Nimbulan tried opening his eyes again. Three concerned adolescent faces stared at him.

"Uuughhh," he groaned again.

"Quick get the chamber pot. He's going to heave." Haakkon lifted his master's head and shoulders so he wouldn't gag on his own vomit.

"Cold," Nimbulan ground out between clenched teeth.

"I know you're cold, sir. You'll feel better as soon as you get rid of whatever's making you sick."

"Cold water. Towels. Need cold." What he really needed was to get rid of the aching pressure in his groin. Lacking a woman, a cold plunge in the river might work.

Powwell scuttled out of the room and returned in moments with several thick towels. He left a trail of small puddles in his wake.

Blessed chill engulfed Nimbulan's face. The throbbing in his head subsided. He held a second soggy cloth against his chest and neck. His hands felt as if he'd plunged them into a snowbank. The cold crept down his body, reducing the swelling.

He sighed in partial relief and turned his gaze to his cold hands. More than just his penis had become engorged by the overdose of Timboor. His fingers were double their normal size. Red splotches ran up his arms, and he guessed they ran onto his chest and face.

"Thank you, boys," Nimbulan said as he pressed the cold towel over his eyes again. "Your quick thinking may have saved my life. I ask two easy chores of you, then leave me to rest and recover on my own." And get rid of the last of the uncomfortable swelling without their curious eyes watching his every move.

"Anything, sir," Zane said. The other two nodded their agreement.

"First, ask cook to prepare a sweet yampion pie for our supper. The sugar in the root restores much of what magic depletes. Remember that as you progress with your magic lessons. Candied coneroot for dessert will help too."

"And the second chore, Master?" Powwell asked, licking his lips with an eager tongue.

"The second lesson is much more important. The basket in the corner is filled with berries. Green-and-yellow-striped, oily berries of the Tambootie tree. Study them carefully so you will know them in any form. Then throw them into the river and never ever touch one again." The essence of Tambootie was too strong in berry form. Too alien in its affects on the body. Power lay within the oils. Power so strong it couldn't be managed by mortals. He had to find a different method for joining thoughts and powers. At least he now knew the first steps toward joining magic.

"But Tambootie is supposed to help magic," Powwell protested, rolling one of the berries between his fingertips.

"When I was a little boy, younger than you three, my father's great-aunt told me that only dragons can eat Timboor and survive."

"Then you must be part dragon, Nimbulan, if you ate the berries and lived to warn the boys about them." Old Lyman stood in the doorway, arms crossed, face frowning in disapproval. "Off with you three. Your master needs rest and privacy." He shooed the apprentices out of the room.

"Part dragon, indeed," Nimbulan snorted as he dragged himself to his knees by clinging to his chair. He must have fallen off of it at some point.

"Do you have a better explanation for surviving a lethal dose? I didn't think you stupid enough to try those berries at all. Perhaps I should have taken you into the void to discover your past existences." Lyman cocked his head as if listening to a voice in the far distance. Then he scratched his neck with fingers longer than normal with purple shadows on the tips.

"Get into the privy, even if you have to crawl. Then we'll discuss your experience." Lyman grasped Nimbulan's arm with the long, long fingers that looked more like talons than human digits.

Myri eyed the rapidly rising waves with skepticism. Amaranth struggled in her arms to be free of the encroaching wet. She held him closer to keep him from escaping. The moon had pulled the tide to its lowest point in many weeks. A storm hovered just over the horizon, sending large erratic waves.

If she and Televarn didn't dawdle in crossing the slippery, broken rocks of the lowest point of the headland they might make it to the next cove unscathed.

Might. Each time a wave rushed to the shore, a deep boom warned her of the dangers. She counted the waves, edging across the sharp rocks, one step for each wave. A ninth wave, bigger than its fellows sprayed water above their heads.

The ninth such wave would signal the turning of the tide. They hadn't much time.

Amaranth mewled plaintively, burrowing his head beneath her arm. His damp tail lashed at her side.

She risked this trip to the next cove and the Rovers only so she could consult a different healer about his bruised back. Myri had given the flywacket strict telepathic instructions to keep his wings hidden. Despite her misgivings about meeting the Rovers, she knew Amaranth needed help. He should have healed by now, with or without her aid.

(You draw your magic from the Kardia. I need healing magic that floats in the air,) Amaranth told her again. He'd been saying that for over a moon. Myri didn't understand what he meant.

If she'd spent more time with her familiar, rather than in Televarn's arms, maybe she'd know how to help him. She caressed the flywacket's fur, feeling guilty for neglecting him. But . . .

Why did Amaranth mistrust Televarn so? The Rover promised her everything she wanted most out of life—a home and a family, people to love and be loved by.

Memory of Televarn's extreme interest in Amaranth and his wings before his fall haunted her for the first time in the moon she'd been with him.

How much of their meeting and his subsequent fall did he really remember?

She banished the thought. *I love Televarn.*

(You love his body and his tender lovemaking,) the voices in the back of her mind reminded her. They had been silent since she'd found the cave—letting her remain there for the winter. Why did they plague her now with doubts?

"Silly cat. Hiding your head won't keep you dry." Televarn brushed his hand along Amaranth's back.

"Hssst!" Amaranth lashed at the Rover with unsheathed claws.

"Dragon's spawn!" Televarn raised his scratched hand to strike back.

Myri reared back in surprise and loathing, pressing her body against a jagged outcropping. The waves continued to pound the land just below them.

At the height of its arc, Televarn stopped his hand. He narrowed his eyes in speculation, then lowered his wrist to his mouth. He sucked on the bloody scratches a moment, never taking his eyes off Amaranth.

"He's in pain. Of course he's temperamental. Watch your step, Myrilandel. That strand of wavebulb will be slippery." A calculating smile lit his face, but not his eyes.

Myri's unthinking count of the waves registered eight. They needed to move or be overcome by the tide. Amaranth needed another healer. She needed to understand Televarn's true motives. She'd never trusted her own judgment before, always relying on the guiding voices.

I need to be strong enough to think for myself.

Did Televarn truly long to return to his own kind for Amaranth's sake? Or had he tricked her with his vulnerability and charm to steal her familiar?

Those couldn't be her own thoughts. They had be echoes of the voices.

Amaranth mewled again, reminding her of the encroaching waves.

Televarn blocked her retreat back to her cove. She'd never survive a swim to freedom among the rocks and vicious surf of this headland. She had to move forward.

A ninth wave crashed two finger-lengths from her already cold and wet feet. She turned her eyes away from the fascinating pulse of pale purple blood through the dominant veins of her instep. She'd slung her winter boots around her neck so her bare feet could find the best toeholds across the broken rocks. She tasted salt and felt the sting of the icy water on her face. The next ninth wave would cover them with enough force to drag them into the churning water. The next ninth after that could crush them against the headland.

She threaded her way through the first low boulders beside the sand and swirling waves. The wind slackened as she rounded the prominence of the headland. A drop in the elevation of the rocks and a stretch of wet sand came into view. The end of the trek was in sight.

Sharp spines of volcanic rock lacerated the soles of her feet as she hurried toward safety. She barely felt the pain due to the cold. Her gray-green cloak flapped in a rising wind. The wet hem of the long garment tangled with her ankles. Televarn pressed his hands against her back, urging her to hurry.

Hurry away from the tide. Hurry toward a camp of Rovers. Rovers who never worked at honest labor; who stole and cheated to make their living.

Amaranth represented a rare prize. How many gold pieces would a magician like Nimbulan pay for a real flywacket?

(Nimbulan would cherish a flywacket as a wonder. The Rovers will only sell Amaranth.) The familiar voices echoed hollowly around her mind.

Tears started in Myri's eyes. She turned to face her lover, desperately needing to know the truth of his motives before she met his people. Why hadn't she listened to her doubts before venturing onto this dangerous headland?

She opened her empathic talent to him, making his emotions her own—something she never allowed herself to do except during a healing.

A flood of greed washed over her, colder than any storm-tossed wave the Great Bay could throw at her. She shivered the full length of her spine down to her toes.

Move, s'murghit. *I don't want to get killed before I have a chance to spend the gold.*

His thoughts came to her as clearly as if he'd spoken aloud.

Pressing her balance forward, her shoulders lifted and her free arm spread away from her body. Her cloak caught the wind like a wing.

Amaranth leaped from her embrace to the cliffside, scrambling up the rocks with agility beyond a normal feline's.

"You lied to me, Televarn," Myri said quietly.

"Not now, *cherbein.* The tide will catch us. Tell me all your doubts when we're safe and dry." He placed a hand on her shoulder in an effort to turn her around and move her closer to the end of their treacherous journey.

"You did not armor your thoughts against me, Televarn. I know your scheme. I know your lies. You compelled me to love you so that you could capture and then sell my familiar. The fishnet that snared him was yours!" She thrust his hand off her.

"Myrilandel, this is not the time. I know you are shy about meeting strangers. But we must get away from the tide. Now." He grasped her arm in a fierce grip. His fingers crushed her skin through the protection of her cloak and clothes.

"Let go of me." She pulled her arm away from him.

His grip tightened. Blood rushed to the bruises already forming on her arm, swelling them painfully.

A wave sloshed their feet. She counted it as the sixth.

Myri pried at his fingers with her free hand. "I said let go."

"When we safely reach the next cove. Now call the fly-wacket and move!" He pushed her toward his goal.

"I will not go with you." She raked her fingernails across the bloody scratches Amaranth had given him earlier.

He jerked his hand away in pain.

The eighth wave wet them to their knees.

Myri reached over her head for the nearest handhold.

"You've come back at last, Televarn. We wondered how much longer you'd allow your new companion to distract you," a man said from behind her. Strange hands clasped her shoulders.

Startled, Myri paused in her instinctive seeking of a high place to hide.

"Come now, we'll carry you to safety. We've a fire and dry blankets in the caves to warm you. Our healer will take care of those rock cuts on your feet." The speaker lifted her free of the rocks.

Myri's hood folded over her eyes, preventing her from seeing who carried her away from the waves.

Or aided Televarn's betrayal?

She batted the cloak away from her face to see who laid hands upon her. An older man with Televarn's intense dark gaze and thin straight nose smiled at her. She squirmed to be set free. His grasp on her tightened and his stride across the sand lengthened.

"Come, now. No need to be shy, pretty lady. We'll take care of you."

His voice washed over her in soothing cadences. Her body relaxed in his grip. Her mind urged her to fight the compulsion to be still.

"Never mind her," Televarn shouted behind them. "Get the flywacket!"

"The creature will come to her when it is ready. We have all winter to wait."

"Let go of me!" Myri struggled to be free of the man who carried her. "I'll not stay with thieves and liars."

"I promised you a home and family, Myrilandel. You belong to us now, and we keep those we claim. Forever, *cherbein*. You and your flywacket belong to *my* clan of Rovers now."

Chapter 16

Nimbulan listened to the rising wind as it whipped around his new School for Magicians. That's what the locals called the old monastery now. The same locals were much more accepting of the school than the people he remembered living around Druulin's tower. But then Nimbulan and his students aided the locals in building and repairing homes. They also helped with minor healing. None of his boys would consider setting fire to fields and homes as part of a lesson or experiment.

His shivers were as much part of his memories as the chill air. Each gust found new cracks and crevices to invade the shelter. Old cold had deeply penetrated the stone walls over generations of abandonment and now dominated every corner of the ancient building. Fires in the large hearths did little to dissipate the frigid air.

"I think it's colder in here than in a campaign tent in midwinter," Nimbulan said to the assembled apprentices without expecting an answer. They were all huddled in the kitchen area, cradling mugs of hot cider between their palms and wrapped in whatever quilts and blankets they had scrounged from the farmers who hid out among the islands. More refugees moved to Lord Quinnault's lands every day, seeking relief from the famine and plague left behind by generations of war.

The islands had a reputation for being sheltered and relatively untouched by the wars. Lord Quinnault de Tanos had earned a reputation for dealing fairly with his people and not conscripting them to serve in any army.

A lot of the settlers had served in one lord's army or another. They were prepared to defend their new homes.

Nimbulan wondered if the influx of settlers wasn't really part of Quinnault's plans to unite the lords in a mutual defense pact against the aggressions of the warlords.

Whatever Quinnault's plans, Nimbulan and his boys were part of the island community now. They were as much a family as any of the more traditional hearth groupings. Old Druulin had never sat with his apprentices around a warm fire with an extra mug of cider before bedtime. Nimbulan cherished these gatherings. The boys shared their little triumphs and frustrating defeats with him. They shared their hopes and dreams as well. He talked of peace and his own dreams of a community of magicians.

If he should die tomorrow, one or more of his apprentices—probably led by Rollett—would pick up that dream and carry it forward. He couldn't wish for more if they were sons of his body.

Lyman had chosen to remain in the library tonight, gaining warmth from his own love of the myriad books still uncataloged. The other war-weary magicians who had come here to teach had retired to their rooms early. They were more than tired of war, they were tired of life and slept away much of their remaining years. The sense of community Nimbulan built with his boys was as alien to these Master Magicians as it would have been to Druulin.

Nimbulan blew steam from the top of his mug, as interested in keeping chilblains from his fingers as drinking the spicy brew.

He'd laced the batch of cider with the last of the dried Tambootie leaves he'd scraped from the folds of a pouch. The boys needed to become used to the effects the tree of magic had on their bodies and minds before they began taking concentrated doses to increase their magic.

He had to find the right dosage and combinations to duplicate the meshing of thoughts he'd attained with the Timboor.

One taste of the brew had set Nimbulan's craving for Tambootie afire. Ackerly had better return soon.

"It's the damp that makes you feel colder." Rollett, the eldest of all nine apprentices and nearly ready for promotion to journeyman, stirred the fire in the small baking hearth with an iron poker. The big roasting hearth had been blocked to prevent further heat loss.

"My da was born not too far from here. He used to say that the river mists chilled his bones so deep it took an entire summer to get warm." An old sadness clouded his eyes. "Da always said the damp would kill him. He was wrong. The wars killed him."

Nimbulan remembered Rollett's father, stoop-shouldered with the joint disease while still fairly young. He had reluctantly handed his youngest son to a magician for training seven years ago. Nimbulan had taken the boy with marginal talent more to give the impoverished farmer one less mouth to feed than because he needed another apprentice. But Rollett had proved his worth time and time again. Eager to please and more eager to learn, he'd mastered all his lessons and improved his talent tenfold. The young man had begun tapping ley lines only a few weeks before the guardian spirit sealed the well.

Nimbulan had expected him to become no more adept than Ackerly, who could hold a spell together and feed Nimbulan strength, but couldn't levitate anything heavier than a small parchment, nor conjure more than a whisper of flame.

Last spring, Rollett had taken a brief respite from his studies to return home for a much anticipated reunion. He'd hoped to help with some of the heavy plowing and planting, maybe use some of his magic to repair the family hut. He could lift a new roof tree by himself with magic, something ten men would have found onerous.

But foraging scouts for one army or another had stripped the farm, burned the buildings, and left the family's bodies to rot in the rain.

Nimbulan grieved with Rollett, then and now. In this case he had truly replaced the boy's birth father. In the moons since that terrible time, Nimbulan had spent many evenings comforting Rollett, sharing memories of his father. Reliving the events of Rollett's loss was the first time Nimbulan had allowed the endless wars to touch him personally. His long road to a quest for peace had really begun there. Keegan's death had been the final catalyst that had brought him to Lord Quinnault de Tanos and this ancient building with Ackerly, Lyman, a few tired Battlemages, and eight apprentices.

"Someone comes." Zane lifted his head, sniffing the air for changes.

"A man. Walking with heavy steps, as if very weary," Powwell added, cocking his ear toward the door. "Two men, one younger and stronger than the other."

"Ackerly." Haakkon closed his eyes and furrowed his brow in concentration. "He's thinking of food and ale and gold. The boatman walks behind with heavy luggage."

He'd expected Ackerly two days ago, before this latest winter storm had made the river a churning cauldron of eddies and wicked currents.

"Together, you three would make one powerful magician," Nimbulan acknowledged the young apprentices' various talents. "Now which of you will be able to open the door for Ackerly at the moment he reaches for the latch?"

The three youngsters looked to each other as if consulting. A grin of mischief crossed Zane's face as he shook free of his blanket and walked to the kitchen door.

"I meant, open it with magic!"

"But you told us just yesterday not to waste our energy with frivolous uses of magic," Haakkon reminded his master.

"Since none of you has mastered levitation with any precision, this is a test and not a waste. Back to your chair, Zane. And no help from you other apprentices." Nimbulan glared at the five older boys who looked as if they wanted to open the door with an easy magical gesture.

Lyman wandered into the kitchen from the interior of the building without a word and moved to warm his hands over the fire, watching the boys with curiosity and amusement.

Zane settled into his blankets once more. The three new boys stared at the door with intense concentration. A blue aura burst forth from each apprentice. The wavering sapphire glows hovered separately. Haakkon's aura took on a hint of red and purple, the colors that would eventually become his magic signature. Zane's yellow and dark red were not as strong, but definitely present.

Nimbulan looked deeper into Powwell's aura for signs of another color. The initial blue swirled and faded. It lost shape, sending out tendrils. Like a river mist, the questing scraps of energy drifted with the air currents, probing this way and that without direction.

Suddenly Powwell's vague blue flared white and engulfed the other two auras. The colors whirled in a bright circle, blending into one riotous rainbow of energy. The book in the library about Rovers said they joined their auras in order to combine their magic!

The door flew open with a flash of eldritch light and wind that smothered the fire in the hearth.

Ackerly stood framed in the doorway, his hand lifted as if to raise the latch. The boatman dropped the small trunk he carried on his shoulder, staring wide-eyed, gape-mouthed at the locked door opening without the aid of a human hand.

Myri huddled in the shadows at the back of the Rovers' sea cave where Televarn's uncle had dumped her without comfort or ceremony. His eyes had glittered with greed as he turned his back on her. No one had offered her any of the communal meal, or a blanket, or a change of dry clothes. All those niceties had been reserved for Televarn, who also ignored her.

She'd tried once to run past them, only to find five brawny young men blocking the opening of the cave. Desperate to be free, she had flashed compulsion spells, sleep spells, invisibility spells at the men. Every attempt had bounced back at her tenfold. She'd crumpled into the soft sand on the floor of the cave, exhausted and humiliated. How could she have been so naive as to fall under Televarn's compulsion to love him?

She fell into dreamless sleep, only to awake, unrefreshed, hours later on the bundle of blankets that retained Televarn's distinctive scent. Would he expect her to continue as his lover after his betrayal?

Hungry and cold, she watched twenty members of Televarn's clan standing in a tight ring around the flickering warmth of a cheery fire, hands linked, bodies swaying, minds in tune with an old woman's chant.

Televarn stood next to the old woman who led the clan in invocation and response. Myri sensed that the strange words they half-sang were in thanksgiving for the man's return. And something more.

A well of power rose with the flames toward the high ceiling of the cave. Each word and sway intensified the spell they wove.

The chant grew in volume. The circle of people dropped hands and shifted into an intricate dance pattern, still going round and round the fire. In and out. Around. Turn back the way they had come.

Myri inched closer to the Rovers, drawn to the magic they worked in unison. She needed to see what they did and how, needed to become a part of it. Memories of other dances performed around Equinox Pylons overlaid the current ritual. Which was she seeing?

Shivering in the darkness beyond the light and warmth of the spell, her feet and hands twitched, eager to join the dance, become a piece of that mighty spell. She reached out to touch Televarn as he passed her. Energy repulsed her hand. Televarn ignored her, intent on some inner beauty she couldn't yet see. His eyes glazed over with the trance induced by the dance—the chant.

Threads of energy bound the entire clan to each other. The intricate web seemed to begin and end with Televarn. Because he had been absent and they welcomed him back? Myri shook her head, trying to clear it of the need to entwine her own life's energy with the Rovers. Her need to join them only intensified.

The web of energy combined with moonlight streaming into the cave and became a dome encasing the Rovers, shutting Myri out.

A flash of movement near the mouth of the cave became a part of the compelling rhythms and dancing energy.

Amaranth skulked near the cave mouth in search of her.

Fear for her familiar sizzled through Myri's mind and body. The spell pulled at her, as if a strong wind dragged her toward the heart of the Rover clan. She resisted the magic, recognizing it for an artificial attraction similar to Televarn's love spell. The compelling need to join the Rover ritual burned out of her system.

Sand, shells, and bits of waveweeds swirled around the edges of the magic. The spell pulled all toward its heart. The Rovers danced *widdershins,* along the path of the moon. Myri resisted the urge to join the debris of life circling *deosil,* the path of the sun.

Amaranth stalked closer to the dancing Rovers, nearly dragging his belly on the ground. He mewled and prodded the invisible wall around the Rovers with nose and paw.

Colored lights sparkled across the spell's armor along a serpentine line. Amaranth's paw marked the beginning and end of the rainbow flashes. Shades of purple and lavender dominated the sparks. The barrier tore open in a ragged hole just big enough to admit the flywacket into the inner circle.

Myri pushed at the armor with her own hand and magic. Burning energy pushed her hand away with a painful jolt. Whirling sand crashed against the shimmering wall and burned in a beautiful array of red, green, and blue sparks.

Only Amaranth was admitted. The spell called him specifically. Amaranth, the rare flywacket who would bring the Rover clan gold, prestige, and honor.

She had to separate her familiar from the ritual and escape with him without disturbing the Rovers. Mind and eyes clear, she stepped away from the magic's influence.

Amaranth took a step closer to the doorway, into the circle.

"No!" Myri screamed. The sound bounced against the barrier of magical armor and echoed about the cave.

Amaranth took another step forward, oblivious to her cry.

Myri opened her mouth again. All of her inborn magic demanded release in defense of Amaranth, her familiar, her only friend, her family. Magretha had warned her against Rovers and their compelling rituals.

She unleashed a wordless *Song* in notes so highly pitched human ears could barely hear them. She *Sang* her love for the pesky black cat. She *Sang* of the freedom of the open skies he so enjoyed. She *Sang* of their life together, the two of them alone and separate from the rest of the world. Then she added notes of powerful love reminding him of how they had never been apart, and never should be.

Amaranth stopped in mid-stride, one front paw lifted to take the next step. The hole in the Rover barrier began to close. The dance inside the magic circle froze; the dancers caught in whatever pose the notes of her *Song* penetrated.

Still *Singing*, Myri grabbed Amaranth and pulled. The

magic tugged him back toward the inner circle. Myri pulled harder, grasping her familiar firmly around his ribs, just behind the delicate fold of his wings.

The old Rover women who led the chant and dance broke free of Myri's *Song*. Her black eyes, so like Televarn's in shape, color, and greedy treachery, locked with Myri's own. The magic compulsion to enter the circle began again.

Amaranth and the magic resisted her grasp.

Myri closed her eyes and *Sang* again, in quieter tones, lulling Amaranth to accept her will as best for them both.

The flywacket collapsed beneath her hands. Myri scooped him up and ran from the cave.

"Stop her!" screamed the old woman.

"She's got the flywacket," Televarn said.

Outside the cave, wind and rain lashed at Myri's face and hands. Cold numbed her fingers around Amaranth. Waves crawled forward, nearly to the mouth of the cave. Escape across the headland was truly blocked. The only way out of this cove was up.

A rude staircase had been cut into the cliffside to her right. That escape route led to a grassy plateau where the Rovers could chase and catch her and Amaranth.

"Can you fly?" she asked the now squirming familiar.

(No.) His entire body shook with reaction to the abrupt release of the compulsion spell.

"Hold tight," she told him as she slung him over her shoulder. Blindly she let her hands and feet find purchase among the jagged rocks. Up she climbed. Up where she could see and survey the terrain. Up where the Rovers couldn't follow.

"Myri, come down from there. You'll fall!" Televarn called. Charming persuasion oozed from his voice. But she was immune to him now. He had betrayed her.

He followed her. He was close. Too close.

She climbed higher, faster, using fingernails and toes to cling to the rocks. Amaranth mewed an encouragement.

"Myri!" Televarn's voice contained a note of desperation. "Myri, I love you. Come back to me."

"You only love the gold my familiar will bring to you," she retorted. Tears for a lost dream and the shattering of her love for Televarn blinded her in her quest for a new purchase among the rocks.

"I love you, too, Myri. We are meant to be together," Televarn pleaded.

"You used me. You used magic to compel me to love you so you could kidnap Amaranth. You don't know how to love for real." She reached higher, found a handhold, and pulled herself up.

"I love you, Myri. I won't ever let you go. Never. You belong to *me* now. Me and only me." Televarn grunted as he pulled himself up the rock face. He seemed to be an adept climber, following her rapidly.

Behind her and to the right she heard other feet scrambling on the staircase. She angled her climb to the next rock outcropping. She'd come out above the plateau, above the Rovers and their treachery.

"Myri, help me. I can't hold on!" Televarn's words trailed off to end on a scream.

Briefly she looked below her. A dark form lay sprawled on his back at the edge of the waves. Frothy water lapped at his feet, rose and covered him.

Her empathy reached out to him, needing to drag him to safety, needing to heal him.

She fought the powers within her. A compulsion stronger than the Rovers' ritual pulled her back to the cove. Pulled her back to betrayal and danger.

"No," she told herself. "I can't risk Amaranth to heal a lying, cheating, thieving Rover." She climbed on, easily outdistancing the men who climbed the staircase.

"Will I ever be allowed to stop running from those I want to love?" Tears fell freely from her face. A home and family seemed further away than ever.

Only the wind answered her with a lonely howl.

Chapter 17

Ackerly stared at the assembly in the kitchen. The five older apprentices stood, chairs overturned behind them, jaws hanging open and expressions of sheer amazement on their faces. The three younger boys, stared at each other in puzzlement, their mugs of cider hanging idle in their hands. They looked as if they hadn't the strength of will or steadiness in their legs to stand.

Nimbulan leaped from his comfortable armchair, splashing cider down the front of his robe. Another stain for Ackerly to sponge out.

"You did it, boys! You opened the door with magic." The Senior Magician patted each of them on the back so enthusiastically the apprentices stumbled out of their chairs.

Ackerly paused, assessing the room before entering. Opening a door and latch with magic shouldn't have elicited so much excitement. A matter of a series of simple levitations opened any lock. Ackerly could do it, with effort. So why all the fuss over the apprentices? And why all three of them instead of one?

"Come in, Ackerly. Don't just stand there. We have cause for celebration. Did you bring the Tambootie? Of course you did. Which pack is it in? We've got to try a new experiment." Nimbulan searched all the bags before the boatman could set them on the floor. "This is amazing. I wonder if it was the combination of Tambootie and cider or something special about the friendship among the boys. They did all come from the same region."

Unerringly, Nimbulan found the parcel wrapped in Ackerly's dirty shirts. Ackerly wondered briefly how his master knew where to find the pottery jug of dried Tambootie leaves.

"Maybe it was the age of the Tambootie. All of the essential oils permeated the pouch and seeped back into the leaves, giving the dose unusual potency," Nimbulan rattled on, heedless of the nonsense of his words.

"What happened, Nimbulan? What makes you so excited?" Ackerly placed a soothing hand on his friend's shoulder. He'd never seen him like this, even when they were boys in training. Even when they sold their first viable fertility spell to a middle-aged couple who had lost their only child and despaired of having another. Nimbulan had been so jubilant when he heard the spell worked he hadn't paid attention to the coins Ackerly had collected and pocketed.

Ackerly prayed Nimbulan would be equally forgetful of the gold left over from buying the Tambootie. The gold was the only triumph left to Ackerly. Nimbulan had all the magic. Why shouldn't his miserable assistant get to keep the gold?

"They did it. The three of them combined their magic to open the door. I saw it in their auras. Is this all the Tambootie you bought for five gold pieces? I had no idea the weed had become so dear." Nimbulan held up the now unwrapped crock.

How had Nimbulan known the exact price of the Tambootie?

Nimbulan had been the magician spying on him in Sambol. Nimbulan had somehow watched him pay over the five gold pieces. They both knew how many were left and should be returned.

A pain stabbed Ackerly in the gut. He wouldn't give up the extra three gold pieces he'd secreted in the sole of his boot. Nor the other five he'd hidden in the lining of his cloak. They were his. He'd earned them! Nimbulan would have paid over the entire twenty coins and more to get the Tambootie. Any price to feed his addiction to the weed. Surely he wouldn't begrudge Ackerly a small commission for saving him so much.

"This crock of Tambootie won't last very long. You should have gotten more. We have a lot of experimenting to do, boys. Come, let's get started." Nimbulan turned toward the stove. "We'll need more cider and a brighter fire. Nothing like a strong flame to focus on while heading into a trance. Will you fix the cider, please, Lyman. You seem to have a special touch with the spices."

For the first time since entering, Ackerly became aware of the old man standing by the hearth. He could have sworn that Lyman wasn't there when he entered. And Nimbulan had asked him politely to make the cider. Not an order. A request. He'd said "please." Nimbulan never said "please," to Ackerly anymore.

"Wait a minute, Nimbulan." Ackerly grabbed the Senior Magician's sleeve. "You mean you've already been giving the boys Tambootie in their cider?"

"Of course. They need to become used to the side effects before they face the trial by smoke."

"But you can't. It's too dangerous. They're too young." Ackerly frantically sought a way to stall the new experiments. He had to find out how much Nimbulan knew about his gold before a deep drug-induced trance took the magician into the void where all knowledge was available to those who knew where to look and what to look for.

Concern for the boys was the only thing that would keep Nimbulan away from the drug tonight. Ackerly didn't care if they all became addicted and stunted their growth. He needed time to hide his gold more securely. Perhaps a tale of bandits. The country was rife with them.

"You are right, of course, Ackerly. I was too excited by the way the boys combined their magic. We are all cold and tired. Time enough in the morning to examine the ramifications of this spell. Off to bed, boys. We all need a good night's sleep."

The three youngsters looked dead on their feet already. The spell they had worked dragged their shoulders down and made them shuffle. They could hardly keep their eyes open.

"Rollett," Ackerly called to the oldest of the apprentices. "See that they wash up and take their clothes and boots off before they fall into bed. We'll need all of you in the morning. Who's on kitchen duty?"

Powwell held up a weary hand.

"Forget it, Powwell. I'll take care of it." Briskly, Ackerly instructed the boatman to bring extra scullions with him at dawn when he brought the cook over from the keep on the big island. In a few moments he'd cleaned up the shambles Nimbulan left behind him with increasing frequency. When they'd both been apprentices, Nimbulan was known for his fastidiousness. This mess was worse than ever, clear evidence that the Tambootie Ackerly always added to Nimbulan's food had impaired his judgment.

Something needed to be done before Nimbulan figured out what had happened to his gold. Something drastic.

"May I help you clean up, Ackerly?" Lyman raised one white eyebrow with his query. "You seem troubled. Perhaps you'd like to talk?"

Not bloody likely, old man. You have a way of ferreting out secrets that I don't want told, he thought. Then he smiled and said, "Not tonight. I have much to think on. Take a hot brick to bed with you, Lyman. You'll sleep better with warm feet."

Nimbulan slumped in his cross-legged position, his shoulders nearly touching his knees. The fatigue of a long session in the void with the boys made him dizzy and nauseated. The elation of one small success sent his heart leaping into his throat.

Combining magic was possible. He'd witnessed it last night with a simple door opening. Today he'd participated in a similar spell to move a chair two hand's widths away from its original position.

I could have done it myself with only minor effort, he thought. *So why this tremendous fatigue?* Rovers wouldn't combine magic if the process were always so tiring. Maybe something in their rituals?

The deliberate vagueness of the book in the library irritated and intrigued him.

He sat up to assess the boys' condition. If they were in as bad shape as he after such a small achievement, he'd have to let them eat and rest. He needed a full meal himself, though they'd all partaken of a hearty breakfast at dawn. The water clock showed only an hour had passed since then.

The workroom spun. Each of his three young apprentices wavered and became three overlapping images. Hastily, he put his head back down. His brief glimpse of the boys had shown them collapsed on the floor in a similar condition.

"Food, Ackerly. We need food," he murmured, never doubting that the ever faithful Ackerly was nearby and ready to supply his needs.

A bowl of warm broth and a mug of cool cider appeared beneath his nose. Shoved there by Ackerly, no doubt. He sipped cautiously until his stomach stopped rebelling.

He peeked at the boys. They, too, were reviving, but still kept their heads down.

"Here, Master. I think you're ready for this now." Rollett handed him a plate of thick bread, meat, and cheese, and a jug of cool fresh water.

"Where's Ackerly?" Nimbulan asked between gulps of water. Using Tambootie always left him thirsty and needing to empty his bladder. As if the drug drained all liquid from his body.

"He said he had an errand to run on the big island, sir. He and Lyman crossed the causeway just after the morning meal. He left strict instructions for you to finish the water and all of the food. Lord Quinnault was here while you were in the trance. He'll be back later. Oh, and a messenger from Lord Kammeryl arrived. He's waiting for you in the courtyard, wouldn't enter the buildings, said they were haunted."

Nimbulan chuckled. The shadowed guardian spirit of the monastery hadn't been seen or heard from since he covered the well of ley lines two moons ago. If he reappeared again, he'd come through the courtyard where the messenger waited.

"Anything else, son?" he asked between mouthfuls. The food had a strange taste to it today. Probably an aftertaste from the Tambootie. He'd used a large dose this morning. He gulped more water to wash his mouth clean. The bitter taste lingered.

"A different messenger from Lord Kammeryl came earlier and left this for you." Rollett placed a rolled parchment into Nimbulan's hand. "He said it was urgent but didn't wait for a reply. He said you'd know what to do when you read it."

Nimbulan unrolled the message. His palms started sweating and itching. He rubbed them on his trews and looked at the sprawling handwriting he didn't recognize. Not Kammeryl's. The lord couldn't read or write for all his brilliance with maps and strategy. Some new clerk probably wrote the missive.

The written symbols blurred and danced all over the parchment, refusing to form words. Nimbulan closed his eyes and shook his head to clear it. He reached for the water again. His system should have cleared itself of the aftereffects of the Tambootie by now. He'd never had the legendary hangovers some magicians suffered.

He put down the parchment and rubbed his eyes clear. When he opened them, he could focus. The pale faces of his three apprentices greeted him. A little color tinged Powwell's cheeks, but blue veins pulsed wildly beneath the skin of his hands and neck. The other two were in no better shape.

"You boys aren't used to the void." The problem with the spell finally hit Nimbulan like a sandbag between the eyes. "I was dragging you through the void by myself as well as holding the spell together. Rollett, put the boys to bed for a few hours, then bring your classmates and Ackerly here, and Lyman, too, if he'll come. You all have some experience in the void. If any of you can get there on your own, besides me, I'll promote you to journeyman immediately."

"About time," Rollett muttered as he led the young apprentices out of the windowless workroom.

A few moments later, Rollett directed Maalin, Bessel, Jaanus, and Gilby to sit on the floor in a circle close enough to hold hands. He assumed the place to Nimbulan's right. A big grin creased his face. "I'll be journeyman before the hour passes," he said smugly.

"Me, too," Bessel chimed in. "I've been practicing and Tambootie doesn't make me sick like it does Maalin and Jaanus."

"Shouldn't I observe?" Gilby looked nervously toward the door. "Master Ackerly and Old Lyman aren't back from the big island yet. There's no one to guide your return if something should go wrong. You always told us, Master Nimbulan, never to go into the void without an anchor to pull us home."

"Correct, Gilby." Nimbulan gulped down a fresh pitcher of water. His tongue felt thick and clumsy. Yet he felt refreshed and fired by his eagerness to complete this experiment successfully. "Step out of the circle and monitor the fire. Try to maintain a light trance without any Tambootie. At the first sign of trouble, grab Rollett and me first. We're the strongest and should be able to help you pull the others back. Not that I'm expecting trouble. This same spell worked this morning. Only the inexperience of the apprentices held us back."

He snapped his fingers. An infusion of Tambootie leaves in hot water brewing in large mugs appeared before each of the six experimenters.

"Drink up, boys. I'm anxious to see how this procedure works."

They all hoisted the dose of Tambootie to their lips and drank deeply of the bitter brew.

"Breathe in, one, two, three," Gilby guided them.

Reality blurred around Nimbulan. People and furniture grew fuzzy around the edges. His heart rate increased with excitement. He was finally going to prove that magic could be combined and thus control any solitary magician. No single Battlemage could defeat the combined might of Nimbulan and his helpers. Only then could magic and magicians remove themselves from war and politics and become neutral servants of all the people of Corònnan.

"Breathe in, one, two, three," Gilby chanted a second time.

The void beckoned Nimbulan, crowding out the lantern light in the workroom. He'd never climbed into the black nothingness so easily. His elation didn't keep him from checking on the boys. All four were still seated in a circle holding hands, but each aura reached for the void individually.

"Breathe. . . ."

Nimbulan lost track of Gilby's chant as blackness enclosed him. He looked around for the others.

Nothing. No one.

The blackness robbed him of sight, hearing, smell, touch. Only the bitter aftertaste of timboor lingered.

Timboor! Poison Timboor, not useful Tambootie.

Chapter 18

Ackerly bent over Nimbulan's crumpled body. He listened carefully with ears and magic for signs of breath or heartbeat.

Nothing.

He pulled his glass from his trews pocket and held it beneath the master magician's nose. No cloud obscured the pristine clarity.

Tall and thin in life, the man he had served since they had both been boys, seemed diminished, shrunken in death.

"In the end we all are reduced to this, regardless of talent," he whispered to himself. "How much Tambootie did he have?" he asked the assembled apprentices. All eight of them who now looked to him for leadership and training.

His heart beat a little faster with excitement.

Grief, he told himself. *Only grief. But now I can make something of this ragtag school. Something important. Something profitable.*

"He took a standard dose with the younglings right after we broke our fast at dawn," Rollett said through the tears he choked back.

"That spell succeeded, but he was greatly fatigued. Once he'd eaten and drunk deeply, he took another standard dose with the older boys," Gilby finished. White-faced with shock and guilt, the young man's hands shook and his shoulders trembled. "I tried to pull him out of the void. Him and Rollett first, like he said, but his soul wouldn't return to his body."

"We followed him into the trance just like always. But when we got to the void, he wasn't there. I saw the others but not him!" Jaanus added. "He wasn't there."

The others nodded their agreement. Something had gone terribly wrong between the first and second dosage. Or perhaps all the years of accumulated addiction had finally taken him.

Ackerly looked at Nimbulan's body once more for obvious signs of why he had died. Beside him lay a wrinkled piece of parchment, partially unrolled and flattened. The writing wiggled and bounced around as he watched. He reached for it then quickly withdrew his hand.

"The guilt is not yours, boys," he said still staring at the parchment. "Where did this come from?" He pointed at the written message.

"A courier from Lord Kammeryl d'Astrismos," Rollett replied, also staring at the parchment. "He didn't wait for a reply but said it was urgent." His mouth remained slightly open, eyes wide, as the implication of the spell contained within the message penetrated his grief.

"Maalin, you are good with fire. Burn the thing, without touching it, as soon as we leave the room. It is tainted with magic and poison. I sense blood in the ink—the work of a Bloodmage!" Ackerly bowed his head and closed his eyes until the gasps and murmurs of the apprentices died away. "I should have been here to guide the spells. I could have intercepted the message and kept Nimbulan from going into the void so soon after the first spell. If he'd waited, the poison in that parchment might not have affected him so strongly."

Powwell sobbed openly. Zane and Haakkon sniffed.

Suddenly their love for Nimbulan irritated Ackerly. *They don't love me!* But he was the one who made sure they were fed and had blankets and firewood to keep out the winter chills. He was the one who did all the work around here.

He suppressed his anger. After Nimbulan was safely buried, he could show these ungrateful boys where their loyalty should lie.

His thoughts kept returning to the possibilities for the future, now that Nimbulan and his ideals no longer hindered him.

"We must dress him in his ceremonial robes for burial. Delay will serve no purpose. There is a crypt beneath the chapel. I can think of no more fitting place for him to take his final rest. We will bury him at sunset." Abruptly, he turned on his heel and exited the room before he broke out in shouts of glee.

Free, I'm free at last! He'd just slip Nimbulan's formal robes over his everyday clothes. That way he wouldn't have to pay the village women to wash and prepare the body. A little delusion spell would make the boys think he'd wrapped the body tightly in expensive shroud cloths, but he'd only use strips from an old sheet. No use spending any more money on the dead than necessary. They certainly weren't in a position to appreciate it.

Only briefly did he wonder at the warmth and suppleness of the body that had supposedly been dead for some five hours.

A tangle of bright umbilical cords knotted and dragged Nimbulan across the void so fast he couldn't comprehend the colors or his destination. He sensed, more than saw, a purpose or design in the symbolic life forces. All seemed to be shimmering crystal tinged with a primary hue. Except the center one. The one driving the others flashed all colors of the spectrum so fast it appeared to be no color at all.

A thought struggled to be born in his consciousness, for he had no body or brain left to house such things. These strange life forces must be guiding him to his next existence. An existence free of his addiction to Tambootie. The drug was necessary to enhance the inborn talent of magic. Too bad it also hastened his next existence. An existence he couldn't yet imagine, but wanted to reach. Now. Without delay, before he regretted leaving Coronnan and his work unfinished.

(The time is not yet ripe for you to leave your destiny behind.) The bright life forces wrapped tighter around him, propelling him deeper into the void, or out of it. He couldn't tell which without a body to sense direction.

Once before that voice had sent him out of the void. Who? What?

His questions and concerns dissipated. The effort to remember was too much. Better to drift with the bright life forces. Red and blue, green and yellow. Red for Keegan. Blue for himself. Yellow for Ackerly. Green for the combined auras of his apprentices. Iridescent crystal all color/

no color reminded him of Myrilandel with her pale blond hair and skin so thin her blood veins shone through it, pulsing purple shadows like bruises. . . .

(Go back, Nimbulan.)

Why?

(Impudence in a human will not be tolerated!)

Was that a chuckle behind the demanding voice? Nimbulan fought the lethargy of the sense-robbing void. Laughter. Humor. Irony. These were the qualities of Life. Qualities he missed greatly, had known too little of these last years. So many of his friends and acquaintances had died. *We should have explored the world with laughter rather than fight each other to the death,* he mentally addressed the spirits of all his fallen comrades.

He appreciated the quirk of fate that he found laughter in the infinite darkness but not in his corporeal life. He laughed with the voices who loved Life and wanted to make the most of it.

What was his life? All he'd known for many years was a driving need to find new magic, better magic to protect his lord. The only lord capable of holding together the volatile factions of Coronnan and ending the wars.

He'd supported that lord—what was his name?—and his father for nigh on twenty years. Neither man had accomplished much in that time.

No lord had.

(Lord Quinnault de Tanos dares to dream of peace when the others are too shortsighted to think farther ahead than the next battle.)

Or the next lover, Nimbulan added, remembering Kammeryl d'Astrismos and his string of younger and younger bedmates. A wave of revulsion flooded his consciousness.

(Does your reaction to that man tell you the value of your loyalty to him?)

Too heavy a question. The tangle of bright life forces danced around him with sparkles of joy, of life, love, and laughter.

Laughter. He'd miss laughter if his next existence proved as full of war and responsibility as the last one.

(Your latest life doesn't have to end. You can fill it with love and laughter, with family and friends. You don't have to be grim and sad all of the time, if you place your loyalty

correctly this time. If your loyalty belongs to peace and not to one man who will betray you, you will know Life to its fullest. Peace. Love peace. Love life. Love the one who draws you back to Coronnan. . . .)

A sinking sensation. Tendrils of pain. Cold. Hands and feet that trembled with weakness and chills. A hard bier pressing against his aching back.

"I'm alive. I have a body," Nimbulan whispered through stiff and parched lips. "I'm thirsty and hungry." Sound echoed in his ears. The kind of sound that bounced against stone walls.

He tried to open his eyes. He thought they were open. Blackness still surrounded him. A different blackness from the sense-robbing void. Sense-cleansing as well. All traces of a Tambootie hangover had disappeared.

The sound of dripping water, steady and rhythmic, awakened his other senses. Mold and something rotten assaulted his nose.

Feebly he snapped his fingers on his right hand, too tired to lift it more than a finger-length above his chest. A tiny flicker of witchlight sat on the end of his index finger. Not much. Enough. He lay on a stone slab in a stone niche— open blackness to his right, solid, damp stone to his left, above and below.

The witchlight vanished, leaving false flashes before his eyes. He'd seen enough. Only the walls of a crypt were lined with open niches the perfect size of a man's body.

He pressed his feet hard against the end of his bier trying to straighten his cramped knees. This burial chamber had been intended for a shorter man.

Men were shorter in centuries gone by.

An old crypt. A very damp and untended one. Where would Ackerly and the boys bury him but beneath the chapel in the old monastery? They must have believed him dead. Perhaps he had been dead for a time. During the time he'd wandered the void with the pretty crystal umbilicals.

For a moment he wanted nothing more than to be a part of the intricate dance of life-that-was-not-Life.

Some force beyond his ken had given him back his life. The destiny planned for him by the Stargods had not yet been fulfilled.

And yet the void was so beautiful, so peaceful. . . .

"Snap out of it!" he admonished himself. The Stargods had returned him to his body for a reason.

Carefully, he turned his head to the open side and flicked another ball of witchlight ahead of him. Crumbling skeletons filled a few of the other niches. Most people avoided these older crypts because of the sight of so many generations of the dead. No one would think to bring flowers to his tomb and rescue him.

He had to find his own way out. Only one niche lay between him and the stone floor. He drew up his stiff knees as far as the ceiling of his tomb allowed and inched closer to the edge. He tried to swing one long leg out, only to discover both legs bound together by a shroud. The same shroud, hastily and scantily wound about his body kept his hands crossed on his chest. He could wiggle his fingers but not move very far. Whoever prepared him for burial used just enough winding cloths to keep him in place, and no more.

He couldn't break the hold the few cloths had on his limbs. Very well, he'd have to roll out of the niche all at once and hope he didn't break any bones during his fall.

As he squirmed and wriggled free of his tomb, the shroud tore and loosened across his chest. He'd been bound in a threadbare old sheet rather than sturdy new linen. He worked his right arm free and felt for the edge. His hand measured the distance and found a small ledge to grasp and ease his fall. Ready to swing his legs out, he paused and wondered why the shroud hadn't completely covered his body and head in tight wraps of linen soaked in preservatives. Surely Ackerly had access to necessary funerary regalia. Lord Quinnault de Tanos would have provided a shroud and servants to wash and prepare the body for burial.

If Ackerly had bothered to ask for them. If Ackerly had informed anyone of Nimbulan's "death." Surely lords and peasants alike would have noticed the lack of proper burial clothes and herbs.

"I thought you my friend, Ackerly. Couldn't you spend a little money for the old women who tend the dead? Didn't you have enough respect for me to provide a proper funeral with shroud and priest and mourners?" Anger heated

Nimbulan's cheeks. He allowed his emotions to fuel his cramped muscles and propel him outward.

With one hand braced on the ledge, he landed safely on his side a few feet below his "final" resting place.

"Why the haste?" he kept asking himself as he stripped off the winding cloths and discovered he was still wearing his everyday tunic and trews beneath his formal robe—not the newest or cleanest one at that.

Why?

(Who?)

Nimbulan looked around, seeking the source of the voice in the far corners of the crypt. Had he truly heard it or was it an echo of his spirit journey in the void? No answers came to him. He aimed the witchlight toward the shaky ladder carved into the wall that led to the trapdoor entrance.

(Hasten not from one death into another.)

This time Nimbulan used the last of his reserves to fill the subterranean crypt with light.

"Are you a ghost? Perhaps the guardian spirit returned?"

No answer. Only the echoes of his own whispers and the lingering memory of the warning bounced in his head.

Hasten not from one death into another, the voice still echoed in his mind.

Who wanted him dead? Who could have arranged it?

The aftertaste of Timboor returned to his mouth. *Timboor.* An overdose of the poison fruit on top of the extra doses of Tambootie he had ingested for his experiments.

He'd destroyed all of the remaining bits of Timboor after his bad experience with it while Ackerly was in Sambol. None of the apprentices would have had the boldness to contradict his orders and give it to him.

Keegan had deserted him when Nimbulan thought the boy well-loved and loyal.

No. Rollett and the others weren't as cynical, nor as ambitious as Keegan. They trusted him.

Didn't they?

Who? Who had been around that day? He had no way of telling how long ago that was. A few hours perhaps or several days? Possibly a week. He was hungry enough for that amount of time to have passed. A murderer could have slipped the Timboor into the Tambootie dosage and left the island before Nimbulan was pronounced dead.

Someone with a boat. Two messengers had arrived from Lord Kammeryl d'Astrismos. One had waited, one had left a parchment. The words written on the parchment had bounced and wavered as if written in magic code. He did remember the pattern of the writing had fallen into verse, like a spell. Could the Timboor have been rubbed into the parchment and combined with a spell? He had just come out of a Tambootie trance. His system was sensitive to all forms of the tree at that point. Perhaps his skin had absorbed the poison.

Or the poison had already been in his system causing his vision to blur.

He had no way of knowing now. If someone had tried to kill him once, they would try again.

He needed more information.

He needed a plan, a place to hide until he knew who had poisoned him and could guard against him.

Who? Who? Who? The question ricocheted around his skull with no answers.

A place to hide. Nowhere on the island.

How to escape from this tomb? He'd lift the trapdoor and find out what time of day awaited him. At night, when all slept unguarded, he'd leave.

He had to get off the island unobserved.

Chapter 19

Nimbulan dragged the little rowboat onto dry land beyond the sucking mudflats of the Great Bay. Winter dormancy made the beach grasses brittle and sparse. A stiff offshore wind smelled of salt and a new storm hovering on the eastern horizon. He needed to find shelter soon.

The night was clear and icy cold. Starlight and a crescent moon lighted his way. He pulled a thick winter cloak tight across his chest and shouldered a pack of provisions.

His raid of the pantry and storeroom had been surprisingly easy. Almost as if someone expected him to wake from the dead and flee the old monastery. He hadn't dared pilfer his private quarters for his staff and glass. Perhaps he should transport them here. No. Someone might witness the disappearance and trace the transport.

He would cut a new staff for his new life and career. What about the glass, expensive and difficult to replace? So many spells depended upon the qualities of perfectly clear glass to work. He'd just have to improvise with a clear pool of water.

He spared a moment to regret leaving his boys. But he had confidence in them. He'd trained them well, taught them honor and respect. He could imagine Rollett gathering all of the apprentices in the dormitory late at night, telling them stories and passing on the message of peace through community. Nimbulan's dream would live a little longer. At least until he came back with Rover secrets and new spells to implement the dream.

Which direction?

(East,) the frigid south wind seemed to sigh.

Rovers lived in the south more often than not. A Rover

spell might give him the clue to combining magic. Because of the curve of the Great Bay, east was the fastest way to the lands south of Coronnan. Once he had information about how Rovers worked their magic together, he'd return to the school and his work to remove magic from battles and politics. And find the man who had tried to murder him.

(*East.*) As good a direction as any. He centered his magic, concentrating on south, the closest magnetic pole. With his left hand up, palm outward and fingers slightly curved, he turned in a slow circle. A slight stab of awareness pierced his palm. South lay up that dune and to the right about twenty degrees. He must have drifted into the great curve of the Bay. If he kept a true course, halfway between east and south, he'd run into the trade road within a mile or two. Rovers traveled the highway.

The well-trod road wandered from village to village offering Rovers many opportunities to sell their distinctive metalwork and earn coins by entertaining the locals with music and dance. Eventually the road crossed the Southern Mountains at a point almost due east from Quinnault de Tanos' islands, and then into Rossemeyer. He had no desire to explore the high desert plateau of that impoverished kingdom. The road went many places before it reached the mountain pass.

Many places. Many choices. The sudden freedom of his situation swamped his senses. His friends and students and patrons thought him dead. He had no obligations. No responsibilities. No expectations.

For the first time in his forty-nine years he could go anywhere, do anything, and not keep a schedule. Giddy laughter sent him to his knees.

"I am free!" he yelled into the wind. Was that a laugh he heard in reply?

Nimbulan stared at the tree on the bluff above the beach. Just an ordinary tree. He tried remembering the last time he stared at a tree for no reason other than to stare at a tree, and failed. For the past thirty years, at least, he'd had to weigh the location of the tree, its height, how much wood it could provide campfires, would it become a rallying point to turn the tide of battle, how many men could hide in it for ambush . . . ?

"You are the most beautiful tree I have ever seen!" he yelled as loudly as he could, throwing out his arms as if to embrace the world. "You are beautiful because you are just a tree."

He drank in the tranquillity of the moment until the winter air reminded him to move on.

A pang of guilt almost sent him back toward the islands. He'd set up the School for Magicians in an attempt to force peace on the lords of Coronnan. The lords didn't want peace. He'd tried. What more could they ask of him?

(Success.)

His only clue to success lay with the Rovers, along the trade road that wound its way east. He set his steps toward his journey. He'd find answers in the east. Maybe he'd find his life there, too.

"Have you hospitality for a lost traveler?" Myri asked the stout woman who hovered in the mouth of an old sea cave. The ocean had changed levels many generations before and left the cave on a plateau a hundred feet or more above the beach. A village had grown up around the mouth of the cave. A fishing village judging by the nets strung out to dry and the boats hauled up for winter repairs.

"A mite young to be out on your own, girl. Where you hail from?" The woman placed her beefy hands on her hips. Her girth and the double doors framed and hung in the mouth of the cave clearly blocked Myri's passage into the domicile behind her. The raucous songs and the smell of spilled ale coming from behind the woman told her a tavern filled the cave.

"I ran away from a great battle. The wars took everything from me, my home, my family. . . ." Myri cuddled Amaranth closer to her face as if hiding tears. In all the places she'd asked hospitality in the past weeks since fleeing Televarn and his searching Rovers, she'd learned to stretch the truth and portray emotions she didn't always feel. Villagers empathized with those who'd been displaced by the war, a fear they all shared. Few trusted aimless travelers. Rovers, thieves, and marauding soldiers made them cautious.

So Myri told them what they wanted to hear. The voices and the circling wind that kept pushing Myri east didn't object to her half-truths and playacting. She couldn't travel East any farther without running into the ocean.

If only she could forget Televarn and the pain he'd left in her heart. She forgot so many things, why not the treacherous Rover?

"Like as not, we'll see more of your kind. Had a whole family through here last week. Thought they'd try their luck in Hanassa rather than put up with the wars here. Living with outlaws and thieves in that hole in the mountain can't be worse than living with armies constantly tearing up fields and scavenging all they can cart away." The woman dropped her arms bud didn't move aside.

"I'm very hungry." Myri's stomach growled loudly of its own volition.

"Bet that cat is, too. Can't afford to give everyone food. You'll have to work for it. You don't look strong enough to fetch and carry here in the pub."

"I know herbs and healing. I can sweeten the stale ale and make your bread so light it doesn't need to be dipped in beer to chew."

"Healing? You a magician?" Suspicion darkened the woman's eyes. Healers belonged with the armies that plagued them all. "We got no use for those bastards. Stealing out harvest and our young women. And if we don't give 'em up fast and willing, they burn us out." The woman crossed her arms across her ample bosom and stared hard at Myri, daring her to claim the extensive training required to turn a person of talent into a magician.

"I'm only a witchwoman. I've never been trained in magic, and I wouldn't accept it if offered. But I know what phases of the moon to gather witchwort." Myri stared back, letting her own fear of magicians shine through her eyes.

"If you want to hasten a birth . . . ?"

"Pluck the freshest leaves of witchwort at the full moon and make an infusion of them immediately," Myri replied to the testing question.

"Every woman knows that. What else can you do with witchwort?"

"Gather the blossoms at the dark of the moon and dry them until they crumble. Sprinkle them on porridge three mornings in a row and your courses will come regular again." Or abort an unwanted baby.

"I heard you had to use them five days in a row."

"Only if you are more than a moon late."

The woman nodded her acceptance of the prescription. "Got me a great, honking boil under my arm. Won't let me raise my arm or lift anything heavier than my drawers. Can't sleep 'cause of it. All Granny Katia's poultices didn't help at all. Reckon you can't hurt nothing if you lance and drain it. Do it proper so's the infection don't spread, then you've got a place to stay, girl. I'm Karry, short for Katareena. You got a name?" Finally, the woman stepped aside, clearing the doorway for Myri to enter.

Warmth and noise blasted Myri's senses the moment she crossed the threshold. The smell of unwashed male bodies nearly overwhelmed the aroma of baking bread and fermenting brews. Amaranth buried his head beneath her arm rather than face the men who halted their songs and stopped eating to stare at her.

"She's a healer, boys, not a whore. Go back to your drinks," Karry said loud enough for all to hear, even in the back corners of the tavern.

"What's the difference between a healer and whore?" yelled a man with broken teeth and long ropy scars on his arms.

"How much she charges!" replied a man from across the room. "Whores are cheaper."

"Ask your wife the difference when she needs a midwife, Timmon. She'll bash your head in for looking at another woman after knocking her up for the ninth time," said a man across the room as he shook his finger at the man with broken teeth.

"Maybe she'll welcome another woman to keep him away from her after the ninth babe gets here." Timmon's drinking companion slapped him on the back laughing.

"Never mind them, girl. It's winter, and they're bored 'cause they can't get the boats out. If the wind dies down by dawn, they'll be out all day and too tired tomorrow night to know their names, let alone bother you. Though with that pale hair and clear skin of yours, you'd best keep your distance from some of them. The quiet ones are the ones you gotta watch. The loud ones are more interested in hearing their own words than doing anything about it. You got a name, girl?"

"Myrilandel, and my cat is Amaranth." Myri followed her hostess along a winding path through the crowded trestle tables toward a curtain draped across the back of the chamber. No man touched her, though she passed quite close to some. Apparently the tavern mistress' word was law here.

"Karry they call me, though I was born Katareena, like my Ma and her Ma before her. Did I tell you that a'ready? Name goes back almost as old as this cave and the pub in it. Always been Katareenas here. Probably always will be. My own daughter has the name and the babe she carries will, too, if this one's a girl. She's got three boys already. But she's carrying this one different. Hope it's a girl. Need another Katareena to carry on the tradition."

"Is she having trouble with the babe?" Myri's healing instincts awakened after weeks of dormancy. She hadn't allowed herself to "feel" anything for the people she treated with herbs and simples along her journey.

Suddenly this little village felt like home. They needed her. They'd welcomed her—after a fashion. Some villages begrudged her the bread and cheese they handed her and made her eat outside for fear of a stranger in their midst. Karry had invited her in. Granted she'd be expected to earn her keep. That was better than being denied admittance just because she was a stranger.

She must have traveled far enough east and south for the wars to have remained a distant threat rather than an imminent peril.

Is this the home you promised me? she asked the voices. No one answered, but the warm and comfortable feeling didn't leave her.

"Nothing much wrong with my Katey, but she's carrying high and all in front. From the back she don't look eight moons along. She's tired all the time and her feet swell, but that isn't unusual so close to her time, especially chasing three boys with more energy than sense." Karry chuckled as she thrust aside a wall curtain to reveal a larger inner chamber that served as home and warehouse for the tavern.

"Has the boil troubled you long?" Myri set Amaranth down on a barrel of ale. He sniffed the rim with grudging curiosity. When he was satisfied the barrel posed no threat, he jumped down and investigated the one beside it. He kept his wings safely hidden. He hadn't flown since he tangled with Televarn's fishing net. She hoped he'd healed, but she didn't know for sure yet.

"This boil started up as a little spot of rash going on two weeks ago. What you going to need, girl. Hot water? Mustard? Cobwebs for a bandage?"

"Lie down and let me look at it first. Two weeks is a long time. I hope I don't have to treat you for more than just the boil."

Karry heaved her bulk facedown on the pallet off to the right. She fumbled with the ties of her gown until she freed her left arm and breast. Her firmly muscled arm showed pale pink in the dim light. An angry red lump the size of Myri's thumbnail glared at her from beneath the arm near the back. Red streaks were beginning to spread outward in a spiderweb of infection.

Deftly, Myri prepared what she needed for the simple procedure. She cleaned her knife and the boil. Then a quick slash of her smallest, sharpest knife across the top and a second cut across it.

Using the side of the knife to press against the eruption, she drained it, catching the pus in a clean cloth, until it bled freely, cleanly red and free of infection.

Should she add a little of her own healing to keep it healthy? Not a full trance; that would make her lose control and drain her of too much energy. Just a touch to make sure all of the infection was gone.

"Mbrtt," Amaranth rubbed against her ankles. *(Trust her. Help her with magic.)*

With her familiar leaning against her, she channeled a little energy through her hand and into the open sore.

"You finished yet?" Karry squirmed restlessly on the pallet. "I've got to get back to my customers before they sneak out without paying up. Reckon you've earned a good meal and place to rest. Stay here. No one will bother you."

"I'm finished, Karry." Myri applied a quick poultice of warmed herbs and pressed it firmly against the wound to keep it open and draining into the absorbent moss. "You'll need to keep this compress on for a few hours. Do you have a bandage?"

"My shift is tight enough to keep it in place." Karry stood, righting her clothes and checking the poultice. "Stargods help me, I get stouter faster than I can make new clothes."

"But you work hard. Your body is healthy." Otherwise the boil wouldn't have cleaned up so easily. A frailer person would have been riddled with the poison.

"Well, the men don't mind a little extra of me when the need is on them and I've got the time. And I'm strong enough to heave barrels around when I need to. Don't have to depend on a man like most women. The Katareenas have always been independent. 'Bitches' some of the men call us when we don't act meek and helpless. They learn to respect us, though."

"Um, Karry, ah . . . I don't think you should sleep with the men for a while. Not until the wound closes."

"You volunteering to take my place, girl? Men get angry when there isn't a woman around to take care of them. A lot of their wives are carrying too heavy to safely lie with their men this time of year. We had a bountiful Equinox festival last Spring."

Televarn's beautiful body flashed through Myri's memory. She'd found great pleasure and satisfaction in their lovemaking. None of the men she'd seen in the pub could compare with the handsome Rover. They would be more honest in their faithlessness.

She couldn't enjoy quick, temporary joinings. She wanted a husband or nothing.

"I'm thinking maybe one of them gave you the infection that started the boil. I've known men to pass all sorts of ailments on to their women."

"Not my men." Karry threw back her head and laughed. "They're clean, and I don't take on strangers. Not that we get many. Moncriith's the only visitor we get. He wouldn't let himself pick up some nasty disease."

"Moncriith?" Myri stilled, all senses alert. Her balance shifted to her toes automatically, ready to flee.

"So you know him?" Karry's eyes narrowed in speculation. "You the witchwoman he's hunting?"

Myri grabbed for Amaranth rather than answer. The pesky flywacket eluded her hands. He stared at her, annoyed and indignant, as only a cat can be.

"Don't worry about Moncriith. He's got a honeyed tongue, but folks around here don't care for him much. He wants them to uproot and follow him to the ends of the Kardia in search of demons. No one in this village has the time or money to leave hearth and home to follow him on some wild lumbird chase. Who cares if magicians are causing all kinds of trouble with the armies up north? Doesn't mean they have demons living inside them. None of them ever comes here to trouble us. Only magic we ever see is an occasional witchwoman seeking a new home. And maybe a Rover or two. But we ain't big enough or important enough to warrant much else."

"You get Rovers here, too?" Myri gulped, trying hard not to dash out the door and keep running until she . . . until she . . . What? *This is the closest place to a home I've found. I have to stay a while to know for sure.*

"Oh, don't worry none about Moncriith. He won't come again until high summer. By then we'll figure out a way to hide you or disguise you. If you're as good a midwife and healer as I think you are, this village needs you. We won't let some crazy Bloodmage take you. Who's to say but him if he's really a priest like he pretends. Yoshi!" She raised her voice on the last word.

A moon-faced young man with light, almost colorless eyes and dark hair peeked from behind the curtain. "Yes'm?"

"Yoshi, get Myri something hot to eat and find her an extra blanket and pallet. Give the cat some milk and a little of last night's fish. They're staying with me a while."

Chapter 20

Nimbulan shivered slightly as rain once more penetrated his cloak and hood. Tonight he'd beg hospitality in a village. If he found one. For several weeks he'd shied away from other people lest they recognize him. His aimless wandering in a generally southeasterly direction had taken him well beyond the usual battlefields and recruiting regions.

As if his thoughts of warm huts and cheerful fires with tasty dinners roasting over them had conjured the aroma, he caught the scent of bread baking. The warm yeasty smell roused his stomach and set his mouth watering. Food. Warmth. People to share the food and the fire with. A place to sleep out of the rain. Magic and lords, battles and schools had no place in his life now.

Following close upon the aroma of baking bread came the clip-clop of steed hooves against the hard-packed dirt road. The light rain was persistent but not intense enough to turn the road to mud. Nimbulan counted the sounds. He heard several steeds plodding along at a slow but steady pace. He guessed they pulled heavy loads rather than bearing riders.

A whisper of caution wiggled into his mind. He stepped off the road, behind a tree and waited.

Voices. Gibberish. Either they were farther away than he thought, or the other travelers spoke a foreign tongue. Curiosity vied with caution.

Down the road, four sledges came into view. Brightly painted cabins perched atop the conveyances. A thin coil of smoke rose from a metal chimney in the last cabin—the source of the baking bread. A team of two small draft steeds, perhaps half the size of the huge sledge steeds used to haul heavy trade loads or army supplies, pulled each of the strange vehicles. Dark-haired men walked beside the teams. None of them carried the long whips customarily used by caravan wranglers. Following the sledges came a host of people, old and young, male and female. All of them dark-haired with olive-toned skin. They wore black accented with bright colors in kerchiefs, vests, sashes, and petticoats. Scrolling embroidery decorated each layer of clothing.

He'd found a clan of Rovers. Old legends and fearful gossip raced through his memory. *Can't trust a thieving Rover. No one crafts metal better than a Rover. Rovers will steal your children. Wild animals love Rovers and obey with little or no training. Rover women have no morals and will steal your soul. Rover women know tricks that will delight you in bed and leave you smiling for days.*

The old whispers lingered, especially the last one.

An elderly man lifted his voice in song.

The lyrics slid over Nimbulan's understanding. Definitely a foreign language. But the tune made his feet itch to walk in rhythm and harmony with these people.

The women picked up the chorus, children chanted the refrain and men hummed a harmony in three parts, unlike anything Nimbulan had ever heard. The haunting rhythm reached out and grabbed him, setting his feet tapping and begging him to join his voice with the others.

He resisted, unsure if he should betray his presence yet. Instead he hummed along, letting the music vibrate from the back of his throat down to warm his belly. A hint of magic drifted in that song. The entire clan sang a spell of joy.

Nimbulan chuckled. Though he didn't recognize the words, he knew their intent: avoid trouble they didn't initiate by robbing troublemakers of their anger.

"You might as well join us, stranger," the lead wrangler said without stopping the caravan.

Nimbulan stepped out of the shadows. He knew the song had robbed him of caution and alarm. He didn't care. "Which way do you travel?" he asked, falling into step beside the man. His face seemed young, though squint lines around his black eyes suggested years and maturity.

"We travel where the road leads us, unless we find a better direction along the way." The wrangler whistled sharply at the steeds who had slowed their pace. The animals picked up their feet with brisk purpose immediately.

"This road looks good to me for now. I'd welcome companionship for a time." Nimbulan scanned the clan spread out behind him. A vague similarity of the shapes of nose and chin told him they were truly a clan and not a motley gathering of outcasts. Who knew what crimes such a group would be capable of if they were immoral enough for Rovers to throw them out.

"Rovers are never lonely and rarely alone. Do you have a name, stranger?"

"Lan," Nimbulan offered the childhood shortening of his name. Rovers traveled everywhere; they probably had heard of Nimbulan the Battlemage.

"Lan." The Rover rolled the name around his tongue as if tasting it. "A good, simple name. Easy to say and remember. You are wise not to reveal your true name."

Nimbulan almost checked his stride in shock. A measure of self-preservation kept him beside the shorter, younger man, matching him pace for pace. "I've heard of that tradition. Some people believe possession of a true name gives one power over another."

"Possession of a true name gives a *magician* power over another." The Rover looked him up and down. "If you have magic, you keep it hidden, Lan."

For the first time, Nimbulan noticed the embroidery on the man's vest. Tiny stitches in silver and gold outlined symbols in ancient writing. The spoken language had died out centuries ago. Some magicians still used the pictorial writing to hide spells. Each glyph became a sigil of power.

"If I had magic, I'd run away from it. Few love magicians in Coronnan these days. They blame . . ." he almost said "us." "Magicians take the blame for winning and losing battles. Whoever wins, the common soldiers and their families lose."

"Aye." The Rover whistled again to the small steeds.

"Do you have a name, fellow traveler?" Nimbulan asked.

A comely woman in her twenties with a babe on her hip moved up beside them before the Rover could speak. An intriguing mole rested near the right corner of her mouth, inviting his gaze to linger on her full lips. She lowered her lashes flirtatiously over luminous dark eyes, watching Nimbulan as she did so. Her breasts nearly spilled out of her bodice when she walked. She'd reversed the lacing so that the garment opened from the top. Probably to nurse the child more easily.

In most societies, most women laced their bodices from top to bottom to indicate their lack of availability.

"The children are cold and hungry. Can we stop for a meal and a rest?" she addressed the leader of the clan while smiling speculatively at Nimbulan.

Nimbulan couldn't take his eyes off her mouth except to peer longingly at her breasts.

"Aye," the Rover chieftain replied. "At the next bend in the road. There is a clean-flowing creek there." He didn't look at the woman's blatant sensuality.

She twitched her hips in invitation as she moved back to the mass of Rovers behind the sledges. Nimbulan licked his suddenly dry lips. He hadn't had a woman in many, many moons. Perhaps more than a year. Women robbed a man of the energy needed for magic. Battlemages habitually made use of the occasional camp follower when they required a quick release of pent up frustrations. That kind of woman didn't expect courtship or lasting relationships. They didn't demand attention that could be put toward the work of saving an army from defeat.

He'd never understood Ackerly's preference for peasant women who clung to him, begging him to return and settle in their villages.

He wasn't a Battlemage anymore. If he succeeded in his quest, there would be no more Battlemages. He could take the time and expend the energy to woo a woman, get to know her, take time making love to her. . . .

"Tell me, leader of this clan of Rovers—I assume you lead, since the woman asked your permission to stop rather than relaying the orders of another—is pursuit of that woman forbidden to me?" Nimbulan continued to watch the woman, hoping he'd read her invitation correctly.

"Maia's man died last spring. He made the mistake of seeking shelter from a brief storm beneath a tree. Lightning killed him and the tree. I trust you'll be smarter."

"Is that permission to accept her advances?"

"She's free. I trust you are as well, or you wouldn't be wandering Coronnan alone." The Rover shrugged.

"I have no woman to bind me to hearth and home." An image of Myrilandel's moon blond hair and lavender-shadowed skin flashed before his mind's eye. More images of his apprentices tugged his heart back to the river islands and the school.

"I have never let a woman bind me." The Rover looked away as if embarrassed. "I find my taste running to fairer women than Maia. My instincts are telling me to spread my seed outside the clan. We become inbred too easily. For that reason, we'll welcome your seed. Take your pick of those who seek you out."

Nimbulan decided not to press the matter. The emotions filling the Rover's eyes could as easily lash out in punishing anger as they could dissolve into tears.

"If I am to rove with you for a time, I must know what to call you."

"Televarn. I am king of this clan and don't fear giving my true name to one and all."

"Televarn." Nimbulan tasted the name in open mimicry of the Rover's reaction to his own name. "An unusual name. Televarn, the one who talks to the Varns—mysterious beings who trade only in diamonds for vast quantities of grain and appear in our ports once a century. They never reveal face or hands or even the shape of their bodies, keeping all veiled and gloved in swaths of rainbow-colored cloths that appear filmy and transparent but hide more than they reveal. You must be a very powerful man if you are privileged to speak to these entities."

"I have more power than you can dream of, Lan. You may be a wandering magician, or a man who has lost all to the wars, though you have not the bearing of grief for such a man. I don't care what you are as long as you tell a good story over the campfire and break none of our laws."

"I have only a few beds left." Ackerly put a sorrowful expression on his face, trying not to look at the few coins the displaced family held out to him. "Alas, many families seek a place of safety for their children. I can only accept those who are truly talented." He allowed a sigh of regret to leave his lungs. The coins were base. Easily ignored.

"But . . . but Kalen has very powerful magic. We haven't had to use firestone to light the rushes since she lost her milk teeth." The mother, a wasted woman worn out by childbirth and hunger, held out her hand in entreaty. A single gold coin glinted against her palm. Her husband closed his fist around the five base coins, removing them from the bargain.

"Fire is an early sign of talent. Tell me, what else does the girl do?" Ackerly tried not to lick his lips in anticipation of handling that single piece of gold. He'd acquired twenty new pieces in the weeks since Nimbulan died. He'd made it known throughout the land that the School for Magicians was offering new apprentices a safe place to learn the one profession that could give a peasant family a guaranteed income and a measure of security against marauders.

The old monastery was fair to overflowing with adolescents and five more weary Battlemages seeking a quiet retirement from the wars.

"Show him, Kalen," the father ordered. He pocketed the lead and copper coins but let his wife keep dangling the gold before Ackerly.

He had been a merchant in Baria on the north coast until Lord Hanic had burned the town. From the ragged and threadbare state of their once finely tailored clothing, the family had been on the road for some time. The gold was probably the last of their former wealth. They must be desperate to be willing to part with it.

Kalen shook her head and tried to hide behind her mother's skirts, being careful not to let any part of her touch the father on the other side of her. Not quite ten, she looked to be a year or more from reaching puberty. If her talent proved true before her body matured, she would be one of the great magicians. Most apprentices didn't show any sign of talent until they were within a few moons of the change. Only the great ones, the men and women who could tap the ley lines and become as powerful as Nimbulan showed talent earlier.

Of course some of the great magicians refused to acknowledge their talents until raging growth sent their emotions awry and they couldn't keep it secret any longer. Minor magicians, like himself, only exhibited talent at or after puberty.

"What is it that you can show me, Kalen?" Ackerly squatted in front of her, making sure his head was level with her own. No use intimidating her into losing control or hiding her talent altogether. He'd learned that much in his recruiting these past moons.

From his crouched position he raised his eyes slightly to look the mother directly in the eye, tacitly asking approval to approach the child. So far, the woman had kept her head down, face in shadow.

As their eyes met, the woman's mouth opened in a silent gasp. "You?" she asked soundlessly. She moistened her lips with a flick of her tongue. Then she firmed her expression into meek subservience. Whatever flicker of recognition had passed across her face was gone, as quickly as it came.

Ackerly shrugged and turned his attention back to the little girl. The mother looked vaguely familiar. Maybe he'd met her in his long years of traveling with Druulin and then Nimbulan.

"It's a special secret." Kalen lisped the esses, not badly, but enough to hint at why she shied away from others.

"Special, yes. I can make fire, too. Does that make me as special as you?" Ackerly snapped his fingers and blinked. A tiny flame appeared on the end of his finger. Quickly he damped it and shook his hand as if the witchlight had burned him. Then he sucked the finger, making a rueful face.

Kalen giggled. "I don't burn myssself," she announced proudly and imitated the trick, holding the flame much longer than Ackerly did.

He watched her face for signs of fatigue. Her gray eyes remained calm and shining long after he would have collapsed from sustaining the spell.

"That's a very nice fire, Kalen. Can you do anything else?"

"Sieur Moncriith says I mustn't. He says the Stargods won't like it if demons find me cause I can work magic."

Curse the wandering misfit. This wasn't the first potential apprentice who'd had magic scared out of them by the wandering preacher. Ackerly had sympathized with Moncriith when it cost him nothing and gained him an ally. But now the Bloodmage stood between him and gold.

"The Stargods only get angry if you use your magic for bad things, like hurting a pet cat or making your brothers look like fools. Surely it wouldn't hurt if you showed me your special secret." Ackerly opened his eyes wide, willing the child to trust him.

"But it's a secret," she protested, looking up at her mother. The woman caressed the girl's hair soothingly. The father glared hard at her, lifting his upper lip in an almost sneer.

"Then perhaps you can show me if we go out into the corridor where no one else can see?" Ackerly held out his hand to her.

Her mother prodded the girl's back with an open hand. "It's all right, Kalen. He won't hurt you, and we won't tell Sieur Moncriith when we see him."

Shyly, Kalen put her tiny hand into Ackerly's pudgy one. Ackerly stood up stiffly and walked her through the open doorway of his office. A few weeks ago this large room had been Nimbulan's private study. Only one of many things Ackerly had claimed as his inheritance from his former master.

Now he was Master of the School for Magicians. He knew how to run a school that earned money instead of draining it from Nimbulan's purse. Acquiring a truly talented child could fill his coffers faster.

In the long echoing hallway, Ackerly sat on the empty bench where supplicants usually waited for him. Kalen's family was the last of the day's applicants. No one else lingered within sight.

Kalen climbed up beside him. She sat with her hands in her lap and her feet swinging above the floor. She looked out the narrow window to the central courtyard rather than at Ackerly.

"Now will you show me what you can do, Kalen?"

Every door along the corridor slammed shut, loudly and without the aid of human hands.

Ackerly jumped at the sudden noise. "Very good, Kalen. Can you open them, too?"

She nodded as each door in turn creaked open, one right after the other, starting at the far end and progressing to his own office. A tiny smile twitched at the corner of her mouth. "Want to see what else?" She didn't lisp now.

Ackerly nodded, trying not to show how impressed he was by the strength of her talent, nor question the sudden confidence in her demeanor. Telekinesis and fire before the age of ten! She'd match Nimbulan in power, if she took to disciplined training.

Kalen closed her eyes in concentration. Ackerly watched her small face scrunch up. Her skin turned pale beneath her muddy brown braids and the spray of freckles across her nose. Was that a touch of auburn in her hair? Red hair usually accompanied a magical talent inherited from the Stargods. Neither of her parents showed a trace of red in their hair.

Suddenly he lost touch with the Kardia. Vertigo sent his vision whirling. His stomach dropped into his feet. The distress passed quickly and he looked down. The bench floated an arm's length above the stone floor. Slowly, Kalen turned the bench, with them on it, around and gently set them back down.

"Very good, Kalen. I think we've found a place for you here in the school." Ackerly jumped off the bench before she sent him flying again.

If her communication spells developed as easily, she could keep him in contact with the far corners of Coronnan and beyond.

Visions of gold piling up as he controlled a network of Battlemages from the school almost sent him into sexual ecstasy. Lords would have to come to him for access to any magician!

"With talent like hers, you shouldn't need quite so much money," her father stated, standing in the doorway. His brown eyes turned cold and calculating. "You'll be able to sell her services earlier than most apprentices'. You should pay us for the privilege of training her."

No sign of gold winked at Ackerly from the mother's hands where she stood beside her husband. She refused to look at anything but the floor. Her posture reminded him of someone. . . . The name "Guillia" jumped into Ackerly's mind. He wondered how he knew that.

Ackerly swallowed, trying to think. He needed that gold, not half memories of a quick tumble in the hay somewhere on his journeys. "Training is very expensive. Kalen must have books, equipment, and a variety of teachers, who must be paid. There is rent and food and firewood to be purchased."

Kalen's father held up a hand to stop Ackerly's protests before he uttered them. "Perhaps we can strike a bargain. You need a steward, someone to deal with suppliers. Someone who can travel and find your books and special equipment, as well as recruit new students who have gold to pay in tuition. Parents will pay more if you provide someone to oversee the raising of your students in matters other than magic. They are, after all, children in need of parents. My wife is an excellent cook. Our other children can run errands. Take in the entire family and you won't need to rely upon Lord Quinnault for servants and supplies. You will be beholden to no one and can sell the services of magicians to the highest bidder rather than give them away to the lord to whom you owe your livelihood."

"I can pay little. The school is not yet large and profitable." Ackerly stalled.

"For now, food and shelter will suffice. In a few moons, when we are all settled we can discuss my salary. A percentage of the profits, perhaps."

Chapter 21

Nimbulan watched Erda, the ancient witchwoman of the Rover clan, strum a lute lightly. The soft notes drifted around the large single-roomed lodge where the extended family had settled for the winter. Beside the central hearth, Maia complemented the quiet melody with a lilting descant on a wooden flute. Her green bodice and yellow headscarf played games with the colors of the flames. Highlights of bronze and gold flushed her face with intriguing shadows and planes.

Ah, Maia. He smiled at the thoughts of her nimble fingers stroking fiery music through his veins as they lay together beneath piles of warm furs each night.

At first he'd been hesitant to indulge himself in her softly rounded body, but privacy was an implied thing in this close-knit clan. Living so close together they simply ignored each other when appropriate. Drifting to sleep with the sounds of other couples making love had quickly dispelled his shyness.

The tune shifted to a more intense rhythm. The melody bounced into a compelling variation that set his toes twitching. Across the fire, a middle-aged woman and her man began a dance. They stamped their feet in counterpoint to the flute. She flipped her skirts, showing off shapely calves and knees. He bumped her hips with his own and clapped his hands over his head. In another quick gesture, his fingers tangled with the ties of her bodice, loosening them. Someone beat a new cadence against a skin drum. Others joined the suggestive bumping dance.

Nimbulan straightened from his recline against a makeshift backrest of packs. Maia grinned and winked at him around the flute. Her eyes twinkled mischievously. The mole at the side of her mouth taunted him as she puckered her lips to blow into the flute rather than into his ear. He winked back, knowing the delights she promised later.

How could he have believed himself content with his semicelibate life before joining the Rovers? To them sex was a open and joyous affirmation of life, not some furtive fumbling in the dark—paid for and quickly forgotten.

He leaned back again, watching the dancers. This clan made their own amusements. Night after night they found something new to while away the long hours of winter darkness. Music dominated their evenings and their days. They all worked hard at assigned tasks, then spent the rest of their time in pursuit of pleasure. He was amazed at the number of hours he had each day for contemplation and enjoyment.

No bickering and passing off of responsibility among these people. Nor any question of authority. They all knew who led them and what their role in the clan was. Sometimes Nimbulan wondered if their minds were all connected, passing thoughts and commands back and forth.

What an interesting idea. If he could figure out how to do that, then his school could train magicians to truly work as a team, even if they never learned to properly join their magic.

An ache of regret formed a knot in his throat. He missed his boys. But he couldn't return to them yet. He had secrets to learn.

Someone had tried to murder him to keep him from pursuing his quest for unity among magicians. He had to be careful.

An image of Powwell's freckles turning darker against his pale skin as he concentrated on a spell, invaded his mind along with an intense wave of loneliness. He pictured Powwell turning his wide gray eyes up to him, begging for an easy answer.

And Rollett, the orphaned apprentice who stood by his side in battle. Without his keen observations of all that happened during the battle, many of Nimbulan's spells might be misdirected. Rollett, who looked to him as a father. . . .

He gulped and pushed the emotions aside. This lazy routine of wandering was his life for now. The Rovers had accepted him as one of their own—mostly. He needed their complete trust before they'd show him the secrets of their rituals.

"My family works together very well, does it not, Lan?" Televarn sat beside him.

"You move as quietly as a cat. You should announce yourself." Nimbulan breathed deeply, trying to quiet his racing heart. People had never startled him before he met the clan. His magic hummed a warning whenever someone approached. How did Televarn avoid his natural alarms? He couldn't detect any countermagic.

How had the Rover known the precise angle of his thoughts?

"Why should we announce ourselves? Enemies could be warned as easily as family."

Without that sense of awareness, Nimbulan would never truly belong to them. Some of the warmth went out of the lodge and his life. His longing to return to his boys and the school intensified. He belonged there.

"There are ways for you to participate in our *Kardiagenea,* friend," Televarn said casually, watching the dancers rather than Nimbulan.

"Kardiagenea," Nimbulan murmured and stroked his new beard. "You make your own Kardia? Impossible." While his words denied the process, his heart leaped into his throat with eager anticipation. Televarn offered him a chance to share in the clan's unique bonding. Perhaps they'd finally reveal some of their magic.

"No, we seek to become the Kardia. All the elements and the cardinal directions combined. We merge with the blue lines that lace the surface of the land, connected by energy to the source of all knowledge, all magic, all life. Think of it, Lan. You could share the most intimate relationship of all. Better than joining your body to Maia's. You would join yourself to all life in your thoughts, your emotions, your very being." Excitement tinged Televarn's voice, infecting Nimbulan with the possibilities.

"How is this done?"

"With magic. Special magic."

"How can you know that I am capable of this magic?"

"You are a powerful magician. I sensed it the first moment we met. I knew it when you refused to give your true name."

"You have not asked for proof of my magic."

"Rovers know when they are in the presence of one who can work our magic. It is part of the *Kardiagenea*. We need no proof that you have Rover blood in you."

"If I have Rover blood in me, then why am I not part of the *Kardiagenea* already?" Part of him screamed a denial that any of his ancestors had stooped so low as to introduce Rover blood into the aristocratic family. He might be only the second son of a second son with no chance to inherit land or title, but he was proud of the lineage traceable back to the time of the Stargods. His dark auburn hair—before gray had faded much of it—proclaimed his pure ancestry.

"You need to be awakened if you are not born among us and exposed to the *Kardiagenea* from the moment of conception. Maia wants another child. Our clan needs more children. Children are the only true wealth of Rovers. You must be truly one of us before the child is conceived."

"You have too many mouths to feed now, Televarn." Nimbulan wasn't about to dash the man's hopes and deny himself access to this new magic. True magicians rarely sired children, and females with magic never carried a child to term. That was a fact of life he'd tried to compensate for with his numerous apprentices over the years, seeking a son or daughter in each one who came to him for training.

He'd lost them all to disease, accident, betrayal. Keegan's death had been the worst loss of all. The emptiness in him yearned to be filled. Televarn offered him the chance. . . .

"Our children are often born sickly. We mate too closely within the clan. Soon we must invoke the ancient laws against incest and banish all the young men to other clans as soon as they mature."

Nimbulan winced at the sense of loss each parent must feel if the boys were sent elsewhere, never to return.

"Your child will be healthy and wouldn't have to be banished," Televarn whispered.

"I would like a child of my own."

"As would I, but all the women of my family are too close to me. Many of the clans who might offer me a bride are also too close, or feuding with us. I must seek a mate elsewhere." A wistful look came over Televarn's face as he looked into the distance.

Nimbulan sensed his mind floating to a different time and place. A woman who eluded him? "How does this magic work?"

Televarn shook himself lightly, as if to banish his far away thoughts. "We have rituals that must be performed precisely. Any variation breaks our contact with the Kardia, and we must begin again. Interrupting a ritual, once we have begun, is death. A horrible death as the forces of sun, moon, and Kardia align and crush the one who interferes with the harmony. Are you willing to risk joining us tonight, as the full moon reaches its highest arc? We must begin soon for the ritual to climax at the proper moment. Timing is as essential as form."

"If the ritual is so dangerous, why do you risk it?" Once he learned it, would he dare teach it to apprentices?

"For the reward of unity. Will you join us tonight, Lan?"

Across the fire, Maia stood up. As she bent to place her flute on the floor beside her stool, her bodice gaped open to reveal the full globes of her breasts. She lifted her head and smiled invitingly to Nimbulan.

"You will join with her afterward, and her thoughts will be yours. You will feel what she feels, know what she knows, and never lose the awareness of her presence again," Televarn whispered.

"What must I do?" Nimbulan swallowed deeply, trying to restrain his desire for the woman and his need to belong to someone. This ritual might prove the beginning of a whole new system of magic that would allow magicians to join their powers. Then, and only then, could they impose ethics and honor on all magicians. He could remove magic from the wars and politics allowing a natural balance of power to bring peace to Coronnan at last.

But once he learned this magic, he'd have to leave the clan and Maia.

"Forget the cold, soon the magic will take you," Maia breathed in Nimbulan's ear. She squeezed his hand and let it drop. Her scent lingered in the frosty air as she moved into her place in the ring of people outside the lodge.

Every adult in the clan gathered in a circle around their winter home. They alternated male and female in even numbers. Televarn was the only unmatched person. He walked around the outside perimeter of people, lost in his own thoughts, mumbling to himself and breathing deeply.

Nimbulan recognized his exercises as the beginning of a trance. The form of magic might be different, but a trance was a universal ingredient, essential for the magic to work with a body.

He, too, inhaled on a ritual three counts, held it another three counts, and exhaled on the same rhythm. The women on either side of him did the same. Visibly their muscles relaxed and so did his. The chill winter night, the hand's span of packed snow, the glittering stars in the clear sky, all receded from his consciousness.

A second deep breath in three counts, hold three, release three, gave him access to the void. The blackness beckoned, urging him to take that third deep breath and release his body.

"Not yet, Lan. Wait for the rest of us," a voice reminded him.

Televarn? Possible. He didn't care. Only the trance and the void tugging at him in opposite directions mattered. He felt stretched almost to the point of dissipating into mist.

The circle of people began moving to his right, widdershins, along the path of the moon. Each left hand held a candle. Every right hand circled in a complicated gesture, fingers weaving. He followed them, imitating every movement.

Televarn wove in and out among them, odd man out and the binding force of the whole.

Erda, who had strummed the lute, uttered the first phrase of a chant in an ancient language Nimbulan didn't understand: the ancient pictorial language represented in the embroidery they all wore. The next person to her right repeated the phrase, then the next, and the next around the circle. By the time the words had reached Nimbulan, they had become a one-note song, sung to the peculiar rhythm of stamping feet and twisting hands.

A web of energy, sparkling white, like snow crystals, followed Televarn's progress through the clan. In and out, around and around.

A thrumming sound rose through Nimbulan's feet, into his body and out his hands along the growing intricacy of the magic. The pulsing energy shifted to match the vibrations of the Kardia beneath him. He looked up to the clear sky and the cold white stars beyond. The web extended up and through their patterns as if the ley lines of Kardia Hodos wound their way through the universe and he was at their center. All of it hummed and danced in tune.

He was caught up in the wonder of the music of life, all connected, all in tune, all one.

The magic spread inward, as well as outward, engulfing the lodge. A dome of shimmering white enveloped the clan and their home. The lodge became a piece of the magnificent web, so much in tune with the clan and the magic that it ceased to stand out as a man-made structure in the midst of the wild creation of the Stargods.

The energy dome magnified before his vision. He saw each filament of magic, woven into the intricate protection. The web began and ended with Televarn's heart, stretching out to each person in the clan, binding them all together. Nimbulan saw the common element in their blood that allowed them to work this wonderful magic. A tiny amount of it showed clearly in his own life force.

Suddenly knowledge of the great-great, multi-great grandmother who took a Rover as a lover awoke in him. Unhappy in her marriage, she cherished her fifth child sired by her lover rather than her husband. Four children stood between the child and inheritance. She had been certain the exotic heritage of the boy would never taint the lords of Baathalzan's pure line of descent from the Stargods. Fate had eliminated all other heirs, war and disease taking them one after another. The Rover's secret child had inherited and survived to sire more children. Much diluted, the *Kardiagenea*, the ability to tap the magic of all life in concert with others of his kind, had come down to Nimbulan.

A wobble in the web of magic filaments revealed imperfections in the inborn talents of many of these people. The ones with the purest Rover blood, the ones who showed signs of diminished intelligence and bone deformations due to inbreeding, had weak and warped talents.

The clan needed the strength of outside blood to strengthen the magical talent inbreeding destroyed.

Nimbulan reached out and traced a filament of this web of life extending from his own body to that of Maia. No weakness showed in her.

His mind melded with hers. He saw through her eyes, sensed the powerful unity of the spell, felt the cold ground beneath her bare feet, knew the longing in her body for the joy of sex tinged with the need to conceive another child now that her first baby was weaned. Her feminine longing, bordering on an ache, returned to him, enhancing his own desire. He explored the sensations with wonder.

Tentatively, he reached beyond Maia to Televarn's uncle and knew the satisfaction of completing the protective ritual properly with exact numbers of male and female. Nimbulan's presence in the clan was welcome if for no other reason.

On and on around the circle, Nimbulan touched briefly each member of the clan. Their personalities opened to him as they never had before. And he knew they would never again be able to creep up behind him in surprise.

Finally he touched the last person in the circle and centered his consciousness on Televarn. The man's thoughts did not open. Nimbulan could not share the sensations of the Rover king's body. Yet he sensed Televarn was totally connected to every person in the circle by a one-way path of communication. Televarn dominated every personality in the clan.

The Rover king completed the ritual by turning three times deosil, sunwise, before the only door of the lodge. The web snapped inward, collapsing into the Rover's body as if he had pulled a flexible string.

The winter lodge was now protected from discovery by outsiders. Would the same protection prevent Nimbulan from escaping with the secret of Rover ritual magic?

The connections to the others in the clan dissolved. Nimbulan's entire body tingled with reserve vibrations. He could increase that humming music of life and recapture the unity within the spell. If the others helped. If they wished. The absence of their minds in his mind left him curiously empty and refreshed at the same time.

He concentrated on his hand, willing the magic to reach out and connect him to Maia once more. Wispy tendrils of magic shot from his fingertips but stretched toward Televarn, not his lover. He retracted the probe and moved closer and closer to Maia until his hand rested on her shoulder. She did not respond to his tentative touch. All her attention was on Televarn.

Televarn, whose mind and intentions had remained closed to Nimbulan's probe. Televarn, who commanded this clan and had ordered Maia to lie with Nimbulan. New blood in the clan was more important than any of their personal desires and emotions. Televarn directed Maia's love affair with Nimbulan as he directed everyone within the clan with direct mind-to-mind control.

Nimbulan shuddered in the cold. If he took this system of magic to his apprentices, would they, too, become totally dependent upon one dictatorial mind? Would the absence of Rover blood in their heritage prevent them from performing this ritual?

A more shattering thought shot ice through his blood. Televarn might have inserted the seeds of mind-to-mind control in Nimbulan's brain without him knowing it. If he had, there was a good chance Nimbulan might not be able to break it, or escape it.

Chapter 22

"**I** don't like you very much, Moncriith." Lord Kammeryl d'Astrismos paced his Great Hall. His fingers twitched as he fussed with the alignment of a bench against the trestle table, then moved on to kick at the fresh rushes and finger a tapestry. "Give me one good reason why I should put up with your preaching and the stench of old blood that surrounds you one more day."

Stargods, can't you stand still one moment! Moncriith clenched his teeth rather than blurt out his thoughts. The lord's constant prowl around the room made him dizzy. Thank the Stargods none of the lord's toadies were present to rush in a new bed partner. The denizens of this dark castle seemed willing to sacrifice anything to avoid one of Kammeryl d'Astrismos' rages. This restlessness was always the first warning sign of an imbalance in his temper. An imbalance caused by his own self-doubt. Only deflowering a virgin returned his self-confidence.

Otherwise, he'd been known to set out on a lightning raid, burning, pillaging, and raping every village he encountered— including some of his own.

Just last week Kammeryl had informed his valet, who informed the sergeant of the guard who informed Moncriith that he "felt like a god," when he claimed a girl's, or boy's, virginity and initiated them into the joys—and pains—of sex. Moncriith wondered if Kammeryl had invented his descent from the Stargods and suffered major self-doubt when he remembered his lies.

The lord's red hair, the visible symbol of his Stargod heritage, was definitely the result of dyes. He'd cropped his hair short to fit under a war helm today. A new, more-vibrant-than-usual shade of red colored it.

"You will tolerate me. Lord Kammeryl, because your retainers would rebel if you threw me out." Moncriith remained serenely still and calm in the face of Kammeryl's increasing restlessness. He had no self-doubts to plague him into rash actions.

Kammeryl stopped in his tracks. He stared a long moment into Moncriith's eyes. Amazement and possibly a little fear colored his expression. Then he threw back his head and laughed, loud and long.

"Do you think my people will honor your prattling warnings of demon possession over their oath of loyalty to me?" Kammeryl asked, wiping tears of mirth from his eyes with his sleeve. The moment he recovered, he resumed his pacing. "No one will renounce their oath to me because they know I will exact a swift and terrible vengeance."

"No, Lord Kammeryl, I don't believe they will follow me rather than you. I *know* they will. Preservation of their souls is more important than any temporal power. They know I may slaughter a goat or sheep in performance of my rituals. I do not lie about what I do, nor do I hide behind threats. One animal is a small price compared to losing an entire village to one of your raids. Are you certain a demon does not possess you? The Stargods desert those who succumb to the lure of demon power." Moncriith sat easily into the chair beside the lord's demi-throne. He leaned back into the depths of the pillows meant to cushion the delicate bones of the lady of the manor.

The chair had been empty for many years and was not likely to be filled by a "lady" ever again. Kammeryl d'Astrismos had an heir by his long-dead wife. He needed no other consort as long as the constant parade of virginal bed partners satisfied him.

"Why? Why would anyone accept you as a leader, Moncriith? You own no land or gold. You have no trading empire. The temple threw you out years ago. The magicians scoff at you. What can you offer the rabble? Not protection, not food, no *tangible* power of any kind." Kammeryl barked, leaning over Moncriith's chair, hands resting on the padded arms. The knuckles on his hands showed white.

"I have shown them the demons who feed upon war—demons who inhabit the bodies of magicians and witches—and possibly lords—and force them to perpetuate wars. The people want relief from war. I have shown them a way to get it. We must kill all of the magicians." Moncriith relaxed into the chair, more certain than ever of his control over Kammeryl d'Astrismos and his followers. "Support of me would prove to one and all that demons do not possess you."

"Relief from war? Bah! Peace is an archaic concept, a myth as unreal as dragons and flywackets." Kammeryl resumed his pacing, glaring at any servant who dared enter the Great Hall to prepare it for the evening meal.

"And yet, at your last battle many hardened soldiers reported seeing both a dragon and a flywacket—evil demons though they are." Moncriith crossed himself. He'd suffered several serious scratches from Myrilandel's flywacket—clear proof of her association with demons. "Think about it, Lord Kammeryl. Think of the power you would wield if you brought peace to Coronnan. Tax revenues. Trade profits. Ambassadors from all over the world bringing you gifts of gold, silk, and slaves."

"Slaves are illegal in Coronnan." Kammeryl paused in his pacing, right hand rubbing his chin in consideration. The florid color in his cheeks intensified and his eyes glowed. Some poor child would end up beaten and bruised when the lord released his emotions in bed.

Moncriith felt a reaching out of his magic talent in anticipation of the unknown child's pain. He preferred fueling his magic with the blood of his enemies. His spells had a sharper focus when combined with anger and hatred. For now he'd settle for absorbing the power of pain inflicted by another.

"As the ruler of a united Coronnan, you would make your own laws. Think of the exotic treasures that could be yours for the asking. Nubile young slaves taught from childhood to please a man of your appetites, without having been touched, waiting for you to tap their erotic knowledge." Moncriith held back a smirk. No sense in letting this lord know he was being manipulated. He had no intention of allowing the likes of Kammeryl d'Astrismos to survive long enough to reap the benefits of peace. His temporal power was necessary now as a catalyst for the populace.

As soon as the mission had been accomplished, all of the demon-possessed lords and their evil magicians would perish in the flames. Just like Myrilandel and her familiar.

"Coronnan can't know peace until it is united. Conquering the other lords is the only way to do that. Quinnault de Tanos and his band of minor landholders can't stand against me in battle." Kammeryl resumed his pacing, deep in thought rather than restlessly seeking a diversion. He clasped his hands behind his back, a sure signal that his restlessness was appeased by serious thought for the moment.

"What if every peasant in the land acknowledged you as their lord, including those who follow de Tanos?" Moncriith dangled the possibility like bait.

"The other lords still have armies to force their tithes and loyalty."

"But if every soldier was occupied enforcing taxes and loyalty, they wouldn't be available to battle you and your armies."

"Some of the lesser lords would have to offer me alliances to maintain order. *Me,* instead of de Tanos," Kammeryl mused, counting on his fingers. He stopped at eight—Quinnault's four and four others who wavered back and forth with their loyalty. The exact number of lords Moncriith figured would flock to Kammeryl's side for protection.

"Alliances lead to unity. Six small lords command more troops and land than any one of the major lords. Begin now, before the campaign season and by the time the fields are planted, no one lord could stand against you."

"What if they band together against me, like de Tanos is trying?"

"They can't if all their peasants desert them for you. Only I can make certain they do."

"Why should I trust you to convert these people to me?"

"You must learn to trust someone, or your reign will never be easy. Trust the Stargods, Kammeryl d'Astrismos. Your family name means 'son of the three stars.' You are the only *legal* descendant of the Stargods. Trust me. Trust the vision the Stargods have given me." Moncriith followed the lord, whispering seductively in his ear. Power, after all, was as much an aphrodisiac as all the virgins in the world.

"You can't carry the true word of the Stargods. The priests threw you out for working blood magic."

"They exiled me from their ranks because they are afraid of me. Afraid that I alone was granted a true vision of the demons that truly rule Coronnan. If they accepted me, they'd have to acknowledge the demons that possess them and kill themselves to be rid of them."

No sense in letting Kammeryl know that the priests had removed Moncriith from the temple because he refused traditional methods of magic. He could use those methods but chose not to. He'd seen how traditional magic caused death and destruction while promising life and healing. He preferred the honesty of drawing blood to fuel magic rather than inflicting murder as a result of magic gone awry.

Priests of the temple were now so sheltered from life that their only contact with magic included meaningless rituals and passing apprentices through the trial by Tambootie smoke.

Moncriith shuddered in memory of his own trial.

"You pursue only a vision born of your imagination, Moncriith." Kammeryl resumed his restless wanderings.

"My vision was born of the Stargods and their desire for peace in Coronnan. When all of Kardia Hodos fell victim to the plague so many generations ago, the Stargods came here, to Coronnan. They gave our people the cure for the plague. We are their chosen people. Think how they must grieve at the way we ravage the land and each other with these endless wars. Think with your heart and your head; not your dick, Kammeryl. Think and know what destiny of greatness the Stargods offer you through me."

"What do you suggest as a first step?"

"First, we destroy the magicians. Lord Quinnault's School for Magicians is a good place to start. Nimbulan is dead. They no longer have a strong leader to rally them against you. And if you kill Quinnault at the same time, his alliance of minor lords will fall apart. Then, we offer a marriage alliance with Lord Sauria. His lands border Quinnault's. He longs for access to the Great Bay. You can divide the islands and the trade profits between you."

"Magic isn't fun anymore," Kalen complained to Powwell.

Ackerly leaned closer to the door that separated him from his two most promising students. The tone in the girl's voice and the absence of her lisp alerted him to trouble.

He heightened his senses a little with magic so he could hear the entire conversation.

"Magic isn't supposed to be fun. It's work. Hard work," Powwell returned.

The children were supposed to be sweeping the floors of the bedrooms in this wing. Powwell had already discovered that brooms pushed by muscles didn't tire him as easily as brooms pushed by magic.

"Well, I don't want to do it anymore. I'm tired, and I ache, and my head spins when *he* gives us those drugs." A thump followed that pronouncement as if Kalen plunked herself down on the floor, arms crossed in her usual pouting position. Ackerly had come to dread the times Kalen resorted to a pout. Underneath the innocent charm, the little girl hid a stubborn streak that taxed the patience of all fifty inhabitants of the school. Not even her doting mother or her coldly calculating father could coax her out of a good pout.

"The Tambootie is necessary to working magic," Powwell said thoughtfully.

Ackerly could almost see the boy biting his lip in indecision. A terrible habit he'd have to make Powwell break. Paying clients wouldn't rent the services of a magician who appeared indecisive.

"I never needed doses of the weed before I came here, and I did a lot more magic than *he* thinks I do now. Besides the drugs make me sick to my stomach. I can't concentrate when I'm about to heave," Kalen said.

"Magic's a lot easier for me when I take the drugs. But it nauseates me, too. What did you mean you worked more magic than Ackerly thinks you do now? Aren't you doing everything he asks?" A clatter of a dropped broom followed Powwell's words.

"Of course not. I never let anyone know precisely how much I can do. Sieur Moncriith used to preach against me and make people throw mud at me for summoning witchlight. Sometimes they threw stones to keep us out of the village before we could ask for food and a place to stay. If Moncriith had known I could levitate things, he'd have demanded people burn me. They would have, too." A touch of fear colored Kalen's voice. Ackerly made a note of it.

He hadn't summoned the Bloodmage in many moons. Perhaps now was the time. He could let drop a few hints about the girl in exchange for a small payment. Moncriith paid well for all information. If Moncriith came back, seeking her, maybe Kalen's fear of him would drive her to throw the destructive battle spells she resisted.

"Master Nimbulan trusted Ackerly with everything before he died. We can trust him, too," Powwell said.

Silence followed that statement. Ackerly wondered what was going on in the girl's head. He didn't have enough magic to break through her natural armor.

"I can't trust a man who gives me drugs that make me sick. I'll just pretend I'm a slow learner."

Aha! so that was why Kalen didn't pick up the principles of distant communication as readily as she had fire and telekinesis. Ackerly smiled as he listened. He wondered what would happen if he reduced the doses of Tambootie and turned the lessons into games. Would Kalen be tricked into stretching her magic for the fun of a game?

He pictured himself crawling around on the floor with a bunch of toddlers.

No. These children were too old for such infantile amusements. He hadn't been around children at all since he left home at the age of twelve to become an apprentice magician. None of Druulin's apprentices had had time or energy for play, unless you considered practical jokes and stealing extra blankets play.

What games had he played at ten and twelve? He remembered vaguely boisterous contests with balls and sticks, of hide-and-go seek, of follow my leader. Yes, he could still play those games—but with a magic twist.

Where? Not outdoors where such rambunctious games were meant to be played. Winter's last storms still raged around their ears with snow and howling winds. When the thaw came, the island would be a sea of mud. He hoped that day was not far off. He'd had enough of chilblains and runny noses. Perhaps he could organize games in the refectory. The trestle tables and benches could be pushed aside after each meal. The center of that long hall would make an adequate ball field. The children would have to learn control to keep witchballs confined and not knock over rushlights and candles. The rest of the school provided infinite hiding places and obstacles to overcome. Yes, he'd start the games tonight.

But he wouldn't eliminate the Tambootie from the curriculum. He needed the apprentices to become dependent on it. Just as Nimbulan had. Then, gifts of the drug—or withholding of it—became tools. Tools to keep his pet magicians performing while he collected enormous rental fees for their services.

He almost tasted the gold as if he were already biting into the coins to test their purity. The weight of them filled his hands and pockets with satisfaction.

Soon. Soon the school would begin to pay. He just had to be patient a little longer.

Ackerly turned away from his eavesdropping, satisfied he had outsmarted two very bright children.

Kalen's voice rose once more, but he didn't pay attention to her complaints. He'd learned what he needed.

"He's gone now, Powwell." Kalen pressed her ear to the door.

"Are you sure?"

"Of course I'm sure. His aura left an imprint on the door. Now it's fading."

"I can't see it."

"Look with your magic, not your eyes."

"You sound just like Nimbulan." Tears filled Powwell's eyes. "I wish you could have known him."

"He sounds like he was more honest than anyone else at this *s'murghing* school."

"We're not supposed to curse, Kalen," Powwell gasped.

"There's no better word to describe this place. I wish Papa had never brought me here." She stamped her foot and plopped down on the floor again, arms crossed over her skinny chest. She scrunched up her face as if trying not to cry. "I want to go home to our house in Baria. It was the most beautiful house ever. I want to go back to the time before Lord Hanic burned the town, before Moncriith discovered me. Before magic was more than a bright, shiny toy."

"You haven't gone hungry since you came here. And you haven't had to sleep in the fields, cold and wet," Powwell reminded her.

"That's true. But before we came, I wasn't sick all the

time from the drugs, and if I got tired, it was from walking and carrying my baby brother, not from forcing strange magic. Magic that could hurt someone if I lose control. *He* can't work real magic, so he doesn't know how bad I feel all the time."

"Master Ackerly is a good teacher. He explains things ever so simply."

"Have you ever seen *him* work any magic?"

"N . . . no."

"That's 'cause he's got precious little talent for magic. What he does is mostly illusion. He makes you think he's doing magic. Like he made you think Nimbulan was dead."

"But he was! I saw him die." Powwell's eyes went wide with disbelief and hope at the same time. "What makes you think the master lived?"

"His niche in the crypt is empty. The body's gone, but his formal robes are there, neatly folded."

"Master always was obsessed with neatness and order when he wasn't too deep in a drug trance. He'd never leave anything untidy after a good sleep and a full day without a dose. Do you suppose the Stargods took him to heaven in their cloud of silver fire?"

"No. I think he woke up from a deep trance and walked away. That's what I'd do. That's what I want to do."

"You're making this up. I saw Master Nimbulan die. I helped lay him in the niche." Powwell jumped up from where he sat on the floor. Suddenly the room was too small, the air too close. He couldn't believe what this little girl . . . this troublemaker, said. If she was right, he couldn't stay here. He'd have to go in search of his true master, Nimbulan. He'd have to leave the security of the school. This was the first place he'd ever lived where the taint of bastardy didn't follow him. Every village his mother moved to, even when she claimed to be widowed—a common enough occurrence these days—someone always found out that his father was a wandering misfit who hadn't bothered to return and marry the daughter of his host. He'd promised to come back. But promises were easily broken.

"I'll show you the empty crypt, Powwell," Kalen whispered as if afraid Ackerly might return and overhear.

Powwell stared at the floor, wondering if he had the courage to follow her and discover the truth.

Chapter 23

Myri poured another bucket of water over the hot rocks in the brazier. Aromatic steam gushed upward, filling the tiny hut with the scent of crushed herbs and a little of the essential oil of the Tambootie. The old woman lying on the thin pallet coughed heavily in the onslaught of steam.

The coughing spasm continued, racking her frail old body with shudders, robbing her of air, slowly choking life from her.

Each time Karry's grandmother gasped for air or clutched her chest in pain, Myri endured the same. Her strength faded almost as rapidly as the old woman's.

(Resist the need to Heal with magic,) the voices whispered to her as they had guided her all night.

"I can't let her die," Myri sobbed. She'd tried every mundane remedy she could think of. Granny Katia's fever and cough only worsened.

(Hold back. Don't waste your strength on her. She will die anyway.)

Myri gritted her teeth and sought the courage to ignore the voices. Resolutely, she placed her hand on the old woman's chest. Blue sparks shot into the air the moment she made contact. She poured her energy deep into Granny Katia, pulling fluid away from her lungs and attacking the fever.

She wished for Amaranth's comforting presence, but knew the superstitious villagers feared that cats sucked breath out of babies and ailing old people. They'd forbidden her to bring her familiar into Granny Katia's home.

Another great spasm of coughs racked the old woman's body. Shudders ran the length of her wasted frame. Myri helped her patient bend over and expel the fluid in her lungs.

"Drink some water now, Granny Katia." She held a small cup to the old woman's lips, still keeping one hand on her back. Strength continued to drain out of Myri into her patient.

Granny Katia tried to push the cup away. Her hands were so feeble she barely touched the cup.

(You can't help her. She's too ill, too weak. Save yourself. Your strength is needed elsewhere.)

An uneasiness in the back of Myri's neck, like an itch that got worse with scratching, followed the whisper in the back of her mind. She knew a sudden urge to pack her few possessions and move southward. She could travel no farther east.

She pushed the compulsion aside. She'd had enough of being manipulated by magic when she was with Televarn.

"Please, Granny. You have to drink." *Karry and the other villagers will never forgive me if you die. They'll blame me, threaten me, drive me away.*

Or burn me. The villagers had heard Moncriith preach. If Granny Katia died, they would blame her.

"I want to stay here. This village feels like home." *You promised me a home,* she accused the voices.

The old woman passed into uneasy sleep before Myri could force more than a few drops past her thin lips. Myri's talent reached out. She poured more magic into Granny Katia, trying once more to draw fluid out of her lungs.

Dizziness scattered Myri's senses. She had trouble concentrating on the healing. Her lungs felt heavy and her breath rattled when she exhaled. Her eyes refused to focus. The walls of the tiny hut spun around her. She dropped her head and scrunched her eyes closed.

"If you don't take the medicine, you'll die, Granny. You have to drink," she said when the room righted itself and she could concentrate once more.

The old woman roused slightly and took two small sips before losing consciousness again.

Myri bathed Granny's fevered brow with a cool cloth. The old woman's skin felt too dry and thin, like a fragile leaf ready to fall in autumn. The fever burned her vitality like fuel in a hearth. Every ragged breath stole air from Myri's lungs as well.

"The cure isn't working, Myri." Karry stood in the low doorway of the hut, arms crossed, grief already dragging down the corners of her mouth.

"I'm sorry. I don't know what else to do for her." Myri bowed her head.

"I can see that you have tried all within your power." Karry looked pointedly at the blue glow of energy surrounding Myri's hand where it lay against Granny's shrunken chest.

Myri resisted the instinct to jerk her hand away and hide the evidence of magic. She tried distracting Karry's gaze by pressing the cup of medicine on Granny once more.

"Leave off with your smelly cures, child," Granny Katia whispered weakly. "Let me die. I'm too old to endure another Festival. 'Tis the Equinox Festival today. A good time to die. Make room for the new lives beginning tonight." She chuckled dryly and coughed again.

This time Myri had to lift her body to a sitting position, so she wouldn't gag. Her lungs gasped in sympathy with the old woman.

Karry rushed to wipe the bloody spittle from her grandmother's mouth. "She's coughing blood now." Fear widened her eyes.

"She's been coughing blood all night," Myri said. She wiped a few drops of blood from her own lips with the back of her hand. Her empathy with her patient had brought the disease into her body already. Would she have the strength to cure herself?

(Leave the woman. Her death is killing you!)

Tremendous heat pushed her hand away from Granny Katia's chest. This time, Myri let the power separate her from her patient.

Karry sat back on her heels. Her face paled, and her hands shook. Amaranth pushed open the door Karry hadn't closed completely and climbed into the pub-keeper's lap. He rubbed his head against her chest, offering his sympathy. She wrapped her arms around the cat, clinging to his body as if he were the spirit of her beloved grandmother.

Granny Katia gasped again as another coughing spasm

gripped her. Myri tried to lift her inert shoulders. A curious rattle replaced the old woman's ragged breathing. Air and phlegm tangled in Myri's lungs, too. Katia's eyes glazed and rolled. Her entire body shuddered once and went limp.

A vital part of Myri's talent wrenched away from her body, trying desperately to follow the dying woman into the void. No amount of willpower could control the need to grab her patient's essence and bring it back to the body that was too weak to support it.

Utter blackness closed around Myri.

With a nauseating lurch she found herself back in her own body. She closed her eyes as the hut spun around her, upsetting her tenuous balance.

Silence filled the too-warm room. Gradually, Myri came back to herself, weak and shaking.

Karry clutched her grandmother's hand to her ample breast.

"I'm sorry, Karry. I have nothing left to try." Gently, she closed the sightless eyes.

"Pass easily to your next existence, Granny," Karry murmured.

They sat in silence a moment. Karry rocked on her heels, still clutching Katia's hand. Amaranth purred gentle comfort in her lap.

"I guess I should leave. This village won't look to kindly upon the healer who lost a favorite patient." Myri bowed her head in regret. She liked the people in this little fishing village. She had almost dared hope they would welcome her, let her stay. Maybe even hide her when Moncriith came looking for her.

Magretha had warned her how often villagers preferred to blame healers for every problem and forget the good they had achieved. Most of Myri's childhood had been spent fleeing one village or another—often with Moncriith hot on her heels.

"You don't have to leave, Myri." Karry reached across her grandmother's failing body to hold Myri's hand. "You saved my Katey and her baby, Katareena. No one else thought to reach in and pull the baby out, ass-backward. If you hadn't, they'd have died and the Katareenas would end with me. And don't forget Yoshi's fever. You cured him last Solstice. We're grateful for those of us you have saved."

"But I couldn't increase the fishing catch. How many of the men blame me for that? They've been drinking heavily for two days, anticipating festival tonight. Some of them get very mean when they are in their cups. We have both broken up a dozen fights a day this winter. Will they turn on me when drink fires their courage?"

After a long and barren winter, the fish had returned to the bay in the last day or two. But many of the men didn't want to believe in the fish. They'd rather drink and complain and fight among themselves.

More and more frequently, Myri heard the men mutter that the village resided under a curse. If Moncriith arrived and pointed to Myri as the cause, the men were ripe to believe.

She forced herself to think about the pretty flowers and the lilting music nine women practiced by the Equinox Pylons. This village could have been home.

(We will give you a safe home.)

"We want you to stay, Myri." Karry pressed her hand reassuringly. You are welcome to join in the Festival dance tonight."

A moment of longing pressed deep inside Myri. She remembered other Festivals. Lilting music guided her steps widdershins around an Equinox Pylon. Men danced deosil in the same pattern. Each pass brought the men and women closer together, brushing suggestively against each other. A hand reached out and loosened the laces of her bodice— all the girls had painstakingly reversed the order of lacing so the simple garment opened from the top. By the end of the dance, several hands had tugged at her clothing, exposing her breasts, heightening the sexual anticipation of the night.

She clamped down on her desire to join the village in the ancient fertility rites.

Amaranth leaped from Karry's lap to prowl restlessly around Myri's ankles.

(Betrayal!) The voices came sharp and insistent. *(You must leave. Now!)*

"Merow," Amaranth agreed with the voices. He twitched his ears as if listening.

Myri walked to the door, looking out at the preparations for tonight's Festival. She sought a glimpse of something out of the ordinary that might reveal who betrayed her.

From the safety of the cliff edge, children watched mandelphs sporting in the warm currents just beyond the Dragon's Teeth, the wickedly sharp rock formation in the center of the cove. Birds danced in the air above them, dipping down to feed among the rich schools of fish. Winter storms no longer drove them into the depths of the bay beyond the reach of men's nets.

Children, flowers, and wildlife burst with energy on this first day of the new season. The entire planet seemed poised for Spring with abundant life.

She needed to belong to the joyous celebration tonight, perhaps find a permanent mate among the fishermen. Instead she would have to run away again.

(Betrayal.)

She stood rigidly staring at the three times three Equinox Pylon, not seeing it or the floral decorations. Awareness of Karry, the dead woman, the village, faded as she listened only to the voices that had guided her so often.

(Go. Now.) Urgency to be out of the village pressed on her.

(Now.) A circling wind began to whip the tops of nearby trees. Her feet needed to follow the wind.

"I can't stay." Disappointment tugged her toward the Pylon. The voices pulled her in the opposite direction.

(Hurry!)

"The men will be disappointed you won't stay to lift your skirts for your partner in the dance." Karry crossed her grandmother's arms upon her sunken chest and brushed her thin gray hair away from her face.

Myri listened for the voices again, ignoring Karry's persuasion. Did she have time to pack some provisions? The sense of urgency lifted. A little. Not much time. Food and extra clothing were necessary. She wouldn't be coming back here soon.

"Look with your FarSight, Lan. Look into the storehouses, look into the fishing nets, look at the fertile fields ripe for the first touch of plow and seed," Televarn whispered seductively.

Nimbulan looked down from their hidden perch on the cliffside above the village plateau. To the west of the village, the fields spread wide, ready for tilling. To the east lay the ocean and a cove pierced by a spreading rock formation. Just beyond the jagged spires of rock, screeching gulls dipped often and plucked squirming fish from the warm currents.

"Look at the Equinox Pylon the women decorate. Three times three poles erected over the place where three ley lines meet. Three is a powerful number. It represents the three Stargods. This village is rich in fertility as well as magic." Televarn pointed at the proud collection of stout poles presiding over the center of the village. Weddings, funerals, and judgments all took place at the base. Three times three granted extra blessings to those events.

"Our people are hungry, Lan. These people deny us sustenance."

"We haven't asked them for hospitality yet. Why do you believe they will deny it to us?"

The Rover chieftain irritated Nimbulan with his broad assumptions. Not just on the issue of prejudice against all Rovers, his clan in particular. Every topic of conversation brought a statement of half-truth that Televarn demanded be accepted as words of profound wisdom. The magical control Televarn maintained over the minds of each of his clan ensured they all agreed with him.

Only Nimbulan remained aloof and untouched by that control. Often, though, he sensed the Rover eavesdropping on his thoughts.

Nimbulan knew that not all women were faithless. Not all children were incapable of behaving, not all steeds were stupid, and not every man lost potency with age. He bristled with indignation every time he heard the last accusation. Just because Maia hadn't conceived yet. . . .

"The lords and magicians teach the stupid villagers to distrust us."

"They have good reason if you plan to steal from them without even asking for food or offering to buy it first."

"Rovers do not *buy* what the Stargods should provide them. Food, sledges, steeds . . . these are ours by right. The Stargods decreed we must rove. Therefore, they must provide for us."

"Then we should remind these folk of their obligation to offer us hospitality."

"The teachings of the Stargods have been corrupted." Televarn spat on the sloping ground. "I know from experience they will give us nothing."

"We could offer to work for the food, trade for it, even sing and dance for it."

"Tonight is Festival. They make their own entertainment. At Festival, all villages refuse outsiders so that no foreign seed spreads to their women." The Rover grinned lasciviously. He had remarked often of late that he fancied finding a woman with fair hair and eyes. One woman in particular who had run away from him.

Myrilandel had pale hair and nearly colorless eyes that reflected whatever color was near.

Strange, he hadn't thought of the mysterious witch-woman in many moons. Maia was the only woman who occupied his thoughts. Myrilandel pricked his curiosity with her wild talent and curious visions. Maia satisfied only his lust. He couldn't converse with her beyond where they would make their bed each night now that spring had arrived and the Rover clan was wandering again.

"Tonight, when the moon is full and the drink flows freely, we can sneak into the village and make off with as much food as we need. Our people won't go to bed with empty bellies for many weeks."

"I still think we should offer to buy the food."

"Coward! No Rover would think such a thing. You can never truly be one of us until you put such craven thoughts aside. You are not worthy of Maia. No wonder her womb has rejected your seed," Televarn backed away. A disgusted sneer spread across his handsome face. His hand reached instinctively for the long dagger he wore on his hip.

"Don't be a prejudiced fool, Televarn." Nimbulan held his hands away from his side to indicate his reluctance to engage in violence. "The safety of the clan should be your first priority. Breaking into that storehouse should be a last resort, after we've tried fishing, or hunting, or asking. What if your men are discovered, and the village turns on them? They have tools and knives that are just as deadly as the pikes and lances of any army." At the end of winter, not much was left in field and forest to glean or gather, or

Nimbulan would have suggested that as well. If the winter storms that had ravaged all of Coronnan had driven away the fish, this village could be as hungry as the Rovers.

"If they see us in the vicinity, they will guard the storehouse. Any attempt to liberate the food will end in violence, perhaps death." Televarn's eyes narrowed as if he expected Nimbulan to lead the raid and be the first to die.

Nimbulan had no intention of taking part in the theft from innocent, possibly hungry, people.

"Do what you must, Televarn. I will go hunting. I will feed our people honestly." Nimbulan turned his back on the village and Televarn.

He took three steps into the depths of the forested hillside and stopped abruptly. He directed his feet to move, but they remained firmly in place.

"Do not walk away from me, magician. I am king of this clan. My word is law."

"Then perhaps I should no longer be a part of your clan." That thought had a strangely liberating feel to it. He hadn't realized how uncomfortable he had become with the lack of privacy, the constant wandering, the uncertainty of each day. Avid curiosity for a different way of life had turned to boredom. No, disgust. He didn't *like* any of the people in the clan, especially Televarn.

He knew a few of the secret rituals now. He could take that information back to school.

His feet refused to move forward. Instead, he found himself turning to face Televarn.

"You cannot leave after you have shared in our rituals, slept with one of our women, broken bread with us." Televarn seemed genuinely confused.

"You said yourself, I was not born to your way of life. I tried to fit in, to learn your customs. But I do not belong. The time has come for us to part." He wore all the clothing he owned, and his knife. He hadn't become used to his new staff yet and could easily cut another. He had no possessions to retrieve. Best if he just walked away, here and now. He couldn't move.

"I cannot allow that. We taught you our secrets." Televarn shifted his balance, eyes searching the surroundings. For observers, help, a place to run?

"Release me from your control. I will not betray you."

But he would. He'd use the secrets to bring unity to magicians all over Coronnan.

"No one outside the clan may share our knowledge. You must stay with us, be truly one with us, or die. You defied me every day when you wouldn't let me into your mind. You deserve to die for that crime alone." Televarn's hand flicked and the long dagger flew out.

Acid sharp pain exploded in Nimbulan's gut. A beautifully decorated knife hilt seemed to be growing from his rib cage. Thick warm blood stained his hand. His blood.

Chapter 24

"**D**o we have to go down there?" Powwell eyed the trapdoor to the crypt with loathing and . . . and fear.

"Yes." Kalen placed her fists on her hips and glared at him.

"I believe you that his body is gone. So you don't have to prove it to me." Powwell mimicked her pose to hide the shaking of his hands. The last time he'd gone into the crypt had been to place the master's limp body into a niche. The darkness and the weight of the Kardia above him had pressed on his lungs until he couldn't breathe. The apprentices and Master Ackerly had formed a semicircle in front of the burial place to say the funeral prayers. Powwell hadn't closed his eyes. He'd been too afraid that the act of diverting his sight from the walls and ceiling would cause them to collapse. As he scanned the other niches, most occupied by decaying skeletons, he'd seen the ghosts of all the other occupants of the crypt rise up to greet Nimbulan and invite him to join them in haunting the ancient monastery.

Powwell hadn't slept well the entire winter, waiting for the ghosts to come for him, too.

Kalen bent to lift the trapdoor hidden behind the altar in the chapel. "You need proof, or you won't run away with me." She grunted under the weight of the door.

Ingrained manners made Powwell rush to help her. "What made you go crawling around down there in the first place?" he asked as she made ready to climb down the ladder carved into the stone wall. He admired her bravery, but he was coming to dread her stubbornness.

She wasn't aggressive and talkative with the others. For

them she put on a mask of starry-eyed innocence and awe, lisping sweetly like a child much younger than her ten years. Maybe he was the only person in all of Coronnan she trusted. His chest swelled with pride and protectiveness. He had to follow her into the crypt to prove to himself he'd earned that trust.

Maybe if he left the door open, the Kardia wouldn't weigh so heavily on him. Still he hesitated descending after her until she sent three balls of witchlight circling her head like a crown of glowing fire.

The directionless light illuminated the small crypt better than a hundred torches. It revealed a small square room lined with shelves, much like a library—only the information stored in those shelves was beyond interpretation. Powwell wondered briefly if learning to read the memories of the dead was like learning a new language. He already knew three. His name meant bright in the oldest tongue known to Coronnan. Perhaps he had the intelligence and intuition to decipher the memories of the men who had lived in the monastery long ago.

He shook his head to rid it of the fanciful thoughts. *Snap out of it,* he admonished himself. *I'm just giddy from the closeness of the walls and the low ceiling.*

Kalen beckoned him to follow her into the far corner. The corner where he and the other apprentices had laid Nimbulan's still-warm body so many moons ago.

The body had remained warm though eight hours had passed between the time of Nimbulan's death and his funeral. Why the haste? Eight hours. Not enough time for decent mourning before putting a beloved friend and teacher to rest. Were Rollett and the other apprentices so grief-stricken they didn't question the premature funeral? Perhaps they were all so used to obeying the orders of a master without question they had obeyed blindly—too blindly.

The wrongness of the situation sent his balance awry. He stumbled over a crack in the paving stones. Ackerly had directed the funeral. What did he have to hide?

Suddenly, Powwell believed Kalen's story from the depth of his heart. Though seeming not to breathe, or have a heartbeat, Nimbulan hadn't been dead, but so deep in a trance ordinary means could not revive him.

Given time, the master magician could have awakened into darkness, hungry, depleted of magic and strength. The winding cloths soaked in preservatives would have bound him so tightly he might not have been able to break free. What terrors had he known? What ghosts haunted him?

Powwell searched the far corners of the crypt for evidence of the spirits of the dead. They had all fled from Kalen's witchlight. Nimbulan might not have had the energy to summon light. Had he gone insane from the haunting?

He looked where Kalen pointed, hoping he wouldn't see what he knew must be. Nimbulan's body, huddled in agonizing terror as he died a second time, alone and friendless in a crypt as a dark as the void.

Powwell swallowed deeply and forced his eyes open.

The second niche above the floor, last row on the southern side, was empty.

"Which way?" Myri asked the voices as she cuddled Amaranth in her arms. He hadn't flown since his injury and she had no idea if he had healed. His wings remained tightly folded and hidden.

The wind pushed her south, around the pub and up a narrow trail toward the top of the cliff. Thick loam of half-decayed leaves and everblue needles muffled her footsteps. No one could hear her passage. If someone sought to betray her, they would have to seek with other senses than sound.

She walked rapidly, not looking back at the gathered faces that watched her. Faces that could betray her as easily as welcome her. She might see Karry's face in the crowd. Karry who had just lost a beloved grandmother.

"Stargods, comfort her," she prayed. "Give Granny an easy passage to the next existence."

No reply, only the shifting wind guiding her away from the village, uphill toward the mountains that formed a near impenetrable border between Coronnan and Rossemeyer. Somewhere in these mountains lay the hidden city of Hanassa, home of outlaws. Rovers, exiles, anyone who didn't belong in the three civilized kingdoms.

"Maybe that's where we must go, Amaranth. I don't belong anywhere within the borders of this kingdom." The

relentless wind increased and pushed her uphill. She set
Amaranth down to walk beside her or fly if he chose. He
walked.

Their path circled around: west, then south again and
finally back to the east until she heard the pounding surf
in the cove below the village. She paused as soon as the
wind let her, looking around. An opening in the trees beckoned to her. She looked out over the village from a perch
well above the milling people.

The bright colors on the Equinox Pylon drew her eye.

(Careful,) Amaranth warned her. He half-spread his
wings, ready to launch into flight if danger threatened.

"So you've had enough time to heal?" She touched the
place where he had been badly bruised.

(Time enough and love enough.) He ruffled his wing
feathers and stretched wide with an almost visible sigh of
satisfaction.

Myri stepped back into the shelter of the trees, but no
one looked up from the daily activities to espy her or the
flywacket.

"Why here? What am I supposed to find?"

"Oooooh. . . ." A moaning sound greeted her.

Was that the wind sighing in the treetops or . . .

Her talent leaped to awareness.

Pain. Blood. Darkness.

She started the long slide into full rapport with the injured one. *Not yet. Don't let me lose consciousness yet. Not
until I find him.*

Amaranth nipped her ankle. The tiny pain kept a part
of her awareness inside her own body. Part of her continued to blend with the one who lay wounded and bleeding.
The encroaching darkness slowed. Certainty that the victim
was male increased as she gained control of the rapport.

Slashing pain, sharp, intense across her midsection. Difficulty breathing. She reached her right hand out, questing
for the source of the agony that ripped her patient and
herself in two.

Not again. Not so soon after losing Granny Katia!

There, stronger to her left, farther uphill. Not far.

One slow step after another she pushed herself closer to
the pain, knowing that running away from it was as impossible for her as for him.

She nearly stumbled over a huddled form collapsed on knees and forehead. His threadbare cloak of mud brown with hints of dark green in the weave blended with the forest floor, making him nearly invisible.

Her hand still reaching out, she scanned his body. Blue sparks of magic arced from her fingertips to him. A vague sense of familiarity touched her. Had she met this man somewhere before?

"Oooooh . . ." he moaned again. His arms convulsed as they clutched his middle.

A desperate need to keep his life's blood from draining into the soft blanket of leaves filled her mind and emotions. She'd just drained herself of strength and stamina in a desperate and futile attempt to heal Granny Katia. What did she have left to give this new patient?

(His destiny is not yet fulfilled. You must Heal him. We will give you what strength we can. Too much of you passed into the void with the old one.)

She touched the man's shoulder. A vision of two men bound together by a nearly tangible bond leaped into her mind. They argued. One threw a knife, then retrieved it and left. Myri tried desperately to see faces. The wound filled her vision. Blood. Too much blood.

She'd treated knife injuries before, but never one inflicted purposely by a friend.

Was this the betrayal the voices had warned her of? Or had the villagers planned some treachery toward her? She'd never know now. She had no future until she healed this man or they both died.

She aimed the magic in her fingertips toward the wound, willing the blood to thicken and slow. She sensed his fading life stall in its progress toward the void. Half a heartbeat later, sensation-robbing blackness swept over her.

(Stay!) Amaranth commanded. His mental voice was backed by the authority of the anonymous ones who guided her, but the love and familiarity of his mental touch broke through her desire to flee outward into the void.

She stayed, half in her body, aware of the magic healing that tied her to the wounded man. The other part of her mind hovered over them both ready to flee into the void with his soul. Another entity lingered, watching, faceless and yet familiar in stature and poise. She examined it.

Blackness shrouded its aura. The man's soul, not ready to slide back into the body until she healed it or released it to death.

Memories of Moncriith's preaching filled her with dread. What if she failed at both and condemned this man to a soulless life?

"I can't let that happen. You won't escape my healing so easily," Myri said through gritted teeth, tears streaming down her face. Numbness weakened her limbs. "I won't lose you without a fight." She rolled him gently onto his back and settled comfortably beside him to conserve as much of her strength as possible. Concentrating on the wound, she placed her hands on top of his at the center of the ugly gash. She didn't bother to look at his face. Time enough later to explore the familiarity—if he lived.

In her mind she saw muscles pulling together, blood vessels closing. She plugged a nick to the left lung and stopped the leaking air.

She ignored the bones. If any were broken, they could wait. She had to stop the bleeding.

Strength drained from her life into his. The opening to the void grew wider. The tie between them grew stronger, pulling the last vestiges of her life into his wound.

Desperate to save herself, she wrenched her hands away from contact with him. The force of her release sent her rolling downhill. The healing magic snapped and recoiled into her hands. Her palms burned. She looked for physical evidence of the pain snaking up her arms to her shoulders. Red and swollen, her hands sparked inside and out. Her magic sought to reestablish contact against her will.

"Forgive me. I have nothing left to give you but my own life!" she cried, burying her hands in the thick loam of rotting leaves and everblue needles. Contact with the Kardia soothed the burning but not her churning talent. The magic demanded she stay with her patient until he recovered. Her sense of self-preservation kept her anchored out of reach.

"I can't give anymore." Tears poured down her cheeks. Relentlessly, she kept her raging talent within her, refusing to check the man and see if he lived or not. Even the hovering shade of his soul was no longer visible to her.

"Ahhck!" the man groaned again, almost coughing. Ripples of the muscles along his body told her of the pain that came with the effort to make even that little noise.

"Do you live, stranger?"

"I'm afraid so." He choked out the words, rolling to his side, hands still clutched to his middle.

Myri looked at him as a person and not as a patient for the first time. An auburn beard shot with silver covered most of his face. His hair, dark auburn streaked with gray, hung in limp tendrils about his shoulders. Tentatively, he brushed a lock out of his eyes. He clenched his eyelids closed as another spasm of pain crossed his face. Finally, he opened them. He took a moment to focus on her. Deep green, the color of Tambootie leaves in spring, before they turned almost black in midsummer.

She'd seen those eyes before. Ages ago, last autumn. That time, the lines radiating out his eyes had shown fatigue, but the eyes themselves had been bright with intelligence and curiosity. Now they were clouded with pain.

"Hello, Myrilandel," Nimbulan said. "I knew we'd meet again someday. But I didn't dream *you* would rescue *me*."

"I had no choice. I don't like you, Nimbulan. I wouldn't have chosen to help you because when you are well you will try to enslave me and my talent. But I have no choice. Until you are healed, I must stay with you." A shiny silver tendril of magic ran from her heart to his. Her talent refused to sever the connection. As long as that cord existed, he had control over her mind and her talent.

Nimbulan awoke gradually to the realization he was no longer cold or lost in darkness. Nightmares of a freezing hell lingered long after he knew he had survived Televarn's knife thrust. He shivered in memory of the ice that had invaded his gut. That slight movement sent sharp pain in a broad band across his belly just below the ribs.

Myrilandel's healing had not been as complete as the miracle she had worked on Sergeant Kennyth last autumn. She'd stopped the bleeding and saved his life, but hadn't done much more to the wound.

He stilled his muscles with conscious effort. The pain receded to a constant but tolerable level. Very carefully, with sensitized fingertips he explored the region. He discovered a bandage wound tightly around him. From the way his skin felt stretched and pierced, he guessed the witch-woman had resorted to fine stitches to close his wound.

Such barbarity! Only the untamed tribes of the northern most regions of Kardia Hodos resorted to such primitive methods of healing. Or a young woman without enough training to control her healing trances. She must have withdrawn from the spells before the work was done in order to save herself.

Where was she now? Had she deserted him again?

Loneliness washed over him, bringing a momentary tear to his eye. Clear evidence of his weakness. Without magic to speed the process Myrilandel had begun, his recovery could take weeks, moons.

Slowly, lest he jar the wound again and bring a new wave of pain, dizziness, and nausea, he turned his head. A small campfire, burned down to coals, gave off a soft glow of warmth to his right. On the other side of the fire Myrilandel's strange cat blinked at him. Its dark eyes looked almost purple in the growing light of early morning.

The creature blinked at Nimbulan several times, then heaved itself up, as if incredibly weary or bored, and sauntered over to him. Without asking permission, it climbed onto his upper chest and settled into a doze. Its paws kneaded gently into the cloak that covered Nimbulan's body from neck to toe. The cat's gentle purr spread instant warmth and calm through Nimbulan's body and soul. The tiny desire he'd entertained of getting up or moving left him.

"If you are here to nurse me, Cat, then your mistress can't be far away."

Then he saw the silver tendril of magic running from his heart and remembered briefly that it had remained after she removed herself from the healing. Had she left him weak and vulnerable so he couldn't break the cord? She'd have almost total control over his mind and body through it.

A moment of panic skittered through him. Moncriith had warned them all about her demons controlling the souls of those she yanked back from their next existence.

"I'm here. Are you hungry or thirsty?" Myrilandel was beside him, sounding incredibly weary.

He turned his head to find her lying with her back against

his side. His cloak covered them both. Her cloak seemed to be beneath them.

The panic receded. He'd watched her heal Sergeant Kennyth. No evidence of a magical connection remained after that powerful spell.

"I'm thirsty, and I need . . . I would like . . . um. . . ." How did he broach the delicate subject of needing a privy? Some things were more important than demons controlling his soul.

"Can you wait until you've had a little broth to strengthen you?" She heaved herself up with more effort than the cat had exhibited.

Upon closer examination, her skin looked so pale it was almost transparent.

"Are you all right, Myrilandel?" Concern for her well-being overrode his pain and he rolled to his other side in preparation of rising. The movement drove spasms of agony from his chest to his gut and back along his spine.

"Merow!" the cat protested, climbing onto his side rather than be displaced. Or was the cat keeping him in place? Nimbulan didn't care anymore. He wasn't going to be moving again soon.

"No, I'm not all right," Myrilandel spat at him. "All my strength is in you right now."

"Thank you for saving me. But my life isn't worth the loss of yours. Why didn't you let me die?"

"I couldn't." She turned her back on him to rummage in a pack. "I'll be back in a moment with water and kindling." She set off into the thick woods, her feet dragging and her shoulders drooping.

When she came back carrying a pot full of water, bright color splotched her pale skin, as if she'd dashed icy water on her face to revive herself. Perhaps fever burned her cheeks. Her eyes looked dull, and she still shuffled as she walked. She poked the fire listlessly. Finally, she set the pot on a rock next to the blaze and sat back on her heels to rest.

"All I have is some jerked meat and dried fruit. I'll boil the meat for a broth for you. I'll eat the meat."

"The fire isn't hot enough to boil the water. We'll need more wood."

Her shoulders drooped further and she dropped her gaze

to the few branches beside her. Clearly the effort to gather more was too much for her. If they were to survive and recover, he had to help.

Bracing himself to endure the pain he gathered his knees beneath him and rose to all fours, back arched to keep his abdominal muscles moving as little as possible. "I can't wait any longer. I'll bring a few sticks on my way back." He gritted his teeth and crawled into the underbrush.

Chapter 25

"**I** suppose it's too late to warn the village," Nimbulan mumbled into the horn cup Myri had fished from her pack.

"Warn them of what?" Myri couldn't muster much enthusiasm for the trek back down the hill to the village she had left . . . was it only yesterday? She'd be content to sit and watch the birds flitting through the branches of the everblue trees. A flock of a hundred or more tiny kinglets had gathered to serenade the world.

"Rovers. They planned to raid the storehouse last night during Festival," Nimbulan said.

"They won't find much but torn fishing nets and broken bay crawler pots. The winter stores have been exhausted and the fishing sparse. The villagers probably didn't notice the raid until this morning. They were quite intent on making a good Festival in hopes of a bountiful summer." They needed a fertile Festival. Nearly half of last year's Festival babies had died within a few days of birth. Several of the mothers had also died despite Myri's best efforts to save them. All of them might have succumbed had she not been there to midwife them. Experience and hard work often worked better at birthings than magic. Not always. She could not save all of them. She hadn't been able to save Granny Katia, beloved by the entire village.

Mourning families tended to remember only the losses. How many of them blamed her for the deaths?

If the villagers followed her, Nimbulan would be in danger, too. She looked at the slender silver cord of magic that connected her heart to his. He'd only crawled a few yards into the woods before the cord stretched thin and tried to yank him back. Her trip to the creek hadn't been much farther away. They were bound together, probably for a long time. Whatever fate followed one, would involve the other. Concern for him overrode her resentment at the implied control he had over her through that cord.

"Televarn seemed to think this village rich, with adequate stores left over."

"Televarn! Stargods, we have to get out of here." Frantically, she gathered together her few possessions. The cooking pot, the water jug, her knife . . . Amaranth!

"Neither of us is in any condition to move, Myrilandel."

"And less prepared to defend ourselves when he comes looking for me and . . ." she almost said "my flywacket."

"He thinks I'm dead. And I would be if you hadn't come when you did. Televarn has no reason to return."

"Unless he questioned the villagers or overheard them talking about me. We have to leave. Now!" This time she stood and kicked dirt over their little fire. Should she scatter the remnants and obscure all evidence of their presence?

"How do you know Televarn?" He grabbed a fistful of her skirt, the only part of her he could reach.

"He covets something of mine he can never have." She wrenched her skirt free of his grasp.

"What?" He stared at the few possessions she crammed into her pack.

Just then a dark, winged shadow fluttered into the little clear space of their camp. Amaranth landed between them, near the remnants of the fire, a gray scurry clamped firmly in his jaws. He left his wings half-furled.

Nimbulan stared, gape-jawed at the legendary flywacket.

"Amaranth!" Myrilandel gasped. "You shouldn't reveal yourself to strangers."

(He's not a stranger. We trust him.) Her familiar dropped the dead rodent near the fire. He fluffed his wings and tail as he paced circles around the two of them, growling and mewling with every step.

"He says I must trust you," Myrilandel said.

(Televarn is in the village. He questions people in the pub. He knows you were there yesterday.)

Myri related that bit of information to Nimbulan. "We have to go. We have to hide."

"I see why Televarn pursues you so relentlessly. Amaranth is a rare prize. Where do you propose we go?" Nimbulan struggled to his feet. His skin paled as pain and dizziness overwhelmed him.

She watched him struggle against the impulse to collapse again. Intelligently, he gathered their cloaks as he righted himself rather than risk bending down again.

"Anywhere away from here. Where do you suggest?" she replied, accepting her cloak from his outstretched hand. She helped him settle his mud-caked outer garment about his shoulders.

The silver cord strengthened. They must flee together or die together. That *s'murghing* connection wouldn't break until he was healed and strong. She couldn't do anything about that now. She hadn't the strength or the time.

"Not back to the road if you are intent on hiding from the Rovers. Though I don't believe he's stupid enough to return to the scene of a murder."

"No, he's not stupid. He's obsessed. If he suspects we are anywhere in the vicinity, he'll hunt me down. I ran away from him once. He can't let that happen again. And if he discovers you still live, he won't rest until he's completed his quest."

"Obsessive. Yes, that describes Televarn well. We'd best rake the leaves and such to remove traces of our camp."

"I'll do it, you start walking. Amaranth, stay with him," she ordered the flywacket.

(Of course.)

"Which way?" Nimbulan cocked one eyebrow up, removing worry lines and lending him an illusion of youth and strength.

Myri remembered his boyish grin touched with mischief last autumn and longed to see it again.

She paused to listen to the wind for a suggestion. A gentle "push" from behind. "Uphill, due south. I'll be right behind you." As if she had a choice with that magical bond holding their fates together.

"Where is Kalen?" Ackerly asked her father.

Stuuvart looked up from counting the sacks of grain in the storeroom. "I have no idea. She's supposed to be in class." He returned to inspecting a ragged corner of one of the sacks. Evidence of mice?

"She is supposed to be with me, practicing communication spells. But she isn't. I thought she might have joined her *family* for some reason." Ackerly took a sudden dislike to the man. Stuuvart managed the school's resources with efficiency and struck bargains with a brilliant flair for conservation of money. But since the day he had arrived, he'd ignored his own daughter, as if she no longer existed—or wasn't his.

"Then ask her mother where she is." Stuuvart moved into the still room filled with crocks of pickled vegetables and salted meat.

"I did ask Guillia. She hasn't seen Kalen since breakfast and she's worried sick for the girl."

All of the children and adults ended up in the kitchen with Guillia at some point during each day. Kalen's mother proved to be a wonderful cook. She was generous with treats and lent a sympathetic ear to one and all. Her homey domain radiated warmth and love along with the wonderful aromas of baking sweets and savory pies. How could such a warmhearted woman have married this cold and unfeeling man?

"You seem to have lost Kalen, Ackerly. A very valuable child." Stuuvart finally straightened from his inventory. He didn't call Kalen "daughter." Ever. "You have also failed to keep the wards around my stores to prevent vermin from stealing us blind. I will require compensation for the damage to my reputation for this. Allowing vermin in *my* storeroom!"

Was the storeroom more important than his daughter? If she was his daughter. Kalen's younger siblings all had blue eyes and blond hair like their mother. Only Kalen had a touch of red in her hair. Stuuvart's hair was dark brown, as were his eyes. Kalen's eyes were gray—like Powwell's and Ackerly's.

His thoughts paused a moment with that realization. A secret smile touched his mouth. Possible. Yes, it was possible. How could he use his blood link to the children, if indeed the relationship existed?

"You are the one who is blind, Stuuvart. The holes in the corners of the sacks have been cut with a knife, not chewed by mice. Only a magician could slip around the wards. One of our own has been stealing. Have you and your wife been keeping *my* students and faculty so hungry they must steal?'' He turned the accusation back onto Stuuvart, the only overt way to maintain control of the man. Would Stuuvart succumb to coercion? His honor would be marred much deeper should it become publicly known that he had not sired Kalen—a very valuable witch-child.

Ackerly hid his revulsion of a man who suddenly seemed as mean and small-spirited as Druulin. His inventories were more important than feeding the apprentices. Ackerly had vowed never to go hungry again.

"Excuse me, Master Ackerly," Rollett said, knocking politely on the doorjamb. His hand went immediately to an open crock of dried fruit and nuts. He popped a handful into his mouth before continuing. "I can't find Powwell, Master. I'm supposed to team up with him today for practice in summoning. Haakon thought he might be with you."

Ackerly looked pointedly from the journeyman's hand plunging into the crock a second time, to Stuuvart. The steward stood his ground, refusing the accusation of short rations. Druulin had done the same thing.

Ackerly didn't have time for this battle of wills.

"Powwell is not with me as you can see. Nor is Kalen. Take Gilby and two others and start searching for them." One gifted child playing hooky from lessons spelled mischief. Two gifted children missing, along with dried fruit, nuts, and grains, and possibly a ham—he'd spotted an empty spot in the orderly rows of smoked meat hanging from the ceiling—smelled of trouble.

"We will discuss this later, Stuuvart, when the children and missing stores are accounted for." Ackerly turned sharply on his heel and left the room before his steward could increase his demands of blackmail.

S'murghit! if Stuuvart weren't so valuable as a manager and accountant, Ackerly would dismiss him, his wife, and the other children as well. *I'm in charge of this school, not him. The profits are mine and I can't afford to share them with another.* As soon as he found Kalen and knew the child and her enormous talent to be safe, he just might turn the rest of the family out. The girl and her talent were all that truly mattered. Couldn't her father see that? If he was truly her father. He didn't think Guillia the kind of woman to stray from her marriage bed. But he knew from experience that any woman could be seduced with the right promises.

Maybe that was why she looked so familiar! He'd visited Baria a number of times over the years and remembered an innkeeper's daughter on the verge of a convenient marriage to a rich merchant she didn't like. . . .

Ackerly didn't need Guillia and her family to make a profit from Kalen. A blood link could be made to keep the child close at hand. Moncriith would know how to do that.

Maybe Stuuvart was hiding both children so that he could demand ransom, a tidy sum of gold for them.

If he was, then Stuuvart had best watch his back. Ackerly had an entire school of magicians to force the truth out of him, very painfully. He'd summon Moncriith to be on the lookout for the children.

He couldn't allow anything to harm those children. They were too important an investment.

"We need help, Myrilandel," Nimbulan gasped as he sank to his knees for the third time. Ruefully he looked back along the path they had come. The crooked rowan growing beside the double everblue that marked the beginning of their trek was still in sight.

"I know." She clung to the trunk of a stout tree as she dropped her meager pack to the ground. Her knuckles were white where she grasped a branch level with her shoulder.

"Perhaps if we went downhill?" He looked hopefully at the easier path.

Myrilandel cocked her head as if listening. "No," she said righting her head and gathering her strength.

That curious habit of listening to the wind bothered him. She reminded him of someone when she did that. What did Amaranth tell her?

"They . . . I said no. We can't take the risk."

"Televarn?"

"He's still in the village." She bit her trembling lip, looking longingly at the downhill path. "I hope he doesn't hurt anyone there." She blinked back a tear, then resolutely shouldered the pack again. She didn't let go of the branch that supported her.

"I don't believe he'd risk hanging around after he raided the storehouse."

Nimbulan thought about rising from his knees and decided to wait a moment more. He'd not lose track of Myrilandel. Not with that pretty silver cord stretching from his heart to hers. What kind of magic had she worked on him? He'd never heard of such a thing.

He should resent the tie she'd established. Strangely, the connection pleased him. He'd wanted her to stay with him last autumn. Now she couldn't run away from him. He had the chance to . . . To what?

"What would Televarn do if he found the storehouse as empty as I know it to be?" Myrilandel looked back at him, as reluctant to move as he. "He'd believe the villagers tricked him, and he can't allow anyone to trick the great trickster. So he'd watch and wait for another chance. He'd ask questions that would lead him to another storehouse. Only there isn't another storehouse. Drinking in the pub is the best place to observe the entire village." She shoved herself away from the tree and took two steps uphill.

"You know him well."

"Too well. Take a drink. You need fluid to replace the blood you lost, then we must move on."

Much later Nimbulan could no longer see the crooked rowan. Blindly he set one foot in front of the other—he was no longer sure which foot moved and which was right or left—and bumped into Myrilandel's back. The silver cord swelled and tugged at his heart when he didn't move away from the warm sensation of her back pressed against the length of him.

"We can stop here." Her teeth chattered as she spoke. "He won't see our fire from the place where he left you. Amaranth says he'll bring us more fresh meat. I think he spotted another gray scurry nearby."

Nimbulan didn't care. If his enemy found him now and killed him again, he didn't have the strength or the will to protest. Anything to end this endless journey.

(No, you must fight for yourself.)

"Who said that?"

Silence.

He looked at Myrilandel. She stood with her head cocked

to the left. Amaranth pointed his nose uphill, to the south, ears alert, tail straight up.

"You heard them, too?" she asked. Curious shadows elongated her face and fingers. Where had he seen that otherworldly image before?

"Yes." He continued to search the small open space for evidence of another being.

"You won't see them. They have guided me my entire life. I have learned to trust them, but I have never known who or what they are." She dropped the pack and began gathering firewood.

"Did they say it's safe to stop here?" He reached to his hip where he should carry a knife, but Televarn had stolen it from him.

"They don't push me forward now."

"I wonder who they are." He sank down and collected the few dead branches he could reach. Her relaxation of her vigilant attention to her surroundings told him that these mysterious voices were trustworthy more than her words had. He'd never seen this strange witchwomen other than wary, almost feral in her desire to remain unconfined by people or places.

"I don't know. But they told me of betrayal and sent me to you. I don't know if they meant I would be betrayed or you would. Now they push me to climb this hill. There is something up there. . . ." She paused and looked in the direction they had been traveling. Her nose twitched and her eyes brightened. "I think I'm going home. But I've never been there before."

Three days passed, three days of struggling uphill along a path only Myrilandel could see. Amaranth brought them gray scurries and an occasional striped lapin. On the second day, Myrilandel had enough strength to dig a few roots. Both of them drank deeply from the numerous streams they crossed.

Finally, at the end of the third day, when Nimbulan was sure he could walk no farther, and could barely lift a hand to push away branches that slapped his face, they both stumbled at the same time, landing flat on their faces. Had the magical cord that bound them together tripped them?

When he had enough strength to raise his head, a wonderful sight greeted him.

"An old woodsman's hut," he murmured. "The roof is intact." Shelter at last.

"A flusterhen coop!" Myrilandel crawled to her feet.

"We'd best check for people." He searched the clearing with his normal senses. He hadn't the strength to look with magic. The place smelled abandoned. But he couldn't be sure.

"Hello!" Myri called.

A flustercock strutted out from the coop in response. He stretched his neck and crowed loudly at them.

Myri laughed and lunged for the brightly feathered bird. He ducked back into the small shelter. She followed and emerged a moment later with two white globes held triumphantly in her hands. "Laying hens. No one has collected the eggs in moons and moons. The hens obligingly laid these two a moment ago just for us. Tonight, we eat properly."

Something snapped behind Nimbulan. With the last of his strength he looked in the general direction of the sound. His eyes saw nothing. A tendril of magic stirred within him for the first time since Televarn had stabbed him. He hadn't the energy or the will to push the magic outward and explore the unusual sound. Yet he had the distinct sensation of something closing, almost as if someone had closed a door with a sigh of relief.

"Did you hear something, Myrilandel?"

She paused in her progress toward the hut. She turned in a complete circle, sniffing the air and cocking her head to listen. A smile lit her face. Joy danced in her eyes. "I'm home. I'm *home!* This is where they need me to be. This is where *I* need to be. We're safe here." She turned another circle, arms outstretched in welcome, head thrown back in laughter.

He'd never seen a more beautiful woman.

His magic stirred again, pulling his hand toward the center of the clearing where Myrilandel continued her delighted capering. Curious to know what power tugged at him, he allowed the little magic stirring within him to sharpen his sight.

Blue! Ley line blue spread before him. Not the intense well of blue hidden beneath the courtyard of the old monastery, but still strong and pulsing with energy. He fine-tuned his focus to follow individual lines. Four, five, six.

Six. Unprecedented except for the well. Six lines equally spaced, coming together at the exact point where Myrilandel danced. There the lines crossed and radiated out again.

A nexus. He'd heard old Master Magicians speak of the legendary points as places of unusual power. Most scholars dismissed the idea as improbable. Ley lines occurred randomly, at irregular intervals. Only rarely did two or three lines cross. No one had recorded more at any time in recent history.

Nimbulan remembered an essay on the subject in one of the books in the library at the school. A major nexus. Six of the phenomena had been recorded in ancient times, one on each continent of Kardia Hodos. No one mentioned the well. The locations of all six of the nexi had been lost to modern magicians shortly after the departure of the Stargods. After a brief skimming of the essay, he'd seen no mention about the well of ley lines as the source of all power. He'd put it aside to read carefully later, but later never came.

Gratefully, he positioned himself directly over one of the lines. Energy filled him with enough strength to crawl to Myrilandel and the nexus. His heart pounded stronger and more regularly, pushing blood to all parts of his body. Warmth filled him to the tips of his very cold fingers and toes. Tingles played with the angry wound across his gut, hastening the healing process and restoring some of his lost strength.

He stood up with only minor dizziness and a raging hunger for food and for Myri.

A smile grew from his belly and spread outward to every corner of his being. He was not satisfied until he held her tightly against his chest, kissing her soft mouth. They continued their spiral dance together, embracing the clearing and each other. The silver cord connecting their hearts swelled and wrapped them closer together.

(We have brought you home. Soon we will meet with you and teach you what you need to know.)

Chapter 26

"**W**hat are we to do with you?" Moncriith asked no one in particular. He stared at the two grubby children from the height of the throne in the great hall of Castle Krej, the ancestral home of Kammeryl d'Astrismos. A conscientious farmer had brought the children to the court after finding them hiding in his barn, stealing milk from his goat.

The lord himself was busy elsewhere and so Moncriith listened to the farmer's tale of woe, as he listened to most petitioners for the lord's justice. Kammeryl d'Astrismos didn't like to sit still and found dispensing justice tedious. He'd almost blubbered in delight when Moncriith showed him the merits of allowing an educated magician to sit in his stead.

"You stole food from an honest man's barn. You milked his goat and stuffed his eggs into your pockets." He looked at the boy, the older of the two, straight in the eye. Most people blinked and stammered when he challenged them with direct eye contact. Not this child. The boy returned the stare and kept his mouth shut. His arm stole about the shoulders of his sister in a protective gesture that said much about them.

Moncriith presumed they were brother and sister. They possessed the same mud-brown hair and gray eyes with incredibly long lashes. The spay of freckles across their noses fell into almost identical patterns. He'd seen those gray eyes before. Where?

The girl kept her eyes lowered. She darted shy glances to right and left. Her mouth opened slightly in awe. Her innocence tugged at Moncriith's heart.

He vaguely remembered meeting her somewhere in his travels. Probably the boy, too. That was why the eyes looked so familiar. Why hadn't they heeded his sermons and become too frightened of demons to ever work magic again?

"This honest farmer also tells me that you frightened his plow steed with witchlight. I have forbidden all witchcraft within Lord d'Astrismos' land." He had to remain stern, make an example of all witches. Their magic would attract demons. He would not tolerate rival magicians in his province, no matter how beguiling the children could seem.

"We didn't know that, Sssieur. We were hungry and cold. We only did what we had to do to thurvive," the girl said quietly, very meekly.

A solitary tear moistened her beautiful eyelashes, threatening to spill over onto her cheek. Moncriith wanted nothing more than to rush forward with a clean handkerchief to brush the tear aside so she could look up at him with thanks. He adjusted his estimate of her age downward.

"Hush, Kalen. He won't listen. He's like all the other witchhunters. He doesn't care about us. Only about his laws." The boy pulled her closer, still protecting her.

"Master Magician Ackerly sent word that two of his students had run away." Moncriith shook his shoulders to rid himself of his foolish emotions. He had to maintain control here. "Witchchildren run away from the witch school, only using enough magic to survive. Perhaps Myrlandel's demons haven't found you yet. I may be able to redeem your souls after all."

Among the d'Astrismos soldiers and retainers he already had commitments from two hundred people—he'd worked hard all winter recruiting those commitments. Soon the weather would allow him to take his crusade farther afield. By the time the fields were plowed and planted and the men could leave home, he'd have control of the lord's army. Control of all Coronnan would soon follow.

The children exchanged a glance. Communication without words.

"Speak with words, not magic!" Moncriith roared.

The farmer backed out of the room with undue haste. Moncriith ignored him, though he should have taken the time to reassure the man he had nothing to fear from Mon-

criith, being an innocent mundane. Only the abominations
who used demon magic had reason to fear Moncriith and
Lord d'Astrismos' justice.

"Sieur?" The boy leveled his gaze on Moncriith once
more. He used the respectful title reserved for honored
priests, but his eyes were more seeking than respectful.

Moncriith had the eerie feeling this child could read him
to the depths of his soul. No one could do that anymore.
No traditional magician could penetrate the armor he'd
erected when . . . when he realized how vulnerable to
demons he'd become. Not even the priests in the temple
with their coercive methods could force their way into his
mind.

"Speak freely, child. I'll not harm you." Moncriith added
another layer of armor to his mind.

"Sieur, we don't think we want to stay with you. We're
on a quest. An urgent quest."

"Now that Nimbulan is dead, the cult of Battlemages will
die out, child. And without the Battlemages, the wars will
cease. You need not worry about quests anymore. Soon I
will return you to your parents and we will all live in
peace."

The children exchanged another of their deep glances.
Moncriith drummed his fingers on the arm of his throne in
frustration. Why did everyone question and doubt the
truth?

"But Master Nimbulan ithn't dead, Sssieur. And we have
to find him. It's important. Very important," Kalen said.
Finally, she raised her eyes to him. Determination overshadowed the innocence and beauty he had seen in her,
leaving only a willful child who must be disciplined. After
she had outlived her usefulness.

"Yes, finding Nimbulan is very important, if he is indeed
still alive." Moncriith leaned forward. His knuckles turned
white under the force of his grip of the chair arms. He
forced himself to remain calm. How could that man still
live to plague him? Nimbulan had to be dead, as reported.
Ackerly wouldn't lie to him, not after Moncriith had paid
out three gold pieces for information. His plans to eliminate
all magicians along with the demons would blow away as
dust if Nimbulan still lived. No other Battlemage commanded the respect of both magician and mundane armies.

As long as Nimbulan lived to direct battles and train other magicians to do the same, Moncriith would remain an outcast.

The kingship of Coronnan eluded him as long as Nimbulan lived to oppose Moncriith.

"I will help you find Master Nimbulan, children. But first you must bathe and have a hot meal. Some new, warm clothing and boots, too." He clapped his hands for servants to see to the children. "We will begin our journey at dawn."

Myri explored the boundary of the clearing with her hands and magic senses. Yesterday, when she and Nimbulan had collapsed into the clearing, she thought she heard a popping sound, as if a door had closed behind them. Now she sought that door again.

Inch by inch, she traced the perimeter of the area around her new home. An invisible wall resisted the pressure of her hand. The thought of being trapped here forever didn't bother her. Within the magic enclosure of several acres, she had about an acre for a garden, access to a creek for water, and a secluded pool fed by hot springs for bathing and laundry. Nimbulan was there now, washing away the blood and dust of his adventures.

A long soak in the warm water would aid the internal healing she hadn't been able to complete. She had probed the wound last night and realized she could do little more for him with magic. Only time and rest and good food would finish the job she had begun.

She hoped he shaved his beard as well. She liked being able to watch his facial expressions. She wanted to see that boyish grin light his eyes again.

It was curious that the silver tendril of magic still bound her to him. She had thought the connection born solely of the incomplete healing and his need to keep her close and controlled until he no longer required her talent. Something else must be maintaining it. She tugged gently on the cord and sent him the message to scrape the beard from his face.

A sense of well-being crept over her at the realization she didn't resent the silver cord or Nimbulan anymore. "We belong together. We belong here. This is home," she whispered, utterly amazed.

Briefly she gave up her examination of the wall to touch her lips where he had kissed her yesterday. The sensations he roused in her still puzzled her. He wasn't as beautiful or as skilled as Televarn, but the raw honesty of his embrace had touched a portion of her heart she thought closed and locked away forever.

Televarn had roused her lust but not her love. What kind of emotions would grow between herself and Nimbulan if she allowed him to stay in her life?

When Old Magretha had died three years ago, Myri had grieved for her lost mentor and companion. If she lost Nimbulan now, she thought she might feel the same kind of loneliness and regret. Or worse.

"You feel it, too?" Nimbulan came up behind her, almost as if she had conjured him with her speculations.

"Feel what?" She was lost in the wonder of examining his bare cheeks and upper lip. Would his kiss delight her as much without the beard tickling her?

He'd pulled his long hair back into a single braid, without the distinctive shorter sides hanging loose, as most magicians did. Now he looked like an ordinary country gentleman, the kind of man who might be willing to linger with her in this remote clearing.

"Feel the wall. I managed to step beyond it and back through it down by the creek, but it took a major effort of will. My magic won't return fully until my body is completely healed. I doubt that anyone else will be able to penetrate the wall without our permission."

"A kind of armor?" She visualized a small opening in the wall and pushed her hand against it. The wall resisted the way a feather pillow compressed under the weight of a head, shaping around it, but not splitting. She opened the image of the door. Her hand slid right through. "Oh, my!" She pulled her hand back in surprise and stared at her palm. Somehow she expected it to burn or at least tingle from the magic. Nothing. Her hand seemed perfectly normal and undamaged.

"Do you think your voices guided you here? Perhaps your guardian spirits prepared this place for us, a place where we are safe from Rovers and witchhunters." He took her hand in his own larger ones, examining it, kissing it, tracing the crease of her heart line across the palm.

Bending over her hand didn't disguise the slight stoop in his posture. The wound must still pain him.

"We are safe from those who would betray us. I know it with the same certainty that tells me the sun will rise in the east tomorrow." Her breathing seemed strangely uneven as his hands moved up her arm to her shoulders, then moved to cradle her face.

"You needn't force me to stay with you, Myrilandel. I want to be with you. This silver cord isn't necessary." He slowly lowered his mouth to cover hers in a long kiss.

Heat rose from her belly to her breasts in a satisfying wave. Her knees nearly buckled with joy.

"I thought you controlled the cord," she said when they came up for air, still locked in each others arms.

"Perhaps neither of us controls it. Perhaps it is a symbol of something deeper that we refused to recognize." He kissed her again, molding her body to fit neatly against his.

"Stay with me, Nimbulan. Please, help me make this clearing our home."

"If we are to stay, we must lay in some stores. There is a sack of seeds and roots underneath the bed in the hut," Nimbulan said. "Magic has kept them in stasis, so they won't spoil. If we're going to be here any length of time, we'd best start planting the garden. Can you dig if I plant? I don't think I have the strength yet to do the heaviest work." He walked slowly back to the one-room home with the very wide bed. Last night they'd slept there, side by side, Amaranth between them or on top of one of them— as they'd slept on the trail. Nimbulan hadn't touched her. Amaranth was too good a chaperone for that.

Tonight the flywacket would sleep elsewhere, Myri decided.

"I don't know if I like it that you are a Battlemage, Nimbulan. But you intrigue me and make me feel safer than anyone has before. You must be a very special man."

Myri's joyful planting song dwindled to a questioning note as a cloud dimmed the spring sun and then passed on.

She looked to the northeast and sniffed the damp breeze. She almost tasted the warm growth and new life abundant in the forest around her. Her song returned to her lips, soaring high. A sense of rightness with the world swelled her heart and added speed to her digging.

Nimbulan looked up from where he dropped triangles of yampion root into the freshly turned earth two rows to her left. He laughed with her and joined her song. They'd made love last night, and the three nights before. Joyous, wondrous, abandoned love, growing in intensity with each joining. She needed to sing about that, too.

"When you stand like that with your face uplifted to the wind, you remind me of someone," Nimbulan said. "But for the life of me, I can't remember who." He shook his head and resumed his planting.

"Someone you know? My family, perhaps?" If he knew her family, she could meet them, talk to them, fill in missing pieces of her memory.

"I must not have known her well, or I'd remember. Don't worry about it. If it's important, the name and the face will come to me."

"I'd like to find my family someday." Someday, when exploring their love wasn't quite so new and fragile.

She'd dreamed of flying again last night. The sensation of wind beneath her outstretched arms felt as natural and as harmonious as singing with this man beside her. She tried to imagine the two of them soaring effortlessly across the bay on a warm current of air; the crisp bite of thin air cleansing her mind and body of old fears and urgencies.

She hunched her shoulders and folded her elbows in memory of tilting wings to catch the next updraft. . . .

" 'Twas only a dream," she sighed. "But it felt like a memory." She pushed the shovel into the ground.

The scent of brine alerted her to the next change in the weather. Tall trees blocked her view of the Great Bay. She blinked three times, a trick Nimbulan had taught her, and found her FarSight ready to scan north, through the forest, and over the horizon.

Dark clouds boiled on the horizon, where the Bay met the open sea. Tonight the rains would soak their small garden and nourish the seeds and roots they planted.

The hair on her arms and the back of her neck bristled. Her sense of safety and privacy vanished. She whipped her head back and forth, sniffing the air for the "difference."

"We aren't alone," Nimbulan whispered.

"We must be. The barrier remains intact," she answered.

"Is someone coming near?" He rose slowly to his knees, still protecting the vulnerable area around his wound. He raised his left hand, palm outward, fingers slightly curled and rotated it.

"I sense weariness and fear. One stumbles and . . . and I share pain with her. Almost too tired to feel the pain. Another helps. But he is tired, too." Awareness of the two lives invaded her empathy.

"They need you. Nimbulan struggled to his feet. Once upright he walked over to the nearest barrier and touched it with the flat of his palm.

The barrier swirled into a dozen visible colors, extending outward from his hand. The trees outside the clearing seemed to lurch and right themselves slightly to the left of where they had been.

Myri closed her eyes. The world returned to the same place as before. She opened them again and the trees continued to shift until an arch opened in the barrier, outlined by a narrow band of the swirling colors. On the other side of the barrier stood two children, a boy and a girl with identical mud-brown hair tinged with red and sprays of freckles across their noses. They both stared at Nimbulan with wide gray eyes.

Chapter 27

Moncriith dragged at the leash of a baying dog. The stupid creature couldn't track its own shit, let alone an elusive witchwoman and two grubby children determined to elude their fate.

He was close to Myrilandel. He knew it, could smell the demon magic in the air. The villagers had said she was nearby.

Where else would those two cursed children run but to the witchwoman? She was the only one in these parts who would give shelter to the brats.

Except possibly the Rover chieftain. He sought Myrilandel, too. Moncriith had to find the witch before the Rover whisked her into Hanassa or some other impossible place.

"Sieur, we've passed that split tree with the boulder growing out of the center three times." The sergeant assigned to Moncriith wiped his brow with his sleeve as he stared at the tree in question.

The other soldiers huddled together behind their sergeant, shoulders tensed as if trying to make themselves invisible by reducing their size.

"Fools! Of course we're going in circles. The witchwoman has laid a dozen false trails. We have to branch out and look for signs of passage beyond this circle." Moncriith pushed his own growing anxiety aside with his forceful tones. He knew the eerie feeling permeating these woods was a cloaking spell. No one would venture closer to the witch's dwelling because of the growing sense of unease generated by her evil.

Magretha had generated the same miasma of impending doom in the woods surrounding her house. A house where she had seduced young men with promises of great magic and never-ending sex.

Moncriith had been naive enough to believe himself the first and only young lad to share her bed.

Magretha had been as false as her foster daughter.

Flushed with lust and newly awakened power, Moncriith had believed Magretha and pledged her his love. His parents had encouraged the match, even though Magretha at thirty—a very beautiful thirty—was fifteen years older and fifteen years more experienced than Moncriith. A magician in the family, particularly one powerful enough to become a Battlemage, offered a chance for a steady income and a way out of the constant grind of hunger and hard work. The entire village hoped Moncriith would be powerful enough to protect them from the marauding armies that had plagued Coronnan for two or more generations.

But Magretha had betrayed Moncriith. She had seduced his father and two of the village elders, as she seduced every man who crossed her path. Moncriith had discovered her lying in his father's arms, both naked, in the throes of passion. While he stood in the woods, aghast and ashamed, the two village elders joined him, awaiting their turn with Magretha. Their lewd jokes had roused Moncriith's youthful anger and righteous outrage. Moncriith unleashed his newfound and uncontrolled magic. He sent a firebomb into the thatch of Magretha's sturdy home. Rain hadn't fallen in nigh on three moons. The dry straw and aged timbers erupted in flames and smoke so fast, the inhabitants hadn't a hope of escape.

Magretha and Moncriith's father should have died, locked in each other's arms at the height of their unbridled lust. But Myrilandel, no more than six at the time, had dragged Magretha from the flames, leaving Moncriith's father to die.

The stench of burning flesh had sickened Moncriith and brought home to his grieving mind the enormity of his crime. He'd run away to the nearest monastery, pledging the rest of his miserable life to repentance and service to the Stargods. At the gateway of the temple he'd pledged never to use again the magic that Magretha had awakened and shown him how to use.

All priests of the Stargods must first be magicians. So Moncriith had turned to blood magic rather than draw power from the ley lines embedded in the Kardia. Most often, he used his own blood, relishing the pain and the power that pain brought him. He should have been the most powerful Battlemage of all time, continuously drawing strength from the blood and death of a battle.

The elders of the temple had banished him on the night of his ordination as a priest. They would not sully their hallowed halls with blood.

But they harbored demons. Only demons could make the elders turn against Moncriith and his vision of the infestation of evil into all traditional magic.

The vision drove him to scour Coronnan free of the pestilence of the demons who used human bodies to house their spirits. Myrilandel led the demons now that Magretha had died—finally purged of her possession by holy fire.

How else had a child so small rescued Magretha? Why else had she rescued the treacherous witch and not Moncriith's father?

"Master Nimbulan!" Powwell flung himself forward, hugging the magician's knees. He wanted to wrap his arms around the older man's waist and hug him tight, but the woman was in the way. "We've found you at last. Kalen said you were alive. I didn't believe her. But she convinced me. We ran away from Master Ackerly and her father. We ran away to bring you back. They searched for us but we hid. Then Sieur Moncriith found us and fed us and kept us warm. He wanted to find you, too, but we ran away again. He wants to hurt you."

"Powwell? Slow down. One thing at a time." Nimbulan eased them into the clearing, toward the little hut at the center. "How did you find me? I've been gone for moons."

"It was Kalen all the time. She knew where to look. She knew we'd find you in the east. You have to come back to the school with us. You have to make it all better."

Only when the heat from the central hearth in the hut engulfed Powwell did he realize how cold and wet he was. How tired he was of sleeping rough and eating rougher. How dangerous Moncriith and his preachings were. But if he was cold and tired and ready for the comfort of a real bed and hot food, Kalen must need it more.

Dark circles beneath her eyes made her look like her

face was always dirty. She didn't smile or laugh anymore, and she certainly didn't play magic tricks on him the way she had back at the school.

Powwell released Nimbulan and assumed a straighter, more mature posture. He wrapped an arm around Kalen's shivering shoulders. He had to take care of her. No one else would.

"Come, tell me your adventures, Powwell. And you, too, Kalen. Then we'll decide what to do with you. Your parents and Ackerly must be frantic about you."

"How did you know to come east?" the woman asked from the doorway. Kalen hovered there twisting her hands in her skirt as if frightened of everything.

Kalen looked up at the woman. Determination firmed her chin and cleared her eyes of all traces of her tiredness. "*They* told me."

"They?" Nimbulan asked, exchanging a worried glance with the woman.

"The voices in my head. They told me to come east and find you."

(*Your family is complete. Come to us. Follow the path only Myrilandel can see.*)

A large black cat stalked into the hut, fluffing his wings for all to see.

Powwell's jaw dropped. A flywacket! A real, live, *fly-wacket!* Nimbulan had found a creature that lived only in legends.

(*I am Amaranth, Myrilandel's familiar,*) the flywacket announced directly into Powwell's mind.

"I . . . I'm Powwell. This is Kalen," he stammered an introduction since it seemed warranted.

(*We must trust the little ones. All of us are needed. The path opens to you at dawn,*) Amaranth told them all.

Nimbulan watched Myri walk up the trail. Her lovely shape was outlined by her skirt with each long, confident stride. He longed to reach out and hold her close, kiss her, love her. The slender silver umbilical that connected them grew stronger every day until he was sure he could reach out and pull her closer to him by tugging on the magical cord.

But they had a long trek into the mountains to find the

mysterious guiding voices, and the children watched every move he made with avid curiosity—when they weren't trying to catch Amaranth and make him show off his wings.

Nimbulan decided to question them once more rather than contemplate Myri and how she found the path that appeared behind them but never before them.

"How did you two meet?" The similarity in hair and eye color, the position of their freckles, and the shape of their tip-tilted noses was too much coincidence for them not to have a common parent or grandparent.

Nimbulan had met Powwell's mother when he recruited the boy for the school. A shy woman who'd been seduced by a man displaced by the wars. She might have been beautiful if loved and allowed to bloom with joy, but years of hard work and being outcast for bearing a bastard child had etched premature worry lines into her face. Hunger had worn her to a thin shadow of the beauty of her youth. She had never taken another lover.

Powwell's mother had been shunned for loving a man not her husband. Rover women regarded children as wealth, regardless of the father or their marital status. The old pagan practice of random matings at Festival and measuring wealth in the number of children hadn't died out with the teaching of the Stargods.

The depredation of war took more lives than the sacrifice to Simurgh had in the old days, before the Stargods. Lives that could only be replaced by numerous children. Powwell and his mother should have been honored rather than cast out by family and village because she slept with a man outside of Festival or marriage.

"Kalen's parents brought her to the school," Powwell said, helping the girl over a fallen log. "Her da was a merchant in Baria and lost everything when the town was sacked. They'd been on the road for months, hungry and down to their last few coins. Kalen has talent, lots of it. So they brought her to the school to have one less mouth to feed. They ended up staying to help run the school."

"A merchant, eh?" Was that the connection? Or had a different man seduced both women? The family resemblance was strong enough that Kalen's father might very well have sired Powwell, too. He'd made promises and never kept them because he was already married. Or about

to marry. Probably Kalen's mother had a hefty dowry,
more attractive than Powwell's mother's small inheritance.
Did Kalen's father have gray eyes and freckles?

"Stuuvart traded for better food, and Ackerly offered
the services of students for healing and soil replenishing.
Sometimes he took money, a lot of the times he could only
get cloth and parchments and stuff. And Kalen's mother is
a great cook." Powwell looked longingly at the pack Nimbulan carried. Undoubtedly his growing body cried out for
food. The lessons Nimbulan had set both children earlier to
test their skills had depleted their energy reserves as well.

Kalen hadn't spoken more than a few words since yesterday. Nimbulan wondered what lay behind her act of wide-
eyed innocence.

"So why did you find it necessary to come searching for
me, if you believed me dead." Nimbulan turned and faced
the children squarely. This was the heart of their desperate
flight from the school.

"Kalen discovered that your niche in the crypt was
empty."

Nimbulan knelt down so that he was level with the girl.
He tried to look her directly in the eye. She suddenly found
a tall everblue tree fascinating and wouldn't look at him.

"Why were you exploring the crypt, Kalen? Surely there
were better places to play," Nimbulan asked gently.

The girl looked at her feet and bit her lip. Powwell had
the same bad habit.

"You can trust him, Kalen," Powwell urged.

"I wanted a place to hide," she whispered.

"Hide from what?" Nimbulan asked.

She darted a worried glance at Powwell then back to
the ground. "Ackerly wanted me to do terrible things with
my magic."

Myri joined them and held the child close against her
side. "If she doesn't want to talk about it, don't push it.
When she's comfortable enough with us to talk, she will.
Don't upset her." She glared at Nimbulan.

Nimbulan returned Myri's stare with love. He recognized
the blooming of her maternal instincts and wished they
could have children of their own. Children with her pale
blond hair and beautifully expressive eyes. They showed
hints of purple now, blue when she was sated with sex, fiery

green when she healed. He longed for children he could teach to carry on the legacy of honorable magic, neutral in the realm of politics. The lack of his own children became a deep and empty ache.

He mentally shook himself free of the delusion. Denied children of their own because of their magic, they could only accept and love the ones the Stargods brought to them. Powwell and Kalen.

"It's important that he knows what Ackerly is doing, Kalen." Powwell encouraged the girl. "If you don't tell him, I will."

Kalen's eyes flashed in anger at the boy. Powwell backed off and dropped his gaze to the ground. The boy might speak for them both, but clearly the girl was in control. Interesting relationship.

"Ackerly was teaching me to work a summons through a glass and a flame. He wanted me to try sending witchfire with the summons. He wanted me to burn whole armies. He wanted me to murder innocent people with magic and then collect gold for it. He's evil, and Moncriith is right when he says demons control magicians. I don't want to be evil. I don't want to hurt people!" Kalen buried her face in Myri's skirt. Huge sobs sent shudders down her small body.

"If Moncriith is right, then why were you so eager to get away from him?" Nimbulan asked. He touched the child's back with a comforting hand. Her sobs eased a little.

"Don't press her, Nimbulan," Myri said, stroking her hair.

"Moncriith is as evil as Ackerly. He wants to burn all magicians, not just the evil ones. He does it to fulfill a vision from the Stargods—or so he says. Ackerly does it for gold. Moncriith wanted to burn me, too, after we found you. That's why we ran away from him. I don't want to be a magician. I wish I'd never been born."

"Don't ever say that, Kalen. Don't even think it!" Myri knelt down and faced her, nose to nose. "Moncriith made me feel the same way. I spent my whole life running away. Now I have found a home and a man who loves me." She reached a hand to Nimbulan and blushed. "Moncriith is wrong, Kalen. Magic isn't evil. It's how we use it for good or ill that matters. As long as you use your magic for good, you are good."

"That's why I started the school, Kalen. I wanted to teach magicians how to act for good, for peace, so that we could end the wars and make magic a tool of Life and Healing, not of destruction. Magic is a wonderful gift. We must use it to help those who don't have the gift rather than for our own power and glory. Moncriith has a magic gift. He think's he's using it for the good of all, but he's not." Nimbulan explained to himself as well as Myri and the children.

"Moncriith thinks all magicians are worthless, except for himself." Powwell spat on the ground. "He wants to be a priest-king of Coronnan. I think he wants to be a god-king instead."

Nimbulan could see the boy's quick mind working, putting pieces together.

"All people have value, Powwell. Those who have magic, and those who don't. All of us were created by the Stargods for a reason. Sometimes it's hard to find the reason and make the most of it. But we have to try." *I have to take the Rover ritual back to the school. I have to continue my work. I can't do it alone. Will Myri go with me, or will she cling to her new home?*

Chapter 28

Myri took Kalen's hand and started forward on the path. Her little fingers felt cold against Myri's palm. Questions clouded Kalen's eyes. She needed time to absorb all the things they'd said about magic and self-worth. Myri hoped the little girl could believe it in time.

Saber ferns, rotting limbs, and rocks blurred and drifted out of Myri's vision to reveal a path of sorts. Kalen kept looking forward and back, off to the side, through wide-open eyes then half-closed lids, straight on and out of the corners.

Myri almost laughed at her puzzlement. She had no idea why none of her companions could see the path.

A broad alpine meadow opened before them. Off to the right, the landscape opened up to reveal peak after snowy peak jutting into the stunningly blue sky. The urge to fly swamped Myri's senses, demanding she let go and soar upward.

Amaranth screeched as he glided past her and pounced on something in the lush grasses. He emerged from the greenery, wings half-furled, shaking his empty paws clean of damp soil. With all of his cat dignity and arrogance, he perched on a rock for a much needed bath. Bright sunlight gave his black fur and feathers a dark purple sheen—a darker shade of the same color of wildflowers that hovered like a mist above the greenery.

He paused in his ablutions, head cocked as if listening. His head reared up, ears flat. He chittered in excitement.

"What is it, my friend?" Myri gathered him into her arms, scratching his ears affectionately.

He nuzzled her chin once and squirmed to face forward, paws resting on her arms in preparation for launch.

"Something awaits us," Myri said.

"Did Amaranth tell you that?" Nimbulan turned a full circle, scanning the meadow with eyes and magic senses. He suddenly stilled. "Something is waiting and watching. In that tumble of boulders and fallen trees." He pointed to the wall of cliffs that enclosed three sides of the meadow. A stream cascaded down over a tumble of boulders at the base of the cliff into a brook that meandered through the grasses. At the edge of the meadow, the stream plunged over the precipice in a wide waterfall.

Amaranth burst upward in a thunderous flap of wings. "Merawk!" he cried over and over. He dove and looped, flipped and soared in a wondrous display of acrobatics. As he swooped down for the third time, claws extended, he grabbed Myri by the hair, tugging upward in an invitation to flight.

"Let go, you silly flywacket. I can't fly," she protested as she laughingly disconnected his talons from her fair hair.

(Can, too!) Amaranth squealed and flew off again.

Dreams of flight. More than dreams, memories lashed through all her senses. She lifted her arms as if they were wings. The wind caught her sleeves. She closed her eyes and relived the sensation of soaring. Had Amaranth's dreams invaded her mind?

Suddenly, the puffy white clouds shifted. A ray of sunlight struck the jumble of rocks. Light arced out and up, filling the meadow with rainbows.

The children squealed in delight and danced about, trying to catch the pretty colors.

"Our oldest legends, before the days of the Stargods, tell us that rainbows are symbols of peace and goodwill," Nimbulan said in wonder. He turned a slow circle, eyes wide with amazement. "This isn't possible. Light doesn't refract through air this way. It needs a prism source. That waterfall isn't big enough to provide enough water for a rainbow. There must be crystal all about his meadow. Only a massive amount of crystal would make this happen."

"Look!" Powwell gasped and pointed above the little waterfall and the jumble of rocks.

Myri looked and saw only water and boulders and a few common plants.

"Dragons!" Kalen whispered. "A full nimbus of crystal dragons."

"I can't see anything but the rainbows," Nimbulan said.

"Who told you there are dragons here?" Myri stared at the little girl rather than the wonder of the rainbows. Memories pushed at her, demanding attention. Memories of . . . The familiarity vanished. "And how did you know to call it a nimbus and not a herd?" She knew a mating group of dragons was called a Nimbus. The dragons invented the word.

How did she know that?

"They told me," Kalen said, eyes open with genuine awe this time.

"Who told you?" Something akin to panic swelled within Myri's chest. She wasn't sure if she let it burst, it would free her of her forgetfulness or push it down again and find solace in not knowing.

"They told me." Kalen pointed to the sky above the waterfall. "The dragons told me, just like they told you."

"How long have the dragons spoken to you?" Myri didn't dare breathe. If she gave in to the longing to join the dragons, she'd have to remember everything, and challenge everything she knew about herself, including her new-found love for Nimbulan and the children.

"They spoke to me right after I discovered Nimbulan wasn't in the crypt. They led me to you and the clearing and your house. The clearing is going to be my home, too. We're all going to live there like a nimbus of humans and be happy."

Finally Myri swallowed the panic in her breast and looked where Kalen pointed. Letting her magic talent flow freely, without plan or push, her eyes followed Amaranth's antics in the sky. He traced the outline of a huge dragon. Glimmers of crystal wings and body outlined in a faint swirl of rainbow colors jumped into her vision.

Amaranth leaped to another point, and she saw a second dragon, silvery in body and outlined in green. Several more creatures appeared before her, each bearing a different hue on wing veins and spinal horns. Only the massive central dragon held all the colors around the edges.

Myri's heart beat double time. Her lungs labored to draw

air. "I see them now," she admitted. Joy replaced her anxiety. Lightness filled her until she thought she could lift free of the Kardia and soar with the magnificent crystal beasts.

(Welcome home, my child. You all have much to learn. Come, eat your provisions, drink from the stream. We will begin to teach you a new form of magic when you are rested.)

Warmth and love folded around Myri as if the dragon had wrapped her in soft wings, like she would one of her own dragonets.

"The dogs have found something," the sergeant blurted out, rushing through the underbrush toward Moncriith. "The trail leads straight through the woods, no apparent path at all, but the scent is strong and the dogs are eager to make up for lost time."

"Then we must be off. The witchwoman and those children must be brought to justice before the spring campaign season begins."

"Yes, Sieur. Children, Sieur?" The seargeant tugged at his maroon-and-green tunic as if it suddenly fit too tight. His face paled and a tightness thinned his lips. "We have never hunted children before, Sieur."

"I will make an example of both of them. They deserted my just cause to warn the chief demon of my pursuit. They forsake the people of Coronnan so that they may enjoy the power of demon magic. They won't enjoy it long. Their deaths will prove to the lords once and for all that they can't go to war with demons in their midst. And without demon magicians to protect their troops, they will think long and hard before entering battles."

"Coronnan will know unity at last." The sergeant parroted Moncriith's doctrine. His eyes remained fixed upon some distant point beyond Moncriith's shoulder. "Freedom from war and freedom from enslavement to demon magicians. Moncriith is the prophet of the Stargods. Only he knows the truth." He saluted the Bloodmage automatically and turned woodenly back to the task of finding Myrilandel and the children.

Moncriith smiled to himself. The guards Kammeryl d'Astrismos had assigned to him were deep under his control. They'd never have a thought of their own again. He'd see to it even if he had to draw their blood to reinforce his spells. All Coronnan would bow to him, unquestioningly, before the end of the campaign season. His followers already regarded him as more god than priest.

(The words you speak matter not. Only that you say them in unison and the words contain the essence of your requirement. Speak together as you shape the magic you have gathered into the form of your spell.) Shayla, the all color/no color female dragon, directed Nimbulan and Powwell. The silvery young dragons with primary colors on their wingtips rested on nearby boulders and clifftops—too old to cavort like children, too young for their fur to be transparent crystal. All four of the dragonets were male.

Each of them sported a different color, no two alike. Shayla, the lone female, maintained the all color/no color crystal sparkles along her spinal horns and wing veins as well as her entire body, each hair as clear as crystal. The spiral horn sprouting from her forehead caught the light, swirled it away from the fine fur of her body, and flung it around the meadow in a dozen rainbows. The prismatic arcs terminated at a spot just behind her. The casual eye swept with the rainbows around the dragon, never seeing her magnificent beauty. Nimbulan found it impossible to look at her long. Yet he couldn't look anywhere else.

He drew a deep breath. Powwell did, too. They released the air at the same time and recited the simple spell formula.

> *"Wisp of flame, burning bright*
> *Travel far beyond my sight*
> *Bring to view the other true*
> *Pass the word of magic might."*

Nimbulan concentrated on the tiny candle flame on the other side of Powwell's apprentice glass, held proudly by its owner. Magic energy pulsed around them in unison with their heartbeat. A visible aura of power blended around both their forms, binding them together. They watched through the glass the vision of the flame skipping across the meadow behind them. Without turning to watch with physical eyes, they monitored the progress of the flame until it burst into the still pool at the edge of the stream.

Through the glass they watched Myri and Kalen from the perspective of the bottom of the pool. Their features took on focus with the slight distortion of looking upward through water. Kalen reared back her head, startled. Myri peered closer, puzzled and curious.

Nimbulan mouthed "I love you." She smiled and returned the silent greeting.

The vision faltered, then cleared. All he could see was a burned-out candle wick standing behind the small scrap of precious glass he held in his hand.

"We shouldn't have been able to do that, Powwell. Myri wasn't using any of her magic senses to channel the flame. And she looked into water, not glass. The spell couldn't have worked with one magician alone using the old magic."

"Let's try it again. I'll work with Myri. You combine with Kalen." The boy dashed across the full length of the meadow to join the women.

A brief conversation ensued that Nimbulan couldn't hear. But Kalen's exhausted posture told him volumes. The new procedure drained her of energy. He didn't understand why. Magic was merely fuel for an inborn talent. Weren't Kalen and Myri gathering the dragon magic at all? He'd already checked that there were no ley lines near this meadow to interfere with the new procedures.

They'd quit soon and have some dinner. He needed to try the spell one more time, to make certain he had the formula memorized. Maybe after Kalen and Myri ate, they'd be more receptive to gathering dragon magic.

The dragon nodded agreement. Nimbulan clutched Kalen's hand as he lit the candle once more with a snap of his fingers. The new magic flared easily from his fingers.

His belly growled with hunger. Dragon magic also demanded more bodily fuel to hone an inborn talent than the old forms. One more time with the summons spell, then he'd eat.

"You've memorized the words, Kalen?" Nimbulan asked.

She nodded, breathing deeply as she'd been taught. They spoke the words together.

The magic remained inert. The flame stayed firmly rooted to the candle.

"Let's switch again, Powwell. Kalen's too tired. Send Myri

over here." Nimbulan called across the meadow toward the streambed where they crouched.

A few moments later, with Myri's hand clutch lovingly in his own, they recited the words again. Nothing happened.

"What's the matter, Shayla? What are we doing wrong?"

The dragon shrugged her massive shoulders in a curiously human gesture. The dragon's long, spiked tail swished impatiently, back and forth in the grass. She had already swept a clear circle around her with the wicked spines. No part of the dragon came close to touching, or harming any of the humans.

"I'm the problem. I can't do it." Myri turned her back on Nimbulan and Shayla.

Nimbulan wrapped his arm around Myri's waist and pulled her head onto his shoulder. "We'll rest a while and try again." He dismissed Kalen and Powwell from their perches at the edge of the brook.

Kalen visibly drooped with fatigue and disappointment as she curled up in the forearms of the now-reclining dragon. Shayla's wings fluttered and stretched into a protective posture—as if Kalen was one of her own offspring. Kalen drifted off to sleep almost immediately, curling into the dragon's warmth. But Powwell looked as bright and alert as ever. He dove into the pack of provisions, pulling out a fistful of jerked meat. He made a face at the dry journey food but bit deeply into the tough fare.

(Fresh meat will replenish your body better than that. *The little ones will hunt for you.)* Shayla dipped her head as her telepathic speech fell to a whisper so as not to awaken Kalen.

"You are all so beautiful," Myri said as she watched the smaller dragons launch into the air. "Why didn't I know before that you were the voices who guided me through life?"

"How long have they been urging you to come to them?" Nimbulan asked, spreading a blanket on the grass near their packs, just outside the circle of Shayla's tail sweep.

"Nearly a year now. I kept delaying while I stopped to help people who needed healing."

"Like you stopped at the battlefield. I'm glad I had the chance to see you work before we were thrust together again by fate."

"By fate or by dragon lure?" She laughed and caressed his cheek with her palm.

"Maybe both. I do remember a voice in the wind telling me to go east. I'd find what I sought in the east. This dragon magic is better than Rover ritual."

(We waited for you both to grow and mature into the vision of united magicians and united mundanes. You had to recognize the need before you could use the tool,) Shayla said, nodding her head at their clasped hands. The pastel colors of her eyes suggested a smile—if a dragon could smile.

Nimbulan kissed Myri's forehead as he eased her down onto the blanket.

A smile lit his mind. Myri's white-blond hair and pale eyes reminded him of Quinnault! The curious elongated shadows he'd seen on Quinnault's face had looked curiously like the muzzle of a dragon.

"You sneaky creatures. You've been priming all of us for this moment. Maybe using us is a better word. How many of Quinnault's words of peace came from you?" He laughed in admiration of their foresight—or precognition. How much of past and future did dragons see?

Shayla nodded her head slightly. A light chuckle of approval and agreement whispered across his mind.

"What if I can't gather their magic?" Myri interrupted his speculation.

"You will. It just takes a bit of searching to find it. The air is filled with it. Breathe it in, like a heady aroma then concentrate and push the air deep into your being, behind your heart."

"I've tried again and again. I can't even smell the Tambootie in the air that you and Powwell can. Kalen can't find it either. What if this new magic belongs only to men?"

(She may be right.) Shayla speared them with her big crystalline eyes. Looking directly at the refracting light drew Nimbulan out of his body, deep into the sparkling colors, so like the colored umbilicals he'd seen in the void.

"We will try again," Nimbulan insisted. "Myri must be a part of gathering and combining magic. You dragons singled her out of all humans to be your link to us. And I need her to be a part of everything I do. In this life and the next." He kissed her again, long and full.

The world drifted away. Only he and Myri remained, their bodies, minds and souls entwining like a spiral of sparkling light illuminating the void.

"Can't you two do anything but kiss?" Powwell loomed over them, hands on hips, a disgusted, but fascinated scowl on his face. "Dinner's here. The dragons brought a deer. They even gutted and cooked it for us. But we'll have to skin it. I'd love to ride a dragon while they hunt. Their fire must reach a hundred leagues!"

(Far less than one league, child. Barely two dragon lengths,) Shayla chuckled.

"Have you something to dig roots with? The dragonets will roast them for us, too. I'm hungry. Can you really throw flames that far, Shayla? I bet you'd end a battle real quick with just one blast." Powwell said.

The dragon stilled and almost faded from view.

(Do not suggest that dragon fire be used as a weapon. We have vowed to teach you to control your magic and your battles rather than blast you away with our anger.)

Shayla came back into view, her rainbow horns and wings glowed brighter than before. She bent her head as if listening intently to the young man. *(Now that you gather dragon magic, you will need dragon food. Enjoy the meat we provide you.)* A curious expression came over the dragon's muzzle, a mirror image of Powwell's hungry gaze at the deer carcass.

Myri laughed, breaking away from Nimbulan. Nimbulan chuckled, too. Adolescence must be catching up with Powwell for him to be so concerned with food. Nimbulan faced his fiftieth birthday next winter. He shouldn't be so hungry his stomach felt like it was wrapping around his spine.

"There are fresh greens growing on the bank of the brook, Powwell. Pick those and eat them raw. 'Tis the wrong season for roots." Myri stood, brushing off her skirt.

"Raw vegetables! Ugh." Powwell stuck out his lower lip and tongue, scrunching up his nose in distaste. A young dragon did, too.

"You ate my ma's greens all the time, Powwell," Kalen informed him. She stretched and yawned from her nest in the dragon paws. "And you liked greens back at the school well enough to ask for more."

"But your ma boiled them in soup stock and dressed

them in vinegar and spices. Myri wants us to eat this stuff raw! A man needs his food cooked."

"A man needs nutrition any way he can get it. We'll eat the greens raw." Nimbulan tried to look sternly at Powwell. Memories of his own childhood view of good food and "women's food" tickled deep inside him. He wanted to bellow with laughter and good will.

His good humor continued through the improvised meal. He and Powwell ate ravenously. Myri and Kalen only picked at their food. "Why don't you and Kalen watch for a while, Myri?" Nimbulan suggested. "Perhaps you can learn something to make the task easier."

"I feel like I should remember how to do it." Myri turned haunted eyes up to him. "I want to remember how to do it, just like I want to remember how to fly. When I don't want my past to touch me, events and people parade before my mind's eye with annoying regularity. When I need to remember, I can't find any part of myself in the past."

"Don't push it, Myri. Memory is like quicksilver. It looks tangible until you touch it. Then it spurts away, breaking into hundreds of sparkling, unrelated entities," he soothed.

(You must remember, my child,) Shayla said. *(Without you, all our efforts are for nothing.)*

Suddenly, the dragon reared her steedlike muzzle in alarm. Steam seeped out of her nostrils. Her eyes shifted rapidly from nearly colorless to a wild array of primary colors, never lingering on one for more than two heartbeats. With a loud blast of sound, almost above human hearing, she burst upward into flight.

Chapter 29

At last the trail dog put his nose to the Kardia and yelped with excitement. Moncriith breathed a sigh of relief. Myrilandel and the children had tried to fool him by walking down the center of a stream, but the dogs had found where they left the water. The dog dragged him through a brambleberry thicket. Thorns snagged and tore his new red robe—bright red, closer to the color worn by priests than of old blood.

"*Simurgh* take you to all the living hells!" he yelled at the dog as his cuff clung to yet another bush. This one was sticky and tried to wrap itself around his arm.

He stumbled and ran, desperately clinging to the animal's leash. A long branch of the clinging shrub detached itself from the main trunk with a sickening slurpy sound.

The dog yelped again and dashed forward.

They were close. Moncriith sensed Myrilandel's presence just ahead. The witchwoman wasn't alone. The evil magic he smelled grew to enormous proportions. She must be hiding in the demon lair! Not far now. After all these years of tracking demons, he would finally rid Coronnan of all of them at once.

A doubt wiggled into his mind. How would he handle several large demons at once? Did he truly know the strength of a demon? He buried his misgivings where he'd hidden his memories of Magretha and his father. The Stargods had chosen him to rid Coronnan of the demons. The Stargods would not, could not fail him now. Not when he was so close.

The dog stopped running so abruptly Moncriith nearly tripped over him. Frantically the animal dug at a hole in the ground. Dirt flew behind him, pelting Moncriith with large clods and small rocks.

"*S'murghin'* useless beast. First you can't find a scent at all, and now you track a path even a striped lapin couldn't follow into a mole hole!"

More frantic yelps from the other four dogs sounded in the near distance. They, too, had caught an elusive scent and converged on the same mole hole.

Moncriith dropped the leash from his sweating palm in disgust. Five dogs digging in one tiny hole in the center of a tangle of brambleberry vines would lead his quest nowhere.

He thrashed his way clear of the thorny vines that reached out and grabbed him as he passed. "What is wrong with your dogs?" he asked the nearest guard.

The young man blushed and stammered, unable to meet Moncriith's gaze.

"I'll tell you what's wrong with them!" Moncriith shouted. Heat flooded his face and sent twitches through his hands. "Your dogs . . ."

The forest stilled. No bird song lightened the heavy air. The tiny rustlings in the underbrush ceased. A pricking sensation sent the fine hairs on the back of Moncriith's neck standing on end.

"What?" Moncriith searched the forest for the source of danger one and all sensed. Even the dogs had ceased their digging and yelping. They stood with their neck ruffs erect and teeth bared in silent growls.

A huge shadow blocked the sun.

"Yikkiiiii. . . ." The lead dog tucked his tail between his legs and ran downhill. The others burst from the thicket, pelting in different directions as if Simurgh himself pursued them.

"A—a dragon, Sieur!" A guard pointed upward. All color drained from his face. His mouth flapped open and shut several times before he could speak again. "It's hunting, Sieur. Hunting us."

"Nonsense." Moncriith tried to present an aura of calm. Lumbird bumps erupted on his skin and his mouth went dry. He followed the guard's pointing finger and nearly fouled his trews.

He saw the outline of a dragon above the trees.

"Stargods, preserve me." He crossed himself again and again. The shadow did not go away.

A sense of peace flooded his mind, replacing his anxiety. The frustration of the past days of searching vanished. He smiled in triumph. He had already killed all the demons and Myrilandel and Nimbulan. He must return to Castle Krej with the good news. Immediately.

Nimbulan searched the skies for signs of Shayla in flight. A few moments after her departure, the female dragon flew back into the meadow with a wild screech that sounded oddly triumphant. She clutched the carcass of a tracking dog in her front paws.

Nimbulan looked questioningly at the bloody animal.

(This creature picked up your trail with its sensitive nose. It led men too close to this meadow. We cannot afford an interruption until you have learned what we have to teach you.)

"How close?" he asked. Televarn? Only a Rover as tenacious—obsessed, Myri had said—as Televarn had the audacity to follow them into the wilderness.

(The one who pretends to priesthood cannot find you. The other dogs have scattered in fear. The men wearing the clothes all alike ran with them at sight of me. Only the one in new red persists, and I have given him a dream that will take him back where he started from.)

"Moncriith!" Myri paled. "He will remember. He has no other reason for living than to watch me burn." She stared at the dragon with less effort than Nimbulan could.

(If he remembers outside the dragon dream, then you can, too. You must remember how to gather dragon magic.)

"Why me? I can't do it, but Nimbulan and Powwell can. Why me?"

(You are the one we trust. We have guarded you for many years, waiting for you to forge a covenant between dragon-kind and humans.)

"If you want her to remember, then she must have done this before," Nimbulan mused. "If she did it before, she would have a memory, but all her memories come and go, as if she were breaking through a spell. A very strong spell that is renewed each time she tries to break free. Did you impose the spell?" Nimbulan forced himself to look Shayla directly in her eye. With effort he maintained his sense of self and kept the dragon within view.

(Dragons have limited magic. Our defenses have always been in our size, our flight, and our fire. Against human magicians these are not always enough.)

An old grief assailed Nimbulan. Reflected in Shayla's eyes he saw men battling across a wheatfield near the River Coronnán. At first he thought he saw the battle last autumn when he had been forced to kill Keegan. Then, he noticed the style of uniforms dated back twenty years—to the time when an out-of-control spell had burned the field and all who stood within it. Druulin, Boojlin, and Caasser had died in the hellish fires that day.

Nimbulan and Ackerly had escaped death only because Nimbulan had finally broken Druulin's binding spell on Ackerly the night before. The cunning old man had known that Nimbulan could break any spell placed upon him. But the spell placed upon another—especially one that held death in the breaking would defy him for a long time. Druulin also knew that Nimbulan wouldn't leave without Ackerly. So the spell had been placed upon the lesser magician. Nimbulan took ten years learning to break the spell. They had run away to take service with Kammeryl d'Astrismos the night before the fateful battle.

His perspective shifted to an aerial view. The Kardia no longer supported his feet. He looked around and discovered himself flying alongside Shayla—arms outstretched like wings, the wind buffeting his face and keeping him aloft. His stomach lurched with the unaccustomed sensation of flight.

A vague tingling ran up and down his leg. He shared Shayla's pain as magic gone awry pierced them both. His belly cramped as Shayla began her premature labor.

Anger at the irresponsible magicians below boiled within them both. They opened their jaws wide, sending forth a blast of dragon, fire. He watched as flames engulfed the people below, spread to the dry wheat, and up the few trees. He heard Druulin and his assistants scream in agony as fire took them.

He took no satisfaction in the revenge. The ghost of dead baby dragons haunted both of them.

Suddenly he was free of the hypnotic contact and knew

who he was and why he stood in this mountain meadow learning a new form of magic.

(We can give you dreams of what has happened or what you want to happen. Rarely, we can give you a glimpse of what will happen. Nothing else that we can tell you is within our power. Yet we are a source of magic for those who choose to accept our covenant,) Shayla said.

Knowing her grief, Nimbulan wanted desperately to be among those who formed the covenant between dragon-kind and humans, to use Shayla's magic for peace and control of those who wielded magic indiscriminately and harmed innocent bystanders. Caasser had thrown the spell that wounded Shayla—a spell Nimbulan had devised and taught his fellow magician.

Nimbulan looked at Shayla and her children with new sympathy. "I take responsibility for those who hurt you. I was not at the battle, but I could have been. I could have woven the spell that cost you the lives of your babies."

(Will you work to end the irresponsible use of magic?)

"I so swear by the Stargods and all I hold dear."

The dragons didn't respond immediately. Nimbulan searched Shayla's eyes for some indication that he had been accepted by them.

He fell into the glittering whirlpool of Shayla's eyes. Dizziness overwhelmed him. Then he awoke, sitting in a thronelike chair padded and covered in blue and silver, the signature colors of his magic. Around him, other magicians sat in similar chairs, each covered in different colors. He recognized none of the men, all much younger than he. Except . . . was that Lyman to his right, his face shadowed by the torches stuck into wall brackets directly above him? In the center of the circular stone room rested a table unlike any he had seen before. One solid piece of black glass. No forge in all of Kardia Hodos could generate enough heat to burn away the impurities of black sand to create true glass of a quality to stand up to daily use. Only one source of clean sand existed that could make the small glass lenses used by magicians.

No man could afford a table of solid black glass.

(No one man could afford the table, but a commune of magicians in covenant with the dragons could request dragon fire to forge such a rare symbol of their combined power.)

Abruptly, Nimbulan was back in the meadow, standing next to Myri, facing Shayla, a live dragon who promised them a way to create peace. His hand still tingled with the cold, smooth feel of black glass. . . .

"Can you give Myri a dragon dream of her past so that she will know how to gather your magic?" He pressed his temple to push away the lingering memory of the magicians working in concert around that magnificent table. The magnitude of the spell they shaped awed him.

Beside him, Myri gasped and shook her head in denial of those memories.

(Myrilandel is not ready. When the time is right, she will know what is important. Her lineage and her childhood will become clear.)

"What about the near past? The days that come and go without my awareness, though I march through them?" She clung to Nimbulan's hand, her sweating palm nearly slipping away.

(The near past is under your control. When you can accept what you have done and what has been done to you, you will remember.)

"But I need to know!"

"Think of the quicksilver, Myri. The images will come when you need them." But Nimbulan wasn't sure. He'd seen several people so traumatized by the wars and the ghastly deeds perpetuated in the name of right that they chose never to remember. Not even their birth name. Some invented exotic pasts that had nothing to do with reality but recreated the person into someone they would rather be than themselves.

Who was Myrilandel? Could Moncriith's delusion of demons spring from his interpretation of the dragons that protected her and guided her? Only the dragons knew for sure. They trusted Myri, believed in her, depended upon her for a most important mission. He committed himself to do the same.

"I still don't know if the dragons warned me that the villagers would betray me. They may have sent Moncriith to follow us," Myri said as she and Nimbulan headed back to the clearing. The clearing, with a small hut they had called home for a time. A home where they could live safely, privately, raising Kalen and Powwell.

"If you don't trust the villagers, we'll have to wait until we reach the School for Magicians to be married," Nimbulan said. "Powwell said that two retired priests had signed on to the faculty."

She didn't want to go with him. The dragons had promised her a home. She'd found that home. But Nimbulan was not destined to be part of her family in the clearing. He had greater things to accomplish at his school.

But if she didn't go with him, she would be alone again.

I am tired of being alone.

Amaranth landed on a branch above her head. The rising wind made him clutch at his perch with fully extended talons. *(You aren't alone. You have me. You have the dragons. We are your family,)* he said.

She looked at Nimbulan, felt the heat of his hand holding hers as they walked. Ahead of them, Kalen and Powwell skipped and capered down the path toward home. Love and joy filled her heart at the nearness of them. The physical pleasure of touching another human being for no other reason than to touch overwhelmed her. She raised her hand, still linked with Nimbulan's and kissed their entwined fingers.

He smiled down at her and returned the gesture. "We will be married at the first opportunity, Myri. I promise."

I need him, Amaranth. Just as I am incomplete without you and the dragons. I must go with him. We must take this new magic back to the other magicians. This is what the dragons planned for us all those years ago. I have to leave my home.

(You will come back.)

Yes, Amaranth. I will come back. We will all come back when we have completed our task. She held out her arm as a new perch for her familiar. The flywacket spread his wings just enough to glide down to her. He retracted his talons at the last moment and landed softly upon her forearm, then siddled up to her shoulder. He wrapped his fluffy tail around her neck for balance and nuzzled her cheek. His purr sent warm comfort through her entire being.

"We're here!" Powwell called just ahead.

"I can see the roof," Kalen added.

"I'm hungry," said Powwell.

"You're always hungry." Kalen punched him in the arm.

Myri looked up at the overcast sky. "There will be rain soon. I can smell it on the wind. We'd best hurry."

(You are needed,) dragon voices invaded her head.

She wrapped her hand around Amaranth's muscular body, strengthening her contact to him. Beside her, Nimbulan stilled, waiting for the rest of the dragon's message.

(Fishermen in trouble.)

"Will the villagers accept my help or betray me?" she asked the sky. She couldn't see any dragon outline against the rapidly gathering clouds. Spring often brought sudden storms—short in duration but violent while they lasted.

A sense of urgency pushed aside her doubts and fears. Men were in trouble. Her feet needed to fly down the steep path to the village right now. Without delay.

What stores of herbs and poultices did she have in the hut? Her mind raced to the few remedies she had left. She lingered over the list, overruling her anxious feet. Was she strong enough to help? Her healing spells for Nimbulan had drained her badly.

"I'll take care of you afterward, Myri. I heard the command as clearly as you did. Go. I'll gather some herbs and the leftover bandages. Don't worry. I'll come as fast as I can," he said, urging her forward. "Remember what I taught you about the ley lines. Stand close to the Equinox Pylon where the lines cross and use the strength of the lines to fuel your healing."

"Follow me, Amaranth." She urged him off her shoulder so that he could fly and not hinder her own run to the village.

(Go. Now. You cannot be late.)

Amaranth launched himself upward, pushing his wings downward with powerful strokes. *(We come,)* he announced.

The wind whispered of small boats swamped by waves and hungry rocks reaching to slash and impale new victims.

Chapter 30

Myri's bare feet found the path into the village without really knowing where she ran. Her mind was with the gale that whipped the waves to a crashing froth. The uncaring air was too busy shifting from here to there to pay attention to the men who were in trouble. Myri found no trace of their life energies. She lifted her arms, letting the wind catch her sleeves. The sensation of almost flight gave her greater speed.

A week ago, when she and Nimbulan were drained of all strength, this same journey in reverse had taken days. Now with her health restored, and the urgency of the dragons pushing her forward, she ran the distance in less than an hour.

Her magic tether to Nimbulan's heart stretched but did not break. For the first time in nearly a week, she was separated from him by more than a few arm's lengths. Loneliness assailed her already.

Her talent pulled her forward. She had to run with it.

The dozen cottages huddled together on the edge of the bluff above a narrow gravel beach looked smaller, shabbier, abandoned since she'd left here a week ago.

She looked out over the bay for physical signs of the men in trouble. Rain squalls and low clouds obscured her view of the waters beyond the cove. Waves rose too high, too fast to reveal what might hide in the troughs. Only small boats with crews of three or four could maneuver through the Dragon's Teeth, the jagged outcropping from the bay floor that changed currents at will and disguised depths.

Myri headed for the dark and smoky pub. All of the

villagers would gather there to organize a rescue or mourn the dead.

Tension hung with the gloomy smoke and the silence in the crowded pub. Doors closed against the storm intensified the stale and murky air. A few men sipped at mugs of ale. Anxious women stared into their cups lest they catch the eye and the worry of another. No stories of daring deeds and monster fish trapped in the nets passed around the cave. No lewd jokes or grumbling of what might have been.

Yoshi, the simple boy, poked sticks into the central fire, silently watching the glowing embers. He was big and strong, in his early twenties, but his mind had never grown after a bout of brain fever when he was ten. The same fever that nearly claimed him last winter. He took orders well, but had few thoughts of his own. He didn't look up at Myri's entrance. A sure sign of his preoccupation.

"Who is missing?" Myri asked as she stood on the threshold. The anxiety of the men and women invaded her heart. She scanned the group, counting heads, lumping family groups together.

"Rory's boat of four," Karry replied. "Kelly has three in his." Years of pitching her voice to be heard over a noisy throng made her near whisper seem a shout.

Amaranth crept between Myri's feet to curl up by the fire. His purpley-black fur absorbed the meager light of the central hearth, draining it from the rest of the cave. A grizzled old man shifted his stool away from proximity with the flywacket. He crossed himself in the manner of the Stargods, then surreptitiously placed his left wrist over his right and flapped his hands.

Yoshi didn't know enough to be afraid of the witch-woman's familiar and reached out a hand to caress the cat. Amaranth nuzzled his outstretched palm, but didn't purr. "Rory be smart," Yoshi told Amaranth. "He'll not try for home in this weather. Knows the Dragon's Teeth won't let him land till the wind slacks and the tide changes."

Karry poured another round of ale from pitchers. Her smile trembled, then reasserted itself, too wide, too fixed.

"Something's wrong." Myri leaned out the door, hesitant to throw herself into the business of rescuing the men, needing to help and obey the compulsion within her to heal. The rising storm and tricky currents threatened her life more than the drain of a normal healing.

"They're coming through now!" Nimbulan shouted as he ran down the cliff path.

"Get ropes and blankets," Karry ordered the men. "Yoshi, build up the fire and find bandages!" Turning to Myri, she whispered, "Who's he?"

"My friend." Myri smiled her love for Nimbulan, then turned and raced for the steps cut into the bluff leading to the beach and the jagged rocks that had claimed more than one life. Karry would organize the villagers here in the pub, but they wouldn't hasten to venture forth into the crashing waves. Could any of them swim? Probably not.

She met cold, wet gravel at the base of the bluff with her bare feet. Spring was barely here. The storm could still contain a last blast of winter. Myri acknowledged the season with a regretful wish for her clogs and woolen socks. But foot coverings would hinger her movements. She needed freedom to rescue the men in the bobbing boat just visible in the trough between two waves. One boat, riding low, not two.

Would they find safety or death in their mad attempt to return home?

She peered through the thickening cloud layer that blended with the sea. Sheets of rain brought the horizon closer. The fury of the sea seemed to push the speck of black that was the boat farther away from the shore.

An opening between waves revealed the much closer outline of the boat, overcrowded with seven men. Too close to the Dragon's Teeth. The stern sank lower yet and the bow tilted in the wind.

Nimbulan appeared at her side. His arm clasped her waist and brought her close to him. The warmth of his body brought a moment's relief from the chill rain. "You can't be thinking of going after them."

"I must. They'll die. I'll follow them into the void if they die before I help them." She closed her eyes against the vision of death that awaited in the waves among the Dragon's Teeth.

"Then let me help the only way I can. I can't swim." He looked regretfully toward the boat. "I'll send a rope to them by magic. They can lash the rope to the bow and we can all pull them in." He indicated the men standing hesitantly on the edge of the cliff. Powwell and Kalen stood in front of the villagers, ready to jump to Nimbulan's and Myri's orders.

Powwell raced down the path to join them.

"The rope will get tangled in the rocks," Myri protested, eyeing the narrow channel between them.

"Maybe I can levitate the boat enough to clear the worst of them."

"Do you have the strength to work?" she shouted above the wind. "Can you and Powwell combine to keep the spell going?"

Nimbulan shrugged. "Like you, we have to try."

She watched them take the regulation three breaths. Nimbulan's eyes went blank and rolled slightly upward. Then he raised his hand high over his head. The rope held by the men on the cliff uncoiled and spun outward, toward the foundering boat.

Myri followed the progress of the rope end with her own talent, willing the fishermen to lash it tight to the prow of the overcrowded vessel. When she sensed the rope in place, she waved her arms to the men who had drifted down the path to the gravel beach. As if with one mind, they pulled, leaning all of their weight into bringing the boat ashore.

She shifted her mind back to the men in the boat. A tall wave washed over them. They clung to the sides precariously. A huge spire of rock loomed directly ahead of them.

"Quickly, Lan, lift them high and to the right!"

He closed his eyes in fierce concentration. Half of Myri's concentration remained with him. The other half monitored the panicky fishermen.

Were the dragons flying nearby, giving the magic power Nimbulan and Powell needed to sustain the spell?

She watched the fishing boat edge past the pinnacle of rock. Their tremendous relief came to her in a rush.

Nimbulan was tiring. Strain whitened the little wrinkles around his eyes. He couldn't sustain the levitation much longer and Powwell was far too inexperienced to take over the spell.

The next massive wave dashed against the boat, carrying it away from Nimbulan's waning spell directly into the rock.

He sank to his knees in exhaustion, clutching his arms across the wound in his belly.

Seven men went under. Their cries of despair stabbed at her heart. Her mind shared the shock of cold, the gulping of too much salt water, the lack of air, the weight against tired limbs and the first hungry bites of the Dragon's Teeth.

Myri shed her bodice and skirt as she dove into an oncoming wave, reaching out in long strokes to carry her toward the drowning men.

Another giant wave rose between Myri and sight of the men. Achingly cold water enfolded her, numbing her limbs and her mind.

The men's fear pulled her forward.

Nimbulan's heart leaped to his throat as Myri dove into the roaring waves. Her slender body, clad only in her shift, took on the sleek form of some water-born creature. She seemed to expand, turn silvery, tinged with purple. The waves parted for her graceful undulating movements. For a moment he lost sight of her. How could anyone— anything—survive the swirling currents that smashed up against the jagged rocks?

He despaired of ever seeing her again, feeling her quiet presence at his side as he woke in the middle of the night, hearing her gentle laughter at his awful jokes, finding the *right* rhyme to accompany his spells. His world emptied of all emotion. He couldn't give way to grief now. He had to be ready to help her at the first sign of trouble.

If he ever saw her again.

There, nearly invisible against the rising blackness of water, he caught sight of a darting form in the water. A white blob of a face appeared at the wave's crest, gasping and choking. Myri's long white arm that looked amazingly like a silvery wing, reached out to curl around the man's neck. The man fought her grasp briefly, then collapsed into the water's embrace.

Moments later, Myri dragged the man up the gravelly shore. Her body once more the same as he had watched dive into the waves; a slender woman wearing a drenched shift that might as well have been as transparent as a dragon wing. Tiny rocks cut into her bare feet. The greedy sea absorbed the thin rivulets of red, sucking them away.

He ran to her, catching her in his arms as her knees crumpled. He clutched her close against his chest, pushing his remaining warmth and strength into her. Others pulled the choking man to safety.

"The others," Myri said as she turned within his embrace. "I must save the others."

"Take some deep breaths. Clear your lungs," he ordered.

"I'll be all right as long as I know you are safe here, on shore. In the water, it's . . . I'm . . . I can't explain. It's like I become the water. The dragons are with me, telling me what to do, how to avoid the rocks and changing currents. I wonder if I am part dragon the way I understand them."

"Merlep mew!" Amaranth screeched as he plunged into the next wave, his wings tight against his body, claws extended.

The sight of his diving body triggered a memory in Nimbulan. He saw again the black creature flying into the column of flame that guarded the abandoned monastery.

Stargods! Amaranth had joined with the guardian spirit to test Nimbulan and Quinnault. Amaranth? Why hadn't he been with Myri?

The spirit had disappeared. Briefly, he wondered if Amaranth was the guardian or had absorbed it.

"I have to go. Amaranth can't keep him above water for long." Myri twisted from Nimbulan's arms and dove into the next huge wave.

In the trough, between crests, the white blob of another face showed briefly. The dark speck that might be Amaranth swam beside the man, front talons and mouth clamped into the collar of his shirt.

Before Nimbulan's eyes, the flywacket grew and faded into transparency. His wings stretched out and out and out, to become life-saving floats.

A dozen terrifying heartbeats later, Myri reached the unconscious fisherman and began the exhausting process of dragging him back to shore.

Lightning flashed across the sky, blinding Nimbulan for an eye blink. When he looked back to find Myri, he couldn't distinguish her from Amaranth. They both seemed half dragon in the weird light. Then Amaranth retracted the spectacular transparent wings and dove into the next wave, once more a black flywacket.

Myri remained silvery and unnaturally buoyant until she reached shallow water. When she stood up, dragging the half-drowned fisherman, she was fully human once more.

Nimbulan shook his head free of the hallucinations and dashed to help her bring the fisherman ashore.

Three more times Myri and Amaranth pulled men from the jaws of the Dragon's Teeth. Three more times, Nimbulan watched helplessly as they performed impossible feats of strength and agility within the crushing currents. Each time they dove, he was certain he'd lost them forever. The emptiness of his life without the witchwoman and her familiar nearly choked him.

The fifth time Myri dragged a fisherman onto the beach Amaranth crawled out with her, bedraggled, exhausted, miserable. They both collapsed against the sharp gravel, in danger of drowning in two inches of water that swirled about their faces. Nimbulan scooped up the flywacket, who now looked like an ordinary half-drowned cat, with one arm while he grabbed Myri around her waist. He tried lifting her clear of the water. Burning pain slashed across his partially healed wound.

Yoshi and Powwell dashed to grab Myri as Nimbulan lost his grasp of her.

"No more, Myri. Don't go into the water anymore." Yoshi said as he carried her to safety.

Powwell tucked a blanket around her. He looked back to Nimbulan. Awe and concern flashed across his eyes in rapid succession.

"Two more. There are two more men out there!" Myri cried.

"You can't save the last two," Nimbulan said as he cradled Amaranth against his chest. Kalen threw another blanket over them both.

Myri struggled briefly against Yoshi's tight hold of her, then collapsed, a limp, dead weight.

"They're dead. It's too late," she said, looking regretfully back to the angry waves.

"You did what you could. You saved five men who would have died without you." Nimbulan brushed wet hair out of her eyes with his fingers. Briefly he regretted Yoshi easily managing her weight. Then common sense asserted itself. He was in no shape to carry her. He'd be lucky to make it up the cliff path without help.

"Five. Only five." Myri moaned her grief.

Villagers rushed forward with blankets and chattering concern. Nimbulan allowed a stout woman to take Amaranth. She wrapped the cat in the folds of rough wool, rubbing his fur dry, pushing her face close to the animal's while she cooed praise and comfort.

Yoshi set Myri back on her feet as Kalen and Powwell draped a second blanket around her shoulders. All three of them rubbed the coarse weave against her arms, back, and legs to stimulate her body's natural heat.

Another woman gave Nimbulan a dry blanket and ushered all of them toward the warmth and shelter of the pub. The smell of hot soup and cider drew him to the pool of light spilling out from the doorway.

"Thank you." Myri kissed his cheek, then rested her head limply against his shoulder. "Knowing you were waiting for me, helping me, almost protecting me, made the job less frightening. I've never had anyone wait for me like that." She looked up as if scanning the ceiling of the pub for evidence of the dragons. They had helped her, too, she had said.

"I will always be here to help you, Myri." He paused at the doorway to the pub. Both of their stomachs raised loud grumbles at the onslaught of the enticing smells and promise of protection from the storm inside the pub.

Gently they laughed, pressing their foreheads together in wonderfully private intimacy.

"Does that mean you will go with her to the cleansing fires?" Moncriith asked from right behind them.

Chapter 31

Powwell trembled at Moncriith's words. How had the Bloodmage found them? The dragons had given him a dream that would take him back to Castle Krej.

Beside him, he felt Kalen go stiff with anger. Her eyes opened wide in her innocent act—something she hadn't done since they'd found Nimbulan and Myri.

"The children led me to you, Nimbulan, so that I can fulfill the vision provided me by the Stargods. When I awoke from whatever enchantment you and the witch put on me and found my men and dogs scattered, nearly witless, I realized I had not killed any demons after all. So I decided to seek the children instead of the witch. Once I remembered that I had kept threads of their old clothing smeared with blood from their small cuts and scratches, all I had to do was link blood to blood and I found them." The Bloodmage chuckled at his own cleverness.

Guilt washed over Powwell. He should have known Moncriith could find them through the clothes they had disgarded at Castle Krej.

"The witch and her consort must be burned to cleanse this land of demons." Moncriith raised his arms to the cave ceiling in a dramatic gesture that Powwell had seen all too often. It had no more meaning to him than if the man scratched his backside. But the people crowding the pub looked up wide-eyed and silent.

Only when he saw the cave ceiling did Powwell realize he was underground again. The smoke and smell of too many bodies crowded together, robbed him of air. He felt the weight of all of Kardia Hodos pressing on his head and chest. All trace of magic deserted his body with his growing panic.

He was defenseless, helpless to join his magic with Nimbulan to oust the Bloodmage.

Kalen took his hand in hers. An image of a flower-strewn field open to sun and wind flashed from her mind to his. He relaxed a little and listened.

"Don't be ridiculous," Nimbulan scoffed. He turned his back on the priest and stalked into the depths of the cave, keeping a half-drowned Myrilandel within the circle of his arms. Powwell noticed how his shoulders had tensed and his grip on her had tightened. Whispers erupted throughout the pub.

"Nimbulan will know what to do. We should stay close to him," Powwell whispered to Kalen as he breathed a little deeper. The ceiling of the cave still seemed awfully close to his head.

Kalen darted a look at Moncriith that Powwell didn't understand. "You need to stay by the door so you can breathe, Powwell," she answered. Resolutely, she eased him through the shadows toward the doorway.

He wanted to rush to Nimbulan. He also wanted to get out of this cave. But Moncriith stood in his way, blocking the entrance.

"You can't ignore me anymore, Nimbulan. I have the authority of Lord Kammeryl d'Astrismos," Moncriith shouted as he stepped past the doorway into the pub interior.

A hush grew outward from his words. No one moved. The only sound in the cavern was the crackling of the fire and the swish of Amaranth's tail against the rough wool of its nest in front of the flames.

"What do you want from us, Moncriith?" A stout woman stepped forward from the center of the crowd. She stood with her ample arms planted on her hips in a defiant stance.

"Out of my way, whore. I have cornered the demon that corrupts all of Coronnan. My vision will be fulfilled. She must burn."

"Not *s'murghin'* likely." One of the fishermen staggered to his feet. "Myri saved five men from certain death. She saved us when no one else could. Every last person in the village will defend her to the death." He coughed heavily then stood straighter. His wet hair still dripped into his eyes, and his hands shook with cold where he clutched a blanket around him. His face looked very pale from shock. Powwell had seen men in his condition after a battle.

Murmurs of assent rippled around the room. One old man even raised his fist in defiance and shook it at Moncriith.

"He's going to lose this time," Kalen whispered in Powwell's ear.

"I have soldiers waiting to follow my orders. Soldiers who will burn this entire town and all of you with it. Will you sacrifice your lives to die with the witch? Will you sacrifice your souls to her? She has already stolen the souls of five men who should have died and joined the Stargods. You think she saved your lives, but she stole them. You will be her slaves in evil for all eternity, never dying, never knowing free will!"

"Steed shit!" the heavy woman shouted above Moncriith's ranting. "Lord d'Astrismos fought hard to win this village back from Lord Baathalzan and the Kaaliph of Hanassa before that. We provide Lord Kammeryl's table with bay crawlers and his troops with bemouths. No other village dares hunt those killer fish, though one will feed half an army." The woman returned Moncriith's stare measure for measure.

Kalen yanked on the woman's skirt for attention. "He's lying. The six soldiers ran away. They won't return from Castle Krej unless compelled by the lord or magic." She pitched her voice to make sure the others heard her as well, then scuttled back to the doorway to hold Powwell's hand again.

"Fetch your soldiers, Moncriith," Nimbulan said, his voice deceptively calm. "Myrilandel and I will be long gone by the time you return." He removed his arm from Myri's shoulders, flexing his fingers. His left hand came up, palm outward, fingers slightly curved, ready to weave a spell—if he needed to.

Powwell walked boldly across the crowded room to stand beside his teacher. The safety of fresh air near the door didn't compare with his need to stay with Nimbulan. He placed his hand on his teacher's shoulder and joined his magic to the older man's. Power welled up within him, ready to burst forth in whatever spell Nimbulan chose.

Myrilandel stood straight and defiant. She seemed to glow from within, like the dragons. Amaranth roused from his nest by the fire and joined her, pacing a protective circle around all of them. His black fur seemed to absorb light where Myri reflected it back.

Moncriith raised a fist in defiance of Nimbulan. He held three strands of Myri's hair, a few bloody threads, and a long splinter of wood, also bloodied. "I have something from each of you four demons. I bind you with magic. You cannot resist my commands!"

A wave of red energy undulated from Moncriith's clenched hand. Powwell suddenly felt heavy and sleepy. He needed to drop his hand from Nimbulan's shoulder to hold up his head. But the decision to move any muscle was too much effort.

Suddenly, a web of light shot from Nimbulan's hand. A giant fishnet of eldritch power wove around and around Moncriith, containing his magic within the web. The pulses of red energy ceased. The heaviness left Powwell.

He stood straighter with no effort.

"You can't do that! Kardia magic cannot defeat blood magic," Moncriith protested.

"We have found a new magic that allows us to combine our powers to overcome any one magician, no matter what source of power he uses to fuel an inborn talent," Nimbulan explained.

"You'll never get magicians to cooperate. This battle isn't over yet, Nimbulan."

"Leave now, Moncriith. Go back to Lord Kammeryl d'Astrismos and tell him that if he goes to war this summer or any summer, he will face the combined might of many magicians and many lords." Nimbulan flipped his wrist and wiggled his fingers in a walking motion. The web of magic pulled Moncriith back toward the door. Wind and rain pelted the Bloodmage as he grasped the doorjamb to keep from being dragged outside.

"You haven't seen the last of me yet. Any of you. I'll be back with an army and the Lord d'Astrismos. You'll all die for your sin of sheltering this witchwoman. She's a demon, I tell you. She plays with evil. Repent now, and follow the path of the Stargods," Moncriith bellowed so loudly Powwell wanted to put his hands over his ears. The

Bloodmage's knuckles turned white where he clung to the edge of the doorway. His feet kept pulling him outside.

"If the path of the Stargods means following your sick hatred, I'll take Simurgh any day." A grizzled old man crossed his wrists and flapped his hands. The waving of his hands imitated the ancient winged god who demanded human sacrifice. His crossed wrists warded against the return of that particular demon.

"Get out of our village and don't come back." The stout woman raised her fist as if she intended to plant it in the Bloodmage's jaw. "Myrilandel is our witchwoman, one of us. She belongs to us, and we'll take care of her. Go meddle in someone else's business, Moncriith."

"You'll regret this. All of you." Moncriith turned and exited slowly, as if his dignity and honor hadn't been questioned.

Chewed up and spat out, Powwell thought. *We'll have to deal with him again. I hope there are more of us then and we know what we're doing with this dragon magic.*

"Thank you. Thank you all," Myrilandel said shakily. Tears streamed down her face. "I was sure you would join Moncriith in throwing me to the flames. The last village where I lived turned against me and my guardian. They burned Magretha while Moncriith laughed. I ran away, but Magretha was too old and ill to get very far. I watched her burn from a distance and couldn't do anything to save her. I truly tried, but I wasn't strong enough to fight Moncriith and the village turned against me. Forgive me for doubting you." She stumbled into Karry's open arms, weeping uncontrollably. All of the fear and strain of the past poured of her in a flood.

" 'Tis we who must thank you, Myri. You saved five good men. Men who will live to fish again, live to provide for their families and the village. Now enough of that blubbering. Time to get some hot soup into you." Karry escorted her to the padded chair by the fire.

Myri looked back to Nimbulan, needing to draw him into the loving warmth of the village. She saw hot brightness in Powwell's eyes. Kalen clung to the boy's hand again. Her chin trembled a little uncertainly.

Nimbulan stood slightly apart from the crowd. He nodded to her then turned to Powwell and Kalen. Myri felt a slight tug on the silvery cord that bound her to Nimbulan with love now, as well as healing. She needed to fold herself within his arms again but knew that would come later. For now she needed to form a new connection with the villagers who had sheltered her all winter and now welcomed her as one of their own.

When the voices had whispered of betrayal, they must have meant Televarn stabbing Nimbulan. These people would never turn on her.

"Where is Televarn?" she asked Karry in a whisper. "I know he was here."

"Left in a hurry after we told him he wasn't welcome and we wouldn't tell him where you were. I think he went to Hanassa. Good place for thieves like him." Karry spat toward the fire.

"Thank you, Karry. You have saved me from him as well as Moncriith. I am glad to call this place home."

(You have work elsewhere, child. Dangerous work that only you can accomplish. We will help you in the coming battle. A terrible battle that may cost you the one you love. Only you can save him, but your talent will be useless.)

Myri fingered the wide skirt of the new gown that molded tightly to her breasts and waist, then drifted loosely around her hips and legs. She'd chosen the fabric from Karry's store because it was the same color as Nimbulan's eyes; the soft green of new oak leaves. She'd memorized every nuance of his eyes, fearful of losing him. The dragons had warned her.

"Since you are heading back to Lord Quinnault's stronghold, you could wait and have a real priest bless your marriage there." Karry smiled hugely as she fussed with the hem of Myri's new dress. "Not that I want to miss this celebration."

Amaranth played hiding games with the hem where Karry lifted it slightly to finish the last few stitches.

"I want Myri and the children to have the protection of my name and rank before we set out on a long journey," Nimbulan insisted. He leaned against the bar of the temporarily empty pub, arms crossed, admiration and love pouring from his glorious green eyes. A brief shadow passed

across his face. He blinked and resumed his admiration of
Myri in her wedding gown.

"I traveled across half of Coronnan on my own, Lan.
The children did, too. I don't have to take your name for
protection. If you want to wait for a real priest, we can."
She met his gaze and nearly lost herself in the intensity of
his stare. She still couldn't believe he had asked her to
marry him. Living with him, following him anywhere across
the continent, would have satisfied her. For as long as she
had him, she wouldn't leave him.

Amaranth pounced from his hiding place beneath Myri's
skirt onto Nimbulan's boot. He batted one cat paw at an
imaginary shadow. Then he curled up on Nimbulan's feet
for a brief nap, clear proof that he had adopted the magician as Myri's equal in his affections. Myri saw only the
flywacket's unwillingness to be separated from him.

Her heart ached with the knowledge that she might lose
him to the next battle. How would she live without him?

She banished the terrible thought, unwilling to let her
fears mar the beauty of the day. Her wedding day.

"The marriage will only last a year if you don't find a
priest to bless it before the next Vernal Equinox," Karry
reminded them as she knotted the last stitch in the hem of
the dress.

Myri prayed they'd have that year together, at least.

"I've not seen any prettier brides, Myri. The color suits
you, though it's the most common of all dyes and most
brides want something different and special for their wedding gown." Karry stood back, assessing the gown and the
bride with a huge smile on her face.

"I want this wedding, Myri. I want the laws of man and
the Stargods to acknowledge what we already hold dear."
Nimbulan stepped to her side and raised her palm to his
lips. They stood together a moment in silence. He kept his
eyes lowered to her palm.

Amaranth circled them both, purring loudly. His looping
path wove an unneccesary binding spell—or was it protection? Myri touched the silver cord that bound her heart to
Nimbulan's. That simple piece of magic pulsed with vitality.
Amaranth merely echoed the bonds already in place.

Myri caressed Nimbulan's face with her free hand, relishing the warm tingles that traveled from his kiss all the

way through her body. Her knees weakened. 'Twas always
the same. She had no control when he touched her. If they
didn't get on with the simple village ceremony soon, she'd
tear his new tunic and trews from his body and make love
with him on the bar. She vowed to herself not to let a day
go by without making love to him and telling him of her
joy in him. She wouldn't let him go to his grave doubting
her feelings.

"Such scandalous thoughts, my love?" he whispered to
her. He raised one eyebrow, as if he also contemplated the
quickest way out of their new clothes—gifts from the villagers in thanks for saving Rory and Kelly and the other
fishermen.

"You read my mind?" she whispered back. He didn't do
it often. He had said that he hated violating another person's privacy, yet every once in a while the rapport between
them was so perfect he couldn't help overhearing her
thoughts. The magnificence of that rapport and the magnitude of his talent still awed her. She suppressed her fears
lest he read those as well.

She didn't deserve to keep him to herself. All of Coronnan needed him and the new magic the dragons gave him.
He must fight the coming battle. She hoped desperately
that she had the strength to save him afterward.

"I could read your mind," Karry snorted, repressing a
laugh. "You'd think you two were youngsters just discovering the delights of Festival." She handed Myri a nose-
gay of wildflowers. Nimbulan settled a crown of similar
posies on her head. He dropped a quick kiss on her lips, a
brief promise of more to come.

"In a way, Karry, we are experiencing our first Festival.
Our first Festival together." Nimbulan offered Myri his
arm.

She clung to him.

"Save the sentiments for the priest who marries you for
all time. He's the one you have to convince that you want
to stay together beyond the first few tumbles in bed." Karry
moved to the doorway, opening it to the morning sunshine.
"Remember, this common law ceremony lasts only a year."

"Its good enough for most people in Coronnan who only
see a priest once a year," Nimbulan replied. "I never considered before what villagers do for religious sacraments or

for healing. We must take magic away from the battlefield and bring it back to the people."

"You'll have a lot of hard work ahead of you, then," Karry snorted. "Not much trust of trained magicians. We like our witchwomen better. They belong to us, not to some lord. Granny Katia told of a time when we had a priest. This village was important because of the triple Equinox Pylon. But the wars came, and the lords took our priest to serve their armies 'cause he was a magician of sorts."

"That must change. Magicians must belong to all people of Coronnan, not just the lords. But we have to start the changes with the lords and end this endless civil war. We'll leave with the children for Lord Quinnault's keep right after the ceremony. He has a priest in residence." He led Myri toward the Equinox Pylon where the entire village, including Powwell and Kalen, waited. Amaranth scampered to join them.

A huge black cloud covered the sun, plunging them all into shadow. Cold darkness descended on the bright morning. Myri shivered at the terrible omen.

Chapter 32

"**M**y Lord Quinnault, I demand justice for the loss of my daughter. These islands fall under your authority. Only you can give me justice." Stuuvart stalked the length of the Great Hall, speaking in tones that demanded attention.

Ackerly hurried in his steward's wake, anxious that his side of the story be heard. He surveyed the hall carefully as he stretched his short legs to keep up with Stuuvart. The lord, his steward, three servants, and five dogs populated the largest room in the keep. The numerous retainers and tenants must be out plowing and planting in the early spring sunshine. He could tell what he knew and hope it wouldn't pass to the general populace.

Ackerly made a mental note to remind the lord how much the presence of the School for Magicians added to his prestige and held together his mutual defense pact. The two lords who had recently signed Quinnault's treaty did so only because Ackerly had agreed to add his magicians to any defensive action needed. He was still looking for a way to make the lords pay him for those services, but Quinnault had reminded him that the school was housed on one of his islands rent free.

Quinnault de Tanos looked up from the parchments he studied with his own steward. The lines around his pale eyes creased with concern. His long, thin face seemed longer yet as he massaged his chin with his left hand. No trace of his pale, blond beard shadowed his face.

"One of my students ran away from my steward, Lord Quinnault, more than two weeks ago," Ackerly explained to his landlord. He wouldn't call her Stuuvart's daughter.

"She was willful and unruly and hated her lessons. Only now does Stuuvart seriously look for her, now when he wants more money from me. Money I do not have to give him. What is of greater concern to us all is Lord Kammeryl d'Astrismos. He has declared himself king and marches his army north to confront any who challenge him. Rumor places Moncriith, the Bloodmage, within his ranks." Ackerly bowed his head in a gesture of humility. Anything to keep Quinnault de Tanos from worrying about that blasted child.

If he'd been able to train Kalen properly, she'd be worth at least a gold piece for each battle. Combined with Rollett and Maalin, he could up the price to about six pieces of gold per battle. Without the girl's ingenuity and creativity with fire, the two journeymen were only the equal of a mediocre Battlemage.

"I know of Lord Kammeryl's pretensions," Quinnault said.

Of course he knew. Ackerly had told him after one of his brief communications with Moncriith.

"D'Astrismos claims the right of kingship from his genealogy," Quinnault continued. "I have always suspected the insertion of the Stargods at the top of his family tree to be false, but that is not important now. The presence of a Bloodmage has yet to be verified. No one has reported lost livestock, prisoners, or pets that could be sacrificed for such an evil magician. How could a man draw power from the pain of another?" Quinnault shuddered a moment. Silence reigned in the room as he looked to each man present for an explanation.

After a moment he returned his gaze to the plans on his desk. "Have you looked for the child before this? Did she have reason to run away?" Quinnault studied Stuuvart in that direct way of his. Practiced scoundrels were known to babble everything they knew under that gaze. If they could remember who they were or what the question was after the lord's rapid leap from subject to subject. Ackerly avoided that gaze whenever possible.

"The child was well behaved, a loving and devoted daughter until we enrolled her in this man's supposed School for Magicians." Stuuvart pointed accusingly at Ackerly. "Almost immediately, she rebelled and fought the use of her

talent. She hated Ackerly, but she remained devoted to her
mother and younger siblings. She would not have run away
unless provoked. I wonder that perhaps Ackerly found a
way to hold her for ransom. He has not mounted a serious
search for her."

Ackerly glared at the steward. He hadn't cared about
Kalen until the question of money came up. Now he was
using her absence to demand coin in redress, coin he should
have offered for her return.

"My lord," Ackerly said with his hands open before him
in a gesture he meant to show his honesty. "Kalen was a
very intelligent child with a great deal of talent. I tried to
teach her the necessity of control of that talent. She was
frightened badly by the impostor Moncriith before she
came to my school. She had been mistreated by Stuuvart,
who claims to be her father but isn't. She had no true
reason to run away after she came into my care. Granted
she was quiet and didn't make friends easily, but she was
more afraid of her talent and Stuuvart than truly rebellious.
If Moncriith does indeed march with d'Astrismos, it's possible he kidnapped Kalen. We both know his attitude toward
traditional magicians—especially females."

The only difference between a female magician and a
witchwoman was the formal training all magicians under-
went to gain control of their talents. Moncriith wouldn't see
that control as a difference. He wanted to burn them all.

"You have a point, Ackerly. I shall send a message of
inquiry to Lord Kammeryl. One of your journeymen can
do the honors. Do you know if Moncriith uses a traditional
method of summons—a flame through a glass?"

"*I* heard that Lord Kammeryl d'Astrismos has de-
nounced magicians and intends to win the crown without a
Battlemage," Stuuvart said. "You'll have to send your message by fleet steed and rider. It will take weeks to get a
reply. I'll go myself. With your permission, sir."

"Don't be ridiculous. No one can win a battle without a
Mage to protect the troops from other magicians," Ackerly protested.

"If only Nimbulan hadn't died. He always seemed to be
able to keep track of what was happening in all corners of
Coronnan." Lord Quinnault shook his head sadly. "He'd

know who marched with d'Astrismos. He'd also know why the little girl disappeared."

"But Nimbulan is dead," Ackerly replied. "He'd never have been able to build up the school as you and I did—to make it big enough to provide defense for your united lords. He'd not have attracted the large numbers of tenants who have settled and will defend your islands. He'd be so lost in a Tambootie trance, he'd forget to eat or teach his classes, or look in his glass for the information we seek. The addiction to the drug of magic ruled him, my lord. Perhaps it's best the weed took him." Ackerly paused a moment in a pose of grief before continuing. "I'll send the message myself. I don't need to know a specific magician's address." He already knew when and where to contact Moncriith, and that Moncriith had found and lost Kalen and Powwell. But he wouldn't let that bit of information slip to Stuuvart.

"That won't be necessary, Ackerly." A strange voice interrupted. A voice from the past that shouldn't have ever spoken again.

"With my head and my heart and the strength of my shoulders, I renounce the presence of this ghost!" Ackerly crossed himself hastily as he mumbled the prayer. Then he looked to the source of the voice and crossed himself again. "Nimbulan!"

The dead had come back to haunt him. Shabbily dressed in peasant clothes, a day's growth of beard, and slightly grubby, Nimbulan alive would never have allowed himself to fall into such dishevelment, unless deep in the throes of his addiction. He must be dead. He had to be dead! The overdose of Tambootie mixed with Timboor had killed him.

Maybe this was an impostor, cloaked in magical delusion?

"Nimbulan!" Quinnault stood so fast his chair crashed backward and skidded across the floor.

"You can't be here, you're dead! I buried you myself." Ackerly found himself backing toward a doorway that led to the interior of the keep. The door to the courtyard was filled with magicians and apprentices trailing in Nimbulan's wake. And right beside him, close enough to be a family unit, walked Myrilandel and the two missing children.

"Apparently, Ackerly, you buried me too hastily and not

deep enough," Nimbulan replied. A wry smile creased his otherwise grim face.

"Where have you been, my friend? Why were you gone so long? What brings you back? How? But . . . ?" Quinnault rushed forward and clasped the Master Magician's hand with both of his own.

He'd never greeted Ackerly with such enthusiasm. Never called him friend. Never acknowledged Ackerly's help and guidance.

"One question at a time, Lord Quinnault." Nimbulan returned the lord's affectionate greeting. "My adventures were long and numerous. Suffice it to say, I have perfected a way for two or more magicians to join their magic, compounding the effect of a spell. Without the Tambootie. I have no more need of drugs to enhance my magic. I have a better way. Henceforth, no solitary magician will be able to stand against those who join me. We will remove magicians from battles and politics. We have a chance for peace." Nimbulan raised his left hand, palm outward, fingers slightly curled, little finger bent almost to the palm, as if ready to capture the threads of the Kardia and weave them into a spell. The habitual gesture confirmed that this was indeed Nimbulan and no impostor. The perfectly proportioned hand with more than ordinary grace couldn't be imitated.

"Stuuvart, Kalen stands before you and you do not welcome her. A moment ago you demanded justice for her disappearance." Ackerly reminded his steward of why they had come to Lord Quinnault's hall. He needed to get back to an ordinary topic, one he could deal with while the rest of his mind worked furiously. Why wasn't Nimbulan dead? The Timboor mixed with the ink on the letter should have killed him if the additional drugs in his cup hadn't.

"My daughter clings to another woman as if she were her mother. She hides from *me,* her beloved father." Stuuvart glared at Ackerly, daring him to contradict his legal claim on Kalen. "What happens here? Who are these people?" He beat his clenched fist against his forehead, effectively hiding his facial expressions.

"Yes, Nimbulan, introduce us to your friends. Then tell us your adventures over food and drink. You must refresh yourselves." Quinnault raised his hand to signal a servant.

Then he clapped the magician firmly on the shoulder, a smile spreading across his face.

"My lord, may I present to you my wife, Myrilandel. My apprentice, Powwell, I believe you have met—and Kalen, Ackerly's apprentice, who discovered I was missing from the crypt and ran away to find me." Nimbulan gathered the three into the circle of his arms as if they were his own children. "And this is Amaranth, my wife's familiar." At last the witchwoman raised her face from the cat she held quite tightly in her arms.

"My sister's name was Myrilandel," Quinnault said as he kissed the woman's hand. "Unfortunately, she died when only two. I thought the name unique to my family."

"I grieve for your loss, my lord. I was an orphan. I have no knowledge of my parents or why I was named Myrilandel, only that I came to my guardian with the name."

Her voice was the same melodic whisper Ackerly remembered from the hospital tent last autumn. He wanted to lean closer to capture every last nuance of her words. He needed to reach out a hand and touch her to make certain she was real, to smell her flowery scent, to follow her anywhere. . . .

No wonder Moncriith thought her a demon. She could enchant the most hardened of hearts.

"Before we settle in for a proper discussion of our mutual goals, I think you should know that the islands are soon to have some rather awesome visitors." Nimbulan spoke with the commanding authority he used only on the battlefield. All within the room heard and turned their attention to him.

"If we are to have guests, I would like to take my daughter home to her mother and give her a good meal and a bath. There is much to prepare at the school before we can offer lodging and meals. How many should we prepare for?" Stuuvart reached to clasp Kalen by the shoulders. The girl shrank away from him, trying to hide behind Myrilandel's skirts.

"Our visitors won't require anything of you, Master Steward." Nimbulan placed a reassuring hand on Kalen's shoulder. The little girl relaxed a little, but didn't move closer to her mother's husband.

"Will they be staying with me?" Lord Quinnault looked as if he were calculating the stores in his cellars.

"No, my lord. Our visitors require nothing from us in the way of hospitality. I doubt they would fit inside either building." That wry smile threatened to break through again. Myrilandel smiled, too.

What was Nimbulan up to? In years gone by, Ackerly was privy to all of his master's schemes. But now he'd been shut out, ignored. He deserved better than this. After all, he'd made the school a profitable and popular business. Nimbulan would never have been able to recruit nearly fifty apprentices and fifteen faculty. Nor would he have found the funds to make the school self-supporting.

"Tomorrow morning, five dragons will grace us with their presence. For they are the secret to combined magic."

Everyone in the room grew unnaturally still.

"Dragons?" Ackerly asked the question for all those present.

"Dragons, Ackerly. I went in search of myths and found my future. The dragons are real and ready to form a covenant with us."

"If this isn't some Tambootie-induced delusion, then the dragons are more likely ready to dine on all of us. Lord Quinnault, I suggest you lock Nimbulan and his wife in your deepest dungeon for their own protection. I ask only that you give me back the children. I am their master and have more legal right to their raising than their mothers." Ackerly stalked out of the keep, heading for *his* school. He didn't truly expect *his* children to follow.

Chapter 33

Nimbulan emerged from the central door of the old monastery at dawn the next morning, still yawning. Myri clung to his arm, barely able to contain her excitement. He looked across the sky for evidence of the dragons. Not that he expected to see the nearly invisible creatures themselves. If he caught a glimpse of a rainbow arcing down from where the sun struck their wings, he'd be lucky.

"I guess we'll have to wait a bit," he said stifling another yawn.

"I don't think so." Myri giggled, pointing upward.

He followed her pointing finger to the top of the residential wing—right over the suite he had appropriated for himself and Myri. Shayla perched on the peak of the roof.

The dragon peered at him with one multifaceted crystal eye. She cocked her head in a listening posture very like the one Myri adopted.

Nimbulan broke the mesmerizing eye contact. He needed his wits about him today, not another dragon dream.

Four smaller dragons—the twenty-year-old adolescents—silvery as moonlight, swam in the river, guarded the causeway, and eyed the fields of fat cows near Quinnault's keep. Five full-sized males sat, reclined, and hovered over other portions of the island. Curious. None of the males had been present during the training session in the meadow.

"Your mates joined you, Shayla!" Myri called and waved.

(The need to control magic brought them out of their solitude. We will see if the covenant we reach is enough to keep them with me. 'Tis not natural for dragons to be together. We will change our society only if you change yours.)

Quinnault ran across the causeway, splashing through the

puddles left by the receding tide. He tucked his shirt into his trews as he rushed to join Nimbulan and the dragons. A servant ran behind him, proffering bread and cheese to his lord.

"I still don't understand why your dragons are suddenly concerned with the affairs of men when they have remained hidden and elusive for centuries." Lord Quinnault stopped abruptly behind Nimbulan. His eyes and mouth opened in awe as he stared at Shayla.

"They aren't my dragons. Myri is the one they listen to. They only tell me what they want me to know. With her they communicate freely." Together they watched Myri caress a young red-tipped dragon's cheek as if she petted a docile steed—a steed as large as a hut.

"He says his name is Tssonnin," Myri said over her shoulder to Nimbulan. "They always accord others the honor of using their names."

"Did I tell you that we rode dragonback from the Southern Mountains?" Nimbulan asked Quinnault, suppressing yet another yawn. "Shayla spoke to Myri the entire trip. They discussed all manner of issues, dragon and human, female and general. Myri rode directly in front of me, and I heard only her words. Nothing from the dragon. I think the young dragons spoke, too. Again, I was not privy to any of their comments."

Quinnault cringed as Tssonnin bent his head to scratch behind his steedlike ear with the barbed tip of his wing. The red-tipped spiral horn on his forehead came dangerously close to spearing Kalen who had crept up to be closer to them. "They will hurt her." He moved to pull her away.

"Doubtful." Nimbulan held Quinnalt back. "They adore children. And Myri has claimed Kalen and Powwell as her own. Myri is the one the dragons trust. She is the one they sought out and waited for."

"But why now? Why not when the wars first started?" The lord looked as if he barely restrained himself from dashing to rescue Myri and Kalen.

Amaranth joined the women and clambered up Tssonin's outstretched foreleg to perch on his shoulder. His long talonlike claws didn't penetrate the tough dragon hide. A few crystalline hairs fell free in the flywacket's wake. They glinted in the early sunlight. Three apprentices dashed forward to gather the hairs as souvenirs.

"Look, my lord, the children have no fear of the beasts. They seem to know instinctively how much the dragons treasure young ones. Now we must get to work. Do you wish to join us in the exercises to gather dragon magic? You might have a talent for it."

"I have so little magic my efforts will add nothing to your schemes."

"Perhaps. Perhaps not. This is an entirely different technique. I find it more exhausting than drawing energy from the ley lines. But you can't see ley lines, so maybe gathering dragon magic will be easy for you. Come. Try, at least. Sharing magic is an exhilarating experience. I just wish Myri were able to join us."

"Nimbulan?" Myri turned sharply. Her spine stiffened, and she looked as if she needed to flee. "Lan, Shayla says there is an army approaching from the south. A day's march away. They move only at night and remain hidden during the day so that Quinnault will have no time to prepare. Moncriith is with them."

> *"Wisp of flame, burning bright*
> *Travel far beyond my sight*
> *Bring to view the other true*
> *Pass the word of magic might."*

Nimbulan listened to the apprentices and masters chant the words of his simple communication spell.

Why did they take so long learning a simple rhyme? He'd never perfect the technique of joining their magic if they took hours on the easiest of spells. Kammeryl d' Astrismos and his army came closer with every tick of the water clock.

He hoped Rollett was able to infiltrate the enemy army soon enough to learn some important tactical information to aid Quinnault in the coming battle. The young journeyman magician would have to be careful and stay out of Moncriith's way.

Patience, he told himself. *You didn't learn magic in a day.* He remembered the years he'd struggled to create his spells. Old Druulin had made him keep his incantations

and pieces of poetry to trigger those spells private, even
from the master and Ackerly, his best friend. Druulin had
stolen the rhyme for a simple invisibility spell and used it
to sneak up on Nimbulan. The old man had knocked his
young apprentice senseless with a mind probe. The lesson
had been clear. Never allow another magician to learn
your spells.

Secrecy among magicians was a major barrier he had to
overcome. Mistrust among the older magicians who had
come to the school might prevent this little communication
spell from working. Only Ackerly seemed to grasp immediately the concepts of this new magic.

If only Nimbulan still trusted Ackerly. The man had
evaded questions about the overdose of Tambootie and
Timboor that had almost killed him, with sly hints and accusations against everyone except himself. He'd even
blamed Nimbulan for endangering the apprentices with his
experiments.

Ackerly was amazingly adept at gathering dragon magic.
Nimbulan hadn't expected his assistant to be more powerful
with the new system than he had with the old. Ackerly grasped
the concept of gathering magic quickly and demonstrated
the technique adeptly to the younger boys, something the
older master magicians couldn't—or wouldn't—do.

They needed speed. Kammeryl d'Astrismos' army marched
closer every minute.

Nimbulan would have gladly excused his assistant from
the practice until he knew for sure who had poisoned him
last winter, but he needed his help.

Journeyman Gilby stumbled over the words of the spell.
The entire circle of magicians and apprentices faltered and
stopped in their recitation.

"Begin again," Nimbulan said impatiently.

When they were all competing against each other, keeping their spells private had been vital, lifesaving. Now they
all must use the same spell, in unison, and work in concert
for the same goal.

The future he envisioned banished all barriers among
magicians. They would share more than power during vital
spells. They would share knowledge and pass it down to
each successive generation.

At last the magicians worked their way through the spell

three times without error. "Hold hands, men. The magic only works when you are in physical contact with every other magician working the spell," he directed.

Twenty bodies shifted and shuffled in embarrassed silence. Men didn't touch each other in their culture. Another custom Nimbulan must banish. Finally they were all joined, old and young, trained and raw. Ackerly, the last man in the line, placed his free hand on Lyman's shoulder, completing the circle. Lyman held his master's glass in front of the flames in the hearth.

"Together now, breathe in on three counts, hold three, release three." A tingle of energy ran up Nimbulan's arms. The room filled with power, begging him to join it. He watched the men's auras blend into one giant pulse. Arcs of many individual colors swirled and shifted until they were all one glowing dome of lavender/white energy. Lavender, Lyman's signature color. If Ackerly led the group, would his yellow dominate the aura?

They knew so little about why dragon magic allowed communal working and ley line magic didn't. Magic was strictly fuel, wasn't it? They didn't have time to puzzle out answers.

Nimbulan stepped back, physically and magically. He wasn't part of this spell. He needed to observe the effects from a distance. So he watched the auara as a reflection of available power. The single united aura grew until it filled the room and pushed outside the stone walls of the room.

"Again, breathe in, hold, release, hold." The united aura began to throb and reach outward.

"Once more. Breathe, hold, release, hold." The level of power in the room grew and multiplied like a living thing, replicating itself faster than they could think. All color vanished as the united aura whirled until it became the nearly transparent all color/no color of a dragon's hide.

"Chant the words of the spell, and send the flame to Naabbon, Lord Hanic's new magician. Send the flame across the island, watch it skip over the river, guide it west by southwest, across the grazing land, through the rich farmland up to the foothills." Nimbulan closed his eyes and imagined the progress of the flame. He'd sent a message along this very route the week before that fateful battle last autumn. Then he had pleaded with Keegan to return and complete his training. His message had been ignored then. Would it be again?

His left hand reached out, palm forward, as if drawing the communal magic into himself. He forced himself to clench his fist and drop it back into his lap. He couldn't participate. He had to observe.

At last he heard Lyman reading the written text of the message Quinnault had worked out. A plea for Hanic to join the united lords in mutual defense against Kammeryl d'Astrismos. United strength to combat those who sought war for the sake of war. If all stood together, they could defeat Kammeryl and negotiate a new government with a new monarchy.

They deliberately left the issue of a monarchy hanging. Hanic had to believe himself eligible for the crown, though Quinnault's alliance had already asked the lord of the islands to rule.

Lyman's words trailed off. Nimbulan opened his eyes to see, what, if any, reaction came back through the glass. Because he was not joined to magicians performing this spell, he saw nothing through the glass but magnified flames. He could only judge the response on Naabbon's end from Lyman's face. A map of time-earned wrinkles around the old man's eyes crinkled. A smile curved upward, revealing amazingly sound teeth.

"Agreed, Naabbon. Your lord will march tonight to reinforce Lord Quinnault as he defends his lands against Kammeryl d'Astrismos and the Bloodmage."

Ackerly removed his hand from Lyman's shoulder. The spell dissolved.

"We did it, Master Nimbulan." Lyman stood up from his crouched position before the fire. "We blasted young Naabbon with so much magic we dragged him out of his bath. He spluttered and gasped, but he couldn't break the summons. He had to stay with his glass, walked it down the corridor—him dripping bath water the whole way and naked as a lumbird—into Hanic's bedroom. Woke the lord up and got the agreement. He couldn't break the summons!"

Moncriith studied the army of Lord Kammeryl d'Astrismos. Far less than the one thousand men the lord advertised as his following. No need. Moncriith could handle any magician Quinnault de Tanos found.

A niggle of doubt crept into his mind. Nimbulan and the boy had overpowered him. He'd had thread from Powwell's cloak, strands of Myrilandel's hair, and a splinter from Nimbulan's old staff—purchased from Televarn before the Rover chieftain disappeared into Hanassa. All of the souvenirs had tasted the owner's blood. His spell should have been more powerful than anything they threw at him.

Except he had nothing from the girl child—Kalen. She'd thrown her old and ragged clothes into the hearth fire rather than let Moncriith have them. Perhaps that was the problem. She had been excluded from his spell and able to help Nimbulan in some way. Either that or the bit of Nimbulan's staff had been false. Rovers were known to lie about everything. Except, Moncriith suspected, the Rover had a grudge against Nimbulan and wanted him dead.

When next Moncriith met Nimbulan and Myrilandel, he would have an entire battlefield of blood and pain to fuel him. They would not survive his next attack. Would not survive long enough to have their marriage sanctified in a temple of the Stargods. Demons couldn't be allowed to profane the sacraments.

When Nimbulan and Myrilandel fell, so would the rest of the magicians and the demons that controlled them. Moncriith would be the only magician left in Coronnan. He would rule through his puppet, Kammeryl d'Astrismos for a time. The self-crowned king would die, too, when Moncriith no longer need him.

His vision had become so real, he reached out a hand as if to grasp the image of himself as anointed priest-king of all Coronnan. No one would dare defy him once he ruled.

He smiled at the army that awaited his command. One of them was Nimbulan's spy. The young man from the school harbored a demon spirit disguised as a magic talent. Moncriith smelled the evil creature on the wind.

Moncriith needed sacrificial human blood to begin his battle spells.

An example must be made now, to all magicians, that their powers and interference would not be tolerated. His army would destroy the one who hid among them. That death would give him tremendous power to neutralize Nimbulan before he managed to summon demons.

"Bring me the demonsniffers," he ordered the young sergeant who stood beside him on the knoll. The two women and one old man who could smell magic in a person, but had no other magic talent themselves, had formerly been called "witchsniffers." Moncriith gave them a more important role in this army—to root out spies and enemy magicians. They would have the privilege of marching at the fore of the army as they massed for battle tomorrow morning, but only after they brought him the impostor. Only after his maddened crowd had torn the magician limb from limb.

Chapter 34

"**M**aster, come quick. We need you!" Journeyman Gilby ran into Nimbulan's study without knocking. He skidded on the smooth slate floor, catching himself on the doorjamb.

"I can't step away from the workroom for five minutes without all of you flying into a panic." Nimbulan looked up from the pile of old journals he'd come to fetch. Over the years he'd kept faithful records of his life, including the numerous incantations and cantrips he used to trigger spells.

"What is wrong, Gilby? Take a deep breath and calm down. Then tell me in simple words." He motioned to his journeyman to sit in the chair beside him. The chair where Myri should be. He missed her company every minute of the day. She was on the mainland with the few girl apprentices, none of whom could gather dragon magic.

Gilby shook his head and gulped air. "A summons, sir. A desperate summons from Rollett. He used a flicker of witchlight and a cup of water. It's all he has while spying on Moncriith. He says there are witchsniffers after him and a mob screaming for blood. His blood."

"Quickly, back to the workroom. This will take a very delicate touch. I pray we have learned enough to help the boy from this distance." Nimbulan snapped his journal closed and reached for an older one from his own journeyman days.

Where was the entry he'd made about delusions? He'd read the rhyming phrases only yesterday. He scattered books across his desk in his haste to find the book. Where?

Three volumes hit the floor with thuds and skids that must have broken the spines of the bindings. He ignored them.

No book was as valuable as Rollett's life.

Why had he sent the boy to spy on Moncriith? He should have sent a mundane, someone who wouldn't rouse the Bloodmage's suspicions, or gone himself.

He couldn't lose another apprentice so soon after Keegan's death. He wouldn't let war take another person he loved.

"Here!" He grabbed the book he sought, rifling through the pages as he hurried down the hall. "We haven't time to memorize the spell. I'll read it aloud, phrase by phrase, the group will repeat each phrase with me. I hope it works. I pray we are in time." He looked out a window as they nearly ran down the corridor. No sign of any of the dragons. They were close—he sensed their presence in the constantly renewing source of magic power. But he couldn't see them. Would the spell be stronger, more easily controlled, if the magicians linked hands around a dragon?

No time to find out.

They found the assembled magicians, journeymen, and apprentices milling about the workroom in confusion.

"In a circle, grab hands. Apprentices stand outside and observe. Break the circle if something goes wrong. A fire and a glass. Where's my glass?" Nimbulan marshaled his magicians.

"An infusion of strengthening herbs, Lan, before you begin. It will help settle your nerves and focus your magic." Ackerly stood at Nimbulan's elbow with a mug of steaming brew. Nimbulan took it from him gratefully. Leave it to Ackerly to think of such a minor thing that could save the entire spell.

The stream drifted past his nose as he raised the mug to his lips. The musky sweet aroma made his muscles freeze. "You put Tambootie in the infusion."

"Yes, Lan. Like always. You need the drug to fuel your magic and channel your energies." Ackerly blinked at him in puzzlement. His wide gray eyes revealed none of his emotions. He'd also found the armor to protect his thoughts from Nimbulan's probe.

"No, I don't need this demon brew. I've broken free of the cursed drug. All I need is dragons. That's all any of us

need to fuel our magic." Impatiently, Nimbulan handed the
mug back to Ackerly. He scanned the group to ensure they
were ready for this important rescue attempt. Their glazed
eyes and vague expressions sent his heart sinking into his gut.

"How many of them drank of your evil infusions, Ackerly?" He grabbed his assistant's tunic at the throat, shaking him in frustrated anger. "They're useless like this!
We're going to lose Rollett to Moncriith's mob because
you dosed them all with the Tambootie."

"We've always used the Tambootie," Ackerly protested.
He surveyed the stain on his tunic where he'd spilled the
infusion. A dark brown stain with green and pink tinges,
just like the fresh leaves of the tree of magic, spread outward across his chest.

"Those flecks and burrs in the infusion. That's Timboor.
Timboor is poison!" Nimbulan jerked away from Ackerly
as if touching the liquid were as dangerous as drinking it.
"You set out to poison us all, just like you . . . You poisoned me last winter and left me for dead in the crypt. You
tried to murder me!" The certainty of Ackerly's guilt hit
him hard. He couldn't believe it, didn't want to believe it.
The evidence lay before him, spilled on Ackerly's tunic.

"Nonsense, Master, your wife gave me the herbs for the
infusion," Ackerly scoffed, backing toward the door, the
incriminating cup still in his hands.

"My wife hasn't been on this island since before sunup.
I'll deal with you later, Ackerly. Gilby, you and Powwell,
Haakkon, Zane . . ." No, not Zane, he couldn't gather
dragon magic. "Jaanus and Bessel, you haven't drunk any
of the poison yet. Join me. Push the others aside. We'll
help them after we rescue Rollett. Maalin, you stand aside
as control and guide."

Three deep breaths brought their talents into concert,
just as they'd practiced.

> *"Shadows and mist gather near*
> *Cloak and shade in pictures clear*
> *Those who seek through smoke and fire*
> *Will not see, through magic's spire."*

Not great poetry. But the intent was there. Nimbulan recited the formula line by line. His five companions echoed

his phrases in unison. The magic built to a whirling frenzy, demanding release. He felt a tiny surge of power from the apprentices, quickly controlled by Gilby's deft blending of energy.

"Steady, men. Hold it steady. With me, through the glass, to Rollett." Together, their minds flew into the image of flame on the other side of Nimbulan's large Master's glass. Like an arrow carefully aligned to a target, they sped with the flame across the leagues to the grassy rolling hills to the south. They bypassed Lord Kammeryl's organized and disciplined troops for the rambling campfires and scattered tents near the perimeter of the army.

The noise of hundreds of angry voices burst through their focus. One magician faltered in the quest. Another pulled him back into the group consciousness. Thoughts, dreams, aspirations—all were available to any in the group who wished to probe deeper, just as in the Rover ritual. But there wasn't the time or malice to invade a man's privacy here.

Rollett? they whispered physically and mentally. *Where are you boy? Rollett!*

An image flickered at the edge of their vision. As the tool of a solitary will, the magic arrow turned a sharp corner and sped to the feeble call of one in need. The mob turned and followed their spell, the three in front sniffing with all their senses.

Hurry, Rollett. Gather the magic in the air. Roll it into a formless mass inside you. Let us penetrate it and make a new you.

Shouts of rage and near recognition drew closer. The witchsniffers moved faster, honing in on the "scent" of powerful magic.

At last the communal magic found a target. Their arrow-like spell penetrated and exploded on impact. The essence of Rollett, his personality, his soul, his magic, burst free of the confines of his body, scattering to the four winds.

Ackerly stuffed his clothes haphazardly into a travel pack. He would be halfway to the mainland before Nimbulan thought to look for him. Anxiously, he flung the pack onto his bed and knelt on the floor by the high narrow window of his solitary cell. He pried at a loose flooring stone with his belt knife. The thin surface of slate lifted free of the square pattern of similar pieces. Beneath it, Ackerly had removed the slab of granite foundation to make a safe hiding place. He thrust his arm elbow deep into the recess until his fingers closed around the neck of a burlap bag.

Using both hands, he heaved the heavy sack onto the floor beside him. Hastily, he untied the knots with a tiny spell. So much easier to do with this new dragon magic. Gathering the ethereal energy from the air made him as powerful a magician as any other single man in the school.

Never again would he have to follow in the wake of a more powerful man, hiding in the background, performing all the menial chores delegated to servants. He had amassed the gold bit by bit for the last thirty years. Between the gold and the dragon magic, he controlled as much or more power than any man in Coronnan.

More. Because he knew how to negate the dragon magic, making Nimbulan and his precious Commune useless.

Kammeryl d'Astrismos would pay much for that knowledge. So would Moncriith. He'd summon the Bloodmage with the nature of the spell seeking to rescue Rollett as soon as he was safely on the mainland.

Ackerly cast aside the clothes he'd already assembled, filling the empty pack with the sack of gold instead.

Should he take Kalen with him? She was now outcast from the school because she couldn't gather dragon magic. She had always been outcast from Stuuvart. A brief longing for companionship with the only child he suspected he had sired almost sent him in search of the girl.

No. She couldn't gather dragon magic, so she couldn't augment his own powers. Moncriith would probably persecute her, too. They were both better off alone.

Looking up and down the corridor outside his room with all of his senses, he slipped outside the ancient monastery and headed to the sheltered cove where he kept a boat. By this time tomorrow he would be the most powerful and respected magician in all of Coronnan.

Myri looked up from her search for a sprig of fennel. A single sprig was all she needed to protect Nimbulan in the

coming battle. A shiver of danger prickled the hair on the
back of her neck.

"Look at all those people running around in circles!"
Kalen whispered to Myri. They and the two other girl apprentices lay flat at the edge of a hilltop overlooking the
army camp. Their baskets overflowing with healing flowers
and leaves—none of them the precious fennel. Myri had
taught them songs of thanksgiving to the Kardia for the
gift of each plant. As they plucked leaf and flower, a second
song sealed the healing properties into it, to be released
only when added to an infusion, ointment, or poultice.

Myri picked out Moncriith's distinctive figure with ease,
below them on a knoll at the edge of camp. His back was
to them as he faced his camp. He always stood on the
highest point around and surrounded himself with people
who stared *up* at him as if he were all three Stargods in-
carnate.

"What do you suppose they're doing?" Kalen asked.

Myri looked for a pattern in the way the people below
them massed behind three figures who held their hands
before them, seemingly sniffing the air.

"Witchsniffers!" Myri nearly choked on her own fear.
Dizziness swept over her, giving her view of the scene a
second layer. She'd watched this scene before. A piece of
a memory fell into place in Myri's mind. She and Magretha,
the old scarred witchwoman, had watched a similar scene
from the shelter of a treetop. The milling throng below
them always looked forward, never up. After an uncomfortable night catching a little sleep wedged into the fork between a stout branch and the tree trunk, she and her
guardian had descended in silence and fled to a distant
village—one that needed a witchwoman, and hadn't yet
learned to blame an ugly old woman with burn scars on one
side of her face and back for every ill that plagued them.

"We'd better run. They'll find us soon enough." Kalen
edged backward on her belly.

"Not yet. They seek someone closer. See how their hands
stay straight out in front of their noses. If they sought someone beyond their camp, their hands would sweep in wide
circles until they found a scent on the wind." Myri held the
girl in place.

Amaranth let out a piercing squawk of distress above

her. His outline looked like nothing more than a large black
raven or hawk in shadow. His cry sounded more birdlike
than cat, but deeper and more resonant than any bird.

Above his circling silhouette she caught the glimmer of
a transparent dragon wing. The larger animal radiated concern into her mind.

Myri, she greeted the dragon, giving her name. Dragon
manners seemed to require free exchange of names.

(Shayla,) the dragon replied with her own name. *(The
one they seek belongs to Nimbulan. We cannot allow the
arrogant one to succeed this time.)*

The female dragon wouldn't dignify the Bloodmage with
a true name. The arrogant one. A good description of
Moncriith.

"Whoever they are hunting needs our help. We have to
come up with a plan," Myri said to her charges. She turned
her attention back to Moncriith and the witchsniffers.

"They keep going back to the same tent, around and
around it. The circles get narrower every time." Kalen
pointed to a small canvas shelter barely large enough to
hold one man.

It wasn't the last tent within the perimeter of the camp,
but very near the edge, as if the owner were a latecomer
or wished a rapid exit.

"And look at Moncriith." The little girl stood up, hands
on hips, an expression of outrage on her face. "He's cheating. Look at his aura. He's amplifying the emotions of the
crowd following the sniffers. He's the one crying for blood
and making them think it's *their* wish."

"Rollett is down there." Myri remembered clearly that
Nimbulan had sent the young man, Lan's most trusted journeyman, to spy on Moncriith yesterday afternoon. Rollett
had been eager to test his skills as an observer, as well as
his ability to disguise himself. A simple delusion, altering
only hair and eye color, required enough magic to alert a
witchsniffer. "How, Shayla? How can we help him?"

A prickling on the back of her neck warned her of danger. She ducked, drawing Kalen and another girl back down
to the grass. An arrow of magic whizzed past them, speeding directly for the tent that must belong to Rollett.

The shimmering spell spun as it flew, sending out tiny
rainbows. It paused briefly, turned abruptly, then plunged

faster and faster toward the tent. The silent impact sent shards of colors radiating into the air like a sunburst. When the tiny points of light drifted to the ground like colored snowflakes, the tent was gone. Vanished in an eyeblink.

Above them, Shayla heaved a sigh of relief.

Myri looked closer with all of her senses. A dome of transparent magic now covered the space where the tent had been. Its presence was discernible only by the distortion of light around it—like looking at a dragon.

The witchsniffers paused in their seeking. Their arms began a new dance of sweeping wide circles. They'd lost their prey and now sought a new direction, following a similar dome of transparent magic that drifted to the east of camp.

"We have to provide a diversion, or they'll find him for sure." Kalen jumped up again. She closed her eyes and frowned in concentration as she drew energy from the Kardia.

Myri felt the pull of a ley line to the north of them. She, too, drew on it to fuel a spell. *Land in the next valley, Shayla, and mount Rollett on your back. No one in the camp will see you. They'll all be looking at us,* she said to the dragon.

(Agreed. Amaranth will guard you until I return for you.)

Beside Myri, Kalen wove a delusion around herself. With each heartbeat she grew taller, broader. Her simple leather tunic and trews shifted toward red tones, stretched into a blood-red robe. Her features took on masculine coarseness. In a moment, an exact replica of Moncriith stood on top of the hill. Then Kalen, beneath the disguise, raised her hands, palms outward in a traditional gesture of benediction. Only the slightly downward curving little and third fingers indicated that she captured threads of the Kardia and wove them together to create her appearance.

The witchsniffers looked up, their seeking arms stopped circling. Fingers and noses pointed accusingly at the new Moncriith on the hill, in a direct line with the original figure. From the vantage point of the mob, the sniffers were pointing at their leader as the source of magic they should seek out and murder.

"Oh, you wicked child!" Myri laughed.

"I can't hold it very long. I don't know how to . . ." The

delusion collapsed. Only a very tired little girl in scratched journey leathers remained, hands to knees, head bowed, panting raggedly.

The witchsniffers faltered again in their quest.

"If you can't sustain the delusion, I'll have to try." Myri gathered the threads of energy in her fingers and spun them around her. From memory she painted a portrait of her enemy on her own face, recreating his signature robes and untrimmed hair and beard.

The seekers found the scent again and marched forward, a confused and angry mob in their wake. They surrounded the knoll where the real Moncriith stood, hands held out in mute appeal. He screamed something at his followers. Fear laced his tones.

Myri fought to sustain the spell. Fatigue threatened to drag the delusion back into the Kardia where it originated. She only needed to hold the spell a little longer. A little longer. Just until Rollett escaped.

Her contact with the ley line drained away. The threads of magic she held within her fingers threatened to tangle.

She gritted her teeth and found the strength to hold the spell. Sweat broke out on her brow. Moisture trickled down her back.

She looked carefully at the scene below her. Moncriith and his three witchsniffers charged up the hill toward her. Shouts of rage filled their voices. Murder glinted in their eyes.

Chapter 35

"**D**id we do it?" Nimbulan asked the magicians who slumped near him. Their hands still linked them together, but the fire in the brazier had gone out and the magic drained away.

"I don't know," Gilby whispered through gritted teeth.

The others shook their heads in confirmation of losing track of the spell. Their stomachs growled in unison. They had used tremendous amounts of energy to throw the magic.

"We have to try again," Nimbulan ordered. "We have to make sure Rollett is safe." Fire burned across his still-healing knife wound. He ignored the nagging pain and re-kindled the fire with a snap of his fingers. He held the glass up before the flames. All he saw was fire, slightly magnified. Frantically, he cast about him for more dragon magic. He sensed none in the air around him. Had they used up the entire supply?

Rollett was still in danger. Nimbulan had to do everything to save him. Ley lines still permeated the area. He reached for the nearest one and ran into a solid wall of resistance.

"No, Nimbulan." Old Lyman placed a surprisingly strong hand upon his wrist. "We must forget ley lines altogether. That is why the shadowed guardian of this place sealed the well of Kardia magic. If communal magic is to succeed, we must never again resort to solitary sources, no matter how desperate the need."

Nimbulan blinked rapidly, trying to bring the old man into focus. "Rollett is still in danger. I can't let him die like Keegan."

Lyman blurred and stabilized, blurred again, mist or smoke cloaked his outline. Finally, his form came back into focus. Nimbulan blinked once more. Slowly. Hard. When he opened his eyes, Lyman had resumed his place on the other side of the circle from him. Had the old man momentarily taken on the form of the shadowed guardian, or had fatigue and pain played tricks with Nimbulan's vision?

"Rollett's life is now in the hands of the Stargods. We did what we could," Lyman said.

"You might add the dragons to your list of thanks. More specially, Shayla." Rollett himself wandered into the room, looking slightly dazed, limping and cradling his left arm in his right hand. His dark curly hair stood out around his head as if he stood in a strong wind.

"Rollett!" Nimbulan flung himself at the young man. Jaanus followed suit, embracing his classmate and his master. "You're safe, boy. You're safe," they repeated over and over.

"Yes, yes, I am," Rollett murmured, amazed at his good fortune.

"How? Tell us all. We need to know the details in case we have to repeat the procedure." Lyman took control of the emotional outbursts.

"I felt your summons. My cup of water throbbed so violently, I thought it would shatter with the force of your demand that I join your spell. I held it up to my flicker of witchlight and suddenly the world seemed to explode with colors. Like lightning growing outward from the water. But it didn't spread very far. When I could focus my eyes, I looked around, and everything within my tent shimmered with that odd iridescent light that you see when you look directly at a dragon and find yourself looking beyond it." He looked around the room for confirmation that they understood.

A twitter of tension-breaking laughter flickered around the room.

"Well, I took a chance and peeked outside the tent,'" Rollett continued. "The witchsniffers and their mob stopped and veered off in a new direction. I slipped out of the tent, and walked as fast as I could in the opposite direction. I wanted to be as far from them as possible. But when I looked back, the tent was invisible. I just stood there in amazement when one of Moncriith's pet sergeants ran past me. He couldn't have been more than an arm's length away, but he didn't see me!"

Nimbulan's heart lightened with relief. He lost a little sensation around the edges as he took in the import of his journeyman's tale. They had used dragon magic to make the boy as invisible as a dragon!

"Then what happened?" Nimbulan prompted, eager to know why Rollett had included the dragons in his list of thanks, other than their wonderful gift of communal magic.

"I ran. I ran as fast as I could over the top of the next hill. I tripped and fell, but I got up and kept running." He winced slightly and shifted his weight off his right foot.

Jaanus rushed to get him a high stool. Rollett sank onto it gratefully, still cradling his left arm. He stretched out his long legs. His torso slumped a little as if he suddenly realized how tired and hurt he really was.

"Halfway down that hill I tripped again and rolled. That must have been how I wrenched my shoulder. I could hear the shouts of the mob. Their blood lust was up and nothing was going to stop them. They were coming my way again, I don't know if they sensed me or not. I thought I was done for, but I suddenly stopped rolling. Something very big stopped me. Shayla."

Everyone in the room nodded. They all knew precisely how big Shayla was. As wide as two sledge steeds and as tall as two more. Several tons of dragon presented a formidable wall to run up against.

"She didn't speak to me, but I knew a compulsion to climb up onto her back. It was a struggle with the ankle and the arm, but I managed to hold onto her spines, and half a heartbeat later we were airborne."

Nimbulan lived again the bunching of dragon muscles between his legs, the tremendous wind generated by the first downstroke of powerful wings. The sensation of his throat sinking to his belly as the Kardia fell away and they broke free of the pull of gravity. Shayla had insisted she and her consorts bring him and Myri and the children back to the island. He hoped to experience those thrilling moments of true flight again some day.

"We stopped on the other side of Moncriith's camp and plucked Myrilandel and the girls from a hilltop. The mob seemed to be pointing at them and getting ready to run after them. But one sight of that dragon and they all turned tail and ran. All except Moncriith. I saw him whip out his knife and slash his forearm to begin a spell." Rollett swayed briefly with relief and pain. "Shayla flew high and fast, and we stayed ahead of whatever he threw at us."

"Let me send for Myri. You need to have her look at your injuries." Nimbulan pressed the young man's uninjured shoulder in reassurance.

"Sorry, she's not here," Rollett replied. "On the way back we flew past Lord Hanic's army. They're on their way here, but I don't know if they can get here before Kammeryl does. Shayla took Myri back that way. Maybe they can hurry them along. I'll have to hunt up Ackerly to look at this shoulder. Maybe Guillia can fix me a poultice for the ankle."

"Ackerly." All thought and movement ceased in Nimbulan. In the rush of the spell and the excitement of Rollett's return, he'd forgotten Ackerly. For a moment, disbelief riddled him with guilt for his harsh words. Ackerly couldn't have betrayed him, tried to murder him with an overdose of Timboor. They'd been friends and colleagues for too long. They depended upon each other for too much. They had saved each other many times. Shared too much of their lives.

"Shall we bring the man to the refectory for judgment or take him to Lord Quinnault?" Jaannus asked reluctantly.

"I suppose we should take him to the lord's hall. These islands still belong to him. He has the right of governance among us. But I hate to turn over a magician to a mundane," Nimbulan said.

"He's Quinnault the Peacemaker, not Kammeryl the destroyer," Lyman reminded him. "He'll understand that Ackerly is still human, with a man's motives and failings and not a demon. We have to obey the laws if we are to set an example for the rest of the kingdom and bring about peaceful living under the law."

"We can't let personal feelings get in the way of the law." Nimbulan hung his head in a moment of grief. "The evidence suggests the man tried to murder me. He must face the law as represented by Lord Quinnault de Tanos."

* * *

"I wish I could fly," Myri said. Idly, she twirled a long stem of grass in her hands while she leaned against Shayla's flank. The grass was very like fennel, but not the precious herb of protection she sought. Maybe if they sought farther north, in a warmer, drier clime, they would find what she needed.

Below the hillside where they perched, Lord Hanic's army hurried along the trader road. If they marched all day and night, they might arrive in time to bolster Quinnault's small defensive force. But then they'd be too tired to fight.

Myri wondered what she could do to prevent the battle as she stroked Amaranth's sleek black fur. He snoozed in the nest of Shayla's curled forelegs. The flywacket seemed more at home there than he did in Myri's lap lately.

"I have dreams of flying." Myri returned to her original thought. If they had one hundred dragons, they might be able to fly the army to the islands. With such a great show of force Kammeryl d'Astrismos would have to retreat and rethink his battle plans.

(You must forget your dreams of flight, my child. Your destiny no longer lies with the dragons,) Shayla replied. *(You are happy with your consort. You must remain with him, not fly with your nimbus of dragons.)*

"I love Lan very much. I don't know what I'll do if he dies in this battle."

(You will survive. We promised you a home and family. You must weave no more magic, to save even the ones you love,) Shayla said.

"The spell I wove to distract the crowd from Rollett was only a delusion. A simple spell," she defended herself.

('Tis not the strength of the spell that will harm your baby. Any spell will change its destiny before it has a chance to make its own. You were victim of one spell too many. Don't do that to your own child.)

"Baby?" Myri sat up straight, her spine rigid, not touching the dragon in any way. Shayla's presumption that she carried a child was much more important than the fleeting glimpse of her past. "Witchwomen cannot conceive, and magicians cannot sire."

(Granted, this blessing is rarely given to those of your kind. Magicians have poisoned their bodies with Tambootie for many generations. This prevents them from fathering

children. But you are not like most witchwomen and Nimbulan has rid his body of the Tambootie. Together you have made a new life. Do not deny what your heart and your body tell you are true.)

"You and your consorts eat of the Tambootie tree, heavily, and produce many babies."

(The Tambootie is a part of dragonkind—both native to Kardia Hodos. Humans came from elsewhere a long time ago. We cannot live without the Tambootie. But what mutates within us to produce the magical energy men may gather is a slow poison when consumed by men and women.)

"I have never taken the Tambootie, and yet I have not conceived before this. Why now?" Gently she touched her belly with sensitive fingertips. Too soon to detect any swelling. She didn't dare probe the life with her magic, not when Shayla had specifically warned her not to weave any spells at all.

(Witchwomen have too much control over their own bodies and do not involuntarily conceive. They have strong instincts that tell them who will be a good father and who will not. Magic and solitude to study and perfect their talent is more important to them than husbands and family. You have that control, my child, and sensed that the time is right. The man is right. Your heart overrode your mind and let you conceive. A new era begins for humans in this realm. Your child will be among those who spread the benefits of dragon magic and prevent the carnage that has plagued both humans and dragons for too many years.)

"Men will always go to war."

(But they will not fight with magic. One last battle will settle the place of magic in your realm. After the last battle, magicians and dragons will control all magic. Mundanes will control the battles and only look to magicians for wisdom.)

"One last battle," Myri mused. She started to stand then sat back down again, leaning hard against the recumbent dragon. "I don't know if I can deal with the aftermath of a battle. I can't throw any healing spells for fear of damaging the baby. How can I not heal suffering men?"

Amaranth awakened with a squeak and moved to her lap. He butted her hand with his head, demanding a caress, offering comfort in the same gesture.

"I have to find the fennel before then. It is the only thing I know that will protect Lan if I can't use my magic to save him."

(Trust Lyman. He is one of us. Amaranth will show you what to do when the time comes.)

"I wish there were a way to avoid this."

(We are too late to intervene. See that man to the southeast of where we sit?)

Myri shielded her eyes from the lowering sun. The silhouette of a man burdened by a heavy pack became visible on the ridge. "I see him."

(That is the gold man.) Shayla gave him no name. That could only mean the dragons feared or distrusted him. *(The man who loves gold more than he loves life.)*

Myri recognized Ackerly's distinctive gait and posture.

(He flees Nimbulan's wrath to the camp of the enemy of dragons. He will make certain there is a battle. Now you must survey this ground and plan ahead. Come, I will take you to the battlefield.)

A short dragon flight took them to a different hillside overlooking a vast plain spreading more than a league toward the river.

"Here?" Myri looked more closely at the flat ground surrounded on three sides by low hills. The rises on the east and west ends of the meadow rose more gently than where she stood. She turned a slow circle, pausing as she looked south where a chain of hills undulated upward in a familiar pattern.

"Here." She resigned herself to the inevitable. "They fought the last battle here. Last autumn, when I first met my husband."

(They fought the same battle here twenty years ago. The battle that loosed uncontrolled magic into the skies and nearly killed me. But this will be the last battle fought on this land.)

"Strange that here I find a single stalk of fennel." Myri plucked the elusive plant and cradled it in her hands like a living baby.

Nimbulan warily eyed a burly lieutenant wearing the colors of Kammeryl d'Astrismos' personal guard as the man marched up to the dais where Quinnault presided over a celebratory meal. The day was nearly finished and they had accomplished so little other than Rollett's rescue. Now the various forces seeking power and control over Coronnan were poised for an inevitable convergence. A very destructive clash.

Tonight the magicians and mudanes gathered in celebration of the successful rescue and one last attempt to make merry before they faced death in battle on the morrow.

"In the name of His Majesty, Kammeryl the First, descendant of the Stargods, King of Coronnan, Master of Hanassa, and Lord of The Great Bay, I demand the surrender of this keep, its surrounding islands, all tenants and leaseholders, boats and vessels, and all buildings," the soldier bellowed for all within Quinnault de Tanos' Great Hall to hear. He held a parchment at arm's length as if he read the document. He allowed it to roll shut with a snap before finishing his statement. Proof to Nimbulan that this man, like all mundanes, had never been taught to read.

"But I do not recognize *Lord* Kammeryl's authority as king. Nor do the seven lords who have signed my mutual defense treaty," Quinnault said. He turned mild eyes up to the soldier for a brief moment, then returned to his meal as if that were much more important than the prattling of the soldier. Only the twitching of his fingers against his table knife betrayed his emotions.

Nimbulan silently applauded the lord for his cool exterior. The soldier had to know that all of the united lords were too far away to send aid in time. Quinnault's only hope for victory in battle lay with Lord Hanic, if he arrived in time. If he decided to help Quinnault and not Kammeryl.

The soldier's face colored briefly. He sucked in his cheeks and squared his shoulders. "Refusal of His Majesty's demands will bring quick and terrible reprisal."

"Tell Lord Kammeryl the united lords will discuss this matter with him directly and not through an underling." Quinnault waved his hand in dismissal. His long fingers made the movement graceful and compelling.

Myri used the same gesture when she finished feeding her flusterhens in the clearing. Nimbulan clutched the little bag of fennel seeds Myri had given him on a thong to wear around his neck. Then he reached the same hand to squeeze her shoulder. Her love protected him more than any plant.

The soldier stood his ground. "No discussion or delay is permitted. Either you accept the orders of your rightful king or you do not."

"Before we can acknowledge Kammeryl d'Astrismos as rightful anything," Nimbulan said, "His Lordship must return the criminal Ackerly to Lord Quinnault for lawful judgment." He stood from his chair on Quinnault's right, pressing his fists against the table until his knuckles turned white. Anger at his assistant's betrayal and his own lack of foresight closed his throat.

Myri covered his hand with her own. Calm spread through him.

The soldier paused, ducking his head and touching his right ear lobe with his right middle finger.

"He's being coached," Nimbulan whispered to Quinnault. "Every word we say is heard by a magician in Kammeryl's camp. They are instructing him now. Every time he touches his ear, he activates the communication spell."

"We must get rid of this messenger.'" A moment of fear crossed Quinnault's eyes.

"How? If we capture and detain him, we have issued a challenge to Kammeryl's authority, bringing immediate reprisal. If we break his contact with Kammeryl, we challenge him. If we stall and send him away we outright deny his right to rule. Your choice, Lord Quinnault de Tanos," Nimbulan said quietly. "Every choice is designed to bring about a battle that will decide our future."

Quinnault deliberately turned his back on the soldier. "I have never fought a battle before. I maintain no army. I have no weapons. But I'll be damned if I acknowledge a warrior who sees war as the solution to all problems as my king."

"Then we must fight a battle. But on our own terms. Kammeryl has made a mistake in not attacking us covertly."

"The islands are easily defended. He wouldn't get very far."

"Then he must draw you into open battle. *We* must choose the time and place. Dismiss the messenger," Nimbulan replied sadly. Myri's hand on his tightened convulsively. Her healing talent would be needed many times over if the Commune of Magicians failed. He worried already that she would kill herself trying to save Quinnault's followers.

Quinnault turned back to face the now-grinning messenger. The soldier's middle finger caressed his earlobe again.

"I believe you already know our answer. Return to Lord Kammeryl at once." Quinnault raised his hand, palm outward in a gesture of goodwill.

Startled by the lord's gracious attitude, the soldier backed out of the Great Hall, half-bowing in respect. Kammeryl d'Astrismos would have executed the messenger bearing distasteful news.

"Now, how do we fight this battle, Nimbulan?" Quinnault stared at his half-eaten meal. "I have no army. Hanic is not here and not a certain ally if he arrives in time. My other allies are spread across all of Coronnan and can't arrive in time. How will I face Kammeryl d'Astrismos and the Bloodmage?"

Chapter 36

The sun had not yet broken the horizon when Myri felt the rush of dragon wings as the great beasts rose into the sky. They circled the battlefield where two armies prepared to face each other with weapons and magicians. Myri and the three apprentice girls waited on a hilltop behind the chosen field of battle.

Where was the third army? Lord Hanic could have been here, if he chose.

She turned her face into the wind, cherishing the power of the moving air. Her shoulders rotated as her arms lifted to grasp the freedom of flight. If she flew with the dragons, she could observe every movement on the field and warn Nimbulan through the silver cord that still connected her heart to his.

(We watch for you. Do not fly. Remember your unborn child,) Shayla warned her.

She picked up Amaranth, needing his purring warmth to replace her need to fly. "Why, Amaranth? Why is the desire for flight so strong in me?" she whispered to the flywacket.

Nimbulan had ordered her to remain well back of the coming fray. At the first sign of trouble for the Commune and the forces of Quinnault, she was to flee with the girls, as far and as fast as she might. She would rather be at his side for every one of his last moments.

"I have to protect the baby from the battle as well as my own magic. The baby may be all I have left of him after today." She hadn't told Nimbulan about her pregnancy. It was still too early for her body to provide proof that she carried a new life within her. Who would believe that a witchwoman and magician had managed the impossible?

She held Amaranth tightly, burying her face in his fur. He squawked at her fierce hug and straggled in her arms, eager to join the dragons in flight. Uncharacteristically, he pushed at her with his back paws, talons unsheathed. Unable to restrain him, Myri released him to the soaring freedom they both craved.

Up and up the black flywacket spiraled in wider circles. He stretched his neck and wings, growing longer, wider, sleeker with each movement.

Myri blinked against the increasing daylight. Amaranth paled. She lost sight of him against the emerging sun. He screeched his joy. She followed the sound of his voice. A shaft of sunlight caught the last of the purple/black fur as it transformed into silvery crystals tipped with lavender.

Memories flooded her. Memories of flight, of diving into the Great Bay to hunt bemouths, the huge fish that terrorized sailors who washed overboard, but could feed an entire village for a week if captured. She remembered watching as her mother, Shayla, brought her and Amaranth, her twin, to the edge of a burial ground in the dark of night—at the site of a human tomb.

Shayla was her mother! A lifetime of seeking her heritage fell into place. Tears streamed down her cheeks. Mixed joy and fear at finally knowing sent her to her knees as she relived the last time she saw her mother in dragon form.

(One of you must choose to inhabit the body of this human child. There can only be one purple dragon alive at any one time. One of you can no longer live with the nimbus,) Shayla had instructed on that long ago night.

Myrilandel—then Amethyst—and Amaranth had quibbled and argued over the great honor to become human, to grow and learn, to guide other humans to live in harmony with dragonkind.

In the end, Amethyst had managed the shapechange faster than her brother. Amaranth was so lonely and bereft without his twin, his otherself, he had taken the form of the flywacket and become the human child's familiar. Shayla had deposited them both near the home of Magretha, a witchwoman with a longing for a child and the magic potential to teach Amethyst all she needed to know.

But remnants of Myrilandel's spirit had lingered in her not-quite-dead body. Dragon memories disappeared in the face of very strong human memories of name and personality. The two spirits in the same body compromised on forgetfulness.

"I remember how to fly now. Amaranth, wait for me." She lifted her arms again, willing the change to overtake her.

(No, my child. Amaranth is the only purple-tip dragon now. You must stay human. You must remain Nimbulan's consort and helpmate.) Shayla said.

"Why? Why must there only be one purple-tip when we were born twins?" Myri almost cried with regret that she could not fly. A small piece of satisfaction also dwelled within her. She couldn't leave Nimbulan. She had to remain human for him, for their child.

('Tis the way of dragons. For as long as dragons have claimed this planet, purple-tips have been born as twins. Their destinies are special and separate. One may remain with the nimbus, the other must seek to fill a vacancy in the world—a vacancy that if left empty will endanger all dragons.)

The need to fly temporarily overrode her emotional bonds with Nimbulan. She'd come back to this human body later. But she *had* to fly now! As a dragon, she'd be able to protect Nimbulan. She spread her arms once more, willing them to form wings. No, the wings must sprout from her back. The pronounced bone structure along her back must elongate into the showy march of purple-tipped spines.

(Do not forget your child, Myrilandel. Purple dragons are very rare and very special, but they are neither male nor female. If you revert now, your child will be lost forever. There will never be another. Will you kill Nimbulan's child so that you may fly?) Shayla asked.

Myri lowered her arms and hung her head. Her hands curved protectively around her still-flat belly. "I can't become a dragon again and aid my husband by giving him dragon magic. I can't use my talent to heal those who will be wounded. What am I to do? I can't just wait and watch and do nothing while men die!"

Kalen reached up and held her hand in mute sympathy.

(You will be needed. Amaranth will show you. Anyone, even a mundane, can gather magic from a purple dragon. But you must be touching him when the time comes. And you must be very careful. Lyman will help you.) Shayla's voice faded as the dragon turned her concentration to the spells Nimbulan and his enemies prepared.

Nimbulan stood on the knoll at the east end of the battlefield. He rested his foot on the magic-blasted stump, one elbow on his raised knee. The view before him was much the same as it had been last autumn—as it would have been to Druulin twenty years past.

Two armies faced each other, each grouped around the slight rise where their Battlemage prepared to direct the course of the battle. Behind the mages, assistants, apprentices and messengers waited to assist.

He didn't need to be an empath to feel the tension roiling through the air. Men on both sides paced restlessly, checked and rechecked weapons, fussed with steed harnesses. They spoke in whispers, then snapped at each other in loud shouts over trivia.

Nimbulan had seen it all before—with and without the magical enhancement to his sight that allowed him to view details across the entire plain. With luck and the help of the dragons, he would never have to see it again.

This time Nimbulan opposed his oldest friend and former assistant, Ackerly, instead of a beloved apprentice. This time he had a nimbus of dragons hovering in the sky above. This time he had Myri to go back to at the end of a long day.

He straightened from his contemplative pose. Instantly his assistants, Master Magicians, journeymen, and apprentices, jumped to the ready. Anticipation fluttered in his belly while apprehension sharpened his already-heightened eyesight and sense of smell. The scent of fear wafted up from the ranks of farmers and laborers hiding behind a delusion of armor and weaponry. A few had fought in battle before. A very few compared to the numbers gathered in the attacking army.

A trick of the light quadrupled the men's shadows in Quinnault's army. Kammeryl d'Astrismos would have a hard time accurately estimating the number and strength of the troops. But would the trick fool Ackerly and the Bloodmage?

"This is the last time," he declared to himself. "This must be the last battle."

Across the way, Nimbulan spied a bustle of activity around Ackerly's robed form. He wore bright yellow today, the signature color of his own magic rather than Nimbulan's blue.

A second magician in formal robes of scarlet stepped to the front. He held up the carcass of a butchered goat for all to see. His ritual knife dripped red. The Bloodmage. Moncriith. Fear, pain, and the spilling of more blood on the field of battle would fuel his magic above and beyond the endurance of most solitary magicians.

Would the combined might of the communal magic be enough to defeat him?

"Never again, Bloodmage. Your kind will never practice magic in Coronnan again," he vowed.

Nimbulan raised his hand, palm outward, fingers slightly curved, little finger crooked in a half circle. The temptation to spin the threads of the Kardia nearly overpowered him. "Force of habit." He shook his hand free of the tingling ley lines radiating over the entire surface of the planet.

> *"Gather dragons,*
> *gather guardians,*
> *magic bright and dear.*
> *Gather power,*
> *gather union,*
> *Join the vision clear."*

He commanded the men and boys assembled behind him. He felt the shuffling and aligning as they all joined hands. Rollett and Lyman each placed a hand on his shoulder to bring him into the chain of mounting power. His hands were free to throw the spells he devised in the course of the battle.

Across the way, Ackerly wove his hands in an ancient pattern to call forth firebombs. The Bloodmage drew an arcane pattern in the grass at his feet with the bloodied ritual knife.

A moment of inadequacy flashed before Nimbulan. He'd done this before as chief Battlemage for a powerful warlord. But never before had he performed this chore with so much at stake.

"Peace," he reminded himself. "We earn peace with this one last confrontation."

A dragon rose up into the sky from behind him. The rising sun caught the crystal outlines, showering the field with rainbows. He scanned the wingspan. Red. Rouussin. Nimbulan had learned all of their names, all of their histories last night. As they had learned his. The magicians and dragons worked today in true communion.

The big male dragon craned his neck, peering directly at Ackerly and the Bloodmage.

The Bloodmage recoiled, throwing his right arm, still holding the knife, over his eyes to shield him from the beneficent light.

Ackerly laughed at the man's fear. The traitorous assistant swelled his chest as he gathered the tremendous amount of dragon magic in the air.

Between the two knolls, the army of Kammeryl d'Astrismos edged backward, bunching up in disorderly knots. They cowered away from the dragon, looking to the officers mounted on their flanks and to their rear for direction.

Good. The space between the two armies widened appreciably, giving Nimbulan room to work his spell.

"You want to play with fire, Ackerly? I'll give you more fire than you bargained for." He wished he'd had time to devise a specific tactic rather than randomly counter whatever the enemy threw at him.

Lyman began the first line of the spell. Then all of the gathered Commune repeated the words in unison. Power built within them. Nimbulan spoke the words by rote, paying little heed to their meaning, concentrating all of the massing energy into powerful arrows that would explode the firebombs into tiny fragments that lacked enough heat to ignite anything.

Ackerly launched his balls of flame. They whizzed over the heads of Kammeryl's army, arcing upward, then descending toward the farmers and craftsmen who made up Quinnault's forces.

Nimbulan threw his probes into the bombs. Tiny arrows of light sped toward the dozen flaming missiles.

Moncriith shouted a chant of discordant sounds.

Nimbulan's probes ran into a solid wall of magic, finger-lengths from their targets. The balls of flame continued forward. Quinnault's men ducked and held their few shields over their heads.

Nimbulan launched a new round of arrows on a shorter flight path. Spell met spell in a blinding flash directly in front of his eyes. He blinked and shook his head, trying to clear it of the dazzle blindness.

Below him, Quinnault's army sagged in relief, but they didn't break formation. Nimbulan let go a tiny sigh of satisfaction. The men were loyal. They wouldn't break easily.

Moncriith smiled briefly in acknowledgment of Nimbulan's quick thinking. He launched a spell of his own. A dense cloud formed above the center of the field. Lightning flashed within the roiling darkness. The mist sent out seeking tentacles toward the ranks of Quinnault's men. Each thrusting coil of blackness was tipped with searing green fire.

Kammeryl's army surged forward in the wake of the cloud. Quinnault's men threw up their hands and shields to protect their heads from the fires and jerked backward in a wave.

Nimbulan countered the cloud with a gush of water gathered from the nearby river. It dissolved and scattered harmlessly. He still had to deal with the seasoned troops rushing forward, weapons raised, battlecries ululating from their throats.

Quickly he levitated a cache of metal throwing stars at the attackers. The razor-sharp weapons faltered in their trajectory and dropped harmlessly to the ground. Neither Ackerly nor Moncriith had countered the spell.

Who? Who else interfered with this battle?

Kammeryl's forces swept closer.

Nimbulan tried to resurrect the throwing stars with a rapid series of hand motions. He had to levitate them before they buried themselves deep in the Kardia, never to be used again.

The throwing stars remained inert.

"Quickly, Nimbulan, shatter their weapons. Do it before they kill anyone." Myri tugged anxiously at his arm.

He didn't stop to question her presence. He didn't dare think about the danger she might be in.

The first rank crashed into Quinnault's amateur defenders.

> *"Metal grow brittle*
> *fragile become*
> *shatter like spittle*
> *dive into the loam."*

He threw the hastily invented poem at the clashing armies.

Swords and pikes, lances and shields all crumbled into thousands of pieces. As directed, the shards of metal sank deeply into the top layer of dirt, just as the throwing stars had.

Men from both armies looked in dismay at their weaponless hands, at missing armor, and finally at their Battlemages for explanation. They shuffled back and forth in indecision.

"Shayla says you can only use the magic for defense. You can't attack," Myri cried, still hanging onto Nimbulan's arm. "The throwing stars couldn't obey your spell."

"Defend?" He looked at her, a little dazed at the concept. He'd always worked for strong warlords who considered the best defense to be an overwhelming offense.

"Look above you, men," Moncriith shouted across the field. Magic augmented his voice so that all could hear. "Look at the demons that force this battle. Do you wish to be slaves of the demons? Do you wish to lose your souls as well as your lives to them? My magic is stronger than theirs. I have neutralized Nimbulan, the greatest Battlemage of our time. I have ended his powers and shattered your weapons! Now I will liberate the souls of all those who have died on this field in times past. They shall no longer be the tools of the demons."

"He's using magic to make all believe his lies," Lyman whispered in Nimbulan's ear. "If we can show the people how he lies . . . *Stargods,* he's doing it!"

Nimbulan looked where the old man pointed. Mist boiled up from the river banks. The dense fog rolled inland too rapidly to be natural. Within heartbeats, the stifling moisture enveloped Nimbulan and his Commune.

Shifting clouds within clouds distorted images within a few inches of Nimbulan's nose. Trees and outcroppings took on engorged dimensions. They seemed to move and shift from place to place as distance and time lost all meaning.

The gray water vapor brightened to green smoke, backlit as if by natural fire. Coiling tendrils writhed and formed faces in the fearsome mist.

"Armies of the dead. They march toward us through the fog," one of the young apprentices screamed. He broke the link with the magicians on either side of him. The power of Communal magic dissipated into the mist.

Ghostly faces solidified, clothed in the armor of twenty years ago. Horrible wounds of lance and fire showed through rents in rotting tunics in the colors of lords long-dead.

Druulin, face and hands horribly burned, stared directly at Nimbulan. Accusing. Demanding retribution for betrayal and desertion.

Nimbulan's body and will froze in the face of his master. He hadn't died with Druulin twenty years ago because he and Ackerly had deserted their master. They had been cowardly and disloyal. They deserved to die now. Die as horribly as Druulin had. . . .

"Stargods, he's conjured the dead from previous battles fought in this field." Lyman's hand jerked against Nimbulan's shoulder as if to ward himself with the cross of the Stargods.

The ward broke the mesmerizing stare from Druulin's ghost. Nimbulan closed his eyes and mind to the horrible accusations of his mentor.

"Stay linked!" Nimbulan ordered. "We cannot fight the Bloodmage individually. We have to stay together."

Above him, dragon wings beat against the stagnating air.

The fog faded but the dead continued to march forward, intent on killing any who stood in their way.

> *"Misty wraiths, lost in time,*
> *Seek your fate in love benign.*
> *Go your way, your life fulfilled,*
> *The void restores your spirits killed."*

He chanted an invitation for the displaced ghosts to find their way back to the void and their next existence. The magicians behind him repeated the incantation.

They recited the spell a third time, together with growing confidence.

The fog thinned. Ghostly faces dissolved. The screams of terror faded in the ranks of soldiers caught between the two Battlemages.

"See the lost souls demons have betrayed and prevented from finding their next existence. I send them away in peace," Moncriith proclaimed.

"A little late, Moncriith," Nimbulan said as he gathered his wits to face the next attack from the Bloodmage.

The slight river breeze that dissipated the mist took on a musky, sweet scent. Real smoke replaced the mist. The smoke of burning green Tambootie mixed with Timboor.

Nimbulan raised his hands to place a barrier between himself and the deadly smoke. No power tingled in his palms. He had no magic left to protect his troops or his magicians. He gasped for breath and took in a lungful of the poisonous smoke. In a moment, he'd begin hallucinating.

He thrust Myri behind him to protect her as much as he could.

Chapter 37

Ackerly fanned the flames higher on his bonfire of fresh and aged Tambootie limbs. The green flames licked hungrily at the fuel. Smoke poured upward in a spiraling column. The wind was already from the west, born in the cold mountain range, seeking the warmer flatter plains of Coronnan. He needed no magic to send the smoke directly into Nimbulan's face.

Years of suppressed resentment for his childhood friend and companion built with each puff of smoke and burning log. "Your respect for me was measured against the size of my talent, Nimbulan." He stabbed at the fire with a fresh stick, building the flames higher, high enough to burn the green wood with the deadly sap still in it.

"You measured everyone against your own magical talent and none of us matched you, so you were superior to all. You used everyone you came in contact with—made them clean up the mess you left behind. You had to be the best, so only your desires, your talents, and your wisdom mattered. But where would you be if I hadn't arranged your business affairs, taught the apprentices, kept you fed, and made sure you had a tent to sleep in? Well let me tell you, Nimbulan, I can gather magic now, as easily as any of your Commune. I can work any spell I want with very little effort. I'm as good as you. Better. Because I also have the gold. Gold to buy people and luxuries and respect. That's something you'll never have. No one will respect you unless you possess gold and are willing to make more gold. Only gold matters to mundanes."

He threw another stick into the greedy flames. The fire burned too hot. The smoke climbed too high before spread-

ing out and engulfing the opposing magicians. He called up
more wind. Harder to do that now. Why?

The dragons, dimly visible above the battlefield withdrew. The magic disappeared with them. Ackerly delved
into the store of magic within his body. The Commune
hadn't figured out how to do that yet. He'd stumbled on it
by accident. Only he knew that unlike the old magic, this
new power could be stored for later use. The dragons didn't
have to be present for him to work magic.

"I'll see you in chains before this day is done, Nimbulan.
And I will rejoice because you will be my servant and your
dragons will help me. Dragons like gold. They hoard and
treasure it. My gold makes me one with them. Only me!"
he chortled as he danced around the fire. He made a full
circle, skipping and hopping, clapping his hands.

Moncriith looked at him strangely.

"You have your rituals, I have mine," Ackerly yelled
back at the man with knife scars all over his face, hands
and body, from where he'd drawn blood to fuel his magic.

Moncriith didn't understand true power either. His scars
marked him as a powerful Bloodmage. He created fear
wherever he went. But he had no gold. Only gold bought
power.

As Ackerly laughed again, the wind shifted. He gulped
a great draught of the smoke. Dizziness shifted and fractured his vision. He covered his mouth with his sleeve and
breathed deeply through the fabric.

Some of the poisonous smoke leaked through. Tears
streamed down his cheeks as he coughed heavily, trying to
rid his body of the smoke and yet still breathe. He felt as
if he'd stumbled into one of Lord Kammeryl's torture de-
vices. Iron bands constricted his chest, pressing tighter.
Tighter yet. Squeezing the life from him. Tighter.

Ackerly tried desperately to erect a barrier between himself and the deadly smoke. His store was empty. There was
no more magic in the air to gather.

His lungs froze in the poisonous smoke.

*(We refuse you the magic. You do not work for unity and
peace,)* a disapproving voice came into his mind.

"Help me!"

(You must help yourself.)

Darkness took Ackerly's mind. Pain kept him awake.

The smoke grew thicker. Dirt pressed into his mouth and nose. Air. I have to have air. . . .

At least my gold is safe. No one will find it in three hundred years.

Moncriith took a whiff of the noisome air. Memories of his own trial by the Tambootie smoke swirled around him like coils of suffocating mist. His visions of demons had been prophetic. They took the form of women, naked from the waist up—voluptuous women with pale skin and fair hair. Magretha, his first love with her lush and welcoming bosom. Other lovers, all whores. All the demons he saw in the smoke had hideous lower halves with numerous snake-like limbs that coiled around throat and heart, crushing him to near death while titillating his male parts to excruciating fullness. At the time, he'd been frightened for his very soul. Now with the wisdom of experience and time, he knew the monsters for what they were. Demons that plagued Coronnan and made magicians their slaves.

Myrilandel was their leader. 'Twas her face he'd seen surrounded by a cloud of pale, almost colorless hair in those smoke demons. She had taken human form, but he knew her and his lust for her could be countered only by cleansing fire.

Moncriith saw her standing next to Nimbulan, slim and beautiful, with hair as pale as moonlight. Her beauty and feigned innocence had been designed to capture men's hearts. 'Twas Myrilandel's demonic influence that caused Magretha to betray Moncriith with other men—his own father. 'Twas Myrilandel's demonic spirit that had driven his anger and hurt at the betrayal into a killing rage. But for her, he would have run away from Magretha and his father. Myrilandel had driven him to use magic to murder them.

But the demon had pulled Magretha from the flaming hut, leaving Moncriith's father to die a terrible death. Myrilandel must suffer the same death by fire. Magretha had. He'd finally tracked her down and consigned her to holy fire. Now it was Myrilandel's turn. She was to blame. She had to be the cause of all his grief. Myrilandel had tempted him. Forced him. Betrayed him. . . . He couldn't have done those terrible things to his own father. He wouldn't. . . .

But he had.

"No more false memories!" He held his head in both hands, driving away the guilt and self-doubt the sight of Myrilandel always brought to him.

He held his breath. If demons took command of his body and mind, he'd lose control of his grand plan for today and tomorrow and a hundred tomorrows. The Stargods had given him a vision. The temple elders were in error.

His eyes crossed and his vision blurred. He blinked rapidly, clearing them of the poisonous smoke. The dragons in the sky multiplied before his eyes, splitting into dozens of small demons that dove straight for his face, talons extended. The colored spines and wing veins blackened. The smaller demons opened their mouths, fangs dripping poison into his eyes.

Weird coils of numbness spread from his lungs to his fingers to his knees and back to his heart. Instinctively, he gulped air. More of the poisonous smoke poured into his lungs. The demons of his hallucination tore at his eyes and lungs, rending his flesh into bloody strips. Everywhere they touched him turned to ice.

He choked and spat. Not enough air! He clawed at his throat and chest to rid him of the things that wrapped cold fingers around his heart and lungs, squeezing. Squeezing the life and the magic from him.

He drew his pain deeper into his body, letting it sharpen his senses and fuel his inborn magic talent. With a mighty effort he drew a spiral with his finger, starting at his mouth and expanding outward. Glowing lines of red magic followed the path of his finger. He willed the magic to draw the killing smoke from his lungs. Two tiny puffs of gray mist exited his body with his next breath.

He needed to inhale. Air, more air! The smoke took the air out of his lungs as well.

Darkness surrounded him. A tunnel of bright light robbed color and definition from his failing sight. He closed his eyes to separate himself from the demons. The world righted. The dragons resumed normal proportions and numbers. Then he knew that Ackerly's Tambootie smoke had created the demons, not the dragons themselves. Air and smoke exploded into a sunburst, blotting out everything else.

*   *   *

Nimbulan kept his arm around Myri as he watched Shayla and Rouussin thrust their great wings up and down. They stirred the air. The Tambootie smoke blew back toward Ackerly, dissipated, faded, mixed with clean air from the river and mountains.

Myri rubbed her eyes, clearing tears away with her sleeve. Nimbulan did the same. Together they scanned the battlefield.

Chaos reigned below them. Hundreds of inert bodies lay in the trampled grass, sprawled where the smoke had caught them. Only Kammeryl's army retained their positions, sagging against their pikes and lances, bleary eyed and coughing, but upright. Quinnault's tenants, pretending to be an army, gradually roused from the choking smoke first. They used pitchfork and shovel handles—now devoid of metal—as braces to hold themselves upright while they coughed their lungs clear. None of the troops, from either army, seemed fit for battle.

On the hilltop to the south, a ragged line of men was outlined. None moved to help or hinder either side.

Lord Hanic had arrived, but he held back, waiting for the tide of battle to turn. Waiting to commit his troops only to the winner.

Nimbulan saw nothing of the Kammeryl d'Astrismos who claimed the crown, or his mounted officers.

The dying fire on the knoll opposite him demanded his attention. Ackerly lay beside the glowing embers, his hands holding his throat. His aura hovered above him, separated by several arm's lengths.

The departing aura proved the man dead. Grief blinded Nimbulan momentarily. Grief for the years of companionship, shared youths, and friendship. He couldn't let his emotions cloud the debacle forming before him. Ackerly had betrayed him and suffered from his own foolishness. The winds were too capricious to use smoke as a weapon. Too many uncontrollable factors influenced the direction and intensity of smoke.

The Bloodmage was missing from the knoll. Hastily, Nimbulan searched the field for signs of Moncriith. He supressed the extra heartbeats that bounced in his chest. Moncriith on the loose, possibly crazed by the smoke, was too dangerous. Nimbulan had to account for the Blood-mage.

Tambootie smoke was debilitating to everyone, magician and mundane. His enemy was out of commission at least temporarily. But where had he gone?

"Thank you for clearing the air with your wingbeats," he called to the dragons. Then he turned to the three apprentices designated as runners between his position and the army command post. "Quickly, send a message to Lord Quinnault. He must ride out in front of his troops. If they see him acting calm, they'll take confidence in him. Tell the lord he must remind the troops not to attack. We are here to defend only."

"A barrier. If you could create a wall to keep the armies separate they couldn't kill each other," Myri said, her eyes lighting up with the idea.

"Of course. But Kammeryl would still seek a way to prove himself the greater warrior. That is the only kind of leadership and rule he understands." Nimbulan closed his eyes and formed the image of an invisible wall running north and south across the entire width of the field. To his surprise, his body responded with a coil of magic ready for forming. He had stored the magic from an earlier gathering rather than dissipating after the last spell. A smile crept across his face as the barrier fell into place.

A few of the seasoned troops on the front lines pressed against the wall and withdrew, puzzled looks on their faces. A mounted officer raced to the front from a clump of trees off to the left. The steed's hooves dug up great clumps of turf as it galloped forward. The beast stopped short, skidding the last few lengths before the wall. The rider nearly plunged over his mount's head in reaction. When he righted himself, he reached out with tentative fingers and pushed against the almost-visible barrier. He jerked it back as if burned.

Lord Kammeryl d'Astrismos emerged next from the clump of trees. He rode a magnificent, white war steed, heavier boned and stronger than standard cavalry beasts. A golden circlet on his armored helm announced to one and all his claim to be King of Coronnan.

"Ah, so that's where he's been hiding," Nimbulan murmured.

"I believe it's called a strategic vantage point for directing the battle," Lyman said, hiding a smile behind his hand.
His extra long fingers stretched nearly to his ear. "It also
makes retreat easier should it become necessary."

Kammeryl d'Astrismos also pushed against the wall. He
let his hand linger, daring the pain to throw him away.

"Fight me!" Kammeryl yelled at the top of his lungs.
"Make this a fair battle. Fight me with weapons and tactics
I can counter."

"We do not attack. We only defend," Nimbulan replied
in a voice pitched for all to hear.

"Then defend yourselves from *ME!* I challenge Lord
Quinnault de Tanos, the traitor, or his champion, to single combat."

"I am the Peacemaker." Quinnault took up the lord's
challenge. "I cannot ask my people to fight for the sake of
fighting. Your quarrel is with me, Kammeryl d'Astrismos.
Let your battle be with me and let the innocent of Coronnan stand aside, free and unharmed by us." He strode out
to face his enemy without helm or armor, only an ancient
sword in his left hand. His fair hair glinted in the sunlight,
as pale and fine as Myrilandel's.

Suddenly Nimbulan saw the resemblance to Myrilandel
in Quinnault's posture, profile and coloring. Could Myri
truly be the lord's long-lost sister? When? How? He didn't
want to think about the incredibly dark forces needed to
reanimate a dead body.

No time for questions, only time to help and guide Quinnault before he lost the entire war in single combat with
Kammeryl d'Astrismos.

Nimbulan withdrew the barrier.

Myri watched Quinnault stride to the front of his troops,
sword in hand, sunlight glinting on his fine, fair hair. A
quick glimpse of his profile, with his long face and proud
nose echoed her own image in the metal mirror Nimbulan
had given her.

"He is my brother. We stole his sister's body to give me
life because there can only be one purple dragon alive at
a time," she whispered to herself and to her mother flying
the skies above her. She didn't know if Nimbulan heard

her words and didn't care. He was her husband and had a right to know.

(Yes. Myrilandel was on the brink of death. Bleeding in her brain from a defect at birth,) Shayla replied. *(Her coma was so deep her family thought her dead and placed her in their stone tomb. Had they buried her, we would not have been able to free her in time. Your dragon vitality awakened the human child's natural talent. Together, you healed the weakness in her brain and stopped the bleeding.)*

"But because she wasn't quite dead, her spirit lives on inside me. That is why I couldn't remember. The two spirits vied for dominance and finally compromised on forgetfulness."

(Yes.)

"I can't let my brother die, Shayla. I have to stop him." Suddenly she knew that her certainty that Nimbulan would die this day was misplaced. Quinnault de Tanos, her only living blood relative, was the one destined to die.

(He makes his own destiny.)

"I must stop him. He is my family. The only human family I have."

(You have your husband and your child. Kalen and Powell look to you rather than their own mothers. Save yourself, Amethyst.)

"I am Myrilandel. Amethyst must die and be forgotten. I cannot be a dragon anymore. Amaranth is the only purple in all the nimbi of Coronnan. I claim Quinnault as family now." Myri ran down the hill. She knew only that she had to stand beside her brother in this most important deed in his life. And when the time came, she would use every resource available to save him, including her magic talent.

Nimbulan caught up with her. Together they ran to help the lord who controlled the fate of Coronnan with his ancient, slightly rusty sword.

Chapter 38

"**D**on't be a fool, Quinnault." Nimbulan grabbed the lord's arm to hold him back from carrying through with his challenge. "You know nothing of weapons and combat. He'll make mincemeat of you in a matter of moments. Choose a champion. Perhaps one of Hanic's men." He pointed to the line of men silhouetted on the hill.

A wry smile touched one corner of Quinnault's mouth. "I'm the son of a lord. I wasn't always intended for the priesthood. I have trained with weapons. But I admit it's been a long time since I held a sword. And never as fine a one as my father's." He surveyed the length of the weapon that had been spared Nimbulan's metal shattering spell. The magic had destroyed only the metal carried by the men on the field, not those who waited and directed from behind.

Intricate runes decorated Quinnault's slender blade. A moonstone glowed in the pommel. Decorative as it was, it was also a working weapon, meant to be used. A telltale line of rust around the pommel indicated how long the weapon had remained idle and how recent was the polishing that made the runes glow in the growing sunlight.

"He outweighs you by fifty pounds, his reach is longer, and he's a practiced warrior," Myri added her own argument.

"Once he was a warrior. Now he's a general. He hasn't engaged in combat in years. And he's used to easy living with his fine wines and fancy food. I've been building bridges all winter, eating the same rough but hearty food as my tenants." Again that half smile lightened Quinnault's set visage. This time the smile almost reached his eyes.

"My lord, I am your sister." Myri clasped Quinnault's hand over the sword hilt, staying his headlong rush into combat. "I wasn't quite dead when the family buried me."

"I guessed something like that happened, Myrilandel. We will talk later. If I survive." He patted her hand lovingly. Again that wry smile lit his face but not his eyes.

"You know something, Quinnault. Tell us why you won't choose a champion to fight this battle for you. Don't lie to us." The man's calm shook Nimbulan, more than Myri's revelation. He kept his hand on the back of Myri's waist to brace himself against the coming shock. He thanked the Stargods she had come with him, yet he was frightened out of his wits that she stood so close to the line that could become a battle front at any moment.

"I know that I have proclaimed my cause as peace, not conquest. If I win, all of the families who have lost men and land and crops and the will to live during a war, will flock to my side. The people are ready for peace. They will grasp it any way they can. Kammeryl has only recently declared himself king. He offers the people nothing but more war. If he wins, they will depose him, and I will still win."

"But you'll be dead." Myri clung to Quinnault rather than wipe her tears away. "I have so much to tell you, brother."

"I know some of it, Myrilandel. I pray that we will have the time to rediscover our mutual past." Quinnault caressed her hair, lovingly, as he would a small child. The child sister he remembered? "But if Kammeryl kills me, I will become a martyr to the cause of peace. We all know that a dead martyr is worth a hundred live rabble-rousers. Make sure the people remember me and not Moncriith and his demons."

He turned abruptly and walked to a place near the center of the field, his troops behind him, Kammeryl's army before him, and the crowds of camp followers and neighbors lining the hillsides around the field. The people of Coronnan cleared a circle for the two combatants, roughly one hundred arm's lengths across.

Kammeryl rode his magnificent steed to one side of the cleared space. He pulled the crowned visor down on his helm and loosed his sword. No king would attend a battle carrying a lance, pike, or ax. Only a sword symbolized the honor of a man who ruled.

A common soldier from Kammeryl's ranks rushed up to Quinnault, offering his own boiled leather helmet. Not much protection, but better than nothing—the offer more valuable considering the source.

"Take it, Quinnault. Please take it. And the breastplate the next man offers," Myri whispered, clutching Nimbulan's arm so tightly she nearly cut off the circulation to his hand.

"Interesting that the offers of assistance come from my enemy's army," Quinnault said, that half smile tugging at the corner of his mouth. He donned the borrowed protection. Three men rushed to help him with the buckles of the chest and back leathers.

Myri stepped forward to help. Nimbulan held her back.

"The Stargods control the outcome of this duel, Myri. We can only watch," he replied, patting her hand, but not loosing her fingers. Somehow he needed that slight discomfort to remind him what these men fought for.

"You can armor him with magic, Nimbulan. A thin bubble that no one else can see," Myri pleaded. Her eyes never left her brother.

"If I could, I would. This must be a battle between the lords. One of them must prove his right to govern by the outcome of this battle. If I help now, then Quinnault's victory or defeat will be mine, not his. If he uses his own magic to protect himself, then the victory or defeat will be for magicians and not Quinnault. No one must interfere." Sadly, Nimbulan pulled Myri close against his chest. "You don't have to watch."

She drew her face away from the protective folds of his formal robe. "I must watch. I must know the moment of his death or his living." She turned within the circle of his arms, resolutely facing the field of combat, filled with anger and fear.

"You will do anything to win, Kammeryl d'Astrismos. Even entering single combat asteed while your opponent has no mount or armor," Quinnault taunted. "Your honor will be in question for as long as you live. As well as your prowess at arms. Every lord with a strong companion will know that you are afraid to face me, an untrained warrior, a former priest, on equal ground."

Kammeryl snarled an incomprehensible animal sound of fury as he kicked his steed into a full charge. The visor restricted his vision. Quinnault neatly sidestepped out of the path of the white steed. At the last moment he dipped his sword and severed the saddle girth. The tip of hammered steel nicked the steed's side. The animal reared and screamed. Kammeryl lost his balance as his saddle slipped and gravity dragged him toward the Kardia. He was too skilled a rider to fall, dismounting lithely at the last moment, sword at the ready, visor pushed back for better line of sight.

Quinnault widened his stance, grasping his sword with both hands. The blade did not waver. But Nimbulan saw the tension in his neck and in between his eyes.

The first blow from Kammeryl came quickly, without warning. A powerful downward stroke meant to split open his opponent's thin leather helmet and his skull beneath. Quinnault blocked the blow, and the next, never having time to recover and strike one of his own.

Slash and thrust, duck and parry. Quinnault led Kammeryl in an exhausting and dangerous dance around the circle. Slash, thrust. Sidestep, jump, and roll. Blow after blow, they wove their way around the circle once, twice. A third time.

The older, stouter warlord breathed heavily, but still he pressed the younger, more agile lord to his limits.

Quinnault parried another blow and retreated closer to the silent watchers. His aura remained closed. Nimbulan couldn't read the man's emotions or physical state. But then, he never could. Kammeryl stepped forward, raising his sword for another strike. His aura seethed with red-and-orange fury. Black spots surged and faded within the envelope of light.

The wry half smile lighted Quinnault's face once more. He must have seen the aura, too, known that Kammeryl's temper would get the better of him; known that the man's inner balance was always precarious.

Quinnault wasn't strong enough to deflect the rapidly twisting blade aimed for his gut. Bright blood stained his tunic across his middle. He staggered, clutching at the wound with his free hand. His sword dangled uselessly from a rapidly weakening left hand.

Kammeryl moved in closer for a killing blow. Confidence slowed him. He wanted to savor the moment of his adversary's death.

Nimbulan wanted to close his eyes, knowing the battle was over. Firmly he made himself watch. For at the moment of Quinnault's death, he would have to begin the campaign to proclaim him a martyred saint in the name of peace.

Quinnault ducked and rolled. Kammeryl's blow barely touched his shoulder. As Kammeryl brought back his sword again, his raised arms lifted his body armor, revealing a vulnerable crack in his middle. Quinnault thrust his sword tip toward the bared midriff, but he was rapidly losing his strength. The blade went no farther. Kammeryl laughed, raising his sword higher.

"You're dead, Peacemaker. You're dead already. I see the light fading from your eyes. I could stand here and watch you bleed to death. But I'll be merciful and make it quick." As he brought the weapon down, he bent forward to guide the blade to the fallen man. Quinnault thrust upward with the last of his strength.

Both men collapsed. Their blood mingled and stained the beaten grass beneath them.

Myri wrenched herself away from Nimbulan's convulsive grasp. The sight of her brother's blood brought her talent into full, insistent preparedness.

(Don't, Myrilandel. Don't risk your child,) Shayla reminded her.

"I must save him. I can't watch him die," Myri protested.

(Then let Amaranth help you. Gather his magic for your healing spells.)

"Women can't gather dragon magic." She ripped Quinnault's tunic open, exposing the wound. Then she pressed a strip from her skirt against the gaping edges of skin, praying the pressure would slow the bleeding.

"Anyone can gather magic from a purple-tipped dragon. Even women and mundanes, provided the dragon in question is willing." Old Lyman, the mysterious magician who seemed to know more about dragons than Myri did, chuckled as he reached pale hands to help add pressure to the wound. "In another existence, I was called Iianthe—the last purple-tipped dragon before Amaranth and Amethyst made a premature entrance into this world. After that I drifted for many years as the guardian spirit of the beginning place until Nimbulan called me forth in the name of peace. Amaranth is willing to give magic to this spell. I must guide you both."

A swoop of wings fanned the air before Myri could question the old man whose fingernails appeared slightly lavender where the blood pulsed beneath them. The crowd pressing close to Myri and her patient gasped and fled backward. A gentle thud behind Myri announced the landing of her familiar, now in full dragon form.

"I am not a healer, but I will direct the flow of magic through you so that it does no harm to your baby," Lyman whispered.

(Give me your hand, Myrilandel.) Amaranth's mental voice came to her, deeper and more mature than she had ever heard him. It sounded very like Lyman's voice did to her ears.

She had no time to reflect on the oddity. Beneath her hands, Quinnault's life hung in the balance.

"Amaranth, you're too big to cuddle in my lap like you used to when I worked a healing." She stretched her free hand to grasp his extended forepaw. "I think I need both hands for this." She studied the red-soaked skirt she still pressed into Quinnault's wound. She sensed his life slipping away. They didn't have much time.

Amaranth waddled closer, not nearly as graceful on the ground as in the air. Gently, he extended one wing to cover her like an iridescent veil while his muzzle rested lightly on her shoulders. The other wing extended to Lyman.

Energy tingled along Myri's spine and into her arms. Stronger than the ley lines, this magic begged to be used for good. Her talent wrapped around it.

Both hands free to hold the wound in place, she let the magic flow freely into her brother. A healing *Song* honed and directed the magic. Her vision followed the healing into the gaping folds of skin, down into the muscles, repairing tears here, rejoining severed blood vessels there. Her mind lost track of what she *Sang,* only aware that a lilting tune hovered near her ears.

She sensed other people joining, adding more and more

magic to the power she felt. The gathered soldiers and commoners must be touching Amaranth, compounding the magic. The spell remained at the same level, not amplifying like Nimbulan's dragon magic. Her husband used rhymes to bring his magicians into a spell. She had no poems ready that described the intent of the spell.

What? What could she use to join these people to the spell?

An old ballad fairly leaped to her lips. She molded it into a *Song* of healing.

A dozen other voices grabbed the melody and joined with her. A deep well of harmony amplified the energy running from the dragon through her into her brother. Other hands grasped her shoulders, hair and back, linking her to the common people of Coronnan as well as the purple-tipped dragon.

Suddenly she was a part of each person who touched the dragon. Their hearts beat as one. Their minds mingled, sharing hopes and plans for the future, all of them centered on the man who lay bleeding to death beneath her hands.

She repeated the melody, uncaring of the words, only knowing that the notes needed to blend and flow in a way that all could sing it with love and hope and unity. As the melody rose and swelled on the breeze, all of them became a part of Quinnault de Tanos and his rapidly healing body, giving him their love as well as the little bit of magic allowed them.

Myri's love for all of them grew with the *Song* and the healing magic.

Soaring on a high note, she directed them all to the core of the wound. Together they patched his internal organs, rebuilt the nicked rib, joined the major artery, then slowly backed out, blending muscle tissue together on their way.

The music turned joyous.

Lord Quinnault opened his eyes.

"Our king lives. Long live King Quinnault!" The shout rippled through the crowd who had given this man back his life.

"I was afraid they'd make me king if I lived. Maybe you should let me die," Quinnault quipped.

"Never, brother. You must live for these people. You

belong to all of them now," Myri replied. Tears of joy streamed down her cheeks.

Hands broke their connection with Myri and Amaranth. The magic dwindled, drained out of her. Movement flickered around the edges of her vision. The people danced and celebrated. One and all they acknowledged Quinnault their king. The wars were over. Peace had won.

Somewhere in the background she heard/sensed Lord Hanic joining the celebration with his men.

"Sorry we were late. Delays crossing the ford. I lost some men who ran from a cloud shadow they swore was a dragon."

She crumpled into the blood-soaked ground, exhausted. Her stomach felt funny, half cramped, partially upset. She clutched her belly desperately, praying she hadn't lost the baby in saving her brother's life.

Chapter 39

Nimbulan gently laid Myri on their bed in the old monastery. He pulled a rough blanket over her. Gradually her shivers subsided as he stroked her hair and held her hand. He checked the silver cord of magic connecting his heart to hers. The gentle bonds pulsed with life and vigor stronger than before.

A breath of relief swept over him. For a few moments, he'd feared that her talent would sever the tie to him in favor of her new patient, Quinnault.

At this very moment, the Lord of the Islands, no, he was now King of Coronnan, was being tended by retainers and healers of all levels of society. Hasty messages of the day's events, especially the proclamation of kingship by the common people, had been sent to all the lords. He sincerely hoped that news of Ackerly's death and the Bloodmage's failure to penetrate the defenses of the Commune would do more for the cause than the death of Kammeryl d'Astrismos. Within a day or two, the leaders of Coronnan—noble and magician—would all descend upon the small keep in the heart of the delta islands to verify that the wars had ended. The lords would probably confirm Quinnault's kingship since he now commanded the loyalty of Kammeryl's army as well as his own islanders. Most of Hanic's men had also sworn their loyalty to Quinnault as king.

Hanic was still wavering, waiting for a consensus from the lords.

While a great fuss was being made over Quinnault the Peacemaker, only Nimbulan remembered Myrilandel, the witchwoman who had saved the new king from certain death. Granted, a great many people had participated in that final spell. But Myrilandel, and only Myrilandel, had known what to do.

"Make sure that Quinnault drinks plenty of water and small beer. We healed the wounds, but magic cannot replace lost blood. He needs fluid to rebuild it," Myri whispered.

"Hush, now. He's in the hands of the best healers in the country. They will see to him. You must take care of yourself, Myri. Kalen will bring you some broth in a few moments. You must promise to drink it all. You must get strong again, soon, for I don't know how I will live without you, love. We will be married by a priest as soon as I can arrange it. A forever marriage, blessed by the Stargods." He traced her cheek with a gentle fingertip, memorizing each plane and angle.

She kissed his palm and closed her eyes with a satisfied sigh.

"Tell me what happened to the others, Ackerly and . . . and Moncriith." She grasped his hand with greater strength than he thought she had left.

"Ackerly is dead, suffocated by the Tambootie smoke and his own strangling hands," he said sadly.

"Commit his body to the pyre with honor and respect. Please, Nimbulan." She held him tightly when he would have turned away.

"Ackerly betrayed me and his students. He tried to kill me, twice. He sabotaged the spell to rescue Rollett from Moncriith's witchsniffers. He . . ." He couldn't go on. Memories of all their years together kept intruding on his sense of outrage.

"For the man you want to remember him as, please, give his death the respect you yourself would want." Her big eyes, almost colorless with fatigue, pleaded with him.

"I promise. He shall go to the funeral pyre wearing his formal robes and carrying his staff—the symbol of his status as a magician." Nimbulan bowed his head, allowing himself to grieve honestly for his old friend.

"And Moncriith?" Myri tucked both her hands beneath the blanket, giving way to a great shudder.

"We don't know. No one has seen him or his body."

"I fear that he lives and will return to plague us all."

"If he does, the entire might of the Commune of Magi-

cians will protect you and all innocents that men such as
he seek to persecute."

She looked at him then with mingled trust and skepticism. "Men like Moncriith will always find a way around
institutions of authority."

"Sleep, now, Myri and don't worry about the future. Or
the past. Sleep and regain your strength. There is much to
celebrate. I want to share the joy with you, as my legal
wife." He kissed her brow and watched as her eyes closed
and her breathing slowed to the easy rhythm of sleep.

Silently, he prayed she wasn't right this time. Coronnan
had enough troubles without worrying about Moncriith.
He'd have to make sure the new government had strong
and just laws for all the people so malcontents like Moncriith had no injustice to use as a springboard to power.

"If you demand I start a new dynasty with a new name,
then I won't make Castle Krej—named for one of Kammeryl's supposed ancestors—my capital," Quinnault said. The
mildness of his tone belied the tension in his knuckles
where he grasped the arms of his chair.

Nimbulan scanned the new king of Coronnan with just a
touch of *Sight*. His normally pale skin carried a tinge of
blue rather than healthy pink and his fine hair hung limply
where it had pulled free of its queue restraint. No other
signs of illness or weakness showed.

"Castle Krej is an easily defended fortress, Your Majesty," Lord Hanic replied. "It is yours by right of conquest.
For your own safety, you must retreat there with an army
combined of all our forces. As general of the united army,
I will guarantee that you are protected."

No one had declared Hanic leader of anything.

"No." Quinnault speared the tardy lord with a glance.
"I will no longer be dependent upon an army, any army to
protect me. Peace and justice will be my protection. We
will build a city here amongst the islands at the head of
the Bay."

"But it isn't safe. The islands can't be defended," Lord
Sauria said.

"I intend to reign over a country at peace. Defense is no
longer my primary concern. We need a new city. Here will
be a center of commerce when we reopen the shipping

lanes in the Great Bay. My home will be a palace, open to lords and merchants and petitioners. I have had enough of fortresses and wars."

"Perhaps we should call the new city Dragonville in honor of the dragons that give us the means to enforce peace without armies," Nimbulan suggested.

"I'd rather call it Coronnan City. The monarch and the capital city must belong to all, rather than the king owning all." Quinnault stood and began to pace, hands behind his back, shoulders slightly hunched like wings tucked up, head thrust forward, sure signs of his returning vitality. No trace of the draconic shadows masked his face. These thoughts were his own. "Don't any of you understand? We are trying to build a united country with laws and justice. No one of the lords will be more powerful than the others. No king will be a despot, but rather a first among the equal lords. And all people, noble, common and magician, shall be subject to law. Therefore, the king can't own more than any other lord, preferably less, to maintain a balance." He paused to look each of the assembled lords in the eye. There were only twelve of them left. A century ago there had been more than twenty.

"I agree to take the surname of Draconis and pass it to future generations of kings. But I insist that the capital be Coronnan City. It is a city of people, the very people who shared in my healing. They are what makes Coronnan great, not me."

Silence hung heavily in the Great Hall of Quinnault's keep. No noble had ever heard of such an outrageous idea. Nobility had always meant privilege and ownership. Nimbulan silently applauded this bold move.

"Responsibility must be the primary tenet of kingship and nobility." Quinnault pulled a small book from the pile of texts, maps, and parchments on the table. "That idea was first put forth by the Stargods, in this sermon, recorded by one Kimmer. He calls himself simply a scribe from the south." The new king looked over the stunned faces of his assembled lords.

"I won't bore you with the entire text. Suffice it to say, I intend to govern alongside you lords with the idea that we are, one and all, responsible for every living creature within our boundaries."

"Does that include the dragons?" Nimbulan asked, ready to move on to the issues Myri had told him concerned the creatures who made this all possible.

"Yes," Quinnault replied. "If we are going to rely on communal magic to enforce our laws and control solitary magicians, then we must ensure the safety of the dragons and their continued presence within our boundaries. Demon hunters like Moncriith can't be allowed to harm them in any way."

"There are only six full-grown dragons in the current nimbus and five youngsters. That figure includes Amaranth the purple-tip." Nimbulan recited the statistics Myri had relayed to him. "Dragons throughout the rest of Kardia Hodos are solitary creatures and may not agree to become a part of the nimbus. Our nimbus needs to increase their numbers to provide us with enough magic to be readily available at all times, no matter where the dragons currently fly. Shayla has requested a provision of livestock to feed them and plantations of the Tambootie tree, the source of their magic." Nimbulan waited, holding his breath to see if the lords would willingly give up parts of their wealth to help the dragons thrive. Previously they considered the beasts to be dangerous predators or demons—if dragons existed at all.

"Will a tithe from each lord be enough?" Quinnault cut through any objections before they could be voiced.

"I think that will do. As long as the herds and plantations are spread out. The dragons must range widely to stretch their wings." Nimbulan hid his embarrassment at the next request behind a cough. "And, ah, the dragons have another requirement to seal the covenant."

Quinnault looked up a little startled, as if he knew the next demand would be outrageous.

Nimbulan signaled the servant at the door to admit the three magicians who waited there. They marched in at a stately pace. Lyman carried a precious artifact, resting upon a wide pillow covered in fine green silk. Cloth of gold velvet shielded the heavy object. They paused beside Nimbulan's chair until he stood and joined them.

"As newly elected Senior Magician of the Commune of Magicians, the nimbus of dragons, currently resident in Coronnan have directed me to offer to the people of Coronnan this crown." Nimbulan whipped off the velvet covering to reveal a crown of precious clear glass, forged by dragon fire in the form of a dragon's head, set with gems—ruby, emerald, sapphire, topaz, and amethyst—the colors of the dragon wingtips.

"It is beautiful!" Quinnault gasped.

"More than beautiful, it is unique and special. No other monarch in all of Kardia Hodos has a crown so valuable, nor so heavy with responsibility. The dragons will be present at your coronation, and the crowning of each of your successors. You and your line rule by the grace of dragons and you will be addressed as 'Your Grace' for that reason. If any man breaks the covenant with the dragons, they will withdraw their grace and the crown—The Coraurlia."

"That is a name I do not know." Quinnault couldn't take his eyes off the glittering crown. Sunlight from the high windows struck the glass, sending rainbows arcing throughout the room.

"The Coraurlia has been imbued with special magic," Old Lyman said as he fiddled with the golden cover cloth, opening it to form a sack with a drawstring and carry-strap. He held the sack open while his two supporting magicians carefully deposited the crown inside.

"You, King Quinnault de Draconis, must keep the Coraurlia on your person for the next three days until your official coronation. During that time, the crown will be imprinted by your aura. Until the day you die, or are deposed by the dragons and the Commune combined, no magic will touch you for good or ill. Mundane weapons can penetrate the spell, but with difficulty. This is the best protection we can give you."

"What about the rest of Coronnan? What will be our protection from magical attack? Your Commune can't be everywhere. In the past decades we have supported numerous Battlemages and their assistants very well. Now that we don't need them, will they retaliate against us, before the Commune has a chance to enforce the new laws?" Lord Hanic stood to make his point, fear written all over his face.

"All magicians will be invited to join the Commune," Nimbulan replied.

"But what about those magicians who can't or won't gather dragon magic?" Lord Baathalzan stood, adding his insistence to the request.

Nimbulan had no answer. He'd assumed all magicians would gladly join him and conform.

"Any magician who practices outside the Commune has no place in the Coronnan we are building," Quinnault said.

"Your Grace." The Lord of Sambol bowed in deference to the new king. "We twelve lords of your Council recommend a law exiling all magicians who will not or cannot join the Commune of Magicians. We recognize dragon magic as the only lawful magic. This law must include all former Battlemages as well as witches and other magicians of minor talent and informal training. *And* they must remove themselves from Coronnan by the time of your coronation."

A general cheer of acceptance resounded around the room. The sound built as it bounced against the stone walls, hammering into Nimbulan's ears.

He sat heavily in his chair, stunned. Myrilandel, his beloved wife, could not gather dragon magic.

"What about the purple dragon?" Nimbulan grasped at the only possibility that presented itself. "Anyone can gather magic from a purple-tip."

"But there is only one purple-tip in all of Kardia Hodos," Hanic said. "I understand one must be in physical contact with it to work magic. It cannot be everywhere and I understand it prefers the form of a flywacket, which doesn't give off magic to be gathered. No. Our definition of dragon magic doesn't include the purple dragon. Exile or death for *all* solitary magicians." Baathalzan resumed his seat with dignified satisfaction that his primary concern had been addressed.

They were right. For the good of all Coronnan, solitary magicians had to be exiled.

Nimbulan stared into nothingness. *Myri, oh, Myri, what will I do without you?*

"I now pronounce you husband and wife, mated together for the duration of your lifetimes. The Stargods acknowledge your vows of faithfulness. Let the people respect them as well." A priest robed in bright red recited the formula of the marriage blessing in some haste. He looked at the long caravan forming outside the School for Magicians before sealing the ceremony with the cross of the Stargods.

All around them steeds stamped, people shouted, sledges groaned with the weight piled high upon them. In the midst of the frenzy, the priest presided over a hasty union. He turned and left the couple without waiting for them to seal their vows with the traditional kiss.

Emptiness washed over Myri. This should be the happiest day of her life, not the saddest.

"Come with us now, Nimbulan. Please," Myri pleaded with Nimbulan one last time, though she knew he must stay in the city. He must help rebuild Coronnan and the create the Commune. Her brother, King Quinnault, couldn't do it all.

She would survive without Nimbulan. She wasn't sure the new Commune, king, and Council of Provinces would.

"The clearing will protect you, Myri, until I can come to you. I moved some lines on the new map so that you will technically be outside the boundaries of Coronnan. I will come to you as soon as I can. I just wish I could find a safe haven for you closer to the city," he said while clutching her hands within his own. He searched her face as if etching the image into his memory.

"I know you will come, my love." She turned her head away to hide her tears. And her guilt. She hadn't told him about the baby. She needed to know for certain that she wouldn't miscarry, as so many witchwomen did. Shayla had told Lyman—he was almost as much a dragon as Myri—but no one had told Nimbulan. At first she waited for the right moment. A quiet time when they wouldn't be interrupted. Then the Council had issued their edict of exile.

To tell him now would divide his loyalties even further between herself and the new government. His dream of peace was too important to all of Coronnan. She couldn't do it now. She would wait until she knew for sure. Then, when he joined her in the clearing, she would tell him. This parting was hard enough on both of them.

Her chin quivered and the ache in her chest choked her breathing.

"Don't hide your tears, Myri." Nimbulan captured her chin between two gentle fingers. "I love you. I'll come soon. Kalen will keep you company." He kissed her tears as they fell.

Stuuvart had blithely abandoned all claim to Kalen as

his child as soon as the edict of exile was made known.
Guillia had hugged the girl fiercely in a tearful embrace
all through the brief wedding. Now she reluctantly let her
daughter lift her pack onto the sledge. Myri tried to summon anger at the absent Stuuvart to replace her lonely
suffering at parting from Nimbulan.

"I'm going with them, too," Powwell announced, marching up to the last sledge in the long caravan headed south
and east. He carried a simple pack bulging with books and
clothes and food.

"Your place is here, Powwell," Myri said. "The Commune needs every magician who can gather dragon magic
to help enforce the laws."

"Stupid laws. I won't be part of a country that forces
you and Kalen into exile. I'm coming with you." He set his
chin in a stubborn attitude that wouldn't budge. "You'll
need a man to help with the heavy work."

"Then I charge you, Powwell, to look after Myri and
Kalen, and to protect them. You must perfect the summons
spell quickly so that you can keep in contact with me,"
Nimbulan ordered the boy. "You are nearly fourteen now.
A man, and I trust you."

"Yeah, sure." Powwell jumped on the back of the sledge
next to Kalen. He crossed his arms and glared at his former master.

"I wish it could be otherwise, Myrilandel. I wish we could
be together." Nimbulan held her close until their hearts
beat in rhythm.

"As do I, my love. I wish we could be together always,
in our own home, with our family." She turned her face
and kissed him long and full, putting all of her regret and
sorrow into her embrace. She tasted salty tears. His or hers,
it didn't matter. If only she could cling to him a little
longer, hold his warmth a little closer, make love with him
one more time. . . .

Shouts and whistles to sledge steeds, and a general shift
of people forward, signaled the beginning of the long journey. Traders and exiles alike settled into the line of march.

Myri flung her arms around Nimbulan's neck, holding
him as long as possible. Gentle hands pulled them apart.
She slid her hand down his arm, caressing his fingers, cherishing his touch for as long as possible.

"I love you, Myrilandel. I'll come to you soon," Nimbulan whispered.

"I love you, Nimbulan." The silver umbilical that bound them together stretched thin but did not break.

Epilogue

*(**T**he Covenant is broken!)* Shayla's last communication reverberated through Nimbulan's ears three days after she and her nimbus had departed abruptly from Coronnan City.

At the same moment as she spoke, Nimbulan's contact with Myrilandel through the silver umbilical snapped.

Now he trudged up the path from the village to the clearing. Footsore and saddlesore, he rested briefly against the split boulder with an everblue tree growing out of the center of it. He'd ridden from Coronnan City at a breakneck pace. Five steeds had floundered under his prodding to move ever faster. The last of the beasts had gone lame two leagues outside the village.

The magical barrier that protected the clearing should be within sight—if the barrier were visible. Winter mud slowed his passage along the trail. More than half a year had passed since he'd said farewell to his wife. Too long. He'd allowed the concerns of the king and Commune to chain him to the capital for too long.

Hastily he finger-combed his hair, trying to make his weary, mud-splattered appearance a little more presentable. Regretting even that delay, he stepped up to the barrier, closed his eyes, and pushed with his left hand. He met no resistance.

Puzzled, he stepped across what should be the threshold of the clearing. No tingle of magical energy. No resistance. Nothing.

He looked through the screening trees. Nothing had changed from the first time he'd seen the place. The thatch on the one room hut sagged in the middle, the door still hung slightly crooked, the kitchen garden was overgrown with weeds. Two flusterhens scratched at the center of the clearing in search of food.

"Myri?" he called. His voice echoed through the emptiness of the clearing. "Myrilandel," he shouted louder with both voice and magic.

No answer.

(The Covenant is broken!) The dragons were gone. He was no longer connected to his wife.

And yet the dragon magic persisted in the air. What was happening?

Why, oh why, hadn't he made sure Powwell or Kalen could work the summons spell properly before they left Coronnan City? Neither of them had perfected the spell in the last three seasons. Myri had never been able to learn it. Communication had been sporadic and incomplete at best.

"Myri!" he cried, desperate to see her again and know she was safe. "Myri, Kalen, Powwell. Somebody please answer me."

Nothing.

"Where are you? You can't be gone." He dashed into the hut, thrusting the door open so hard he nearly jerked it off its frame. *"Myrilandel!"*

Empty. The hut was as empty as the clearing, with no sign it had been inhabited at all in the last year.

"Where are you?" he whispered into the emptiness. "Were you ever here?"

Loneliness landed on his shoulders like a lead-weighted cloak. A headache pounded in his temples. He tried to remember her face, her tall, slim body and fine hair so pale it looked like colorless dragon fur. The purple shadows under her fingernails. The way she buried her face into the fur of her black flywacket.

All the images faded from his mind. He forced them back, holding on to them with the desperation of a deserted lover. The memories slipped through his grasp as if they'd never been.

His heart ached as tears choked him.

"Were you real, Myrilandel, or just a dragon dream?"

THE
LAST
BATTLEMAGE

For Karen, the logical one.
For Linda, the flamboyant one.
For TJ, the action one.
Thanks. I couldn't write without you.

And to the patient staff of Applebees, thank you for putting up with the critique group from outer space, who never order anything but half-price snacks, and monopolize too much room for hours on end. At least we tip well.

Chapter 1

"**A**nother moon before your babe is ready," Karry announced to Myrilandel, holding her hands expertly on the younger woman's swelling abdomen.

"I've midwifed enough babies, you'd think I'd know how my own baby progressed," Myri replied to her friend. She rubbed the lower portion of her enormous belly where the baby kicked vigorously. While she looked at her ungainly bulk, she checked the magical cord that bound her to her husband, no matter how far away he was from her.

A pulse beat against her fingertips. Nimbulan's life force remained steady and true. She had never been able to delve deeper into the meaning of the unique phenomenon.

Amaranth, her familiar, mewed at her feet. He rubbed his black cat head against her hand as if adding his caresses to the unborn child. He kept his falcon wings carefully hidden beneath protective folds of skin and fur. No sense advertising that he was a rare and magical flywacket.

She'd never been separated from Amaranth, not since they'd been born twin purple-tipped dragons twenty years ago. Dragon lore demanded that only one purple-tip could be alive at any time. Either Amaranth or Myrilandel had to take another form or die. Myrilandel had chosen a human body. Amaranth had transformed into his flywacket form to remain near her throughout her life. She had seen him grow into his true dragon form only once.

Myri scratched his ears. "Sorry, there's no room for you in my lap, Amaranth. Not that I have any lap left."

"Mbrrrt," Amaranth purred loudly, in rhythm with Myri's stroking of her belly.

"At the first sign of labor, you send that boy you adopted

to me. I'll come and help," Karry ordered, just as she ordered everyone in the small fishing village.

"I'm ready for this baby now," Myri laughed. "I want my magic talents back, so I can help in the village again. I need to repay you for all your kindness to me. I've never had a home like this before," Myri whispered. If only Nimbulan would return from the capital city, her family would be complete. She had many friends in the village now, but they weren't family.

"What do them dragons of yours tell you about the babe?" Karry asked, setting her simple home to rights.

"Shayla only tells me it's a girl." Myri smiled every time she thought of her dragon family.

Her only family, other than the two children she had adopted. And Amaranth.

She refused to dwell on depressing thoughts about her human brother, King Quinnault de Draconis, who had exiled her, reluctantly, for her rogue magic talent. A talent that had decreased as her pregnancy increased. Her husband, Nimbulan, had remained in the capital serving her brother as adviser and Senior Magician. She might have been born a dragon, but in this body she couldn't gather dragon magic—no female could. Without the ability to work in concert with other magicians through dragon magic, she had to accept exile along with every other solitary magician.

Nimbulan would return to her soon. He'd promised.

(Danger!) a dragon voice screamed into Myri's mind. *(Danger to you and the younglings!)*

Raised voices and pounding feet filled the village square.

Amaranth leaped to the doorway, back arched, fur standing up. The tips of his wings poked free of their protective skin folds in his agitation.

"Raiders!" Powwell, her adopted son, shouted.

Kalen, Powwell's half-sister, dashed inside. "Myri, come, the storage sheds are burning. We have to flee, now! They are coming closer." She tugged anxiously at Myri's arm.

"Who?" Myri barely had time to ask as Kalen pulled and Karry pushed her outside.

In the open space around the Equinox Pylon, dozens of villagers rushed madly from hut to hut. Smoke filled the air with an aura of menace.

"This way," Powwell half-dragged, half-carried Myri's bulky body toward the path leading up into the hills and their magically protected clearing. Amaranth kept close by her side, refusing to fly until she was safe.

(Not that way!) Shayla announced into Myri's head. *(Evil men await you near your clearing.)*

The carpenter's hut at the edge of the village exploded in flames. Three people, faces blackened with smoke, ran out the door, coughing. They beat uselessly at the bright green fire with blankets and cloaks.

The greedy flames ate at the dry timbers and thatch. The entire autumn had been unusually dry and bright. Very little rain had soaked into the homes to protect them from the flaming arrows that sped through the air. A fisherman's home, near the cliff path to the beach, caught fire with the next barrage of arrows.

Powwell tried a magic spell to douse the fire. The flames shot higher, feeding off his magical energy as well as the thatch.

Smoke filled Myri's lungs. She nearly doubled over from coughing. Moisture streamed from her eyes. Cold autumnal air chilled her skin.

A tiny cramp in her belly sent panic and new energy shooting through her veins. The baby wasn't ready to be born yet.

Amaranth circled her ankles, mewing anxiously. She almost tripped over him. Her senses distorted. She needed a moment to grab a hold on up and down, right and left, safety and danger.

Black-clad men appeared at the edge of the village. A dozen or more. They carried torches, swords, and bows with full quivers on their backs. Something seemed familiar about them—brightly colored vests and kerchiefs covered in silver embroidery—Rovers!

"Into the forest. They can't find us in the trees!" Karry yelled.

(To the trees. I will guide you to safety,) the dragon said. Amaranth agreed.

Instantly, Myri's vision spun upward. From the perspective of a dragon flying overhead, she saw the villagers running aimlessly in all directions. Some of the humans ran afoul of the black-clad men who approached from the north with fire and sword. Others disappeared amid the towering trees that spread up the hills to the south of the village.

She forced control over her double perspective. She'd done this with Amaranth many times. Part of her consciousness had to remain anchored to her body so she could flee from the danger.

Myri's empathic senses roared into life after many moons of dormancy. She stopped her running steps to absorb the full impact of her talent. The essence of every life around her slammed into her consciousness. She needed time to sort through them, to know who was friendly, who intended harm, who needed help, who could help.

Suddenly she knew that the lives who hid among the towering trees awaited the villagers with clubs and knives.

"We've got to hide." Powwell slipped his adolescent arm about her waist, guiding her. She sensed his magical armor dissolving as fast as he erected it. What magician led these raiders? She didn't think the Rover chieftain powerful enough to interfere with Powwell's magic.

"No, it's a trap! There are more Rovers in the forest." Myri reeled, not knowing where to turn.

Shayla circled the gathering of humans, screeching her distress. She spurted flame at the edges of the milling villagers, then withdrew it. She endangered the innocent along with the raiders.

"Yiheee!" a black-clad man screeched, running toward Myri with club raised.

"I need her alive," another voice shouted. "Catch the witchwoman and her familiar *alive.*" A voice she recognized. She should have known he was behind the raid the moment she recognized the attackers as Rovers.

"No," she moaned. "Not him."

Amaranth screeched and launched into the air. He extended his talons to rake Piedro, the man with a club. He threw his hands over his face, ducking beneath the flywacket's assault.

Amaranth raked the man's scalp and circled back for a new assault. Piedro came up swinging his club, blood from his scalp dripping into his eyes. He caught Amaranth on the tip of his wing.

"No!" Myri tried to rush to her familiar. Powwell dragged her back into the mass of villagers fleeing into the forest.

The flywacket faltered. Out of nowhere, a fishing net flew through the air, trapping him. He fell heavily to the ground, thrashing and hissing. He bit the knotted ropes that covered him.

He stretched and paled. His black fur shed light. His wings grew larger, forming wicked hooks on the tips and elbows. The net parted at one knot, then a second.

"Transform, Amaranth. Transform into a dragon," Myri cried with relief. She needed to stay and make sure he was safe. Powwell pulled her away, toward the trees.

An old woman flung herself over Amaranth's struggling body. She enfolded the enraged flywacket in a thick canvas sack, cutting off his access to sunlight. Without light, he couldn't transform into his dragon body. He had only cat claws and teeth to fight the net and the sack.

The cramp in Myri's belly intensified. She panted, trying desperately to regain control over her body and the people running and screaming around her. The line of trees loomed closer. Sanctuary. She knew how to hide in trees. But she couldn't climb anymore. The bulk of the baby kept her bound to the land.

A dark man stepped out from the concealment of a fallen tree. Myri tried to run from him. Kalen and Powwell dragged her in a different direction.

Help us, Shayla!

(If I flame those who threaten you, many innocents will be killed. You must flee and hide. Flee into the trees.)

The dragons' Covenant with the king and the magicians forbade dragons harming any human for any reason. If Shayla broke that Covenant, even to aid her daughter Myrilandel, many dangers to every dragon would follow. She had only dragon dreams as weapons against murdering humans.

Shayla broadcast the vision of a blazing desert into their midst: Wave after wave of rolling, red sand hills met the raiders. Sun burned through their clothing, parched their throats, and drained their bodies of sweat.

Myri saw what they saw, but with a curious transparency. None of the illusions of heat and arid air touched her. But her empathic talent forced her to share their emotions and pain.

Desperately she clasped the silver cord attached to her

heart with both hands, trying to communicate with her husband. It had never worked over this great a distance before. Maybe danger would fuel her pleas.

Nothing. She looked around for another avenue of escape from the raiders and from her own empathic link to them.

One man stood free of the illusion. He grinned at Myri and stalked toward her, swinging his club and whistling a jaunty tune—the same tune he'd whistled as he thrust a knife into Nimbulan's gut last spring. Televarn. The Rover chieftain who oozed lies and tricks with every word he spoke, every magical spell he wove.

Shayla added the image of a blessed oasis with a creek to her illusion. The people stumbled into a real creek, pressing their faces into the refreshing water. Shayla pushed the image of a shallow pool, no more than half a finger-length in depth.

The true creek ran nearly as deep as half a man. The dragon increased the sun's temperature in the vision, urging the evil men and women to press their faces deeper, deeper into the water. Relentlessly she pressed the dragon dream into their minds.

Air evaporated from Myri's lungs in empathy with the men and women around her. Fleeing villagers as well as the dark-haired, dark-clad raiders staggered in the imagined desert heat. Only Televarn remained upright. He continued his approach toward Myri.

She tried to run. A new cramp stopped her. Powwell and Kalen weren't there to help her. They, too, rushed toward the creek to drink.

Shayla! Myrilandel shouted. *Stop the dream. They die. They will all die.*

(And so they should. They dared harm you. They must die, by their own foolishness.)

If they die, then I will share their deaths. I am linked to them by my talent. I feel what they feel.

(You will be free of them in a moment. You need not share their fate.)

Televarn, their leader, is immune to your visions, as am I. He continues his pursuit of us. The children can't flee with me because of the dragon dream.

The vision evaporated.

A harsh blow to the back of Myri's head shot pain down her spine. Black spots crowded her vision. She stumbled. Powwell recovered enough to catch her. Kalen dragged her forward.

(Not that way. Evil men await you there!)

"Yes, this way, it's safe. I know it's safe," Kalen insisted.

Myri tried focusing on the trees around her and the path Kalen followed. Two of everything swam before her.

Two Televarns grabbed her harshly by the neck. She flailed against him. He tightened his grip, threatening to choke the life from her.

Other men bound Kalen and Powwell with stout ropes. Powwell kicked at his captor. Piedro punched him in the jaw, smiling vilely. Kalen screamed and thrashed. Abruptly she ceased, staring ahead with blank eyes.

Myri lurched forward, trying to get to her daughter.

"One more move, and I slash your belly open. I have no use for another man's child, Myrilandel," Televarn hissed in her ear.

She stilled her struggles.

"That's better, *cherbein.* I always knew you loved me best. As soon as you are rid of Nimbulan's brat, you will be my mate again. For all time."

The trees seemed to double. The colors shifted and swirled into a mighty vortex. Had Shayla superimposed another form of vision on her eyes? What did it all mean?

"I can't have you remembering the way to your new home, *cherbein.*" Televarn laughed as he pounded something into Myri's temple.

The silver cord connecting her heart to Nimbulan's dissolved. Just as blackness enveloped her, she heard Shayla bugle her distress to every mind that could hear.

(The Covenant is broken!)

No, Shayla. Don't break the Covenant, she sobbed. *Don't desert us when we need you most.*

Chapter 2

Intense magical power swirled around Powwell in ever tightening eddies. Pain assaulted his joints. A great roaring filled his mind.

His talent cried out for the opportunity to tap the surging power and use it. Almost instinctively he drew the power into himself as if gathering dragon magic. The special place behind his heart where he stored magic couldn't hold the energy. It coursed along his nerve endings and erupted from his fingers and toes and the ends of his hair to rejoin the force that generated it.

Then abruptly the sensation of being caught in an airless vortex ceased. Powwell's ears continued to ring in the sudden silence. His body ached as if he'd been dragged through the surf of the little cove by the village.

An enticing melody hummed within his mind. He knew a compulsion to turn around and reenter the vortex.

Intense fear of the unknown kept Powwell rigid, with his back to the alluring song.

Inside his tunic pocket, Thorny, his hedgehog familiar, gibbered in fear. The little animal's bristling spines pricked Powwell's chest through his layers of winter clothing.

With Thorny's help, Powwell oriented himself to the planet. He located the South Pole of Kardia Hodos. With that position firmly anchored into his consciousness, he knew up and down, right and left, night and day. Only then did he became aware of moving his body.

Pain throbbed behind his eyes. He tried to raise his hands to press his fingers against his eyelids.

Something held his arms at his sides, at the same time

pulling his hands forward. He twisted a little and winced as scratchy rope bit into his chest where it pinned his arms at his sides. More rope bound his hands in front of him. A dark-skinned man dragged him forward by his wrist bonds. His skin chafed and burned beneath the constant pressure on the ropes.

Powwell risked opening his eyes a little and stumbled over rubble on a rough path. Black and gray surrounded him.

He was *underground*. The entire weight of Kardia Hodos seemed to press upon his head and chest, robbing him of air.

No. Only his imagination and fear made him breathe so shallowly, fighting for every scrap of air.

A new noise rushed toward him like surf over the Dragon Teeth rock formation in the cove. *Yeek, kush, kush. Yeek, kush, kush.* The sound grew with every step forward. It echoed and multiplied until it overshadowed the sound of Powwell's heart throbbing in his head.

The air heated until it rasped against Powwell's throat. He longed for a drink of water—even the sulfurous stuff in the hot spring near the clearing.

Despair washed over his emotions like a living entity, compounding the heat. He began to sweat.

He wanted to roll himself into a ball, just like Thorny did, and ignore the world until all this strangeness went away and he was safely back in Myrilandel's clearing.

He thought of cool green trees, shaded saber ferns, and clear mountain streams. The heat intensified.

"Move, move, move. We haven't much time!" Televarn whispered hoarsely. He prodded the man dragging Powwell with a stick—as if herding cattle.

Memory returned abruptly to Powwell. Televarn had raided the village with fire and sword. The Rover chieftain had kidnapped the pregnant witchwoman and her fly-wacket. He'd also snared Powwell and Kalen. Why?

At least their captor was Televarn and not Moncriith the Bloodmage. With Televarn, they had a chance to live and maybe escape. Moncriith didn't want any magicians or politicians left alive except himself.

Powwell hoped the Rovers hadn't brutally murdered anyone in the village. Moncriith would have burned them all in his obsession to burn Myri at the stake and thus rid the world of demons.

Quickly, Powwell checked the line of marching bodies in front of him. An older Rover woman, clad in black highlighted by red and purple, pulled on Myri's bonds, somewhat more gently than the Rover man dragged Powwell.

Ahead of them, a younger Rover woman, also in black but wearing a fire-green vest and blood-red trim on her skirt, yanked at Kalen until the little girl fell flat on her face.

Powwell almost cried out in protest of the rough treatment.

Kalen appeared nearly unconscious as the Rover dragged her to her feet. Myri moved in the same disjointed daze.

Televarn ignored Powwell, as if he expected his captive to be unaware as well. The Rover wanted them dazed and obedient for a reason. Just before the massive field of magic had engulfed him, Powwell remember Televarn saying something about not knowing the way to their new home.

Powwell kept his eyes half-closed. He could still see, but Televarn couldn't tell that he was awake. He needed time to gather information and plan.

A dour-faced older Rover yanked on Powwell's bonds. He stumbled forward on nearly numb legs. Two half running steps later, full sensation returned abruptly to his body. His legs felt like tree sap in the grinding heat. His head pounded more fiercely than before.

"I said 'move,' *s'murghit.* We have to get to the surface before Yaassima finds us," Televarn hissed through his teeth. Impatiently he moved beyond Powwell. He strode ahead of the dozen Rovers to the first man in line who carried a heavy sack over his shoulder.

Amaranth was in that sack. Powwell remembered how fiercely the flywacket had fought imprisonment within the dark canvas. From the wriggling within the sack, Powwell guessed that Amaranth still fought for freedom. But his talons and teeth didn't seem to penetrate the heavy canvas.

"Follow me, Piedro. I don't want you getting lost down here and betraying the entire plan," Televarn said.

Piedro—the man who carried Amaranth—flashed the Rover chieftain an evil sneer, but he yielded the lead. His scalp wounds from Amaranth's claws had clotted messily in his sleek hair.

The black-and-gray landscape resolved into a long tunnel broken by small caverns. Powwell didn't know of any cave system near the village and the clearing, other than Shayla's lair. The big female dragon would never allow Televarn to hold them hostage in the lair.

Powwell tested the strength of his bonds with a small magic probe. The ropes remained firmly knotted, sealed with a magic he couldn't understand. They didn't move against his sweat-slick skin. If he could break a single strand of rope, he could wriggle free and take care of Myri and Kalen. He'd promised Nimbulan he'd protect them. He'd never broken a promise before!

Who would help Myri when the baby decided to enter the world? He had to get her back home before then. Nimbulan depended upon him to protect the family while the Senior Magician was detained in the capital.

"Quickly. They'll change shifts in the pit in a moment. We have to cross the big cavern in just a few heartbeats," Televarn directed his people.

Powwell took a longer than normal step so that his hands were closer to his chest without changing the pressure on the lead rope. *Thorny,* he probed the hedgehog with his mind. He knew better than to touch his familiar without warning. Thorny hunched and rolled in response to the mental caress. Then he relaxed his spines and wiggled his nose. He relayed a series of scent impressions to Powwell. This place was strange beyond new. The hedgehog had never smelled anything like this before. No plants. Few insects. A lot of fear. And too much noise. *Yeek kush kush. Yeek kush kush.*

Thorny, can you talk to Kalen's familiar? Have the beast wake her up a little. He couldn't see Kalen's pet on her shoulder; perhaps it was hiding beneath her skirts.

Thorny hunched again and remained firmly locked in a defensive ball. He wanted water and quiet. So did Powwell.

A flicker of white moved at the edge of Powwell's vision. Lumbird bumps raised on his arms and back. He risked turning his head to see what threat he and Thorny both sensed.

Nothing. Just more black and gray stretching in all directions. He almost gave in to the feeling of hopelessness. For Myri and Kalen, he had to fight the emotions that pressed against him from the outside. He had to appear bewitched for a little while longer.

The tunnel walls narrowed again 'and lowered. Powwell resisted the urge to duck beneath the heavy ceiling. Myri didn't duck in her unconscious movement. Televarn didn't either and he was only a finger's length taller than the witchwoman. To maintain the illusion of sleepwalking, Powwell couldn't cower away from the rocks that seemed ready to drop and crush him.

They passed through a large cavern. The path seemed clearer, well-trodden. He breathed a little easier, less aware of the tons of dirt and rock above him.

Televarn pointed toward another narrow tunnel. Piedro stepped confidently into the darkness with the now quiet Amaranth still in the sack upon his back. The older Rover woman yanked Myri's rope and followed. So did Kalen's leader. Powwell gulped uneasily.

"They'll wake up soon." Televarn inspected Kalen. The girl swayed as she walked. Her head bobbed. "We have to be aboveground before they come to. We can't have them suspect the dragongate exists." He prodded the lead Rover harshly in the back.

Dragongate? What was that? The alluring, unknown song lingered in his memory. He needed to go back to it, to join with the intense forces that threatened to tear him apart— at the same time the vortex hinted at joining with the great secrets of the universe. Secrets beyond comprehension to mere mortals.

Powwell risked a tiny turn of his head to search the cave system for something unusual. Only gray rock walls shadowed with black met his gaze. Where was the light that produced shadows? He didn't see any torches, 'nor did the light flicker like a natural flame. A steady glow seemed to come from the ceiling. But darkness followed them, engulfing the light soon after they passed by.

Where are we? He tried touching Kalen's mind. Their rapport was strong; she should respond to the lightest probe. She remained blank and unresponsive. Then he tried to bring his TrueSight to the front of his awareness—a harder task. His head throbbed and he lost focus. No magic responded to his quest. He reached deeper into his being in search of stored dragon magic.

Nothing. He was empty. He'd used it all trying to get Myri safely into the forest. There must be a ley line nearby. He could tap the energy embedded in the Kardia to fuel his magic. The clearing was full of ley lines and so was the village.

Nothing. Wherever they were, the land and the air were devoid of energy to fuel his talent.

He must have been unconscious for longer than he thought. But his inner awareness of the planet and the passage of time insisted that he'd only lost his senses for a few heartbeats. Thorny agreed with him. The tiny hedgehog gibbered of dark magic and holes in time.

Televarn urged them up the steep incline, increasing his pace with each step. Everyone breathed faster and more shallowly. Sweat poured down Powwell's face and back. If only he had a drink of water, he could think straight.

A gate of crossed iron bars blocked their path. Televarn touched the lock with a strange metal wand. It unlatched silently. Where did he get the magic to do that? Rovers supposedly had strange powers, but they had to have fuel like any other magician whether it be dragons, ley lines, or blood. Could Televarn tap the heavy emotions that pressed against Powwell?

Televarn pushed the gate open. The hinges didn't protest. It was well maintained by someone.

At last they emerged into broader tunnels that looked as if men had attempted to smooth the walls with tools. Even without magic, Powwell knew that other lives drifted close by, possibly in adjacent tunnels. The air became sweeter and more plentiful. Each breath came easier. They neared the surface.

With the release of the tremendous weight on his senses, Powwell began to hope. He sought landmarks and avenues of escape within the limited range of his half-closed eyes. He stretched his hearing, praying for some hint of where Televarn had brought them.

He saw a flamboyant tapestry draped across another tunnel opening. Some private apartment?

If only he had some magic to reach out with. He needed to know how extensive this cave system was and how many people inhabited it.

They paused by a very large tapestry. It would more than cover all the walls of Myri's little hut. Red, blood red, dominated the scenes depicted here. Executions and terrible tortures filled the weaving. Beheadings, hangings, dozen of arrows piercing a naked man. Racks and hot pokers, victims writhing in agony. Powwell almost had the impression he was watching the horrible events unfold before his eyes.

Then they moved on. Televarn thrust aside the next tapestry. It was as large as the previous one. Powwell stared at the amazing pictures of naked men and women coupling in bizarre and obscene combinations.

He closed his eyes in disgust. Where were they that misery and perversion dominated the walls?

Embarrassed heat wanted to flood his face all the way to his ears. He fought for calm, breathing evenly, looking elsewhere. Desperately, he hoped his flushed face could be attributed to the unnatural heat of the lower caverns.

Televarn peered behind the tapestry, seemingly unaware of the obscenities he held in his hand. Odd yellow light poured out from a vast open space beyond the woven wall covering.

Sunlight? No. Too yellow, like the glow in the lower caverns that brightened and dimmed in response to the passage of people. Powwell couldn't see any hint of the normal green firelight. Thorny wouldn't be able to help him figure it out. The hedgehog's eyesight was terrible.

Televarn beckoned his troop to enter the room beyond. He pressed his finger to his lips, signaling silence. All of them moved cautiously on the balls of their feet.

They entered a large room with a dais running the length of one wall. In front of the dais rested a rectangular stone of dressed granite. It stood about as high as a tall man's waist. Powwell had the impression of an altar, except . . . except a sturdy metal spike was jammed into the rock of each of the four corners. Manacles dangled from each of the stakes.

An altar all right.

But the benevolent Stargods had never been worshiped

here. This had to be a temple to Simurgh, the ancient demon who demanded blood sacrifice. Powwell had seen descriptions of similar underground temples during the moons he studied at the School for Magicians.

That hideous religion had been outlawed in all of the Three Kingdoms almost a thousand years ago. The temples to Simurgh had been destroyed and filled with rubble. But not here. Where were they?

"What pretty prizes have you brought me this time, Televarn?" an oily feminine voice asked from the center of the dais. No one had been there a moment ago.

A tall woman with white-blond hair and almost colorless skin, similar to Myri's, stood at the exact center of the raised stage. Another tapestry, this one of a remarkably lifelike, rippling waterfall hung behind her. Not a thread on the wall covering fluttered to indicate recent movement. The woman wore a simple gown of glittering sapphire blue. Diamonds glinted in her nearly colorless hair, picking up the yellow of the uncanny light and the blue of her gown. She seemed to sparkle all over, sort of like a dragon standing in direct sunlight.

Powwell couldn't tell how old or young she was because of the odd light. She flicked her very long, talonlike fingers in an elegant gesture. The hideous altar groaned and slowly descended into the floor until it became another paving stone. With another gesture the woman sent the stakes into hiding as well.

No wonder the Stargods hadn't been able to find and destroy this altar!

"Yaassima!" Televarn opened his eyes wide in feigned innocence. "I did not expect you to be in residence today."

She smiled with a slight twist of one corner of her mouth.

Powwell didn't like the menace that remained in her eyes.

"Tell me about your prizes. I see you have found a relative of mine." The woman glided forward to the edge of the dais. A dozen black-clad guards appeared on the platform behind her. Each man wore at least three weapons. Four of them carried strange metal wands that appeared to be hollow.

The same kind of wand Televarn had used to open the gate.

"Bring the woman closer," Yaassima ordered.

"My petty hostages are not worthy of the attention of the Kaalipha of Hanassa." Televarn eased toward the doorway on the opposite side of the room. He dragged Myri's rope behind him. She had no choice but to follow.

Her eyes flickered slightly. Her hands moved instinctively to rub at her belly. She must be nearly awake.

Powwell sensed movement in the stretched skin that protected the baby. He hoped the unborn child merely kicked and this was not a portent of early labor. The baby wasn't due for another moon.

So far, Kalen had made no sign that her mind stirred beneath whatever spell Televarn had placed upon her.

"Nonsense, Televarn. Obviously you have found another descendant of dragons, one I did not know about. Who are you, child?" Yaassima seemed to float down the two steps to the main floor. Her sparkling gown hid all traces of her feet. She stopped directly in front of Myri. The guards followed her.

Powwell watched as awareness returned to Myri's eyes. She darted glances all around her, opening and closing her mouth in silent protest. Her shoulders hunched and she bent her spine as if protecting her belly—or withstanding a pain.

"She's just a simple witchwoman from the hills," Televarn replied.

"Is the child yours, Televarn?" Yaassima placed her hand familiarly on Myri's bulging belly.

Myri hunched again. Her hands fluttered and clutched again. She groaned slightly.

Danger screamed from the last remnant of Powwell's magical senses. He struggled within his bonds. He had to get Myri home. Now. Before the baby came. Nimbulan needed him to take care of Myri and the baby.

No one paid any attention to him. All eyes seemed glued to the Kaalipha.

"No, the child is not his. I would never allow him to father a child of mine," Myri spat. "Release us immediately. I will have retribution from him for this outrage." She gritted her teeth and held back yet another groan.

"Such defiance. A worthy descendant of dragons!" Yaassima stepped back. A true smile spread across her pale features and her eyes opened wide in delight. "If Televarn has no claim on the child, then where is its father?"

"My husband had business in Coronnan City. Televarn waited until we were alone and then kidnapped us."

"The husband of a witchwoman with business in the city? Magician Nimbulan is the only man that could be. And you must be Myrilandel—the witchwoman who saved the naive king of Coronnan. He's your long-lost brother, I believe. You saved him from death, and then he exiled you. And your husband allowed it. Not only allowed it, but he stayed in the city to serve the Peacemaker rather than follow his pregnant wife into exile. What a delicious scandal. Name your reward, Televarn. You have brought me a rare prize indeed."

"The Kaalipha is too generous." Televarn dipped his head in a gesture that resembled humility. But Powwell saw him bite back a protest.

"Then I give you the commission to assassinate King Quinnault, Myrilandel's worthless brother. I need control over Coronnan, and he stands in my way. There is a reward of one thousand gold pieces for confirmation of his death. And if his pet magician Nimbulan is caught in the backlash, I will add an additional five hundred gold pieces in Myrilandel's name. She will be free of the blackguard."

"Never!" Myri cried in protest. "I will never countenance . . . uuuugh," she ended on a groan of pain. Her hands pressed against her belly once more.

"Oh, and take these hideous children with you, Televarn." The Kaalipha ignored Myri's outburst. "I have no need of them." She flicked her wrist again, and a small knife appeared in her hand. Myri's bonds seemed to dissolve at the touch of the blade.

"You can't kill my husband!" Myri screamed. "I'll kill you myself, Televarn, before I let you harm my husband." She lunged for the Rover. Before she had gone two steps, she doubled over in pain. Her hands clenched at the sides of her belly.

Powwell lurched forward, needing to cradle her, protect her. The Rover who managed his ropes held him firmly in place.

"Now see what you have done, Televarn. She has gone into labor prematurely. You'd better hope the baby lives.

I have never found another person who looks as much like a dragon as me. Therefore, we are related by spirit if not blood. Go now and complete your commission." Yaassima reached to cradle Myri in her arms. She beckoned to the older woman who had led Myri through the tunnels. "You there, Erda, you are a midwife. You will stay and see to her. Ease her pain with drugs—whatever will keep her quiet. Nastfa," she waved at the guard in the center of the phalanx, "carry Myrilandel to my private suite. Gently."

"Powwell, Kalen," Myri called weakly. "You must warn Nimbulan and my brother, the king. Kalen can talk to dragons, have her tell Shayla. You have to warn them."

Televarn yanked harshly on Powwell's rope. He resisted, trying desperately to guide his steps toward Myrilandel. Televarn smiled, squinting his eyes with malice. This time he yanked so hard on Kalen's rope that she fell to her knees. She cried out in pain as the paving stones tore patches of skin from her knees.

"You'll warn no one, Powwell," Televarn said through clenched teeth. He whipped out a knife and held it to Kalen's throat. "So much as a weak cry in the night, and I shall kill the girl and make you watch while I slit her throat. I have uses for you now, but they are not so strong I must keep you alive if you defy me. Murder is quite legal here in Hanassa, the City of Outlaws."

Chapter 3

"**D**on't touch that wine, Your Grace! It's poisoned." Nimbulan rushed into the Great Hall of King Quinnault's keep. He was breathless, and his heart raced from his run across the bridge from School Isle. The sense of danger intensified the closer he came to the king. Lumbird bumps stood up all along his arms and his hair stood on end at his nape.

Silence descended upon the busy hall. Servants stopped their endless routines in mid-step. Courtiers and petitioners halted their babbling in mid-sentence. Two architects stared at him as they poised over their intricate drawings. Ink dripped from their pens. Even King Quinnault's pack of hunting dogs ceased their constant yapping and quarreling.

"What do you mean, Nimbulan?" Quinnault, King of Coronnan by the grace of the dragons, sat back in his demithrone at the high table. He left the golden goblet where the understeward had placed it moments ago. The servant still stood beside the king, jaw flapping, carrying tray clutched to his chest as if a talisman.

"It's poisoned, Your Grace. I saw your death and that cup in a vision through my glass." Nimbulan waved the gold-framed piece of precious clear glass. He'd been looking for a clue to his missing wife's whereabouts when the premonition of danger intruded.

Three weeks had passed since Shayla had announced to one and all that the Covenant with dragons was broken. No dragon had been seen in Coronnan since. The amount of dragon magic available to the magicians diminished each day.

Soon they would have to resort to illegal solitary magic
to perform everyday tasks of communication.

Nimbulan guessed that the dragons' withdrawal coincided
with the disappearance of his wife, Myrilandel, and the sev-
ering of the magical cord that bound him to her.

Nearly two weeks had passed since he had returned to
the capital after discovering her absence from the clearing.
The villagers had been extremely reluctant to tell him anything about her disappearance. They were too busy rebuild-
ing after a disastrous fire.

Not a day had passed since that Nimbulan hadn't searched
for her. Fruitlessly. Every spell went awry. He couldn't
sleep. His concentration wavered at the most inopportune
times. He had to find Myrilandel soon.

Quinnault and the magicians wanted Myri found, too.
They needed to restore the Covenant with the dragons. But
Quinnault had ordered Nimbulan to remain in the capital
while they monitored an attack fleet from Rossemeyer
gathering in the mouth of the Great Bay. The quest to find
Myrilandel should go to a younger man. No one doubted
that she must be found and the Covenant with the dragons restored.

"Who wishes me dead, Nimbulan?" Quinnault pushed his
heavy chair farther away from the table and the tainted
goblet.

"I didn't do it, Your Grace," the understeward protested.
"I only carried the cup here from the cellar. I didn't . . ."
He looked pleadingly toward his king.

"Who prepared the cup?" Nimbulan approached the
high table from the front, below the dais, never moving his
eyes away from the suspicious goblet. Moisture condensed
on the outside of the cold metal. Quinnault's favorite red
wine was always served at room temperature, not chilled.

Nimbulan didn't have much time. If the poison came
from magic, it would dissipate quickly, leaving no trace of
the assassin or clue to the nature of the spell.

"Did you ask for wine, Your Grace?" Nimbulan raised
his left hand, palm extended toward the goblet, fingers
slightly curved. The sense of danger stabbed his palm. Re-
flexively he jerked his hand away from the cup.

"No. But when it arrived, I welcomed it, not realizing I

was thirsty until then," Quinnault said as he slowly rose from his chair. His eyes remained fixed upon the cup.

"The new girl in the scullery told me to take it to you, Your Grace," the understeward said. "I don't question things like that, sir. The steward could have asked her to take the prepared cup to me. The order could have come from any number of people. I didn't do it, Your Grace!"

"A new servant?" Nimbulan raised his eyes to the understeward. The man's aura radiated layers of blue truth shot with the nearly white energy of fear. At least he could still sense auras. If he'd had to throw a truth spell over the young man, who knew what his magic would do.

"There are always new servants, Magician Nimbulan," the understeward explained. "They start in the scullery, and if they last, they move up to more respectable chores. I've been with His Grace five years. I would never think of harming him."

"You might not think of it, but a rogue magician could plant the idea in your head and you'd never know it. Describe the girl." Nimbulan moved his raised hand in a circle, wrapping the dangerous cup in a web of magical containment. When he saw the noon sunlight sparkle against the magic, he relaxed a little. He'd managed at least this simple spell. Time would not touch the poison and humans could not touch the cup.

"Short." The understeward held his hand up to his chin, indicating the maid's height. "A delectable little mole just to the right of her mouth. Dark hair and eyes. Beautiful eyes . . ." He drifted off in contemplation of the new scullery maid.

"How dark? Olive skin tones or fairer—more pink?" Nimbulan transferred his gaze from the cup to the understeward in alarm. *A mole to the right of the mouth.* No. Televarn wouldn't dare send Maia to do his dirty work.

Nimbulan hadn't thought much about Maia since he'd met Myrilandel. He wanted to remember his brief affair with the Rover girl as a time of spontaneous joy. But his mind told him the entire sordid mess had been manipulated by Televarn, the head of Maia's clan.

A wrongness grated against his mind. Televarn was a power-hungry, manipulative bastard, but he had courage.

If he wanted to kill someone, he'd do the deed himself; as he had tried to murder Nimbulan with a knife.

"Rover-dark hair, I think. Her skin was so smooth and clear, except for that delectable mole. . . ." The understeward fell back into his reverie.

"Guard, dunk his head in a steed trough, a very cold one," Nimbulan ordered the men who hovered close by, hands on short swords. "He's been bewitched, and I think I know by whom. Bring me the biggest bowl you can find—crockery not silver, filled with fresh creek water. Remember, a free-running creek, not a confined well." A Rover spell to catch a Rover assassin.

Fortunately, Rover magic required multiple magicians. Nimbulan wouldn't have to depend upon his increasingly erratic magic for accurate results.

He searched the pockets of his everyday working trews and tunic. The wand he sought eluded him. *S'murghit,* he'd have to levitate the wand from his private chamber. He pictured within his mind the necessary tool with the faceted crystal suspended from the end by a reinforced spiderweb, right where he'd seen it last, on his desk. He'd locked the door to his chamber with a mundane key to keep the apprentices on housekeeping duty from disturbing his research. No need for magic on the seal.

From this distance he couldn't guarantee the levitation or the unlocking of his door.

"What do you need, Nimbulan? I can send someone to fetch it," King Quinnault offered.

A guard appeared with a bread bowl, large enough to hold several pounds of rising dough. Beside him stood a second man with a pitcher of water, still dripping from having been dunked into the creek or river.

Nimbulan patted his pockets one more time in search of the wand he wanted. He fished a small rock out of his pocket instead.

"I've found what I need, Your Grace." Not a faceted crystal that had been made perfect by men, but a naturally beautiful stone polished by water and sand. Like the free water and the crockery bowl, this natural stone was a tool a Rover could use.

Carefully he set the bowl on the floor in the middle of the Great Hall. The rushes had been scraped clear of the stone flooring and the assembly of people and dogs hugged the wall, giving Nimbulan space to work. Sunlight streamed through the high windows, illuminating the bowl in a glowing warmth. Three hastily summoned magicians, including his senior journeyman Rollett, knelt beside Nimbulan, linked to him in trance and by touch. They encircled the bowl.

Gently Nimbulan adjusted his magic to match the compounded energy his assistants gave him. They'd keep the spell aligned and focused, even if he couldn't.

Where in Simurgh's hell had Myri gotten to? What had happened to the silver cord that connected their hearts?

He filled the bowl with the fresh water. Then, together, he and the magicians levitated the poisonous cup into the bowl until it rested snugly upright, surrounded almost to the rim by fresh creek water.

Only then, did Nimbulan dissolve the web of magic wrapped around the cup. It fell apart much more easily than it had gone together.

"The clay that formed the bowl is the Kardia." He raised his voice as if chanting.

"Sunlight is Fire," Rollett picked up the chant.

"The source of our question rests in Water," Lyman added.

"The magic we add comes from Air," Gilby, the fourth magician continued.

"We stand at North, South, East, and West. The four elements combined with the four cardinal directions form the *Gaia*. All is one. One is all," Nimbulan finished. Subtly he shifted his body so that he stood at the south of the spell—the direction of the nearest magnetic pole. The forces of the pole should keep his magic under control even if his mind strayed.

Myri had to be safe, wherever she was. The dragons would have done more than announce that the Covenant was broken if anything had happened to his wife.

His wife. She should be at his side, not exiled, not missing.

Nimbulan forced his mind back to the problem of poison and Rovers, looking deep into the mystery of sunlight sparkling against the clear water. He dropped the agate into the bowl close to the golden cup. Ripples moved outward from the stone, spreading the sunlight up and out.

He whispered a spell in the most ancient language of all Coronnan. The words of the dead language fell clumsily from his tongue.

The water clouded, dark mists boiled up from the bottom where the agate lay touching the base of the cup. He blinked away the ominous portent symbolized by the clouds, willing the mist to part and reveal the image of the one who had poured poison into the wine and sent it unbidden to the king.

Lightning crackled across the surface of the water. The clouds roiled and grew as black as the void between the planes of existence. More lighting flashed before his eyes. He dared not blink away the brightness lest he lose whatever brief glimpse might be granted. Streamers of color coiled and tangled in a giant knot in the air above the water.

The assembled men in the Great Hall gasped with awe.

Another blinding flash of light, bearing all colors of the spectrum, cleared the surface of the water.

Nimbulan peered eagerly for sight of the one he sought.

A face rose up from the depths of the bowl. The beloved face of Myrilandel. Her white-blond hair streamed out behind her, unbound and uncovered. Her long face with its straight nose and high cheekbones reflected the generations of aristocratic breeding overlaid with a feminine softness. Her eyes searched right and left with an anxiety that filled Nimbulan's gut with fear. Behind her, desert-colored buildings rose in a tall circle, trapping her within their midst.

NO! Myri couldn't be responsible for this assassination attempt. He wouldn't believe it.

Chapter 4

Nimbulan placed his gold-framed glass between his eyes and the water, moving it back and forth for better focus. He had to see the truth. Myri could not poison Quinnault. She valued family too highly, and the king was her only blood kin.

He had to believe that his lack of concentration had brought him the image he had sought in a previous spell rather than truth in this one.

The image faded until only Myri's pale eyes remained, pleading with him for . . . A scratch in the bottom of the bowl jumped into view, magnified many times its size by the glass.

Nimbulan stood up from his crouched position. His knees didn't want to unfold. They creaked and groaned for every one of his fifty years.

Myri had made him feel like a teenager again. Her youth and beauty sparked his vitality as well as his intellect. Every day without her weighed heavily on his soul and his heart. And now he didn't even have the magical silver cord that had bound them together.

He'd allowed that bond to suffice for too long. And now he couldn't find her at all.

"I saw the face of a Rover woman," Lyman, the eldest of all the Commune of Magicians, said. "Very pretty in a dark, exotic way. A man could get lost in those deep, dark eyes . . ." His voice trailed off, very much like the understeward's had. Then, abruptly, he roused himself with a visible shake. "She had a mole to the right of her mouth—positioned perfectly to entice a man to kiss her. I watched as she poured a very cold liquid into the cup and whispered words over it. I could not hear the words, but I recognized the lilting pattern of them. She spoke in an old language. A language that is almost forgotten within the Three Kingdoms. As she said the words, the liquid in the cup foamed and nearly boiled over the rim, yet I knew it to be a cold boil. Unnaturally cold."

"I saw her, too!" Gilby and Rollett agreed. As senior journeymen magicians, they often worked in concert with Nimbulan and Lyman. Nimbulan trusted them. Rollett's quick eye for detail was unfailing. Gilby was particularly adept at delving into symbolism for patterns that reflected truth.

"The image faded very quickly. As quickly as the poison in the cup." Lyman looked at the clear water in the bowl as if he could pull more images from it.

"Maia. The woman is Maia," Nimbulan said. But Maia had never had an original thought. None of her clan did. Every thought, every action was manipulated by Televarn. Nimbulan had experienced Televarn's direct mind control during the season he lived with the clan.

I heard a baby cry in the background of the vision, Nimbulan, Lyman said directly into Nimbulan's mind. *I knew instantly that the baby had pink skin and auburn hair. The same color hair as yours.*

"Maia has a baby? My baby?" Nimbulan whispered, praying that only Lyman heard his conjecture. The emotional blow almost sent Nimbulan staggering. A child of his own loins? Magicians rarely sired children. He'd given up hope of ever having a child of his own. He had to find Maia and claim his baby. He had to find Myri, his beloved wife.

How? When? Which first?

"You know the Rovers, Nimbulan." Lyman cocked his head as if listening to something in the distance. But he didn't take his eyes off of Nimbulan. "Did you see who you sought in the vision? Can you find these people again?" Mischief danced behind the old man's eyes. His words had more than one meaning. Possibly many more than two.

What was Lyman up to? Had he seen Maia or Myri in the vision? "Maia may have been the instrument of the delivery of the poison. But Televarn directed the assassination attempt, as he directs all within his sphere." *I will not have him in charge of my child's welfare. I must find them. Now.*

Where was Maia? Was she truly involved in the assassination plot against the king?

Where was the child? Why hadn't Maia told him she carried his baby? She could have sought him out after he left the Rover clan, or sent him a message. She must know that he had survived Televarn's knife.

Think, s'murghit. He had to think clearly. Relying on information given him by others grated against his nerves. but all he could think about was Myri trapped within a bowl of red sandstone walls.

"A search across the void would tell us for certain who tainted the cup, and where they hide," Quinnault offered. He'd had some training as a magician and priest before becoming lord of his clan and then king. While he knew magic theory well, he had very little talent and knew nothing of dragon magic. Though the dragons had partially awakened the king's telepathic powers, he shared them with none but the dragons.

"No, Your Grace, we can no longer access the void. By law, we cannot use rogue methods even to serve our king," Lyman replied. The old man clutched Nimbulan's arm, offering him unspoken support and confidence; taking charge until Nimbulan sorted his thoughts and could speak without blurting out his true vision.

Myri couldn't be involved. Quinnault was her birth brother though they'd been separated when Myri was two. Somehow, Maia was involved. Maia, the mother of his child. Myri, the love of his life.

His thoughts refused to settle on one idea.

Later. We will discuss your vision later. Trust me to know that Televarn and his Rovers are your enemy in this and other matters, Lyman said into Nimbulan's mind.

Nimbulan forced his circling thoughts into some kind of order. Rovers had been banned from Coronnan, along with all magicians who could not or would not gather dragon magic. Myri had been among those forced to leave. Myri and her two adopted children, Kalen and Powwell. Why hadn't he seen the children in the vision? Only Myri. Only the one he truly sought with his heart as well as his mind.

Suddenly Nimbulan's mind brightened. Myri was a healer;

she would never harm anyone, especially not Quinnault. The king had been brother to the little girl Myrilandel. When the girl-child nearly died, Amethyst, the purple-tipped dragon had taken over the weakened body and healed it. The two personalities had fought for dominance and compromised on forgetfulness until Myri had grown into the knowledge of both her heritages. She would never harm her only living blood relative.

I must go in search of Myrilandel. She is in terrible danger. I sensed it in the vision, now I know for sure, he whispered to Lyman telepathically—the only way he could be certain no one else overheard. Rollett was capable of eavesdropping, but he wouldn't. The boy respected privacy too much. Gilby found telepathy difficult and relied on his other talents.

I must add Maia to this quest, Nimbulan decided. He had to find her before Televarn tainted the baby's upbringing.

"The Rovers are a race not known for their forgiveness, or short memories," Quinnault mused. "Guard Captain, send all available men to search for the assassin. Any Rover found within two days' walk of the capital must be arrested and brought here for investigation," he said to the officer who paced anxiously behind his chair.

The guard practically ran out of the hall, gathering armed men as he went.

Nimbulan nodded his approval then turned his thoughts back to the problem at hand. He had last lain with Maia the night before Televarn tried to kill him with a knife between his ribs. That had been in early spring, nearly three seasons ago. The babe would be newborn about now.

"You can't go in search of your destiny yet, Nimbulan," Lyman whispered, drawing Nimbulan aside as if to consult on the assassination issue "Soon, though. Wait until we can make arrangements in private. King Quinnault has ordered you to remain in the capital rather than search for Myrilandel. He won't take kindly to your leaving on this quest either. He needs you to counter whatever ploy the attack fleet from Rossemeyer plans."

They stared at each other in a moment of complete understanding. They barely heard the commotion at the entrance to the Great Hall.

"Your Grace, you can't be considering this draft of the

treaty. The conditions are preposterous!" Lord Hanic burst into the room, oblivious to the tension surrounding the bowl of water and the cup of wine still sitting on the floor.

"Lord Hanic to see you, Your Grace," a servant squeaked from the doorway somewhat belatedly. He straightened his stiff tunic in the new green-and-gold livery of the royal house. A stylized dragon was embroidered over his heart.

"Calm down," King Quinnault soothed, not at all flustered by the lack of protocol. He hadn't been king long enough to expect the elaborate courtesy that plagued other kingdoms. "All of those 'preposterous' clauses are negotiable. However, we should at least pretend to consider them so that Ambassador Jhorge-Rosse can tell his king that he presented them. We might also lull him into the belief that we are incredibly stupid because we do consider them. His natural feeling of superiority might make him stumble into a mistake in our favor." Quinnault ambled back to the demithrone at the table, ready to return to business as usual.

"Your Grace," Nimbulan interrupted. "You don't need me further. Allow me and my assistants to clear away this mess and join the search for the assassin." If he stayed, Quinnault would drag him into yet another endless discussion about the blasted treaty.

"Stay, Nimbulan. The weather has been clear for two days. The Rossemeyerian fleet could attack at any moment. We need to plan our defenses. Now." Quinnault glared at his magician with an expression that tolerated no defiance. A new expression for the king, learned within the last year.

"His Lordship, General Jhorge-Rosse, Ambassador from the Serene Kingdom of Rossemeyer," the harried servant at the door announced.

Quinnault turned his attention from Nimbulan to the tall desert dweller who swept into the room in his all-concealing black robes. An elaborate black turban added more height to his imposing figure.

Rossemeyer's primary export consisted of mercenaries. Mercenaries, not assassins. No desert warrior would stoop to the dishonor of magical poison when a knife duel worked as well or better. Every member of the government in Rossemeyer had to have earned leadership on the field of battle before entering the battle of politics. The "Rosse" suffix

added to the ambassador's name was the highest honorific
allowed his people. Only members of the royal family made
the name a prefix.

Nimbulan motioned to the two journeymen to dispose of
the bowl and cup on their way back to the school. He
dispatched Lyman to organize the search for Televarn.

Was Rossemeyer's desert sand as red and black as Nimbulan had seen in the vision?

Rovers were known to seek refuge in the desert wastes
of Rossemeyer.

Concentrate! he ordered himself. *Find out what you can
and then leave quickly. Leave and follow your heart. Myrilandel.*

"Your Grace." Jhorge-Rosse dipped his head and perhaps one knee in a brief gesture of respect to the king. He
glanced sideways at Nimbulan and ignored Lord Hanic.

Nimbulan wondered briefly if his mud-stained leather
working clothes, dyed a common blue, earned him respect
or dismissal in the ambassador's eyes. He didn't allow himself to dwell on it. He had to find Myri and Maia.

"Your Grace, I have read your proposals and find them
nothing less than insulting," Jhorge-Rosse continued. "Are
you aware that our fleet is assembled in the Great Bay
ready to descend upon you if I do not report progress in
these negotiations *daily?*" The ambassador's calloused hand
rested near his hip, where a sword or dagger might be concealed beneath his robe.

"You remind me of that *daily,* General Jhorge-Rosse.
What precisely do you find so insulting in our proposal for
a resumption of trade? We are making concessions in buying large quantities of beta'arack, a noxious alcoholic brew
that we don't need and your only export, in exchange for
food which you cannot grow." Quinnault leaned back in
his chair, chin lifted, eyes cold and calculating.

"You and your magicians want my people to starve.
Your tariffs are absurd." Jhorge-Rosse's upper lip lifted in
a snarl.

Nimbulan edged closer to his king, fully aware of how
dangerous a man Jhorge-Rosse could be.

"You have fertile valleys rotting from the neglect of
three generations of civil war while my people starve, and
yet you demand added export tariffs before selling us the

food you would otherwise throw away!" Jhorge-Rosse's hand remained on the hilt of the concealed weapon.

"Tariffs and taxes are a natural means of earning income for the crown so that I may pay my troops to defend my borders, or hire your mercenaries from Rossemeyer if necessary." Quinnault narrowed his eyes. He made a point of placing both of his hands flat on the table. Jhorge-Rosse would earn no honor in murdering an unarmed man.

Nimbulan's magical armor snapped into place around his own body. He consciously extended it to wrap around his king, praying it wouldn't dissolve at his first stray thought. Quinnault was the one man who could hold together a government, demanding and getting the cooperation of all twelve lords of Coronnan. If Jhorge-Rosse killed or seriously wounded King Quinnault, the chaos and civil war that had plagued Coronnan for three generations would erupt once more. The bachelor king had no child to inherit the Coraurlia and the Covenant with the dragons.

The Covenant was broken. Shayla had proclaimed it. Because Myri was missing. He had to go after his wife, now.

He wrenched his attention back to his king and the volatile ambassador.

Jhorge-Rosse sniffed in Nimbulan's direction. He wrinkled his nose as if the magician, or his magic, smelled bad. "You are a coward who hides behind magicians. I refuse to deal with a man who cannot defend himself. Prepare for invasion! We will have unrestricted access to your rich farmlands." The ambassador stalked out of the room, robes flapping indignantly.

"Be prepared for your ships to run aground in the mud, General Ambassador Jhorge-Rosse!" Quinnault said. He exhaled sharply as if he'd been holding his breath.

Lord Hanic collapsed into the chair beside Quinnault. "Am I mistaken, or did that man just create an excuse to invade?"

Quinnault nodded in silent agreement. "I'm surprised he waited so long. We've been trading insults for weeks. He could have invaded two days ago, as soon as the last storm settled."

"Now what?" Hanic raised troubled eyes to Nimbulan.

"The tide turns as we speak." Nimbulan sensed the subtle shift in the position of the moon in relation to the poles.

"By sunset we will have a flood tide pushed by a storm still two days off the coast. The full moon will also raise the tide. The Rossemeyer fleet might very well negotiate the mudflats without mishap. That is why he chose today for his ultimatum."

"That is not an option, Master Magician." Quinnault leveled his gaze on Nimbulan. "We have six hours to block that armada. Three half-built warships and a scattering of fishing vessels won't stop them."

Chapter 5

Myri concentrated on Amaranth. Her mind blended with her flywacket familiar's as he flew to freedom with her message to Nimbulan.

She had only a few moments of privacy to send Amaranth on this desperate mission.

Warn him of the danger. Stay and protect him! She urged the flywacket above the bowl of the volcanic crater that formed the city of Hanassa. Deep within the Southern Mountains, this haven for outlaws, rogue magicians, and mercenary soldiers was lost to casual searchers. Only Amaranth could fly over the protections and lead rescuers back to Myri and the children. *After* he warned Nimbulan of the plot against him. If only she wasn't too late. She'd lost so much time and consciousness from the drugs Erda gave her—still gave her—and the concussion she had suffered during Televarn's kidnap.

(Who will guard you and the babe? I don't want to leave,) Amaranth replied even as he flew higher.

North. Fly north until you find my husband. Her shoulders hunched and her arms spread slightly as if she could catch the wind and fly with Amaranth.

She could sprout wings and fly with him to freedom—ending forever Kaalipha Yaassima's enslavement of her.

What if she couldn't transform back into her human body once she took dragon form? Her tiny baby, barely three weeks old, depended upon her for life and nurturing. Powell and Kalen were also captive. She couldn't leave them behind in this city of cutthroats and thieves. She didn't dare escape—yet.

For the moment she and her children lived. She could

extend her thoughts and cares beyond the immediate circle of her daily routine.

She had to warn Nimbulan of Televarn's treachery before Yaassima returned to the suite and prevented Amaranth's escape. Myri hated the decadent opulence of the rooms she shared with Yaassima. She might have rich food, lovely clothing, and comfortable furnishings, but it was a prison nonetheless. Nor did the two separate bedrooms with a large common room between offer the privacy and solitude Myri craved. Someone, a guard or a maid, always hovered nearby.

She hadn't been allowed outside the suite since that horrible day Televarn had kidnapped her and brought her to Hanassa. The baby had been born the day she arrived.

How long had Televarn kept her mind blank while they traveled here? How long had her husband suffered, not knowing her fate?

If only the silver cord of magic still connected her heart to his, she would know if he lived.

Myri turned her attention outward again. She established contact with Amaranth's mind. A sense of free soaring overtook her. A cold wind blasted Amaranth's face and lifted his wings. Freedom!

Through her familiar's eyes she saw the wide curve of the Great Bay, the mudflats on the western shores, and the braided delta of islands that made up the growing capital city.

Almost there. *Quickly, Amaranth. Yaassima comes.*

Her breath shortened in anticipation. Within a few heartbeats she would see the beloved face of her husband. "Nimbulan," she whispered. "How I miss you, husband. What made you stay away so long?"

Deep within her mind, she heard Amaranth cry out. He'd spotted the palace where King Quinnault lived. New construction gave the ancient keep an untidy look. She didn't dwell on the changes that had occurred in the last three seasons. The island next to the palace was her destination; the island where a vast pool of magical ley lines slept, hidden beneath compacted mud and silt. She honed in on the quiescent power in the pool.

She directed Amaranth's vision in an anxious search for

the man who had given her love and trust and a child when no other could.

Together, she and her familiar picked out the window of the room in the ancient monastery, now the School for Magicians, where Nimbulan slept. She had shared the room with him for a few precious days before her exile from Coronnan. Her baby had been conceived there. Conceived in love.

And now the baby's father didn't even know she existed. Myri had never told him, waiting for him to come to her so that she could relay the joyous news to his face. She had waited impatiently for him to come, always hoping that tomorrow . . . Neither she nor Powwell nor Kalen had perfected the summons spell. The road between the capital and her clearing was still too dangerous to trust a messenger to get through.

Pain stabbed her neck and chest, hot and fierce. Amaranth had been stabbed! He faltered from the wound. Myri's inner vision darkened as the pain swelled to encompass her entire being. Amaranth's agony pulled her mind deeper into his pain. Each heartbeat spread the burning acid through his veins.

Poison. Magic poison pierced them. His pain became hers. A deep wound beneath his left wing, perilously close to his heart, made him falter and lose altitude.

Myri clutched the baby to her breast. The warmth of the tiny body anchored her to the reality of her physical existence. The familiar pressure of milk swelling in her breasts kept her from following Amaranth deeper and deeper into paralysis.

Voices in the corridor warned of Yaassima's approach. Abruptly the pain ceased. Myri's vision swirled and brightened.

"Amaranth!" she screamed with her mind. Her voice remained a whisper. "Where are you?" Frantically she searched for some contact with her familiar. The door squeaked open. Myri couldn't allow Yaassima to break her precious contact with Amaranth.

Amaranth, fight the wound. Fight the magic. You have to live, Amaranth. You have to warn Nimbulan, Myri screamed again with her mind. The pain returned. Not the hot stabbing wound Amaranth suffered, but a dull aching loneliness that threatened to squeeze the life from her.

Don't die, Amaranth. Oh, please, don't die.

"We have no fleet of warships, Your Grace." Nimbulan said. "But we have an army of wily fishermen who work the mudflats every day of their lives." Nimbulan retrieved his gold-framed glass from inside his tunic. He walked to the nearest candle on the high table.

"The tariff on trade was merely an excuse to trigger an invasion," Quinnault said as he cleared the table of current projects with one sweep of his arm. "The warriors of Rossemeyer thrive on war, not food." The king summoned a map with a snap of his fingers. Two servants dashed to obey his order.

"My magicians, your fisherman, and every able-bodied person we can gather will have a long hard day ahead of them, but we have a chance, Your Grace." Nimbulan breathed deeply, seeking calm. He had a battle to organize, when he'd thought his days as a Battlemage were over.

He had to stay and fight when he'd rather leave on his quest to rescue his wife.

When his thoughts fell into order, he continued the breathing exercise—in three counts, hold, out three counts, triggering a light trance for the summons spell. No time to return to the school for magical tools and a treatise on naval warfare. He'd have one of the apprentices bring them from his private study. He couldn't levitate them through the locked door. Stuuvart, his steward, had a key.

Nimbulan finished his summons, then marched into the courtyard and the stairs to the top of the palace walls and the roof of the keep. He didn't bother to pocket his glass. He'd need it often in the coming hours. His head spun with ideas and plans, as it had in the old days when he prepared for battle nearly every week of the campaign season.

"Merawk!" The sharp cry of a large bird screeched through the glass, piercing Nimbulan's ears and mind.

"Mewrare."

"That sounds like Amaranth." Nimbulan ran up the stairwell. As soon as he opened the trapdoor to the watchtower he looked to the partially cloudy sky for signs of the half-cat, half-falcon he'd last seen in Myri's arms.

"Perhaps your wife's flywacket responded to your seeking vision, coming to you with word of Myrilandel." Lyman poked his head through the opening right beside him. Nimbulan scanned the bowl of the heavens rather than question how the old man had appeared so suddenly.

They both searched through a long moment of silence. Only a few fluffy white clouds broke the unending blue sky. Cold and crisp now. Beyond the horizon, a fierce winter storm gathered energy. The tide raced ahead of the storm, swelling the bay so that even the deepest-keeled ship could sail into Coronnan City.

At last, Nimbulan spotted Amaranth's silhouette, far out over the Great Bay, black against a white cloud. Wings stretched wide, Amaranth could have been any large black bird outlined against the sky.

"Merawk," the flywacket cried. He banked and circled lower.

Nimbulan triggered his FarSight with a tendril of stored dragon magic. There wasn't much of it left. He had to conserve it.

The flywacket's cat-face came into focus within his glass. Amaranth searched back and forth as he flapped his falcon's wings, seeking the air currents to keep him aloft. His black fur seemed to absorb light, robbing the clouds of their share of sparkling sunshine.

"Here, Amaranth. Come to me." Nimbulan held out his arm as an inviting perch.

"Merew," Amaranth acknowledged the command. He stretched out his legs in preparation for landing.

"He'll tear your arm to shreds with those talons." Lyman draped his cloak around Nimbulan's outstretched arm.

"No, he won't. He's very gentle when he lands," Nimbulan protested. But he didn't remove the cloak. His fine linen shirt and sleeveless leather tunic wouldn't offer much protection if Amaranth didn't retract his raptor's talons to normal cat claws in time.

A shaft of light off to the right distracted Nimbulan. He peered in the direction of the next island in the Coronnan River delta. Movement in a pattern contrary to the passage of wind in the shrubbery betrayed a presence. No unnatural colors revealed a silhouette, only the movement and the light.

"Someone is hiding over there." Lyman looked through his glass, aiming it at a shaft of sunlight to trigger the magic. "A man, dressed in green and brown and maybe black. I can see his aura but not his face or a signature color."

"Not a magician, then." Nimbulan turned his gaze back to the flywacket.

The light flashed again.

Amaranth screeched and faltered.

Nimbulan covered his ears against the high wail of sound that assaulted all of his senses, physical and magical. But he didn't shift his gaze from the flywacket.

Amaranth grew at an alarming rate. His black fur and feathers paled as he seemed to explode into a dazzling display of silver and purple. All of his black fur and feathers released the light they had absorbed until he reflected the sunshine away from his crystalline skin and hair.

"He's transforming into a dragon!" Nimbulan cried. "Why, Amaranth? Why go back to your natural form?" Once before he'd seen the flywacket burst free from the confines of his familiar shape. He'd flown to join the dragon nimbus as they hovered over the last battle of the Great Wars of Disruption—last spring.

"He's hurt. He's dropping fast!" Lyman shouted. "The light. It must have been some kind of magical arrow. No normal shaft would penetrate his hide at this distance." The old man began searching the other island, looking through the glass into a wisp of witchfire on his fingertip. "Nothing. No aura, no silhouette, just a ferret running in circles. It's as if the man vanished into the void. Or took the animal's form."

The silvery dragon wings caught an updraft. Amaranth stretched and banked into the soft air, slowing his descent. Only then did Nimbulan see the black spot on his hide, near his heart. The wound spread rapidly across the dragon's chest.

"We haven't time to investigate the assassin. Send Quinnault's guards. We have to take care of Amaranth," Nimbulan said, stretching his arm wide again in invitation.

"They search for one assassin already. Perhaps it's the same one." Lyman turned back to the trapdoor and called something down the stairwell.

Nimbulan kept his eyes on Myrilandel's familiar. "Easy,

Amaranth. Land slow and easy." He turned to Lyman. "Get a healer. Quick. We have to save him. He's our only link to Myri."

"There isn't enough time," Lyman replied, already hastening down the stairs to the wide courtyard in front of the ancient keep. Nimbulan followed.

"Will Amaranth talk to you, Nimbulan?" Lyman cleared the courtyard of guards, servants, and courtiers with a gesture and a stern look.

"I hope so. He knows me. He's my wife's familiar."

"But do any of the other dragons talk to you?" As they emerged into the courtyard, Lyman whistled sharply, encouraging Amaranth to come to him. The noise pierced Nimbulan's ears like dragon speech. "That's right, Amaranth, come to me. I'll help you," Lyman coaxed.

Amaranth seemed to heed the man's advice and aimed for the court. He faltered and rocked.

Nimbulan sensed his pain and uncertainty. "He's losing consciousness. Moments of dizziness, then a brief recovery."

"You're in rapport with him. He'll let you touch his wound. Maybe he'll let you heal him. I'll seek his thoughts." Lyman stepped back as the wind from the dragon wings blasted dust into their faces.

"Do you speak with the dragons?" Nimbulan asked, amazed. He only heard the telepathic communication from the great beasts when they had something specific to say to him.

"My link to the dragons is—different from Myri's," Lyman said. He offered no further explanation.

Amaranth landed bellyfirst, scraping his muzzle on the packed dirt of the courtyard. The almost mature spiral horn on his forehead bent at an odd angle near the blunted tip. Wearily he lifted his nose a little and collapsed, wings half furled.

Nimbulan rushed to the dragon's side. Gingerly he probed with his fingertips to the center of the spreading black spot, over Amaranth's heart. With his left hand, palm up and fingers slightly curved, he pressed under the wing joint, seeking a major blood vessel. Almost instantly his mind moved inward, seeking the source of the wound. Dimly he watched with physical eyes as Lyman placed both hands flat against the creature's skull at the base of his single spiral horn.

This spell has to work. Stargods, please help me do this right.

The silver cord that bound him to Myri sprang to life. It tugged at his heart almost painfully. The hair on the back of his neck stood up, sensing danger. He didn't have time to reflect on its sudden reappearance. Amaranth was dying.

Blackness as deep as the void between the planes of existence invaded Nimbulan's inner vision from Amaranth's wound. He pushed it aside, seeking healthy blood and energy to combat the growing infection. Down, down, he sought a beginning place. He needed a fragment of healthy tissue near the wound to strengthen and begin pushing back against the disease-ridden magic. He hadn't the specific healer's gift, but a lifetime as a Battlemage had taught him much about field surgery for physical and magical wounds.

The blackness raced ahead of him. Propelled by magic, the evil grew thicker as it spread, slowing his probe. He pushed harder. Like wading in freezing honey, he forced his vision forward to the strong wing muscles, hoping the magic would follow him there and stay away from the vulnerable heart.

Thicker and thicker, the black magic encapsulated him, crushing him, robbing him of air. His heart flailed against his chest, fighting against the taint spreading from Amaranth's body into his own.

The void opened before him. Nimbulan searched the black nothingness for a trace of Amaranth. He might be able to separate the essence of the purple-tipped dragon from the magic that killed it, then return them both to their physical bodies.

(The void is forbidden to users of dragon magic.)

Nimbulan ignored the warning. He had to save Amaranth.

A tiny amethyst jewel winked at him in the distance. Purple, like Amaranth's wing veins and horns. He dived after the spirit-light. It eluded him, always keeping just ahead of him.

Nimbulan concentrated and reached forward with senses that dissipated in the void. Closer. He came closer to the dragon spirit. A black aura surrounded the jewel-toned light. The blackness of evil magic.

He fought his revulsion and tried to push the blackness aside with his mind.

A blinding flash of pure white crystal erupted between him and Amaranth's spirit. Thousands of shards of all color/no color light blasted his senses.

Don't die, Amaranth. Oh, please don't die, Myri's unique mental voice pleaded. Each fragment of crystal seemed to vibrate with her need to save her familiar.

"Break it off, Nimbulan!" Lyman shook his physical body. "Let go of Amaranth. He's gone, you can't help him anymore. Amaranth is dead."

With a jolt that nearly robbed him of consciousness, Nimbulan dropped back into his body. The blackness receded from his mind, a little. Pain exploded from every pore in his body. He pressed his fingertips against his eyes. Starbursts of light appeared on his eyelids. He pushed the pinpricks of light together until they filled his vision.

At last the blackness fled out of him, unable to withstand the light.

"Myri! I have to go to her. She's in the void. I heard her. I have to go back to her."

"No. The void is forbidden to users of dragon magic. You have to wait and find her by other means."

Nimbulan shook his head in denial. The movement broke his void-induced thrall. The reality of battle preparations crashed into his frayed senses. The need to stay and protect the city warred with his need to go to Myri.

He prayed to all three Stargods for his wife's safety.

"Amaranth, *Stargods!* What did they do to you?" he cried.

"He lived long enough to tell me something of Myrilandel."

Lyman's words broke through Nimbulan's emotional dizziness. "Where? Where is my wife, Lyman?"

"In Hanassa."

Chill raced up Nimbulan's spine. Hanassa lay deep in the Southern Mountains, within a dry caldera. There, hidden from the rest of the world, outlaws, Rovers, rogue magicians, and other criminals had built a city. Secret passes and tunnels were said to lead into the heart of the mountain. Few people who entered Hanassa, who weren't invited by one undesirable sect or another, left it alive.

"Myrilandel was twin to Amaranth before taking a human body." Nimbulan shivered in distress. Myri's plea across the void haunted him. "She was happy enough to remain human while Amaranth lived because there could only be one purple-tipped dragon at a time. Now that Amaranth is gone, her instinct will be to return to her dragon form.

"Believe me, I know the instincts that drive her!" Lyman replied. He closed his eyes tightly. The thousands of lines around his eyes deepened.

"I have to find her before she abandons her body and joins the dragons," Nimbulan whispered through his grief. "I have to leave tonight—no, now. There are others who can lead this battle. Myri is in Hanassa. Televarn was headed for Hanassa last year. Maia and her baby are probably with the Rover clan, too."

"*You* have to organize this battle and save the kingdom first," Lyman reminded him. "As much as the dragons need you to rescue Myrilandel, they also recognize your responsibility to maintain peace in Coronnan. You are the only one with the experience and the wits to win this battle."

Chapter 6

"**W**ater, the last of the four elements. Equal in strength to its three brothers," Televarn murmured. He stroked the surface of the small pool in the marshy ground of the small river island near Palace Isle. Kardia and Air were feminine elements. Fire and Water belonged to men. He'd rejected Fire as his source of magic today, too obvious, too visible.

The spell he'd put on Quinnault's wine had been Water based—though he'd been wearing the delusion of Maia's face and body at the time. Quinnault should be dead by now. Televarn had delivered the poisoned wine to the understeward over an hour ago.

He chuckled at the image of Quinnault dying. The moment the water in the wine hit the king's belly, it would freeze. The ice would grow so cold it, in turn, would freeze everything around it, growing steadily outward until the entire body was one sold block of ice.

Televarn thought about how he would spend the Kaalipha's reward for Quinnault's death. Gold. One thousand gold pieces to buy mercenaries and bribe the Kaalipha's loyal protectors. Her own gold would be the instrument of Yaassima's downfall and Televarn's rise to power.

Nimbulan would feel less pain than Quinnault from the spell Televarn planned for him. He would have a few seconds to realize that the wall of water engulfing him would cause his death before life and intelligence vanished in a massive struggle for air.

Nimbulan and the meddling old man had seen him when he killed the flywacket. They knew who orchestrated today's devastation. True to character, Nimbulan had devoted his attention and his magic to the dying animal rather than searching out his enemy. He didn't deserve to be the father of a Rover child.

By Rover law, Maia's son belonged to the Rover parent. Televarn planned to make Myrilandel's child a Rover, too. His clan needed the new blood to expand and grow healthy again. He needed a large and healthy clan to support him when he became Kaaliph of Hanassa. Myrilandel wouldn't reject him then. She'd come back to his bed willingly when he made her Queen of Hanassa.

Televarn cupped his right hand slightly as he swirled his entire hand in the pool of water. The ferret, Wiggles, crept out from his hiding place in Televarn's pant leg and sniffed at the circling water. "Come. Share the spell with me."

Wiggles oozed back toward his dark hiding place.

"Your mistress ordered you to obey me," Televarn commanded the ferret. He clamped his free hand on the animal's neck to keep it from retreating further.

Wiggles plopped down on Televarn's arm reluctantly.

"My name means 'The one who speaks to Varns,'" Televarn muttered. "I was given that name when I rid my clan of its previous chieftain because I am gifted with persuasion. So, why can't I persuade you to cooperate, Wiggles?"

The ferret ignored him.

"I have met true Varns and struck bargains with them, a feat few can claim. You will obey me, beast, as your mistress commanded!" Televarn hated having to remind the creature that its loyalty to another bound it more tightly than his own magic and gifts.

He drew circles in the water with his hand, finding the element more cooperative than the ferret. A small whirlpool followed his movements. He continued the circling motion until he knew he had captured the essence of Water. Slowly he removed his hand from the pool, drawing the swirling vortex up with him. He chanted the ancient words that bound the element to his will.

Water resisted. It did not want to leave the pool where it rested before flowing into the gentle creek, then into the racing river, and finally into the Great Bay. Televarn pushed with his magic; not so easy without the support of his clan and only the ferret to aid him. His family had to remain in Hanassa for now. If they should be discovered in Coronnan, all his plans would fall apart. He'd had enough trouble keeping himself hidden for two weeks while he watched and waited for an opportunity.

Yaassima must not know that he had discovered the dragongate. He had to wait and assassinate his victims after he'd had enough time to journey from Hanassa to Coronnan City by mundane means.

He'd used the time well, observing, planning.

"Come!" Televarn commanded Water. A thin trickle leaped to his hand, trailing back into the pool. Wiggles touched the Water with a tiny paw, bonding with the magic and the element. Televarn took two steps away. Water remained connected to himself, the ferret, and the pool. Two more steps. Water stretched the connection and continued to follow.

"Good." He nodded his satisfaction. Now the hard part of the spell. He had to get the continuous stream of Water into Nimbulan's private bedchamber.

The thought of Myrilandel sharing that chamber with Nimbulan churned acid in Televarn's stomach. His jealousy nearly broke his connection with Water. He forced his emotions down into a cold knot of anger. Water was cold. Water would end the life of his rival.

He walked toward his hide canoe, following the little chirping noises Wiggles made—one chirp meant a step right, two chirps a step left. The ferret instinctively found the easiest pathway.

At the point where the island became more water than Kardia, Televarn steadied his small canoe with one hand; his awkward left hand, not his dominant right where Wiggles clung and they both maintained the thin stream of water trailing back to the pool.

Slowly he levered one knee into the boat. It rocked and slid beyond the reach of his leg. He overbalanced and fell into a cold blanket of mud. Wiggles wrapped tighter around his arm in an undulating wave of fur that mimicked laughter.

"*S'murghit!* Stay still," Televarn ordered the boat and the ferret. He pushed himself up onto his knees and elbows, never letting go of Water or of Wiggles.

Wiggles subsided. The hide canoe bobbed and thrashed

under Televarn's hand, more responsive to the buoyancy of the water beneath it and the air above than to Televarn's command.

His fine black trews and shirt looked ruddy brown with the mud. Ruined. His green-and-purple vest embroidered with sigils of power was equally covered in goo. He'd never hear the end of Erda's displeasure for such carelessness. The ancient wisewoman of his clan held too much power over Televarn's Rovers. Power that should be his.

He stilled his growing frustration. Water pulled him back toward the pool of its origin. Perhaps Water had turned the canoe against him.

How to make his tools work with him? What could he promise an element and an inanimate object to pacify them?

(Freedom,) a voice whispered in the back of his head. *(Release them.)*

"Enough," he shouted. "You are mine. You will obey." He pushed more of his waning strength into the binding. Physical contact with Wiggles helped. But the creature wasn't truly his familiar, only borrowed. Their rapport was incomplete. Another annoyance. He'd never been able to bond with a creature so that its senses enhanced his magic and made it totally responsive to his wishes. They'd all escaped his net of control, like Water was trying to do.

The weight pulling his arm back to the pool grew to enormous proportions, then abruptly eased. He nearly fell into the mud again with the sudden release.

The canoe rested easily against its tether. Water remained in his hand.

Not willing to tempt the capricious canoe, Televarn knelt in the mud as he steadied the boat with his hand. More brown-and-green goo soaked through the fine cloth of his trews. He gritted his teeth against the seeping cold and caking stiffness to his vest. Then he slid one knee into his vessel. The canoe wobbled again. He forced it quiet until his other leg rested comfortably in the bottom. He balanced against the mild rocking his entry triggered. Then the canoe subsided, almost with a sigh of resignation. Wiggles slithered off his arm and undulated around the boat, sniffing every fragment. A few drops of Water trailed from the creature's paw back to Televarn's hand.

"Just keep me afloat until I reach School Isle and I'll set you free," he whispered to the boat.

Water quivered, wanting to be included in the promise. Televarn glared at the rebelling element. It stilled. "You'll be free when you complete the task I have for you and not before. Nimbulan won't survive the day. Then Myrilandel will be free of the spell he holds over her and she will come to my bed gratefully—as she did when first we met."

The darkness of the void faded from Myri's senses. Amaranth's cries faded from her mind. An irresistible urge to leave her body and fly to her familiar made her stretch her arms wide again to catch the wind. But she was deep within the Kaalipha's palace on the leeward side of a volcanic crater. No wind stirred to lift her dormant wings. The elongated bumps on her spine didn't stretch into horns to act as rudders while in flight.

Over and over she relived the moment Amaranth died. His pain and terrible loneliness swamped her awareness of everything, even the cries of her daughter.

"Make that child stop crying!" Yaassima ordered. Her eyes grew wide in growing frustration. Then her tone softened and her eyes narrowed. "You are making us late for the ceremonies assigning commissions to my followers."

Myri only half heard the older woman's verbal caress. *Amaranth!* her mind screamed.

"We must plan the Festival of Naming for your baby. All of Hanassa will rejoice when I name the child my heir." Yaassima clapped her hands together in delight.

How long had she been in the void, unaware of Yaassima's entrance into the common room of the suite? The Kaalipha had obviously been prattling for some time.

Myri fought the urge to transform. She had to stay aware and keep Yaassima away from her baby. Her best defense against the bloodthirsty Kaalipha of Hanassa was to stay out of her way and her thoughts until she found a means to escape Hanassa.

Oh, Amaranth, I'm sorry. I didn't intend for you to fly to your death. When she escaped, would she share the fate of her birth twin?

"Only my husband has the right to name my child," she reminded the Kaalipha of the tradition so old it had become law. Her need to fly faded a little with her efforts to control herself.

Amaranth! How will I live without you. Did you warn Nimbulan?

"We are kin, you and I." Yaassima caressed Myri's unbound hair. "Your husband abdicated his rights to the child when he exiled you. Now I claim the right of kinship and naming. Come to the Justice Hall now. 'Tis your duty to observe how I delegate the commissions and the fees. You and the child must grow into the heritage I give you."

"The rich and powerful of Kardia Hodos come to you only when they need the death of a rival and the disruption of trade." Myri kept her back turned toward Yaassima, hiding the tears that gathered in her eyes.

"I will not deal in death and destruction, Kaalipha." Myri stiffened her spine and her resolve to escape. Amaranth's death would not be in vain. Until then she had to maintain rigid control of herself and her emotions. Grief for Amaranth must wait. She could betray no trace of weakness before Yaassima.

Like a dragon, she must remain invisible while she watched and waited for the best opportunity to escape.

"You are thinking too fondly of your treacherous husband, Myrilandel. I can tell." Yaassima sounded petulant. "He is but a distant part of your past. Better you should think about how to control Moncriith the Bloodmage." Yaassima licked her lips. "I have given Moncriith permission to gather mercenary forces against Coronnan. His planned invasion of your brother's kingdom won't keep him busy long once he learns that you are here. He is so very single-minded in his obsession. I find his rants about blood and fire and the demons *you* control quite amusing."

Myri felt all the heat leave her face. The man she feared most in the world, the one who had stalked her from village to village all her life, lived. Lived here in Hanassa. He wouldn't stop with burning Myri at the stake. He'd murder her baby as well. At least her other enemies, Yaassima and Televarn, wanted her alive.

"Remember this, Myrilandel, if ever you step outside my palace, into the city, I will make certain Moncriith hears about it. He will seize and destroy you. So you see, all your pretty plans to escape Hanassa are for naught. Only I can protect you. Only I can become the family you so long for." She stroked Myri's hair with possessive hands.

Never! Myri vowed to herself. She would have her family back. Her true family of Kalen and Powwell, the baby, and Nimbulan.

But never again would she be able to include Amaranth in that tight circle of love and kinship.

The threat of Moncriith seemed trivial against the loss of Amaranth and the danger to Nimbulan. She had to escape, now.

She needed to fly free, to breathe the sparking clear air of the mountains. The heat haze and dust of Hanassa was all she'd been allowed since Televarn had kidnapped her and brought her to this cursed place.

If only she could fly!

The baby's whimpers kept her firmly anchored to her wingless human body.

"Come, Myrilandel. We mustn't keep my people waiting much longer," Yaassima ordered. Persuasion fled her voice, replaced with deadly impatience.

Myri knew she couldn't ignore the Kaalipha. Yaassima executed those who defied her. She'd executed her consort. Rumor also claimed she'd killed her daughter who had disappeared right after the unlucky consort had lost his head to Yaassima's sharp sword.

Myri caressed the sleeping baby on her shoulder, needing contact with her life to counteract the death that assailed her senses at every turn.

"I have no blood kin, Kaalipha Yaassima. Only my daughter," Myri replied. "I can't claim King Quinnault as kin anymore. He exiled me." Nimbulan had agreed with the edict.

Why had she risked Amaranth to warn Nimbulan? *Amaranth!*

"You should hate your husband for what he did to you. Yet you cling to his memory as if you expect him to defy his king and join you," Yaassima sneered.

"I love him." He was the missing piece to make her family complete—once she escaped.

"You and your daughter carry the blood of the dragons

in your veins," Yaassima reminded her. "That is a heritage that must be perpetuated. Not your paltry emotions toward a treacherous husband and those two grubby children."

"Show me that Powwell and Kalen are safe, and I will not question your wisdom in separating me from *my* children." Myri kept her eyes locked on the blue desert sky above the crater. Clean and clear, untainted by Yaassima's need for blood and destruction. The Kaalipha perverted her dragon hunting instincts, just as her ancient ancestor Hanassa had when he went rogue and deserted the dragon nimbus.

Yaassima twined her fingers in Myri's fine hair. The sexuality behind the gesture made Myri shiver with revulsion. The baby fretted. Myri cooed at her daughter and turned toward her bedchamber, on the inside wall away from the window, without looking at the Kaalipha.

"I rescued you from Televarn's ungentle clutches for the sake of our kinship," Yaassima snarled. "His jealousy knows no bounds. He would have killed your daughter as soon as she was born, rather than admit that the child isn't his. If he let *you* live, Moncriith would have found a way to destroy you. You owe me your life, Myrilandel, as does everyone who seeks refuge in Hanassa."

"I did not seek refuge. Televarn kidnapped me and brought me here against my will."

"Forget the magician who forced marriage upon you. Forget the children not of your body. Only I am your kin. I will protect you as Nimbulan and your brother, King Quinnault, refused to do." Yaassima's voice swelled with pride. As absolute ruler of Hanassa, none of the thousands of criminals who lived in the city questioned her authority.

Myri had been forced to witness three executions in as many weeks. Each time she feared the offender would be fifteen-year-old Powwell or eleven-year-old Kalen, adults responsible for their actions in this vicious society.

After each beheading, Yaassima dipped her hands, with their preternaturally long fingers, into the blood of the dead man or woman. The symbolic gesture, that the death was her responsibility, paled in comparison to the look of nearly sexual glee that dominated Yaassima's eyes for an hour afterward.

Myri sensed Yaassima's hand dropping away from yet another caressing stroke of her hair.

"Let the child sleep, Myrilandel. Put her back in the cradle and come to the Justice Hall," Yaassima ordered.

"She's wet. By the time I change her, she will be hungry, too."

"It is time we found a wet nurse for her. Women of quality do not feed their own children. One of Televarn's women has just lost her baby—Maia, I think, is her name. I'll send for her." Yaassima spoke to the guard outside the door of the suite.

"I will have no Rover woman taint my child!" Especially not Maia, Nimbulan's former lover. "Rovers steal children from their lawful parents."

"Your daughter deserves a name," Yaassima continued without acknowledging Myri's protest. "She needs a name of power; a name that will resound through history as does the name of our ancestor, *Hanassa*. Tomorrow we shall hold the Festival of Naming."

This time Yaassima caressed the baby's hair, only a shade darker than Myri's. Just a trace of silver gilt had appeared in some of the strands with the last few days.

"Dragon hair. We all have it. You, me, the dragons. My daughter didn't have it. Crystal fur on dragons, crystal hair on us. It reflects light away from us so that none may penetrate our thoughts and actions. Mystery is power."

"She's just a baby. Her hair and eye color will change within a few weeks. She will grow into her long fingers and toes. She has no trace of the elongated spinal bumps." Myri denied the kinship her protector pressed upon her daily. "Did you hear me when I said that Maia will not touch my child?"

"I shall present the baby to the people of Hanassa at her naming. They must see that the dragon blood continues. No one will dare oppose me if they know for certain that another dragon waits to exact retribution. They wouldn't have respected my daughter. She was weak, too like her father." Yaassima continued to touch the baby, delaying Myri's retreat to the privacy of her bedchamber. "Her name must be Hanassa."

Never! Myri kept her protestations to herself. She had to persuade Yaassima rather than defy her.

"Rovers steal babies," she repeated. "So few of their babies live that they must rob others of their children to bring new blood into the clans. If you allow Maia near my baby, she will find a way to kidnap her—or substitute her own dead child for my healthy one."

"She wouldn't dare. I am the Kaalipha, and the child is my heir."

"*My* baby is very wet. Do you wish to change her?" Myri asked coyly, knowing fastidious Yaassima would have nothing to do with the rather messy process of rearing an infant.

"Go." Yaassima fluttered her fingers in disgusted dismissal.

Myri dodged around the older woman and walked toward the door to the inner room of the suite.

She waved her hand across a metal plate set into the wall by the doorway. The light panels in the ceiling came to life, activated by some spell only Yaassima understood. The clear panels gave off a directionless glow, like witchlight, but yellow instead of the more natural fire green.

The Kaalipha came no farther into Myri's chamber than the doorway.

"Where is the pywacket?" Yaassima asked. She used the ancient word for a familiar, from a language that had died out from all of Kardia Hodos except here in Hanassa.

"I . . . I don't know," Myri stammered, halting her quest for a clean diaper. Grief nearly felled her again. "Perhaps he hunts rats in your kitchens."

Amaranth! You can't be dead. Knife-sharp pain stabbed her heart and brought tears to her eyes again. The void beckoned for her to follow Amaranth into his next existence.

"Did Televarn kill Amaranth, too?" Yaassima asked. A half smile creased her face and her eyes lit with lustful glee. The Kaalipha didn't read minds often, but when she did, she always found her victim's vulnerability. "I wondered how long that jealous Rover would allow your nasty creature to live. He could never possess it, so it must be eliminated. Just as he will never possess you. I can protect you from him, Myri. But only if you mind your duty to me. I will expect you in the Justice Hall as soon as you clean up the child. You may feed her there. Maia will take over as wet nurse this evening."

"I will not allow another to nurse my child—especially a thieving Rover. Never. And I will not nurse the child in front of your amoral criminals and perverts. Do you hear me?" So much for remaining invisible. But, *s'murghit,* some issues she had to fight.

"My people must see the child and know her for my heir. If they see your breasts and lust after you, all the better. Their uncontrolled emotions give me control over their desires and power over their lives. Just as I have the power of life and death over you."

Chapter 7

King Quinnault made his way through the groups of people in the palace courtyard. He didn't have enough to do. Dedicated underlings jumped at every task he created in the battle preparations. As king, he was supposed to be free to make decisions. So far, he didn't even have that chore.

Nimbulan, as the experienced and respected Battlemage, directed the defenses today.

Common citizens filled the courtyard. Quinnault smiled at them as he strode away from the confines of the palace. The corpse of the purple-tipped dragon had been cleared away from the busy courtyard. Later, after the battle, they would hold some kind of remembrance and consign it to the funeral pyre.

Two of the Master Magicians had fought the formal burning of the dragon body. They needed to study it, dissect it, learn the secret of generating magic. But Nimbulan had insisted. The dragons deserved the same respect as any human—especially Amaranth who had aided in healing King Quinnault last spring. All of the magicians respected Nimbulan enough to bow to his demands.

Quinnault's magical ties to the great beasts went beyond affection. He grieved with the entire dragon nimbus over the loss of the little purple-tipped dragon. Amaranth had been one of his family.

He sorely missed his telepathic communications with the dragons. He'd never shared that level of intimacy with any human. He strongly doubted he ever would.

He moved through the crowd of his bustling citizens, making his kingly, but distant, presence known to them. He couldn't do much else.

Some of the women bent over a huge cauldron, boiling bandages. They paused in their work only long enough to dip him a curtsy. Most of the men acknowledged their king with a nod of the head.

A year ago, he had worked alongside these people building bridges among the islands. Then, he'd been only a lord, the Peacemaker. Now he was king, less useful and more removed from the people he served.

A gaggle of children piled stones together by the gate. Useful weapons, should the enemy manage to attack the palace itself. A five-year-old waddled toward the pile with a stone far too heavy for his skinny arms. He dropped the rock off balance. The entire mound began to spill backward on top of the boy.

Quinnault dashed forward to pluck the child out of the way. He held him against his chest until the rocks stopped tumbling all over the courtyard.

"Can't you stay out of the way, Mikkey!" an older boy scolded. He had been supervising the arrangement of the stones.

"I only wanted to help," Mikkey blubbered.

"We need all the help we can get." Quinnault set the boy down and wiped his tears with the hem of his tunic. "Next time, Mikkey, why don't you give your rock to him and let him place it on top of the pile." He indicated the older boy with a thrust of his elbow.

"Yes, Your Grace." Mikkey executed an awkward bow.

"We're all working together today. No need for bows among battle comrades." Quinnault ruffled Mikkey's hair. The older boy stared at the familiar gesture with wide eyes and dropping jaw. Quinnault reached over to offer him the same rough affection. Then he showed the boys how to arrange the rocks for better balance.

He moved toward the riverbank and the men who wrestled with small boats to float felled trees into the bay. Over half of these people had been refugees from the war a year ago. He expected them to pack up and leave at the first signs of trouble. Instead, they worked side by side with the long-time residents of the islands to defend their new homes—to uphold his kingship.

"All I really wanted was to be left in peace," he said to himself. He turned a full circle, watching all of them work together for a common defense. His heart swelled with pride. He needed to work with them, show them how much their loyalty meant to him.

"Excuse me, Your Grace." Another child tugged at his tunic. "Lord Konnaught requests you attend him." The little girl, not more than five or six, hesitated on her esses but managed to push them out without lisping.

"Where is Konnaught?" he asked her, looking about. The son of his former rival for the crown wasn't among the workers in the courtyard. Quinnault thought he'd ordered all of his fosterlings to help with the defenses.

"His lordship is in the armory, Your Grace." The little girl bobbed a sketchy curtsy and ran off.

"He should be out here, learning who we fight for." Konnaught had made his belief in his superiority over all of Coronnan well known. His father, Kammeryl d'Astrismos, had claimed kinship to the Stargods and therefore felt he needn't dirty his hands with normal people.

Quinnault had killed Konnaught's father on the field of battle. He owed the boy more than he could repay. But the boy also owed him obedience and loyalty in return for protection and an education.

Quinnault sighed and wondered what kind of temper tantrum would result if he ignored Konnaught's demand for attention.

"Mikkey," he called, waving the rock toter to him.

The little boy relinquished his latest burden almost gratefully and ran the few steps to stand before Quinnault. "Yes, Your Grace?"

"Lord Konnaught is in the armory. Go tell him to bring me a short sword and sheath. Make sure he comes himself and doesn't give you the weapon to carry for him."

"Yes, Your Grace." Mikkey bowed again, a little less awkward this time.

Quinnault ambled over to stand at the foot of the palace steps. The jumble of people cleared around him, giving him a semblance of privacy, acknowledging his separateness. He had no doubt that at least a dozen ears would overhear his conversation with the troublesome young lord no matter where he conducted the interview.

Konnaught approached several long minutes later. He carried a sword far too big and heavy for his twelve-year-old frame. His father's sword. The sword that had nearly split Quinnault in two until the people of Coronnan joined with Quinnault's sister Myrilandel and a purple-tipped dragon to heal the man they proclaimed king.

The weak sunlight of late autumn highlighted the blond in Konnaught's sandy-colored hair—blond, not the red inherited from the Stargods. Just before his father's death, rumors had abounded that the name of one of the Stargod brothers at the top of the d'Astrismos family tree had been inserted by Kammeryl. The warlord had also dyed his hair to resemble the bright locks of the three divine brothers.

"Why do you demean yourself by consorting with peasants?" Konnaught kept the heavy sword firmly at his own side.

Quinnault couldn't see any evidence of the short sword he had requested.

"You are the king! You should be giving orders from your throne, not out there working with peasants." Konnaught nearly spat the last word.

"The 'peasants' are Coronnan. Without them, I would have no one to rule, and my kingship would be meaningless. We've had this conversation before, Konnaught. I do not agree with your father's views of authority and responsibility," Quinnault said mildly, refusing to let the boy rile him.

"You would have the land. Land is more important than peasants. If my father were king, you wouldn't see him out hugging ruffian babies and hauling rocks like a mule."

"The Stargods did not see fit to let your father be king." Anger began to heat Quinnault's skin. He wanted to turn this malcontent over his knee and spank him.

There had to be a better way to deal with him before he became a bully like his father. Kammeryl d'Astrismos had used pain and intimidation to prove his superior power.

Quinnault refused to do that. He had found a way to bring peace to Coronnan without forcing his followers into submission, with Nimbulan's help. And the dragons'. And the help of all those dozens of people working around him.

"Since I am your king, and you are my fosterling until you come of age, you are required to obey my orders." Quinnault placed his hands on his hips and glared at the boy.

Konnaught stood up straighter. He darted glances about him in alarm.

Quinnault made a decision. He'd allowed his fosterling too much freedom.

"Konnaught d'Astrismos, you will accompany me on my rounds today and lend a hand wherever I deem fit. Come." Quinnault turned toward the battlements. "But first you must fetch me the short sword I asked for earlier. And put away that weapon. It's too big for you and too unwieldy for me to carry in a boat."

Konnaught caressed the jeweled hilt of the sword. Reluctantly he returned to the armory, a circular stone building on the far side of the courtyard. His steps dragged until he was halfway to his destination. Then he stiffened his back in defiance.

"You won't be needing a weapon for yourself, Konnaught," Quinnault called.

"A lord must always appear a lord. A sword on his hip displays his authority for all to see."

"A king must learn other ways to earn his authority," Quinnault reminded him—again. "If you keep me waiting, I'll double your time tomorrow studying the history of Coronnan." Quinnault smiled to himself. That was a chore he would enjoy, but he knew Konnaught hated reading and ciphering, thought them demeaning skills.

Today, Lord Konnaught would do something else he hated.

The boatmen could always use an extra pair of hands on the oars. Nothing like rowing against the tide all day to make a man out of an arrogant stripling.

From the top parapet, Nimbulan watched the teams of men, nobles and common laborers, mundanes paired with magicians, as they felled trees from the nearest mainland forest. Every magician carried a few threads of Nimbulan's formal blue robe, or strands of his hair, to connect them to him—a trick of illegal rogue magic. But the mundanes didn't need to know that. None of the magicians had enough dragon magic left to survive this battle.

Through those connections Nimbulan monitored the sharpness of the blades and the positioning of the fallen trees.

His palms burned with sympathetic blisters. He rubbed his tender hands against his tunic. The new dye rubbed off the worn leather. Now his hands tingled with the coloring chemicals as well as the raw nerve endings.

At least the magic was working. He could keep the channels of communication open and think clearly enough to make decisions. As soon as this battle was over—win or lose—he would leave in search of Myri.

Sighing heavily, he turned his attention back to supervising the defense preparations. He hoped the actual battle progressed more favorably and swiftly than the hard work of the day.

Teams of magicians and fishermen levitated the felled trees into the river where local boatmen guided the untrimmed timber out into the mudflats.

Would they be able to fell enough trees to fill the mudflats with traps? Aching shoulders joined his smarting palms as evidence of their attempt. Nimbulan prayed to the Stargods they had enough time and strength. There wouldn't be much magic left in the kingdom after today—dragon or rogue. But they had to use it all to save the kingdom.

Several nobles joined the numerous soldiers and farmers in the hard work. Quinnault had been among the boatmen earlier along with the arrogant brat, Konnaught. Master magicians and apprentices worked as hard as the men more used to using the strength of their bodies than the power of mind and magic.

Hanic and a few other nobles had suddenly found other places to be—a long way away from the city. Nimbulan was surprised Konnaught hadn't managed to find a way to join them.

Nimbulan was the Battlemage once more, responsible for all the lives that surrounded him. *Never again,* he vowed. He'd sworn the same oath a year ago when he organized the final battle of the civil war that had crippled Coronnan for three generations. *There has to be a better way. If only I can find it.*

"Such a waste of timber," King Quinnault groaned as he climbed the last few steps to Nimbulan's parapet. They watched a fifty-foot tree tilt and smack the ground. "I had plans for those trees, building, export. . . ."

"Books." Nimbulan regretted the loss, too. "Trees will

grow again, given time. The cleared area can be plowed and planted. New trees can be started in old, worn-out fields. As long as we save the kingdom tonight, all will work out. Somehow."

"I certainly hope so." Quinnault shaded his eyes and peered out toward the bay.

"I thought you were helping with the trees, Your Grace."

"I was. I got tired of Konnaught's whining. And I thought some of the others would work themselves into heart attacks if I remained down there much longer. They seemed to have to prove they could work harder, longer, and faster than me." The king flashed a wide grin at his magician.

Both men chuckled. A year ago, those same lords were more interested in murdering each other than striving for a common defense.

"They seem to forget, I spent this autumn hauling loaded fishnets to help feed our growing population. Last winter I built bridges among these islands. I'm used to hard work. They aren't." Quinnault rubbed his shoulders lightly, more an easing of tightness than a massage of an ache.

Together, they watched two fishermen—and surprisingly, Konnaught—in a flat-bottomed skiff ram the first tree into the mud beside one of the few channels that keeled ships could negotiate. With the help of a magician, they embedded the trunk deep enough to hold it upright against the rising tide. The top branches remained above the waves for now.

Too soon the tide would flood the traps and the fleet would enter the channels.

Too soon. They wouldn't be ready in time. But the sooner this operation was over, the sooner Nimbulan could leave in search of Myri. And Maia's child. How was he going to persuade the mother to allow him access to the baby, help in its rearing, keep Televarn away from it?

"At least you persuaded Konnaught to do more than complain, Your Grace."

"Ordered, threatened, more like. I told him I would try him for treason against his dragon-blessed monarch if he didn't work as hard as everyone else out there. If he whined once more about how his father would have fought this battle, I think I might have strangled him. Spanked him at the very least."

"You'd have to stand in line for the privilege." Nimbulan kept his smile contained. If he'd had his way, Konnaught would have been shipped off to a foreign monastery the day after his father had been defeated in battle.

A large wave slapped at the boat Konnaught rowed, turning the flat-bottomed craft sideways. The log he was towing slipped free of a magician's control.

"If I still had access to ley lines, I could transport the *s'murghing* tree directly into the mudflats," Nimbulan muttered. Dragon magic only allowed levitation, not instantaneous transportation. He was letting the ley lines fuel his magic, but he couldn't advertise that with obvious rogue spells.

A second fishing boat snared the loose log as it towed its own tree farther out into the mudflats. An errant wave caught the sprawling branches threatening to rip it away from that journeyman magician, too.

Lasso it with magic, Rollett. Use your talent, Nimbulan urged the young man telepathically. The tendril of magic connecting them was weak. He'd used too much already today. He'd also thought of Myri too often and lost his usual firm control over the expenditure of power and energy.

Carefully he stilled a special place deep within his belly, preparing it for an influx of magical power. New energy, dragon energy, trickled into the vacancy. Not enough. Not nearly enough.

Were the dragons with Myri, guarding her while he couldn't? They had cared for her and guided her through her entire life. He had to believe they continued to do so. They had to fill the void in her life left by Amaranth's death until he got to her. She'd be so lost and alone, so vulnerable. . . .

Out in the bay, Rollett waved his arms in acknowledgment of the help. Nimbulan relaxed a little. His stomach growled. He'd skipped the noon meal to direct the preparations for battle. Now he was using up his energy stores in surges.

A little girl with muddy brown braids brought a tray filled with mugs of steaming cider and slabs of bread and meat. "Thank you. Please, extend my thanks to Guillia." He bowed formally to the child as he reached for the nourishment. "And would you have someone at the school fetch my text on naval battle strategy from my desk. The door is locked and Master Stuuvart has the key." The book hadn't come with his earlier request.

Nimbulan drank down the spicy brew gratefully, as did Quinnault.

"I'll fetch the book, Magician Nimbulan." The child dipped a shy curtsy, then scampered down the stairs. She looked a lot like Kalen, probably one of the magician girl's numerous sisters. All of the family had been tested for magical talent, but only Kalen seemed to have it—unless one counted Guillia's ability to sense the nutritional needs of every magician living at the school.

Kalen could transport anything. She'd make short work of this chore. But she wasn't here. The now familiar ache of loneliness drove Nimbulan to tear a furious bite from his bread. Kalen had been exiled along with Myri, and he couldn't go find them until the invading fleet from Rosse-meyer had been repelled.

"You realize, of course, that the obstacles in the Bay won't be enough," Quinnault asked. "Some of the ships will get through." He pointed where some of his men set up a fire pit in the center of the courtyard. Huge cauldrons filled with oil sat nearby, ready to be boiled and thrown on invaders who managed to come ashore.

"What do you suggest?" Nimbulan ignited the kindling with a snap of his fingers without leaving the parapet. He breathed a deep sigh of satisfaction that the simple spell worked. Then he levitated the first cauldron onto the frame above the fire. He controlled it until it was firmly settled. His mind whirled as he withdrew from the levitation. Thirty years as a Battlemage and he couldn't think beyond the first assault. Where was his mind?

(With Myrilandel,) a voice in the back of his head reminded him. *(Think long. Think like a dragon. Myrilandel is part of the whole.)*

"If we still had some catapults, we could fling burning oil at the ships," Quinnault suggested.

"Witchfire would be better. Only a new spell can extinguish it. It can be guided more accurately than oil and will also give us enough light to pinpoint the ships." Nimbulan's mind started working again. He latched onto familiar patterns of strategy and battle plans. "But we don't have any catapults. We dismantled our siege engines after the last battle. We thought the wars ended, so we used the timbers in the new wing of the palace as a reminder of the devastation we brought on ourselves."

The two men stood in silence a moment, remembering that awful day when Quinnault had been forced into single combat with his archrival, Kammeryl d'Astrismos. His priestly training hadn't prepared him for the dirty fight that ended with Kammeryl dead and Quinnault nearly so. Only Myri, with Amaranth's aid, had brought her brother back from the brink of death.

Now Amaranth was dead, and Myri was missing. Nimbulan cursed himself for letting his mind drift from the coming battle. He couldn't do anything about Myri until this battle ended.

What would he do once she was safe? She couldn't return to Coronnan. He had responsibilities here. Magicians weren't meant to be family men. He had no precedents to latch onto.

"Some of Kammeryl's engines were abandoned and left to rot," Quinnault mused. "I wonder if they're still usable? Who can you spare to go check? The old man?" He pointed out Lyman's white head amidst the younger men at the edge of the forest.

"Old Lyman might surprise all of us before the day is through. But you're right. He'll be more useful locating a couple of catapults than wearing himself out hauling trees."

Nimbulan checked the level of the sun. The red-yellow orb of light eased past high noon toward the horizon. The turning tide hummed in his blood. His sensitivity to the planet told him precisely how long before the flood tide allowed passage across the mudflats. He looked downriver toward the Bay and the line of ships hovering offshore. Dared he waste a little precious magic to check the decks for signs of activity? No. The armada would hoist sail at sunset. Not before.

He watched the waves a moment, noting how high they reached on the mudflats. Each one drowned more of the shore than the previous one.

He and his teams hadn't nearly enough time for all that needed to be done.

Chapter 8

"**R**emove that squalling child from my presence if you cannot control her," Yaassima screamed. The Kaalipha wrenched a handful of her own white-blond hair, as if tearing it from her scalp could ease the headache the baby's fretful crying caused.

Shyly, Myri covered her breast and rose from her chair at the head of the Justice Hall. She'd endured today's Dispensation of Favors for as long as she could tolerate it. Moncriith stood at the back of the former temple to Simurgh, glaring at her while she nursed the baby.

"Whore of Simurgh!" he mouthed a curse at her. The hatred in his eyes dominated all of the emotions swirling about the Justice Hall. Myri's distress at his presence must have reduced her milk and upset her child.

Nursing a baby in public was one of the most natural and proud acts a woman could perform. But the assassins and thieves, including Moncriith, who looked to Yaassima for work and pay, were a hardened lot who viewed any woman's breasts as objects of unbridled lust. Even the women among the outlaws stared at her with moist lips and wide eyes.

Myri wondered how long Moncriith would feign obedience to Yaassima. He didn't usually accept anyone's authority but his own. Unless he wanted to use Yaassima in some convoluted plot before he murdered her. And drew magical power from her pain and death.

Myri had almost reached the stairway leading to the royal suite when Yaassima's words stopped her cold. "Take the child to the wet nurse, then return to help me preside over the Dispensation of Favors."

"Maia's babe has been dead two days. Her milk has probably dried up," Myri said, thinking furiously for a way to prevent separation from her child. She had never met Maia, only knew her from Nimbulan's memory of her and a few rumors the servants had related.

"Maia is a Rover. Everyone knows that Rover women make the best wet nurses."

"Rover women hire out as wet nurses so they can steal the babies and raise them as their own. Will you risk this child to Rover theft?"

"No one steals from the Kaalipha of Hanassa." Yaassima gestured to Myri to withdraw. Then she sat back in a high thronelike chair with a deep sigh.

Myri knew the Kaalipha would wait patiently for her return. *You will have a long wait, Yaassima,* she thought.

Back in the privacy of her own bedchamber, she slammed the door that separated her from the common room. Yaassima's chamber was adjacent to Myri's. A thick wall of stone separated them, but Myri had no doubt Yaassima had spy holes and listening spells to observe Myri.

No one awaited her in the suite. Maia must not have come yet.

"You may watch, but you won't enter this room easily," Myri whispered to the absent Rover. The door had no lock, so she pushed a heavy blanket chest in front of it. The dark wood scraped aside the colorful rugs scattered across the stone floor. The screeching sound reminded Myri, painfully, of Amaranth's cries of distress just before he died.

She blocked the sound from her mind as she stacked two chairs on top of the chest. Then she stood a clothes chest on end in front of the pile. Not satisfied, she shoved the bed against that.

"I will rest undisturbed until my milk comes back," she said to the blocked doorway.

She needed liquid to replenish her milk while she rested. Greedily she drank from the pitcher that always sat on the stand beside her bed. As the water slid down her throat, she tasted copper and salt, different from the usual sulfur tang that permeated everything in Hanassa. Drugs.

The same drugs Erda had given her during the baby's birth. Yaassima must have ordered them, needing Myri docile and obedient.

Myri almost sobbed. She couldn't plan her escape while drugged. This was the last dose she'd take. From now on, she'd test all her food and drink. For now she must rest, must fight the grief that threatened to overwhelm her.

She threw herself across the bed, cuddling her baby close. The infant whimpered, still hungry.

"Soon, Baby. I'll feed you soon," she promised her hungry child.

She pressed both hands into the delicate flesh above her heart. The magical dart had penetrated Amaranth in the same place. Tenderness beneath her fingertips told her a bruise formed there, whether from her own hands or in sympathy with Amaranth's wound, she didn't know.

Tears of loneliness slipped down her cheeks.

Time lost meaning. The baby cried herself to sleep.

Voices in the outer room of the suite startled Myri awake from heavy dreams of crashing to the Kardia from a great height.

"When Televarn returns from his mission, I must send you back to his slave pens," Yaassima said sternly from the other side of the door.

Had Maia finally arrived? Myri wouldn't stir until she knew whom the Kaalipha addressed.

Her breasts ached, too full of milk. Her arms were damp from where her milk had soaked through her shift and gown. It still smelled sweet. How long had she slept? Beside her, the baby cried again. Silently, she reached for the infant, determined to feed her herself. Maia would have no tasks awaiting her.

"For now you may tend to Myrilandel. I fear for her health. Do what you must to get her to open the door and see that the child stops crying." A note of desperation entered the Kaalipha's voice.

"Yes, ma'am." A different voice. One Myri hadn't heard in a long time. Kalen. Her adopted daughter was safe. She would have to open the door to see her. Would Yaassima use that moment to take the baby from her?

She clutched the baby, urging her to feed more quickly. All her latent desire to transform into a dragon and fly away faded as she nurtured her young. Purple dragons had no gender. As a dragon she couldn't care for a baby. This was a task only she could perform. Maia—and through her, Televarn—would never get her hands on this baby.

A loud squalling sound told her she held the baby too tightly. Still, she couldn't let go. If she released her grasp, even a little, *they* would steal her baby. Myri knew that *they* had kidnapped her, betrayed her, exiled her, separated her from Nimbulan and her other children. *They* wouldn't stop until she was utterly bereft and destroyed.

They took form in her mind. Moncriith's face dominated the form, surrounded by the flames he claimed would cleanse her and Coronnan of demonic control.

Vaguely, she knew the drugs clouded her mind.

"Myrilandel, let me in, please. Let me stay with you." Kalen pleaded from the other side of the door. Last spring, the girl had said the same words to Myri. Kalen's father had disowned the girl when all magicians who could not, or would not, gather dragon magic were exiled from Coronnan.

Kalen's mother had cried out at the girl's expulsion, but would not defy her husband or abandon her other children to stay with the girl.

"Myri, if you don't let me in, I'll have to go back to Televarn. He . . . he's made slaves of Powwell and me. He forces us to . . . he forces . . ." She broke off in a sob.

Kalen was adept at lying and wearing the emotions people wanted to see in her. But Myri had never known her to cry.

"Give me a moment. I'll let you in, but not the thieving Rover woman." Myri began dismantling the barricade. She cursed and muttered under her breath, knowing Yaassima had found a way to force her into the action.

Several minutes later, Myri focused her gaze on Kalen. The little girl stood in the doorway, wringing her hands and looking over her shoulder toward the center room of the suite. The girl's auburn-tinged braids swished with her movements. Concerned gray eyes met Myri's above a small nose with a wide spread of freckles strewn across the bridge.

"Kalen." Myri drew her adopted daughter into a tight hug. Kalen was safe. The baby was safe. Where was Powwell?

"Yes, Myri, I'm here to take care of you. Can you tell me what happened?" The girl urged her toward the padded rocking chair near the hearth. She slammed the door behind her, putting a barrier between them and the Kaalipha.

"You've grown in the last few weeks. But you still can't keep your hair bound up properly." Myri smoothed a stray strand of hair from the girl's face.

The musky smell of Kalen's familiar was absent. Myri didn't like the weasel like creature that had adopted Kalen soon after they settled in the clearing. "Did your ferret follow you from the clearing?"

"I . . . um . . . my familiar isn't in Hanassa." Kalen buried her face against Myri, clinging to her tightly. "Will you brush my hair later? Do you remember the hours you spent brushing it when we lived in the clearing? What made you shove all this stuff in front of the door? Is the baby all right?"

"Her name is Amaranth. My baby must be Amaranth." Myri gently disengaged Kalen's fierce hug and settled into the padded chair, the baby feeding greedily.

Kalen froze. "You'd only allow that if Amaranth had died."

"I felt him die. I almost died with him. The pain. Oh, Kalen, the pain was terrible . . ." Tears gathered in her eyes at last. "We have to find Powwell and get out of here, Kalen," Myri whispered so that Yaassima, safely in the other room, couldn't hear. "We have to keep Amaranth away from the Kaalipha and away from Televarn's people. We have to warn Nimbulan. Amaranth didn't have time to tell him that Televarn plans to kill him as well as my brother."

"Maybe we should let him. What did Nimbulan do for you after he'd seduced you, left you pregnant, and then exiled you?"

Powwell slipped from the shadow of the cave mouth into the slightly lighter blackness of the open street. The Rover guards dozed before their fire within the cave, seemingly unaware that one of their slaves was escaping. Where could he go? There was only one known exit from Hanassa—a gate controlled by the Kaalipha's magic.

He wasn't certain enough of the way Televarn had brought the captives into Hanassa to be sure there was a true exit beneath the palace.

If he had to resort to drawing blood to find enough magic

to open the regular gate tonight, Powwell would—after he found Kalen and Myri.

You have to get me out of here! Kalen had called to him telepathically shortly after the Kaalipha's elite guards had removed her from Televarn's slave pens.

I'll get you all out, Powwell had sent back to her.

Myri's too ill. We'll have to leave her behind. But you have to get me out. Soon, Powwell. Soon, please.

That last message had bothered Powwell. He didn't want to leave Myri behind. He'd promised Nimbulan he'd take care of the witchwoman. He'd promised.

Thorny, he alerted the hedgehog before reaching inside his pocket to pet the miniature hedgehog. The timid creature kept his spines relaxed and soft. Calming energy soothed Powwell's fears and firmed his resolve.

Time had run out. He had to get Kalen and Myri out of Hanassa tonight. This morning he'd watched as two of the Kaalipha's personal guards, uniformed and sober, had slapped chains and a gag on Kalen and dragged her into the palace. Usually such rough handling preceded an execution.

He placed each foot soundlessly in front of him. He'd make less noise if he ran barefoot along the baked mud roadway. Impractical at best, even in warmer weather. No one maintained the roads here. Cracks, stones, and refuse littered them, traps for the unwary.

At the next cave mouth, Powwell paused, listening with every sense available to him. Thorny wiggled a little, adding his senses to Powwell's. Light snores filtered through the darkness. Two, no, three people slept within. He peered with his Sight beyond Sight into the interior; an easy spell that didn't require much strength. The fire had burned down to a few shapeless coals. He should be safe crossing in front of the opening. If anyone were still awake, they'd have built up the fire on this freezing night. At least there wouldn't be snow. This high desert rarely saw any moisture at all.

He looked up through the tunnel-like opening of the city walls to check the stars. The great wheel had turned past midnight. The guards should be dozing. He ran soundlessly toward the first of seven rock outcroppings strewn across the bowl of the crater that housed the city of Hanassa. Mud huts clustered around each of the outcroppings. The jumble of buildings and pathways created a mapless maze.

The setting moon hid behind the crater walls. Faint starlight glimmered just brightly enough on the minerals embedded in the rocks to show him a rough outline of obstacles. He paused, wrapping the deepest shadows around him like a cloak. He checked landmarks, orienting himself to his memorized path. The escape had to succeed tonight. If he was caught, he'd never get another chance.

He counted his heartbeats. One hundred. The sentry should pass in front of him now. He detected no movement, no sound. Where was the man? The next leg of Powwell's journey across the outlaws' city was the most exposed. He had to wait for the sentry to pass before proceeding.

At last he heard a faint trickle of water. Ah! The sentry taking a piss. Couldn't he use the latrine at the beginning of his patrol route?

Powwell wrinkled his nose in disgust. He couldn't get out of this hole in the mountains soon enough. He'd wasted too much time learning Hanassa and its routines. During those weeks of patient observing, he'd become so frightened by the violence and cruelty of the outlaws that he would resort to blood magic to get Kalen and Myrilandel out of here.

Yaassima had killed her consort because he was *liked* by the outlaws of Hanassa and therefore threatened her control over him and the inhabitants. Then she had killed her own daughter because the girl refused to dip her hands into her father's blood.

He shuddered in revulsion. He'd seen Moncriith in the city yesterday. Moncriith also reveled in blood. If he and Yaassima teamed up, no one in the city would live long.

A little blood magic paled in comparison to the river of death Powwell imagined running through Hanassa.

Thorny puffed up inside Powwell's pocket.

Not you, Thorny. I'd never sacrifice you, he soothed his familiar. *Moncriith is hanging around. He'll slaughter anyone or anything to bolster his magic. But I won't. All I have to do is prick my hand a little.* If he had to resort to blood magic, maybe he should use one of Thorny's spines. Involving his familiar might increase the effectiveness of the hideous procedure.

The sentry burped loudly. Stale ale fumes wafted past Powwell's nose. He grimaced and held his breath until the man responsible for the security of this portion of the city staggered past, hiccuping and bleary-eyed. From his ragged clothes Powwell surmised he must be one of the common road bandits. The patrols were bands of outlaws who paid part of their rent to Yaassima with sentry duty. Rarely did they perform their jobs sober.

After another one hundred heartbeats, Powwell resumed his trek across the city to the palace—which was little more than another jumble of mud huts piled on top of each other on the outside. Rumor claimed the palace had been carved out of a vast cave system and reached far and deep into the ancient mountain.

So far the Justice Bell had not tolled within the converted temple to Simurgh, summoning the populace to witness the Kaalipha's judgment. Kalen wouldn't be executed yet.

Powwell had to arrange the escape tonight. Yaassima preferred dawn executions.

At the seventh and last outcropping of volcanic rock, Powwell waited for the next sentry to pass. The guards were more alert here, members of Televarn's clan. Rovers seldom drank enough to dull their senses. This man had to be neutralized quickly. The sentry's next circuit would take him to Televarn's slave pens where he would make a head count. Any other night the chore would have fallen to a different enclave of outlaws and Powwell could have slipped past his sleepy guards at any time.

He couldn't wait another night. The Kaalipha had taken Kalen.

Using all of his senses, physical and magical, Powwell listened to the sounds of the dirt and rocks shifting and whispering to themselves in the nighttime chill. When he heard a pebble roll and strike another, he knew the sentry approached. Three breaths later a shadow within a shadow shifted.

Powwell rolled his balance to the balls of his feet. The sentry probably weighed twice Powwell's slim adolescent body and stood a full head taller. Powwell needed the advantage of surprise and speed. His magic was too limited in this desert. No ley lines crossed through the ancient volcano, and the dragons shied away from the area. He had no source of power other than his own growing body. Rovers had their rituals, which Powwell didn't know or understand. The Bloodmages drew strength from pain. Powwell would save that for a last resort.

He closed his fingers around a jagged rock he'd tucked into his pocket this morning. With every fragment of strength he possessed, he threw the rock at the passing sentry.

A grunt followed by a thud against the baked mud street told him his aim had been true. Only one more obstacle to overcome, the very alert team of guards at the palace portal.

Powwell paused long enough to thump the Rover more soundly on the head, making certain he wouldn't wake up soon. From the squishy sound of the rock hitting flesh, the guard might never wake again. Televarn would seek revenge. But Televarn was already Powwell's enemy.

Then he grabbed the man's sword and spear. He hefted the weight of each weapon. The sword seemed awkward and heavy in his grasp. It would hinder his stealthy movements and weigh him down if he needed to run. The spear, though, was made of wood, long and slender; just the weight and length of a fighting staff. He ran both of his hands the full length of the shaft, hoping he could imprint it with some of his magic personality through such brief contact. This was a tool he knew how to use.

He pointed the staff at the entrance to the lower levels of the palace, pushing his Sight beyond Sight along the smooth grain of the wood. The fibers within the core of the shaft vibrated in tune with his magic. Details jumped to the fore of his vision. He saw the precise outline of the cave mouth, lopsided, jagged, obscured outcroppings that could knock an unwary man senseless. Inside, one man fed the small fire contained within a circle of stones. The other paced from the fire to the entrance and back again, brushing past a gaudy tapestry on the right-hand wall.

Powwell's instincts told him the tapestry was a blind. The passageway behind it led to a dead end, possibly through several lethal traps. A separate cave mouth with a heavily guarded gate off to the left was the only access to the inner caves and the palace above. This smaller cave housed only the Kaalipha's brothel.

While the pacing guard checked the narrow opening to the brothel, Powwell crept closer. He gripped his newly acquired staff tightly, channeling his magic through the wood. A barely visible cloud of gray mist surrounded him. With luck, he'd be invisible to the guards. He couldn't tell for sure. He'd never tried this spell before without Kalen at his side, guiding him through it.

Holding his breath, he stepped into the cave mouth. Neither guard stirred. Powwell circled the perimeter, careful to stay between the guard and the light of the fire. No sense in betraying his presence with a moving shadow.

He slid into a short corridor. The sound of soft snores and restless bodies shifting beneath bedcovers greeted him. Now all he had to do was find Myri and Kalen among the dozen women Kaalipha Yaassima kept for the guards' pleasure, and an equal number of children belonging to those women. Myri should be among them. He hadn't seen her since the Kaalipha had removed her from Televarn's custody three weeks ago. She must have had the baby the first night here. Would the Kaalipha send her to be made available to the guards so soon? She had to be in this dormitory. Except for Yaassima's private maid, women weren't allowed to sleep in the palace proper. The Kaalipha surrounded herself only with men she could manipulate and control.

With his back against the rock wall of the inner corridor, Powwell sidled into the women's chambers. He dropped the spell of invisibility before it drained too much of his energy and waited for his eyes to adjust to the minimal light cast by the still active fire in the central hearth of the cave.

Whoever had built up the fire might still be awake.

Powwell froze, willing himself to blend into the rock wall. He scanned the dark forms upon the scattered pallets for signs of movement or a glimmer of Myri's white-blond hair reflecting the firelight. One of the figures, larger than the rest, grunted and shifted. The blanket rose up.

A lump choked Powwell's throat. He heard his heart pounding in his ears so loudly the women must surely awaken at the echoes.

"Got to get back to work, love." The rising figure resolved into a naked man. He pinched his partner's bare backside and replaced the blanket. Then, as he reached for his discarded clothes on the floor, his gaze locked with Powwell's. They both froze in place.

Chapter 9

"Fifty ships to sabotage and barely one hundred obstacles embedded into the mudflats," Nimbulan pounded the ramparts of the old keep with his fist. "Not enough. Not nearly enough."

Exhausted and filthy with soot and sweat, he watched the small fishing fleet, King Quinnault's poor excuse for a navy, launch into the swollen tide.

Not once during this very long day of frenetic activity had he forgotten that Amaranth had died trying to summon help for Myri. She must be in terrible danger for the familiar to leave her.

He needed to be with his wife, protect her, comfort her in her grief.

Myri would feel Amaranth's death, possibly try to share it. That agony would only compound whatever she suffered in Hanassa. He had to go to her. Then what?

"At least I know she's alive," he reminded himself. The slender cord of silver magic connecting his heart to hers pulsed with life. Amaranth had restored it somehow.

Myrilandel lived, in Hanassa, the hidden city where nightmares were born.

Nimbulan rested his head on his arm. Fatigue weighed heavily on his eyelids. He didn't dare give in to it. In a few moments full dark would be upon them, and he'd have work to do.

Behind him, the glowing sun sank below the rim of the western mountain rage. With the loss of heat and light from the sun, an easterly breeze sprang to life.

Out in the bay, fifty ships hoisted sail, catching the increasing wind that now favored their invasion of Coronnan City and the rich river delta.

Nimbulan focused on the small boat leading the defense of Coronnan. King Quinnault's pale blond head shone in the dying sunlight as he stood in the prow of the boat he shared with Journeyman Magician Rollett and a fisherman, a beacon to rally his people.

Lord Konnaught wasn't in the second boat, as Quinnault had ordered. Where did the brat get to? He was probably tucked snugly into bed with a hot posset on this cold and clear night.

You shouldn't be out there, Your Grace. Konnaught is right this once. The kingdom can't spare you. Nimbulan hoped his telepathic call reached the king. Quinnault had so little natural magic, the chances of him hearing, much less heeding, the message were slim. The dragons were the only ones who could engage his telepathy—and they had left Coronnan.

The Covenant is broken.

Nimbulan hoped he had enough tricks up his sleeves to convince the mundane lords he hadn't yet resorted to illegal solitary magic in order to hold the kingdom together. He hoped he had enough strength, magical and physical, to get through the night.

The fisherman who guided Quinnault's boat rowed eagerly for the rapidly approaching fleet. A large wave lifted them nearly level with a larger ship's deck. The tide neared flood stage; another hour would mark the highest water.

Aboard the looming vessels in the invasion fleet, sailors leaned over the rails, pointing and laughing at the myriad small boats sent to deter them.

Armor, men. Don't forget the armor! Nimbulan ordered the magicians among the fishermen. The threads from his cloak and splinters from his staff kept the lines of communication open since they didn't have any of the communal dragon magic left.

Two heartbeats later, the invading sailors pelted the small boats with ballast rocks, spears, and debris. Much of it bounced off bubbles of magical armor and fell harmlessly into the waves. Two boats wobbled precariously as the flying objects forced men to lose control of their oars.

Nimbulan sent hasty reminders to magicians in nearby boats to protect the faltering ones. They couldn't afford to lose a single man or boat.

The glowing reservoir of witchfire in the cauldron beside him picked out the sparkling magical shields now in place over each of the boats.

One of the foreign vessels listed badly to port as it scraped the first of the submerged trees. Immediately Quinnault, in the lead boat, let loose a flaming arrow into that ship's sails. Dozens more archers followed his lead.

The ship veered off course. The rushing ride embedded the keel in the sucking mud. The ship's captain frantically swung the wheel, trying to regain his course. The rudder jammed and refused to budge.

"One down, forty-nine to go." Nimbulan dropped his arm, and Lyman released the catapult that dominated the keep's courtyard. A great ball of green witchfire flew through the air, almost faster than the eye could follow. As it sped over the bay, the millions of flamelets that made up the mass separated but did not lose intensity. Sails burst into flame when the witchfire found additional fuel in the canvas sails.

Three ships lost control of their sails in an instant. They, too, ran aground as all hands rushed to douse flames that could not be extinguished by mundane means.

Behind the vessels, half the tiny fishing boats moved close to the sterns of the ships still under control and heading for the islands. Nimbulan watched Quinnault fling a net outward, toward a ship's rudder. The net spread and landed in perfect position to tangle in the steering rod.

The king's long hours of fishing paid off. He hauled the net tight. The ship swung sideways to the waves. The helmsman spun the wheel uselessly, further tangling the net.

Other fisherman weren't so lucky. They needed the extra guidance of the magicians before their nets ensnared more rudders.

Nimbulan signaled for another catapult. Lord Konnaught appeared beside the war engine, seemingly rested, clean, and well fed when every everyone else showed the effects of a long day of hard work. Nimbulan repeated the signal. The boy pointedly turned his back on the magician. He spoke quietly to a grimy man wearing a blacksmith's apron. The catapult remained firmly in place.

Angrily, Nimbulan sent a line of communication to Lyman who monitored the cauldron of witchfire. The old magician limped over to the catapult. He grabbed Konnaught's shoulder with his extra long fingers and forcibly turned the boy around.

"I do not take orders from underlings," Konnaught protested.

Lyman tightened his grip and propelled the rebellious young man to the catapult. Konnaught jerked his hand forward—as if acting only under compulsion—and snapped the trigger. Then he looked up at Nimbulan. Hate filled his expression.

Nimbulan couldn't spare him a thought.

Fire filled the sky. The nearest sail exploded in heat and unnatural light, dropping living flames upon the deck. Sailors and heavily armed mercenaries scrambled away from the blaze. Some jumped ship. A few remained behind, beating uselessly at the fire with heavy tarps and water.

"Witchfire is created by magic. Only magic can douse it," Nimbulan recited to himself. Silently he mourned the men who screamed out their dying agony aboard the ship. Some of the men fled to the sea. They flailed about in the heaving waves. Heavy robes and armor dragged them down. The deepening tide that allowed ships to sail through the mudflats now made the water deep enough to drown the men. The storm that pushed the tide intensified the swells.

The witchfire continued to burn underwater. The few men who managed to shed shields and swords and all-concealing robes couldn't shed the flames that burned clear to the bone.

Nimbulan bit his lip, suppressing his own agony as many men died. Each death diminished him as a man because he was the instrument of their destruction. He'd organized similar scenes too often. There had to be a better way.

Once again he had proved himself the best Battlemage in all of Coronnan. Hundreds of men died at his command. *Enemies,* he told himself.

(Men,) a voice in the back of his head reminded him.

"Never again," he vowed. "I will not do this again. Somehow we must find peace from invasion as we found an end to the Great Wars of Disruption. I have to make Battlemages obsolete."

(You need Myrilandel to complete yourself and your work.)

Myri trudged into the Hall of Justice on the ground floor of Yaassima's palace. She stifled a yawn behind her hand. True sleepiness, not a stupor induced by drugs this time. She tucked away the tiny vial of powder she'd stolen from Haanna, Yaassima's maid, before the woman could sprinkle it over Myri's supper. She had substituted plain salt for the drugs. Her meal had tasted vile with too much salt, and she'd been thirsty all night. But her mind was clear of the drugs.

Myri's arms felt strangely empty without Baby Amaranth. She'd placed the sleeping infant into a back cradle while she and Kalen answered the peremptory summons of the Justice Bell. She would never leave Amaranth alone with Maia, who now slept on a pallet at the foot of Myri's bed.

The Rover woman had not roused in answer to the loud bell. She and Myri hadn't exchanged a single word since her arrival.

A sense of dread pushed away the last of Myri's predawn sleepiness. A crowd of men in various states of undress huddled near the doorway, awaiting Kaalipha Yaassima. Their unease became Myri's as she absorbed their fears.

She recognized some of the elite guard who owed loyalty only to Yaassima. The Kaalipha tended to overlook infractions of her arbitrary rules among these guards. The same action from someone else brought swift execution.

Myri's attention centered on a slouched figure in the center of the group. A man on either side seemed to be holding him up by the arms. His head bent nearly to his waist, hiding his face. Myri knew the pain in his belly where he'd been punched with a fist or the butt end of a spear.

Behind her, Kalen gasped and clung for balance to a tapestry wall covering. "Powwell." She mouthed the name.

Myri snapped her attention back to the prisoner. Other than the auburn-tinged hair, she had no clues to the man's identity. Too much of her talent was bound up in her baby to extend beyond basic emotions broadcast by others. She trusted Kalen's instincts.

She had all her children in view. Now all she had to do was lead them out of Hanassa. Getting Powwell safely away from Yaassima would be the hard part.

'What crime did this boy commit?" Yaassima appeared on the dais without warning. She hadn't been there a heart-beat ago. Where did she come from?

The Kaalipha clapped her hands. The torches dimmed. Panels in the ceiling came to life, replacing the flickering green flames with a brighter, more golden glow.

"How'd she do that?" Kalen asked, eyes wide.

"I don't know, and she won't tell," Myri replied, keeping her eyes on Powwell. Other than the ache in his belly he seemed healthy and fit.

Where were the exits? She marked each visible portal into the Justice Hall.

"Tell the man's crime so that I can dispense swift justice." Yaassima's voice swelled to fill the room over and above the babble of fearful men.

"Kaalipha." A man stepped forward and knelt, touching his forehead to the floor.

Myri recognized him as Nastfa, the guard who had carried her to Yaassima's suite that first day in Hanassa. He wore black trews less ragged than some inhabitants of Hanassa, and an almost clean linen shirt. If he dared speak, he must have some authority over the men assembled behind them. Myri already knew that Yaassima trusted him more than most of the elite corps that always surrounded her. Some of them were fully clothed, as if they had just come from guard duty. The others wore bits and pieces of hastily donned uniforms.

"Speak, Nastfa." Yaassima granted him permission to continue.

"The prisoner was found in the brothel. He is one of Televarn's slaves and has no right to the women there," Nastfa said, maintaining his subservient position, with his backside in the air.

"Who found him?" Yaassima stepped down from the dais and circled Nastfa. She caressed his upthrust bottom, not with affection, more like appraisal, as if he were a haunch of pork.

"I arrested the prisoner, Kaalipha." A second man assumed the position beside Nastfa. He wore only trews of fine black wool that he'd buttoned so hastily they fastened askew with gaps.

"Was the prisoner attempting to partner with one of *my* women?" Yaassima widened her circle to include the second man.

"No, I was not." Powwell raised his head as he spoke and shook off the hands that held him up. He could lose that head for speaking to the Kaalipha from an upright position. Just like Yaassima's consort and daughter had.

Myri broadcast caution to him. She didn't have her husband's easy command of telepathy, only her emotions to project to another.

"I was searching for my adopted mother, Myrilandel." He spotted Myri and Kalen beside the dais at that moment. Brief joy lit his face, then he masked all his emotions.

Kalen took a step toward him. Myri held her back, uncertain of Yaassima's cruel whims. Safety and escape lay in avoiding Yaassima's notice.

How could she distract the Kaalipha from Powwell without drawing unwanted attention to herself and Kalen?

"Do I understand this report, that you were found *in* the brothel, rather than attempting to enter?" Yaassima turned her gaze on Powwell. Her long fingers moved from the guard's rear end to Powwell's chest. She traced a glowing design over his heart, her talonlike fingernails snagging on the rough cloth of his tunic. Myri couldn't read the design, but she suspected it was a sigil of control.

Yaassima snapped her fingers. The sigil disappeared as a knife appeared in her hand. She repeated the symbol with the tip of the knife, slicing Powwell's tunic and shirt but not his skin.

"Yes, Kaalipha, I was inside the brothel," Powwell answered when the other men looked at the floor and shuffled their feet.

"How did you get past the guards?" Yaassima's eyes narrowed as she scanned the motley array of half-dressed men. Her gaze halted on the second kneeling man.

"I used a spell of invisibility."

The Kaalipha's gaze whipped back to Powwell.

Myri cringed. If she ran and pushed the Kaalipha aside, she might be able to drag Powwell and Kalen through the primary entrance. Where would they go once they were free of the palace?

She didn't have enough information!

"A magician. How lovely. Were you trained by Nimbulan? Or perhaps Myrilandel's Rover lover was your teacher?" The knife disappeared. Yaassima's extraordinarily long fingers flexed and opened repeatedly.

"I received some training from Myrilandel's *husband,* Kaalipha."

"Can you work dragon magic?" Yaassima's voice became too sweet. Myri waited in dread for the vicious blow to follow.

"When there are dragons present," Powwell said.

"Can you work dragon magic now, child?"

"I sense no dragon magic. Nor are there any ley lines near. I have only limited reserves of magic available. I'd rather not waste them on parlor tricks."

"No dragon magic!" Yaassima screeched. "No dragon magic! There has to be dragon magic. I am *The Dragon,* that's what Kaalipha means in the old tongue—dragon. I am descended from dragons. You will take your magic from me. Show me, boy. Show me this dragon magic, or I'll know you for a liar and execute you at dawn for the crime." The torches flared high, adding their green light to the yellow ceiling panels.

"You may have the blood of dragons in you, Kaalipha. But you are not in dragon form. I cannot gather your magic. Nor can I gather Myrilandel's while she resides in a human body."

Yaassima glared at the boy. Color rose in her pale cheeks. Torchlight reflected green sparks off her white-blond hair. She stood almost a head taller than he. Powwell had grown these last six moons to be equal in height to some of the men present. Yaassima seemed to swell taller yet. Her arms stretched away from her sides for balance as if she expected them to become wings.

Surprised, Myri stepped forward to watch the Kaalipha more closely. She thought the gesture to be unique to herself. Would Yaassima transform?

Could she transform?

All the men except Powwell backed away from Yaassima, recognizing her posture as a threat.

"I have not the time to test your magic right now. Tell me, though, if you were invisible, how did my men find you? Careful of your answer, boy, your fate resides in my good wishes." The torchlight faded along with Yaassima's temper.

Cold sweat broke out on Myri's back. This was the moment when Yaassima was the most dangerous; when cold calculation replaced hot temper. Life or death. The Kaalipha of Hanassa controlled them both.

"I dropped the spell as soon as I passed beyond the guards. I did not want to use so much of my energy until I had to."

"The guards were in the anteroom and you were in the brothel?" Yaassima turned back to the two men who continued to kneel with their foreheads on the floor.

"One of them was with a woman, Kaalipha. He caught me." Powwell pointed to the second man. The one who had barely had time to pull on his trews.

"You have done me a favor, boy. I must deal with this man's disregard of my rules. I grant you life, Powwell. Today. Guards, take this fledgling magician to the pit. A few moons sweltering in the heart of the volcano will either cure him of his desire to escape or kill him."

Chapter 10

Yaassima fluttered her hand in a dismissive gesture. Two fully-dressed guards hastened to haul Powwell away. The other men regrouped in a tighter knot, unwilling to be singled out by the Kaalipha.

Yaassima did not shift her gaze from the kneeling men.

Myri swallowed deeply. No execution for Powwell. While he lived, she had a chance to help him escape, along with herself and her daughters. The longer she delayed, the more dangerous Hanassa became.

"Who was on duty?" Yaassima caressed Nastfa on his buttocks. She reached between his legs and fondled his genitals through the rough wool of his trews. Her palm remained cupped, ready to squeeze with the extra strength of her long fingers. Nastfa gulped. His dark skin paled.

"Bjorg and Evaar, Kaalipha." His voice rose in an unnatural squeak.

Myri smelled his fear and anticipation of pain. She clutched Kalen's arm for support. Yaassima had been known to prolong her tortures when she sensed Myri's loathing, as if she needed to punish Myri, too.

Beside her, Kalen licked her lips. Myri couldn't tell if she moistened them in reaction to her own fear or anticipation. Her swirling emotions bewildered Myri.

"Kalen," she whispered, clutching the girl's arm tighter. "What are you feeling?"

"They betrayed Powwell. They deserve whatever *she* gives them. I want them to suffer for betraying Powwell." This time, Kalen's eagerness to watch the men writhe in pain broke through her armored emotions.

Myri recoiled in disgust.

"There should have been a third man on duty. Who was he?" Yaassima's grip on the man's balls tightened a little.

"Golin shared the duty, Kaalipha." Nastfa's voice rose again in fear, anticipating Yaassima's grip. His greasy black hair trembled from his reaction. He had nearly Rover-dark hair and skin. But his face bore tinges of yellow and his eyes slanted slightly. He must have been one of the elite assassins of Maffisto before Yaassima brought him into her guard. What power did Yaassima hold over him to make such a ruthless man subservient and quaking in fear?

"Golin, the man who discovered the magician in the brothel, was also on duty?" Yaassima removed her hand. Nastfa nearly collapsed in relief. His companion began to shake, though. "Golin, who was supposed to be patrolling the entrance, shifting the torches every few minutes to cast new and different shadows so an invisible magician would be betrayed by his shadow falling in the wrong place. Golin, who was, instead, naked in the bed of one of my women!" Yaassima slipped her fingers beneath the man's belt. Her long fingernails tore the fine black cloth of his trews. She yanked the fabric with all of her strength. The cloth tore in three straight lines so that the fabric fluttered to the floor in rags.

Golin's shaking increased as the cold night air shriveled his genitals.

"You are not free of guilt yet, Nastfa. You lead this sorry band of murderers. Yours is the responsibility to keep them in line."

Nastfa nodded and maintained his pose. He gulped in air and stared briefly at Myri before dropping his forehead to the stone paving once more.

That one long look spoke of many secrets that had to remain hidden. What did the man try to tell her?

"Tell me, Golin," Yaassima cooed with unnatural sweetness. "In return for refuge in *my* city, you have the duty to protect *my* women certain nights of the moon. On any other night you are free to take one of those women back to your quarters. Yet you forsook your duty to me to lie with one of those women tonight. Do you do this often?" Yaassima placed both hands between his legs.

"You provide for us quite generously, Kaalipha. I had to make sure the women slept soundly. Kestra couldn't sleep,

she claimed she was too cold. She asked me to warm her."
Golin stammered.

"Kestra. One of Televarn's women. She dissatisfied him,
so he gave her to me as part of his tithe. I should have
known a Rover woman couldn't resist a man. Any man, at
any time." Yaassima looked up at Myri as she continued
to stroke and fondle Golin. He grew with her now gentle
ministrations. His magnificent proportions would entice
most women.

Myri tried to look away. Something in Yaassima's eyes
compelled her to continue observing Golin's humiliation.

"Kestra, isn't she the one who bore a half-caste child
two moons ago? I believe the father was a magician from
Coronnan, the one who betrayed Televarn. The one who
also fathered Maia's baby. He did spread his seed far and
wide. What was his name?" Yaassima continued to look at
Myri. A malicious grin spread over her face.

Myri swallowed heavily. She knew her husband, Nimbulan, had lived with Televarn's clan for a season before their
marriage. He'd been invited to mate with Maia. Televarn
had arranged the union and manipulated their emotions
with magic. No other woman of the clan was offered to
Nimbulan.

" 'Twas Televarn who betrayed my husband, Kaalipha,"
Myri said through clenched teeth. "Televarn's tales change
with the wind. He cannot tell the truth."

Yaassima smiled again. "Nimbulan's infidelity is not the
issue here. I could have you castrated, Golin, for neglecting
your duty."

Every man in the room blanched. Myri grew hot, then
very cold in her mid-region. She knew Yaassima was manipulating her through her empathic talent.

"There is no call for that, Yaassima." She firmed her
chin and stared at the woman. She had to stop this. Her
own safety paled in significance to the violence that permeated Hanassa. Kalen had already been tainted by it. She
had to stop this here and now.

"You wish to deprive me of justice?" Yaassima raised
one eyebrow in speculation. Her hands tightened on Golin
as a reminder that her attention wasn't totally on Myri's
distraction. He shrank again.

Every eye in the room rested on the Kaalipha. Would

she dare perform the torturous procedure with her bare hands, using her fingernails in place of a knife?

"Golin will be useless to you if he lives. You will destroy his courage and clear thinking. What good is a guard afraid to confront men who challenge him?"

"Perhaps, perhaps not. I need loyal men. Men who know I hold their lives and their deaths in my hands. Men who know that to fail me will bring worse punishment than my enemies could inflict upon them."

She squeezed Golin harder, then abruptly released her grip. He groaned and collapsed, clutching his still intact groin. Yaassima laughed and wiped her hands on the rags of Golin's trews. "It would be a pity to lose a man who is hung like a sledge steed in rut. I have a better idea. Stand up, both of you." She kicked at the two kneeling men.

Nastfa scrambled to his knees. Golin managed to get his legs under him but remained slumped over and groaning.

"For your punishment," Yaassima continued, "both of you shall stand guard over the women every night for the next moon. All night. And you shall watch as they service the guards I send to them, every night. You shall help undress the women. You shall help them bathe. But you may not lie with them. If you succumb to the temptation, and they will tempt you mightily, I will castrate and then execute you both. Do you understand?"

"Yes, Kaalipha," Nastfa and Golin whispered with relief.

"Louder. I want all of your crew to hear you and understand that they are to make sure you know what you are missing." The torches flared again, a sure sign of her rising temper and a possibly worse fate for the men.

"Yes, Kaalipha," they nearly shouted.

"Good. Then we will begin now. Someone fetch the women. We will watch the sport together."

Golin bent to retrieve the tattered remnants of his clothes and his dignity.

"No, Golin. No clothes for you. I need to know that you suffer torment and understand why you must endure." She rubbed him with her dangerous hand. He didn't fill it.

Yaassima laughed.

"He's so scared he'll be lucky to get it up again," Kalen muttered.

"Precisely," Yaassima replied. "Come, Myri. You might enjoy this. You haven't been with a man for many moons. Choose a partner, or several, whatever you desire. If you like, I can provide the means for you to play at being raped." Her tone told everyone in the room this was an order rather than a suggestion.

Yaassima clapped her hands. The floor groaned and shuddered. Slowly, the huge altar stone rose from its subterranean hiding place. Stone scraped on stone until the long slab of granite stood a little higher than Yaassima's waist. A metal stake poked up from each of the four corners. Manacles for wrists and ankles dangled from each spike.

Yaassima's victim would rest in the place of sacrifice formerly reserved for offerings to Simurgh. Did Yaassima subject her own daughter to this humiliating torture before murdering her?

"The tide is nearly out," King Quinnault shouted with glee as he bounded up the steps to Nimbulan's post on the battlements. Quinnault cradled his right arm in his left, rubbing the bicep and shoulder.

Nimbulan raised his head from his crossed arms upon the wall. He blinked grit from his eyes. His deep concentration on the individual ships within the battle had also kept him from noticing the world beyond the tangling fishnets, broken hulls, his aching body, and the death of too many men. He had supervised the entire battle and left the throwing of magic to others. Still the exhaustion of maintaining communications dragged him close to unconsciousness.

A gentle tug on his back, a lower pitch to the humming in his ears, a sense of weight in his knees, all told him of the shift in the forces of moon and water.

He sensed no trace of the special stillness in the air that heralded dawn. He longed for the red-gold sunshine to bake the ache from his joints. His eyes were tired of straining through the green light of torches and witchfire.

"You saved Coronnan this night, Magician Nimbulan." Quinnault bowed deeply in respect, still holding his arm close to his body.

"Thanks should go to you and your comrades, Your

Grace," Nimbulan replied as he surveyed the wreckage of the Rossemeyerian armada. "Are you hurt?" He reached a hand to touch the injury. Quinnault shied away from him.

"I twisted or pulled something out of place." He shrugged and winced painfully.

"More than a muscle strain, Your Grace." Nimbulan probed the tender spot with insistent fingers.

"Some flying debris broke through the magical armor and bruised it. Then I had to grab the oars in a hurry when Leauman, my boatman, ducked too hastily. The strain pulled something," Quinnault said through gritted teeth.

"I don't think you dislocated anything. Maybe a bruise to the bone. We'll get a healer to look at it. I wish you hadn't endangered yourself out on the Bay tonight. If you had been killed, Coronnan would be in dire straits, victory or no. You have no heir to succeed you."

Quinnault dismissed Nimbulan's concern with a wave at the destruction out in the Bay. "My people needed to see me leading the charge. They fought harder alongside me than they would have if I'd been safely protected by stone walls—remind me later to reinforce that lesson with Konnaught. I'm tried of his scowls of disapproval."

"Lord Konnaught should have been exiled upon his father's death," Nimbulan grumbled.

"He deserves the chance to grow into his rightful inheritance. I'd rather teach him to nurture the land and the people than punish him for his father's tyranny," Quinnault replied.

The king stared out at the wreckage strewn across the moonlit bay before continuing. "We won't be bothered by Rossemeyer again for a while. Ambassador General Jhorge-Rosse must now respect me as a warrior as well as a peace-maker. We'll present a new treaty to him after we've slept." He yawned hugely, then seemed to shake off his fatigue.

"We should let him cool his heels for a day or two," Nimbulan said. A day or two while he and his exhausted magicians slept and ate and slept some more. "We don't have to make the trade treaty now; we've proved we can defend ourselves. The ambassador must learn that the treaty is an offer of friendship more than trade advantages. We also have many prisoners of war to ransom back to Rossemeyer. We bargain from strength this time."

Fifty ships had sailed into the mudflats of the Great Bay. Perhaps twelve managed to hoist enough sail to catch the wind that shifted to an offshore direction. Thirty-some ships rested at bizarre angles with their hulls run aground on mud and lethal debris. Five had burned to the waterline, their sailors captured as they jumped for the relative safety of the water. Some of the refugees managed to swim toward departing ships and save themselves. Many more died in the pounding waves and the witchfire that continued burning on the surface of the Bay. Hundreds of men had surrendered to the crews of the fishing boats.

Nimbulan closed his eyes and concentrated on the flames that bounced and separated with each wave of seawater. When he looked again, all traces of witchfire had winked out. The sudden darkness soothed his eyes but not his soul. He'd cleaned up the last spell of the battle. He could rest now.

"Speaking of treaties of friendship, there are several offers of marriage alliance to consider." Quinnault changed subjects in mid-thought—not uncommon for his keen intelligence. "I'll need your help with a letter to King Lorriin of SeLenicca. I really can't marry his sister. She's ten years older than me and a barren widow. But we have to word the rejection to sound like I am not worthy of her beauty rather than that she is inadequate to be my queen."

"And how old are you, Your Grace?" Nimbulan raised one eyebrow skeptically.

"You know, as well as I, that I'll see my twenty-eighth Winter Solstice a moon hence."

"A mere infant." Nimbulan frowned at his king. "That makes the Princess of SeLenicca thirty-eight. She's been widowed for many years. Perhaps she hasn't had the opportunity to bear children."

"I can't take the chance. I need a young and fertile princess. And I won't have just any well-born lady with the proper dowry and political connections—there are three offers for those. She must be intelligent and have a sense of humor. If she's easy on the eyes, so much the better." Quinnault paced, left hand behind his back, shoulders hunched. With his long face and hair in wild disarray, his silhouette resembled that of a young dragon.

How many of his draconic mannerisms were natural?

Some of them could be a result of his magical link to the dragons established at his coronation. Nimbulan didn't know how much of the link remained since Shayla had declared the Covenant broken. King Quinnault didn't talk about it.

Every thought of dragons brought Nimbulan back to his missing wife, Myrilandel. *Shayla, please take care of her for me,* he pleaded with the sole female dragon in the nimbus and Myrilandel's mother. *I miss her more than I thought possible.*

Nimbulan's age and loneliness weighed heavily on his shoulders. He had to convince his king to allow him to leave the capital immediately so he could begin his search for Myri. He'd forsake the much needed rest if he had to. But not his meal. He'd get nowhere fast without food. And soon.

"We'd best get busy. I'm certain General Ambassador Jhorge-Rosse will be demanding an audience at first light." Quinnault turned sharply on his heel at the end of his serpentine route.

"You seem to have a disgusting amount of energy left after a full day of work and a full night of battle, and an injury, Your Grace." Nimbulan surveyed his king. He smelled of salt spray and sweat, of tar and fish. The grin on his face rivaled the setting moon in brilliance.

"I have won a battle on my terms, with weapons I know—the cunning of men and small boats. I respect myself much more tonight than I did when I ran my sword into Kammeryl d'Astrismos' gut." King Quinnault frowned slightly at the mention of that grisly battle. "Time to eat and rest, my friend. Then it's back to work for both of us." He slapped Nimbulan on the back in comradely affection.

Friend, indeed, Nimbulan thought warmly. Surely Quinnault would recognize Nimbulan's need to go in search of Myri and grant him permission to leave. The quest should be his own. No other man had the right—or the desperate need—to find Myrilandel no matter his age or responsibilities in the capital.

Jaanus, the journeyman who had been dispatched on the search for Myri didn't know how to look for the elusive witchwoman. Only Nimbulan could find her. He was sure of that now.

"You must see a healer before you begin reorganizing the world, Quinnault. Coronnan can't afford for you to be laid low by some hidden injury that flares up later."

"I'm glad I made you my chief adviser, Nimbulan. I can't envision governing without you at my side. Why don't you move your quarters into the palace where you are close at hand?"

And under the king's constant eye.

Nimbulan sighed, wondering if he'd have to risk losing the king's friendship and trust by running away. The Commune's influence in the new government had been based upon Nimbulan's relationship with Quinnault.

Surely the new king wouldn't remove the Commune from advisory positions because he was angry with Nimbulan. Quinnault was fairer minded than that. Several of the lords on the Council weren't so generous. Konnaught led a faction that preferred the old way of ruling where personal privilege of the lords was more important than the welfare of the country.

Nimbulan shuddered in memory of the chaos that had run rampant through Coronnan when Konnaught's father had proclaimed himself king.

The ties keeping him in Coronnan were almost as strong as the ties that pulled him to search for Myri.

Chapter 11

The Kaalipha and her guard stared at Myri from a frozen tableau. The flaring torches and uncanny yellow ceiling panel lights cast conflicting shadows around the room. An aura of evil followed the shadows.

"Promise me, Kalen, that if Yaassima kills me, you will care for Amaranth. You will keep her from the clutches of the Kaalipha. And if—no, *when*—you escape, you will keep her away from Moncriith and Televarn. Guard her with your life." Myri clutched at her daughter's sleeve. Her long fingers wound around the girl's thin arm, clenching with a grip as tight as the one Yaassima had used on Golin.

"Let me take your place, Myri. They won't kill me." Kalen looked up at Myri with her wide gray eyes, all innocent and trusting.

Behind the familiar mask of naïveté lurked cold calculation. Myri wondered when in the last three weeks Kalen had lost what remained of her innocence. What went on in Televarn's slave pens? Had her virginity been stolen, too? She feared so and grieved that her daughter hadn't had the opportunity to learn joy in sex at an Equinox Festival.

Too early Kalen had figured out that every adult in her life used her—and her talent—for their own benefit. She used her mask of childish trust as a blind while she thrust her own will upon those around her. Myri doubted she had ever been innocent and trusting.

Myri addressed her adversary rather than her daughter. "No, Kalen. This is not about sex or punishment. It is about control. Yaassima cannot control my love for Nimbulan, so she seeks to destroy it by making me feel soiled and unworthy. If I allowed you to take my place, I would feel even more worthless. I refuse to be manipulated by her."

Yaassima maintained her steady gaze at Myri, saying nothing. A malicious smile crooked one corner of her mouth upward. Her eyes showed no trace of amusement. The manacles lay between them in mute challenge to both their wills.

"But in raping me, or watching you, Kalen, become her victim, my sense of self-worth would shatter. That is not in her plans. She no longer has an heir of her body, and so she seeks one who bears dragon blood to rule this city when she is gone. Dragons are long-lived, but they do die. Sometimes they are killed. Amaranth and I are her only possible heirs. I do not think she will live long enough to see my baby grown and ready to assume the title of Kaalipha. She is older than she looks. She has many enemies who lust for her power, including Televarn and Moncriith." Myri didn't drop her gaze from Yaassima.

"Your logic is very good, Myrilandel, but not perfect," Yaassima said. "Have you forgotten that dragons always mate with three or more consorts? The more fathers, the larger and stronger the litter. I should think you ready to welcome the attentions of these men." She gestured to the incorruptible guards who watched the battle of wills between Myri and Yaassima. None of them had left to fetch the women.

"Dragons can only mate once every two years. If conditions are not perfect, they will wait longer, much longer. They choose their consorts from among the males they can tolerate dealing with day after day. And they never mate while still suckling their young. I will not allow you to control me, Yaassima. Seek your sport with another."

"Your foster daughter is willing."

"Kalen is barely eleven summers. She doesn't know what she offers."

Some of the guards shuffled their feet a little. Myri sensed their embarrassment. Elite assassins they might be, but they maintained their own rough code of honor among themselves. Raping young girls violated even their code.

"I think the child knows precisely what she risks." Yaassima narrowed her slightly uptilted eyes. An extra lid fluttered down, obscuring the pupil from external view while she looked out on the world from a different perspective. Myri didn't have that extra dragon eyelid. Her body hadn't been born dragon—merely borrowed by a dragon. The dragon personality had forced the body to exhibit some draconic characteristics, but not all. Her spinal bumps were barely noticeable compared to Yaassima's.

"Kalen has been Televarn's hostage for over three weeks now," Yaassima said. "He always samples his female slaves before selling them to traders in SeLenicca within a few weeks of capture. But only after he tires of them. He likes training young girls for life in the brothels. The male slaves, he sells to the mines. But he has not sold this girl, nor her foster brother. Why? What sport do they offer him?"

"Televarn captured hostages, not slaves, when he laid a trap for us among my villagers," Myri replied. "He hoped I would come to his bed willingly in return for their freedom. You thwarted his plans by claiming kinship with me."

Myri closed her eyes briefly, trying to banish the images of the nightmarish day when Televarn had burned an entire village, murdering those who stood between him and Myrilandel.

Yaassima threw back her head and laughed long and loud. The sound rose in pitch and shrillness, echoing around the Justice Hall. Myri was reminded of the deafening sounds made by dragons when they communicated among themselves.

"Your defiance speaks well of your ability to lead the ungovernable filth who inhabit this city," Yaassima said when she gained control of her mirth. "You must be strong of will and ruthless of action to remain alive. I will find another, more willing, victim for my men tonight. Kestra, I think, since she was willing to break my rules to have a man inside her." She waved her hand and the ceiling panels dimmed. The flickering shadows of the torchlight replaced the too bright directionless glare.

The band of guards visibly relaxed. One of the black-clad men slipped out, presumably to fetch the woman.

Stiffly, Myri turned to leave. Wariness overshadowed any sense of relief.

"Tell me, Myrilandel," Yaassima called to her. "Do you reject these men because you loathe them specifically or do you prefer the touch of women?"

Myri froze in her tracks. Truth had served her well so far on this dangerous night. Would it be strong enough to continue to defend her?

She looked over her shoulder at the tall woman with white-blond hair and unnaturally long fingers and toes. Her instincts told her to find safety in a high dark place, become invisible and slip away unnoticed. Alone.

She couldn't. Baby Amaranth, Kalen, and Powwell all depended upon her.

The sense of belonging to her children banished her lingering thoughts of becoming a dragon. She wasn't a solitary creature anymore and she never would be again.

(Nimbulan must be part of the circle.)

A dragon thought? She hadn't heard the guiding voices in her head since the kidnap. Why now? She didn't have time for questions, only relief that the dragons hadn't completely deserted her.

"No dragon would ask that question, Yaassima. Mating is for the purpose of begetting young. The rest of their lives are solitary, without thought of another of their kind. Why waste the effort of a mating flight on a fruitless passion?"

"Yet Moncriith tells an interesting story of how you murdered his father when you caught him in the arms of your guardian, Magretha. Why would you kill the man with witchfire and permanently disfigure Magretha if not out of jealous rage? You were eleven at the time, the same age as Kalen." Yaassima raised one eyebrow. The gesture often replaced a laugh or a smile.

"Moncriith manipulates history to suit his purpose. *He* threw the ball of flame while waiting in line for Magretha's attention. I was but six and saved the woman who raised and protected me."

Myri clutched Kalen's hand and left before the Kaalipha could think of another dangerous question.

"Do you think she takes women to her bed?" Kalen asked as they hurried back to Myri's bedchamber. Her eyes reflected a fascinated revulsion.

"I do not believe Yaassima shares passions with anyone but herself. In that, she truly is descended from dragons. She loves no one and lives her life alone. But unlike dragons, sex has become a weapon for her, or a tool to control and intimidate people."

Myri slammed the door of her chamber closed as soon as she and Kalen were safely within. She leaned on it, needing to reinforce the barrier between herself and Yaassima. Maia stirred on her pallet to look up at the disturbance. Myri gestured the Rover woman back to sleep.

"I must walk carefully in my defiance of Yaassima. She must believe me under her spell until after I'm gone. Our only hope of escape lies in her belief that no one dares defy her." Myri placed her daughter in the cradle. She lingered there, touching the baby's fine hair and delicate skin.

"I wish, Kalen, you had your familiar, Wiggles, with you now." Myri drew a long breath.

"So do I. I miss him." Moisture gathered in Kalen's eyes in true regret. "But you didn't like him. Why do you want him now?"

"I didn't like his sneaky ways. He stole eggs and hid in strange places. His smell was almost enough to drive me out of the cottage. But if you had him with you now, you could use him to make contact with Powwell. We have to get him out of the pit. Soon."

"I think I can link my mind to Powwell's without a familiar." Kalen's eyes wouldn't meet Myri's, a sure sign she was telling the truth. Only when she turned the wide trusting gaze upward at an adult did she lie. Except for a moment ago when she allowed tears to gather.

"Good." Myri was too tired to figure out Kalen's complicated behavior and motives. "Please, Kalen, find out where he is being held. Tell him not to worry or give in to despair. We'll plan our escape after the next sunset when the guards are sated and sleeping heavily. Yaassima may have done us a favor with that horrible orgy in the Justice Hall." She shuddered at the thought of how close she had come to falling into the Kaalipha's trap and becoming another victim of her "justice."

Powwell stumbled over the rough ground leading downward. Pain lanced through his shoulders as a guard on either side of him grabbed his arms and hauled him along in their rapid course to the pit. The uniformed men before and behind didn't check their stride or look at him.

The pit was death, as certain as the executioner's ax. If

the narrowing tunnel didn't kill him first. The lowering ceiling seemed to push all the air out of the cave complex. Powwell thought he felt the weight of several miles of Kardia piled on top of this tiny, tiny cave.

He gasped, willing his lungs to breathe in more air. Each inhale became more painful and shallow.

A blast of heat hit him in the face. Unnatural yellow light glowed along the tunnel walls.

He stumbled again, falling to his knees. Fear set his chin quivering and his limbs shaking. Televarn had led them through the pit from the dragongate to the palace that first day in Hanassa. Powwell remembered only heat and noise and overwhelming despair. No one survived the pit for long.

Not the pit! Not the pit, his mind played the words over and over. *The fire is burning up all the air.*

The people of Hanassa told him of the undead who walked the endless labyrinth of caves deep within the Kardia. They never died, couldn't live, and so they haunted the caves and bled the life from the living guards who were unlucky enough to draw a shift guarding the pit. Hellfires burned day and night. The Kaalipha's magic grew there.

He'd suffocate from his own fears before the undead and the magic robbed him of sanity. He was sure of it.

He was dying already from lack of air. Underground places never had enough air for him. Thorny tried to climb out of his pocket. His ruffled quills poked Powwell's chest. Powwell broke the defeating circle of his thoughts long enough to urge his familiar back into hiding. No one knew he'd brought the hedgehog with him from the clearing. No one suspected that the animal's keen sense of smell might lead him back to the dragongate and home. He had to keep Thorny hidden from the guards.

A guard prodded him with a boot to his lower back. Powwell fell to his knees, careful to protect Thorny. Another boot connected with Powwell's ribs. He collapsed onto his other shoulder and side. The pain barely registered in his mind. Better to die here than face the pit. Thorny could escape and seek out Kalen. She would need a familiar since Wiggles had deserted her about a week after they arrived in Hanassa.

The guards grabbed his arms and roughly pulled him to his feet. Somehow he found the strength to stand on his own. They resumed their march forward to doom.

Take heart! a voice whispered into his mind. The brief contact slithered in and out of his head. He heaved a momentary sigh of relief and filled his lungs with air.

"Kalen?" he asked aloud, wondering if, in his despair, he had imagined her voice. But he had air to breathe. Kalen knew of his problems when underground. Her presence helped his lungs relax and use what little air he found.

"Shut up, prisoner," the guard to his right shoved a fist into his damaged ribs. "You can gibber all you want once we deliver you to the pit." Quickly he unlocked the gate with one of the hollow wands.

Kalen? Powwell cast out with his mind in search of the girl's light mental touch.

Stay alive. At all costs stay alive. I will rescue you!

Definitely Kalen's voice. There and gone again before he could latch onto it.

"How, Kalen?" he whispered with mind and voice.

"I said, shut up." The guards lifted Powwell off the ground and heaved him toward the menacing red glow.

Powwell slammed against the uneven ground. His already bruised ribs exploded in agony. The noise of the clanging gate rivaled the awesome sounds rising from the pit. He barely heard the guards running away, their bootheels echoing along the tunnel walls.

Chapter 12

"**L**et's go eat. I feel as if my stomach is wrapped around my backbone," Nimbulan said. "Then I *must* sleep. The ambassador from Rossemeyer and the one from SeLenicca can wait until you have seen a healer, Quinnault."

Quinnault looked back across the Bay at the destroyed armada. A touch of wonder crossed his face. "I can't say I want to do battle like this again. I want Coronnan to be respected for trade and peace and wise councillors, like you. But I can't see how we can avoid more battles as long as other countries lust after our land and the fish in this Bay. I've listened to proposals for dredging a couple of channels to let trading ships in. Where traders can sail, navies will follow."

"What we need is a protected ferry service from the deep waters to the city," Nimbulan mused, following Quinnault's gaze to the mudflats glistening in the starlight.

Midnight, his body told him. The tide would be at its lowest within the hour. Perhaps he'd manage a few hours of sleep before Quinnault and his boundless energy dragged him out of bed at dawn.

Maybe he should leave on his quest for Myri before then. Before the king could once again deny him permission to depart. Myri was worth the loss of a little sleep.

But how far would he get before the depletions of his body stopped his quest?

"There are a couple of little islands out there." Quinnault pointed east with his uninjured left arm. "We could set up loading docks there to transfer cargo and passengers. What I wouldn't give for some Varn diamonds now to pay for building a port city out there."

"Good plan. We'll find the money somehow. The Varns aren't due to come trading for another fifty years or so. Can we eat now?" Nimbulan took two long steps toward the stairs, dragging Quinnault away from his contemplation of the Bay. The king winced as he sidestepped to retain his balance.

"Time for you to see a healer. We'll find one faster over on School Isle. That's where the wounded are being taken." Nimbulan offered a supporting hand to guide Quinnault down the steep stairs.

"I'll row you over to School Isle. We collapsed the bridge in case we were invaded. The old causeway isn't stable since that last series of winter storms undercut it." Quinnault shrugged off any hint of assistance.

Once before, Nimbulan had ventured out in a leaking boat with Quinnault. They'd both nearly drowned before they crawled ashore on Haunted Isle. Now the locals called it School Isle.

"I'll guide you across the causeway. The tide and the river are low now. It's not that dangerous," Nimbulan said.

"You're still a total novice around boats, Nimbulan. You'd rather trust the causeway than a rowboat." Quinnault accused with mock severity. They both smiled in recollection of their first misadventure together—the first in a series of events that had led Nimbulan to the dragons and a kind of magic that could be combined and controlled by the Commune.

"I think we owe the dragons a large thank you for tonight's victory," Nimbulan mused. "We have to do everything in our power to bring them back," he hinted as a prelude to leaving.

"Don't even think about deserting the Commune, or me, Nimbulan. You are much too valuable to retire. As soon as you have a direction to send them in, dispatch every journeyman in the school to search for Myrilandel and the dragons. But you have to stay here. Coronnan needs you too much to risk you on such a dangerous quest." Quinnault cocked his head, listening for any glimmer of communication from the elusive dragons. Myri's gesture.

"Coronnan needs the dragons more than me. My wife is the key to the dragons. *I* must be the one to go in search of her."

"No, it's too dangerous. I can't afford to lose you." Quinnault replied flatly.

"Even if Shayla herself ordered me to search?"

"Only if Shayla orders it. But none of the dragons have spoken to me since they broke the Covenant." Quinnault turned and walked down the stairs toward the rivergate. Then, looking back over his shoulder, he smiled a brief apology. "I depend upon you for much more than magic, Nimbulan. I need your wisdom and your experience to guide me. I am, after all, only a priest at heart, and now I find myself a king trying to pull together a fractious rabble that calls itself a government. Don't desert me, my friend. Please."

Nimbulan shrugged. He had no words to counter such an argument. Quinnault had reasons not to trust any of the lords or other magicians.

In short order, Nimbulan stepped off the rotting causeway onto School Isle. Two guttering torches provided enough light to see six boats tied up to the adjacent dock. Six boat teams, at least, had returned from the Bay.

"Come, join us for a meal, Your Grace," Nimbulan invited. "I'm sure we'll find a healer in the refectory. They, too, will be seeking rest and refreshment between sessions with the wounded," Nimbulan said as he hauled his weary body toward the boat dock and the path back to the school. His knees protested the incline of the path, and his back didn't want to straighten. He groaned, pressing his hands against his lower back. The stretch felt good. He rotated his shoulders and grimaced at the knots in his muscles. "I'm getting too old for this."

Quinnault whistled a merry tune as he joined him, pointedly ignoring the last comment.

Nimbulan's spine needed a longer stretch. He bent and grasped his knees, arching his back before the muscles could spasm.

A thin trail of water caught his attention. No wider than three drops, but a solid flow. Strange, no rain had fallen for three or four days. Until three weeks ago, when the dragons left, the autumn had been unusually dry and bright. Why would the puddles and marshy pools overflow now with just this thin trickle when creeks drained the water through more normal routes?

His orientation to the spin of the planet, the tides and the cycles of sun and moon told him something was terribly wrong with this stream of water.

"It's flowing uphill!" Nimbulan looked back toward the dock. The line of water ran beside the structure, down the embankment into the water. No clues that way.

In the other direction, toward the school buildings, the water trickled beside the footpath, over hummocks and rocks. He placed his left foot gently on the path, leery of any magic that might spill over from the unnatural trickle. The water continued to move slowly uphill without disturbing his magic.

Quinnault followed him, placing his feet in Nimbulan's footprints. "This reminds me of the first time I rowed you to this island." The king hefted an oar like a quarterstaff, ready to knock heads should anyone menace them. He couldn't seem to grip it with his right hand. He put the oar back into the boat with a shrug of regret and drew his short sword with his left hand. "Good thing I'm Varn-handed."

"Have you ever noticed that a dominant left hand usually accompanies magic talent in a person—even the little talent required of a priest?" Nimbulan mused. "I wonder if the mysterious Varns were also aided by the Stargods."

"Varns are probably myths," Quinnault reminded him. "Wishing for Varn diamonds in return for grain surplus is just that, wishing. But then, we used to believe dragons and flywackets were myths, too."

Both men shrugged at the mystery and turned their attention back to the trickle of water.

"This little Water spell is probably the work of one of my more adventuresome apprentices." Nimbulan rotated his shoulders again to ease the muscles in his back. He automatically checked his store of magic for a counterspell.

Nothing. Until he ate and slept, his magic was as inert as the Water trickle he followed. The spell would have to be triggered by some direct action or word.

Controlling the essence of an element—Kardia, Air, Fire, or Water—was usually a spell that required subtlety and deviousness. Elements didn't willingly allow mortals to chain them. Who in the school had the time and knowledge to practice with an elemental?

He paused in his progress toward the nearby building,

picking out the figure of Stuuvart, steward for the school, standing on the front steps. Stuuvart's scowl extended from his face into his posture. His cloak swished behind him with his restless movements, mimicking his attitude. The impatient administrator waved his arms as he shouted orders. Apprentices scurried in all directions at his bidding.

Nimbulan scowled, too. Stuuvart loved his meticulous recordkeeping and full storerooms to the exclusion of his wife and family. But he couldn't send the steward packing without dislodging the entire family—Kalen's family—including Guillia, the cook.

An apprentice ran past Nimbulan. He grabbed the boy's arm to stop his pelting progress toward the unstable causeway to Palace Isle. "What's the hurry, Haakkon?"

"Master Stuuvart says we can't afford to feed all the wounded and the peasants. He wants additional stores from the palace, sir. He's madder than a penned lumbird 'cause you sent everyone here after your battle." The boy gasped for breath as if he'd already run to the palace and back over the dangerous passage several times.

"Have any of you boys slept since yesterday's battle preparations?" Nimbulan studied Haakkon's face for signs of fatigue. Gray tinged the edges of his flushed cheeks, and his eyes seemed overly bright.

"No time, sir." Haakon shifted his weight as if he needed to continue his errand.

"Have you eaten?" Nimbulan held tight to the boy's sleeve.

"After I've fetched the palace steward, sir."

"It's past midnight! Stuuvart can't expect to refill the storeroom now." Nimbulan suppressed his anger at the steward's obsession. When he could control his words, he said, "All of these people worked very hard to defend this land. Feeding them and caring for the wounded is the least we can do. They have earned their meal and a rest, and so have you."

His mouth watered at the smell of savory bacon and fresh bread emanating from the kitchen wing. Stuuvart's wife always provided just the food that Nimbulan craved most, right when he needed it. The two snacks she had sent him during the battle were all that kept him going now. Guillia mothered everyone at the school. Why couldn't her husband give a little care for their daughter, Kalen? If Stuuvart hadn't disowned her, the little girl might not have gone with Myri so readily.

If Kalen had stayed, Powwell would have as well, her devoted friend and possibly her half-brother, and Myri would be alone now—wherever she was. Why did it seem as if what was best for the school, best for his wife, and best for himself were always in contradiction?

The emptiness of his life rose up before him like one of the stone walls of his school. Only a day ago, he had seen a vision of Myri in the bowl of water. Yesterday morning, Amaranth had died, imparting a cryptic message that Myri had been kidnapped to Hanassa. Yesterday, Lyman had told him that Rover Maia had a baby—Nimbulan's baby, the only child he was likely to sire.

Nimbulan pounded his left fist into his right palm in frustration. He'd wasted a whole day that he might have been journeying toward his wife, his former lover, and his child.

Not wasted. He'd helped save Coronnan from invasion. Another contradiction of priorities. When would he ever be able to put his own needs above those of others?

"But Master Stuuvart said . . ." Haakkon's protest brought Nimbulan out of his loop of self-defeating thoughts.

"I run the school, Haakkon. Now get into the refectory and take your classmates with you. Oh, and have someone fetch parchment and pens from my room. His Grace and I have some plans for ferries and loading docks to organize while we eat." He clapped his hand on the king's good shoulder. He needed to appease Quinnault's enthusiasms, or he'd never take the time to see a healer. Nimbulan wanted the king's health in good order before he left on his quest.

He half smiled to himself, realizing he'd already made up his mind to leave on his quest today. Before dawn if possible.

"I'll bring you the supplies myself, Master Nimbulan." Haakkon ran up the narrow stairs that curved toward the residential wing.

"Wait, Haakkon, the door is locked," Nimbulan called to the boy. Stuuvart's younger daughter had never arrived with the treatise on naval warfare so many hours ago when he had requested it. Why not?

Stuuvart had probably found other more "important" chores for the child. More important to Stuuvart and no one else.

Nimbulan eyed the pesky trail of water where it crossed the threshold of the school. Tiny, damp pawprints ran beside the water. Where did the tracks go from here? How long had the water been trickling toward its destination, perhaps filling some unknown reservoir?

A glint of moisture on the stairs told him.

"Haakkon, come back! Haakkon?" he called anxiously. He mounted the steps without thinking.

A sleek form slithered past him, brushing against Nimbulan's leg. Then, the creature—a ferret?—was gone, so quickly it might have been only his imagination.

A scream split the air.

"Haakkon!' Nimbulan rushed forward.

Darkness streaked down the stairs in the wake of the animal. The thin trickle of water swelled to the width of the stairs. His foot slid on suddenly wet stone. A loud roar echoed through the stairwell. Torches sputtered. Darkness filled his mind and his eyes.

The water swelled and rose in a wave, washing over him. He forced himself to relax in the surge of water, as Myri had taught him.

Myri! He couldn't die without seeing her again.

He kicked upward, striving for air. Iron bands crushed his chest. *Only water,* he told himself. *Heavy water seeking its home.*

Air. He needed air. Fight one element with another.

I can't swim. I'll drown. Then his head broke the surface and life-giving air filled his lungs. He almost sobbed with relief.

Hard stone jabbed into his back, nearly knocking the blessed air from his laboring lungs. Walls. Steps. Air. He lay half on the first stair, half in the landing, still breathing. Water exited the building and retreated along the path of the original little trickle.

Nimbulan shook wet hair out of his eyes and waved the torches back to life. He surveyed the damage. Water dripped from every surface, traveling with some urgency back to the primary stream. Every last drop left the stairs and landing. Definitely the work of an elemental.

Nimbulan wiped his face with shaking hands. "Quinnault, are you all right?" The king sat against the wall, somewhat dazed and very damp.

A quick survey revealed the corridor to the refectory remained dry. The trapped element sought only to return to its home, not to spread.

"Haakkon!" Nimbulan turned over, ready to crawl up the stairs. "Answer me, Haakkon!"

Only then did he become aware of something heavy resting against his shoulders, crosswise on the steps just above him.

Haakkon lay there, eyes wide open, limbs tangled, skin pale as the underside of a fish.

Chapter 13

"**S**o many deaths. When will it stop?" Nimbulan cried as he cradled Haakon's slack body. In his mind he saw Keegan's face replace Haakon's immature features. Nimbulan had been forced to kill Keegan, his former apprentice, almost two years ago. The boy had run away to become a Battlemage before his training was complete. He had known his new patron would challenge Nimbulan's patron in battle. Keegan had come close to defeating his teacher in that battle. But inexperience had made him more bold than wise. In order to keep the boy's spell-gone-amuck from destroying most of Coronnan, Nimbulan had been forced to kill the boy.

Ackerly, Nimbulan's assistant and childhood friend, had died in battle opposing Nimbulan the following year, this time from his own spell, not Nimbulan's.

Now Haakkon had drowned because some unprincipled magician had chained an element. Water had only been rushing to return to its natural state. The apprentice had been caught in the trap and drowned.

Trap?

Haakkon had triggered a trap set for Nimbulan. Under normal circumstances, only Nimbulan would have gone into his private, locked workroom. Why hadn't Stuuvart's younger daughter gone in there earlier when Nimbulan requested the treatise on naval battles? Did Stuuvart know about the trap?

Someone had put Water under a compulsion in order to kill the Senior Magician.

Who? Who had the power to compel an element? He needed to think clearly, not let his grief turn him in circles.

If only he had his journal to hand so he could sort his thoughts into a logical order. He didn't have time to sit and ponder, writing ideas and crossing off the scattered thoughts. He needed answers now.

Who? Not one of the apprentices. Dragon magic didn't lend itself to compelling an element. Without the ley lines to power the spell, Water would not comply. No junior magician, dependent upon dragon magic, could have carelessly set the spell to see if it could be done.

That left the master magicians or a rogue. He didn't think any of the men he'd hired to teach at the school bore him a grudge worthy of such complex magic. Besides, they'd all been employed in the battle and its preparations yesterday.

A rogue could have slipped into the school during yesterday's chaos. A rogue who had a different source of magic. Perhaps Moncriith, a Bloodmage who found energy in pain and death, had returned to Coronnan and targeted Nimbulan. Moncriith's body had never been found after the last battle. Could he still be lurking around Coronnan, seeking to destroy the demons he saw in anything he disagreed with? He had preached against Myrilandel as the source of all demons for many years.

New chills raked Nimbulan's spine at the thought of Moncriith pursuing Myri.

Televarn and his Rovers had reasons to hold a grudge against Nimbulan as well. Devious traps were more Televarn's style than Moncriith's. The poison spell on Quinnault's wine yesterday—was it only yesterday?—might not have been the only mischief they organized. Rovers tapped the energy of every living thing surrounding them, including the elements. Their intricate rituals usually required several members of the clan.

Televarn had aspirations to be king of his people. He had tried to kill Nimbulan once before and failed because Myri intervened. Lyman had seen Televarn in the questing vision. Nimbulan had seen Myri.

Myri had admitted to an affair with Televarn. She'd run away from him when she discovered his duplicity. Someone had kidnapped Myri and held her captive in Hanassa. Rovers often sought refuge in the city of outlaws, as did Bloodmages.

"Send out search parties, quickly. Rovers hide in the region. Find them and bring them to the king's hall for justice. Take soldiers with you," he called to the men he sensed gathering around him. "Your murder will be the last, Haakkon. I swear it. If I have to follow Televarn all the way to Hanassa, I will stop these senseless deaths." He clutched the limp body to his aching chest. Hot tears gathered in his eyes.

Televarn fed sticks into his little fire, idly watching the green flames consume the wood. If only he dared burn some Tambootie branches, he could watch the progress of the sea battle in the flames with his FarSight. But the aromatic smoke of the tree of magic would alert Nimbulan's people to his presence. This opening in the mainland forest west of Coronnan City was too close to the capital. He couldn't afford to be found. Not until Nimbulan had triggered the trap and drowned in a wall of water. Water should have had time to fill the magician's private chamber to the ceiling by now.

Televarn shivered as a moist breeze rose up from the river. He smelled the richness of the lush forest and the chill ran deeper into his body. "*S'murghing* damp," he cursed the river, the mud, the islands, and the battle that kept Nimbulan from returning to his bed. Televarn needed to be back in Hanassa, breathing the clean desert air, letting the intense sun bake the damp from his bones.

S'murghit! He needed to get back there, monitor Yaassima, and gather his forces to resist her rule. He needed to wrest Myrilandel away from her manipulations.

Perhaps Myrilandel could spy on Yaassima for him and learn the Kaalipha's weaknesses. He had control of one of the Kaalipha's secrets. But he needed more.

How much longer could Nimbulan linger on the battlements? The tide had receded hours ago. If the Senior Magician didn't go home soon, someone else might enter his private chambers and drown instead.

Bare luck had put Televarn in the path of the little girl sent to fetch something from the room earlier in the day. She had the only spare key and knew that no magic seal locked the door. He had pocketed the key and sent her off to her other chores, promising to take the book to Nimbu-

lan himself. He hadn't, of course. He'd left Water alone to
do its work.

He checked the section of woods where two trees leaned
together to form an arch. That was his exit to safety. At
certain times, the dragongate shifted time and distance to
open portals to different locations. This was only one of
many such destinations. All of the portals led back to Hanassa and nowhere else. During the past night of waiting,
Televarn had watched the dragongate open and close once,
when the full moon created an arch-shaped shadow between the trees. The interval between access times shifted
randomly. He had no way of knowing when the opportunity
to return to Hanassa would present itself again. Today, tomorrow, within the next moment? He knew that it would
only happen when there was enough light to cast the
proper shadows.

He didn't dare leave until Wiggles returned to him. He
owed the ferret's owner the return of the smelly little beast.
He owed more than he wanted to admit.

A hot blast of wind and a faint tingle of power made the
hair on his arms stand up straight. The dragongate was
getting ready to open again. His own fire had created
enough of a shadow between the trees to suggest an arch.

Where was Wiggles?

If he lingered much longer in this opening, barely two
hours' walk from the capital, he ran the risk of being discovered. Should he take the chance of returning without
the ferret?

Underbrush rattled off to his left, close to the riverbank.
He stood up, ready to kick dirt over his fire and flee the
open circle. Once amid the Tambootie trees, with their dormant magic embedded in leaves, sap, bark, and fruit, he
could hide indefinitely.

Nimbulan's people would want revenge for the death of
their leader. Wiggles might lead them directly here—if they
had the sense to follow the creature once the trap was
sprung. Perhaps Televarn should flee now and save himself.
Simurgh take the ferret.

The rustling grew louder.

The air between two leaning Tambootie trees shimmered. The dragongate wouldn't stay open long. Now—or
wait for the next opening?

Wiggles burst through the thick saber ferns that marked
the path to the river. The animal ran with the strangely
efficient undulations of his kind, tail up, middle down,
shoulders up, nose down. Then his entire body shifted forward by trading ups and downs. He streaked across the
circular opening in the woods almost faster than Televarn's
sight could follow.

Three men carrying clubs followed Wiggles, barely two
steps behind the ferret. One look at their blue tunics with
the dragon badge over their hearts and Televarn knew they
were Nimbulan's magicians, bent on revenge.

"Come," Televarn commanded the ferret. He snapped
his fingers and the creature leaped onto his leg, clinging to
his trews with needle-sharp teeth and claws. Never mind
the pain and the rents in the cloth. He had to get back to
Hanassa. Now.

The shimmering light between the two trees faded.

Televarn closed his eyes and dove for the remnants of
the strange light just as the first club caught his hamstring.

"You must hurry, Nimbulan. Quinnault's messenger is
on his way to summon you to court. You must be well
away before he comes or you will never be free to leave
the capital." Old Lyman hastily buckled the straps of the
half-filled pack on Nimbulan's bed.

"I feel strange leaving without the king's permission and
without resolving Haakon's death. I should say the prayers
at his funeral." Nimbulan resisted a jaw-cracking yawn.
He'd snatched a few hours of sleep and a meal. Other than
that, he hadn't slept in a day and a night.

He needed to replenish his reserves. Lyman had brought
food, meat and bread, and a huge pitcher of water.

He gulped down as much as he could, then hesitated in
the doorway of his private chamber, longing to return to
his bed. All traces of the water that had filled the room
mere hours before had fled when the essence of the element rushed back to its place of origin.

A few of Nimbulan's books had been damaged. But everything had dried so quickly, so completely, the essence
of Water might not have filled the room hours before.

"There are plenty of people who can say the prayers for
Haakon." Lyman bowed his head in a moment of silence.

"I will say a few for Amaranth, too. The purple-tipped dragon died trying to tell you where Myri is held captive. Will you waste his death in the endless talk that surrounds a government striving for peace?"

Nimbulan recited a brief prayer remembered from his childhood.

"I need my journal. I must record the events and the plots that threaten to disrupt Coronnan and the Commune," he said, searching his desk for the little book filled with blank paper. He cast aside six books from earlier years. He couldn't think straight. Where had he put the new one? He found it open on his desk, the ink from his entries two days ago smudged and blurred from Water's presence. "I must stop the murders of my apprentices. They were like sons to me, Lyman."

"You have a son of your body now, Nimbulan. You must find him and save him from Televarn. But you must leave immediately, before the king and your suffocating sense of duty chain you here for all eternity." Lyman handed him the pack.

"I wish I knew how that man escaped in the woods. Even with fully active ley lines, a magician can't transport a living being. Have an apprentice and a journeyman camp there if they must while they examine every grain of dirt for evidence of magic." Nimbulan shouldered the pack and reached for his journal to tuck into his pocket. His staff jumped to his hand.

"The answers lie at the end of his trail, not the beginning." A far-off look came into Lyman's eyes. He cocked his head as if listening to something beyond human understanding. "Go, quickly. The messenger from Quinnault crosses the bridge as we speak. You can't delay even a moment. Myrilandel and the children are in terrible danger."

"Are you in communication with the dragons?" Nimbulan halted with his hand on the door latch. This revelation might take him on a direct course rather than chasing in circles after an assassin or running blindly to Hanassa to rescue Myri.

"All I can say is that a dragon awaits you. A young one who wants to explore more than he wants to obey Shayla. But you must hurry or he will fly away with the rest of the nimbus. You can't afford the delay of walking to Hanassa. If you do, you will lose Myrilandel forever."

"Be sure you give my letter to King Quinnault. He deserves an explanation."

Lyman pushed the Senior Magician out the door. "I'll look after things here, in your absence, but keep in touch."

"I'm going with you." Rollett, the oldest of the journeymen magicians stood in the doorway. He, too, carried a pack of provisions, and a journal poked out of his pocket. His eyes looked hollow and black, as if sleep had eluded him longer than it had Nimbulan.

"No, Rollett. I can't risk losing you as well. This trip is dangerous enough." Nimbulan grasped the younger man's shoulder affectionately, but firmly.

"I'll follow if you don't take me with you. You need someone to watch your back, Nimbulan. There is treachery here as well as on the road. I am coming."

"Hurry, Nimbulan." Lyman took both Nimbulan and Rollett by the arm and guided them toward a back staircase. "The dragon won't wait long. Take the boy. He's right about treachery. Lord Konnaught is with King Quinnault's messenger. He's planning something. Something dire for you and for the king. Now get out of here before someone else dies."

Chapter 14

Powwell opened his eyes and slammed them closed again in the bright glare. A sharp ache pounded in his right temple and spread to his neck and shoulders, down to his lower back.

A bizarre noise pulsed around him in rhythm with the pain in his head. It sounded like a threshing machine, but louder and harsher. Much louder.

Yeek, kush, kush. Yeek, kush, kush.

Over and over the noise pushed aside rational thought and self-awareness. It smothered him, wrapping him tighter and tighter, until he was the heart of the terrible sounds. Nothing existed but the noise.

He'd heard those sounds before.

"You'll get used to it," a husky voice penetrated the noise and Powwell's mind.

He opened his left eye a slit. If he opened his right eye, the noise and the light would stab it out.

A dirty face looked back at him. Hard to tell if it was a young male or female. The voice gave no clue to gender either. A dirty kerchief knotted over the left ear, Rover style, covered the person's hair entirely.

"Pretty soon you won't notice the noise at all. Even the heat will seem tolerable after a few moons. I'm Yaala." A feminine name. She held out a hand in greeting, palm up. A masculine gesture.

"Powwell." He raised his left hand slowly to place on top of Yaala's. His right arm seemed to be pinned beneath his body. Every muscle in his back and shoulders protested. He winced. Sweat poured off his body in the tremendous heat.

Thorny was in his right pocket! He rolled over, groaning with the movement. He probed Thorny's hiding place with his thoughts and fingertips. His tunic pocket was empty. *Thorny!*

Chip, chip, mmmblr, grmmmblr, came the muffled gibbering reply from nearby. Powwell couldn't understand his familiar's emotions, only that the little hedgehog hadn't been hurt.

"Did they beat you?" Yaala seemed to be squatting in front of him, quite comfortable on her heels.

"Not much." He mentally inventoried the sorest points on his body. The dull ache in his gut and jaw where the guards had punched him to subdue him, and the sharper throb in his right temple made themselves known right away. The rest of his misery seemed to be reaction to those pains.

A small biting irritation on his right calf told him that Thorny clung to his flesh with his tiny claws. The hedgehog must be trying to find a safe hiding place in Powwell's trews pocket. Powwell's discomfort eased a little. His familiar was safe for now.

"Here, drink this." Yaala pressed a metal cup to his lips.

Powwell drank greedily, unaware of his thirst until he swallowed. The taste of rancid eggs fouled his mouth and set his eyes and nose to running. He spat out the tainted water. Some of it sprayed on Yaala's thin shirt.

"Drink. You'll get used to it." She laughed at his discomfort. "It's all you get down here. The heat leaches the sweat from you in no time. You've got to drink a lot or die."

"We're dead already," Powwell grumbled. Cautiously, he sipped at the awful tasting water. He clung to his last communication from Kalen. If anyone could get him out of the pit alive, it was Kalen. He'd have to make the effort to stay healthy and vital until she got here, despite the water.

"Depends on how you look at things." Yaala twisted her legs beneath her and sat on the rough ground. And who's on guard duty this shift."

"Enlighten me." Powwell laid his head back on the ground, urging Thorny into the pocket. The effort of sitting up seemed too much in the oppressive heat. His ribs throbbed painfully. He wanted to bathe them in cold water to reduce the swelling. The hot, red light only aggravated them. He couldn't see any colors, only shades of blacks and grays, overshadowed with the strange red-yellow haze. The light and heat drained everything of vitality and color.

He had to fight the despair that radiated from the pit. Kalen would rescue him. *Come quickly!* he urged her.

"Yaassima never comes down here," Yaala said. "She trusts her elite guards to keep us in line. Not all of her guards are trustworthy."

"That's something positive," Powwell replied.

"The assassins she sends down here either treat us nice or they wind up having an accident."

"They might not kill us, but heat and neglect will," Powwell replied. The feeling of hopelessness wiggled in his gut. Thorny pricked his thigh with his sharp spines, jolting Powwell out of accepting the defeating emotions.

"You'd be surprised how long people can live down here, as long as they remember to feed us." Yaala looked back over her shoulder toward the next chamber. "I make sure they do remember."

Powwell sensed movement in there. He struggled to sit up again. "Is there a chance they'll forget to feed us?"

Kalen had told him to endure. She'd find a way to get him out. But if he starved to death in the meantime . . .

"Not *s'murghing* likely. There are too many of us with family and friends on the outside. They see that we get fed. Besides, Yaassima needs us—me—alive and well." Yaala stood up in one fluid motion. "Drink your water, then I'll show you to your work station."

Powwell shifted onto his left elbow preparing to roll to his knees. As he moved, his shirt stuck to his side where a guard's boot had broken the skin. The coarse cloth prickled against his sweat-dampened back.

"How come you aren't sweating?" he asked. For the first time he realized Yaala looked as cool and fresh as if they were lounging in the clean mountain air of Myrilandel's clearing. Except her clothing was gray. Everything down here was gray or black.

"I guess I'm used to the heat and don't need to sweat now." She shrugged.

Two men wandered toward them, seemingly from the heart of the fire. They, too, looked thin and worn, with dirty sweat masking their features. Their gray clothes hung damp and limp upon stooped shoulders.

"We're ready for the ceremony, Yaala," one of the men said, his voice barely above a harsh whisper. She nodded and started walking toward the brightest point of red light.

"What ceremony?" Powwell asked as he balanced, first on his knees and then on his feet. Thorny poked his nose out of the pocket and wiggled it, rapidly digesting the scents of their new home. He didn't like it and rolled back into a sharp ball. Powwell wished he could do the same.

"You might as well watch with the rest of us. You're one of us now." Yaala beckoned him to follow.

The blinding glare resolved into a single tunnel in a maze of black openings. Powwell spent several moments trying to memorize landmarks—a triangular outcropping here, a rockfall there. Flickers of white movement teased his peripheral vision. He kept looking for the source of those brief glimpses of white rather than for distinctive features.

The heat increased, and he mopped his brow with his sleeve. Maybe the sweat dripping into his eyes blurred his vision. He wished he'd drunk more of the water; as bad as it tasted, he needed the liquid.

"Don't waste time learning the route. All the tunnels lead to one place eventually." Yaala paused where the tunnel opened up into a large cave. She stood at the edge of a precipice. Below them, far, far below them, molten rock churned and boiled, shooting flares up hundreds of feet. None of those huge flares came close to where they stood. A thousand feet or more separated the ledge from the core of the volcano. Still, the roiling lava dominated the scene. The ceiling soared so far above him, Powwell couldn't see the top.

How deep below the crater's surface had they come?

The temperature rose higher yet. Powwell staggered back two steps away from the edge. Vertigo tempted him forward into the boiling heart of the volcano. The Kardia seemed to press heavily against his shoulders. The air left his lungs in long gasps. He couldn't inhale. He imagined all the air was concentrated in the molten rock. If he wanted to breathe, he'd have to throw himself into the next flare that nibbled greedily at the flimsy ledge where he stood.

"Don't look at it. Keep your eyes on the walls." Yaala grabbed his arm and pushed him hard against the tunnel archway. "The pit will eat your soul if you let it. Just as it eats away at Hanassa."

Powwell closed his eyes and absorbed the solid feel of the rock pressing against his back. His feet still tingled with the vibrations of those flares slamming against the ledge. Almost like waves running against a cliff.

Slowly he opened his eyes, keeping his gaze away from the hypnotic fires of the pit. To his right and left people stood in other tunnel openings in groups of four or five. Gray-clad denizens side by side with black-clad guards. All around the immense pit, they stood and waited in respectful silence. Powwell tried counting the faces. He lost track at one hundred and seventeen.

"How many people live down here?" he whispered to Yaala.

"A couple hundred, maybe more. No one counts."

"That's a lot of people to feed without getting any work out of them."

"Oh, we work for our keep. *She* needs us to keep her magical toys active. She also needs us alive as hostages for the good behavior of her followers." A half smile quirked at the woman's mouth, as if she knew something Yaassima didn't.

"Hostages? Can we be ransomed? If there are so many of us, we could break the lock on the gate and charge the guards. It would be easy to storm out of the palace in a group."

"I'm not ready for that." She waved him to silence as two men carried a third to the ledge three tunnels to the left. Silently, they heaved the inert body into the boiling mass below them. The body fell a long, long way, diminishing in size to a pinpoint before it touched the boiling rock. Instantly the internal fires of Kardia Hodos consumed the body.

Powwell's heart leaped into his throat as he imagined how the flames would burn away his own flesh and dissolve his bones. He knew the man must have been dead before being consigned to the pit. His fears kept seeing himself down there—alive, forever dammed to be eaten alive by the fires.

No one said a word for one hundred heartbeats. Then Yaala raised her voice in a curious ululation, high-pitched, wordless, sad, and triumphant at the same time. Around the pit, the other watchers took up the strange sound until they drowned out the constant roar of the boiling lava and the *yeek, kush, kush* behind them. Powwell's throat worked convulsively. He had to add his own cries to Yaala's.

A curious sense of relief and completion came to him as soon as he let loose the ancient mourning cry. He continued the wail almost eagerly.

At last, Yaala held a single high-pitched note for several heartbeats.

Abruptly, all the inhabitants of the pit fell silent. The absence of sound hovered for a moment, then the roars of the pit rushed back, louder than ever.

As one, the people of the pit turned and walked back into the tunnels.

"For now, that is the only escape from the pit," Yaala said.

Myri pressed her back against the cave wall near the ground level exit of Yaassima's palace. Smooth rock formed most of the corridors, almost perfectly circular tunnels with packed dirt on the floor. Black dirt, black walls, bleak and lifeless. Outside, the crater was filled with redder dirt and rocks—equally bleak but filled with life-giving sunlight and fresh air.

Irregular shadows draped the curving passageway in darker shades of black and gray. Beneath the torches, mounted into iron brackets at regular intervals, the shadows crawled away into a bilious gray green—real fire, burning green as it should. The Kaalipha didn't waste her bizarre magic on light panels in the passageways and rooms where she seldom appeared. She saved her tricks for the times she could make a great show of her power.

A black-clad guard rounded the curve from the direction of the main doorway into the palace. Myri recognized him as one of the men who usually patrolled the interior corridors closest to Yaassima's suite. He whistled a jaunty tune. A satisfied smile relaxed the lines around his eyes that usually betrayed his acute wariness. As he walked, he tossed his belt knife in the air, watched it spin, and caught it again by the hilt. Then he grasped the tip with the other hand and repeated the trick.

All the elite personal guards of the Kaalipha practiced this movement whenever their hands were idle. Few in Hanassa doubted their expertise with the weapons. Those few usually ended up dead.

The guard didn't look right or left as he passed Myri, still whistling, still tossing his knife as if it were a harmless child's toy.

When he moved out of her line of sight, Myri headed toward the main door as silently as she could, letting her soft indoor shoes whisper across the packed dirt-and-stone floor. Kalen was off exploring the kitchens and possible servants' entrances. Myri needed to know the routine of traffic in and out of the main entrance. She had to find a way out of the palace once they rescued Powwell.

Recovering from Amaranth's birth, Erda's drugs, and staying out of Yaassima's way had kept her close to the royal suite for the past three weeks. Without the mind-clogging potions she had found a gap in Yaassima's watchfulness in the suite. But here . . . ?

Myri kept to the shadows beneath the torches. All of the brackets marched along one side of this passageway rather than alternating sides to eliminate shadows. This was a security lapse she didn't expect of Yaassima.

She touched the dark kerchief hiding her hair. In her old leaf-green gown over a simple shift, she hoped to pass as another servant. Any glimpse of her white-blond hair, so similar to Yaassima's, or the jewel-toned silks Yaassima had given her to wear, would identify her to the regular inhabitants of the palace. She needed anonymity to scout an escape route.

Multiple footsteps echoed loudly around the tunnel walls. A shimmer of reddish orange light signaled the infiltration of sunlight, so different from the green flames of the torches.

Sunlight, air, freedom. She longed to dash forward and experience life once more. She couldn't. Not yet. Not until she knew she could take all three of her children with her.

A side passage opened in the wall opposite her. She dashed across the widening tunnel and secreted herself in the unlit corridor.

A merchant laden with bolts of fabric spilling from his arms staggered past her. A laughing guard walked beside him, picking up brightly colored silk that trailed behind the merchant. New clothes for Yaassima. Good, she would be occupied for several hours while making her selection from the fire-green, bay-blue, and blood-red cloth.

Right on the heels of the merchant and his escort came three women. They wore ordinary sturdy gowns and kerchiefs over their hair. They must be part of the huge staff of servants Yaassima maintained. The Kaalipha never allowed a servant to perform the same chore in the same rooms as the day before, except for Haanna. Yaassima's mute personal maid seemed to love her ruthless mistress blindly. Mealtimes and menus varied widely. No one had an opportunity to detect patterns and routines for laying traps against the only person in Hanassa who maintained any degree of power: Yaassima.

Myri watched a continuous parade of people in and out of the main entrance for a few more moments. Servants, guards, merchants, and outlaws in search of favors all passed through the same portal. Would so many people come this way if there was any other way in or out of the palace?

Her heart sank.

Keep yourself safe from Televarn, Nimbulan. Please be careful. I can't come to you yet. She checked the magical umbilical that connected her heart to her husband's. It appeared stretched and thin, as if the distance between them had grown beyond the physical separation. The pulses of her heart and his counterbeat pushed strongly back and forth, though, with little delay. She wished she understood the nuances of the connection better. The strength of the cord and the heartbeats told her only that Nimbulan lived, and that he loved her.

Was that enough to rebuild their marriage? She didn't know. She'd answer that question when she saw him again, and gave vent to her anger at his leaving her alone and vulnerable. First, she had to find a way out of this horrible city of crime and death with her three children.

She edged closer to the cave opening that formed the main entrance. If this truly were the only way in or out, she had to know what security measures Yaassima employed. She kept her eyes on the floor and her extra long fingers folded within her skirt. No one looked at her twice.

Through her lowered lashes she watched as the black-uniformed guards stopped each person entering the palace. Two guards stood to the side of the portal, hands on their swords. They wore three or four other, shorter knives stuck into their belts, their boots, and protruding from their cuffs. Chains crossed their chests and slings dangled from their shoulders. Two other men carried metal tubes the length and thickness of one of Nimbulan's small wands, in addition to the multitude of weapons.

An outlaw swaggered up to the entrance. Myri recognized him as a cutthroat who had stood in line for a job yesterday in the Justice Hall. Yaassima had denied him any assignment, especially his request to waylay a caravan from SeLenicca bound for Rossemeyer.

The cutthroat flashed a broad smile to the guards, revealing broken teeth beneath his drooping mustache. Myri knew a moment of recognition. Where had she seen him before yesterday?

Casually he saluted the guards and stepped into the cave as if he had every right to enter without scrutiny.

Before he had gone a second step, Yaassima's trusted men clapped their strong hands around his arms.

"You know the rules, Piedro," one guard growled, not releasing his grip.

The two men with wands placed themselves in front of and behind Piedro while the other two maintained their hold on the outlaw. They waved their wands over Piedro's entire body.

The wands blasted out an ear-piercing shriek. Myri clapped her hands over her ears. Every person within sight froze in place. They remained locked in position as if the shrill sound had numbed their will as well as their hearing.

Sweat broke out on Piedro's brow, and he lost much of the high color beneath the dirt and beard shadow on his cheeks.

The four guards shoved the outlaw's face into the cave wall. They stretched his arms painfully over his head. One of them tore the rough black shirt from Piedro's back. He shook the fabric hard. Another guard poked and slapped the prisoner's body. He pressed his fingers into every fold and crevice of Piedro's trews until he came up with a small knife concealed between the prisoner's legs near the groin.

He held up the palm-sized knife triumphantly. Grinning, he slapped his wand twice against a rock by the entrance. The metal chimed against stone but didn't screech as it had earlier. The guard shouted: "Send two escorts. We've got one for the pit."

No humiliating trial in the Justice Hall. Obviously, taking a weapon into the palace meant immediate punishment.

The crowd of people surrounding the entrance began moving again, talking quietly among themselves. A few cast sidelong glances at Piedro, still held hard against the wall.

One serving girl tried to slip outside without being searched. The vigilant guards grabbed her, too. But the wands remained silent, so they let her go.

Two more guards ran up and took custody of Piedro. The criminal screamed pleas and protests as they dragged him roughly into the dark interior of the palace.

Myri turned. They would lead her to the pit. If she remained silent and unseen behind them. She'd spent a lifetime eluding pursuers. The dragons had taught her many things, especially how to avoid detection.

"There you are, Myrilandel," Yaassima said sweetly. She clamped her long-fingered hand firmly on Myri's shoulder.

Chapter 15

"**Y**ou seem restless today," Yaassima said. A satisfied hum followed her words. "Perhaps you should have joined us last night. I found the spectacle of Kestra being raped—invigorating."

Myri turned slowly under her warden's hand, to face her. Yaassima's emotions were dominated by sexual satisfaction. Nothing else reached Myri's empathic talent. Yet she sensed dissatisfaction in the older woman.

"Did you need me for something?" Myri asked. She didn't want to touch on the subject of Yaassima's orgy or Kestra's pain and humiliation.

"You need new gowns. The mother of my heir must appear as regal as I. I thought we burned that hideous peasant gown you're wearing."

The gown had served Myri well for a long time. Most of the people she dealt with in her normal life considered her choice of attire graceful and attractive. Yaassima's clothes were too bright and clumsy for everyday wear.

"The people need to see you suitably clothed. I can't decide between the ruby and the emerald for you." Yaassima started walking toward the interior of the palace. She kept her hand firmly on Myri's shoulder, compelling her to accompany her.

"I prefer the colors of the Kardia to jewel tones," Myri said. She walked slowly, making the Kaalipha adjust her long stride to fit hers.

"Nonsense. You fade into the background. I want you to stand out in any crowd."

Dragons prefer to remain unnoticed. Myri bit her lip rather than voice the thought. Safety lay in making Yaassima believe she took the drugs and didn't have the will to defy her.

"Always remember the tremendous honor I do you in making your daughter my heir." Yaassima threw her hands wide as if embracing all of Hanassa in her enthusiasm. "I think the red for the baby's naming ceremony. Hanassa has such a majestic ring to it. She will grow into the name with proper training.

"My daughter's name is Amaranth." This was something she had to fight Yaassima for. She couldn't allow the Kaalipha to engulf her identify or her daughter's in grandiose delusions. Yaassima had no concept of reality beyond the walls of Hanassa and her own imagination. "If I must wear your fancy silks in brilliant colors, then I will wear purple."

"Nonsense. There are no purple dragons. We wear only the colors of our kind. I have decreed it." Yaassima's eyes narrowed as she glared at Myri, trying to impose her will.

Myri stopped short. Rage boiled within her. "There are no purple dragons now." Amaranth was dead and Myri dared not transform. There would not be another purple dragon until Shayla bred again. Even then, dragonkind might have to wait several generations for another purple.

(Purple dragons have special destinies determined by forces beyond the wisdom of dragons.) Shayla's statement rang through her memory. That special destiny had fallen to Myrilandel. She had become the link between dragons and humans so that human magic could be controlled and used only for the benefit of all.

"I will wear purple, or I will wear my old gown," Myri said. While she remained in Hanassa, she had no other link to the dragons. She must wear purple, the same shade as Amaranth had worn on his wing veins and spinal horns.

Yaassima stopped on the first step up to their private suite. Her eyes narrowed and her fingers flexed convulsively. "You take your independence and defiance too far, Myrilandel. You will wear the gown I provide or you will wear nothing at all. And the baby's name is Hanassa."

Myri stared into the Kaalipha's eyes, shoulders rigid and jaw set. They were bound together by that gaze for long moments, neither bending to the other's will.

The sound of running footsteps down the steps broke Myri's concentrated defiance. She dropped her gaze but

kept her posture. Yaassima looked up, severe annoyance
showing in her tightly compressed lips and the deep lines
around her eyes.

Kalen skidded to a halt three steps above Yaassima. She
clung to the walls of the narrow staircase to keep from
falling forward from her abrupt stop.

"There you are, Myrilandel. Amaranth is crying. I think
she's hungry," the girl said, out of breath. *I found him,*
she sent to Myri telepathically. *I know where Powwell is
being held.*

Myri shook her head, wondering how Kalen dared use
mind speech in Yaassima's presence. The Kaalipha might
overhear.

*She doesn't have real magic, only gadgets and toys that
make her seem all-powerful. That's what Powwell says.*

"I must go to Amaranth." Myrilandel shook herself free
of Yaassima's hand that still rested on her shoulder.

"You may watch Maia nurse your child if you must. A
monarch does not stoop to such messy, peasant activities."

"Yaassima, you claim dragon heritage in one breath and
deny it with your actions. Dragons nurse their own young
for many years, until they are old enough and strong
enough to hunt on their own. Yet you seek to deny me
that same nurturing, instinctive to me. Which are you,
Yaassima, dragon or self-serving outlaw?" Had she over-
stepped the line between safety and strength? Myri pushed
away her fear of the older woman.

The Kaalipha's lip curled upward in a snarl. Her fingers
flexed as if tearing the flesh of her prey. "You have no
need to explore the palace, Myrilandel. You must learn to
keep the air of mystery and power, so the *people* we govern
don't lose their fear through familiarity. I have set boundaries within the palace. You will soon learn them. Maia
and I will take complete control of the care of *my* heir,
Hanassa."

Myri looked hard at Kalen, wondering if the Kaalipha
had overheard the girl's telepathic message.

"Oh, and, Myrilandel, do not consider defying me on
this." Yaassima adjusted her tone to one of mild pleasant-
ries. She pulled a long golden chain from the pocket of her
gown. From the chain dangled a dragon-shaped pendant
cut from a single crystal. "You will wear this amulet at all

times, and I shall know where you are and who you talk to. I have assigned Nastfa and Golin to watch over you day and night.''

Curiosity glimmered in the back of Myri's mind. Nastfa and Golin had been humiliated and tormented by Yaassima last night at the orgy. Their resentment toward the Kaalipha might be turned to help Myri escape with the children.

"Nastfa and Golin have a vested interest in staying close to you now, Myrilandel," Yaassima continued. "They entertained me so well last night with their embarrassment that I have commuted their sentence. My women are still forbidden to them, but if you stray beyond the boundaries I have set, they may do with you as they wish. I promise you, they will not be gentle or kind.''

"You aren't a very good king," Konnaught d'Astrismos said matter-of-factly.

King Quinnault looked up from a copy of the newly drafted treaty with Rossemeyer to stare at him. The boy returned his gaze, stone-faced and unreadable. But the way he cleaned beneath his fingernails with his belt knife—the small tool every man carried—was too casual. Konnaught sought to pick a fight. Why?

"What brought on this absurd accusation?" Quinnault refused to allow this *child* to unnerve him. But he wanted to just thrash the boy and exile him to the kitchen until he came to his senses, or of age, whichever came later.

Unfortunately, the d'Astrismos line was the closest thing to an heir Quinnault possessed. Konnaught held the grudging loyalty of four of the other lords. They had supported the boy's father and only swore fealty to Quinnault because they were outnumbered by the remaining seven lords. Their oaths came with the proviso that Konnaught be next in line of the throne.

Everyone agreed that an heir must be greed upon before the death of a king to avoid another contest that led to civil war.

Until Quinnault found a suitable wife and sired an heir, he was stuck with Konnaught. He also had to deal with four disapproving lords on his council who prompted Konnaught's disrespectful attitude no matter what discipline Quinnault imposed.

"I thought you had the makings of a real king when you exiled your own sister as a rogue magician. But not now."

Quinnault froze. He'd hated exiling Myrilandel. For Konnaught to hold up that action as laudable revealed an evil core to his personality. Was there any way at all to exorcise that evil? He doubted it. He began to wish he had heeded Nimbulan's advice and exiled Konnaught the very day his father died.

The boy sheathed his knife and picked at his cuticles with his free hand. A bad habit Quinnault had every intention of breaking—if he let Konnaught stay in Coronnan City.

"Don't you have chores or lessons?" Quinnault asked, keeping a bored edge in his voice. "I don't have time to listen to your childish fantasies."

"My father would never have allowed Nimbulan to leave without permission. My father would have locked him up before he fled."

"What do you mean, Nimbulan has fled?" Disappointment landed heavily on Quinnault's shoulders. He'd told Nimbulan not to go, confided in the magician how much he depended upon his advice. The chore of retrieving Myrilandel from Hanassa should be delegated to younger men. The dragons insisted only that she be rescued, not by whom.

"Nimbulan has disappeared. I was with the messenger you sent to fetch him. He couldn't find your chief adviser anywhere. You should exile Nimbulan now, too. He left, so he's a rogue now."

(Do not allow this child to guide your actions. We guard Nimbulan as we guarded our daughter, Myrilandel.)

Quinnault lifted his eyes to the open window by his desk. He hadn't heard a dragon speak to him since Myrilandel's kidnap. And yet . . . was that slight tingle behind his heart that signaled his awareness of the guardians of Coronnan becoming stronger?

I need Nimbulan, he thought back at the voice in his head.

(You need to put this child in his place.)

"What are you going to do about the outlaw Nimbulan? He called off the search for the Rover who murdered the apprentice. He's in league with the Rovers. My father wouldn't . . ."

"Your father made the mistake of outlawing Nimbulan when the magician left his protection. If he'd allowed Nimbulan the freedom to pursue magic as he needed, then welcomed him back, Kammeryl d'Astrismos might very well be sitting here now evaluating this treaty rather than me. But your father wasn't all-wise or all-knowing." Quinnault lost a little of his hope that Konnaught could be redeemed by care and good examples. "Your father's mistakes are the reason I am here and you are my fosterling—owing me allegiance and obedience. You act more like an exiled rogue than an heir." Quinnault raised one eyebrow at the boy, hoping to intimidate him.

"Dungeons with stout locks were made for men like Nimbulan," Konnaught replied, undaunted.

Quinnault had to make one more try at breaking down Konnaught's dogged hero worship of his misguided father.

Part of him argued that no child deserved to know the depth of evil a father like Kammeryl d'Astrismos had stooped to—the torching and pillaging of his own villages merely to soothe a temper tantrum. Quinnault refused to think of his dead rival's perverted sexual practices that eased his increasing periods of black self-doubt and reinflated his belief in his descent from the Stargods.

Quinnault decided to point out Kammeryl's lack of judgment before he enumerated the man's evils. "There isn't a lock made that a competent magician can't open. Nor a prison they can't break out of if they choose to. Your father underestimated Nimbulan. That is a mistake I shan't make. Now I am through explaining myself to you. You have chores and lessons. I don't want to see you again until they are complete."

Konnaught looked as if he wanted to argue, then turned sharply on his heel and stalked out of the room. "You'll pay for this, little king. I'll make you pay when I rule this land," he muttered as he slammed the door behind him.

Quinnault vowed to find a wife quickly. If only there was someone else he could name his heir in the interim. Konnaught d'Astrismos must never be allowed to rule, even for a heartbeat. In the meantime . . .

"Guard!" he called the sentry posted outside his door. "Have my steed saddled. I join the search for Nimbulan and for the Rovers. I don't want a stone left unturned anywhere in Coronnan. They can't have gotten far without leaving a trail."

"Thank you, Seannin." Nimbulan saluted the young blue-tipped dragon. He rested both hands against the animal's side as his feet reaccustomed themselves to the Kardia.

Nimbulan hadn't wanted to leave Coronnan just yet. There were still clues to be gleaned from that strange clearing by the river where Televarn had disappeared. The little girl who was supposed to have fetched a book for him needed to be questioned. But Seannin had insisted he fly Nimbulan and Rollett away now. The dragon couldn't delay any longer. Shayla awaited him. No dragon dared disobey Shayla.

Few humans did either.

Rollett clambered down from the animal's back, also unsteady. He looked as if he wanted to heave his last meal.

"The flight was gentle, boy," Nimbulan said. He gripped Rollett's shoulder affectionately. "Last time I rode a dragon, we hit a high crosswind. I thought I'd be blown off."

Rollett turned a little green and gulped.

(I can take you no farther, Nimbulan,) Seannin sounded apologetic.

Nimbulan looked down a steep escarpment from the ledge where the dragon had landed. The air was thinner and drier at this elevation than he was accustomed to in the river valleys. He didn't recognize the sparse, low-growing vegetation with thick needlelike leaves and tiny flowers.

"You have brought us farther than we could walk alone in a moon or more. For that I thank you, Seannin. You and all of the nimbus of dragons." A moon closer to finding Myrilandel than he was this morning when he left Coronnan City. Hopefully he was closer to some answers as well.

(You may not thank us when you face Hanassa.) The dragon bunched his muscles as if eager to be gone from this hostile environment.

"Seannin, why didn't the dragons tell me before this is where Myrilandel was hidden?"

(You didn't look for her. We will not show you something you do not seek, not even in a dragon dream.)

Nimbulan dropped his head and closed his eyes. Seannin was right. He'd let Quinnault keep him in the capital for too long before he tried returning to Myri's clearing. Only when Shayla had broken the Covenant between dragons and humans had he actively looked for his wife and their two foster children.

But he'd looked with magic, not with his heart.

Amaranth had died because Nimbulan hadn't sought Myri earlier. If Nimbulan had gone to his wife, might he have prevented her kidnap into Hanassa?

Now he had to make that search his primary quest. He wouldn't rest until he found Myri, Kalen, and Powwell. Kings and treaties and magic schools had to wait—or find a new Senior Magician.

Could he willingly give up all he'd worked for just to be with Myri for the rest of his life?

He'd think about that later. After his wife and children were free of Hanassa.

"Where must I go from here?" Nimbulan searched the mountainside for signs of a trail.

(Follow your heart to Myrilandel. Only you do we trust to save her. The youngling will help you, but only you can find her. We can do nothing more to help. Hanassa is forbidden to true dragons.)

"I don't understand. Myri was one of you. Dragons can fly anywhere. Why can't you go into Hanassa?"

(We do not fly over or near Hanassa.) Seannin bunched his muscles again in preparation for flight.

Nimbulan stepped out of the way of the powerful wings. Seannin launched himself off the ledge and into flight. He thrust down with his wings and rose above Nimbulan's head.

The channel of communication from the dragon's mind snapped shut. Nimbulan felt curiously empty and alone without the few words the dragon had given him. As alone as Myri must feel, cut off from her family and from the dragons.

He turned in a full circle, looking for a way off this narrow ledge and into the hidden city.

"There's a staircase of sorts." Rollett pointed to crude indentations in the cliff wall.

Nimbulan was suddenly grateful for the company of his

senior journeyman, a young man he had raised since the age of ten. The bleak mountainside reminded him just how dangerous and lonely this quest would be.

At the same time he feared that he would have to watch this boy die as he had watched so many of his friends, companions, and students pass into a new existence. He clamped his hand on Rollett's shoulder with affection, reaffirming the bonds that had grown between them for more than eight years.

"Looks like someone tried to carve the steps. The intervals are too regular to be natural," Nimbulan replied. Not much of a road, but it was the only exit other than the one the dragon had taken. He peered down the mountain slope once more. Something akin to Myri's dreams of flight invaded his senses. If only he could spread his arms wide and launch himself into the thin air. . . .

"Careful," Rollett warned, grabbing Nimbulan's collar and dragging him backward on the ledge. "After experiencing flight on a dragon, it seems only natural that we should be able to do the same."

Nimbulan shook himself free of the need to fly. That way led only to death. He was not a dragon and never would be. But Myri could be a dragon again, if she wished. Had she transformed in response to Amaranth's death?

Not yet. He'd know if she had. He'd know in his heart. The silver cord pulsed too strongly between them. His loneliness increased at the thought of losing her. But if that were the only way she could save her life . . .

"Someone must use this route regularly," he commented as he placed his boots along the width of the step. It was too narrow to take more than his toes straight on, so he climbed sideways. The stairs up the mountainside fit his feet better than he'd expected on first glance.

"With these hand notches beside the steps, the route seems almost comfortable." Rollett hauled himself up the steep path.

The magical tendril connecting Nimbulan to Myri pulsed stronger with each step. His heart lifted a little. He climbed higher, taking time to breathe the thin air. No sense in arriving too out of breath to act.

One hundred twenty-two steps above the ledge, Nimbulan paused on a shallow plateau that spread right and left.

Rollett crawled up, landing on his belly. He clung to the level area with both hands dug into the sandy soil. "No wonder Hanassa is such a mystery. No one in his right mind would seek this place just to explore," Rollett panted. His eyes were squinted nearly shut, keeping out the bright sunlight and hiding his emotions. His trembling chin betrayed his uncertainty. He never looked down. "I hope there's a different way out. Those steps will be really treacherous on the way down, especially in a hurry."

"Agreed. You are good with detail. Memorize everything, particularly anything that seems odd or out of place." Nimbulan searched the plateau for signs of the trail continuing.

"Something that is repeated too often might be a delusion." Rollett's gaze followed Nimbulan's around the open space.

The plateau measured perhaps fifty long paces wide. The cliff continued to reach for the sky above it. Nimbulan walked a few steps to the right. Around the curve of the plateau, nearly one hundred average paces away, cut into that otherwise impenetrable wall was an archway. Smooth symmetrical sides and the top a perfect half circle proclaimed the opening as man-made. Metal bars filled it with an intimidating crosshatch pattern. Two guards, bristling with weapons, stood on either side of the archway. Two more held positions behind the bars. A long dark tunnel stretched from the barricade into the mountain.

Nimbulan stepped back hastily, out of view.

The guard spotted Nimbulan at almost the same moment.

"What brings you to Hanassa, stranger?" The guard on the right slapped a rock beside the archway with a curious metal wand.

A high-pitched ringing sound attacked Nimbulan's ears. He scrunched his eyes closed in a painful grimace. The sound continued inside his head long after it had ceased vibrating from the hollow metal tube the guard carried. Rollett curled up on the ground—which he still hugged—hands over his ears.

"Have you hospitality for a stranger lost and alone?" Nimbulan recited the formal words accepted throughout Coronnan. The customs of hospitality were ancient and ingrained in the culture.

"Hospitality!" the guard laughed. "No one seeks hospitality here. Who are you, and what do you truly want?" The guard held up the wand, as if he expected it to shoot a debilitating spell from the empty end.

Nimbulan backed up a step, being very careful not to fall off the edge. He kept his hands open at his sides when he really wanted to grab his staff and shoot a counterspell. He'd disguised the staff as a waterskin and lashed it to his pack, knowing it would identify him as a magician. He just had to be careful when he moved, not to knock the long tool against anything that would betray the disguise.

Rollett had accepted the same delusion for his own staff. He looked up as the guard motioned them closer, still holding out the wand. The journeyman magician remained where he was, out of sight from the other guards because of the curve of the plateau. Nimbulan took two steps closer.

The guard slapped the rock again, much harder, with the wand. The high-pitched ringing tortured Nimbulan's eardrums louder this time. He resisted the urge to cower behind his hands.

"Only magicians cannot tolerate the wand," the guard said when the ringing ceased abruptly. "You are not welcome here. Leave immediately or face the wrath of Yaassima, Kaalipha of Hanassa and Dragon of the Mountains."

Chapter 16

"**I** need your help on Old Bertha," Yaala said to Powwell. Her husky voice was packed with authority. All of the men milling around the central living cavern stopped what they were doing to listen to her, including the guards. Some—the younger and healthier prisoners—glared at her in resentment. The guards showed fear. Most of the others obeyed without question, without thought, incapable of making decisions anymore.

Powwell mopped his brow with the kerchief she'd given him last night. He still felt strange wearing it on his head, Rover style, so he stuffed it back into his pocket. His shirt and trews were soaked with his own sweat. He had no way of knowing how long he'd been down here. A day? Two? He'd survived three work shifts of cleaning and lubricating the giant machines that filled various rooms of the cave system.

Through each waking moment, the vision of the dead man falling and falling into the pit haunted him. While he slept, he dreamed he was the falling man, the heat eating away at his soul long before the fires consumed his body.

He awoke from those dreams shaking with fear. The sense of gaining release and freedom by jumping into the fires frightened him more than pain and thirst and despair.

And overlaid atop those dreams was the sense of being watched by the white wraith that drifted around the caverns, never closer than the periphery of his senses.

Come for me soon, Kalen. I don't know how long I can keep my life and sanity down here.

In the time since the guards had kicked him into the pit, he'd eaten six small meals of thin gruel. The covered pot of food was lowered down a narrow chute only marginally wider than the pot. When the denizens of the pit had eaten—after much squabbling on the part of the healthier citizens—they reattached the rope to the pot, and it was hoisted back up by unseen hands. Yaala's presence kept the stronger prisoners from gobbling all the gruel, leaving the weaker ones to starve.

Everyone down here acknowledged Yaala as their leader, as above they acknowledged Yaassima as their Kaalipha.

Even with Yaala's supervision, no one got enough to eat. When they weren't working, the men and women congregated in the living cavern, watching the chute for any sign of more food dropping down, kicking and fighting to be first to delve into the pot.

An older man related a tale of many years ago when loaves of bread appeared in the chute every day for a week. He thought a relative of one of the prisoners might work in the kitchen. But the bread stopped coming as abruptly as it started, never to be seen again.

Powwell's mouth watered at the thought of bread—even stale unleavened bread.

The lack of food only hastened the time until he, too, was consigned to the fires at the heart of the Kardia. Since the guards seemed to walk in fear of Yaala, and the accidents Powwell was certain she could arrange for them, maybe they could be coerced into bringing more food into the pit. Maybe . . .

"How do you know so much about the machines?" he asked Yaala as she led him unerringly through the labyrinth of caves and tunnels.

"I hung around the engineers when I was a kid. When the last of them died last year, I was the only one who knew enough to take their place."

"Does Yaassima know that you, a prisoner, are now the—engineer?" Powwell stumbled over the unfamiliar word.

"No." Yaala closed her mouth firmly, refusing to elaborate.

"Which one is Old Bertha?" he asked, just to keep words flowing above and around the sounds of the chugging machines. Each of the monstrous noisemakers had a personality and a name. Yesterday he'd worked on Liise, a small placid machine who only needed a little attention to purr along quite happily.

"Old Bertha is the oldest and crankiest of the Kaalipha's generators," Yaala replied.

The strange name for the machines rolled easily off her tongue. But she'd been in the pit for several years since her imprisonment as well as much of her childhood on a voluntary basis. Powwell couldn't quite form the strange words without thinking.

"What can I do to help?" he asked. "I don't know anything about the machines." He'd been taught to squirt an oily liquid onto various moving parts and wipe up the excess that spilled onto the casing.

"You have a good memory, part of your magician training. I need you to remember where every part goes and what condition it's in when I pull it out and find out why Old Bertha is wheezing and not producing enough 'tricity."

Another strange word, this one for the power that came out of the generators. Magic was much easier to understand.

"You're the only one smart enough to become the next engineer. I'll not trust anyone from aboveground with *my* machines."

As Yaala led Powwell deeper into the cave system, closer to the pit, he examined the tangle of metallic conduits that channeled the 'tricity from the generators to an unknown "transformer" in the Kaalipha's palace. Maybe these conduits were like a staff, and the transformer was a magician who had learned to use this strange power. He'd learned to gather dragon magic to fuel his talent after he'd used the ley lines. This might be another kind of fuel.

The steam that powered the generators came from a lake that filled one of the lowest caverns. Pipes channeled the water above a glowing pit of lava, heating it past boiling into steam. The steam moved inside Old Bertha in some mysterious way, churning out energy that was captured by a turbine—some of the smaller satellite machines. Flexible conduits Yaala called "wires" snaked out of the turbines and disappeared into narrow lava tube tunnels.

Maybe the ley lines were just another kind of wire for naturally generated 'tricity.

Steam from Water becoming Air. Fire from the heart of

the Kardia. All four elements were present in the 'tricity.
That made it magic. He'd understand how to use it eventu-
ally, just as he'd learned to use ley lines and dragon magic.
If he lived that long. If Kalen didn't come for him soon.

Yaala ducked beneath a low-hanging slab of black rock
within the dim tunnel. The only light came from that
strange color-leeching yellow glow produced by the 'tricity.
Powwell ducked, too. Behind the slab the roof remained
low. He had to crouch to keep from banging his head.
Yaala was short enough, so she only had to bend her head.
She seemed to know the way and moved adroitly around
other obstacles as the tunnel narrowed.

The noise grew louder the smaller the tunnel became.
Powwell resisted the urge to cover his ears. He'd almost
accepted the noise level back in the passageways. Here the
sounds of Old Bertha chugging and wheezing echoed and
compounded within the confines of the lava tube.

Yeek, kush, kush. Yeek, kush, kush. The sound assaulted
his senses as it had during the trek with Televarn from the
clearing. Powwell opened his eyes wider, looking around
him for something familiar.

If Televarn had brought them through the pit to the palace, there must be another entrance from outside Hanassa.
He turned a circle, peering at everything. Automatically he
reached into his pocket to touch Thorny and see if his
familiar remembered any of the smells down here.

His pocket was empty. The little hedgehog had found a
nest of insects he liked up near the living cavern. He'd left
Powwell alone sometime ago while he hunted a meal.
Thorny would find him when he'd eaten his fill and napped
a little.

S'murghit. He'd have to figure out the connection to
Televarn's route by himself.

Yeek, kushshshshs. Yeek, kush, kush.

"It sounds like Old Bertha has a blockage. A big
blockage," he yelled at Yaala. He'd learned that much
about the generators in his three shifts. The tiniest buildup
of mineral deposits from the water supply or rust on old
metal created problems.

"I know that. But we've got to blast it clean with this
probe before she conks out, or we'll never get her started

again," Yaala replied, holding up a long flexible wand type tool. She moved swiftly around an old rockfall that nearly blocked the passage. "Bertha is *very* old."

Powwell squeezed around the loose debris and nearly stumbled into the largest cave he'd seen down here. He could have built at least two buildings the size of the School for Magicians within the cave. Nearly filling the open space was the largest, rustiest, and loudest machine he'd ever seen.

Encased in black metal, Old Bertha rumbled and groaned and belched steam through rust holes in time with her vibrations. The rattle of the conduits going into and out of the generator gave the impression of a crotchety spider of immense proportions crouching over her latest prey.

Powwell immediately crossed himself in the Stargods' ward against evil as he remembered Moncriith's sermons against demon magic. The Bloodmage had gathered numerous followers to eliminate all magicians tainted by demons, starting with Myrilandel and including every person of talent except Moncriith. If demons did exist, they surely inhabited Old Bertha.

"It's just a machine." Yaala laughed as Powwell crossed himself a second time.

"Then why do you give them all names and treat them as if they were sentient beasts?" Powwell circled the grunting monster, keeping as close to the walls as he could and as far away from the machine as possible.

"Because these machines make Yaassima appear to be a magician. All of her tricks begin and end with them. She can't be overthrown until I know everything about these machines, how to turn them off and how to restart them keyed to a different frequency. She'll be powerless without her toys."

"You mean the lights and appearing out of nowhere? That's magic. My teacher, Nimbulan, could do that." Powwell stopped his circuit when he came to a narrow archway that opened into the pit. The swirling colors of the molten rock beyond him upset his balance and reminded him of the weight of the mountain pressing on top of this cave. He kept to one side of the archway.

"But he performed those feats with an inborn talent," Yaala argued. "He didn't have to rely on machines he inherited through fifty generations of Kaaliphs."

"Fifty generations?" Powwell added up the years in his head, then added them again. "That's nearly a thousand years. These machines can't date back to the time of the Stargods!"

"Maybe not these machines, but the technology comes from the time when Hanassa, the first Kaaliph, broke away from the dragon nimbus and took human form. He created the city named for him, and it became a refuge for the scum of Kardia Hodos who weren't welcome anywhere else."

Powwell's brain reeled with that information. Myri had been a purple-tipped dragon before taking a human body. Did that make her related to Yaassima in some way?

"Hanassa used knowledge he stole from the Stargods to build the machines," Yaala continued. "Maybe he stole the machines themselves from the Stargods. At first, the Kaaliphs knew how to replace old and worn-out machines. Now we can only clean and patch them. We've lost so much knowledge." Yaala pounded her fist into her thigh.

She turned her back on Powwell and gave her attention to a quaking water pipe running from Old Bertha back to the lake. Hot water leaked from the pipe where it joined the machine's belly. Flaking rust spread outward from the join. "I think there's a blockage in this pipe."

Powwell walked toward her, ready to watch how she inserted the probe. The shifting reds and greens of the pit, visible through an archway, kept drawing his focus. He looked over his shoulder repeatedly, watching the play of colors within the frame of the opening. He tried to break the compulsion to shift direction and walk through the colors into the pit.

Suddenly he watched not the boiling molten lava within the heart of the volcano but a secluded glen within a lowland forest. Tall trees bordered a nearly perfect circular clearing with a small campfire in the exact center. A moment later Televarn ran across the clearing and dove into the archway. Two men from the School for Magicians chased him, brandishing clubs.

The Rover chieftain landed in the cave on his belly just

as the colors swirled again and changed to the boiling lava in the pit.

Hastily, Televarn picked himself up and limped past Old Bertha. He looked around quickly, but Yaala was on the other side of Old Bertha and Powwell ducked into the machine's shadow. The Rover whistled a jaunty tune as he brushed caked mud from his trews and vest. Then he strode into the nearest exit cavern, dragging his right leg slightly.

"Did you see that, Yaala? It was Televarn, I swear it, he walked out of the pit into this cave."

"Illusions, Powwell. The heat plays tricks on you until you get used to it. Take a long drink, then help me disconnect this valve."

Quinnault cantered slightly ahead of his escort on Buan, his favorite fleet steed. A year ago, he had ridden the length and breadth of Coronnan without a servant or bodyguard. Back then he was merely one lord trying to persuade, coerce, or browbeat the other lords into accepting peace. No one cared if he fell victim to the marauding armies or packs of outlaws that roamed the countryside at will. Today he was king. Many people surrounded him, guaranteeing his safety.

But these mundane guards hadn't stopped the Rover form poisoning his cup. He wished Nimbulan hadn't gone on his dangerous quest. Quinnault didn't really feel safe without his chief adviser and Senior Magician.

Why hadn't Nimbulan told him he was leaving? He hadn't even left a note or message for his king and friend.

Quinnault missed the solitude of his former life. Long rides between strongholds had offered him periods of intense meditation. Now he only found time to ride after supper or when on business as king. He never rode alone. So he kneed Buan into a slightly faster pace. The dozen soldiers who rode behind him urged their own mounts to keep up. But they stayed a discreet two-dozen steed-lengths behind him.

He'd left Konnaught behind with a long series of sword exercises to perform. The brat wouldn't allow him this brief illusion of solitude. What could he do with the boy?

Quinnault wouldn't arbitrarily exile or imprison Konnaught. Execution was out of the question for all but the most violent crimes. He wouldn't allow himself to become the kind of tyrant who made up laws to suit his whims and then broke them when convenient. The new laws required a crime proved to judges before such a sentence could be considered.

Konnaught was too smart to let himself be caught in an active plot to overthrow Quinnault.

The road curved ahead of him, just before it entered a stretch of woodland—a former haven for outlaws. Heedless of possible ambush, he rode without slowing into the evening shadows gathering beneath the trees.

He needed to think, and think hard before full darkness forced him to return to the palace. An apprentice magician rode with the soldiers. He could provide torches of witchlight, but that wasn't enough illumination to ward off predators and light their way home.

He pelted around the next curve, completely losing sight of his escort. The last of the afternoon sunshine dropped into deep twilight. Shadows stretched out to enfold the road in mystery. Buan faltered a step as the road became muddy. Huge clods of the sloppy road sprayed behind him. The sun rarely reached this deep into the woods to dry the trader's road.

Buan slowed of his own accord. Quinnault loosened his short sword as he searched for whatever bothered the steed.

Something light and wispy fluttered across the road. Buan shied. Quinnault fought the beast with knees and reins. He needed all of his skills to stay mounted.

Buan circled and snorted. His skin rippled and twitched nervously. He pranced and circled.

Quinnault curbed him, resenting the concentration required to control the steed. He needed to know what had startled Buan. The now familiar short sword fit his hand comfortably. Stargods, how he resented the need to carry a weapon when Coronnan should know peace from violent crime as well as war.

"What is it, boy? You don't usually fuss about a bit of evening mist." He soothed Buan with a quiet voice and a gentle hand upon his glossy neck.

More drifting mist gathered in the woods around him.

Short columns of lightness stood in a half circle across the road, spreading to his sides, blocking advance. He kneed Buan to prance in a circle, checking behind him. The road back to his escort remained open.

He turned to face the tallest column that stepped forward from the line of its companions.

"What manner of ghost are you?" Quinnault asked, not liking the slight quaver in his voice. He'd faced the shadowed guardian of Haunted Isle with less uncertainty than he felt now. But he'd had Nimbulan, a powerful Battlemage, at his side then.

Where was the Senior Magician of the Commune now when his king needed him?

"We are not of this world." A deep, melodic voice drifted out of the central ghost. Masculine in timber and authority. His outline fluttered in a slight breeze. "We need conversation with you, King Quinnault."

"You have my attention." Where was his escort? They should have caught up to him by now.

"Your companions await you at the edge of the woods. They are not aware that time passes or that you are not with them. We will restore them when our conversation is finished."

"Are you magicians, that you read minds?" Quinnault's nervousness transferred to Buan. The steed stamped and tried to break free of his master's control.

"Not magicians as you define them. But we have powers similar to them. We seek a bargain with the King of Coronnan. We usually pay in the mineral substance you call diamonds. This time, we trade something more valuable."

"Varns! You're Varns." Fantastic legends surrounded the mysterious merchants who appeared in the marketplaces of Kardia Hodos once each century—always in a year of bounty. They bought enormous quantities of grain and fresh food, paying in diamonds.

Quinnault's grandfather claimed to have met a Varn about forty years ago. They weren't due back in Coronnan for another sixty years or more. This wasn't a year of plenty either.

The king's senses shifted into full alertness.

"Your people call us Varns because we prefer to trade in the city of Varnicia."

"How may I be of service?" A large quantity of diamonds would go a long way toward stabilizing Coronnan's economy after three generations of war.

"Coronnan needs more than diamonds to bring stability, King Quinnault."

Disconcerting how these amorphous beings read his thoughts.

"You need a bride who can give you many heirs. You also need a way of keeping greedy enemies from invading through the Great Bay. We can give you both."

"At what price?"

"We are dying. The tree you call the Tambootie offers the only cure."

"How much will you need?" Quinnault thought of the dragons who used the foliage of that tree for food. Previously, magicians, too, had eaten of the tree to enhance their magic. The addictive qualities of the drug made the Tambootie almost as dangerous as it was beneficial. Now that magicians gathered dragon magic, they had no need of the Tambootie. Dragons were as essential to Coronnan as the promised wife and heirs.

"The new leaves of many acres of the tree will allow us to distill enough medicine for our immediate needs."

"That is a lot. I don't know that we can spare that much." Quinnault sent out a silent plea for advice—permission—from the dragons.

"Raw Tambootie is toxic to humans. What possible reason do you have to hoard it when we need it so desperately?" A note of pleading entered the otherwise emotionless voice.

"Tambootie feeds our dragons. I need the dragons, and the dragons need the Tambootie as much as you do."

Chapter 17

Televarn paced the perimeter of the Rover cavern. His cavern. He was *THE* Rover. Every member of the nomadic tribes who dwelt within the city looked to him for leadership. He controlled their movements, their thoughts, their beliefs.

So why couldn't he find Kalen among them? Wiggles squirmed impatiently inside his vest. The animal sensed that Kalen was near enough that it should be able to join her.

"Be still, beast." Televarn batted at the ferret's paws where it tried to claw through his shirt to his skin. "We'll find her if we have to tear this city apart." The city, not the Kaalipha's palace. He intended to make the palace his home as soon as he deposed Yaassima.

Swallowing his pride and gritting his teeth in distaste, Televarn decided to ask questions when he should have been able to pluck the information from the mind of any one of his followers. Why?

Erda, the old wisewoman of his clan—every clan possessed an Erda, but this one was the oldest, most powerful and *HIS*—shuffled past him into the slave pens. She carried a pot of gruel, the standard meal for captives. As soon as the slaves had eaten, they would be linked together by ankle chains and led to the lush plateau northwest of the city to work the only fields near enough to Hanassa to provide some food for the inhabitants.

Televarn's obligation to lend his slaves to Yaassima for this work irritated his pride. *He* should make the decision where and when his slaves worked. *He* should be the one running the city and raiding rich caravans for food and other necessities rather than supervising work parties.

"Erda, where have you hidden Kalen?" He grabbed the old woman's sleeve to detain her.

Erda glared at his hand, reminding him of the effrontery of touching an Erda without permission.

Televarn's irritation made him reckless. He left his hand in place.

"Televarn seeks the one who is dangerous. Your death I see in her eyes." She didn't pull away from him, just continued to stare at his hand on her arm, reminding him of his trespass.

Televarn jerked his hand away from her arm as if she offended him, rather than the other way around. "The girl child is important to my plans. Where is she?"

"Seek her where you want her to be," Erda spat at him and continued into the fenced area where twenty hungry slaves awaited their meal.

"What is that supposed to mean?" His words echoed in the cavern. He'd broken the oldest rule of etiquette within the clan by shouting at Erda.

Erda shrugged and plodded on.

"Stubborn old bitch. I'll find Kalen and make her my chief adviser and wizard. There will be no place for old crones who spout nonsense and call it wisdom when I rule Hanassa."

Erda didn't reply.

"Seek her where I want her to be," Televarn mumbled to himself, stroking Wiggles into submission as he paced the cavern once more.

"I want her at my side, reading minds and magically lifting weapons away from my enemies. Kalen isn't by my side. But she might be reading minds and lifting weapons away from my enemies. My biggest enemy is Yaassima, in the palace. Myrilandel is also in the palace. I've waited too long to claim her." He ran his hands through his thick hair, grooming it for his imagined reunion with his former lover.

"Erda, is the witchchild in the palace?" he asked politely.

The old woman pretended not to hear him. He knew she had. She heard everything that happened among the Rovers.

"I can't get into the palace. I don't know that you could either, Wiggles," he mused.

He took a deep breath, reluctant to admit he had only one way to contact Kalen. He had to touch her mind. When she'd first become his ally—back in Coronnan before he'd taken Myrilandel through the dragongate—Kalen had made him promise never to read or control her mind, like he did with all the members of his clan. She had never participated in the rituals designed to bind every Rover to him.

Promises had never bothered him before. Why did he consider respecting this one to Kalen?

Because the child was dangerous. The promise was for his own safety as well as her whims.

He had to risk it. He'd completed the first stage of his plans with Nimbulan's death and the elimination of Amaranth. Myrilandel was now alone and vulnerable, ripe for his plucking. She had nothing left to bind her to her old life in Coronnan. But he had to get her away from Yaassima before he could reclaim his lover and bind her to his will.

Myrilandel had to see him as her rescuer. She had to witness how tenderly he cared for Kalen, her adopted daughter, how he planned to honor the witchgirl and allow her the freedom to maximize her talents—something Nimbulan couldn't do for her in Coronnan where witchwomen were exiled. He expected loyalty from Myrilandel. He knew better than to expect anything from Kalen that didn't suit Kalen.

He and the child were well suited to each other.

He sought his dark and quiet corner of the cavern, way in the back. Years ago he'd scraped away the debris and made a soft meditation nest of furs and pillows. Plain colors, without Erda's distracting embroidery, soothed his eyes and comforted his body. In one fluid motion, he crossed his legs and sank to the floor.

Wiggles squirmed out from beneath Televarn's vest and stretched along the length of his right thigh, head resting on his knee. He stroked the ferret's fur as he breathed deeply.

A light trance settled over him. Resentment churned in the back of his mind. He shouldn't have to work this hard to touch the mind of one of his own. Every member of the

clan was connected to him, mind, body, and soul, by the
magic rituals unique to Rovers. Only Erda could dissolve
bits and pieces of the control.

Kalen had steadfastly remained outside of those rituals
for several moons before Televarn laid the trap for Myrilandel. Even Nimbulan had been easier to control than that
willful child.

He suppressed his anger before it rent great holes in
his trance.

Slowly he released a thin tendril of magic. It resonated
against the mineral deposits in the volcanic rocks of the
cavern. He heard the magic shift its vibrations until it
hummed in harmony with the Kardia. He matched his voice
to the solid note. Maintaining the one-note chant, he built
a picture of Kalen in his mind. Her brown braids laced with
auburn came easily to him. He traced an outline of her hair
in the air before him.

Bright green lines followed his finger, leaving a bare
sketch of a head behind. He added wide, gray eyes and a
snub nose. With tender care he dotted a spray of freckles
across her nose. The last detail eluded him. How to draw
her mouth and chin? They faded from his memory. All he
could see in his mental picture of the girl were her eyes,
big, innocent, gazing up at him with awe.

Enough. The eyes were more important in identifying her.
They were also a place of entry for his probe. He withdrew
his tracing finger and attached his magic to the drawing.

Then he willed the magic to find the one whose image
he had drawn.

The magic uncoiled into a slender arrow and darted
through a crevice in the cave walls. Wiggles leaped from his
lap, following the probe into the depths of the mountain.

"*S'murghit!* There goes my only true link to the girl."

Myri tugged at the heavy necklace Yaassima fastened
around her neck, careful to make her movements sluggish.
The gold links, each the diameter of her little finger, settled
against her collarbones and wouldn't move from there. The
dragon pendant rested firmly between her breasts, tightening the fabric of her gown to outline their shape. She
started to lift the necklace over her head. A painful whistle
sounded deep within her ear.

She dropped the necklace and grabbed her ears, trying to block the sound that stabbed at her mind like a knife.

The dragon pendant glowed brightly.

The whistle and the pain ceased as soon as Myri dropped the gold links. All traces of eldritch light faded from the crystal dragon as the gold links quietly caressed her neck.

An audience of guards and servants paused in their routes through the palace to watch the spectacle of the Kaalipha's favorite receiving an unprecedented gift. Yaassima grinned at them, obviously enjoying her display of power over Myri. Kalen was nowhere in sight.

Myri looked at the pendant where it settled between her breasts as if it belonged there. With one finger she flicked it until it swayed. Her skin burned through her shift and bodice as if pierced by a branding iron wherever the beautiful jewel touched her. The only time she was comfortable was if she ignored it.

"You needn't bother trying to remove it." Yaassima draped Myri's hair over her shoulders, creating a frame for the jewelry. "My great-great-grandfather had it made for his mistress after she tried to run away. The next time she attempted to escape, the necklace kept shrieking inside her mind until blood vessels in her brain burst and she died."

Myri ceased moving, stopped thinking. The purple-tipped dragon, Amethyst, had only been able to take over Myrilandel's body because the little girl was thought dead from bleeding in the brain. The dragon's vitality had allowed the little girl to heal the broken places. Myri's innate healing talent knew the vessels were still weaker than normal. The necklace would kill her quicker than most humans.

"Now that the necklace has found a home on your beautiful neck, Myrilandel, no one will be able to remove it until you die." The Kaalipha let her hand linger on Myri's cheek.

Myri forced herself not to jerk away from the caress. Yaassima had trapped her with a magic-infested slave collar. No matter how beautiful the jewelry, it still branded her the Kaalipha's possession, without freedom or control over her own life. She'd never taste fresh air and open skies again.

She had to. The necklace was just one more obstacle to overcome.

She looked frantically right and left. The gathered servants blocked any route of immediate escape from Yaassima.

"Don't consider killing yourself, Myrilandel, by deliberately crossing my boundaries. Suicide is forbidden by your Stargods," Yaassima cooed, reaching to run her hand across Myri's breast.

The corridor wall pressed against Myri's back. No place to run.

Yaassima squinted her eyes nearly closed. Age lines, spraying outward from her slightly uptilted eyes marred her otherwise flawless complexion. "I think you might welcome my gentleness when Nastfa and Golin finish with you. Just remember, they will do you no harm until you try to escape. And don't try to make friends with them so that they will aid you. Through the crystal dragon, I will hear every word you speak. Don't give me a reason to have the jewelry stab into your brain until you die an ugly death."

The Kaalipha flipped her hand in a quick rotation. She pressed her thumb against the ring on her little finger. The whistle shrieked inside Myri's head once more.

Myri fought to keep from cringing from the pain.

Darkness encroached on her vision from the sides. A white tunnel opened before her eyes. At the end of the tunnel she saw Coronnan, beautiful, cool, green Coronnan. Blue skies invited her to soar free through the fresh air. Her home. Numbulan's home. Freedom!

But she had to transform to win free of Hanassa. Once a dragon, she wouldn't have a human body to come back to. Amaranth would have no mother—only Kalen and a Rover wet nurse.

She allowed the blackness to overwhelm her, praying that Yaassima wanted her alive. Her knees buckled.

Abruptly the whistle ceased. Her eyes cleared. Hot, desert air filled her dry mouth and lungs. Her tongue tasted sour from fear.

"Remember this little lesson next time you defy me." Yaassima stalked back toward the staircase that led to their suite. "Nastfa and Golin are waiting for you in your chamber, Myrilandel."

Nimbulan hastened away from the gate into Hanassa before the guards changed their minds and arrested him. He searched the mountainside for an alternate route up the steep slope above the gateway. He had to find another way into the city. Myri needed him. Old legends and a few unreliable reports from Televarn said that Hanassa was within the crater of an extinct volcano. The ridge line above him should actually be the rim of the crater. Once up there, he'd try dropping into the city from above.

He spotted a scraped stone next to a prickly bush that seemed to be missing four branches. Upon closer examination, he decided the missing branches had been nibbled off by some browsing animal. The scrape marks came from hooves.

He dug his boot toes into the rocky soil and stood beside the bush. Above it, he saw a line of other plants that might have been lunch for the same animal. He followed the grazing pattern upward, finding footholds that weren't visible until he was almost on top of them.

Rollett angled farther north to see if a better trail existed.

The sun rose higher, more intense here in the desert than it ever shone in the river valleys of Coronnan. Sweat dripped down Nimbulan's back and between his thighs, despite the winter season. His hands and neck sunburned rapidly in the thin mountain air.

He drank from the waterskin Seannin had made him fill before leaving Coronnan. He wanted more, but the top of the mountain seemed very far away. Perhaps he'd best conserve his supplies until he was inside the city.

Rollett? He sent a query to his journeyman. *Any luck?*

Nothing, came back the reply.

Conserve your water. We may be out here a long time.

They had to remain strong enough to rescue Myri once they managed to drop below the crater rim. And Nimbulan hadn't slept more than a few hours since before the battle. For weeks before that his rest had been troubled by worry over Myri. He wondered if Rollett's more youthful body had rebounded after the grueling battle and the preparations before that. The young man had been almost as depressed over Haakkon's drowning as Nimbulan had, further depleting energy resources.

Hopefully the crater's slope into the city would be climbable or not too far a drop to the roof of some building.

Myri. Oh, Myri. I miss you so. Stay safe until I can come for you, he pleaded with every scrap of telepathic talent he possessed.

An hour later, the top of the mountain seemed no closer. Rollett was out of sight around the curve of the slope. Flies pestered Nimbulan's face, crawling into his ears and nose. He swatted at them. Five flew off, replaced by ten more. His pack grew heavier with each step, and he longed to drain the waterskin. He dragged out his staff and used it as a prop to pull himself up one more step.

A small puddle of shade beneath a narrow outcropping enticed him forward. His eyes welcomed the protection from the glaring light, though the temperature didn't vary significantly. The flies continued to plague him as his sweat dried to a salty crust.

Go home. You're too old for this kind of an adventure. Go home where life is safe and comfortable, a small voice in the back of his mind whispered.

"Not without Myri. I won't leave this place until my wife is by my side once more. And not without finding an end to the murdering of my apprentices," he called to the four cardinal directions and the four elements. When he finished this quest, he'd make a home for Myrilandel on one of those little islands in the Great Bay that Quinnault wanted to use as a ferry station and loading dock. That would put her outside of Coronnan and still allow him access to his work in the capital.

He crouched within the shallow confines of the shade until his back protested the unnatural hunch. He sat, curling his legs tightly against his chest and rolling his hips slightly toward the back of the overhang. If he stretched out so much as a hair, the sun beat down, burning him through his clothes. Extremely uncomfortable, he closed his eyes and thought of Myri and the clearing.

He thought about recording his impressions of Hanassa in his journal, but didn't want to waste his energy. His eyes were very heavy and the sun too bright.

He awoke to find the shadows had lengthened. Rollett stood in front of him, hands on hips, trying for an intimidating posture. But the weary sag of this shoulders and neck belied his expression.

"Take a drink, and we'll be on our way, Rollett. Our entrance might be safer after dark," Nimbulan said.

"Cooler anyway. We'll need our cloaks within minutes of sunset. And there isn't much twilight in this desert air."

Rollett continued to look around, seeking a way up to the top.

The water refreshed Nimbulan enough that he thought he could finish the climb before full dark. He stretched cramped and aching muscles and stood up slowly.

Thoughts of holding Myri in his arms once more filled him with determination. *A few more hours and I will be with you, beloved.*

Stretching shadows obscured the faint game trail he had followed earlier. Rollett picked it out, feeling for it with the tip of his staff—a trick Lyman had taught the young man—to seek the lingering life-vibrations of the last being who had climbed this way with the sensitive staff. They plodded upward, grasping bushes and rocks for balance as the slope steepened.

Nimbulan dug his staff into the sandy soil as a prop when the bushes weren't close enough. His thighs grew as heavy as his pack, and his head felt as light as the waterskin.

The shadows deepened. The sun set behind the mountain. Chill air dropped dramatically upon them. Stars burst alive in the blue-black sky all at once. The tangy smell of desert plants sharpened in the cool air.

Nimbulan looked up to the rim of the crater. Starlight glimmered against a shiny network running along the crest. He narrowed his eyes, looking for signs of magic. Nothing extraordinary met his gaze. He dragged himself up the last few steps and reached with his left hand, palm outward, fingers curled, for the source of the now sparkling obstacle.

He jerked his hand back, pain stabbing his fingertips. Close inspection revealed tiny punctures where he had met the obstacle. Blood oozed from the cuts He inspected the barrier again, more cautiously, with all of his senses.

A long line of rusted metal fencing, barbed with sharp wires twisted at close intervals, ran the full circle of the crater rim. It stood nearly double Nimbulan's height.

"This fence stretches for miles," Rollett whispered. "I can't sense an end to it, as if it makes a full circle with no beginning and no end."

Two hundred feet below them, down a nearly straight precipice, Nimbulan saw the city. The rising moon, just past full, illuminated the haphazard streets and jumbled huts.

Even without the fence he'd not be able to climb down the cliff into the city. Too steep to climb, too far to jump.

The barred gate was indeed the only entrance and exit to Hanaassa.

Chapter 18

*(**W**hen in doubt, stall!)*
      The idea persisted in Quinnault's mind. He dismounted slowly, thinking furiously. As he slid down Buan's side, he was briefly out of sight of the Varns. He palmed his belt knife and loosened his short sword in its sheath. He'd never undergone the intense weapons training of a warrior. But he knew the business end of his blades.

His years of studying to become a priest, before his entire family was wiped out by the wars and the plagues and famine that always followed in the aftermath of war, had trained him to negotiate.

"Tambootie has become a valuable commodity since the advent of Communal magic."

The Varn leader turned his head region to the column of fluttering mist on his left. A moment of silence ensued. Quinnault wondered if they consulted telepathically, as magicians sometimes did.

The Varn beside the leader reached up and removed a flowing headdress. Like breaking free of a cocoon, a red-haired woman shook herself free of the coverings. She dropped the elaborate veils to the ground.

That's all the cloaking mist proved to be—many layers of soft, translucent cloth. The woman concealed beneath the drifting draperies seemed to be human.

Quinnault gasped. He'd never seen a more beautiful woman. Her small heart-shaped face was framed by a cap of short curls. A snub nose gave her a look of youth. Big green eyes seemed to sparkle with humor and mischief, another hint of youthfulness. Her full-lipped mouth twitched as if suppressing a smile.

"Am I valuable enough?" Her voice lilted over him as if she sang a sweet love ballad. Her accent hinted of exotic lands.

Fascinated, Quinnault stepped forward. He needed to be closer to her, make certain she was truly human and real. The heavy swathing veils still hid her figure. Below the neck she could be a many tentacled monster.

He didn't care.

"The ladies of my court will frown at your hairstyle while they rush to mimic it. There will be an abundance of shorn locks for the gentlemen to collect as talismans of luck and favor." He felt himself smiling and wanted to burst out laughing.

"I . . . I am not used to dealing with court ladies." She gnawed at her lower lip with small perfect teeth.

A sense of panic invaded his mind like a telepathic probe from a dragon. He looked at the woman, stunned. No other human had ever been able to awaken his dormant talent.

Are you reading my mind? he asked her.

Not intentionally, she replied. Her eyes opened wide, startled.

He nearly lost his balance gazing into their green depths.

Many of the women in my family have green eyes. It is considered a sign of inherited intelligence. Her mental chuckle told him that she didn't believe the family superstition.

And suddenly he realized that with the lines of communication open in his mind this woman couldn't lie to him. He relaxed a little.

I don't want to lie to you, ever, Your Grace. Please don't lie to me. She gnawed her lip again in uncertainty.

This crack in her composure struck Quinnault deeply. He needed to reach out and protect this woman. He didn't even know her name, and yet he found himself dreaming of long years with her, of children and shared memories.

Katie. The name came to him without a deliberate probe.

The woman shifted her shoulders as if pushing aside her doubts. She extended her hand in a masculine gesture to shake his. "I am Mary Kathleen O'Hara. My friends call me Katie."

So her companions didn't know that he had established a telepathic link, and she didn't want them to know.

"Quinnault Darville de Draconis at your service." He

lifted her hand to his lips and pressed a gentle kiss to her fingertips. When he lifted his head, he couldn't let go of her hand. "My friends call me Scarecrow, but don't tell anyone at court."

Scarecrow? The mischief returned to her eyes. "I can think of many names better suited to a handsome bachelor king."

"I haven't been called Scarecrow since I was a teenager, actually, all arms and legs and clumsy as a newborn colt."

"Does that mean you haven't had any friends since?" Concern touched her voice and her smile. *I would very much like to be your friend.*

Quinnault fell in love.

(Offer them half the Tambootie.)

Sense reasserted itself into his brain. "If we can negotiate a treaty, you may have half the Tambootie requested, harvested in thirds. We will deliver the first load when the marriage banns are posted, the next when the marriage takes place, and the final third when our first son is born." He had to keep his eyes closed to keep from giving them everything up front without a thought for the future. If he looked at Katie any longer, he'd give away his entire kingdom without regret.

"We need the Tambootie now," the leader asserted. He tried to push his body between Quinnault and Katie.

Neither of them yielded to him. Nonetheless, Quinnault dropped her hand. "I have a marriage treaty waiting for my signature that promises me a perfectly good princess. My people know her lineage and will welcome the alliance. Her family will secure my entire western border."

"And leave you more vulnerable to the south and east."

"Do you have a name? Perhaps we could retire to my palace for refreshment. These negotiations could take some time. I will need to consult my Council and my magicians." Quinnault cocked one eyebrow, trying to appear as if his sanity didn't depend upon grabbing Katie's hand again and never letting her go.

"You may call me Kinnsell, Scarecrow. And we can finish this here and now if you are reasonable. Katie could be your wife by tomorrow night."

"You may call me *King* Quinnault, or Your Grace. I rule by the grace of the dragons and I will not hesitate to call

them up to dispose of my enemies." He glared at Kinnsell.
He didn't need to tell these Varns that no dragon had been
seen in Coronnan since his sister had been spirited away.

Behind him Buan snorted as if amused. Quinnault cursed
the steed under his breath.

"Magicians and dragons," Kinnsell snorted. "I guess you
use the Tambootie to induce hallucinogenic trances that
make you see dragons and believe in magic."

"If that is what you believe, then we have nothing to
discuss." Quinnault turned on his heel and grabbed Buan's
reins. He didn't want to go. Didn't want to leave Katie.
But he had to show strength, knock some of the arrogance
out of these beings.

"Your Grace, there is no need to go through the lengthy
process of banns and an elaborate marriage ceremony,"
Kinnsell said mildly, almost politely. "A simple exchange
of vows is all we require. Your laws do say that when marrying a foreigner the bride's customs prevail at the
ceremony."

"But I am a ruling monarch. My people must accept
Maarie Kaathliin," he repeated her name with the softer
intonation of his people, "as their queen as well as my wife.
We must all know her lineage and her dowry." Maarie
Kaathliin. The name had a familiar ring to it. Where had
he heard it, or read it. Kinnsell, too, sounded familiar. . . .

Kinnsell! the servant of the Stargods. Kimmer, Konner,
and Kameron O'Hara. No. The Varns couldn't be delegates
of the Stargods. The three red-haired brothers who had
saved Kardia Hodos from a plague and given the people
justice and magic belonged to the people of the Three
Kingdoms, not to the Varns, who hailed from some unknown, unnamed location.

"I assure you, Quinnault," Katie said. "I am the daughter
of an emperor, descended from seven hundred years of
emperors. I believe you value people descended from your
Stargods? My family dates back to them. My lineage is im-
peccable. We would not press you to hasten our union if the
lives of many millions of people did not depend upon access
to the Tambootie." She captured his gaze with her own.

He fell into their green depths and knew she spoke the
truth.

We need you as much as you need me. But be careful of

Kinnsell. He has his own agenda aside from the issue of the Tambootie.

(She will do.)

Quinnault almost laughed at the amused voice in the back of his head. He had no doubt that Shayla eavesdropped on both conversations, spoken and telepathic.

"Half the Tambootie, delivered in two batches—at the marriage and half when our first son is born." He felt an odd reassurance as well as a chuckle of approval behind his heart where the dragons dwelt. "But we must have a public marriage and posting of the banns."

Kinnsell and Katie exchanged another of those meaningful glances. The leader turned away first, sighing heavily.

If this haughty leader bowed to her demands, she must be very strong-willed. Quinnault was glad she was on his side. She couldn't lie to him. He'd know it in his mind and in his heart. So would the dragons.

"You need to protect your shipping channels without challenging your neighbors by building an extensive navy." Kinnsell removed the elaborate headdress of veils and shook his head as if freeing it of the weight. Taller and older than Katie, he, too, bore a head full of red hair, cut short. His complexion and green eyes matched hers. A similarity of jaw and mouth shape suggested close family ties. Father and daughter?

"Agreed," Quinnault said warily. These people knew too much about his situation and he had no bargaining tools other than the unacceptable marriage treaty with SeLenicca. He clamped down on those thoughts lest the Varns read them.

You have the Tambootie. He cannot harvest it without your permission. Our family covenant requires your permission and trade of equal value.

"The mudflats of the Bay offer a natural protection for your harbor but prevent shipping into the harbor," Kinnsell continued. He drew the arc of the bay in the ground with a stick. He marked the mudflats with squiggles. "We will build a series of jetties and bridges among the islands at the beginning of deep water. Flat-bottomed barges can transport people and cargo from the port into your city." He finished off the drawing with the exact placement of the four islands.

Nimbulan had suggested the same solution to the problem. It would work. Quinnault forced himself to reply levelly. "Such a venture will take many moons to construct. Possibly years. Plenty of time to post the banns and prepare a great marriage ceremony."

Kinnsell sighed again as if incredibly weary. "We have the technology to build the port in the space of one long night."

"My boatmen will need many seasons to learn the changes in the currents to guide the barges through the mudflats safely."

"We will lend one, I repeat, *one,* of your boatman a device that will show him the shifting currents and channels. Marry the girl tomorrow and while you conceive the first child, we will build your port. But we must have the Tambootie. Three quarters of the original demand delivered in halves."

Can you spare that much Tambootie? he threw the question at whatever dragon might be listening, and he had no doubt they heard every word of every conversation he conducted.

(Not all at once.)

"Two thirds. Half of it this season. The remainder next year. Too heavy a harvest will cripple the trees and prevent them from leafing out properly next year." Quinnault didn't know where that information came from, but he sensed it was true. "If you destroy the trees, you won't have a source for your medicine should your plague break out again."

"You will marry the girl in the morning?" Hope colored Kinnsell's voice for the first time.

"My western and southern borders are still vulnerable." How much could he trade for the Tambootie?

"Ties of friendship and trust will protect you better than anything we can give you. Will you marry Katie in the morning?"

"In the evening. We will have to prepare a gown and a feast." And convince the Council. Soothe the ruffled feelings of the Commune. Placate the ambassador from SeLenicca . . .

A candlelight wedding in an ancient temple. Her mental sigh of delight filled Quinnault with deep satisfaction.

And the fairy tale gown of your dreams, white satin and

pearls. He completed the mental picture for her. Seamstresses would have to work all night and all day tomorrow to alter his mother's gown to fit this slight woman.

Katie smiled at him, only for him, and he knew the bargain was worth going to war with SeLennica. The dragons had said she would do. He agreed.

Nimbulan eased behind a tumble of boulders near the gateway into Hanassa. He fished some oddments from his pack for a disguise. Behind another jumble of rocks, Rollett squatted and made similar preparations. No sense in risking a magical delusion slipping if they had to hold the spell too long. Nimbulan loosed his hair from its queue restraint and tangled it into a rat's nest with his fingers. Then he slipped an old black patch over his right eye. The molded fabric was threadbare and ragged around the edges. An equally ragged robe, similar to the one General Ambassador Jhorge-Rosse wore, covered his ordinary shirt and trews. The last item in his pack looked like more rags. He wound these around his head in a slipshod turban. Durt on his face and a stooped posture, dependent upon his staff for support, transformed him into an out-of-luck mercenary from Rossemeyer, seeking employment with the gangs of mercenaries headquartered in the city.

Rollett looked a little firmer of step, but equally ragged in his black robe and disintegrating turban. His own dark beard hadn't been shaved since the morning before the battle and effectively covered the lower half of his face in shadow.

Nimbulan worked his way around the back side of the boulders so he could approach the gate from the direction of the stairway. Rollett followed silently. The sound of shuffling feet and a mournful dirge sung by a few male throats brought them to a hasty halt.

Nimbulan peered over the cliff edge toward the staircase. Nothing. The sounds echoed in the thin mountain air, defying direction. He extended his FarSight with the few reserves of dragon magic he'd gathered from Seannin.

Around the side of the mountain, on a narrow trail, level with the gate, marched several dozen people. An aura of despair, hunger, and fatigue hung over the marchers. Their emotions beat against Nimbulan's heightened sensitivities.

Beyond hatred and anger, they plodded through a routine guided by heavily armed guards.

As the group came closer, Nimbulan saw with his normal eyesight heavy, iron collars around their necks. *Slaves!* his mind screamed in outrage. No one had the right to own another human being. *No one!*

The Stargods had outlawed slavery a thousand years ago, likening it to the horrible human sacrifices demanded of the ancient demon Simurgh.

Outrage and disgust almost pushed him to confront the guards and free the captives. Where would they go in these trackless mountains without supplies, a leader, and a destination? How could he get into the city to free his wife if he disrupted the routine so boldly?

Breathing deeply to calm his rapid pulse, he clung to his hidden position, observing the sentries and their curious wands.

As he expected, the troop of slaves with their eight guards halted abruptly on the little plateau by the gate. The slaves ceased walking in unison, almost as if minds and bodies were controlled by a magician. Televarn's Rover magic could do that. Nimbulan had barely escaped the man's magical manipulation. He'd been looking for it and blocked the spell with his own magic. What could these poor slaves do against so insidious a master?

The rear guards set aside a pile of pitchforks, hoes, and rakes. None of the slaves carried the tools. They might use them as weapons on the march back from the fields. How were they controlled in the fields?

The two sentries with wands slapped the instruments against a rock—the same rock they'd used before. Instantly the high-pitched ringing assaulted Nimbulan's ears. He resisted the urge to hide his head and block the sound with magic. He had to know how mundanes reacted to the noise.

Every one of the slaves froze in place. The guards with the wands moved among them, passing the magical instruments up and down, seeking. Seeking what?

As the guard approached a tall man in the center of the slave group, his wand glowed hot green, as if lit by fire within. The guard's partner searched the immobile slave with his hands, slapping the man hard. He lingered in the region of the slave's waist. Then he pulled a metal belt buckle out from under the man's loose shirt. The wand faded back to its normal black iron color.

Farther down the line, the guards discovered an assortment of metal buttons and eyelets among the slaves' ragged clothing. None of the slave collars or leg shackles reacted with the wands.

Curious. The iron must be specially treated. Nimbulan wondered if he could analyze the shackles and fabricate weapons of a similar material.

"They're clean," the sentry announced. At last the obnoxious humming ceased. The slaves roused from their stupor and shuffled forward, through the gate as if they hadn't been standing frozen in place for several long minutes. Nimbulan longed to dash forward and cross the threshold with them. The sentries resumed their watchful stance. He'd never get past them.

He had to divest himself of any metal not part of his disguise. Reluctantly he removed his glass from his pocket and directed Rollett to do the same. Unwrapping the layers of silk protection, he revealed the large square of precious glass framed in gold. Rollett's journeyman's glass was smaller and framed in bronze. Apprentice glasses were little more than a shard without a frame.

Nimbulan dented the gold rim with his belt knife until he could slip a broken fingernail beneath it. He stripped away the expensive casing, ripping his fingernail further.

The thin rim of gold weighed heavy in his hand. What to do with it? Rollett squeezed his bronze frame into two small coins. With magic, he imprinted them with a fuzzy image similar to the coins of Rossemeyer. Nimbulan chuckled to himself as he formed his gold into three slightly larger coins. What mintage should he mimic? A mercenary from Rossemeyer might have coins from a dozen countries. He settled on the image of the king of Jihab, a country that hired many mercenaries to protect their jewel merchants.

Slowly, Nimbulan counted one hundred heartbeats. Then another one hundred. The slaves were well within the city. The sentries assumed a pose of casual wariness. Rollett offered Nimbulan a supporting arm. They dragged themselves toward the gate, leaning on their staffs, as if incredibly weary.

"Who are you, and why do you approach the Dragon's

City of Hanassa?" the first sentry asked when Nimbulan shuffled to a stop in front of him.

"Dragon's City?" he returned the question in a weak and shaking voice. The dragons, the real dragons, had said they wouldn't approach the city. "I hope the dragons inside need another soldier for hire."

"You don't look strong enough to wield a belt knife, let alone a sword." The guard with a wand stepped forward.

"Lost my sword to the bay in the *s'murghin'* battle with Coronnan a few weeks past." It had only been two days since King Quinnault and Nimbulan won that battle, but the guards wouldn't know that. "Had to jump ship to avoid the witchfire. *S'murghin'* unfair of that upstart king to fight with magicians. An honest soldier ain't got a chance against 'em," he grumbled.

"We haven't heard of any battle." The guard raised the wand above the striking rock.

"You'll hear soon enough. King Quinnault wants all of Kardia Hodos to know no one can defeat his magicians and their new powers. . . ." He trailed off and froze his body as the wand and the rock resonated with that horrible sound.

It took all of his willpower to keep from clutching his ears with both hands. His muscles twitched for release as the guard lingered over searching his body for concealed weapons. He didn't even dare flick his eyes toward Rollett, to see if the boy remained as rigid as the mundane slaves.

The guard found Nimbulan's little belt knife—an eating tool more than a weapon. He ran his thumb along the length of the blade, testing for sharpness. It barely creased his skin. Grunting, he returned the blade to its sheath.

Nimbulan sucked on his cheeks to keep from flinching as the guard's hand patted his groin. Did his hand linger overlong? A test or personal perversion?

The guard found another knife, a longer blade inside Nimbulan's boot and a few base coins tucked inside his shirt. Then he searched the multiple folds and pockets of Nimbulan's all-concealing black robe.

"Gold!" The guard's eyes widened as he felt the weight of the three coins.

"A good day's haul. Drinks are on you when we go off duty," the other guard laughed.

"He's clean," the first guard said as he pocketed the coins.

"This one is clean, too," said a second guard, straightening from searching Rollett. The horrible humming ceased abruptly.

Nimbulan wondered if the word "clean" triggered the release. He rotated his shoulders and looked up at the guards. "You gonna search me?"

"Already have. Aander here will carry your knives to the far side of the tunnel and give them back to you there. Enjoy the Kaalipha's protection for two days. After that you have to find a sponsor and join normal work details or leave." One of the guards opened the gate.

Nimbulan moved past the iron bars. A strange tingle snaked across his skin. Some kind of magic, but unlike any he'd encountered in all his years as a Battlemage. He willed his body not to shiver at the alien touch. Nor did he look at Rollett to see if he felt the same tingle. Aander watched them too closely.

A long dark tunnel stretched forward, perhaps three hundred long paces. Lanterns at the far end revealed another barred gate and four more guards. Would they have to go through the same search again? Nimbulan sighed wearily, preparing to ignore the horrible ringing noise and the humiliating search one more time.

The next guard nodded briefly to Aander as he flashed his wand across the proffered knives. Then he opened the second gate. Apparently the Kaalipha trusted her guards enough to forgo a second test.

At last he stepped out of the tunnel, into the city proper.

"No weapons inside the palace or the tunnel. The wands remember the people and weapons, so don't try sneaking anybody out. You have two days to find a sponsor or get out—the two of you together and no one else with you. Without any other weapons. Other than that there aren't a whole lot of rules in Hanassa. There's lots of hiring of mercenaries right now. You'll find a sponsor easy, if you really want to stay." Aander handed the knives back to Nimbulan and Rollett. Now to find Myri and get her past these vigilant guards and their magical wands.

Chapter 19

"**D**o something, Kalen. Oh, please help me get this chain off my neck!" Myri begged her daughter when the girl finally returned to their quarters. She couldn't take a chance that the next time the bizarre whistle stabbed her brain the weakness left over from her infancy might rupture.

Then sun was nearly down and the air stifling. Even sight of the dark blue sky above the crater rim didn't ease her near panic.

Breathe deeply. In three counts, hold three, out three. She remembered Nimbulan's patient coaching from their first days together. He'd been teaching her to trigger a trance. She had to be relaxed before the trance would work.

She inhaled deeply on three counts, trying desperately to still her racing mind and scattered thoughts.

"Don't you want to hear my news first?" Kalen stuck out her lower lip in a good imitation of a pout. Her eyes opened wide and filled with moisture. She hadn't resorted to that expression in Myri's presence for nearly a year.

"News?" Memory of Kalen's errand to discover Powwell's whereabouts broke through her anxiety about the necklace. Hard on the heels of her elation about news of Powwell's whereabouts came awareness that Yaassima listened to every word she said through the dragon pendant.

"I . . . I can't listen now, Kalen. Can you do anything about this necklace?" Yaassima would expect her to try to break the necklace. Myri didn't feel safe telling Kalen about the Kaalipha's eavesdropping. She did look pointedly at the two guards who stood so stiffly by the door, also listening.

Kalen's expression closed. She dropped her gaze with all

the innocence and shyness of a normal little girl. "I don't know how to do it." She waved at the offensive necklace biting her lip. "You'll have to free yourself."

Kalen never looked directly at someone when she told the truth. She used her wide-eyed innocence act to cover deceit.

And yet, Myri's magical senses picked up defiance. What was happening inside Kalen's complex thoughts?

She had to trust the girl. They'd been close for a long time. Kalen had learned to trust Myri, though Powwell was the only male she would allow past her defensive barriers. Kalen wouldn't betray Myri, her foster mother.

"I can't break the magical hold the necklace has on me, Kalen. I've tried. It chains me to Yaassima and this place. I have to get it off!" Myri intended to tell the listening woman precisely what she expected to hear and nothing more.

Kalen shrugged and moved toward Amaranth's cradle near the window, rocking it idly with her toe. The baby cooed and gurgled in response. Kalen sneered and turned her head away from the baby.

Myri caught jealousy and resentment from the girl's unbridled emotions. How could she resent an innocent baby?

Because little Amaranth devoured all of Myri's attention. She had little left to give Kalen. "Babies require a lot of attention," Myri said to her older daughter. "But just because my attention is on the baby doesn't mean I love you any less."

Kalen sniffed and refused to look at anything but the blank wall.

Myri reached out to touch the girl, fearful of losing all of the emotional stability they had built together.

Suddenly Kalen looked up, eyes alert, shoulders back and spine stiff. A trance of some sort. Myri had seen the posture often enough in her husband. But she'd never seen Kalen bother with the altered mind state that made a magician receptive to weaving or receiving spells.

"What is it, Kalen?"

The girl remained silent. A streak of dark fur sprang from a crack in the wall and slithered up the girl's leg, clinging to the fabric of her skirt until it reached her shoulder where it wrapped around her neck.

"Kalen!" Myri shook her daughter's shoulder. She had to break the trance. "Wiggles is back. Wake up and listen to your familiar."

The ferret might very well carry a message of danger. Both Kalen and Myri were vulnerable to magic here in this city filled with Bloodmages, Rovers, and other malcontent magicians. The trance could blind Kalen to magical manipulation.

"Nimbulan is dead," Kalen whispered through stiff lips. Her hand crept up automatically to caress Wiggles. The ferret chirped ecstatically.

"What?" Shock rooted Myri in place. All thought deserted her. "I won't believe it." Kalen didn't know about the magical link between Myri and Nimbulan. No one could see it but themselves.

Kalen lied.

"Believe it. Wiggles brought me a vision. I saw Nimbulan in a great battle on the bay. Drowning. Waves and waves of water. Water pushing him down and down. No air. No strength. Blackness." Kalen barely roused from her trance.

"He can't be dead. I'd know it," Myri protested. Kalen and the eavesdropping Yaassima would expect her to say that.

How had Wiggles observed a battle on the Great Bay when he'd last been seen in the clearing, several days' ride south of any access to that body of water? He had no reason to go north to Nimbulan—whom he'd never met. Myri presumed the ferret had either sought Kalen out or come with her and then gotten lost in the city and the maze of tunnels that made up the palace.

Myri clutched her chest, trying to calm the frantic pulse. But her panic came from the knowledge that Kalen lied and Wiggles was her partner in deceit. She had no reason to grieve yet over the loss of her husband.

The silver tendril pulsed a normal heart rhythm. It grew stronger and thicker beneath her fingers, as if . . . as if Nimbulan had suddenly come closer.

Perhaps Kalen had been misled by her sneaky ferret—could the animal have been tampered with? Not likely. The bonds between a witchwoman and her familiar were strong and convoluted, but exclusive.

She opened her mouth to ask the girl for details, to find the source of the deceptive message.

The half curl of satisfaction on the right side of Kalen's mouth told Myri more than she wanted to know. Even if she knew the information to be a lie, Kalen wanted Nimbulan dead and Myri lost in grief for him. Why?

Powwell swallowed his fears. Televarn *had* stepped from somewhere else into the tunnels. This was the same route they had taken from the clearing, through the pit and into the lower levels of the palace.

Yaala said it was a hallucination, induced by the heat and dehydration. Powwell knew what he had seen. Knew what he had experienced during the kidnap and his first few moments of awareness.

Thorny confirmed his impression as he waddled up to Powwell and begged to be picked up. As Powwell cradled the little hedgehog in his palm, his familiar replayed scents through Powwell's memory. This tunnel branching off from Old Bertha's cavern smelled different than any other tunnel in the pit.

If Televarn could come and go from this hellhole, then Powwell could, too.

He tucked Thorny into his tunic pocket, letting his familiar's nose work with him. With one hand on the wall and the other extended, palm outward, as a sensor, he crept forward. At each step he stopped and extended his senses as far as he could, looking for something different about this particular tunnel. Thorny had poor eyesight but keen smell. All he could tell Powwell was that this place was different and he didn't like it.

Powwell rotated his left hand, much as Nimbulan did when seeking information or weaving the magic of the Kardia. His palm was sweating, as it had almost continuously since he'd been thrown down here. Nothing else infiltrated his searching senses.

One more step brought him within sight of the heaving lava at the core of the volcano. The churning mass seemed quieter, grayer, less liquid today.

A hot wind blasted his face. Power tingled along the fine hairs of his arms.

Suddenly the view lurched and shifted into a circling vortex of vivid red, green, yellow, and black.

Powwell's head spun. His stomach bounced. He slammed his eyes closed. The Kardia righted. Only his eyes sensed movement.

Slowly he pried open first one eye then the other. Before him lay a desert. Rock and soil—more rock than soil—lay bare in the brilliant sunshine, bleached of color by the bright light. He sensed reds and yellows beneath the glare. Strange arched rock formations sprang up out of nowhere. Mountains rose in the distance, more desert. The only vegetation in sight were stunted grasses growing out of rock crevices in the shade of larger rocks.

Just as suddenly as the view came to him, the scene lurched back into the swirling vortex. The hot wind died and the crackling energy faded.

Powwell grabbed the wall for balance, trying desperately to keep his vertigo in check while he kept the unknown desert in view.

The circles of colors and light faded and the pit returned to its normal place below the tunnel opening.

"Powwell, what are you doing down here? Staring at the pit will only mesmerize you into joining it. That is an honor reserved for the dead," Yaala said from right behind him.

Rather than answer the woman, he examined the edges of the tunnel opening, seeking a spell or other anomaly that would explain the sudden vision of distant places.

"Did you hear me, Powwell?" She tugged at his arm, attempting to draw him back through the tunnel. Behind her, Old Bertha belched and chugged in a normal machine rhythm.

"I heard. I also saw another place. I think this archway is a portal to other places." He didn't take his eyes off the opening.

"Nonsense. I told you you were hallucinating. I saw all kinds of things down here when my . . . when Yaassima first banished me. You'll get used to the heat eventually."

"How long have you been here, Yaala?" Powwell finally shifted his gaze from the portal to her face. Her heavy-lidded eyes masked her emotions, almost fading into her pale skin. He wondered briefly if he would take on the same ghastly pallor after an eternity away from sunlight.

Her high cheekbones nearly poked through her skin, revealing a long face with a determinedly outthrust chin.

No one in the pit was overweight. Most of them were gaunt skeletons, wasted away from short rations, debilitating heat, and hard work. Yaala was the healthiest of the lot and by the reckoning of some of the old men, had been here longer than most.

How much of that time was exile and how much her own choice? Powwell was suddenly fascinated with this strangely competent and self-assured woman. Almost beautiful underneath the dust and gauntness. The first stirring of interest tingled in his body.

"What use counting time when there is no sun to mark the passage of days?" She kept those heavy eyelids lowered as she turned her gaze to the boiling lava in the pit.

A spurt of lava flared up. She opened her eyes wide in the sudden red light. Powwell had never noticed the color of her eyes beneath her normally heavy lids. He couldn't see it now. A film covered her iris.

"Are you blind, Yaala?" He touched her back with a gentle hand as he looked more closely at her eyes. She dropped her gaze to her boots and wrenched away from his touch.

The pronounced bones of her spine brushed against his palm. The bumps were much bigger than those of a normal person and sharp, very sharp. He jerked his hand away, then tentatively replaced it, needing to make contact with another human being in this hellhole.

"No, I am not blind." She paused and swallowed heavily. "Come. We have work to do. Old Bertha still isn't working properly, and some of the pipes are corroded. They'll have to be replaced."

"I don't want to stay down here, Yaala. I've got to get out of here. I can't live like this."

"Get used to it. Death is the only escape from the pit, and you've seen how we dispose of the bodies." She turned on her heel and marched back toward the machinery.

Powwell looked once more to the portal, longing for a vision of the green trees that had surrounded Televarn just before he stepped into the tunnel.

The vortex lurched again, spiraling green, red, yellow, and blue—the blue of a summer sky above Coronnan. His

mouth longed for the taste of fresh, sweet water. His skin
clamored for relief from the heat. His heart begged for
freedom.

"Look, Yaala. It's doing it again!"

"Hallucination born of desperation. I've seen it before."
She kept walking away from the portal, one hand on Powwell's sleeve, dragging him with her.

"Trees! It will take us to Coronnan." Powwell pulled his
arm free of her grasp and took two rapid steps toward
escape.

Don't leave me alone, Kalen's mental voice pleaded with
him. *You have to take me with you. You have to get me out
of here. You are the only one who loves me.*

He slumped sadly against the wall. He had to wait.

Come to me soon, Kalen. I can't endure this much longer.

Chapter 20

"**I** will have to lie through my teeth to convince these hidebound lords," Quinnault said quietly. He patted Katie's hand where it rested on his arm. Since the conclusion of the negotiations with Kinnsell, he had been in constant touch with her. He kept a gentle hand at the small of her back, her hand on his arm; he brushed a stray curl from her brow; or brushed his leg against hers as they walked.

At each touch her mind brushed his, and he knew completeness. He didn't know everything about her yet. But he knew enough. She still had secrets from him, but she couldn't lie to him.

If she stepped beyond his reach for more than a heartbeat, or withdrew her mind from his, he felt cold and awkward and terribly, achingly alone.

They paused outside the Council Chamber where the lords in residence had been hastily summoned to approve the royal marriage.

"I was told that your government is new. How can these men be hidebound?" Her humor sparkled in her eyes like green stars. A mature humor despite her childlike stature. The top of her head only reached his shoulder. Her figure was hidden beneath her old-fashioned gown with a long train. The heavy woolen fabric must weigh a ton. And she'd worn it beneath the now cast-off draperies. Why wasn't she suffering from the heat generated by the thick cloth?

He wished she'd share the joke with him.

"My lords come from a long tradition of caution. Some of them believe that we have recreated the government by the few for the few. My sense of responsibility for the people and the land is new to them. They will see you as a disruption of their carefully protected privilege. Each has a candidate for my bride. They seek only to bind me closer to them and away from others rather than thinking of the security of the entire kingdom."

"Then we will have to convince them that I am precisely what they want me to be, a foreign princess who brings trade to make them rich and you grateful to them for their wealth." Her full lips pouted, and she bit her cheeks trying to hide a smile.

"They will want to see a signed treaty."

"I will have Kinnsell draw one up in the morning." This time the smile burst through her attempts at restraint.

Quinnault lost contact with the Kardia and his head as he stared at her mouth, longing to kiss her.

"We are to be married tomorrow and you haven't kissed me yet. Isn't it customary to seal a betrothal with a kiss?" She looked up at him, mouth slightly parted, eyes completely serious.

"Did you read my mind again?"

"I didn't have to. Kiss me, Scarecrow. Kiss me and make me forget my fears."

"You are a princess. Diplomatic marriages are expected of the offspring of an emperor."

"Diplomatic marriages among our own kind, among cultures that are similar to our own. Marriages that bring close alliances and the chance to visit home once in a while. You need to know that I will never again be able to contact my family or friends. I have sacrificed myself so that my people can have the Tambootie."

"Your plague must be decimating your people terribly."

"Worse."

"Do you have this mysterious plague?" Caution chilled his ardor. "Will your people bring it here, by design or chance?"

"No. I have been one of the lucky ones. The plague is one of the reasons we have disguised our appearances. The veils have been specially made to act as a barrier for the plague. If I should carry the dormant virus and pass it to our children, I know how to distill the Tambootie for a cure. Your people are safe from us."

"Then your people will be saved by the Tambootie and my people will gain a defensible port as well as a queen.

When the succession is secured, Coronnan will finally be able to put aside the fear of civil war, provided our marriage doesn't start a new one. I have worked for this moment a long time. I didn't expect to find a wife I could love and cherish, too."

"Will you kiss me to seal the bargain, then?" She reached up to pull his face down to hers.

He brushed his lips tentatively over hers, tasting the butterfly softness of her mouth. He deepened the contact. Passion exploded in him. He pulled her close against him, cherishing the way she filled his arms so naturally.

"Your Grace!" Lord Hanic exclaimed from the doorway. Shock colored his voice.

"Have the lords assembled at my request?" Quinnault asked, reluctantly lifting his head. He wanted to go on kissing Katie forever.

"Your order, more like," Hanic grumbled. "The ambassador from SeLenicca has come as well. He has that secret smile that tells me he expects you to ratify the marriage treaty with *his* princess." He eyed Katie suspiciously.

"I have accepted a better offer, Lord Hanic. Come inside, I will introduce the Council to my betrothed," Quinnault said. Nervousness assailed him. He'd hoped to break the news to the ambassador in private.

He took a deep breath and felt Katie do the same beside him. Suddenly, he knew that he couldn't tell the entire fantastic story to the foreigners. They'd take it as simply a wild tale made up to explain away an inappropriate passion.

"Whatever I say, Katie, please play along with me."

She pressed his hand in agreement.

They entered the crowded Council Chamber together, arms linked. Quinnault took the high-backed dragon throne, gesturing for Katie to sit next to him, in the chair usually reserved for Nimbulan, his chief adviser.

Five magicians sat among the lords, along with three ambassadors. In the center of the table, surrounding the Coraurlia—the fabulous, magical glass crown provided by the dragons—lay five marriage treaties. SeLenicca, Rossemeyer, and three lords all had eligible daughters. Clearly, all thought tonight's announcement would confirm one of them.

"My Lords, Master Magicians, may I present to you Princess Maarie Kaathliin of . . ." He couldn't claim she was from Varnicia, the usual trading point for the Varns. The king and his bevy of sons were well known to these men. Where could she be from? "Of Terrania." He named a remote and little known country way to the north of Varnicia.

Katie looked at him strangely. *How did you know?* she asked.

Quinnault didn't respond, sensing mental barriers crashing down between them. He'd have to ask her later about Terrania. Later. He plunged on with his speech, almost babbling in his nervousness. "My Lord Konnaught, I cannot accept your offer of your half-sister, the illegitimate daughter of Lord Kammeryl d'Astrismos, as my bride. Five years old is just too young to marry. Coronnan needs a queen now." He handed the rolled parchment to his fosterling. The fragile sheepskin was tattered on the edge, signs of much scraping clean and reuse. The boy probably didn't understand the insult this represented. His sister and the marriage weren't worth a new piece of parchment.

"My lords Hanic and Balthazaan, I must also decline the offers of your very beautiful and gracious daughters. Either one would make an admirable queen. But we are striving to set up a delicate balance of power here in Coronnan. The twelve lords representing the twelve provinces are equal in wealth and authority. I, as your king, must be a neutral binding force among you, a tie-breaking vote, dependent upon you for revenue and all but the most rudimentary warband. If I marry within Coronnan, the alliance will upset that delicate balance."

The ambassador from SeLenicca smiled smugly and crossed his arms in front of him. He sat back, satisfied. Only a frequent flicking of his gaze toward Katie betrayed any questions he might have.

"My Lord of SeLenicca, please inform His Majesty that I cannot in good conscience marry his sister. She deserves a chance at happiness, to marry the man of her own choice rather than an arranged alliance in which she has no say." He picked up the SeLenese treaty and handed it to the ambassador.

The diplomat's face turned purple with barely controlled rage. He grabbed the treaty out of Quinnault's hands, almost tearing the new parchment. "My king will not be happy about this."

"I am sorry. But my decision is made." Quinnault kept his gaze level, daring the ambassador to stalk out and declare war.

The foreign emissary reclaimed his chair, tapping the rejected treaty against the council table angrily. "Moncriith warned us you would reject us. We are prepared to defend the honor of our princess," he said. His eyes narrowed as he held the treaty out to Quinnault for reconsideration.

"If Moncriith the Bloodmage guides your king and princess, then I have even greater reason to seek elsewhere for my bride." Quinnault stared at the ambassador, challenging him to look away first.

At last the man slid the rolled parchment of the treaty into the wide sleeve of his robe.

Quinnault took a deep breath and continued. "My Lord of Rossemeyer, I must also reject the offer of your king's daughter." Quinnault directed his attention to the next issue. "The Three Kingdoms of Coronnan, Rossemeyer, and SeLenicca occupy this continent in an uneasy peace. If I marry a princess from either of my neighbors, I will again upset the balance of power."

"I understand, Your Grace." Ambassador General Jhorge-Rosse nodded his head graciously. He shot a victorious glance at his counterpart from SeLenicca. For the moment, neither one had won over the other.

"Your Grace!" Hanic protested. "You have just given King Lorriin of SeLenicca an excuse to invade us."

"He will seek war anyway. Making their princess my queen would not guarantee our safety. Read your history—or consult with the Lord Sambol about the number of times his border city has faced invasion."

"Reading is a waste of time for all but priests," Hanic scoffed.

"Reading skills may be reserved for priests and magicians, but it is not a waste of time!" Quinnault replied, holding his own anger in check. "I studied history when I trained to be a priest. I know that SeLenicca tries to take our resources by force every fifteen years or so. They refuse to nurture their own land and see ours as their rightful pantry when they can't buy food elsewhere. Marrying the

Princess of SeLenicca will give us a few seasons of peace, nothing more."

The ambassador narrowed his eyes as if he hadn't expected Quinnault to be so well informed.

"Your Grace, you must marry and get an heir," Lord Balthazaan reminded them all. "Do you remember what happened the last time a king of Coronnan failed to do so? We endured three generations of civil war trying to find a successor!" He stood, leaning his knuckles on the table. His eyes blazed with fear. He had suffered large losses during the war. His lovely dark-eyed daughter was the only asset he had left beside a badly damaged keep and nearly ruined farmlands.

"You have rejected all viable offers, Your Grace. Where do we look for a new candidate?" Hanic nearly screamed. He stared at Katie. Questions and fear swept across his face in rapid succession.

"Her Highness, Maarie Kaathliin of Terrania, will be my bride," Quinnault said quietly.

All eyes in the room turned to Katie. She blushed slightly and lowered her eyes in maidenly modesty.

"The treaty I have negotiated with her father, King Kinnsell requires that I marry her tomorrow evening."

"Your Grace!" every lord in the room protested.

"This haste is most unseemly," Hanic said. His eyes narrowed as he scanned the princess, looking for flaws.

"Forgive the interruption, Your Grace, my lords." Old Lyman stood from his chair near the corner. "I realize that magicians are supposed to be neutral advisers in this new government, but I have some pertinent information."

The lords turned their malevolent glares to the aging magician.

"Senior Magician Nimbulan has been in secret negotiation with King Kinnsell for nearly a year." Lyman looked at Quinnault, his eyes twinkling and his mouth twitching at the obvious lie.

Katie coughed delicately into her tiny hand. Quinnault recognized her failing attempt to keep a straight face. Were the two conspirators in this lie?

"Even now, Nimbulan is working with King Kinnsell in completing the treaty. This marriage has been planned for a long time. But we feared news of it would jeopardize the rather delicate negotiations. A wedding tomorrow will not be in quite so much haste as you imagine." The old man paused while he swallowed deeply. He cocked his head as if listening.

Who gave him orders?

Quinnault hoped desperately that the dragons spoke to him directly.

"Look at our king, my lords!" Hanic turned his attention away from Lyman's almost plausible explanation. After all, Nimbulan wasn't present to confirm or deny the lie. "He's head over heels in love with the chit. He can't have met her more than once. In love after *one* meeting. She's worked some form of enchantment on him. She's a witch or a demon. Who is to say that the legendary country of Terrania even exists? She's a demon, and we cannot allow this marriage!"

"I will marry Princess Maarie Kaathliin tomorrow," Quinnault said through gritted teeth. "The choice is mine and I have made it."

"We will not crown her queen until she proves she is not a demon!" Konnaught stood up so fast he knocked over his chair. "Moncriith predicted this would happen. He was my father's Battlemage. He warned us all about demons—including the king's exiled sister."

"Moncriith would have been exiled or executed, had he lived, because he refused to gather dragon magic. Moncriith drew his power from blood and pain. We don't know how long he would have contented himself with his own blood and the death of small animals. His next victim would have been human, probably one of us," Quinnault reminded them.

"This unknown, possibly false princess, can't gather dragon magic—no woman can. But she might be a magician working in secret to undermine our peace and stability." Hanic sat down, seemingly calm. "She must prove that she is indeed a princess of Terrania and not a rogue witch."

"How?" Cold sweat broke out on Quinnault's brow. The magicians couldn't access the void with dragon magic to test her talent. All of the usual witchsniffers who sensed magic in others but had no other talent of their own had been exiled with the other rogues. Only magicians could survive the other tests for magical talent—fire and water.

The only way Katie could prove herself innocent of Hanic's accusation was to die.

He wouldn't abuse her trust or the wonderful gifts from her people by allowing these men to murder her in the name of protecting Coronnan from rogue magic.

"The dragons will tell us if she is the right queen for the king they blessed," Lyman said quietly from his corner.

All eyes turned to the Coraurlia in the center of the table. The glass crown shaped like a dragon head and embedded with costly jewels had been a gift from the dragons as a symbol of their tie to the wearer of the crown.

Quinnault relaxed. The dragons approved of Katie. He knew that in his heart.

An evil smile crossed Hanic's face. "Yes, the dragons. She must face a dragon at dawn. Shayla will eat her alive."

"Dragons don't exist. How can they test me?" Katie whispered. Bewilderment erased the smile from her eyes.

"A demon will become hysterical and flee in its true form when faced by a dragon." Hanic's smile spread with confidence. "If this so-called princess of Terrania can remain in human form in the presence of a dragon, we will accept her as your bride, Your Grace."

But no one had seen a dragon in almost a moon. Shayla had announced to one and all that the Covenant was broken. The amount of magic in the air had dwindled. Would she come in answer to this summons?

If she didn't, would Katie survive another test dreamed up by these superstitious lords?

Chapter 21

"Those, 'wires,' as you call them, barely fit through that conduit. How do you expect me to crawl in there and find the broken one?" Powwell asked Yaala. He eyed the narrow tunnel skeptically. He'd just begun to get used to the miles of Kardia above his head and breathe almost naturally within this extensive cave system. The bottom of the conduit rose man height above the cavern where he stood. It couldn't contain enough air for both him and the bundle of wires.

An eerie sensation crawled over his skin; it felt as if he were being watched. He looked hastily in all directions. A flicker of white moved beyond his peripheral vision as fast as he turned his head.

More hallucinations. Or so Yaala said. But she said that Televarn's portal was imaginary, too.

"The conduit is wide enough. I've crawled through it a number of times," Yaala said as she cupped her hands to boost Powwell up.

"You're thinner than I am. And some of the others are narrower in the shoulders than I. Why me?" Powwell kept both feet firmly on the ground, lungs laboring mightily at the thought of entering that tiny tunnel. He'd already discovered that, in the pit, Yaala gave orders and everyone obeyed her without question—except the new man, Piedro, and he'd learn soon enough. Yaala was the Kaalipha of the pit, just as Yaassima was Kaalipha of the city above them.

"You haven't lost your intelligence, so you will recognize the broken wire when you find it," she said, motioning for him to place his foot into her hands.

"You've been here longer than most everyone else. Why haven't you lost your intelligence?"

"Because I haven't given in to my fears and panic. Because I love the machines. I'd rather live here with them than aboveground with Yaassima."

"Then why don't you go into that conduit? You know these machines—you love these machines as if they were your familiars."

"You will go, Powwell, because I'm training you to know and love these machines as if they were more than your familiars. They are family. The day will come when you will need them. They will need you. I need another engineer to keep things going."

"Yaala!" a man's voice echoed down the corridor from the upper levels of the pit. "Yaala, they need the engineer to fix something above."

Powwell jumped at the words. *"Above!"*

"Coming," Yaala called back. "You'd better come, too. You need to know how Yaassima's toys work." She strode toward the passage out of this small cavern. A very deep cavern. "Oh, and as soon as we get beyond the gate, I'm no longer Yaala. I'm the Engineer. Yaassima doesn't bother with names as long as the job gets done. She thinks I'm dead. I want her to continue thinking that until . . . until I'm ready."

"We're getting out of here? Yaala, if I get out of this place, I won't come back." Powwell could only think of clean sweet air and natural light.

"Yes, you will come back. There isn't anyplace else to go, and I'm not yet ready to kill Yaassima. I have to know everything about these machines before I'll have the power to murder my mother and take her place as Kaalipha."

"I see that the dragon bitch gave you one of the better pieces of jewelry," Maia sneered as she sorted laundry in Myri's bedroom. "Televarn won't like it."

"I don't care what Televarn likes and doesn't like," Myri replied. She sat rocking in the nursing chair. Amaranth suckled greedily. Her tug against Myri's breast sent a deep wave of satisfaction through her entire being. The faint milky scent of the baby and the smell of fresh sunshine in the laundry almost made her content. Almost.

The weight of the necklace and her own lack of freedom preyed on her mind. How was she to escape if the necklace killed her as she left the palace? Nastfa and Golin had already shown their sympathy with her by escorting her politely around the palace rather than molesting her as Yaassima promised. They hadn't said anything the dragon pendant couldn't relay to Yaassima. But Myri sensed their emotions. Nastfa in particular. He didn't belong here and wanted out as badly as she.

Every time she was with the proud member of the assassins guild, she had more questions about him than before. All she knew for sure was that he'd help her escape if she could break the necklace. If . . . how?

She sent the chair rocking faster to absorb her emotions before the baby sensed her disquiet and became fretful. The old wood of the chair creaked in time to her movement.

She and Maia moved around each other in cautious, untouching circles, sharing the room, the rocker, the laundry—but never the baby. Maia didn't push the issue of nursing Amaranth unless Yaassima was present. Since the Kaalipha had given the necklace to Myri, she left the two younger women alone a lot.

Neither Myri nor Maia seemed to want to openly antagonize the other. Equally, they were unwilling to offer friendship.

"Well, you'd better start thinking about what Televarn wants. He won't leave you here for long. He never gives up something he claims as his own," Maia said bitterly. She snapped the diaper she was folding so hard the air crackled around it.

"Including you and Kestra?" Myri asked. He'd surrendered both women to Yaassima's brothel as part of his "rent" here in Hanassa.

"We are only on loan until he's ready to reclaim us," Maia said weakly. She dipped her head, suddenly very busy folding a mountain of diapers.

"You don't say that as if you believe it."

"I say what I am told to say."

"Told by Televarn. I know something of the way he controls your actions and your mind. You don't have to put up with him."

"You don't know anything." Maia closed her mouth with a snap and turned her rigid back on Myri.

"I know that Televarn has to control everything he touches—including the minds and thoughts of his clan. You don't have to go back to Yaassima's brothel. You have other choices. Other men are not so selfish. Another man will give you a healthy baby. Your baby died because its father was too closely related to you. My husband didn't father your child. Televarn did." Myri repeated the rumors she'd overheard in her exploration of the palace. She longed to say more. The necklace reminded her that Yaassima heard every word spoken in Myri's presence.

"For women in Hanassa, there is no other choice. I accept Televarn's orders or Yaassima's, and they both want me to be the toy of any man they choose. Any other action brings death or the pit." Maia gulped, then firmed her chin.

"As soon as any child I bear is weaned, Televarn will take him from me, just as he took my first son from me," Maia continued. "I thought that Nimbulan was strong enough to change things in the clan, but he deserted me. He deserted you, too. We're both Yaassima's whores right now. That jewelry marks you as clearly as the tattoo she put on my butt." Angrily Maia flipped up her skirt and dropped her drawers enough to reveal the outline of a dragon drawn in blue ink spread across her left cheek. "The dragon bitch enjoyed every scream I let loose. She watched while her men did this to me, and she drooled while they did it. I couldn't sit or lie on my back for over a week afterward.

"Does Televarn know?" Thankfully Amaranth drifted off to sleep, little milk bubbles caressing her puckered lips. The baby wouldn't know the horror Myri felt at the evidence of Yaassima's continued cruelty. Some of her resentment of the Rover woman drained away. They had both been used by Televarn. They were both victims of Yaassima's complicated plans.

"I don't know. He wasn't there when they did it to me. He won't like it if he sees it. It marks me as Yaassima's property, not his."

Myri longed to reassure the woman that she would include her in the escape plans. She couldn't promise. Kalen, Powwell, and Amaranth had to take priority.

"Neither Televarn nor Yaassima will give up anything they possess," Maia reminded her. "Remember that when you try to escape. They'll kill you rather than give you up. Your children, too."

"What makes you think I plot escape?" Myri asked mildly, remembering that Yaassima listened.

"Because you're a dragon just like the Kaalipha. You have to try, and you will die in the process."

Nimbulan and Rollett wandered into a wineshop—one of a dozen or so scattered throughout Hanassa. So far they'd discovered no inns. People either slept in the cave of their sponsor or sat up all night, drinking and gambling. All of the businesses seemed to be owned by the Kaalipha and run by people loyal to her. How deep that loyalty ran, Nimbulan couldn't tell without a great deal of money for bribes. The guards at the gate had stolen his only valuable coins.

Perhaps they'd get a little information in this hovel built out from the back side of a large rock formation. He assumed that all life within Hanassa took its orientation from the palace which dominated the south wall of the crater. The outcropping stood between the wineshop and the palace. The gate—the only gate into or out of the city—lay on the west side of Hanassa. This place was dirtier and more decrepit than all of the other wineshops combined. The Kaalipha's authority seemed less present, out of sight of the palace.

The stench of unwashed bodies, spilled wine, garbage, and refuse assaulted Nimbulan's senses. He shuddered in revulsion beneath his enveloping robes. He thought he'd become inured to the filth in the city. This shop was worse, much worse, than he'd thought. Information might come cheaper here.

Rollett loosened his belt knife. His eyes shifted restlessly in the gloom. Instinctively he stepped behind Nimbulan, guarding his back.

No one seemed to notice their entry. Strangers must not be that unusual here. Nimbulan sat down on a backless stool, the only empty one, near the center of the four-table room. One leg was shorter than the others and he teetered precariously, grabbing the table for balance. The crude planks wobbled when he braced his weight. Five cups of wine already on the table sloshed onto the stained and scarred surface.

Rollett remained standing, wary and alert. Nimbulan had never fully appreciated the young man's ability to observe and absorb detail until now. By the time they left, Rollett would know much more about the people in this wineshop than Nimbulan could have found out in days of conversation.

Five pairs of eyes glared at him with anger and distaste. The owners of those eyes all wore the uniform loose black robes and turbans of Rossemeyerian mercenaries. Dangerous men to offend.

He shrugged and held up his hand to order his own drink and one for Rollett, though he knew his journeyman wouldn't drink it until he had finished observing.

After several long moments of silence, Nimbulan raised his eyes from his cup of rancid wine to confront his equally silent companions. "Where does one find a woman in this town?" he asked.

The man across from him smiled so that the scar running temple to temple across the bridge of his nose whitened. His eyelids didn't shift. "Depends on what kind of woman you want," he replied.

"The Kaalipha keeps the best ones in the palace for her private guards. Our sponsor has a few for his men. Lots of hiring right now. You interested in hiring on?" asked the fair-skinned teenager to Nimbulan's left. His skin wasn't dark enough for him to be a native of Rossemeyer.

Nimbulan schooled his face to keep from betraying his questions.

"How's your sponsor pay?" This was the most information Nimbulan had been able to glean from a night of drinking in every shop in Hanassa.

"One Rosse a day during downtime. Two while on campaign. A share in the loot if we win," Scarface answered. "And free access to his women. They aren't the youngest or the prettiest, but they're all pros and you don't have to tip unless you really want to." He grinned again, revealing several gaps in his teeth.

"What's he hiring for?" Nimbulan asked.

"Big invasion of Coronnan from SeLenicca. Every sponsor in Hanassa is looking for experienced men. Your robes and turbans mark you as veterans."

Nimbulan nodded. "I'll think about it."

"You want to look at the women first?" The teenager laughed and slapped Nimbulan's back.

"I like blondes myself," Nimbulan said.

Everyone in the room stilled.

Nimbulan's heart beat loudly within his chest. What had he said wrong? Rollett shifted his body closer to Nimbulan, so that their backs touched and no one obstructed their peripheral vision.

"Only true blondes in the city are the Kaalipha and her heir," the teenager whispered. He hadn't removed his hand from Nimbulan's back. "Don't talk about them, and don't ask to see them. Kaalipha Yaassima sells all blonde captives within a day."

Nimbulan's skin crawled. How else would one describe Myrilandel's almost colorless hair other than blond? One of the two women had to be his wife. The vision had shown Myri to be in Hanassa. What was she doing in the palace, the Kaalipha's designated heir? He believed she had been kidnapped by Televarn.

Reluctant babble broke out across the room as the drinkers recovered from Nimbulan's stated preference. He knew the Kaalipha was respected, almost revered, she had the power of life and death over all within Hanassa and dispensed her favors liberally, with conditions. He hadn't known the depth of fear she inflicted upon her people.

"We need the work. Blondes or no blondes in the brothel." Nimbulan decided to change the subject. Maybe he could work his way back to Myri and the Kaalipha later.

"You got into Hanassa, you can't be a spy for Coronnan. Spies get murdered in the entrance tunnel. Our captain needs men willing to commit for a year. His Majesty of SeLenicca put out a call for every mercenary company that's willing. Paying well, I hear. No questions asked. Seems there's to be no restraint on looting and slaves when he wins the war." Scarface's mouth twitched as if savoring a fine delicacy. He placed his hand on the teenager's shoulder. Indirectly, he was in contact with Nimbulan.

Magicians did that to read a stranger's mind. Was he overly suspicious or were these men magicians in disguise? That would account for the pale skin.

Nimbulan gulped back a retort. He had to get back to Coronnan fast. Quinnault needed this information to mount a defense. What had the new king done to precipitate an invasion? Nimbulan had only been gone a few days.

He couldn't leave Hanassa without Myri and Powwell and Kalen. He had to find Maia and her baby, too.

"Moncriith's coming!" a man shouted from the doorway.

Several drinkers scrambled out the door. Rollett took one step away from Nimbulan, as if to follow them. When Nimbulan didn't immediately run from the pub, Rollett resumed his protective stance.

Why not run? Moncriith will recognize you, he asked telepathically.

Nimbulan didn't answer immediately. His senses reeled with this second blow. Moncriith. The Bloodmage who had stalked Coronnan from one end to the other preaching against demons. He saw Myrilandel as the source of all demonic evil in Coronnan.

Our drinking companions look wary but not alarmed, he replied finally. Then out loud he asked, "I heard Moncriith died a year ago. Struck down by King Quinnault's magicians in battle."

"Take more than a dragon to kill that one. Better hide your magic deep, stranger," the teenager advised.

Nimbulan raised one eyebrow in question.

"The dragon bitch has her knickers in a twist about foreign magicians. She gave Moncriith permission to sponsor his own mercenary camp if he'd root out a foreign magician with a blue aura," the young man continued.

Dragon bitch? Myrilandel carried dragon blood in her veins.

"New law announced three or four weeks ago, right after the Rovers delivered the heir to the Kaalipha. Seems some foreign magician was holding the woman hostage with magic. Most crimes, the Kaalipha gives a man a trial before she lops off his head. For the crime of being an unidentified magician with blue in his aura, it's immediate death and a huge reward to the accuser. That's when we became mercenaries instead of Battlemages for hire."

"But there's no blue in your auras," Nimbulan protested.

"Why take the chance?" Scarface replied. "Moncriith can't be trusted. He sees auras, the Kaalipha doesn't. He could accuse anyone and she'd be happy to execute the man just to see the blood spill. We're safe as long as we don't work magic in Hanassa. You, on the other hand, radiate blue in all directions."

Chapter 22

Televarn tapped his foot impatiently. Wiggles raced around his toes in sympathy. Kalen had sent him a message by way of her familiar to meet her in this narrow corridor near the palace kitchens. She was late.

Why was it that in the outer world women jumped to his command and took no action without his permission? But here, in Hanassa, he did nothing but wait for women to make up their minds?

It was all Yaassima's fault. She'd pay dearly for giving women ideas of power and independence.

Soon. He was almost ready to depose the Kaalipha and yank her dragon throne right out from under her skinny bottom.

He smiled slightly. Yaassima had done him a favor without knowing it. She had placed Kalen in a position of trust within her household.

He had to watch Kalen closely. He'd spent several moons corrupting her before he'd kidnapped Myrilandel into Hanassa. Why the girl had chosen to betray Myri, the only adult who had not used Kalen and her talent for their own ends, he had no idea.

Televarn had promised Kalen power in the new regime. That promise had granted him cooperation—not trust or loyalty.

The girl owed loyalty only to herself and could betray him at the least offense. When she did, Yaassima's retribution would be terrible and swift.

When she betrayed him. Why hadn't he thought "If she betrayed him?"

He expected betrayal, just as Kalen did. Better the snake he knew than the viper he didn't.

Wiggles stopped playing with Televarn's foot. The creature ceased all motion in mid-ripple. His back fur stood up. Then he darted along the corridor to the next bend. He seemed to flow around the imperfections in the tunnel like liquid fur.

Televarn held his breath. Why had the ferret deserted him? His hand shifted to his belt knife without conscious thought. The fine blade he had stashed at the entrance to the pit rather than risk the searches at the palace gate.

Piedro guarded the growing stash of weapons in the pit. He also sought the secrets of the monstrous machines Yaassima seemed to cherish.

Two heartbeats later, Kalen appeared. She bent to gather the ferret into her arms. A smile lit Kalen's eyes as she nuzzled her familiar.

Wiggles joyfully slithered up to her shoulder and draped himself around her neck like a lover. His needle-sharp teeth chattered perilously close to the great artery in her neck.

A lump of apprehension formed in Televarn's throat. What if the animal had turned rabid? He kept his hand on his knife wondering if he could move fast enough to kill the ferret without harming Kalen.

He pushed aside his concern for the girl. She was a tool. Nothing more. Tools could be replaced.

"You're late," he snapped out his words more harshly and louder than he'd intended. It might be the middle of the night, but the nearby kitchen bustled with activity all day, every day, without stop. The staff never knew when the Kaalipha might order a meal for one or a hundred. Any one of them could spot him talking to Kalen and report to Yaassima.

"I don't have the freedom of the palace like some people," she returned, just as harshly.

"Where is Myrilandel, and will she help us overthrow Yaassima?" He started pacing, pointedly not looking at the little girl. She'd grown in the two weeks since he'd seen her. Her body was losing its boxy shape and had started showing signs of the curves she would eventually develop. But she was still a little girl and he was not interested in her. Myrilandel was the only woman he lusted after.

"She will help. I have made certain of that. But she refuses to believe Nimbulan dead. Tell me again how you accomplished it so that I can give her the grisly details. Maybe then she will accept my word as truth," Kalen ordered. She continued to caress Wiggles rather than direct her gaze to Televarn.

Televarn looked at her through narrowed eyes, resenting her lack of respect for him. He had to play his hand carefully with her or trigger betrayal.

He turned his thoughts to the problem before them. Myrilandel had to be convinced that her husband had died. She would never become his queen as long as Nimbulan lived. She'd made vows before a priest, vows that could only be broken by death. Once released from her miserable husband, she would welcome Televarn again as she had for a brief time a year ago.

"I didn't see Nimbulan die," he admitted.

"What do you mean, you did not see him die? He has to be dead!"

"I set the trap. Wiggles was part of it and returned to me when it was sprung. Ask him how the magician died." Televarn resumed his pacing. A niggle of doubt thrust its way into his brain. Nimbulan had to be dead. Wiggles had slithered under the sealed door. But he couldn't leave the magician's private quarters until the door opened—the magic of the spell bound him there as it did the Water. The Water had supported Wiggles, kept him from drowning. Nimbulan had the only key to the door.

"Someone drowned in your trap," Kalen muttered, gazing deeply into the ferret's eyes. A look of rapt joy softened her features while she communed with her familiar. Hints of adult beauty—cold and austere—showed in the planes of her face and the luster in her clear gray eyes.

The only other time he'd seen her look so happy, so vulnerable was . . . never. Televarn wondered when she had become so bitter.

"Wiggles ran past a male, with Water following close behind in an angry wave. As he exited the building, he brushed against two more males, taller men. They smelled mature. The first one's scent wasn't as strong." Kalen looked up, startled. "Nimbulan might not be dead. The male who triggered the trap was just a boy."

"*S'murgit!* That man has more lives than a cat. What do I have to do to kill him?"

"Nothing. All that is important is that Myri believes he is dead and that Yaassima ordered the assassination."

"The Kaalipha put out a contract, and I accepted it. But she won't pay up until I can prove he's dead." He slammed one fist into the palm of his other hand. He needed that money to pay men to storm the palace. Hundreds of men fighting alongside every Rover he could secretly gather into Hanassa. They wouldn't do it without money. A lot of money.

But if Myrilandel or Kalen could be coerced into killing Yaassima first, his plan would prove much easier to carry out.

"Tell Myrilandel what you know. Tell her how Wiggles witnessed the death of the only person who could open Nimbulan's sealed door. Remind her that Yaassima controls the reward for the death of Nimbulan and Quinnault. Tell her whatever you have to so that Myrilandel demands revenge. Revenge by her own hand. Yaassima will die and Myrilandel will be my queen. I will give her children she can adore, children who have no connection to the magician who enslaved her for her talent."

"If either woman lets you live long enough to rule." Kalen smiled sarcastically with one corner of her mouth. She continued stroking Wiggles.

"I've never heard of a magician hiding his talent before," Nimbulan said around a very dry throat.

"Then learn to do it in a hurry." Scarface grabbed Nimbulan's wrist on the table. "I'll take you into a trance and show you where to look."

Nimbulan didn't have time to ask why these men were cutthroat mercenaries in Hanassa when they might be employed as honest magicians elsewhere. The void opened before his eyes as Scarface breathed deeply in the first stages of trance. Nimbulan followed him, sensing the urgency. Rollett moved closer, placing his hand on top of Scarface's. Nimbulan wasn't certain if his companion joined the trance or merely monitored it.

Three deep breaths brought him into rapport with Aaddler, Scarface. The void revealed true names, ideals, and

faults. Nimbulan scanned his companion carefully, seeking
a source of trust. Before he could examine more than the
constant pain behind his eyes from the old wound, Aaddler
said, "Nimbulan, I know you from old. We faced each other
as Battlemages. I know you to be honest and true to your
oaths. Trust me. Look into your heart's aura. Look for
the beacon."

Nimbulan had never heard of an individual organ having
an aura, he'd always looked at the layers of energy that
enveloped the entire body. Those layers had to begin somewhere.

Another's colors were always easier to see than one's
own. He searched Aaddler in the region of his heart. Sure
enough, a tiny flare of dark green light pulsed there. Dark
green suited Aaddler—suppressed fire hiding behind logic
and reason. He remembered him now. They had fought to
a standstill fifteen years ago. Both patrons had withdrawn
from the battle. Aaddler had saluted Nimbulan in respect
for his talent and retreated honorably.

*Find your own beacon. This is the core of your magic.
The beginning and the end. Find it quickly.*

Do it! Rollett added. *I sense Moncriith is very close. His
thoughts revolve around destroying every magician he en-
counters.*

Nimbulan looked deep within himself. He knew his signature color was blue, had identified it long ago when still
an apprentice. The layers of his own energy flared and
blinded him.

Follow the life-cord backward! If a mental voice could
hiss, Aaddler hissed. *I can't afford to be caught with you,
Nimbulan. Your guilt will become my guilt. You are the
magician Yaassima seeks to eliminate. You are the husband
of her heir and the only person who can take the heir and
her baby away.*

The news of a baby slid into his awareness. Did Yaassima
have control of Maia's baby as well as Myrilandel?

With a deep breath, Nimbulan found the blue-and-silver
umbilical that trailed from his corporeal body into the void.
Wrapped tightly around it was a crystal-and-pale-lavender
umbilical. *Myrilandel!* He'd found her at last. If he followed
her umbilical, he'd be beside her in an instant. But only in
his mind. Living bodies couldn't traverse the void.

He traced the umbilical back into his own body. Each layer of energy was thicker, more resilient. He pushed harder until he faced a blazing blue light like a thousand sapphires sparkling in sunlight.

There. Now grasp the beacon and place it atop the physical table.

Nimbulan followed instructions. The pulsing blue energy didn't want to leave his body. His magical talent had defined his life for so long it had become entwined with his very soul.

Yank it out. Now. We haven't time to waste. The Bloodmage enters this abode, Rollett ordered as his own blue-and-red beacon slid into the wood grain of the table's surface.

Reluctantly, Nimbulan thrust the beacon out of his body. Once free of his personal energy, the light dimmed. He needed all of his willpower to keep himself from rejoining with his talent. His body was but an empty shell without it.

Drop the damn thing onto the table. Aaddler nearly deafened Nimbulan's mental hearing.

He obeyed. His talent spread out into a gentle puddle with clearly defined edges. His talent filled a space shaped like a hand, fingers slightly curved—the gesture he used to gather magic. Aaddler's puddle took on the shape of an open mouth, tongue tasting the air. Rollett's looked like two eyes connected by a furrowed brow.

Let your talent merge with the wood. The Bloodmage can't find it embedded in an inanimate object. Good. Now lighten your trance so that you are aware of your body and the room around you. You will have to react to Moncriith as if he is no threat. Aaddler withdrew slightly from the rapport he and Nimbulan shared.

"Don't take your hands off the table." Scarface nudged Nimbulan's knee with his boot beneath the wooden surface. "You have to stay in contact with your talent, or you'll lose it forever."

Chapter 23

Nimbulan kept his eyes glued to his wine cup. He waited for the hair on the back of his neck to bristle as a warning that Moncriith approached. His body remained inert. The faint sensory tingles on his skin that told him much of what happened around him evaporated with the removal of his talent.

Colors faded before his eyes. A general numbness began to creep through his body. He bit his lip to control his panic.

He pressed his hand harder against the table where his talent lay. The wooden surface contained six other puddles. None of the five mercenaries, nor Rollett, seemed overly concerned with the separation from their talents.

Nimbulan's knuckles turned white where he gripped the table.

"He'll leave soon enough." Scarface grinned in sympathy. "He's single-minded enough to ignore anyone without an obvious talent."

"He could get us into the palace, Nimbulan. He has the Kaalipha's ear," Rollett whispered.

"I won't risk becoming his ally," Nimbulan replied. "He's too dangerous."

Nimbulan heard footsteps behind him. Heavily booted feet. He couldn't detect any other clues to the man's identity and nearly panicked. He needed his talent to survive.

Moncriith would sense the talent and condemn him on the spot.

"Stand up, soldier," Moncriith ordered. He pressed a knee into Nimbulan's back as a prod.

Nimbulan resisted the urge to turn and look at the man,

see how he had changed in the last year. He wanted to demand how the man dared survive the last battle in Coronnan when Ackerly, Nimbulan's assistant and oldest friend, had died. Instead, he said defiantly, "You ain't my officer."

Scarface nodded ever so slightly in acknowledgment of the tactic.

"Yaassima, Kaalipha of Hanassa, gave me the authority to sponsor my own troop of mercenaries. Lorriin, King of SeLenicca, marches into Coronnan as soon as I have gathered my forces. I can gather soldiers any way I choose to. I choose all of you present."

"You'll have to debate that with our captain," Scarface said. "We have signed blood oaths to follow him to the death."

Nimbulan gulped back a protest. He couldn't sign an oath like that. He had no intention of staying with these men any longer than he had to. As soon as he found Myri, he would leave and never return.

"Your captain fell to my blade less than an hour ago," Moncriith boasted.

All heads turned to stare at a man's severed right hand. Two rings glinted on the lifeless fingers. Blood dripped from the stump onto the floor. Even if the owner of the hand lived, he'd never wield a sword again.

Moncriith held his bloody trophy up in his left hand while he twirled a long knife in his right. Traces of blood lingered on the blade.

"I'm surprised he didn't bring the man's head," Scarface muttered bitterly.

"The head would involve an instant kill. No more pain. As long as he has the hand and the victim lives, he can fuel his magic with the pain," Nimbulan replied. Outrage at Moncriith's casual dismissal of life boiled up from his gut.

Briefly, Nimbulan noted the new scars that creased the Bloodmage's face and arms. He hadn't given up his vile magic that required blood and pain for fuel. If he was recruiting mercenaries, his war would be a crusade. With the new invasion of Coronnan by SeLenicca, Moncriith could carry his demon hunt right back to the dragons that now protected King Quinnault and the Commune of Magicians—presuming they would return now that he actively searched for Myri.

What had he said? King Lorriin marched when Moncriith was ready! Who organized this campaign, the king or the Bloodmage?

Stargods! He had to get back to the capital soon, with his wife, Kalen, and Powwell. He didn't know either of Myri's adopted children well, but he'd not leave behind anyone she loved.

"By your oaths in blood you must now follow me, the man who defeated your captain in single combat." Moncriith kicked the stool out from under the teenager to Nimbulan's right. The boy lurched sideways, keeping one hand on the tabletop.

Nimbulan bit his lip to keep from crying out. The boy's fingers had slipped away from the puddle of his talent. He darted a look to Scarface to see if this condemned the boy to a mundane life or not.

Scarface replied with a tiny shake of the head, then lifted his chin ever so slightly toward the teenager's puddle. It had spread within the grain of wood to reach his fingertips.

Nimbulan relaxed a little. As long as he touched some portion of the table, his talent was safe.

"By my vision from the Stargods and the authority of the Kaalipha, I claim your loyalty. I have the power to make you obey me." Moncriith touched the partially coagulated blood on the hand and chanted a string of unrecognizable words.

Even without his magic, Nimbulan recognized the spell the Bloodmage wove—a compulsion to follow him blindly.

"We have to get out of here, fast," he whispered to Scarface.

"Not without my talent. If I grab it and run past the Bloodmage, he'll know me for what I am."

"Is there another way out of here?"

"Not unless you want to dig a hole through solid rock into the volcano."

"If we let him capture us, we'll get into the palace. We can turn on him once we're inside," Rollett reminded them.

Moncriith increased the volume of his chant. All around them, men's faces took on glazed looks. Already the need to obey pushed at Nimbulan. He willed it aside.

"On my count of five, grab your talent and run for the door, don't try to attack the Bloodmage, and don't look back," Nimbulan murmured to the men closest to him. "Whatever you do, don't touch Moncriith or that bloody artifact. If you do, you will be marked by magic, and he'll be able to follow and command you anywhere."

Five men nodded. Nimbulan kept his eyes on Moncriith, waiting for the crucial moment between partial awareness while he set up the spell and a full trance when he had total command of everyone within reach of his aura.

"One . . . two . . . three, four, five!" Nimbulan closed his eyes, wrapped both hands around the tiny sapphire beacon on the table and dashed for the door.

Moncriith ended his chant and spread his arms to gather the auras of all the men in the room.

Nimbulan ducked and rolled past the Bloodmage. Moncriith's hand brushed his shoulder. He opened his eyes wide, fully aware.

"Nimbulan! There. Grab the foreign magician. Yaassima will reward us greatly for his head!" Moncriith shouted.

Rollett stumbled into Moncriith, knocking the heavier man off balance. He fell against the table Nimbulan and the others had just vacated. The bloody hand flew out of Moncriith's grasp and landed flat against Rollett's chest.

The young man's eyes glazed over. His mouth gaped slightly. He turned and faced Moncriith, obedient and docile.

In unison with the men in the wineshop, Rollett unsheathed his sword and marched after Nimbulan.

Sweat broke out on Televarn's brow and under his arms. His legs twitched restlessly beneath his sleeping furs. He flung out his arms seeking his bedmate. His mate. His bride.

Myrilandel.

He clutched only cold air within the Rover cavern in Hanassa. Thirty-three days she had been his in that secluded cove on the Great Bay. His, body and soul. Over a year had passed since he had possessed her unconditional love.

Over a year since she had deserted him. Myrilandel, the only woman who had ever left *him*. He couldn't rest until he bedded her again and wiped the memory of Nimbulan from her mind.

Enough! He thrust his sleeping furs into the corner. He'd

not wait another day to wrest control of Hanassa from Yaassima's hands. By the time the sun set again, he would claim Myrilandel as his wife, and together they would dip their hands in the Kaalipha's blood.

"Get up." He kicked his uncle in the small of the older man's back. "Marshal all of our people and give them weapons. We storm the palace from within and without at dawn."

"Where are you going?" Uncle Vaanyim groaned and pressed his hands where Televarn had kicked him. Then he sat up and rubbed his eyes sleepily.

"To claim some favors a scar-faced mercenary owes me."

"What about the slaves, do we arm them, too?"

"Why not? We need numbers of people to overwhelm the guards before they can slap their wands and freeze us all."

"The slaves may turn on us and try to escape."

"So what? They will cause more chaos at the gates. Arm everyone you can find. If you run out of weapons here, you know where we have stored the extras in the pit." Another advantage of the dragongate. Over the past two years, he'd brought in large numbers of swords, spears, and clubs from outside and hidden them in the rabbit warren of tunnels that led beneath the palace to the pit. The means of the Kaalipha's destruction had never passed her guards with their detection wands.

He reminded himself to force the secret of those wands from Yaassima before he lopped off her head with her own execution weapon.

"Televarn, tell Scarface to bring all of his magician companions." Uncle Vaanyim rolled stiffly to his knees. "We'll need them to neutralize the wands at the palace gate."

What to do with the loose talent in his hands? Nimbulan wondered as he ran from the filthy wineshop.

His table companions ran past him, also holding their magical abilities in their hands. They all needed a moment of quiet privacy to reabsorb the talents.

Rollett. What had the boy done with his talent? Nimbulan needed his magic to break Moncriith's spell upon the journeyman magician. But his talent made him an easily recognizable target.

The sound of marching feet behind him spurred Nimbulan to run faster in his companions' wake. He stumbled over an imperfection in the ground. His knee twisted under him with an audible crack. He resisted the urge to brace his fall with his hands. His face met the Kardia. A sharp rock stabbed his chest. Fire ran up his leg from the wrenched ligaments in his knee.

"Spread out, men. Bring me that magician alive!" Moncriith ordered.

The Kardia reverberated beneath Nimbulan's body from the force of the men marching in unison. Probably thinking in unison, too. Televarn's spells did that to his followers as well.

Nimbulan turned over, still cupping his hands around his talent. He needed a place to hide it and himself. An inanimate object he could hold.

His staff! Where in Simurgh's hells was the thing?

As he thought about his valuable tool, a long stick rolled toward him, resting against his hands where he held his talent. The staff had found the magic talent that had molded the grain and shaped the knobs and bends in the once straight tree branch.

Quickly Nimbulan thrust the tiny blue beacon into the staff, a nearly inanimate object that Moncriith should not sense.

He still had to break the Bloodmage's hold upon Rollett. Perhaps there was a mundane method. What? Villagers used them all the time to break curses, real and imaginary. He'd never paid enough attention to the lives of people outside the army and the training of Battlemages. Myri would know.

The footsteps came closer. Nimbulan tucked his miserable knee beneath him. He bit his lip until he tasted blood to keep from crying out in pain. Awkwardly he scrunched into the nearest shadow. His staff seemed to melt into the darkness with him.

A blazing light illuminated the stretch of path he'd just measured his length against. He stared at the bloody hand that held aloft the witchlight. Moncriith. The Bloodmage had slashed his own palm to fuel the light.

Nimbulan ducked his face deep within his folded arms to keep the light from reflecting off his pale skin. Through his closed eyelids, he sensed more light. Had Rollett added his own abilities to Moncriith's?

Stargods, he wished his talent was intact. But Moncriith would seek it out. Slay him on the spot and collect a huge reward for the deed.

More light crept through his closed eyes. Moncriith must be flooding the area with balls of witchlight. The glow dimmed as the Bloodmage's spell faded.

He heard a cry, and the light blazed once more. Nimbulan winced in sympathy with whichever man suffered the slash of Moncriith's wickedly sharp knife for the sake of a little more magic light. He had to rescue Rollett before he became a victim.

If ever Moncriith's compulsion on these hardened mercenaries fell apart, they'd turn on him. Nimbulan didn't have time to wait for that, nor the privacy and peace to set a counterspell to Moncriith's terrible compulsions.

The footsteps moved on, more slowly as the men searched for Nimbulan with mundane senses. Or were they searching at all? Maybe only Moncriith looked. The mercenaries could be just following him. In which case, the Bloodmage would use his magic to seek Nimbulan's magic. That brief touch in the wineshop had given Moncriith a glimpse of Nimbulan's magical signature, all he'd need under normal circumstances.

But Nimbulan's magic was now embedded in the staff, not his body.

Slowly he stood up, using the staff to brace his painful knee.

"I'm getting too old for this kind of adventure," he muttered as his back resisted straightening and his shoulder revealed another wrenching injury.

He limped in the direction Scarface had taken. He needed help finding Myri and getting out of here. The magician mercenaries seemed his only chance.

"There, grab that man! He was with the magician we seek," Moncriith commanded ahead of Nimbulan and to the left.

Nimbulan swallowed back his instinct to run in the opposite direction. He couldn't. He needed Scarface. The man had befriended him with cooperation and an important lesson in magic. Battlemages weren't known for sharing anything magic. If Scarface could gather dragon magic, he'd make a valuable contribution to the Commune.

If they could escape the city. If they found Myri.

He limped forward as quietly as he could. One hundred paces from his hiding place, he encountered the backs of the men from the wineshop. They stood in a half ring around Moncriith. Rollett stood in the exact center of the lineup. Backed up against the wall of a small building, Scarface and one of his compatriots defended themselves with their staffs. They batted off the fireballs and truth spells Moncriith flung at them.

Nimbulan ducked one of the repelled balls. He almost smiled at the image of turning this bloodsport into a game. He presumed the magicians had also embedded their talents into their staffs. How else could their tools combat Moncriith's magic so accurately?

A crowd of noisy gawpers drifted closer. Nimbulan needed to get his new friends and Rollett free before the locals realized the reward attached to his capture. He had no doubts any of them would gladly sell him, alive or dead, to the Kaalipha.

Nimbulan tapped Rollett on the shoulder. He took one step to his left. Nimbulan slipped into place beside him, directly behind Moncriith. The Bloodmage didn't take his attention off Scarface and his comrade.

From this new vantage point, Nimbulan surveyed the faces of the mercenaries standing shoulder to shoulder in a near perfect half circle. Their faces remained blank and unresponsive. A few revealed muscle twitches of resistance in their shoulders and fingers. Nimbulan didn't need his talent to recognize their reluctance to remain in thrall to Moncriith any longer than necessary.

Despite the danger, Nimbulan felt a small smile flicker across his cheeks. Without bothering to weigh the consequences, he hefted his staff in both hands and swung with all his strength at the back of Moncriith's head.

The Bloodmage crumpled to the dirt. The mercenaries raised their swords over their heads as one.

Rollett's blade pressed sharply into Nimbulan's spine.

Chapter 24

"**S**wear loyalty to our new captain!" Scarface shouted to the assembled mercenaries as he lifted his sword to join the others in salute to Nimbulan.

"What?" Nimbulan looked right and left in amazement. He'd been prepared to flee or defend himself against the trained warriors. Instead they looked to him for leadership.

"Moncriith defeated our old captain. You defeated Moncriith and broke his spell over the men. Therefore you are our new captain," Scarface said with a wide grin. He prodded the Bloodmage with his toe.

Moncriith groaned and tried to raise his head, but he collapsed onto the ground again with a sickening splat that meant a broken nose. Blood gushed over his face.

All traces of blank enthrallment had left the men's faces, including Rollett's. The dark-haired young man grinned.

"Before you wake that piece of bloody garbage," Rollett said, holding Scarface back from kicking Moncriith again. "We need a plan. He can get us into the palace. He has the ear of the Kaalipha. He can get us all past the guards and their wands without a search."

"He'll have to think he's taking Nimbulan to Yaassima for justice," Scarface added. "You willing to risk that, Captain?" He looked at Nimbulan, eyes wide with speculation.

"I'll have to. I have to rescue my wife and the children. I presume Powwell and Kalen are with her. She wouldn't willingly separate from them."

"After that, these men and I will decide what to do with our lives. There's always the invasion of Coronnan. You can take on our sponsorship, Nimbulan, and collect the money from SeLenicca's recruiting agents. They leave at dawn and plan to launch the first strike within a week."

"No." Nimbulan cast about for ideas. He had to either stop that invasion or get word to Quinnault fast. What had the boy done to precipitate a major invasion in only a few days?

But he couldn't leave without Myri.

"Quickly, Moncriith is coming around," Rollett ordered as if he were the new mercenary captain. "Scarface and Nimbulan, on the ground. The rest of you, put those blank looks back into your eyes."

"Some of you will have to secure the gate so that we can escape later. Drift away now, before Moncriith knows you are gone," Nimbulan added.

"If we all work together, with magic and mundane weapons, we have a chance. But we won't be able to hold the gate long," Scarface replied.

"Then take a moment to reabsorb your magic." Nimbulan held his staff upright in front of him while he anxiously took the usual three deep breaths. He'd been without his talent too long. He felt diminished, half a man. He lost sight of his quest to free Myri while he reached to restore the lost talent.

The staff shimmered in the moonlight. A pulsing double aura spread outward from it. Deep in the core of the wood grain lay a throbbing blue light, dimmer than what he remembered it should be.

He willed the blue light to return to his heart where it belonged. Slowly, too slowly, the blue crept out of the staff into his hands. It found his veins and merged with the blood flow returning to his heart.

A sense of completeness pushed up his arms like the taste of cool water after a long day in the hot sun. His fingers tingled with renewed sensitivity. The ache in his wrenched shoulder and scraped knee faded. His heart beat faster, truer, more powerfully. Awareness of every cell in his body returned.

The beacon of light settled into place with a satisfied wiggle that felt like a sigh of relief.

Scarface pointed to Nimbulan's left. "There's a commotion at the gate. Maybe something we can take advantage of."

Two men faded into the shadows in the direction of the gate. Nimbulan had no doubt they'd return shortly with a report. He and Scarface stretched out on the ground as if Moncriith had felled them with his last spell.

Almost as if cued by their preparations, Moncriith raised himself up on one elbow and shook his head clear.

Nimbulan watched him through half-closed eyes. As the Bloodmage rolled and heaved his body upward, the prominence of his bones was sharply outlined beneath his bright red robe. For all the breadth of his shoulders and square-ness of his shape, the man was not well fed. Or something ate away at his innards. Disease or fanaticism?

"Bind those two with magic and mundane means. We will take them to the Kaalipha for judgment," Moncriith grunted before he was fully erect.

"There is a disturbance at the gate, Captain," one of the mercenaries said in a monotone as he slipped back into line. "There is information to be gained, sir."

Moncriith looked into the eyes of each of the men who surrounded him, then back to the inert bodies of Nimbulan and Scarface. "Bind them and bring them along. I would know who disturbs the Kaalipha's peace." He shuffled off in the direction of the gate, confident that his men would follow. He shook his head repeatedly, as if trying to clear his muddled thoughts.

By the time they reached the solitary portal into or out of Hanassa, Moncriith had regained much of his poise and his habitual confident stride.

Nimbulan kept his head down. Impatiently, he tested the ropes Rollett had placed around his wrists. They slipped easily over his hands. He pushed them back up again before Moncriith could turn and test them.

When a milling crowd around the gate came into view, Moncriith halted his men. They stopped moving in unison, continuing to stare straight ahead without expression. Nimbulan had no doubt they saw everything.

A troop of twenty palace guards stood squarely in front of the gate, swords drawn, wands aimed at the crowd. Behind them, several figures crouched by the slapping rock.

"Hey, butt-licker, them wands don't work without the slapping rock. Can you defend yourself without them?" a slightly built man taunted from the depths of the crowd.

"Get some good use outta that there rod. Ram it up the Kaalipha's butt instead o' ours," a drunken woman yelled. he threw an overripe fruit at the rigid guards. They didn't flinch.

"Ain't seen you fight with those swords before." A half-dressed woman swiveled her hips and bent forward so the guards could see the fullness of her breasts. "They're stiffer than the ones you usually wield on the Kaalipha's orders."

The guards didn't move. Their sword tips remained at the ready.

The crowd oozed forward one step.

Someone else lobbed a sulfurous smelling egg at the unmoving wall of guards. The bloody yolk splattered against one man's clean, black uniform. He didn't flinch.

The milling people pressed closer yet to the lethal sword tips and hated wands.

"Do my eyes betray me, or are they in some kind of trance?" Nimbulan whispered to Scarface.

"I believe they are being controlled by a magician. They are well disciplined and very loyal, but I've never seen them so unresponsive before," the mercenary magician replied.

Moncriith whipped his head around, silencing them with a glare.

"I'd like a closer look at the slapping rock and what those people are doing to it," Nimbulan whispered.

Rollett surreptitiously nudged Nimbulan with his confiscated staff. The journeyman grounded the butt of the staff and leaned it against Nimbulan's hands, without shifting his gaze or moving his body. In full contact with the staff and the Kardia, Nimbulan called his TrueSight up from the depths of the little bit of dragon magic left within him.

The shape of the slapping rock jumped into his vision in precise detail. The brown lump, so unusual in this black and gray landscape, lay on its side, revealing a deep hollow place inside it. A tangle of hair-fine tentacles grew from the middle of the rock. But it wasn't a true rock.

What kind of strange creature is this rock? Surely it must be alive in some manner. No natural mineral grew appendages. The wands responded to the sounds it made, like dogs trained to a whistle.

"Look at the girl crouched beside the rock." Scarface pointed to the figure closest to the creature. His tones couldn't reach much beyond Nimbulan's sensitive ear. "That's Yaala, Yaassima's daughter. Everyone thought she was dead after the Kaalipha killed her consort—the girl's father—when she tired of him. Made the girl watch. When Yaala refused to wash herself in her father's blood, Yaassima threw a fit and condemned her, too. Said she didn't have enough of the dragon in her. I wonder how she managed to stay alive. She seems to be doing the chore of the Engineer, the only one Yaassima trusts to work on the wands and the slapping rocks. Maybe she's been hiding in the pit."

Nimbulan's blood froze in his veins. Myri had a lot of dragon spirit within her. What did the Kaalipha have planned for his wife?

The young woman removed one of the long red appendages inside the "rock." She pulled an identical snakelike piece from inside her tunic and placed it where the discarded one had been.

"Wh . . . what is the pit?" Nimbulan kept his eyes on the young woman and the other person in ragged and filthy clothes who handed her metal tools upon command. Something seemed familiar about the shape of his skull and the way he braced his legs . . .

"The pit is the heart of the volcano. Yaala is the only person other than the Engineer I've ever seen leave it and live."

"What about the young man beside her?"

Scarface shrugged. "I've never seen him before."

Just then, the young man turned his head to scan the crowd. His eyes lingered on Nimbulan, then opened wide in recognition.

"Powwell!" Nimbulan breathed the name, barely loud enough to hear. "My foster son. He must have come here with Myrilandel and . . . and Kalen. I've got to rescue all of them." His heart turned over at the sickly pallor of the boy's skin, the shoulders bowed in defeat.

The young woman, Yaala, rolled the rock back into place. She stood and dusted the knees of her trews. All of the guards relaxed from their enchanted vigilance. Six of them broke away from the half circle and prodded Yaala and Powwell in the back with the wands. Reluctantly they trudged back toward the palace and the pit.

Nimbulan took one step as if to follow.

"If you go after him into the pit, you'll die, too," Scarface said.

Myri carefully untangled her legs from her sheets. She moved slowly so the soft mattress wouldn't shift and awaken Kalen who snored softly beside her. Baby Amaranth cooed and blew bubbles. Myri lifted her from her cradle, automatically checking her diaper. Nearly dry for once.

Maia shifted on her straw pallet at the foot of the bed but didn't awaken. She slept with her arms pressed tightly against her breasts. The front of her shift was wet and smelled of sour milk.

Myri's empathic talent shared the aching pressure of too much milk with no child to suckle. She hugged her own baby tightly, cherishing Amaranth's life. Maia had only memories of the children she had lost.

Myri left the bedchamber rather than think about Maia's loss. The door to Yaassima's room remained firmly closed.

Singing softly to Amaranth, Myri wove her way around the heavy furniture Yaassima favored to the window in the common room. Dull light glowed behind the ceiling panels, never totally extinguished. Tonight, they didn't seem to give off as much of a glow as usual.

As she did so many nights, Myri stared out at the dark sky above the bowl of the crater, longing to fly to freedom. If she transformed into her dragon form, would the necklace choke her to death before it destroyed her brain, or would she break free of Yaassima's bondage?

She blinked back the moisture that filled her eyes. For the sake of the baby in her arms, she didn't dare transform. But she had to put her half-formed escape plans into action tonight. Kalen had fallen prey to the vices of lies and deceit so prevalent in the city. The girl had to be taken away from here now or she'd be lost forever. Powwell, too, was in terrible peril in the pit. Yaassima's demands for the baby chilled Myri to the bone.

How to subdue Yaassima long enough to steal the trigger for her necklace? The questions spun around and around her brain, a lot like the dancing harlots in the streets below.

No one in the city seemed to sleep tonight. Crowds of people gathered around pubs and wineshops, or danced serpentine patterns around the city, shouting and singing with a kind of desperation Myri couldn't understand. She'd heard Nastfa and Golin say that this kind of revelry only happened the night before large companies of mercenaries left the city on campaign. Tomorrow Hanassa would be nearly deserted. Fewer crowds for her to hide among.

Myri had caught an emotion of regret from Nastfa. He needed to leave the city, but not with the mercenaries. His roots and his heart belonged elsewhere. His need to be gone was reaching the point of desperation.

Would Moncriith leave with the soldiers? Now that he knew Myri resided in Hanassa, he might elect to stay and seek a way to destroy her. He'd hounded her for as long as she could remember, driving her from village to village. His preferred method of execution of witches was burning.

Why did villagers always believe his sermons against the demons only he could see and not the healing and helping she gave them?

Only the nameless fishing village near her clearing had resisted Moncriith. She missed her friends there. She missed her home nearly as much as Nastfa did.

"I want to go home," she sobbed.

First she had to get herself and her children out of the palace. Then out of Hanassa without Moncriith or Yaassima seeing her.

A disguise for herself and the children as mercenaries perhaps. Could they walk out with the armies?

Suddenly the silver cord of magic that connected her to Nimbulan glowed brighter with a more rapid pulse. She looked from the cord tugging at her heart out the window to the closest knot of men, near the gate.

One figure stood out among them. He stood tall and proud, a long twisted staff in his left hand, a faint blue aura gave him an air of command. She didn't need to follow the cord to know her husband.

I come, beloved, he called to her with his mind.

Your daughter and I await you! she nearly shouted back to her husband in triumph. *Be very careful, Lan. Yaassima binds me with magic and mundane traps.*

Nothing will separate us once I reach you. Not even the terrible Kaalipha of Hanassa, Nimbulan replied.

She breathed a deep sigh of satisfaction. She had known

he would come for her eventually. The silver cord wouldn't let them remain separated too long. She was so relieved at his appearance she couldn't resent his delay.

He'd need help getting them out of the palace. She thought she could trust Nastfa and Golin. How far would they go in their revenge against Yaassima? Or would their own fears restore their grudging loyalty to her?

Her mind refused to think beyond holding Nimbulan in her arms again. She drank in the sight of him. The men around him began to take on individual characteristics in the wild torchlight that filled the city tonight. That could be Rollett standing to Nimbulan's left and slightly behind him. Another teenager and a middle-aged man also stood nearby. Then her gaze lingered on the back of the man that seemed to be in front of the group. He turned his face to glare at Nimbulan.

Moncriith. She'd know him anywhere.

What was her husband doing with their archenemy?

The hairs on the back of her neck prickled a warning before she heard a soft footfall. Carefully she shut out the telepathic communication from Nimbulan. All these weeks as Yaassima's pampered prisoner and she still wasn't sure of the extent of the Kaalipha's powers.

A heavy hand rested on her shoulder. Not Yaassima. She turned her head to look at this new companion.

Nastfa, her constant guard, stood beside her. Golin slept somewhere else in the suite. Nastfa held one finger to his lips to signal silence.

That brief moment of physical contact told her more about Nastfa. He had never been loyal to Yaassima. He'd only used his position among the elite guards as a way of saving himself when he found himself trapped here. When he'd completed his spying mission for the King of Maffisto.

Myri nodded her head once in compliance, eager for this man's help. She shot one more glance out the window. Moncriith still stood with Nimbulan. She had to set her escape into motion by herself.

The senior guard squeezed her shoulder gently, reassuringly. He held both hands together and rested his cheek on them, pantomiming sleep, then he pointed to Yaassima's private chamber. Abruptly he looked up, almost startled. A moment later he laid his face back onto his hands.

The Kaalipha slept lightly.

Myri nodded again, uncertain what the man wanted of her.

Nastfa fished a small vial from his pocket. The enameled metal tube was sealed tightly with wax. He pointed again to Yaassima and pantomimed a deeper sleep. Gently he placed the vial into Myri's hand and closed her fingers around it.

The moment of physical contact relayed his emotions to her empathic talent. He hated the Kaalipha as did his king. Even before Yaassima's humiliation of him in the Justice Hall the other night he had hated her. But he feared her also. Feared that if he tried to kill her himself, he would fail. He didn't know where the loyalty of his men lay. His years of entrapment had eaten away at his confidence.

"When?" Myri mouthed the word, lest Yaassima awaken and overhear through the dragon pendant.

A tiny bell rang within the Kaalipha's bedchamber. Myri looked toward the sound, startled. The door to Yaassima's room opened and her sleepy-eyed maid—the only servant Yaassima trusted near her regularly—shuffled out, headed for the carafe of wine and cups that always sat on the side table.

Yaassima must have drained the carafe by her bed already. Most nights the wine was all that allowed her to sleep. She frequently ordered Myri to bring the wine so the Kaalipha could regale her with bloodthirsty tales of her dragon ancestor Hanassa.

"I'll take the wine to Yaassima. Go back to sleep, Haanna." Myri waved the woman back to her pallet in a tiny alcove.

She could trust only herself. She had to get the children out of Hanassa tonight.

Haanna flashed Myri a grateful smile and stumbled back to her bed.

With shaking hands, Myri poured the bright red wine into a goblet of fine porcelain. She stared at the vial a few seconds, indecisive.

Yaassima rang her bell again. "What keeps you, Haanna. I'll send you to the pit if you don't hurry," the Kaalipha called querulously.

Smiling slightly, Myri pocketed the vial and withdrew

powders left by Erda to make Myri docile and obedient. She hadn't taken any drugs for days. There should be enough here to send Yaassima to sleep for days. Or forever.

Chapter 25

"There is nothing of import happening here." Moncriith signaled the mercenaries to follow him. "Back to the palace. The Kaalipha will want to be a part of the execution of these foreign magicians."

The troop of mercenaries wheeled as one man and marched back toward the palace. Nimbulan and Scarface had no choice but to follow them. They needed Moncriith to get them into the palace without a search for weapons or magic.

"I have to find access to the pit, after we rescue Myri," Nimbulan whispered as they neared the palace entrance.

"You'll have to give the boy up for dead. No one survives the pit. You saw how pale and wasted he looked. He won't live long even if you could get him and yourself out," Scarface replied.

A line of dancers snaked out from a side path. They alternated men and women, each holding the waist of the person in front of them. The lead reveler was too drunk to stand on his own. He swayed and stumbled into Moncriith.

Moncriith backhanded the man across his face. Blood spurted from the man's nose. He fell backward, throwing the entire line off balance. "*S'murghin'* wastrels. I'll sacrifice you one and all before I let you join the ranks of my army!" Moncriith screamed at them.

A woman burst out laughing at the Bloodmage's posturing—too drunk to be afraid. Her ragged red gown drooped off her left shoulder, revealing most of her breast. She caressed herself, taunting Moncriith to join her.

Moncriith turned back the palace. His deliberate path took him through the line of mercenary magicians. He shoved Rollett out of his way. The journeyman magician stumbled and fought for balance. His flailing arms and shifting steps broke the blank expression of numb obedience to Moncriith.

Nimbulan gasped silently. Every one of the mercenaries stopped and slid silent hands toward their swords. *Don't break rank! Keep your weapons sheathed until HE orders you.* Nimbulan directed his warning into the mind of each man. The Bloodmage had to believe himself in control of this troop until they were well within the palace.

The dancing woman sidled in front of Moncriith, continuing her drunken taunt. He slammed his fist into her face. She fell backward over the jumble of collapsed dancers. Her leg twisted under her as she fought for balance. With an audible crack, the bone broke. She stopped laughing abruptly. Her jaw quivered and pain filled her eyes. But she didn't cry out. The drunken dancers found this hilarious. Insults to the woman joined their off-key song of celebration. Nimbulan caught a few derisive comments about Moncriith as well.

"Doesn't anyone in this city sleep?" he asked Scarface out loud. Moncriith whipped his attention back to the magician and away from the revelers.

"Not the night before half the town leaves for a major war." Scarface spoke a little too loudly, demanding Moncriith listen to him and not be sidetracked by the dancers.

"Silence, demon spawn. You won't live long enough to join these people in the glorious campaign to stamp out the demon-led king of Coronnan," Moncriith said. He raised his fist as if to slam it into Scarface as hard as he had the drunken woman.

"You like preying on helpless victims, don't you, Moncriith? People who can't fight back and prove just how weak you really are," Nimbulan sneered. He inserted his bound hands between his new friend and Moncriith.

The Bloodmage's face darkened with rage. "I don't have time to waste trading insults with you, Nimbulan. I shall have my revenge when Yaassima and I both dip our hands in your blood. I shall carry your severed head into battle as a symbol of the end of the demons that control you."

The troop of mercenaries stepped forward as if propelled by a single will. Nimbulan ground his teeth together trying to keep from ending this charade and murdering Moncriith there and then.

Rollett nudged Nimbulan with his staff, reminding him to keep his thoughts under control as well as his actions. Nimbulan forced his frustrations away from the front of his mind.

The palace loomed ahead. The jumble of buildings piled on top of each other spread across a good portion of the southern arc of the crater. Four guards stood in front of a smoothly rounded arch, just broad enough to admit two men walking side by side, very close together. Off to the right of the gate was another opening, less regular, shorter and narrower yet.

Nimbulan touched Scarface with his elbow and tilted his head in the direction of the smaller entrance.

"The brothel for Yaassima's guards. It doesn't lead into the palace," Scarface replied under his breath.

Nimbulan wondered if he should look there first for either Myri or Maia.

Two guards stepped forward, challenging Moncriith's right of entrance. The Bloodmage spoke a few words in an ancient language and wove his hands in a complex sigil. The eyes of the guards glazed over.

"No need for your wands and your searches," Moncriith said smugly. He waved aside the first two guards. They stepped back to their accustomed sentry position.

"The Kaalipha has given me the freedom of the palace, and I vouch for my men. None of them would betray me."

Moncriith turned and glared at the phalanx of men behind him.

All of them thrust a clenched fist forward in salute. "Death to all demons. Long life to Moncriith the demon slayer," they chanted as if in thrall.

The guards nodded acceptance.

"Alert the Kaalipha. I have found the foreign magician she seeks and brought him here for justice," Moncriith ordered. The guards nodded again in compliance.

A long tunnel widened inside the entrance. Torches placed at random intervals along one side of the rock walls lit the way. They rounded a curve and marched into a side tunnel. A particularly long stretch of shadowed darkness stretched before them.

The palace gate and the four guards were out of sight. This walkway seemed deserted.

Nimbulan grabbed his staff away from Rollett's custody. Scarface retrieved his own staff from another mercenary.

"Now!" Nimbulan shouted. His bonds fell away from his hands.

Moncriith turned to see what disrupted his march forward. Seven men held swords at the ready, all aimed at his gut.

"You won't get away with this, Nimbulan," Moncriith warned. He flicked his wrist. A long knife slid down his sleeve and into his palm.

"I think I will." Nimbulan leveled his staff to counter any spell the Bloodmage might weave.

Moncriith took a step back as his hand closed around his naked blade. The Bloodmage flinched slightly as his sharp knife sliced his palm. Blood dripped onto the weapon.

"Watch him, he's got the power of blood to fuel his magic," Rollett warned.

Nimbulan matched Moncriith step for step, pushing him toward the shadowed wall. The other men pressed closer. Eagerness to end Moncriith's tyranny showed in their bared teeth and determined grip on their weapons.

A bubble of armor draped around the Bloodmage. Nimbulan could barely sense it with his own diminishing reserve of magic. Moncriith stepped back again and ran into the wall.

Nimbulan closed his eyes and brought forward the last of his dragon magic. Rollett placed his left hand on Nimbulan's shoulder. Power swelled and multiplied within him.

Quickly, before the reservoir of magic was used up, Nimbulan pierced Moncriith's armor with the end of his staff. He flipped the tool horizontal again and rammed it across Moncriith's throat.

The Bloodmage's face turned dark with rage. He grabbed the staff with both hands and pushed against the magic and the staff with all of his might.

Nimbulan pushed back with the amplified dragon magic.

"You can't do this!" Moncriith croaked.

"I just did it," Nimbulan replied. "You are no match for communal magic. Take his weapons and bind him with mundane and magic ropes."

Carefully, he kept his enemy pinned to the wall with the
choking staff while Scarface and the other men bound
Moncriith.

"You're going to leave him alive?" Scarface asked.

"If Yaassima has enough magic to control this city, she
will be able to sense his death. We can't afford to alert her
to our presence." Nimbulan clenched his fist and rammed
it into Moncriith's jaw. The Bloodmage slid to the floor.
"Hide this trash in the next alcove. Add another blow to
his temple to make sure he's out. Then wrap him in armor
so he is invisible to mundane guards. We have to find Myrilandel before the guards alert the Kaalipha that we are in
the palace."

Quinnault paced the long corridors of the new wing of
the palace. He couldn't sleep. Every time he thought about
tomorrow, his heart raced, heat filled his veins and his head
felt like it floated.

Tomorrow he would wed Katie.

After she passed judgment by the dragons.

After the Council recognized this marriage would benefit
the entire kingdom.

The palace was quiet tonight. Usually someone was about
at all hours, checking torches, using the privy, raiding the
kitchens. He met no one on his prowl past Katie's bedchamber. If only he could see her, watch her sleep for a
while, he might be able to relax enough to snatch a brief
rest before dawn.

He eased closer to her door. No one stirred within. He
pressed his ear to the heavy wooden panels, hoping to catch
the sound of her soft breathing. A murmur of voices, anxious and intense rose behind the panel.

Who? Who had invaded Katie's bedroom in the dead
of night?

He reached to lift the latch, barge in, and demand explanations. Shouted words stopped him.

"I am in charge here." Katie's voice rose, became shrill.

Quinnault backed away. He bumped up against the protruding alcove wall that masked this corridor's join with the
older, central keep. He smiled. His architects had incorpo-
rated older tunnels and hidden passageways into the new

building. Escape routes in case the keep fell to invasion or treachery, they had insisted.

The secret panel yielded to the pressure of one hand and slid inward on recently oiled hinges. Cold, damp river air gushed out of the tunnel. He stepped inside and closed the door behind him.

He kept his right hand against the wall, counting stones until he reached the twenty-seventh. He identified it by tracing its outline, rougher and larger than its neighbors. At the bottom right-hand corner he found an extra knob, no larger than his little fingernail. He turned it three times to the right. Half the wall swung inward a narrow slit. He stepped through and found himself behind a full-length tapestry between a wardrobe cabinet and the inside corner of the room.

The loose weave of the wall hanging allowed him to see the majority of the room. Princess Maarie Kaathliin paced anxiously at the foot of the four-poster bed. The bed hangings were thrown open to reveal rumpled sheets and blankets. Katie was fully dressed in her heavy woolen gown. She kept her hands folded inside the full sleeves and hunched her shoulders as if warding off a chill.

A large fire blazed in the hearth, heating the room well beyond what Quinnault thought comfortable. Kinnsell stood before the fire, warming his hands above the flames.

"I am still your father, Mary Kathleen O'Hara, and you will obey me in this. We owe it to the Empire."

"I will not discuss this. We do it my way or not at all." Katie ceased her pacing abruptly. "And stop trying to break down my shields. Isn't it bad enough their magicians will be playing games with my mind and my memories tomorrow?"

Kinnsell stood firm, staring at his daughter with fierce concentration.

"Get out of my mind and this room, Kinnsell. Get out or I call the guard, and all of your fancy weapons and technology won't get you out of their dungeons. I'll see to it." Katie matched him stare for stare. "Go back to Terra, Daddy, and make a new desert. You are very good at that."

Kinnsell stalked out of the room, back rigid. The cords on the back of his neck stood out from the tension in his jaw.

Katie slammed the door behind him.

Quinnault shifted his balance to his toes ready to flee or dash forward, whatever seemed called for. Unsure of what he had just witnessed, he braced himself with one hand against the wall and breathed deeply. Dimly he was aware of Katie wrapping a brick from the hearth in a wad of cloth. She placed it beneath the covers on the rumpled bed and climbed in, fully clothed. He could hear her teeth chattering and wondered how hot the climate of her home was—truly Terrania?—that she found this warm palace so cold.

Katie tossed and turned for several minutes before curling up in a ball and drifting to sleep.

Quinnault waited several more minutes before stirring. He longed to stand closer and watch his bride. He hesitated, unsure of what he had witnessed between Katie and her father and if it boded ill for his kingdom.

His mind spun furiously. He hadn't found contentment watching Katie, only more questions.

The latch clicked. Quinnault pressed his back against the wall. Katie didn't stir.

He watched the door inch open, half expecting Kinnsell to reappear with some new argument. A Rover-dark man of medium height and lithe build crept into the room. He looked all around and closed the door behind him. It didn't latch.

Before Quinnault could catch his breath and leap out to question the man, the intruder moved forward with three long strides. He pulled a long cord from his pocket and wrapped it tightly around both hands.

Quinnault dove out from behind the tapestry as the Rover tightened the cord around Katie's slim neck.

Chapter 26

Where is Scarface hiding tonight? Televarn asked himself. He'd already checked the wineshops the magician haunted. The man spent a lot of time drowning his physical pain in wine. Tonight he seemed to be occupied elsewhere. No one had seen him.

Some of the shopkeepers were lying. Scarface had been there, but wasn't there when Televarn looked. He checked with magic as well as mundane senses.

Lacking the magician, Televarn decided to return to the palace and alert his spies to the impending revolution. He'd also get Piedro out of the pit with the huge stash of weapons. Piedro was a good man to have watch the Kaalipha's apartments. He was patient and ruthless. He'd enjoy killing anyone who went into or out of Yaassima's private quarters without permission.

I'll have to warn him not to touch Myrilandel or Kalen, Televarn reminded himself. Piedro was as dangerous as he was useful.

The palace guards searched Televarn with efficient speed and sent him on his way. The Rover chuckled to himself. He'd had several blades made of the special iron the Kaalipha used on slave chains. The wands were not tuned to that substance. He had enough weapons on him to murder all four of the guards at the gate and they never found them.

Just inside the main tunnel, he ducked into a dark side passage that would take him to the Justice Hall and then down into the pit. He stumbled over something large and inert. It groaned and shifted away from his boots.

Televarn stared at the crumpled figure lying prone on

the ground, hands bound behind his back. Dim torchlight reflected off scar tissue on the man's face.

"Are you alive, Moncriith?" he asked. Best if he kept his distance until the man was fully awake. One blast of a defensive spell thrown when the Bloodmage was half awake could kill any innocent bystander.

"Of course, I'm alive. Nimbulan didn't have the guts to kill me or even do me serious harm," Moncriith said as he spat dirt from his mouth. "Untie me."

"Nimbulan?" Cold raced up and down Televarn's spine. Kalen had been right after all. The Water spell had claimed a different life from the one intended.

"Yes, Nimbulan. You failed in your assignment. I don't intend to disappoint the Kaalipha in mine. Untie me!"

"I can't. He's wrapped magic into the rope that binds your hands and ankles."

The knots were very professional, the work of a mercenary and a magician. Scarface wasn't the only magician disguised as a professional soldier, but he was the best of the lot. If he had allied himself with Nimbulan, there was trouble brewing this night. More trouble than Televarn could invent.

His plans began to evaporate. Maybe he should just grab Myrilandel while she slept and flee through the dragongate.

No. He'd worked too long and too hard to depose Yaassima. Everything was in place. He just needed to rearrange his plans. Maybe he could use the chaos created by Nimbulan's rescue attempts.

"Use your magic to break the bonds," Moncriith ordered. "If we time it right, Yaassima will execute Nimbulan for us."

"Yes. He will try to free his wife. I can arrange for Yaassima to discover him," Televarn replied. He continued to examine the knots, but didn't try to release them.

"You can turn Myrilandel's anger toward Yaassima to your advantage," Moncriith coaxed.

"What will you gain? You want to kill Myrilandel, too." Televarn didn't trust Moncriith. No one did.

"I want revenge against the Commune of Magicians and I want the Crown of Coronnan. I can't successfully invade with my mercenaries as long as Nimbulan lives to guide

Quinnault. If you keep the demon Myrilandel here in Hanassa, I have no need to seek her death."

"I thought you were recruiting on behalf of SeLenicca." Televarn began working on the knots. The spell on them was hastily constructed and easily broken down.

"I'm using SeLenicca just as you have been using Yaassima."

"We'll need to coordinate our plans. Timing will be everything. Nimbulan has to be dead before we attack the palace. But Yaassima has to still be enthralled with his blood. She's usually senseless for half an hour after an execution." Televarn sat back on his heels, thinking.

"I will sense his death." Moncriith licked his lips as if savoring the taste of death already.

Televarn resisted warding against evil with gestures and spells. Moncriith would interpret them as fear—or worse—cowardice. Televarn had no intention of appearing weak and therefore vulnerable to this very dangerous Bloodmage.

"Nimbulan's death will be my signal to dismantle the slapping rock at the palace gate. I saw the girl Yaala work on it earlier. This is the first use the girl has been since Yaassima refused to execute her when I ordered it. Yaala showed me how to put the rock to sleep without knowing it. You must hurry, Televarn. Nimbulan has had enough time to make his way through the palace to Yaassima's quarters with Scarface and the other mercenaries."

"Scarface owes me his life. He will have to help us. I have weapons stashed inside the palace. I'll kill Yaassima while she's still in thrall. You'll come in with your mercenaries and my Rovers. Hanassa will be mine."

"Ours."

Quinnault grabbed the intruder by the wrists, forcing him to release the pressure on Katie's throat. He gritted his teeth, putting all of his strength and leverage into his efforts. The Rover only leaned back, pulling the corded silk belt tighter about Katie's neck.

Her eyes popped open, and she clamped her fingers around the garrote. The fibers were too fine and slick for her to get so much as a fingernail between it and her vulnerable throat.

The Rover laughed at her efforts. Quinnault shifted his grip. If he could only find the one vulnerable nerve beneath the man's arm. He closed his eyes, remembering the trick taught him by his tutor in the monastery. Sometimes a priest had to defend himself without weapons. He fought the loose folds of the man's black shirt and the thick embroidery on his vest, seeking, probing. Pressing.

There.

The Rover's hands went limp.

Katie rolled out of the bed and away from her assailant in one panicked movement. She gasped and pried the cord away from her throat.

"Call the guard," Quinnault ordered as he shifted his grip once more. This time he captured the Rover's head with his left arm and controlled his right wrist with the other.

"Your name," he demanded.

The Rover laughed again in response.

"I'll have your name now or by torture later." He twisted the man's arm back and up. A grimace of pain crossed the man's face but he kept silent.

Quinnault twisted harder. Another fraction of an inch and the arm would break.

"My chieftain calls me Piedro," the intruder said through gritted teeth.

Quinnault relaxed the pressure on the arm a fraction. Dimly he was surprised at his lack of revulsion in causing the man pain. His priestly training to preserve all life seemed to have fled the moment Katie was threatened.

"That tells me that you answer to another name." Quinnault reasserted the pressure on the man's arm.

"Don't we all?" Piedro shrugged within Quinnault's tight grasp. A desperate gesture to twist free. Quinnault didn't let him. One of the small bones of Piedro's wrist slid out of place under the fierce grip.

Piedro dropped his head. His defiant pose melted. But the tenseness in his thighs belied his acquiescence.

"Who sent you?" Quinnault gestured with his head for Katie to call for help.

She just stood there, the bed between herself and her assailant. She held her tiny hands to her throat, gently prob-

ing for injury. She stared straight ahead, wide-eyed, mouth
working silently.

"Katie, get help. I can't hold him forever." At the same
moment he pushed upward on the arm he held while pulling back on Piedro's throat.

"Yihee!" Piedro screamed as his shoulder dislocated.

Katie moved at last, staggering slightly as she hastened
to the door and yanked it open. "Guards!" she croaked.
Then she swallowed deeply and repeated her call, louder,
more confidently.

"I estimate you have less than one hundred heartbeats
to tell me who sent you before I turn you over to my very
efficient guards. They were not trained as priests and have
less respect for life and pain than I do." He tightened his
grip on the man's throat.

"Can't talk if you throttle me," Piedro said calmly. Too
calmly.

"I'm not letting go. Who hired you? I don't think you
are smart enough to think up this plot on your own."

"I have my reasons for killing your bride with the belt
to your own dressing gown, Your Almighty Supremeness."

"Cut the sarcasm. I know who would profit from such a
plot to bring down my kingdom." Too many people.
"Which of them hired you?"

Piedro laughed as the sound of heavy boots pounding in
the corridor foretold the entry of the household guards.
"Oh, they are properly embarrassed that you captured me
in the middle of the crime. You who they are pledged to
protect. They never suspected I walked right past them."

"A magician. I know how to control you now. Throw
him in the dungeon. Have three magicians working together seal the door. I'll interrogate him myself. When I
have time. In a week or two. If you think of it, you can
feed him in the interim. That will give me time to import
a professional torturer from Maffisto." Quinnault stared at
the wall, fighting his urge to become as vengeful and violent
as Kammeryl d'Astrismos had been. He would not succumb
to his base urges and destroy the peace and harmony of
Coronnan with his own bad example.

Piedro put up a little resistance as three burly guards
wrestled him through the doorway. He dug in his heels.

"There isn't a dungeon made that can hold me, Your Supreme Loftiness. I am a Rover."

"Make sure three magicians seal the dungeons. And don't leave him alone until they do," Quinnault returned. "Tell them it needs to be a spell that even Nimbulan couldn't break."

"You'd best look to your own house before you start throwing accusations far afield, and trusting every magician, lord, and peasant in the land," Piedro called over his shoulder.

"What does that mean?" Quinnault grabbed a handful of Piedro's thick black hair and yanked backward.

Piedro laughed. "All of your tortures are nothing compared to what my chieftain doles out every day. I have no reason to blab."

The tunnels within Yaassima's palace wove an intricate pattern through the ancient mountain. Nimbulan could never be sure how many times they doubled back on themselves. All of the passageways seemed to lead back to the large hall that had once been a temple to Simurgh. He shuddered with residual pain and terror every time they neared the place.

Finding Myri was proving more difficult than expected. His heart cord pulsed strong and true but gave no indication of which direction led to his wife.

Few guards patrolled the corridors. The first one they encountered, a dark man in an ill-fitting uniform, turned Nimbulan around and pointed back the way they had come, without being asked for directions. "The Justice Hall is along that tunnel, take the first left then the second right." He moved on his rounds without checking to see if they complied. Obviously, if they had gotten into the palace they weren't considered dangerous.

The next guard, also Rover-dark and uncomfortable in his clothes, gave them the same directions.

"Some transgressor must have been caught. There will be a trial and execution shortly," Scarface whispered.

"We have to find Myri and the children, my children, fast." Nimbulan paused at the first turning. He savored the taste of those words, *my children*. Firmly he pushed aside his need to stop and wonder at the beauty of such a simple phrase. Since his brief mental contact with Myri he'd finally come to believe in those words. "My children."

"I don't know where the Kaalipha's apartments are," Scarface admitted.

"We need to split up. But we'll keep a light telepathic contact all around." He directed the gathering of mercenary magicians to follow three different tunnels. "Rollett, I need you to dismantle the slapping rock at the main gate."

"Easy." Rollett grinned. "I can disrupt the magnetic fields with mundane tools and no magic."

The observant young man had sensed more about the slapping rock than Nimbulan had.

"I trust you, Rollett, to be thorough and remain unobserved."

"With pleasure, sir. I'll have an exit ready for you." The young man's white teeth flashed through the accumulated dirt on his face. He stepped backward and faded into the shadows, a trick Nimbulan had taught him.

Nimbulan and Scarface took a fourth tunnel that he could have sworn they had not tried before. Within two dozen long strides they found themselves back at the still empty Justice Hall.

"How long a march to the staging area in SeLenicca?" Nimbulan asked to keep his mind off the memories embedded into the rock walls of the Justice Hall. Myri's empathic talent would center on this horrid room and trap her in a useless whirl.

"A week at the most. We're scheduled to march through an obscure pass in the Southwest while King Lorriin advances through the pass at Sambol at the same time. Rossemeyer will try a new invasion of the Bay." Scarface gestured them forward along a major passageway.

"Rossemeyer tried the Bay a few days ago and lost the battle. I don't think they have enough ships left to try again."

"That was last week. The summons spells have been flying fast and furious for two full days. Rossemeyer is itching to avenge their reputation as the fiercest fighters in all of Kardia Hodos. They will find more ships and mercenaries even if they have to buy them from the Varns."

Nimbulan chuckled briefly. The mythical Varns weren't due to appear in the port cities for another fifty or sixty years. Even then, no one ever bought anything from them. The Varns bought food, vast quantities of grain, produce, and livestock. The only currency the mysterious beings recognized was diamonds.

Rossemeyer wasn't likely to find a source of shipping from the Varns—or anywhere else.

One less worry. He still had to get back to Quinnault and avert this new threat to Coronnan. After he rescued Myri.

"You said that Yaassima appears magically upon the dais after everyone is assembled?" He prowled around the stage, carefully avoiding the hideous altar in front of it.

"One minute the space is empty. The next moment she appears in all her glittering cold beauty."

Nimbulan pressed against the tapestries covering the back wall. His first encountered resistance long before he expected. He stepped back and examined the perspective of the woven pictures of a mountain meadow ringed by mountain cliffs. A waterfall seemed to tumble over a pile of boulders near the center.

He'd been there before. That was the meadow Shayla, the female leader of the dragon nimbus, had chosen to educate Nimbulan and Myri into the mysteries of dragon magic.

Something was wrong with the angle of the water spilling down into a creek that meandered along the meadow.

He touched the threads depicting the water with a single sensitized finger. Harder to do that now. His reservoir of dragon magic was gone. He had only the strength of his body to fuel his inborn talent. His stomach growled, reminding him he needed more fuel, and soon.

The silvery threads of the tapestry parted as he thrust his finger, then his entire hand through the weaving. He stepped back in surprise.

"Come look at this," he called to Scarface. He plucked at the loose threads hanging free of the woven picture. They parted to reveal another tunnel snaking up a spiral staircase.

"I bet this leads to Yaassima's private quarters," Scarface said. A grin twisted the straight line of the scar.

Nimbulan looked at his heart cord. No clues. "Up those stairs," he whispered.

Scarface shrugged and hurried toward the narrow staircase. The steps were shallow and well worn, the edges rounded and slippery. They spiraled sharply around a metal center post. Damp residue clung to the black metal. It had been in place a long time. The passage became narrower and each step higher.

"Are you sure this is the right way?" Scarface asked. his low tones echoed in the confined space.

"Yes." The silver cord tugged at Nimbulan now, urging him to climb faster. Myri awaited him at the end of that cord.

He remembered the days right after she had partially healed him, almost a year ago. The cord had sprung to life, keeping them close together and dependent upon each other. They had both resented the bond, thinking it sprang from the other as a means of control. Gradually Myri had recovered from the draining healing spell. Nimbulan had healed enough to function on his own. The cord hadn't evaporated, merely stretched. They had found love then, and the cord strengthened each day as did their emotional bonds.

Until it snapped moments before Shayla announced the covenant with dragons was broken.

That must have been the moment Televarn kidnapped Myri. Despite Nimbulan's wrenched knee and aching shoulder, he increased his pace, taking the stairs two at a time. He stretched his legs and his love to reach forward to his wife.

He rounded the final curve. A long corridor with many doors stretched before him. One door at the far end was taller, broader, than all the others. Heavy bronze panels, embossed and hinged with gold, blocked the entrance to an important suite. In front of the majestic door stood a grim-faced guard in black. Nimbulan counted at least six knives and a cudgel on him.

The guard hunched his shoulders and widened his stance a fraction. His hands flexed, ready to grab a weapon.

Nimbulan stopped abruptly, holding his staff ready to focus whatever defensive spell came to mind. If he had the strength to throw it.

That's Nastfa, Scarface whispered in his mind. *He was kicked out of the assassins guild in Maffisto. Then Yaassima recruited him to lead her personal guard.*

He probably knows six dozen ways to kill us before we get close enough to launch a spell, Nimbulan replied.

So close. He'd gotten so close to Myri. If he could just get through this one last obstacle she would be in his arms again.

Nastfa smiled. His full set of white teeth shone in the yellow light of the dim ceiling panels.

Nimbulan's heart leaped to his throat. That grin could only mean that Nastfa enjoyed killing people. Why else would he become a professional assassin?

Slowly, Nastfa raised his hand.

Nimbulan blasted him with paralysis.

Nastfa's grin froze. His hand remained poised over the hilt of a small throwing knife.

Nimbulan took one step forward. Nastfa didn't move.

The door behind Nastfa creaked open a slit.

Nimbulan saw Myri's incredibly long fingers curve around the panel.

"Careful, that's the Kaalipha!" Scarface said, aiming the end of his own staff at the door.

"No, that's my wife," Nimbulan asserted. He pushed past Nastfa and yanked the door open.

"Lan!" Pale and beautiful, Myrilandel stood framed in the light of the ceiling panels. Her nearly colorless hair reflected the strange light in a halo of gold.

"Myri!" Nimbulan threw caution to the wind and rushed forward. She came into his arms, fitting against him as living water.

Her sweet smell filled him—different than he remembered, better. His heart beat stronger, truer. More completely than rejoining with his talent. A sense of rightness washed over him. He bent to kiss her, tasting her differences and her familiarity. Her curves molded against him with the ease of belonging.

He came up for air, then bent to claim her mouth once more. He seemed to have waited all his life to hold her this close.

A resounding slap stung his cheek before he could complete his kiss.

"What was that for?" He reared back his head in alarm and found himself staring into Myri's livid eyes. Normally very pale blue, they'd lost more color in her anger.

"That was for forsaking Powwell and Kalen when you

promised to aid and guide them. And this . . ." She slapped him again, "is for deserting me and leaving me vulnerable and never even coming close enough for me to tell you about . . . about . . ." Tears pooled beneath her eyelids, bringing the iris closer to their normal color.

A soft whimpering sound drew his attention into the room behind him. Kalen stood, dressed and ready to flee, with a baby in her arms.

Nimbulan cocked one eyebrow upward. "Do you have Maia's baby?" he asked. His task would be much easier if he didn't have to go looking for yet one more person.

"*We* have a daughter, Nimbulan. I have named her Amaranth. I hope you approve," Myri snarled. "Maia lost her baby son—Televarn's child, not yours. She sleeps soundly in the other room. We mustn't let her betray us to Yaassima—if the Kaalipha ever wakes up from the drugs I gave her—or to Televarn."

Nimbulan kissed her again, long and hard, before speaking again. "We must be on our way immediately." He had no doubt that Televarn, Moncriith, and Yaassima would follow them with murderous intent.

"We have to get Powwell out of the pit," Myri reminded him.

He snatched another quick kiss from Myri to keep him from doubting the outcome. He trusted Rollett to secure the gate. Once beyond the city, Myri could call the dragons. Shayla must restore the Covenant then.

"How sweet. The lovers reunited just in time to die together," Yaassima said, coming into view from one of the rooms within the suite. Televarn stood beside her, holding the sagging woman up with one arm around her waist. His other hand held a beautiful goblet of delicate porcelain.

"You really should have used some of your own magic in the sleeping potion, Myrilandel. My mixtures are so easy to counteract," the Rover chieftain said. His wide smile nearly interfered with his words. "Scarface, relieve the magician of his weapons and wake up the traitorous guard. We're going to have a party in the Justice Hall."

Chapter 27

Televarn continued to hold Yaassima up on the long trek from her apartments to the Justice Hall. The bell clanged harshly again and again, summoning the entire city to witness judgment. Maia stumbled behind them, while Scarface and the guards herded Myri, Nimbulan, and Kalen ahead of them. Why was Scarface still holding Nimbulan's staff? He should have discarded the powerful tool rather than keeping it close to the magician. So close that Nimbulan could grab and use it in a heartbeat.

Scarface honors his debts. Especially a life debt to me, Televarn reminded himself. *He won't dare betray me. Stop worrying.* Still he wished the staff had been discarded elsewhere. He needed someone to intervene between Scarface and Nimbulan.

The guard, Nastfa, was still frozen by Nimbulan's spell and useless to Televarn's plans.

He'd known the guard was a spy for the King of Maffisto since he arrived in Hanassa six years ago. Why Yaassima hadn't discovered this truth remained a mystery. Maybe she believed Nastfa had switched allegiance to her. Maybe her own arrogance blinded her to the possibility of spies and traitors within her ranks.

Nastfa was immune to the promise of a route back to his home country in return for his group siding with Televarn and the Rovers in the rebellion against Yaassima. At least he was until he awoke from the trance. The offer couldn't be made in front of the Kaalipha either.

Patience, he reminded himself. Everything was falling into place. *Patience.*

Yaassima stumbled frequently on the route to the Justice

Hall. She cursed at each false step. By the time they encountered the back door to the circular room, she could almost stand upright by herself. Televarn kept his arm around her, needing her weak and dependent.

"I'll reward you for delivering Nimbulan to me, Televarn. But I won't reward you with the woman as you requested. She defied my laws. She must die with the man she calls husband." Yaassima struggled to stand upright on her own two feet.

Televarn adjusted his grasp to keep her off balance. She was so tall—taller than Myri, who stood eye-to-eye with him—his shoulder felt dislocated by her weight.

"What of the babe?" Televarn asked casually, as if Myrilandel's life or death meant nothing to him. He shifted his stride, keeping it uneven so Yaassima would have to concentrate on her steps and not her plans.

"Hanassa is my heir. I will raise her properly to control the power bequeathed to us by the dragons. I see now that Myrilandel would interfere too much with the raising of the child. She must die." Yaassima shrugged off his arm and straightened her long, bumpy, back. She glared at him, as if she knew his intentions. But she didn't reprimand him. "Open the door for me, Televarn. I must confront my people with justice."

Hundreds of people would witness the execution. Televarn had made certain his agents prepared the populace and the palace denizens while he crept into Yaassima's bedchamber by a secret route. Some of the tunnels he had crawled through not even the Kaalipha knew about. Certainly, she wasn't aware of the opening in the interior wall of her bathing chamber. The laundry bin covered it. Maia had discovered it when she overturned the bin in a fit of rage just yesterday.

Maia's uncontrolled thoughts were easy to read at a considerable distance.

"Nimbulan must die first, Yaassima." Televarn tried to keep the begging quality out of his voice. "Myrilandel must watch him die and know that she brought this on herself."

"Yes. She must suffer by watching him die. I give you the privilege of holding her head so that she may not turn away." Yaassima shook off the last effects of the sleeping potion.

Televarn smiled to himself. Little did the Kaalipha realize that the drugs and spells he'd used to counteract the
potion had left her mind open and vulnerable to his sugges-
tions. The enthralling ecstasy she always experienced after
an execution would seal her doom. A true Bloodmage, like
Moncriith, drew power from blood and death. Not Yaassima. She used them like sex to satiate her bizarre appetites. When she dipped her hands in Nimbulan's blood,
she'd be powerless to defend herself from Televarn's
poison-dipped blade.

Yaasima stepped through the narrow bronze door—
miniature duplicate of one of the panels that sealed her
private suite. The lights blazed as the doors swung forward.
Smoke swirled and thunder clapped. The audience hushed,
then gasped in awe as the Kaalipha of Hanassa, descendant
of dragons, stepped through the tapestry and appeared as
if by magic.

"I'll wrest the secret of that trick from her before she
dies," Televarn said as he followed Yaassima through the
doors. He watched with the crowds as Scarface and a cor-
tege of mercenaries escorted Myrilandel and Nimbulan
through the other door, below the dais. The couple held
hands and looked proudly ahead of them. Kalen stumbled
behind them, weeping loudly. She hugged the baby to her
chest, clinging to the squalling form as if her life depended
upon never letting the infant go. But no tears marred her
innocent looking face. Wiggles wrapped his nearly boneless
body around Kalen's neck like a fur collar. Only his nose
twitched, seemingly investigating the baby Kalen clutched
so tightly—a sure sign that the animal communicated with
Kalen. They were followed by members of Yaassima's private guard, dressed in black and keeping their eyes glued
to the floor. Was that Nastfa hidden in their midst? The
head of the elite guard wasn't where Televarn had left him,
behind Nimbulan and Myri. No time to worry about him.

Maia slipped in behind them, eyes searching the shadows
of the huge Justice Hall. Televarn doubted that Yaassima
saw her. The Kaalipha's eyes were riveted on Myrilandel
in pure hatred.

"Nimbulan, Magician of Coronnan, you conspired to
steal my most precious possession from me. My heir and
her child," Yaassima said. "Myrilandel, you conspired with

this foreign magician to abandon your true heritage. I took you in, treated you like a daughter, made your child my heir!" She screwed up her face in anguish.

Televarn wondered if any of her outrage and sense of betrayal were real. Yaassima didn't give in to emotions that couldn't benefit her.

"Do either of you have anything to say before lawful execution by beheading?" Yaassima recovered her poise and glared at her prisoners.

"If I swear in blood to be your obedient heir and raise my child to follow the dragon heritage of Hanassa, will you allow my husband to live?" Myri held her head high, proud and defiant.

Televarn had never wanted her more. Her strength and courage were worthy of the Rover Queens of legends. With her by his side, he could rule the world.

"No, Nimbulan must die!" Televarn hissed into Yaassima's ear. The magician had to die once and for all. Otherwise Moncriith wouldn't know when to launch his attack. Myri would never be his while her marriage vows bound her to Nimbulan.

"Myri, are you sure you want to do this?" Nimbulan asked. He tilted her face toward him with a gentle finger. She seemed to melt into his touch.

"I will do anything to spare your life, beloved. I'm still angry that you deserted me and the children, but I do love you." Myri kissed his palm. Her bottom lip trembled and tears overflowed her beautiful eyes.

Angry heat flooded Televarn's face and chest that she should express so much sentiment for *Nimbulan*. Nimbulan, the aging magician who forsook the power of his Commune, refused to lead Coronnan, and stood behind a king when he could have been king himself with more power than any three monarchs in the rest of Kardia Hodos.

"He's a sniveling weakling, Myrilandel. Why waste your love on him when . . ." At the last minute, Televarn closed his mouth over the words that would proclaim his intentions.

"You love her, too!" Yaassima's eyes grew round and wide; their colorless depths took on a dark purple shade that did not bode well for him.

"As do you, Yaassima. You want her body in your bed

as much as I want her in mine. Kill Nimbulan, and we can share her."

"An excellent idea. But I do not share what is mine, Televarn. Send the magician to the pit and take Nastfa and Golin with him. I see them hiding behind their friends. I want to know that they suffer a long time before they die."

"Never! Nimbulan must die now," Televarn screamed. "All my plans are for naught if he lives. Kill him." He thrust his knife into Yaassima's back, waving for his followers to do the same to his rival.

Two dozen Rovers cast off concealing cloaks and hoods. They drew swords in unison. Yaassima's guards reacted quickly, extending their own weapons in mute challenge.

Shouts and cries and the clash of weapons wielded in anger erupted throughout the Justice Hall. Myri grabbed Amaranth away from Kalen, desperate to know the child was safe. Her head spun with the rapid shift of emotions and her knees nearly buckled with relief when she saw Yaassima sag under Televarn's knife. At the same time her healing talent burned within her, trying to drag her to the victim and heal her.

Between two ribs. Not mortal. Televarn's aim was off. The painful wound evaporated from her consciousness. Yaassima would survive without Myri's attentions.

"Run, both of you," Scarface directed as he tossed Nimbulan his staff. He blocked an attack from a Rover with his own staff. Three quick moves sent the dark-haired man reeling backward. He fell over one of the elite guards. Their limbs and weapons tangled, bringing more men into the heap.

Myri's talent relayed the pain of the blow from one man's chin to her own jaw. She had to blink hard to keep her balance. She shifted forward to keep from falling.

Nimbulan fended off another Rover with his staff and his fists.

The blow to the side of his head sent pain pounding into her temple. She clutched the baby tighter, trying to block her talent. Her jaw ached as she ground her teeth together. She concentrated on biting the insides of her mouth rather than thinking about the chaotic pain generating emotions around her.

Nimbulan wrapped one arm around her waist, holding her up. The warmth of his body and the strength of the cord that pulsed between them gave her a measure of new strength and stability.

On the dais, Televarn and Yaassima struggled. The Kaalipha raked the Rover's face with her talonlike fingernails. At the same time, Televarn pushed against her jaw, trying desperately to keep her from gouging out his eyes.

Myri cried out in pain as he twisted the blade in Yaassima's back—the same way he had twisted the knife in Nimbulan's wound over a year ago.

Life and death hung in the balance. The void stretched wide before Myri. She held back. Saving Yaassima would not gain freedom or peace for the children or herself. She had to deliberately turn her back on a life that needed healing.

Suddenly the Kaalipha wrenched the bloody knife from her own side. She thrust the blade into Televarn's throat. Her gleeful laugh rose shrill and piercing above the chaotic noise of dozens of other individual brawls. Triumphantly, she withdrew the knife, twisting it. Then she plunged it deep into Televarn's heart.

"You need more than a poisoned knife to kill a dragon, Televarn," Yaassima sneered.

Breath left Myri's lungs in a sharp spasm as her talent changed focus from Yaassima to Televarn and back again.

She had to get out of here before someone died and took her with them into the void.

"Bring me my child. Return Hanassa to me!" Yaassima screamed to any who could hear.

A guard lunged for the precious bundle Myri carried.

She whirled sideways and back out of his reach. He took two running steps closer, stretching his arms to grasp the baby.

"No one will take my baby away from me!" Myri cried as she pivoted and kicked. Her foot landed squarely in the man's stomach.

"Ooof," he grunted, expelling air as he stopped short in surprise.

Protective triumph replaced Myri's empathic sharing of the man's pain.

"This way." Kalen pulled at her sleeve. "We have to

save Powwell." Her eyes lost the feigned wide-eyed innocence she'd been portraying since Myri had awakened her.
Only desperation shone through. Her ferret chittered anxiously on her shoulder.

"Lead the way, Kalen." Nimbulan knocked a black-clad
palace guard senseless with his staff. With his free hand he
herded them toward the interior doorway.

"Not that way," Scarface called behind them. "Rollett
has dismantled the gate. We can get out of the city." He
gestured toward the exterior of the palace.

"Not without our son," Nimbulan said. He saluted
Scarface. "Tell Rollett we'll join him soon." With a few
swipes of his staff, he cleared a passage for Myri and Kalen.

Scarface shrugged and followed. Maia grabbed his arm.
"You've got to protect me. My people will kill me if I do
not bring them the child," she panted as she ran to keep
up with him.

Myri reluctantly nodded to Maia, knowing the truth of
her statement. But she'd have to watch the woman. She
couldn't be allowed the opportunity to steal Amaranth.

Scarface blocked an overzealous Rover as he shifted the
aim of his throwing knife from Nimbulan to Maia. "Come,
then, but if you betray us, I'll kill you myself," he grunted
as he tripped one of the black-clad guards.

Pain and fear receded as Myri separated herself from the
two dozen or more individual fights in the Justice Hall. No
one seemed to know who to fight for or against.

She'd last seen Nastfa and Golin and some of the other
black-clad guards fighting with the Rovers against Yaassima's more loyal followers. Moncriith and his followers entered the fray, surprising Nastfa from the rear.

Good-bye and thank you! Myri thought toward her val-
iant ally. *Escape by the gate if you can. Ask for Rollett.
He'll let you through.*

She ran with her companions through the twisting interior tunnels. Her senses insisted the way was familiar, but
she'd never been in this portion of the palace before. Or
had she?

No time to wonder. She had to find Powwell. She had
to get out of Hanassa. Now. Before the guards organized
themselves and closed the gates.

Down. Down into the heart of the volcano. The heat increased.

Nimbulan was sweating, too. Amaranth fretted, kicking at her blankets.

Darkness pressed against Myri's eyes. Nimbulan lit the end of his staff with soothing green witchlight.

Kalen seemed to know the way. In this matter, Myri trusted her. Kalen loved Powwell as she loved nothing else in this life.

The tunnels took on an unholy red glow. Myri stumbled and caught her balance against the rock wall. Heat seeped through her clothes from the living stones.

Pressure on her back told her of a dozen or more men who followed her. Desperation pushed them to stop her flight before Yaassima's rage turned on them.

Myri ran faster. Down. Hotter. Her mouth went dry. The baby slept, whimpering with discomfort.

At last, light appeared at the end of the tunnel. Red light, pulsing and flaring brighter, then dimming a fraction. Myri felt like she was staring at the sun after the darkness of the tunnels.

"That's the beginning of the pit," Kalen said. She pointed to a massive gate of crossed iron bars straight ahead. Footsteps and shouts echoed against the tunnel walls behind them. Many men, heavily booted. Their anger twisted inside Myri.

"They mean to kill us," she gasped.

They stumbled forward. Nimbulan and Scarface fumbled with the lock. Finally a blast of magic from Nimbulan's staff broke the latch.

"Rollett was right. Disrupt the magnetic fields and everything falls apart," Nimbulan said with a wry smile.

They all ran forward. Nimbulan closed and latched the gate behind them with more magic. Myri hoped the spell would hold against whatever bespelled keys Yaassima's men had.

Another dozen steps forward and around a bend in the tunnel, a broad cavern opened. They all stopped short.

Dozens of people, clad in filthy rags, turned to stare at them. Some held bizarre metal tools. Others dipped water from a sulfurous smelling stream. A few lounged against rough pallets made of more rags, staring listlessly at an empty pot that sat in a niche with a rope attached to the handle.

Six black-clad guards sat in a far corner of the cavern, playing a game of dice. They looked briefly toward the newcomers and returned to their game.

In the background a loud chugging noise beat against Myri's physical senses. Pain lanced from her ears across her eyes. She felt Nimbulan and Scarface wince, too. Amaranth whimpered, too exhausted from the heat to cry loudly.

Maia seemed to accept the heat and noise as natural. Had she been here before? How and when? No one had been known to escape from the pit and live.

Hopeless resignation weighed heavily upon Myri. The people who had been consigned to the pit trudged through their days waiting for death to release them from the heat and the drudgery. The guards didn't care about anything except the end of their shift. They feared something down here almost as much or more than they feared Yaassima.

Myri stretched her senses, counting the lives she encountered. Hundreds of despairing personalities blurred together. Her talent couldn't sort them.

"I can't sense Powwell," Kalen cried. "I can't find him anywhere in the pit!"

Chapter 28

The shouts and clanging of men beating their weapons against the gate echoed down the tunnel. Nimbulan only hoped the lock would hold against them.

"Powwell!" Kalen darted off into a side tunnel, calling anxiously.

Myri set off in a different direction, stretching her senses as far as she could.

"We can't afford the time to aimlessly search." Nimbulan pulled her back. "We have to do this right or we'll never get out of here. Kalen, Myri, come back. We'll do this with a plan!"

"I fully intend to get out of here, if for no other reason than to make you pay for deserting the children and me, love," Myri replied. A half grin mocked the severity of her words.

Kalen returned grumpily, frowning at Myri's gesture of affection.

Nimbulan had no doubt he'd hear about his intense sense of duty for the rest of his life. In that moment he vowed to make up for every slight he'd given her since their first meeting. "I love you, too. Now stay with us, both you and Kalen, and let's get on with the business of escaping this hellhole."

"Where are Powwell and Yaala?" Nimbulan addressed the prisoners in the command voice he usually reserved for the battlefield.

All of the denizens of the pit turned back to whatever they were doing, without bothering to answer. The guards cowered deeper into their private thoughts and fears.

"The Kaalipha has been stabbed. There's a riot in the

Justice Hall. You are free. We can open the gate for you," Kalen added.

Two men near the entrance who rubbed oil onto strange metal tools looked up again. A flicker of interest crossed their eyes. Two men darted furtively up the tunnel toward the gate.

"Armed men are coming closer with every heartbeat. Tell us where we can find Powwell, and we'll help defend you," Nimbulan added.

Some of the people heard him. Dully they shifted toward the interior cavern. The guards looked up with a spark of interest and . . . and hope?

"*Powwell!*" Kalen screamed.

"Pwl, pwl, pwl," the caverns called back to her.

"Follow those people into the next cavern." Scarface gestured with his staff. "We have to find a hiding place. Those guards will break the lock any minute now. They don't usually go beyond the gate. This time, I think they will."

"Did anyone see what happened to Golin and Nastfa?" Myri asked. "They helped me. If they lead those guards, we'll be safe."

"They are hardened assassins, Myri. Their fate is their own and not your concern," Nimbulan said, drawing her farther away from the entrance.

He tied his ratty black robe into a sling for the baby. The heat building in his skin knew a moment of relief. They'd all be shedding layers of winter clothing before long.

As he draped the carrier around Myri's neck, he glanced at the tiny red face drawn into a whimpering pucker. A sense of wonder nearly paralyzed him. He'd helped create this tiny morsel of life.

He traced the line of the child's cheek. Amaranth turned into his caress, seeking comfort and nourishment. She waved her tiny fists in delight.

A wave of possessiveness engulfed him. "My daughter. We have a daughter." Finally he looked into Myri's eyes for confirmation that this was indeed his child. His wife smiled and time stopped around them.

"You also had a son," Maia said defiantly. She crossed her arms across her breasts, drawing her shoulders down.

"But he died before he had lived a full moon. He might have lived if you had taken me back to the city with you. There are plagues in Hanassa that kill the innocent and leave outlaws and misfits untouched."

Nimbulan pitied her. She was as much Televarn's victim as Myri was.

"Neither of you told me about my children," he said. A bit of anger crept into his tone. "I couldn't meet my responsibilities to them if I didn't know they existed."

Did either woman consider him fit to help raise the babies? His shoulders felt tremendously heavy with the conviction that Rollett was the only young person he had successfully helped raise—he'd only had a few moons with Powwell and no time at all with Kalen. He hoped Rollett was managing at the gate and could hold it long enough for Nimbulan to get back there with this motley group.

Quickly he sent a telepathic message to his journeyman. His mind met only confusion, no specific identity. Perhaps the depth of the cave system and the configuration of the rocks blocked his talent.

"You weren't around to tell about babies or anything else," the women replied in unison.

"I would have been if I'd known."

"Hmf," Myri snorted and centered her attention on her squirming child. Maia turned her back on them.

"I promise I'll protect you both," Nimbulan said to the women. "You and the children." Possessive protection welled up in him.

"Time enough to play proud papa later," Scarface nudged him forward. "We've got to get out of here. With or without the boy you seek."

The chugging sounds grew louder as they passed through a low, narrow tunnel to the next cave. Nimbulan resisted the urge to cover his ears. He had to absorb every sound, lest he miss some trace of Powwell.

Beyond the threshold of this cavern lay a huge black metal monster, chugging and belching. *Yeek, kush, kush. Yeek, kush, kush.* Long, thick tentacles ran into the beast from the floor and out of it into tiny tube tunnels high up on the wall. He was reminded of the mass of wire-thin lines within the hollow slapping rock.

"What's the fuss?" The woman Scarface had called Yaala approached them from yet another cavern, deeper and lower into the volcano.

An older man of scarecrow proportions gestured mutely toward the gate and the guards. Yaassima's men were scrambling to their feet, pretending to look alert and concerned as the noise from their approaching comrades increased. Yaala lifted her eyes to the newcomers. Puzzlement crossed her face.

"Are you new prisoners? I've never known Yaassima to send a baby down here," she said approaching Myri.

"We flee the Kaalipha." Nimbulan addressed her. "But we can't leave without Powwell."

"You can't escape Yaassima." She shrugged one shoulder and turned back toward the inner cavern.

"Yaassima is dead," Kalen insisted. "We saw Televarn stab her with a poisoned knife."

"Truly?" Yaala turned back, interest animating her face. Nimbulan noticed the draconic characteristics then, in the long straight nose and high forehead. But her fingers weren't overly long and the strands of hair that strayed below her knotted kerchief were darker, more yellow. Her eyes were a definite blue, not the pale, nearly colorless orbs of Yaassima and Myri. He wondered if she had the pronounced spinal bumps of the vestigial dragon horns like Myri did, or if that trait was tied to the long fingers and nearly transparent skin.

Myri looked as if she was about to protest Yaassima's death. None of them knew for certain who lived and who had died in the Justice Hall.

"The child speaks the truth," Myri said. "We saw Televarn stab Yaassima and twist the knife as he pulled it out."

"We must hurry," Nimbulan added. "We don't know how long the guards will be disorganized and allow us through the gates." *Rollett, are you safe? Did you succeed?*

No answer.

"I . . . I'm not ready to take control of Hanassa. I don't know how to use all of Yaassima's toys. I need more time!" Yaala looked anxiously from the noisy monster to the chain of passageways back to the surface.

"Hanassa isn't worthy of you, Yaala. Come with us." Powwell entered the cavern from the same interior room

Yaala had come from. His skin had taken on a ghastly gray pallor that didn't bode well for his health. He touched the woman's shoulder affectionately, staring at her.

Myri reached out a hand to him. Powwell grasped it and pulled his foster mother into a tight hug, baby and all. Then he reached to gather Kalen close, too. The little girl edged between Myri and Powwell, effectively breaking their embrace.

Through the cord connecting him to his wife, Nimbulan sensed her need to touch the young man with healing and strength. Strength she couldn't spare until they were all safe. He also sensed her puzzlement over Kalen's obvious jealousy.

"There isn't time to waste arguing," Nimbulan intervened. "The guards are close on our heels. We don't know their loyalty. We have to hide, then sneak past them."

"They won't cross the threshold. They'll barricade it and starve us out rather than risk ambush in the pit. I've seen them do it before, the first time I organized a rebellion," Yaala said bitterly. "Now I know better. There is no escape from the pit until I know how to shut down every machine and deprive the Kaalipha of her so-called magic and her weapons. But I also have to know how to restart them, so I can take control away from her. I'm not ready!"

"Machines?" Nimbulan stepped forward, curious. He needed to examine the chugging black monster. His fingers itched to sketch the machine and record it in his journal. Only the Stargods could have built so fantastic a device that gave an individual the power to mimic magic.

"Yes, machines. Yaassima doesn't really have any magic. It's all tricks, powered by 'tricity," Powwell explained. "I know how to stop them. And I know another way out, if you are willing to trust me." He looked Nimbulan squarely in the eye; no longer a boy, hardened into a man, making a man's decisions.

"I trust you, Powwell," Nimbulan replied. "I always have."

Rollett! Answer me, boy. We're going out another way. Escape now, while you can.

No answer, nothing but the confusion of a dozen minds in chaos.

He'd just have to come back for Rollett. It wouldn't be

easy, but he couldn't leave his journeyman. He'd lost too many friends, students, and colleagues.

But he had his wife and children back. His quest was partially complete.

"I'm sorry to deprive you of your staff, but I need it. And yours, too." Powwell turned to Scarface, holding out his hand for the tool.

"No, Powwell," Yaala screamed. "I can't let you destroy them!" She launched herself at the young man's back, fingers flexed as if trying to claw him.

"You can't stop him!" Kalen stepped between Yaala and Powwell. "We have to get out of here. The only way to do that is to destroy the Kaalipha's power." She clenched her fist and slammed it into the woman's jaw.

Yaala teetered in her tracks, disoriented and confused. Scarface rushed to catch her.

Sounds of a scuffle broke out in the cavern behind them. Shouts of triumph and pain rang out louder, then the clash of iron weapons against stone. Screams of terror echoed through the cavern system. Underneath the sounds of battle, the rhythm of the machines beat discordantly.

Flickers of movement, a wisp of white, caught Nimbulan's attention. He looked right and left and saw nothing. The guards wore black, not white. The prisoners' clothing was mired in gray filth. Who watched them?

"This way," Powwell called to them as he retreated deeper into the cave. He looked over his shoulder, shuddered slightly, then crossed his wrists and flapped his hands—an ancient ward against evil. What did he fear?

"We don't have to destroy all the machines, only Old Bertha," Powwell said. Determination hardened his jaw. "She is the key to all the little ones that feed power into the palace network of wires."

"No, not Old Bertha. If you shut her down, we'll never get her started again," Yaala protested weakly. "Bertha is sick. I have to take care of her." She rolled her head against Scarface's shoulder, then her eyes closed and she went limp.

"I'll carry her," Scarface said. "I want out of Hanassa as badly as you do. I've had enough of thieves and cutthroats and rule by terror." He gestured with his chin for Nimbulan and the women to follow Powwell.

They passed through four more caverns, each containing a machine identical to the first one they had encountered. The sounds of fighting behind them faded. Nimbulan breathed easier. Powwell stopped looking over his shoulder.

Nimbulan wished he had time to stop and examine the exotic machines. Powwell pressed on through an empty cavern and then into the largest chamber they had yet encountered. Here resided a monstrous machine, easily four times the size of any one of the others. Arrhythmic coughs and wheezes accompanied the regular chugging he had almost become used to. Clearly, this machine was sick. Possibly dying.

"Well, Old Bertha, time to put you out of your misery," Powwell addressed the black monster. "You've served the dragon lords of Hanassa and that white wraith well. Now it's time to rest." Grimly he took Nimbulan's staff and thrust it deeply into the machine's belly, through an open panel.

Old Bertha whirred and clanged. Bright green sparks shot out from the open panel. The lights around the cavern flickered and dimmed.

A curious emptiness tingled in Nimbulan's right palm where he usually carried the now dead staff.

Powwell thrust Scarface's staff into a second opening. More sparks, louder whirring and bright flashes of fire belched from the dying machine.

"This way," Powwell called, indicating a narrow tunnel. "She'll explode in about five minutes, just about the time the guards arrive to kill us."

Nimbulan hurried behind Powwell. He herded Myri and Maia before him. He had no need to direct Kalen, she stuck closely to Powwell's heels, making certain Myri and the baby never came in contact with the boy. Scarface flung the unconscious Yaala over his shoulder and brought up the rear.

At the end of the short passage, Nimbulan saw the roiling mass of fiery lava and no other exit.

Chapter 29

"Let me get this straight. I have to face a dragon, and if I don't freak out or transform into a demon, then your Council will consider me human?" Katie asked Quinnault. She turned her big fire-green eyes on him.

Residual fear lay behind her innate humor and optimism. And her mind remained firmly closed to him.

Quinnault searched for signs of bruises on her lovely throat. Only a little redness lingered to remind them of the assassin.

The Rover, Piedro, was safely confined to his dungeon cell. Quinnault had checked only a few moments ago to make certain his prisoner hadn't slipped away.

He knew how to deal with physical danger to himself and Katie. He didn't know how to ask what had transpired between Katie and Kinnsell before Piedro had entered her room. They would have to discuss it before the wedding. First he had to make sure there would be a wedding.

"The dragon will determine if you are fully human and worthy to be our queen," he replied, not knowing how to address the other problems facing them.

The maids had dressed her in a simple white shift that hung lightly on her body. The fine linen fabric revealed tantalizing hints of curves. He could see the outline of her legs and wanted more.

"One of your magicians is going to create an illusion of a dragon, to make me think I face a monster worse than that assassin last night," Katie continued, mulling over the problem. "I can deal with that, though I don't like other people messing with my mind." She shook her beautiful head, the soft curls bouncing and catching glimmers of torchlight.

Only you, Scarecrow. You're the only one I trust with my thoughts.

Then let me in. Let me see what truly frightens you so that I can combat it for you.

Her mind snapped shut once more.

I can't let you see my secrets until we are wed, until you can't send me home.

"I've seen into your mind, Katie. You have secrets, but that doesn't make you a monster. I know that you are good, and kind, and honest. You care for me. What more do I need to know?"

A tear touched her eye, and she blinked it away quickly.

"Kiss me, Scarecrow. Quickly before I lose my courage."

He bent his head, savoring the warmth of her trembling mouth. She stood on tiptoe to bring him closer yet, clinging to him with a kind of desperation. He enfolded her into his arms, keeping her close to his heart.

"I won't let anyone hurt you, Katie. Not my people, or your father, or the dragons."

"I can deal with your monsters, Your Grace. I expected primitive plumbing and no central heating. Assassination and kidnap are facts of life for the nobility of my world as well as yours. What bothers me is the lack of privacy. Am I never going to be allowed to be alone?" She gestured with her head to the bevy of maids who stood behind her, respectfully looking away from their new mistress. The almost smile was back in her eyes.

When he had left her last night, Quinnault had ordered two of them to sleep in the room despite Katie's protestations. They should have been there before the Rover tried to strangle her. But Katie had sent them away. Had she wanted merely to guard her privacy or to have a moment to argue with her father? And how had Piedro known she would prefer to sleep alone? Most noblewomen always kept a maid in their beds if their husbands were not there to warm them.

"Servants, courtiers, and pests are a way of life for nobility on this world, I'm afraid." Quinnault spoke quietly into her ear so that none of the hovering servants, courtiers, and pests could overhear. He didn't trust his telepathy to penetrate her barriers. A few more kisses and no barriers would stand between them. Not even their clothes. "There will be moments we can steal away from them, but not often. All these people are a sign of respect for my authority as well as part of our security."

Assassination and betrayal had been a way of life for three generations in Coronnan during the Great Wars of Disruption. He liked to think he'd eliminated those factors. True power lay in maintaining peace not imposing war. But, he knew, many people—including some of his Council—hadn't accepted that premise yet.

Piedro had made it clear that he intended to end Quinnault's reign by making it look as if he had murdered his own betrothed.

But Piedro hadn't acted alone. Who had hired the Rover?

Quinnault checked the shadows for signs of unwanted intruders. There were a lot of shadows. 'Twas barely dawn outside. The interior of the keep was still dark and damp with night chill. Quinnault shivered inside his heavy tunic and cloak. Katie must be freezing in the simple shift that symbolized purity and her maiden status.

His thoughts jerked to a halt. He hadn't thought for a moment to inquire about previous lovers. Somehow, it hadn't seemed important until now. Customs might be different in her land. Some societies didn't value virginity. Coronnan seemed strangely ambivalent on the subject. Festival in the more remote regions initiated youngsters into the joy of sex by the age of twelve or fourteen. A population depleted by war made the begetting of children more important than virginity at marriage. Noble lords sheltered their offspring, enforcing sexual innocence, to artificially inflate their value in the marriage market—insuring there were no bastard children to claim titles and lands.

Quinnault had refrained from joining with a woman throughout his teenage years while he studied for the celibate priesthood. Once he assumed the leadership of his family and responsibility for his lands he indulged in the random partnering of Festival, but so far had not found a woman he was willing to repeat the experience with.

Somehow, he knew that life with Katie would be different. With her in his bed, he wouldn't need to think about any other woman.

"Uh . . ." he heard himself make noises, but he'd forgotten what she said in his speculation about the wedding night to come.

If the dragons found her worthy.

If the Council accepted the decision of the dragons.

"I know how to block illusions if I have to, but I suppose that would be impolitic," she repeated.

"The dragons are not delusions cast by the magicians, Katie. They are real. They are wise. And they won't hurt you, no matter how frightening they are the first time you encounter one. I remember the day they arrived at the School for Magicians. I thought my heart would stop beating before they ate me." He almost smiled in memory of that fateful day when magic in Coronnan changed for all time. "Now I know better. Dragons are meat eaters, but they don't like the taste of humans. And they like their meals cooked. Why else were they blessed with fiery breath?" He grinned, trying to relieve her fears.

"Your magicians must be very good indeed, to fool the entire populace." She smiled and tucked her little hand into the crook of his elbow. "Come. Your 'dragons' await us. Or should I say, the Council and the magicians await us."

"Katie," Quinnault said as he halted in mid-step. "You have to understand the dragons are real, now, before you see them and run away screaming in fear."

"Princesses from Terra—Terrania—are made of sterner stuff than you think. I have faced worse terrors than an illusory dragon." Impatience crossed her face, erasing the humor that normally danced across her features.

Suddenly, Quinnault feared for her life as well as their future—more so than when he wrestled Piedro into submission. Dragons had made a pact never to willfully harm a human so long as humans did no harm to the dragons and offered the tithe of Tambootie and livestock to the creatures. Shayla had announced the end of the Compact more than three weeks ago when Myrilandel had disappeared.

What if Katie, with her strange Varn powers and technology took it into her head to harm the dragon? The pact would be shattered beyond mending and communal magic would dissolve forever with the loss of the dragons. Quinnault's reign of peace would be more effectively ended than if Piedro had succeeded last night in implicating the king in murder.

"Your Grace," a page greeted them as he hurried up the corridor to fetch them. "The Council awaits in the Grand Courtyard." The boy bowed deeply, sneaking a peek at Katie as he bent his head.

"We haven't time to argue about the reality of dragons, Katie. Just stand still and let the dragon judge you."

"I don't like the idea of being judged by an imaginary beast." She set her jaw determinedly, an expression she had assumed when confronting her father. She'd won that argument.

"You are as stubborn as my sister," he muttered. "I hope you aren't as foolish and earn the condemnation of my lords."

"I didn't know you had a sister. When will I meet her?"

"Most likely you won't." He clenched his teeth together, firmly closing the issue of Myrilandel and why she couldn't be a part of his life.

Thoughts of his brief reunion with the sister he thought had died at the age of two, brought him to Myrilandel's husband, Nimbulan. Why had the Senior Magician of the Commune defied orders and gone in search of Myrilandel himself, without so much as a note of explanation? A younger man would have a better chance of succeeding. Nimbulan should be here now to guide Quinnault and Katie through the coming ordeal.

And prevent complex plots involving Rovers and traitors close to home. If anyone could ferret out the hidden motives and traps in the Varn's offer, it was Nimbulan.

His Senior Magician had a lot of explaining to do when he returned.

He wouldn't think about Nimbulan not returning from his dangerous quest.

A blast of cool air from the open doors of the palace onto the Grand Courtyard sent lumbird bumps up Quinnault's arms. Katie shivered slightly beside him. He patted her hand in reassurance, but couldn't look at her. Not now. One look at her skeptical face and he'd drag her back inside the palace, away from the ordeal by dragon.

Seven of the Twelve Lords awaited them, standing in a rough circle around the edges of the circular paving. None of their ladies had joined them. By their own choice or a decision of the Council? Quinnault didn't like the implication that the women needed to be protected from this ceremony.

Master magicians from the Commune filled in the spaces between the lords. Every man in the court looked grim and unforgiving. The walls and risers intended for this outdoor arena hadn't been constructed yet. The dais, left over from Quinnault's coronation last spring, stood in the exact center of the circle. Only Old Lyman stood at the foot of the dais.

Quinnault looked up into the lightening sky for signs of a dragon. He wished he knew which one would answer the summons put out by the magicians last night. He'd prefer docile old Ruussen, the red-tipped male who viewed all humans as beloved children to be coddled and indulged with humor.

"There is still time to change your mind, Your Grace," Lyman said as Quinnault and Katie approached the dais. "The ambassador from SeLenicca is prepared to send messages of reconciliation to his king if you renounce this woman in favor of the princess of SeLenicca."

"I suppose he sent messages by magician last night, authorizing an invasion?" Quinnault stared at the top of the western wall, wondering how long a reprieve from invasion such a reconciliation would buy him.

"Every magician was busy last night, sending messages through the glass to all interested parties. I intercepted a particularly interesting one aimed at a *Bloodmage* in Hanassa," Lyman replied. The last statement was almost whispered.

"Moncriith," Quinnault said through clenched teeth. "I wonder who really rules in SeLenicca, King Lorriin or the Bloodmage? Is their drought so terrible they will engage a Bloodmage to win a few acres of grain from Coronnan?"

"I fear it is so, Your Grace," Lyman replied sadly. "Food is short all over Kardia Hodos. Our rain and the acres left fallow during the Great Wars of Disruption incite jealously and greed among those whose bellies are slack and whose children are dying of hunger."

"I feel for them. But I cannot feed the world. If they

invade, I won't be able to spare the men to plow the extra land to provide food for those in my own country let alone theirs."

Katie squeezed Quinnault's arm, reminding him of the instant rapport they had shared. "I can give you a few new seeds that will multiply your yield per acre. But it will take time for those seeds to grow and produce enough more seeds to sow all your fields. The rest of my dowry must be enough to defend Coronnan for now," she whispered.

Quinnault looked out over the Bay, a sight that would be obscured when the palace and this courtyard were finished.

"Use your FarSight, Lyman, and tell me what you see on those distant islands." Quinnault pointed to the small dark specks that were just barely visible on the horizon.

Lyman's eyes crossed slightly as he took the regulation three breaths to trigger the spell. "I see a great many men on four small islands. They are very active, but I cannot tell what they do."

"Kinnsell and his crews," Katie said. "They uphold their part of our bargain, Quinnault."

"And I must uphold mine. Summon the dragon, Lyman. Katie, my love. You must stand in the center of the dais, alone, and wait for your destiny." His heart in his throat, Quinnault disengaged her small hand from his arm and stepped back into the circle of nobles and magicians who waited on the judgment of a dragon to determine their future queen.

"Wait a moment. The gate will open soon. I can't control it," Powwell said. In a few sparse sentences he explained his observations to the others.

Nimbulan nodded slowly with each sentence. His hand came up, palm outward. Scarface peered at the opening through squinted eyes as if testing the truth of Powwell's statements.

Powwell hoped, desperately, that the portal chose that circular opening in the forest of Coronnan as its next destination. Too many of the scenes he'd viewed wouldn't support life for long.

"Yaassima!" Myri choked. She grabbed her ears, scrunching up her face in agony. The crystal dragon pendant glowed eerily in the dim cavern. Powwell thought he heard a high-pitched whistle in the back of his head, but couldn't be sure.

She stumbled closer to the tunnel entrance, relaxing a little as she put some distance between herself and the pit—or did she move closer to the palace and Yaassima's controls?

Nimbulan grabbed for the pendant. He jerked his hand away from it as if burned.

"Televarn threatened me with a necklace like that if I didn't spy for him in the palace." Maia slunk away from Myri in fear. "I didn't want to be chained to him. It's bad enough that he's in my mind all of the time."

"Yaassima is the only one with the key to that necklace," Kalen said matter-of-factly. "Myri can't take it off while the Kaalipha lives. Nor can she set foot outside the palace perimeter and live." A small secret smile crept over her face.

Powwell looked at her, alarmed at her attitude, almost as if she wanted Myri dead, or to remain Yaassima's captive. He didn't like the way that smile lit her eyes with mischief, nor the fact that she kept shifting her expression from eyes wide open and innocent looking to hunched over and closed. She only did that when she was plotting something more drastic than her usual deviousness.

"What do you know?" he whispered to his foster sister, the one anchor in his rootless life.

She turned that false smile of hers on him, as bright as the sparks that had shot from Old Bertha.

A blast of hot wind rose up from the churning lava.

"It's happening," Scarface announced. "Amazing. The gate is opening!"

They all looked at the arched opening as the boiling red-and-yellow lava turned to a vortex of red and green and black and white. A lot of white—like the wraith that haunted the caverns. Powwell shuddered in cold fear.

A vast arctic plain, covered with drifting snow and frozen grasses stretched before them. The shadow of a massive ice flow at the edge of the plain formed an arch. Beyond it stretched miles and miles of frozen wasteland without a hill, shelter, or sign of people.

"We can't go there," Nimbulan said.

Myri moaned as she pressed her fingertips against her

temples. Her pale skin blotched with purple flushes high on her cheekbones and deep on her throat, spreading downward onto her chest.

"What kind of spell is this?" Nimbulan wrenched at the necklace. All color drained from his face.

"It's Yaassima's magic. Myri can't leave Hanassa as long as both she and the Kaalipha live," Kalen repeated. "This is proof that Televarn failed . . ." She turned as if to flee the tunnel. Powwell grabbed her around the waist to stop her.

"Yaassima doesn't have real magic," Yaala said from where Scarface had sat her inert body against the wall of the narrow tunnel. "Every power she mimics begins and ends with the machines. When they explode, so will the necklace."

"Then how does she control the necklace?" Nimbulan turned on her. Anger brought color back into his face. "We have to get if off Myri before it destroys itself and her with it."

"If the necklace lives, then Yaassima does, too." Yaala seemed to crumble in on herself. "She'll kill me this time, just like she killed my father. Then she'll dip her hands in my blood and taste it as if it was the sweetest ambrosia. My own mother . . ." She shuddered and shook herself as if ridding herself of the hideous memory. "I might have a key to the necklace." Yaala levered herself up from the ground.

"The gate is closing!" Scarface said. The hot wind from the pit died with the gate.

"Wait a few moments. It will come around again to a different location," Powwell reassured him. "The wind comes just before the swirling colors."

Yaala peered closely at the clasp on the back of the chain and the crystal pendant on the front. "Can I have more light?" she asked.

"The guards are very close," Powwell reminded her. "Light will alert them to where we are. Right now, they are stumbling around half blind. Torchlight doesn't go very far in these caves." He peered out into the larger cavern.

A man with a torch rounded Old Bertha. Strange shadows danced around the flames. Powwell ducked back into the cavern. "Hurry. They are close," he whispered harshly. His throat nearly closed on the words. He hadn't seen the wraith, but the hair on his arms and the back of his neck stood up as it did when it was near.

Yaassima would kill him this time. She'd kill them all without a trial or explanation or anything.

Yaala pulled a small black box out of her pocket. " 'Motes work on the wands and the slapping rocks. Yaassima has several of them stashed in her pockets and hidden in her jewelry. That's how she triggers her special effects. This one might work on the necklace, if it's connected to the same frequency." She pressed the box against the clasp.

A soft whirring buzzed around the tunnel followed by a loud rattle. The necklace fell into Nimbulan's hands. Myri nearly collapsed against him. She rested her head on his shoulder.

"Gate's opening again," Scarface whispered.

"Hurry, the guard is coming." Powwell risked a quick peek into the cavern. The guard investigating Old Bertha and the two staffs jammed into her innards looked up at the sounds from the 'mote.

"It's a desert this time. Hotter than the wind portending it. Weird arching rocks," Scarface said, disappointed.

"I've counted one hundred heartbeats between cycles," Nimbulan said.

"They aren't regular," Powwell told him. Sometimes faster, sometimes slower. I've counted ten different locations and they don't come in the same order every time. The snows-cape is new to me."

"We've got to get out of here. There are twenty men with torches out there, coming this way!" Kalen wailed. "I think Televarn is dead." Big tears rolled down her cheeks.

Kalen never cried. Powwell's heart felt too heavy to stay in his chest. His beloved Kalen cried for a murdering Rover when she wouldn't cry for anyone else.

"Stargods, I wish I had a dragon," Nimbulan whispered. "I wish Rollett were here, or would answer my calls. Can anyone else reach him?"

Scarface and Myri both shook their heads.

"Wish all you want, we have to take the next gate out. No matter what the location," Powwell whispered, moving away from the tunnel opening. Kalen remained, peering out. She dried her tears with her sleeve and stared grimly at Old Bertha.

"There they are! Get the Kaaliph," a guard yelled. His words echoed around the cavern. His footsteps sounded like thunder as he ran toward Kalen at the tunnel entrance.

"Gate opening," Scarface sighed at the first puff of the wind.

"Pray for green trees or a dragon," Nimbulan tossed the necklace into the still visible pit. The portal seemed to explode in a shower of every color in the spectrum.

Green trees materialized before their eyes. Trees and rough grass and round mountain peaks behind. More slowly, the outline of a shimmering dragon flickered into view.

"Go, go, go," Powwell shouted. He grabbed for Kalen's hand to pull her through the gate with him.

"Wiggles!" she screamed and pulled free of Powwell's grasp. She chased after her familiar as it scampered into the main cavern.

"Kalen!"

"No, Powwell, we have to leave, now. She made the choice." Nimbulan grabbed his arm. His teacher dragged him away from the cavern opening. Kalen disappeared into the darkness beyond.

"Kalen," Powwell called. "I can't leave you."

"You must. We have to escape now. She made her choice," Nimbulan insisted. "She'll follow us when she can. If she wants to. She's a survivor."

The constant whining coming from Old Bertha raised in pitch to the intensity of a dragon scream. "Kalen, get away from the machine!" Powwell yelled.

Metal screamed against metal as pieces ripped free. A single boom and thud that shook the ground beneath them. Red fire, brighter than the pit, blazed within the cavern. A fissure opened in the wall, running horizontally from the pit into the cavern. Lava glowed behind it. Then another explosion was followed by the screams of dying men.

Blazing lava flared from the pit through the vision of the gate's destination.

Nimbulan yanked him harder. Powwell felt as if he were flying. . . .

"Kalen," he sobbed.

The hot wind followed him, a sure signal that the gate closed behind him. Cool green caressed his eyes while a fresh breeze smelling of Tambootie ruffled his hair.

Chapter 30

Nimbulan shook his head and blinked his eyes several times. The Kardia didn't boil and move beneath his feet. Fresh green grass, trees, and blue skies replaced the sense-destroying landscape of the gray tunnels beneath Hanassa. Cool air caressed his face. Air that smelled of life and dragons. Instinctively he gathered dragon magic. Like taking a deep gulp of air after holding his breath underwater for a long, long time. How many days ago had he nearly drowned in Televarn's Water spell? Two? Three? It seemed a lifetime. How long ago since he'd filled himself full of dragon magic without fear of depletion?

"We're free of Hanassa," he said. "But I don't know where we are."

He let Powwell collapse against the ground, stunned and crying over the loss of Kalen. The boy needed some time alone. Nimbulan turned his back to give Powwell privacy while he checked his companions and indulged in his own grief over Rollett. If only he'd thought to keep his journeyman close beside him . . . If only he'd tried a little harder to reach the boy.

A journeyman must travel alone to complete his quest.

Can you hear me, Rollett? he broadcast the message far and wide in all directions. He could focus it better if he knew where he was.

Nothing responded to his call. *S'murghit, Rollett, answer me!*

Still nothing.

He decided to concentrate on those he could help and guide. He trusted Rollett in many things. He'd just have to trust him to take care of himself. But he ached to return for the boy. Young man. He's a man now. On his own.

The dragongate remained firmly closed.

Yaala plopped down beside Powwell, not intruding on his grief, just there if he needed her. A valuable friend. Maybe more, in time.

Rollett had been a valuable friend as well as student and assistant. Almost more a son than Powwell whom he and Myri had adopted but he'd never had the chance to get to know.

Myri stood beside Nimbulan, a small smile spreading across her face. "I'm free!" she whispered, as if she couldn't quite believe it. "My baby is safe."

Nimbulan reached over and brought her tight against his side, where she belonged. She snuggled into him, filling the emptiness he'd lived with for too long. He lowered his head to kiss her once more. He'd never get enough of her. He pushed aside thoughts of Rollett, so he could appreciate the warmth of his wife.

Amaranth fretted once more and Myri lifted her from the sling onto her shoulder. "I think she's hungry. It has been a long night."

"It has indeed," Nimbulan replied. The first glow of false dawn shimmered on the frosty hilltops. A bird chirped a sleepy query to the sun. At least it wasn't raining or snowing. "I'm hungry, too. We need to find food and shelter. Warm clothes. *S'murghit,* where are we?"

"Uh, would you care to greet our host?" Scarface stammered through clenched teeth.

Nimbulan looked ahead of them to the emerging outline of a nearly transparent dragon. The growing light reflected off of wing veins and spinal horns in an iridescent display of all color/no color.

"Good morning, Shayla," he greeted the only female dragon in the nimbus. "I have rescued Myrilandel. I hope this restores the Covenant between humans and dragons. Can you tell us where we are, perhaps take us back to Coronnan City?"

The dragon dipped her head.

"She returns your greeting," Myri said. She cocked her head as if listening intently. "She wants to meet the baby. She doesn't say anything about where we are or taking us away." Myri separated herself from Nimbulan's embrace and walked over to the crouching beast.

Shayla stretched her neck to peer at the infant clutched in Myri's arms.

"Do you trust that monster with your child?" Scarface took a step forward, alarm radiating from his body. He clenched and flexed his fingers as if ready to launch a defensive spell.

"Of course I trust her. No dragon would deliberately hurt a human, especially children. They adore children."

"If you say so." Scarface's expression betrayed his inborn fear as well as his attempts to master it. "Damn cold out here. We need help."

Maia didn't look reassured at all. She backed up until she stood within the arched shadow cast by a rock outcropping. Her hands beat at empty air as if pounding on a firmly closed door.

The dragongate didn't open.

"So that's what Yaassima wants to be—wanted me to be," Yaala whispered. She turned her eyes away from the beautiful dragon to look at the grass.

"Yaassima didn't understand true dragonkind," Powwell replied, still wrapped in his grief. "She created a myth in her own mind and then tried to change reality to fit her version. She failed." He kept looking to the place where they had emerged from the pit. The shifting vortex of time and distance remained closed.

Nimbulan knew he'd have to go with Powwell if the boy decided to return for Kalen. But he had to get back to the capital, too. He had to take care of Myri and her baby. He probably owed something to Maia as well. She had borne him a son, though the baby had died. His responsibilities weighed heavily on him at the moment.

Rollett would understand. Wouldn't he?

Ah, Rollett, what have I done to you?

"Ask Shayla again where we are, Myri. I need to get back to Coronnan City and warn Quinnault of the impending invasion," Nimbulan said. He kept looking at the round tops of the hills that stretched into the distance. "You might ask when we are as well. Those hills look much older than the sharper peaks of Coronnan."

"I don't think I want to hear this." Scarface held his

temples and sat heavily on a nearby rock. He began gathering loose sticks and branches, piling them into a fire stack.

A mental chuckle invaded Nimbulan's mind. The humor behind the brief communication was definitely draconic in nature.

"Shayla says we are in the time you expected to be. The dragongate folds distance not time." Myri straightened her neck and peered at the dragon with a touch of concern creasing her brow.

"Something calls her. She must leave." Myri looked around, rapidly shifting her focus from the nearby trees and grass to the far hills.

Shayla bunched her shoulder muscles and spread her wings in preparation for flight.

"Where are we?" Nimbulan asked hurriedly. His transportation was leaving. "We have to get back to the capital! We need warm clothing and food."

"Shayla says to beware of the massing men in the valley below." Myri's words were nearly drowned out by the downthrust of mighty wings.

"Massing men?" The sense of many lives pressed against his mind. "Hundreds, no thousands of men," he gasped.

"Angry men," Myri echoed his tone of concern.

"The army of mercenaries, preparing to invade Coronnan from SeLenicca," Scarface added. "We're in one of the mountain passes between the two countries."

"Mercenary patrols there, to the west with arrows nocked and swords drawn," Yaala gasped, jumping up and pointing.

"The gate is opening," Powwell shouted. "We can go back for Kalen." He jumped up and pointed to the rapidly shifting colors within an arch shaped shadow between boulder and tree.

"No!" Nimbulan stared at the partially opened portal. Moncriith is there waiting for us."

A hazy vision of the people behind the gate kept shifting out of focus, never solidifying. Blood pounded in his ears at the sight of Moncriith pushing Yaassima and Kalen into the pit. Huge tongues of lava reached up greedily to enfold them.

"Kalen!" Powwell rushed forward to catch the little girl. The gate dissolved before he reached them.

Chapter 31

Myri ran downhill as fast as she could. Nimbulan carried
Amaranth. Yaala dragged a reluctant Powwell away
from the dragongate.

Soldiers followed them, close on their heels. She sensed
more men running beside them. Still others moved to cut
off their retreat.

Nimbulan and the others stopped short before the barricade of soldiers that appeared in front of them without
warning.

"Don't move." One of the mercenaries stepped forward
from the dozen men who aimed weapons at the party of
refugees. He held his arm straight out in front of him.

A witchsniffer. He'd followed the scent of dragon magic
to capture Myri and Nimbulan and the others.

Myri looked from the drawn swords to the eyes of the
soldiers holding the weapons. Their fanatical hate nearly
blistered her empathic talent. "They are Moncriith's men,"
she whispered to Nimbulan, choking back her fear of the
Bloodmage who had stalked her nearly all her life.

She wouldn't allow her fear to keep her from protecting
her children and her husband.

"Moncriith?" Yaala mouthed the name without sound.
"He helped persuade Yaassima to murder my father and
exile me. He always meant to take over Hanassa. Now that
he has killed the Kaalipha, he can." Her words were soft
and bitter.

"Be quiet. Bind them." The mercenary leader gestured
for his men to come forward. They hesitated and shuffled
their feet.

"We have to get out of here, Nimbulan," Scarface said

under his breath. "Moncriith is smart enough to follow us through the gate." He deepened his breathing in preparation of a spell.

"Not yet. We have to know the battle plans," Nimbulan said harshly. "Then we have to relay the information to King Quinnault. We can't fight King Lorriin if we don't know his tactics."

Myri gripped his arm with both hands. Her long fingers clenched and released spasmodically. The swordsmen fumbled with ropes that hung from their belts rather than approach magicians.

She absorbed and understood their hesitation. Moncriith wasn't there to protect them from magic they didn't understand. The archers wavered in their aim a tiny fraction. Their uncertainty could make them release their arrows without thought or true aim. She retrieved Amaranth from her husband. The baby's best protection lay in keeping Nimbulan's hands free to work magic.

Maia tried to slink behind the nearest tree. Another soldier with nocked arrow met her at the side of the tree trunk. She backed up, joining the troop of refugees.

Myri deliberately gathered the soldiers' malice and compounded it with uncertainty. When the negative emotions churned in a heavy knot in her gut, she swallowed her misgivings and broadcast them back on a tight line to the aggressors. Her talent rebelled, bouncing back to her, compounding the negative emotions within her. She wanted to whimper and cower behind any cover she could find.

She had never used her empathy for anything but healing. This attack was against everything she had ever hoped to achieve with magic.

To protect her children, she swallowed the rebounded emotions and added fear to her broadcast.

At the first sign of wavering arrows, she turned, putting the baby between herself and her husband.

"Demon magicians!" The lead soldier hissed through his teeth. His still outstretched arm shook slightly. "Lord Moncriith ordered death to all demons." He raised his arm to signal the archers to fire.

"Wait!" Nimbulan commanded.

Myri had heard that tone of voice before—on the battlefield when an entire army and the full Commune of Magicians looked to him for leadership. She dropped her replay of bad emotions. The lead soldier's hand wavered in the up position. Myri held her breath.

"When I left Hanassa, Moncriith had just hired my band of mercenaries to join your ranks," Nimbulan said. "Kill us and you risk the wrath of your leader."

Myri peered closely at Nimbulan's face and aura. Untruth flickered around the edges of his statement. Not a total lie, but not the truth either.

"*Lord* Moncriith don't hire no magicians," the soldier averred. "And where's your band if you be a true captain? Women and babies can't fight a war."

"We merely seek shelter for our families before we join our band." Nimbulan dismissed the man's misgivings.

The witchsniffer didn't look as if he believed Nimbulan.

"What makes you think we are magicians?" Nimbulan asked in a reassuring tone. "We carry no staffs, nor do we wear the blue robes of the Commune, *Lord* Moncriith's true enemy." He held his arms out to his sides, palms out, as if inviting trust. At the same time, his arms came in front of Myri, urging her to seek protection behind him. His fingers curved slightly over his palms, he prepared a spell with that habitual gesture.

Myri sensed no ley lines in the immediate vicinity. Had Nimbulan gathered enough dragon magic when Shayla was here to neutralize the dozen or more men? She looked at Powwell and Scarface. They also prepared to defend with magic but waited for Nimbulan's lead.

Yaala and Maia huddled together as far away from the magicians and the mercenaries as they could. Carefully they inched toward a tree that might give them cover. If the mercenaries didn't stop them.

"You still haven't told us where to find your band of mercenaries. If you truly have one, *magician*," the sergeant accused. He looked back down the path he had recently traversed. No reinforcements seemed to be approaching.

"You didn't answer my question, sergeant. Nor did you salute a captain. Insubordination. I could have you flogged." Nimbulan's voice turned iron cold. Myri shivered from the implied menace behind his words.

"I smell the demons in you." The sergeant looked right and left hastily, betraying his nervousness.

"Moncriith makes witchsniffers sergeants over men with better leadership qualities," Scarface mumbled under his breath. Then louder he said, "Hanassa is rife with incompetents like him stumbling over their own feet, changing orders almost as fast as they make them. Any true mercenaries Moncriith hires will be demoralized and in disarray by the time they get here."

"I am a good leader!" the soldier protested. "I earned my rank."

"Did you truly?" Nimbulan pushed doubt into his words. He lifted his hands, still palm outward, still holding his magic tightly bound.

Beside him, Scarface did the same with a gesture of fluttery finger weaving. Powwell eased himself to stand next to Nimbulan. The toe of his boot touched the Senior Magician's foot. Their auras combined as did their magic.

Myri sensed the doubt growing in the archers. Their bow strings lost a little of their tension. The men holding swords dropped the tips a fraction.

Nimbulan and Powwell built upon the results of Myri's emotional attack.

Amaranth opened her eyes, focusing on her mother's face. The baby's emotions came through to her clearly. She feared the death of the men.

Your daughter is an empath! Myri screamed mentally to her husband. *Kill them and you will kill her.* Carefully, she clamped down on her own talent. She had the closest ties to the baby. Amaranth would know everything she felt, everything she absorbed, everything she broadcast—for good or for evil. All of the turmoil and chaos of the past night must have awakened Amaranth's talent early.

What of you, beloved? Nimbulan asked. The silver cord between them raced with their combined heartbeats.

I will survive. I have control over my talent now. The deaths of these men will hurt me, but not slay me. Our daughter will follow them to the void if they die violently in her presence.

"What do you mean to do with us?" Nimbulan asked evenly to the soldiers who still confronted him. "You're renegades, out to kill all strangers rather than save your energy and your weapons for the campaign you were hired to join."

Before the mercenaries could react, Nimbulan pointed the index fingers of both hands at the men. Faint blue sparks sizzled along his skin, shooting out of his fingernails. He directed the compulsion magic to engulf the mercenaries in a cloud of glowing blue sparkles. The cloud spread over the entire patrol.

He couldn't have commanded that much magic on his own. He nodded his thanks to Powwell for the boost to his magic.

Scarface aided him with his own spell, binding the men in place while Nimbulan questioned them.

The sergeant stared straight ahead, eyes glassy, barely breathing. His men froze in place. The blue sparks caught their expressions of horror.

Amaranth wailed as if stuck with a pin. Myri shied away from the freezing pain that bound the men's muscles in knots.

"Get this over with. Quickly, before Amaranth stops breathing," she ground out through her nearly paralyzed jaw. She edged over to Yaala and Maia, putting a little more distance between the baby and the paralyzed men.

Nimbulan nodded briefly to his wife. He forced down the panic of haste. He'd only be able to complete the task safely if he mastered his own emotions.

"When do you march across the border into Coronnan?" he addressed the mercenaries.

"Tonight, as soon as word arrives that King Quinnault has married the Princess of Terrania," the sergeant replied in a monotone.

Terrania! Was Quinnault totally insane?

"What about the troops coming to join you from Hanassa with Lord Moncriith?" Nimbulan forced out the words while keeping his rage and fear under control. If he vented his emotions, his daughter would suffer.

"They will have to catch up with us in Coronnan."

"Why not wait?" Nimbulan asked coolly. Through the silver cord, he sensed Myri using his emotional control of his magic to counteract the overwhelming fear within the mercenaries. Her muscles relaxed a little. Amaranth's breath continued uneven and difficult.

"We raid and pillage randomly. No pitched battles until we confront Quinnault's army near the capital. By then he won't have a populace to draw troops from."

S'murghit, how did one fight dozens of small battles without a single man directing the whole? Nimbulan needed masses of men to direct in an overall plan. He had no skill interpreting battle on the level of a single patrol.

"King Lorriin, when does he march?"

"He takes the city of Sambol tonight. Then he sails down the River Coronnan to take the capital, raiding as he goes."

"S'murghit!" Nimbulan said aloud this time. Guilt began to creep upward from his gut to his mind, clouding his thinking. "When did Quinnault have time to woo a princess and sign a marriage treaty? I knew I should have sorted through the offers for him before I left the city."

"The marriage negotiations took place in secret over many moons, led by Nimbulan, the king's magician," the sergeant replied as if the question had been addressed to him.

"That is interesting news to me." Nimbulan raised one eyebrow, biting his cheeks to keep from laughing at the ridiculous rumor. Nervous laughter.

"Quickly. We have to leave now. I don't like Amaranth's breathing." Myri bounced the baby in her arms, trying to break the empathic link between the infant and the men.

"Yes, we will leave. Scarface, can you arrange a delayed release from the thrall for these men? Powwell, set up a summons to Lyman at the Commune."

Powwell looked at his feet. Red tinged his cheekbones.

"I'm sorry, Powwell. I forgot you never mastered that spell before Televarn kidnapped you. I'll do it, as soon as we are away from here." Nimbulan, too, looked at his boots. If Powwell had been able to work the spell well enough to keep in contact with Nimbulan during the first few moons of Myri's exile from the capital, Nimbulan would have known of her pregnancy. He would have broken away from his responsibilities in the capital to be with her.

Instead, he had deluded himself that all was well with her because he did not hear otherwise.

That thought sobered him. Did he love her enough to sacrifice his work in the capital and with the Commune to be with her for her own sake, or only for the child of his own body he had wanted so desperately?

He'd waited until Shayla had broken the Covenant between humans and dragons to seek out the cause.

"Maybe the gate has opened again," Yaala said, still staring at the grouping of rocks and trees that had been their portal from the heart of the volcano. "I've got to find out what happened to Yaassima. Hanassa should be mine, not left to whatever riffraff decides to step in."

"The sequence and the timing of the dragongate are random," Powwell said harshly. Embarrassment at his failure to work a basic communication spell still tinged his face. "It needs an arch shape to solidify—even if only a shadow. Maybe the sunlight changed the opening. Maybe Kalen fell into a different location when the gate couldn't open here." Hope brightened his eyes.

"We have to get safely away before these men recover," Nimbulan reminded him. "I have to get this information back to Quinnault immediately, before he enters into this disastrous marriage. I won't leave you behind like I left Rollett. It's a long walk back to the capital." He stretched his arms as if gathering his little band into a herd.

"You won't leave me behind, but you'll desert Kalen. You'll let her die because you won't budge to help her. Just as you deserted Myri when she was pregnant and needed you most," Powwell said bitterly.

Chapter 32

Quinnault watched Katie march up the three steps of the dais, rolling her eyes in disbelief. His gut turned cold in despair. Visions of his solitary life stretched before his imagination. Having given his heart to her, he couldn't imagine marrying anyone else. Without this marriage he'd lose the port, he'd lose his credibility with his Council. He'd lose the stability of an heir.

She had to pass this test. She had to survive and become his wife!

He had fended off assassins last night. He only wished he could intervene with the dragon for her.

"Where is Nimbulan, Lyman? He should be here, presiding, advising. Helping," he whispered into the old magician's ear.

"He's off being a daddy and restoring the Covenant with the dragons. We'll know if he's done that if a dragon responds to my summons."

"Myrilandel had a baby? Why didn't Nimbulan tell me he's a father? I'd have given him leave to go to my sister moons ago. But I need him here now." Joy for the new life warred with his irritation that no one had told him.

"He didn't know himself until after he left." Lyman continued to scan the skies.

"Then why didn't you tell me? You seem to know more about it than Nimbulan. You always know more than you tell."

"It wasn't my secret to tell." The magician shrugged enigmatically.

"You also seem to know more about the dragons than anyone, including Myrilandel—who is half dragon—and myself with my magical bonds to them through the Coraur-lia. How, Lyman? Tell me now." Quinnault studied the old man.

"Because of Myrilandel, you know that purple-tipped dragons have special destinies. They are always born twins but only one may remain a dragon, the other must seek a different form to fulfill its destiny. My twin deserted dragonkind and sought his own life path, forever separated from dragonkind. It was left to me to live both lives."

"You were born a purple-tipped dragon!" Quinnault stared with his mouth half open. Quickly he recovered and checked the ring of lords and magicians to see if any of them had heard the astonishing confession.

"Look. There. Nimbulan must have succeeded in saving Myrilandel and her baby." Lyman pointed eastward, toward where the sun rose over the Great Bay.

"We will discuss this later, Lyman," Quinnault said, also looking across the bay.

A small shadow blocked the growing sunlight for a moment, then the light burst forth brighter, shimmering with rainbows. A dragon approached.

Quinnault shaded his eyes with his hand and looked toward the east for signs of the huge beasts that had blessed his coronation by flying over this courtyard at the moment the priests placed the Coraurlia on his head. His eyes slid right and left, dazzled by the light. He breathed a sign of satisfaction that warred with his concern for Katie. The dragons were as much a part of him now as Katie.

"There, look!" Lyman pointed higher than the rising sun on the stretch of the bay. "Lords of the Council, you should be able to see the dragons now."

Gradually the rainbows faded and revealed a vague outline of wings and spinal horns. All colors swirled into no color around the outline. The male dragons sported a primary color along their wing veins and horns. This, then, must be Shayla, the female leader of the nimbus. Quinnault's eyes wanted to slide around the flying form, giving the dragon an illusion of transparency.

At this distance she appeared no bigger than his sister's flywacket. But Quinnault knew Shayla would fill the courtyard. Her head was as high as two sledge steeds and her body as broad as two more.

A harsh judge who had announced the breaking of the Covenant. Quinnault knew the heat of guilt. He had exiled his sister, Myrilandel, the chosen intermediary between dragons and humans. Did Shayla hold a grudge?

He shifted his gaze to Katie. She, after all, was the point of this demonstration. She stood in the exact center of the dais, slim and tiny against the larger backdrop of the unfinished courtyard and the Bay beyond. The morning breeze pressed the thin fabric of her pure white shift against her body, outlining her breasts and legs. She seemed unconcerned by the immodest revelations of the simple garment. Her gaze wandered across the Bay, not focusing on the dragon even after she shaded her eyes with her hand.

She probably couldn't see the rapidly approaching dragon because she didn't yet believe in Shayla's existence.

Resentment rose in his throat against the men of his Council who had arranged this test to satisfy their own lust for power. Quinnault recognized their motives now, not caution against an unknown princess, but the desire to prove their king in error and thus increase their own power within the Council.

The assassin must come from a different source—someone less subtle, more desperate.

Who stood to gain from the death of this unknown princess?

He dragged his gaze away from Katie to survey the reactions of the men in the court. Lyman, still at the foot of the dais, seemed unmoved by the approach of the dragon. Indeed, a small smile played across his ancient mouth as if this entire exercise was a big joke. The other magicians smiled, too. But differently. They experienced a great joy at the sight of Shayla, much as Quinnault did. They almost swelled with pride and happiness as they filled with dragon magic. He'd seen them do this before whenever a dragon was present.

The Lords of the Council reacted differently. Most with the slight cringing of men faced with their fears but too prideful to run. Some closed their eyes and mumbled prayers. None of them reacted to the dragon with joy—though they had called Shayla to preside over this test.

Slowly, as if moving in a world that measured time differently, Shayla dropped into the courtyard. The bulk of her massive, crystal-like body barely fit between Quinnault and the dais, yet somehow she managed to land gracefully with only a minor breeze to ruffle the king's hair. Lyman scuttled adroitly out of her way, moving much more quickly than a man of his years should.

Good morning, Shayla, Quinnault greeted the dragon. *I hope the demands of my Council did not disrupt your day too much.*

(The selection of your queen is important, Quinnault Darville de Draconis. Unlike dragons, humans are not meant to live alone.) Shayla dipped her head in greeting to him. Then she turned her steedlike muzzle toward the small woman on the dais.

Katie stood stiffly, unmoving, as if frozen in time. Her mouth hung partly open in awe. Quinnault saw her perfect white teeth and pink tongue caught in mid-gasp. He was enthralled by her vulnerability. He hadn't recognized that quality in her before. Her small frame was filled with so much strength and humor there shouldn't have been room for this weakness. His heart swelled with the need to protect her.

(So, this is the thing you humans call love,) Shayla chuckled in the back of Quinnault's mind. *(My daughter possesses almost too much of it. I can no longer expect her to live the solitary life of a dragon. You must not force this on her.)*

He wanted to smile with the shared emotion. He didn't quite dare. Katie was still vulnerable to both Shayla and the Council. *I will do what I can to make sure that my sister, your daughter, is no longer alone.* Why had he promised that? He had no idea how he could reverse the edict of exile for Myrilandel and not other rogue magicians.

(Tonight, I will mate with my consorts as you mate with yours. The nimbus will be strong once more. 'Tis the wrong season, but a necessary symbol of our ties to you.)

What I feel for this princess is more than lust of the body, Shayla. I need her at my side every day of my life. I need to share the big decisions and the small daily trivia with her. My life is incomplete without her.

(It is the same, King Quinnault. I am no longer a solitary dragon, but part of a greater whole. Without my consorts

*and my children, I am less than I am now. Myrilandel has
taught me this.)* Shayla cocked her head as she examined
Katie.

Quinnault sensed puzzlement in the dragon. Then, Shayla
turned her attention to Lyman.

"Princess Maarie Kaathliin of Terrania," Lyman said in
a stern and commanding voice.

Katie shook herself free of her paralysis and flicked a
glance at the old magician. Her eyes returned quickly to
the dragon before her.

"Princess, the mental armor you have erected to block
out any chance of illusion is very strong. If we cannot poke
holes in your barricades to communicate with you telepathically, then we cannot create an illusion for you. The dragon
is real. Touch her and know the truth."

Katie paused indecisively a moment, shifting her gaze
from Lyman to the dragon, over to Quinnault and back to
the dragon. After an interminable moment, she lifted her
hand and stretched it forward, stopping a finger's length
from Shayla's muzzle. She bit her cheeks and closed her
eyes. Then, resolutely, she stretched the extra distance. Her
fingertips brushed the soft fur, then jerked back as if
burned. She opened her eyes wide and collapsed into a
heap of white linen and tangled limbs.

Quinnault leaped for the dais. In two strides he crossed
the distance, shouldering Shayla out of the way. Mutely he
lifted Katie's limp wrist.

His hands shook so badly he couldn't find her pulse.

Powwell stumbled over a tussock walking backward. He
had to keep watching the portal to see if Kalen found her
way through it. Nimbulan watched it as well, as if he expected Rollett to walk through it, too. The gate should
reopen again soon. The air remained still, without trace of
the hot blast from the heart of the volcano.

Ahead of him, the others walked close together, hurrying
away from Moncriith's mercenary patrol.

Myri and Maia pointedly ignored each other. Myri strolled
at an easy pace. Her longer legs kept her physically closer
to Nimbulan than the Rover woman. Neither of them ever
got close enough to the Senior Magician to allow him to

touch them, or help them over the increasingly cold and rough path.

At least they'd been able to take warm clothing and a few supplies from the patrol. They would survive in this low pass through the Western Mountain Range. If they stayed ahead of Moncriith's men.

What about you, Kalen? Where are you now? Do you live? Powwell prayed that the dragongate had sent her elsewhere at the last minute. He couldn't forget the sight of the hungry lava burning through the bones of a dead man his first day in the pit.

No, Kalen. I won't believe that happened to you.

He turned his gaze back to the top of the hill where the trees leaned together to form an arched shadow with the pile of weathered rocks. The sun continued to rise, shrinking the shadow to a slim line.

He stumbled again. Moisture gathered in his eyes. Even if Kalen escaped the pit, she couldn't come here until the sun rose again in the morning to create that arch. Desperate to get away from the boiling lava, she might plunge into one of the hostile environments of desert, storm-tossed sea, or frozen wasteland and perish before she could get back to Hanassa.

His mind kept shying away from those last moments in the dark and close tunnel. He didn't want to think of the weight of the Kardia pressing on his shoulders or of the way Kalen had run after her familiar, finding the smelly ferret more important than her own safety. He forced himself to remember all the details, as if he memorized a spell he had read in one of Nimbulan's many books. He reached for Thorny, forgetting to speak to his familiar before touching. The hedgehog hunched in startlement. His spines pierced Powwell's hand. Five drops of blood oozed onto his palm. He sucked at them, letting the sting draw more tears from his eyes.

"Just before we stepped through the portal, the guards said 'There they are! Get the Kaaliph.' " He muttered quietly, dredging the memory out with difficulty along with all of the others. "He said 'Kaaliph,' not 'Kaalipha.' Yaassima must have been captured or killed by Moncriith." This time he let the others hear his words.

"I think I would have felt her death," Myri said, stopping abruptly. "Hers or Televarn's. I . . . knew them both very well. I watched the pit engulf her in that vision, and I sensed nothing."

"Moncriith as Kaaliph of Hanassa," Nimbulan said, tasting the words as if seeking poison in them.

Myri lost all color in her normally pale face. She shuddered.

Kalen! Powwell shouted through the void to his friend. *Kalen, please live. You have to live.*

No one answered. A cold ache started in his throat and spread outward. "I have to go back! I have to know what happened to her." Powwell started running back up the hill toward the portal. Scarface blocked his passage. The strange magician held his shoulders tightly, preventing him from going any farther.

Powwell beat at him with clenched fists. Desperation turned his breath to sobs. The hands on his shoulders remained firm but gentle.

"The gate is closed and the patrol is waking up, Powwell. You can't go back through the dragongate." Scarface shook him slightly, forcing him to think beyond his immediate desire. "I know what you are going through. I lost my family during the wars. They were attacked by the troops of our own lord. He suspected he harbored an escaping soldier from the enemy. Their Battlemages made me watch, wouldn't let me help my family. I was spared because I was too valuable as a magician. Later I escaped to Hanassa. It's a pain you never get over, you just learn to live with it."

"I can't leave Kalen in Hanassa!" Powwell added mental blasts to his attack on Scarface.

Scarface only shifted his hold to encircle Powwell's throat from behind.

"Think, Powwell," Nimbulan soothed. Think with your head, not your heart. Getting yourself killed won't help Kalen."

"She loved that damned ferret more than me!" Powwell cried. All of his strength dribbled out of his limbs. "And Wiggles got her killed by Moncriith."

"You know the bond between a magician and a familiar is very special, Powwell," Myri said. "Imagine how you would feel if Thorny left you for more than a few moments.

Kalen must have been separated from Wiggles for all the weeks since we left the clearing, until yesterday. The ferret wasn't with her while we were in the village and was still missing when she came to me in the palace. He found her yesterday. Those special bonds brought him through hundreds of miles of mountains to reclaim her. Her sanity might not have survived another separation so soon."

Powwell stopped his struggles, aghast at Myri's words.

"What do you mean, she and Wiggles were separated?"

"He wasn't with her when Yaassima first brought Kalen to me, right after . . . right after Amaranth died and I was so distraught I couldn't care for my own baby. Kalen must have felt much the same when she first arrived in Hanassa without Wiggles to comfort her."

"She had the blasted ferret tucked into her sleeves when Televarn pushed us into the dragongate near the village. Wiggles was with her the first week we were in Hanassa. I didn't see him again, but you know how he hides." Every muscle in Powwell's body froze with fear. Fear that what he had perceived as the truth was false. Fear that Kalen had indeed deserted him by choice.

Thorny gibbered at him from his tunic pocket. Powwell couldn't understand all of the rapid ripples of emotions broadcast by the hedgehog. He did catch a sense of being told to run, *Run quickly, back the way we came.* Then the memory of being dragged through the dragongate.

Silence echoed in Powwell's ears.

He fought the conviction that Thorny had heard Kalen tell her familiar to run away so she could avoid leaving by way of the dragongate with Powwell and Myri and Nimbulan—her family.

"Where . . . where was the ferret when Kalen came to me? She said Wiggles wasn't in Hanassa." Myri, too, seemed afraid to move lest she discover an ugly truth.

"I don't know." Powwell shook his head in denial of the entire issue. But Kalen's duplicity wouldn't go away.

"When I first discovered evidence of Televarn's Water spell, I saw tiny pawprints beside the trickle of water," Nimbulan said. His left hand came up, palm out. The habitual gesture told Powwell that he sought information. "A moment before the trap crashed over me, I saw a small animal dash past me. At the time I thought it one of the rat-catching ferrets Quinnault keeps in the palace who was running from the wall of Water. Later, the guards searching for Televarn also reported a ferret in the clearing with the Rover. They disappeared together."

"Kalen and Televarn? I won't believe it." Powwell cringed inside, wanting to run far and fast—run from the idea of Kalen corrupted by the slimy Rover.

"I caught Kalen in a terrible lie at the moment Wiggles returned to her. She told me Nimbulan had drowned." Myri clutched at her husband's hand as if to reassure herself that he lived indeed.

"Kalen hated Televarn. She hated Hanassa and . . . and . . ." Powwell choked on the next thought. "And yet she thrived there. I watched her daily as she blossomed. I wanted to believe it was womanhood coming upon her and her love for me."

"The brat thrived on power, not love," Scarface added, spitting into the dirt. "I saw her often enough in the city. The first week you arrived, she was always with Televarn. Even after the Rover chieftain left the city on his assassination commission, she never went out to the fields with the work parties, but she carried messages for the Rover clan."

"What do you know about it? You never met her!" Powwell wrenched free of the magician's now gentle grasp. Anger exploded in his mind. He needed to slam his fist into something. Scarface's ugly visage was the nearest satisfactory target.

Scarface caught his wrist easily, restraining his blow.

"Televarn used the girl as a messenger. She came to me and my men several times. I owed Televarn—some favors, favors that I resented and he never let me forget. I watched the girl manipulate people with words and with magic. She inflated men's self-esteem with promises of sex with herself or the Rover women. She hinted at influence with Televarn and Yaassima's growing dependence upon the Rovers. She was using Televarn's plans to depose Yaassima to elevate herself to a position of power in the new regime."

"I loved her," Powwell said. Defeat weighed heavily in him. He knew Scarface spoke the truth. He had watched Kalen's manipulations. She had told him that she wanted to be in a position so that no one could use her for their own gain. Her parents had sold her talent for food and shelter. Ackerly, Nimbulan's former assistant, had tried to sell her talent for gold that he kept himself. She had pleaded with him to forget his plans to help Myri. She was jealous of the baby, thought Myri had deserted and betrayed her by having another child, as she thought her mother had betrayed her for staying in Coronnan City with Kalen's brothers and sisters.

"She wanted to be in control of herself and everyone around her." Powwell didn't realize he'd spoken until her heard his own words. "I thought it merely a childish dream. No one has that kind of power over people."

"Yaassima did," Yaala said in her deep voice, so husky he could never tell if she verged on tears or not.

"Kalen and Televarn would make quite a pair." Nimbulan shook his head sadly. "With his ambition and her plots, they could have ruled all of Kardia Hodos in time."

"If either of them lives," Powwell added. He didn't think Kalen was dead. But where could she be and still live? Their bonds had been close before they had been kidnapped with Myri. After that she had changed, and the closeness, the whispered confidences in the slave pen, the shared tears, holding each other to keep out the cold and the terror, were all a sham. On her part. "I love her. I would have taken care of her. I wanted to marry her as soon as she was old enough."

"You do realize, Powwell, that Kalen was your half-sister? The physical resemblance between you is too strong to be coincidence," Nimbulan said.

"She wasn't!" Powwell screamed. "She couldn't be. I won't believe it."

"I doubt that Stuuvaart sired her," Nimbulan continued. "He has no trace of magic in him, neither does Guillia or your mother. I believe a magician seduced both women and then abandoned them. Not an uncommon occurrence in the war years."

Powwell took a deep breath and released it. Stuuvart, the self-serving steward at the School for Magicians, was the last man he wanted to acknowledge as his long-lost father. But who? He didn't want to think about it. Was afraid to believe it.

"The physical resemblance between you and Kalen is too remarkable," Myri reinforced her husband's statement.

"Your speech patterns and gestures are also too similar. It is right that you should love each other and be friends, but you can never be intimate with her, never make her your wife."

"You have no proof that Stuuvart isn't her father."

"When we get back to the School, I will find a way to prove it to you, Powwell," Nimbulan said, resuming his trek eastward, toward Coronnan. "Now would be a good time for the dragons to return."

"That won't stop me from finding a way to go to Kalen."

"Somehow, I don't think your sister will appreciate your efforts, any more than my brother will welcome my return to Coronnan," Myri mumbled.

Chapter 33

Shayla! Myri called into the vastness of open sky.
Her mind and her heart remained empty of the dragon's presence. She huddled closer to Nimbulan and the small fire they allowed themselves while she nursed her baby and they all ate of the dry journey rations. The absence of the dragons left a chill deeper in her heart than the winter wind that whipped through the pass.

"I can't hear Shayla at all!" Myri tried again to summon a dragon—any dragon. "This is as bad as when I was in Hanassa. I can't hear the dragons." All her life she had listened to the voices in the back of her head, guiding her through life when no one else cared for or trusted her.

She understood they would not go near Hanassa in any way, even to reassure one of their own trapped within the boundaries of the volcanic crater. Their vows of separation from the stronghold of the renegade dragon, Hanassa, who had taken human form, had lasted for centuries. Dragon memory was long.

She wondered briefly if Old Lyman who had been, in his previous existence, the last purple-tipped dragon before Amaranth and herself, had known Hanassa.

This emptiness was something more than the dragon's avoidance of Hanassa. The dragons roamed free over this land. Shayla had been calmly munching on a stunted Tambootie tree when Myri and the others emerged through the dragongate. Almost as if she expected Myri to emerge there and wanted to make sure her daughter was safe.

Now Shayla shunned her call for help and reassurance.

"I can't raise Lyman at the school," Nimbulan said, staring into the fire. He held his glass, minus the gold frame, before his eyes, magnifying the flames and his spell. "We have to get news of the invasion to Quinnault before he marries the temptress. I wonder where she really hails from and who planted her in Coronnan. I have a lot of questions about the princess who appeared as soon as I had left the capital."

Myri looked closely at his bland expression. He had locked away his emotions from her gentle probes since Powwell's terrible accusation.

"Talk to me, Nimbulan," she pleaded.

"I just spoke to you about the summons spell." He continued to peer into the fire through his glass.

"You said words, but you haven't talked, haven't reacted to the terrible hurt Powwell dealt you with his words."

"He didn't hurt me. He spoke the truth. I hurt myself with my regret and my guilt."

"You won't heal, Lan, until you talk to me."

"There is nothing to talk about. I valued my apprentices above you and Kalen. 'Tis my shortcoming. I must learn to live with it."

A chill ran through Myri. "Do you mean to abandon me again? Me and Amaranth, your daughter?"

"I don't know what I will do after I get word to King Quinnault about the invasion. I don't know if I'm capable of loving anyone enough to . . ." Without another word, he traded his glass for a journal and began writing with a black stick he kept tucked inside the book.

Myri looked at the intricate marks on the page, wondering what he recorded. She'd never learned to read and hoped Nimbulan would remain with her long enough to teach her.

"Why do you ask where the princess comes from, Lan?" Myri asked. "I've heard of Terrania in old legends."

"Do you remember the landscape of the desert with red sand we saw through the dragongate?"

Myri nodded.

"That is Terrania," he replied grimly. "No one has lived there for many thousands of years. Quinnault's bride is a fake." He returned to his journal.

Scarface watched from the edge of the rock overhang that sheltered them in a mountain pass from any mercenaries patrolling in the area. The ones they'd left behind should have recovered by now. They had no way of knowing if the witchsniffers would pursue revenge for the massive headaches the paralysis spell would leave with them and the loss of their cloaks and food, or if they would retreat to nurse their injured emotions and minds.

"Could Televarn have planted the princess?" Yaala offered. "He thrives on convoluted plans. He sold his women to the brothels for politics as well as money. Perhaps he plotted with this woman for the purpose of inciting a war. If he can create enough chaos, then he can step in and take over for lack of leadership."

"That sounds like Televarn," Myri agreed. During the moon she had lived with the Rover more than a year ago, he had proved false in his protestations of love and loyalty.

"Televarn doesn't need to be sneaky. He just needs to read your mind once, and he'll never leave you alone," Maia said bitterly. "He uses people like candle stubs. When they are used up, he throws them away."

"I left him before he could discard me. So he has to pursue me. No one else may possess me until he decides he is finished with me." Myri added.

She checked the now sated and sleeping Amaranth rather than dwell on the Rover chieftain. Satisfied that the baby was safe from the blazing emotions that had run rampant a few hours ago, she shifted her attention to Powwell. The boy sat, sullen and staring into the distance. He systematically stripped a long stem of grass, then plucked another, stripped it, plucked another. Myri wondered if he knew what occupied his hands.

"Maybe I can summon Kalen," he said quietly. "She was always receptive to communication spells, though she hated sending them." His words barely reached across the fire to Myri.

"Even if she answered, Powwell, we can't help her yet. We need to get to the capital, fast," Nimbulan said. He stood abruptly and scanned the skies. "But I promise you, as soon as I have arranged for the safety of my king and the kingdom, I will return to Hanassa for Rollett and Kalen. Maybe if we join our magic, Powwell, we can catch someone's attention in the capital."

Powwell stood up, lethargic, his attention still on the distant hilltop and the dragongate.

"I would be interested in this new magic," Scarface said.

"Before I can even test you to see if you can gather dragon magic, I must have your life's oath of loyalty to the Commune, Aaddler."

Myri raised her eyebrows at Nimbulan's use of the man's real name. Involving a real name among magicians seemed a gesture of intimacy or intense seriousness.

"I understand." Scarface nodded his acceptance. "I must think on this. A lifelong commitment like that cannot be taken lightly."

"I respect that more than a hasty agreement that might be regretted later. I find the fellowship and ideals of the Commune easier to live with than the constantly changing rules and loyalties of solitary magicians and rogue mercenaries," Nimbulan replied. He turned his back on the stranger as he took Powwell's hand in his own.

By some unspoken agreement, Scarface also turned his back on the two communal magicians, continuing his watch of the low mountain pass—a narrow but easy passage from SeLenicca into Coronnan.

Myri observed, through the magic cord that bound them together, Nimbulan's preparations for the next attempt at a summons. Desperately she hoped that this time she would comprehend the secret of dragon magic. If she could figure out how to gather and use the special energy. Then, and only then, could she return to Coronnan legally with her husband, never be separated from him again.

Once again the elusive process passed by her so quickly she missed the essential ingredient. Once again she was shut out of the special bond of communal magic.

She sank back onto the ground beside Amaranth and Yaala. The need to open communication with someone prompted her to speak to the young woman. "Why did Yaassima exile and disown you? You seem like a woman who could lead."

"I don't look like a dragon." Yaala shrugged and shifted uncomfortably. She pulled her back straighter, away from the hard rock surface they had been leaning against. Her light blond hair had more color than Myri's or Yaassima's. Broken nails and encrusted dirt on her fingers couldn't hide their slender length. But they weren't extraordinarily long like Myri's or Yaassima's. Or baby Amaranth's.

"Do you have the spinal bumps?" Myri asked.

"Very prominently." Yaala wiggled her back again, trying to find a comfortable position.

"Mine aren't very obvious," Myri volunteered. "I borrowed a human body for my dragon personality. Myrilandel was blonde and long boned already. My fingers and toes grew to accommodate Amethyst's instincts to grasp and climb. I guess Amethyst also bleached the color from my hair and skin. But I couldn't grow the extra eyelid that protects dragons from dust and the super brightness of the sun in the upper atmosphere."

Yaala stared at the flames, much as Nimbulan did to work the summons. A light film dropped over her eye.

"Which person are you, Myrilandel or Amethyst?" Yaala shifted slightly, putting a few more finger lengths between herself and Myri.

"Both and neither. Myrilandel was only two when her human body was on the verge of dying. Amethyst gave her the vitality to use her natural healing ability to correct the weak blood vessels in her brain. The two personalities were so strong that they compromised on forgetfulness, neither of them dominant, until I met the dragons and found a husband who loved me enough to let me explore my past without prejudice. I like to think I developed a personality all my own." Unique, worth preserving. Yaassima had forced her to fight for what she held important in life rather than running away. Did she have the strength and will to continue the fight for Nimbulan's love?

Yes. She had to. Her family wasn't complete without him. She wasn't complete without him.

"Yaassima can't allow anyone that kind of freedom and individuality." Yaala pushed the words out through clenched teeth. "She has to control every thought, every gesture, every moment of their lives. I fought her. My father encouraged me. That's probably the real reason she executed him and exiled me to the pit."

"And yet she is very lonely," Myri whispered. "She needed to love you. Since you didn't meet her expectations, she transferred her need to Amaranth and me. If only she had recognized that the strength you found to fight her was the strength you need to rule Hanassa, you . . ."

"But she did recognize it. She hated it and saw me as a

rival rather than a partner." Yaala stood up, ending the conversation. "I think the summons is working."

Myri felt Nimbulan's growing excitement through her talent. The silver cord vibrated in tune with the magic pulsing through the glass.

"Lyman, you have to warn the king," Nimbulan said into the glass. He looked tired and hungry from his efforts to contact his friend at the school.

"Not now, Nimbulan. We're all very busy." Lyman's voice was so strong they all heard the message. "Shayla says you are safe. That is enough for now."

The communication ended abruptly, leaving them alone on the vulnerable mountain pass.

Chapter 34

"**G**et a healer!" Quinnault bellowed. He lay Katie flat against the wooden platform of the dais and began breathing into her mouth.

(She will be difficult to live with, Quinnault. Are you sure you wish to mate with her for all time?) Amusement tinged Shayla's voice.

"Be quiet, I'm trying to save her life, Shayla."

(She lives. Your efforts are redundant.) Again that irritating chuckle invaded his mind.

Beneath his hands, Katie stirred. Relieved that the dragon was correct, he raised his head enough to glare at Shayla. "The shock could have killed her."

"It very nearly did," Katie whispered. Then she raised her right hand and slapped him soundly across the face.

"What was that for?" He reared back, dropping her back to the dais with a thump. He fingered his right cheek delicately. He'd be lucky if it weren't bruised for the wedding ceremony and banquet. Not a good precedent to set for the beginning of a lifelong commitment.

"That was for every man in my life who presumes to know what my duty is and what is best for me. And since my father and brothers, and esteemed royal grandfather aren't here to collect their share, you get it all." She sat up, pushing away from his hovering presence. An angry flush replaced the paleness on her cheeks.

Some of her fears leaked through to his mind—the chill morning breeze against her nearly naked body, and the hostility of the lords and magicians surrounding her. He smiled, realizing that only he stood between her and all those terrible things. Things he could protect her from.

Shayla pushed her enormous muzzle closer.

Katie slapped her away—somewhat more gently than she had Quinnault. "Go away. I told you I don't like other . . . beings mucking about in my mind. That goes for you too, Daddy!" She directed her last words toward the islands in the Bay. "Telepathy made me special back home. Here, it's a nuisance. I don't want any more of it." Anger banished all those fears. But the faintest tremble touched her lower lip.

Quinnault wanted nothing more than to kiss it back into stubborn firmness.

"She's a magician. We can't have a rogue magician for a queen. The marriage treaty is voided!" Lord Hanic shouted across the courtyard. The other lords pressed closer, along with the magicians to look more closely at the angry princess.

"You can't break a dragon-blessed treaty, Hanic," Lyman reminded the Council member. "Nor can you depose a dragon-blessed monarch. You wrote that law and forced it upon the Council."

Lord Hanic glared at Lyman, standing his ground. He opened his mouth to issue another pronouncement. Shayla turned her gaze on the man before he said anything. Quickly he closed his mouth with an audible click of his teeth and backed away from the dragon.

"I'm not a magician, and I don't want to be one. I can read minds a little, and that's too much,' she retorted. "For seven hundred years, the only telepaths we've been able to find in my—um—country are in my family. Kinnsell wanted to take some of your magicians home to study them. I wouldn't let him. Telepathy is a curse. From now on, I swear to keep my thoughts to myself and stay out of everyone else's!" *Except for you, Scarecrow. I couldn't keep you out if I tried.* "I'll take drugs to suppress my talent if I have to."

Quinnault sat back on his heels, amazed at the transformation of his gentle princess into this spitting spotted saber cat. Some of Shayla's humor spilled over into him.

"You are the most beautiful woman in the world!" he laughed uproariously.

"Stifle it, Scarecrow, before I pack my bags and run far, far away from this dirty backwater."

He ended her tirade with a kiss. She pummeled his chest with her fists. He captured them and deepened his assault on her full lips, savoring the taste of her on his questing tongue at last. Slowly she relaxed her struggle but did not respond. He enfolded her in his arms, pulling her into his lap, twining his fingers in her silky hair.

Her mouth opened a fraction as her arms stole around his neck.

Heat invaded every pore of his body, filling him with passion.

"Are you two going to come up for air?" Lyman asked.

"No." Quinnault stole a quick gulp of air and renewed his kiss.

(Are you certain you wish to spend the rest of your life with this headstrong woman and no other?) Shayla asked.

Quinnault looked the dragon in the eye as he breathed deeply, trying to control his raging passion for the woman in his arms.

Shayla's penetrating gaze made him squirm as she examined his motives. He looked from the dragon to the islands in the Bay, back to Katie, then returned once again to the port, thinking furiously all the time. He had so many questions. Was his love for her enough to overcome them?

Katie drew his eyes like a lodestone to iron. Finally he had his emotions under control and could speak in a normal tone of voice.

"I have no choice, Shayla. I have to marry her."

Thwack! Katie slapped him again as she squirmed to be free of him.

"I thought I didn't have a choice either. But I'll be damned if I put up with this. I thought we could care for each other, but you are as selfish as every other man in my life." She fought his grasp with fists and kicks.

He clung tighter to her, desperate to rectify the misunderstanding. "Katie, I meant that you are the only woman I want. I can't choose another after meeting you." He put all of his feelings into his eyes, staring at her. Willing her to believe him.

She glared at him. He held her gaze. Gradually the truth penetrated her stubborn mind.

"Oh, Scarecrow," she sighed and kissed him as passionately as he had kissed her only moments before.

(You have my blessing, King Quinnault Darville de Dra-conis. Enjoy!) Shayla bunched her muscles, took two running steps, and launched herself into the sky. *(Tonight I shall fly with my consorts as will you. We will both conceive, though the seasons are not quite right. The future of Coron-nan and of the nimbus is assured.)*

"Where are you going, Shayla? Won't you stay for the wedding?" Quinnault asked. He kept a tight hold on Katie, afraid she'd disappear in a puff of smoke now that she was his.

(I have my own celebration to attend.) The dragon blasted their ears with a high-pitched screech that announced her triumph and her passion. As she circled the courtyard, the outlines of five male dragons joined her.

Quinnault picked out red, blue, green, yellow, and orange along the wingtips and veins of the consorts.

"The more fathers, the big and stronger the litter," he quoted.

"Not for this princess, King Quinnault. You are the only one allowed in my bed," Katie retorted. She reinforced her statement with a resounding kiss that left him light-headed.

"Well, at least wait for the nuptials and some privacy," Lyman laughed. "Don't we have a banquet to prepare?"

"Go ahead. We'll be right with you," Quinnault waved them away and pressed his mouth to Katie's once more.

Nimbulan walked closer to Myri, slipping his arm around her waist, a subtle support before she stumbled again. She didn't lean into him, but she didn't pull away either. He was too tired to think about the tangled mess he'd made of his personal life.

Maia still presented a big problem.

What to do with her? He owed her a home. She'd never be allowed to return to her clan. Without them, she had nothing. Unless Televarn was still manipulating her through his mind link.

How far away must Maia be to get beyond Televarn's reach? Had the Rover Chieftain survived the knife thrust?

He turned his mind back to watching his steps rather than thinking about how much women complicated his life. The bachelor life of most magicians seemed inviting.

But if he hadn't married Myri, loved her so desperately, he'd not have his daughter. His very beautiful daughter.

"Let me take the baby, Myri. She must be very heavy for you." He lifted the tiny bundle of life out of her makeshift sling.

Myri's hands grabbed for her child, resisting separation. Nimbulan saw her emotions play across her face even as he sensed them. "You won't lose her if you let me hold her for awhile. I'm not Yaassima. And I'm not a Rover who will steal any child for the sake of new blood in the clan," he reassured her. He refused to look at Maia while he spoke. Did the Rover woman still seek to kidnap Amaranth for the benefit of the clan and Televarn?

Myri relinquished the burden of the baby's weight reluctantly. As he cradled Amaranth in the crook of his right arm, he draped his left around Myri's shoulders. The sudden warmth that filled his soul almost stopped him in his tracks.

In many ways, Nimbulan was an unknown to her. Their courtship and marriage had been brief before her exile.

He had allowed her to become the victim of an edict that put the fears and prejudices of the Council above the needs of the individual. *He* had become so involved in politics he hadn't followed through with the sporadic communication with her and Powwell.

He kept walking, trying to figure out his emotional upheaval. He thought again of the four islands in the Great Bay. He'd take Myri there, and they would live together for the rest of their lives. He couldn't leave her again.

But he couldn't tell her about his plans in case they came to naught. There had to be a way to keep her close without breaking the laws of Coronnan.

The low mountain pass twisted and turned back on itself a dozen times, leading into box canyons and across surging creeks before descending the hills into Coronnan. Nimbulan didn't know how to use the terrain to their advantage. He needed a broad plain with two opposing armies. That he could plan for.

They'd walked for hours. They were all tired and hungry. They all watched the sun march progressively closer to the horizon and the time for Quinnault's wedding.

Lyman and the other magicians continued to ignore a summons spell. Without a dragon to carry them to the capital, Nimbulan had no hope of preventing the union of his king and the false princess before the invasion.

"We need to stop and eat," he said though his mind urged him to continue forward.

What had gotten into Quinnault that he would risk his fragile peace? Where had the Princess of Terrania come from? More important, who was behind the plot?

"I'm sensing a mass of people behind us," Scarface replied warily. "I don't think this is a good time to stop."

Nimbulan scanned the canyon to his left. A small creek joined a slightly larger one at the mouth of the opening. He guessed the easy game trail led into yet another dead end, hopefully one that offered numerous hiding places, possibly caves where they could light a fire and rest.

Powwell turned automatically up the trail, without argument. He'd been so depressed since leaving Kalen behind that Nimbulan wondered if the boy was capable of independent thought.

Yaala trudged after the boy, bound to him by their shared experiences in the pit and yet apart from them all.

Myri reached to take back the baby.

"Please, Myri, let me carry her a little longer. I know I don't deserve this special blessing, but . . ." How did he make amends for all those lonely moons of exile that made her vulnerable to Televarn's kidnap and Yaassima's cruel imprisonment of her?

She nodded slowly, maintaining eye contact with him.

"Our daughter is very precious. I vow before you and the Stargods that I will never do anything to harm her or you again." He touched his heart, then hers to seal the vow.

Myri rewarded him with a weak smile. Her hand lingered tentatively on his as he supported Amaranth against his shoulder. Yet he feared every moment she would withdraw from him.

Maia's face turned bronze-red beneath the olive tones of her skin. "I was your first love. I gave you a *son*. You never promised me anything."

"Myrilandel is my love and my wife. I will provide for you, Maia, do what I can to protect you from Televarn and the rest of the clan. But I do not love you, I doubt I ever did. We were both victims of Televarn's manipulations. We did not enter that union of our own free will."

"They're getting closer!" Scarface hissed, urging them into the rugged canyon. "Can't you feel their malevolence beating against the rocks? They want blood. Our blood."

Cradling Amaranth in one arm, the other supporting Myri around the waist, Nimbulan increased his stride. He left Maia to Scarface's ministrations. Yaala guided Powwell.

They needed a hiding place, someplace with wood where they could separate from their talents. Only then would they be safe from the witchsniffers.

"Not that way, Lan. I feel people up this canyon. Lots and lots of people!" Myri held him back.

Nimbulan turned to retreat. Two dozen archers faced them, arrows nocked, bowstrings taut.

"So we meet again, Nimbulan. This time on my terms, on my battleground, without any of your dragon demons to defend you or your witch," Moncriith said mildly, working his way through the ranks of soldiers to face Nimbulan.

Chapter 35

Doubts nagged at Quinnault. He didn't have enough to do to keep them at bay. Katie was closeted with the women, preparing for the wedding. His servants and stewards bustled about the palace, preparing for the ceremony and the banquet to follow. Even the magicians all seemed to be occupied, looking for omens in arcane spells and rituals.

More often than not, he was in the way—just like the day they had prepared for battle. This time his chief steward and the senior ladies of the court had become the Battlemages.

He chuckled at the idea of viewing a wedding in the same light as a major battle.

Memories of Katie and her argument with her father came back to haunt him. *I am in charge,* she had said. They'd do it her way or not at all. Do what?

Kinnsell had left, accepting her edict that the Varns would harvest the Tambootie, build the port, and leave, never to interfere with Kardia Hodos again. What rare qualities of leadership did Quinnault's bride possess that allowed her to command meek obedience from her father?

Quinnault wondered if she'd order her husband around with the same authority. The telepathic bond between them meant that she could manipulate him with a thought. Would she? Or would she keep her vow to suppress her talent? He didn't know if that was possible. He'd never heard of any drugs that effectively masked a talent without putting the patient to sleep for days on end.

And what about Kinnsell's plot to kidnap magicians for

study? Katie claimed that was the core of their argument last night.

Quinnault had no doubt that Kinnsell had the means to remove several powerful magicians from Coronnan without detection. Would he obey Katie's edict or appear to accept her orders and then do precisely what he wanted later?

Kinnsell hadn't been seen all day. Would he come for the wedding? As Katie's father, he had every right to participate in the ceremony.

Too many questions and no answers.

Too many people rushing about the Great Hall, including Lord Konnaught. Quinnault's fosterling stood in the center of the dais, hands on hips, lower lip thrust out belligerently. No one paid him any attention.

Quinnault decided he'd ignore the brat, too.

Since he couldn't talk to Katie or her father, Quinnault decided to talk to someone else. Piedro, the Rover assassin. He'd feel a lot better about the ceremony if he knew who had hired Piedro. Nimbulan had told him often enough that Rovers were incapable of independent thought, all were manipulated by the clan chieftain who was always the dominant mage. He wondered if last night's attempt to strangle Katie and place the blame on Quinnault was part of the aborted poison plot arranged by Televarn.

"Bessel," he called to the journeyman magician who directed apprentices on the placement of witchlight torches around the great hall. "I need your assistance."

The young man detached himself from the younger students almost eagerly.

"Do you know who sealed the dungeon cell last night?" Quinnault asked as he guided Bessel toward the cellars.

"Gilby and I did it, Your Grace, along with Master Maarkus." Bessel thrust his shoulders back proudly.

"Can you undo it by yourself?"

"I can let you in and out of the cell, sir. But since the three of us set the spell, only the three of us can break it and allow the prisoner out. Do you wish to interrogate the prisoner now?" Bessel loomed back over his shoulder at the hectic preparations for the wedding.

"Yes, now. Before his employer tries something else." Quinnault signaled two guards to follow them.

Together they wound their way through a series of cellars, then down another spiral staircase into the chambers cut from the bedrock of Palace Isle. A long corridor broken by the doorways of a dozen cells stretched before them. All the doors except one stood ajar. Quinnault hadn't jailed anyone but Piedro in years.

"Are you going to torture the prisoner now? Can I watch?" Konnaught asked as he hurried down the steps behind Quinnault and Bessel. He pushed his way between the guards who followed the king everywhere. The men stepped away, hands on the hilts of their swords, eyes wary.

"This is none of your concern, Lord Konnaught. Return to your lessons at once." Quinnault stood firmly in place, refusing to move any closer to Piedro's cell until the boy had left. With a flick of his head upward he gestured for the guards to remove the pest.

"But I must know how this is done when I am king." Konnaught glared at him, mimicking his hands on hips posture.

"I have no intention of dying prematurely so that you can be king. Tell me, did you arrange this assassination so that I would?" Quinnault grabbed the boy by the neck of his tunic. He wanted to shake the brat but restrained himself, as a king must.

"I'd be more direct, if I were to do something so stupid. And I'd hire a more intelligent assassin," Konnaught snarled back, not intimidated by Quinnault's superior size or his barely restrained anger.

"Then why are you here?" Quinnault asked. He kept his eyes focused on the stone steps behind him rather than the boy who incited such anger in him.

"Because I want to watch the Rover-scum squirm under torture."

"Did you ever watch your father beat his lovers until their faces were bloody pulps and they bled from the inside?" Quinnault bared his teeth as he moved his face closer to Konnaught's, maintaining his fierce grip on his collar.

Konnaught shook his head. He closed his eyes and gulped.

"What about the times your father pillaged and burned entire villages for no reason other than to soothe his temper? Did you watch then as innocent men and women burned alive? Did you enjoy watching their skin melt away and their hair becoming torches as their lungs clogged with smoke?'' Renewed anger at the depredations of his now deceased rival burned within Quinnault. In this moment he put aside his regret that he had wielded the sword that killed Kammeryl d'Astrismos, Konnaught's father.

''No—no, Your Grace,'' Konnaught stammered and sagged within Quinnault's grip. Then he stiffened. ''But they were peasants. . . .''

''They were innocent *people*. I refuse to argue with you anymore, or put up with your insolence and your idolization of your father's evil. Pack your possessions. You sail at dawn for the Monastic School in Sollthrie.''

''You don't dare exile me. I—I'm your only heir. I—I hold the allegiance of three other lords who think your view of government is stupid. And I think you are stupid,'' Konnaught blustered. But his chin quivered as he spoke.

''Then you must learn to think differently. I know of no better place to do that than Sollthrie.''

''But . . . but there's nothing there!''

''There is the finest school in all of Kardia Hodos.''

''But no one ever leaves there. They . . . they stay and become celibate priests.''

''Precisely. I should have sent you there last spring, but I was too kind and expected too much from you. Guard, take him back to his room and supervise his packing. He won't need much.''

The guard on the left took Konnaught's elbow, somewhat more gently than Quinnault had grabbed his collar, and led him back up the stairs.

''Now, Bessel, let us see what this Rover knows.'' Only a tiny bit of regret niggled at Quinnault's brain. He'd failed with teaching Konnaught responsibility, justice, and concern for others. Maybe the boy was incapable of learning such concepts. Mostly he felt a tremendous relief at having made a decision.

He turned to face the sealed prison door.

''I'm afraid we are too late, Your Grace,'' Bessel said, peering through the slitted window of the heavy wooden cell door.

''What do you mean?'' Quinnault shouldered the young

journeyman aside to look himself. The cell appeared empty.
"He was here this morning. His guards reported him
screaming to let him out not an hour ago."

"He's gone, Your Grace. The Rover has escaped and left
my seal and the mundane locks in place."

Powwell nearly jumped out of his skin at Moncriith's
words. He'd been so preoccupied with his own misery he
hadn't watched his steps until he nearly stepped on the
Bloodmage.

"Where's Kalen?" he blurted without thought.

"Silence, demon spawn!" Moncriith intoned, raising his
hands in the same gesture priests used to denote a benediction.

Blood dripped from Moncriith's fingers and a gash across
his forehead. Behind him lay the corpse of a man wearing
the black uniform of Kaalipha Yaassima's personal guard.
His throat had been slit. His mouth was frozen in a scream
of horror.

"Nastfa!" Myri choked at sight of the man.

"I name him traitor," Moncriith replied. "He fell victim
to the seduction of the demons within you, Myrilandel. He
had to die. What better way than as sacrifice to give me
enough magic to stop you once and for all?" He cocked
his head and smiled almost amiably.

The Bloodmage was insane, Powwell realized. Moncriith
had murdered a man and mutilated himself, again, to fuel
his fanaticism.

"With my head and my heart and the strength of my
shoulders, I reject this evil." Powwell signed the cross of
the Stargods. Beside him, Yaala did the same.

"The Stargods can't protect you. They are with me,"
Moncriith proclaimed. "Prepare to die!"

Nimbulan's hand landed on Powwell's shoulder. The familiar blending and surging of power pulled the last remnants of dragon magic out of Powwell. He fought the light-
headed emptiness. He had to stall while Nimbulan prepared
a defensive spell. The dragons wouldn't allow an attack
fueled by their magic, only defense.

But an attack might very well bring a dragon to them
posthaste. He hoped Nimbulan realized this or read his
thoughts. He had to stall.

"Where's Kalen?" Powwell asked again. "You came through the dragongate in Hanassa. Kalen was the only one left there who knew its secrets."

"She and Yaassima died opening the gate for me. Their deaths shifted the vortex to take me directly to my troops. I was the last person through before the tunnels and caverns collapsed behind me. The *demon's* gate is closed forever."

"You bastard!" Powwell launched himself at the Bloodmage. Rage turned his vision red. Vaguely, he heard Nimbulan protest the separation between them and the division of the magic.

He didn't care. The only thing that existed for Powwell was Moncriith and the need to kill the Bloodmage. Fingers flexed, he aimed for Moncriith's eyes. Soft skin squished beneath his jagged and dirty fingernails. He felt a satisfying gush of hot blood against his palms.

Inside his tunic, Thorny hunched. Sharp spines penetrated Powwell's clothing to prick his chest. His emotional contact with the hedgehog strengthened his anger and his determination to kill Moncriith.

He kicked back at the men who tried to pull him off of Moncriith. He heard screams and closed his ears to them.

Someone pressed a dagger against his throat. He didn't care. Moncriith had killed Kalen. Moncriith had to die. Powwell would gladly die with him as long as the Bloodmage died. Painfully. Messily.

"Powwell, no." Myri's quiet command penetrated the red blur of pain and fury. "He's not worth murdering."

Powwell didn't release his grip on the now screaming Moncriith. Thorny relaxed his spines. Powwell refused to follow his familiar's lead.

"Amaranth isn't old enough to separate herself from the victims around her. Kill Moncriith and you kill the baby." Nimbulan reminded him quietly. "Do you want my daughter's death on your soul as well as his?"

Moncriith roared triumphantly as he broke Powwell's grip on his face with a mighty thrust. Powwell flew backward, landing on his butt with a harsh jar that sent his head spinning.

The note of exultation in Moncriith's pain shook Powwell more than Myri's words or the spine numbing fall. How could the man revel in the pain?

Then he knew. As soon as Moncriith's blood had touched his hands, Powwell had felt a surge of strength and power. His own pain from the prick of Thorny's spines added to it. He had tapped blood magic without thinking. The rage drained out of him. His stomach twisted into a knot.

"To me, Powwell. I need your magic," Nimbulan called. His hands rose up, palm outward, fingers curved, to catch the magic hurled by Moncriith.

Powwell struggled to get his feet beneath him. They wouldn't cooperate. Yaala's hand grasped his belt and propelled him in Nimbulan's direction. He landed facedown in the dirt, one hand touching his teacher's scuffed boot.

Tingles worked their way up from the ground, through him. He lay across a ley line that begged him to tap its energy.

Useless.

Nimbulan couldn't combine with ley line energy. They needed dragon magic. Powwell's store was empty.

Nimbulan faltered in his defense. His own store of magic must be dangerously low as well.

Where were the dragons?

Moncriith yelled something in the old language as he hurled a massive ball of witchfire at Nimbulan and Myri.

Nimbulan extinguished the flames before they reached the band of refugees.

Powwell pressed his face deeper into the dirt. He had never taken an oath to the Commune to forsake all other forms of magic. Nothing prevented him from drawing the ley line into himself. He could throw some kind of barrier between Moncriith and his friends. He had to protect them, make up for his lapse in tapping blood magic.

A barrier. He needed a barrier. He dredged a half memory up from somewhere. Nimbulan had thrown a wall in front of Moncriith's attacks on Quinnault's army a year ago. How had he done it?

Powwell didn't have time to remember. In his mind he created a picture of a brick wall rising up from the ground between himself and the Bloodmage. He pushed the magic outward with all of his strength.

Moncriith's next volley of magic darts, meant to enter the mind through the eye and destroy all thought and memory, crashed through Nimbulan's defenses.

Chapter 36

"**O**pen that *S'murghing* door, Bessel," Quinnault ordered. "Guard, fetch Old Lyman. Carry him here over your shoulder if you have to. I don't care what he's doing or which dragon he's talking to, I need him here. Now."

"I don't know how Piedro could have left without a trace. No one can transport a living being from place to place and live," Bessel protested.

Quinnault recognized the young man's deep breathing as preparation for a trance. He stepped out of the way to let him work. Questions whirled through his mind. He drew his belt knife just in case the assassin was somehow hidden in the cell and planned to rush them as soon as the door opened.

"Maybe we should wait for the Master Magician," he suggested.

"Yes. That isn't my seal on the door," Bessel said. His eyes crossed in puzzlement. "I don't recognize the signature or style of the spell. No one from the School set it. I know all of them." He sounded almost relieved.

"We are dealing with rogue magicians as well as Rovers and assassins. On my wedding day! Piedro warned me to look to those I trust for his employer. Who? I wonder if I dare go through with the ceremony until I know for sure who wants me not only dead but discredited as a murderer."

"Lord Konnaught?" Bessel offered.

"I doubt it. He doesn't have the forethought or the money to plan such a thing."

"The style of magic will tell us much," Lyman said, bustling down the steep stairs. He rubbed his hands together in excitement. "An interesting puzzle. I love puzzles almost as much as I love books. Wonderful treasures, both. They make a man think."

"You didn't have time to be summoned from School Isle unless you flew or transported," Quinnault growled, ready to suspect anyone of Piedro's escape.

"Of course not. I was in the Great Hall helping arrange tonight's entertainment. We have five apprentices who are quite talented with delusions and fireless lights. They'll put on quite a show during the banquet," Lyman replied. He bent to eye the lock on the cell door without further ado.

"What do you see, old man?" Quinnault pressed him.

"Not as much as Nimbulan would. These eyes are aging and less interested in detail than I could wish." Lyman frowned as he straightened to peer through the slit window.

"Which is another complaint I have with the world today. I wish Nimbulan would get back here. He never should have left. Not even a note," he bemoaned.

"But he did leave a letter of explanation. I gave it to the messenger you sent to fetch him." Lyman looked around the dank dungeon as if he expected to find the errant courier hiding there.

"I never received it!" Quinnault barked. "Guard, bring me that courier!" Heat stung his cheeks and his fingers tingled with the anger building inside him.

Nothing was going right. Bad omens for the wedding ceremony and his life ahead with Katie.

"Unnecessary, boy." Lyman looked at Quinnault as if the king were indeed an errant child. "Lord Konnaught was with the messenger that day. Who told you that Nimbulan had departed on a personal quest?"

"Konnaught." None of Quinnault's anger dissipated. "That demon spawn child deliberately interfered with a royal messenger. More reasons to exile him. Guard, Konnaught is to be confined to his room and watched. He is not to attend the wedding or the banquet. See to it immediately."

One of the men retreated. His haste up the slippery stairs suggested he was happy to remove himself from target distance of Quinnault's temper.

"Open the damn door, Lyman. I'm getting tired of this.

I want explanations now, even if I personally have to break every bone in Piedro's body. Nimbulan has a lot to answer for when he gets back. He'd have known a way to make sure this Rover didn't escape."

"All in good time, my boy. Nimbulan's errand was necessary. You'll see that when he gets back."

"Which will be. . . ?"

"When he gets back."

"Stop with your riddles, Lyman. Who released the Rover?" Quinnault began to pace, hands behind his back, shoulders hunched. He couldn't think standing still.

"Not any magic I know firsthand," Lyman replied.

"Varn magic, perhaps?" Quinnault had to ask the question that had been hovering in the back of his mind since he'd witnessed the argument between Katie and her father. He trusted Katie, but not her father.

"Closer to home, I think," Lyman said. He pulled his glass from a deep pocket of his blue robe and looked closer at the entire doorjamb.

"How close?" both Quinnault and Bessel asked.

"Kardia, Air, Fire, and Water are present. Smell the urine? That's what he used for Water." Lyman wrinkled his nose.

"That sounds like a Rover spell. Piedro must be a clan chieftain, so he can't be working with Televarn," Quinnault mused, as he continued his pacing.

"Perhaps. Perhaps not." Lyman wiggled his fingers in an arcane pattern. "Bessel, help me with this." He signaled the journeyman to come closer. The young man placed his hand upon the old man's shoulder. Together they took three deep breaths.

Quinnault sensed the power building between them. But he didn't have enough magic on his own to see their auras merge and expand.

"The original seal was broken from the outside and reset from the outside. Our Rover had help. Someone who could come and go without question. Your guards wouldn't let just anyone down here, would they? I wish Nimbulan were here. He knows more about Rovers than I do." Lyman continued his trance as he lifted the latch on the cell door and pushed it open. The empty room showed no signs that anyone had been there in many years.

"Whoever helped Piedro had to have Rover blood in him," Quinnault mused. "Nimbulan told me that much. That's the only way their magic works is in combination with other Rovers. Someone close to me, someone trusted, with Rover blood. Who could that be?" He stopped pacing as stared at the empty cell.

"Nimbulan is the only person I know with Rover blood. Some distant ancestor. That's how he learned about Rover magic," Lyman whispered.

"Nimbulan?" Quinnault didn't dare breathe. "I refuse to believe that Nimbulan was part of this conspiracy." But the evidence suggested the possibility.

Powwell's ears roared with the strain of pushing the wall to intercept the rapidly flying magic darts. The roar grew louder. He needed to cover his ears. He wanted to throw up.

The roar increased, ululating up into a screech so high-pitched he barely heard it.

A wall of flame split the ground between himself and Moncriith. Instinctively Powwell pulled himself into a fetal ball, protecting his face and neck from attack.

Moncriith screamed in frustrated rage. His magical darts dropped to the ground, repelled by Powwell's wall of flame.

Something heavy shook the ground beneath Powwell. He risked peeking in the direction of the vibrations.

Another body joined Moncriith's sacrificial victim. This one still breathed, though its eyes stared sightlessly upward and the mouth hung slack. Gender and personality were lost in hideous burns across half the face and burned clothing hanging on the frame in tatters. All trace of hair had been burned away, leaving a naked skull. The straight nose, high cheekbones and thin mouth were marred by the oozing raw meat of massive burns. The person curled and shrank against the cold air of the mountain pass.

"Kaalipha?" Yaala gasped.

Powwell raised his head a fraction higher. "Where did she come from? Where's Kalen? If Yaassima survived the pit, then Kalen might have, too. Where were you?"

Hope blossomed inside his chest. Kalen might still live.

"She was in the void," Myri whispered. "Tssonin brought her out."

Powwell looked further. A young dragon—red-tipped but still silvery along his wing veins and horns—perched on an outcropping halfway up the canyon walls. He breathed steam. Outrage swirled in his multicolored eyes.

"What does Tssonin say?" Nimbulan asked Myri.

"He says he found Yaassima in the void alive and still anchored to this existence. She is not welcome there. The secrets of past, present, and future lives do not belong to such as she. She hasn't the magic or the wisdom to use the information. She must die in this existence before entering the void again." Myri's words took on confidence as she spoke. She cocked her head slightly, listening to the telepathic commands of the dragon that only she could hear.

"Impossible!" Moncriith spluttered. He poked a finger toward the still flaming line that encircled Nimbulan and Myri and the others. "I threw her and the witchchild into the boiling lava before the gate fully formed with the landscape of hills just above the main camp of my army."

"We know," Nimbulan replied. "We watched through the partially open gate. Where is Televarn?"

"I killed the traitor," Yaassima croaked. "I killed him with the knife he poisoned for me."

"He can't be dead!" Maia screamed clutching her head between her fists. "He's still whispering in my mind how he'll punish me if I don't tell him everything that's happening."

"Another mystery we cannot solve," Nimbulan said.

Powwell crept a little closer to Yaassima. He needed to talk to her, find out what happened to Kalen. The wall he had erected blocked him. He dismantled the spell. The wall of dragon fire remained, a clear line separating Moncriith's people from Nimbulan's.

"See her burns?" Moncriith continued to rant. "They are her just punishment from the pit. No one could live through that inferno. I watched her hair and clothing ignite. I drew power from her pain."

The thought of Kalen suffering the agony of that fire hot enough to melt rock, while still alive, nearly made Powwell ill.

"If Yaassima survived, where is Kalen? Tssonin, where is Kalen?" Desperate hope propelled him upward to face the dragon. "You've got to tell me what happened to her."

"Tssonin says that he only found Yaassima because she doesn't belong in the void. If your sister remains there, then she is fated to learn something important from the life forces that shroud her from dragon senses."

"What does that mean? Tell me what that means." Powwell turned on Myri. All his frustration and anger and fear pulsed in his throat. He needed to lash out at something. The dragon was an easy target. Suicide to try.

Tssonin opened his mouth and breathed fire, renewing the wall between Moncriith and the refugees. Powwell shrank away from the evidence of the dragon's power.

"We don't know what Tssonin means, Powwell. Dragon communication is usually cryptic." Nimbulan placed a gentle hand on his shoulder.

Powwell shrugged it off. "I have to go find her."

(That route is dangerous. You have much to learn before you can enter the void and learn with safety.) A young blue-tipped dragon joined Tssonin on the ledge above the canyon. *(Seannin,)* the dragon announced his name.

The dragon's words rocked within Powwell's mind. A headache pounded behind his eyes. "Then teach me what I need to know," he demanded. "I have to find Kalen."

Moncriith raised a mundane bow and shot an arrow through the dragon flames that separated him from his quarry. Wood, metal, and feathers penetrated where magic couldn't.

Seannin breathed a new stream of green fire. The spinning shaft exploded and dropped to the Kardia in a flutter of ash.

"We seem to be at an impasse, Moncriith," Nimbulan said. "The dragons protect us from you. But they do not protect Yaassima. We will depart."

"Seannin and Tssonin, will you fly us to the capital?" Myri asked politely.

"We may still be in time to stop the wedding," Nimbulan said, heading toward Seannin, dragging Myri and Yaala with him.

"It's already too late," Moncriith called. "King Lorriin will invade anyway. We want more from Coronnan than just a marriage treaty. He needs your arable land and farmers. SeLenicca can never be nurtured by any but the Stargods. I intend to give him what he needs—for a price—once I rule Coronnan as the Stargods dictate I must."

Tssonin breathed a new ring of flames around Moncriith and his men, preventing them from menacing the refugees as they clambered aboard the dragons.

"Do you suppose we really conceived a child this night?" Katie asked, pressing her hands against her flat belly.

Quinnault looked at the pale skin beneath her hands. An occasional freckle enticed his eye, beckoning him to search her entire body for more. He'd found most of them in the hours since midnight, after the wedding banquet.

"If we haven't made a child tonight, we'll have to keep trying until we get it right." He couldn't stop smiling. He felt like an idiot, grinning until his face hurt. Loving Katie was the most natural, satisfying thing he'd ever done. The casual liaisons he'd indulged in paled in comparison to the joy he knew with Katie.

Questions and problems of kingship faded whenever he thought of Katie. Her father had arrived for the wedding, suitably clothed as befitted the Crown Prince of Terrania. He hadn't renewed his argument with Katie. When asked about progress on the new port he had nodded curtly and replied, "Before dawn." He hadn't said much else the entire evening.

"I never thought I'd be lucky enough to have a child," Katie said wistfully.

"Why not?"

"Pregnant women and small children are particularly vulnerable to the plague that attacks my people. It comes in waves every few generations. Usually it goes away, naturally, after three or four years and tens of thousands of deaths. This time it has lasted ten years and doesn't look as if it's waning. Any woman healthy enough to have children is afraid to have them. That is why we need so much of the Tambootie. We have to get the plague under control before our population dwindles to nothing."

Quinnault kissed the smooth skin just above where Katie's hands still pressed against her stomach. "Your people will have as much of the tree of magic as the dragons can spare. The plague will be stopped," he promised. A delicate quiver across her skin followed his trail of caresses upward. She reached to bring him higher, matching his passion in yet another long kiss.

Her response to him delighted and awed him.

His Katie.

He released a satisfied sigh. "Wherever you come from Maarie Kaathliin, you belong here now, in Coronnan. With me."

"I never thought I'd be happy calling any port home except where I was born. But this certainly feels like home now." She rested her head against his shoulder.

For a moment they lay silent, enjoying the contented closeness. Her mind brushed his in a momentary deepening of their mutual joy. Then she withdrew, slowly, as if drifting into sleep, not the quick closing of a barrier.

"I feel as if I've known you all my life," Quinnault murmured sleepily. It had been a long day.

"One day can be a lifetime," she replied softly.

He drifted on the edge of sleep, reluctant to give in to the clouds that pressed against his brain, lest he awaken and find Katie a mere dream.

"I'm cold, Scarecrow. I'd like to get my shift." She squirmed away from him.

Reluctantly he let her go. The room seemed no cooler than usual for this time of year. "There's an extra quilt in the wardrobe cupboard." He rolled to his side, one arm draped across the empty space where Katie had been a few moments ago. Her scent lingered on the sheets. He inhaled deeply, anxious for her to return, too sleepy to follow her movements about the dim room.

"Mind if I blow out the candle?" she asked from behind the privacy screen that led to the water closet.

"Mmmmm . . ."

The soft rumble of voices hovered just below his hearing. He shut out the brief annoyance. The palace never slept. Servants found chores and duties at all hours of the day and night.

The rumble came closer, louder. A touch of anger colored the tones. He should get up and see what the fuss was about. No one was supposed to disturb him tonight, except for the most dire emergency. He'd had enough of those yesterday to last a lifetime.

He half-opened one eye, willing the disturbance to go away and Katie to come back again. The tiny night lamp didn't cast enough light to see her moving about. He hadn't heard the wardrobe door open or close, nor the curtain to the water closet swish on its sliding rings, only the distant but angry voices. Kinnsell again? Where was Katie?

He sat up, suddenly alert and alarmed.

The voices grew louder, more insistent.

"You can't go in there!" the steward protested.

"I must. The kingdom is in dire danger." A new voice. One he hadn't heard in several days. Hoped not to hear again until he had some answers. Nimbulan.

"Open the door, Your Grace!" Fierce pounding followed the magician's words.

"Gently, Lan. We need calm and wisdom now," a feminine voice soothed. A voice he barely recognized. But only one person alive used Nimbulan's childhood nickname. A woman who had no business being in Coronnan at all.

His exiled sister, Myrilandel.

Nimbulan had broken the law by bring the witchwoman back to the capital. He'd been implicated in attempted murder and conspiracy. He'd deserted Quinnault when the king needed his advice.

The door nearly buckled under fierce pounding.

"Wait a minute, Nimbulan," Quinnault yelled back angrily. He reached for his robe. "Katie?"

She didn't answer.

"Katie?" he asked a little louder.

"Just a minute, Scarecrow. I'm . . . um . . . busy." Her voice came from his dressing room. Not hers. Not the water closet.

"*S'murghit*, Katie what are you doing?" He swung his legs over the edge of the bed.

"This won't wait!" Nimbulan replied as the cross bar on the door flew across the room, toward the shuttered window. The door crashed to the floor. Light spilled into the room from the corridor revealing Katie leaning over a strange black box no bigger than her tiny palm, tapping a code into the bizarre apparatus.

Chapter 37

The door to Quinnault's private chambers, in the center of the old keep, had landed on the stone floor with a resounding *thunk*. Nimbulan stared at the offending barrier with a glimmer of satisfaction. Some of his frustration echoed down the spiral staircase with the collapsing door.

Some. Not all.

The entire day had been one thwarted plan after another, followed by a series of long delays. Seannin and Tssonin had been the engineers of many stops along the journey to the capital. Granted, they were young dragons, unused to carrying the heavy load of six adults. Granted, they had all needed a bath and meal while the dragons rested. Granted, Nimbulan had benefited from an aerial view of King Lorriin's troops hidden in the mountain pass near the border city of Sambol.

But each stop and detour had pushed them past the time when Quinnault would wed the false princess from a nonexistent country. Now he had arrived too late to prevent the marriage, or the consummation of that marriage.

He needed to smash something. The door hadn't been enough.

"What is the meaning of this?" Quinnault asked in outraged tones. His gaze flicked back and forth between Nimbulan and the princess—queen now—crouched over a strange black box.

"That looks like one of my 'motes." Yaala pushed past Nimbulan and crossed the room to the other woman in six long strides.

"'Motes?" Quinnault and his bride asked in unison.

"Yeah, they turn 'tricity on and off. The Kaalipha uses—

used—them all of the time," Yaala said with unusual enthusiasm. She hadn't shown so much animation since Powwell had sabotaged the monstrous machines that powered Hanassa.

" 'Motes and 'tricity . . ." Queen Maarie Kaathliin murmured. "Remotes and electricity!" Her eyes brightened. "You have generators and remote controls? That's impossible. The family covenant forbids technology on Kardia Hodos."

"If that was indeed what the Kaalipha of Hanassa possessed, they work no longer," Nimbulan reminded them. He didn't understand what the queen talked about. Maybe he could use her arcane knowledge to discredit her and end this marriage. "What were you doing, Your Grace?" He pointed at the black box.

"This is none of your concern, Nimbulan," Quinnault said sternly. His kingly dignity was severely impaired as he flipped the sheets back across his lap. "But there are several questionable matters that you need to answer for." He stretched for a dressing gown, just beyond his reach on a nearby chair, while trying to keep himself covered.

Beside Nimbulan, just inside the doorway, Myri sucked in her cheeks to keep from giggling.

"The security of this kingdom is my concern, Your Grace," Nimbulan said, trying very hard not to yell at his king. "I have reason to believe that your bride is a spy planted here by your enemies."

"This breech of . . . um . . . protocol is almost enough for me to label treason, Magician Nimbulan. On top of the charges of willfully bringing an exiled criminal within the borders of Coronnan. And suspicion of several charges of conspiracy and attempted murder." The king glared at his sister, Myrilandel. The harshness of his gaze softened as his eyes lingered on her face, so similar to his own and yet different, changed by the dragon spirit that inhabited the body. Then he caught sight of the bundle she carried.

His mouth opened slightly, and he almost reached to see the child.

"My only crime, brother, is that I was born female and unable to gather dragon magic," Myri said softly.

"The presence within my borders of magicians who cannot or will not gather dragon magic is a danger to my government and the peace we are trying to build. And so all solitary magicians had to be exiled or executed. I cannot make exceptions for you, sister. I fear you must leave Coronnan."

"I know that. And I will, as soon as you are safe from the invasion that threatens you." Myri bowed her head in acceptance of her fate.

"An invasion prompted by your marriage to this woman, Quinnault," Nimbulan said. He looked again at the woman in the corner. He didn't know what conspiracies Quinnault was talking about, so he chose to ignore them in favor of threats he could unravel. "Terrania is a desert wasteland that hasn't been fit for human habitation in thousands of years. Even the lizards and flies have abandoned it. She cannot be the Princess of Terrania."

"You may leave, Steward. This discussion must remain private." Quinnault nodded to the servant who still stood in the doorway. He had followed Nimbulan and the others, wringing his hands and protesting disturbing the king on his wedding night.

The steward sidled past Scarface and Powwell, eyes wide, feet reluctant to move him out of earshot. He stopped in front of Maia and pointed to the mole on her cheek just to the right of mouth.

The woman in the vision spell questing the source of poison had a mole in the same place. So much had happened in the last few days, Nimbulan had difficulty remembering how short a time ago that was.

Quinnault nodded acknowledgment gestured the man out of the room. "These other people are not necessary to this discussion either, Nimbulan." Quinnault nodded toward Yaala who still peered over the bride's shoulder, trying to examine the black device, and Scarface and Powwell who stood by the door in a guarding stance. "The Rover woman will have to be questioned regarding her relative who tried to murder my queen last night with the tie from my dressing gown."

A sly smile that Nimbulan didn't like at all stole across Maia's face.

"Maia's clan is all in Hanassa, Your Grace. I don't see how any of them could be involved," Nimbulan said.

"Unless . . . Maia, were any of your people sent to the pit?" He whirled to face the woman.

"Piedro?" Powwell interrupted. "A Rover-dark man was sent to the pit right after I was. He never did much, just wandered around like he was lost in a dream."

"That was the man's name!" Quinnault said. He almost jumped up, then remembered why the sheet was tangled around his hips and sat back on the mattress again.

"When was the last time you saw him, Powwell? Did he know about the dragongate?" Nimbulan asked.

"Maybe. I think he was part of Televarn's gang when they kidnapped us and took us from the village into Hanassa. He looked like the man who had Amaranth in a sack over his shoulder," Powwell replied. He stroked something just inside his tunic pocket as he spoke.

"Televarn again. He must have followed Piedro and helped him escape my dungeons. Lyman said that Rover magic opened the magic seal from the outside." Quinnault eyed the dressing gown, just out of reach.

"Televarn couldn't have done it," Myri said, dropping her head to stare at the floor.

"Don't defend the man, sister, just because you lived with him for a while," Quinnault said harshly.

"I am not defending the man who betrayed me twice." Myri raised her head to glare at her brother. Her eyes lost most of their color as her emotions tumbled across her face.

Nimbulan touched her arm before she broadcast all of her fears and anger into their daughter. She relaxed a little at his touch.

"Televarn did not leave Hanassa," Nimbulan informed his king. "We saw him last with a poisoned knife sticking out of his throat. If he survived, he was in no condition to follow us. Moncriith was in charge of Hanassa by then. He is dead, isn't he, Maia?" He whirled to face the Rover woman who cowered near the door.

She nodded mutely, too frightened to do more.

"Who is in your mind now, Maia? Which Rover has picked up Televarn's reins of manipulation?" Nimbulan pressed her for an answer.

"I don't know," Maia wailed. "A voice, a control. The same as always. It could be Televarn. It might not be. We are all so closely related, many times over-related, its hard to tell one slave master from another."

"If not Televarn, then who? Lyman insisted the magician who opened the cell door and resealed it had to have Rover blood. You are the only magician I know who has a trace of Rover blood in his heritage," Quinnault accused.

Nimbulan's face went hot, then cold. His frustrations returned and he wanted to plant his fist into someone's face. Right now, his king looked to be a fine target.

He took a very deep breath in an effort to control himself. "Your Grace, every one of my relatives carries the same remote trace of Rover blood. That makes them vulnerable to mind manipulation by a Rover mage. I think I know this Piedro from my days in the Rover camp. He had the makings of a powerful mage if he ever broke free of Televarn's control. He could easily have used the dragongate a number of times to subvert my cousins or brothers, or a number of others with a tiny trace of Rover heritage. He could have been working in Coronnan for moons, or years."

"The same way Televarn subverted Kalen," Powwell whispered.

Myri shifted her attention from her brother to Powwell, taking the boy into her arms and his grief into her heart. They would both heal in time.

Time they might not have.

"You have not explained this 'dragongate,' Nimbulan," Quinnault reminded him.

Nimbulan briefly explained the strange vortex created by the combination of heat and pressure within the volcano. Their escape from Hanassa, the vision through the partially open dragongate, and their encounter with Moncriith took only a few more sentences. He didn't consult his journal. The events were embedded deeply in his memory now.

"All these refugees risked much to help me rescue Myrilandel. I only wish I had had time to fetch Rollett, too. I'll have to go back for him. Soon."

"We have nothing to fear from them, Scarecrow," the queen said proudly. She continued to tap the device with her right index finger.

"Scarecrow?" Nimbulan lifted one eyebrow.

Quinnault met him stare for stare with no further explanation. But his gaze kept flicking to the black box held by the queen.

"For the Stargods' sake, allow the man some dignity." Myri rolled her eyes and finally tossed the king a silken robe from the chair near the bed. Her cheeks worked in and out, but she couldn't suppress the grin on her face.

Nimbulan was glad to see her sense of humor returning after the dramatic events of the past few weeks.

"It's nice to see that your legs are nearly as long and shapely as mine, brother," she said around her smile.

Quinnault gave her a brief smile of thanks and returned his attention to the false princess from Terrania. His mouth clamped shut on a question. He was probably waiting for privacy before questioning her. Nimbulan had to shatter the man's illusions now, in front of witnesses, before the royal bride subverted the king's mind further.

"Your wife is probably a foreign agent planted here in order to precipitate an invasion," Nimbulan reminded Quinnault. "I have learned that King Lorriin leads an invasion of Sambol as we speak. He's been poised for weeks, waiting for an excuse to seize valuable farm land to feed his people."

"I know about Lorriin. The marriage treaty with his sister would not have kept the peace between us beyond spring planting." Quinnault shrugged into the robe. He turned his back briefly as he stood and belted the garment. "I knew it when I agreed to marry Maarie Kaathliin and give her people half a ton of new Tambootie leaves in exchange for a port city and jetties built on the Bay islands."

"A half ton of Tambootie? What strange magic requires that much of the weed?" Nimbulan's mind spun with the possibilities. His entire Commune wouldn't use that much of the fresh leaves bursting with essential oils—if they used Tambootie any more, which they didn't. The trees were reserved for the dragons. "A half ton will strip many trees to the danger point. They may never recover enough to feed the dragons. Dragons are more necessary to your peace than a precipitous marriage just to get an heir."

"My wife's father assured me they will spread their harvest across all of Coronnan and take the leaves in two batches so they don't endanger any of the trees. Besides, Shayla personally approved of our marriage."

"Shayla?" Myri asked. "She left us in a hurry before she could carry us to safety. Did she come here? She wouldn't respond to my call afterward."

"I faced your dragon at dawn." Maarie Kaathliin shuddered and finally ceased her tapping. "Then she flew off. We haven't seen her since."

"I had a message from your dragon, sister. You are not to worry, she will be with you after she rests from her . . . er .. exertions." Quinnault flicked a shy glance to the bed.

"Oh!" Myri clasped a hand over her mouth. Then she cocked her head as if listening, a sure sign that the dragons spoke to her and her alone. "No wonder Shayla ignored me. Only two of my brothers, barely half-grown dragons, could be spared to fly us home. All of the adults were—engaged. Congratulations, brother. You'll be a father by the Autumnal Equinox."

"Really?" the queen stepped closer to Myri, hands pressed against her belly as if seeking confirmation.

"You still haven't told me what kind of illegal magic your wife's people intend to work with the Tambootie. I can't believe the dragons would willingly give up so much of their necessary food supply.'"

"Not magic," the queen said, clutching her husband's arm. Her voice carried a note of desperation that made Nimbulan want to believe her. "My people need the Tambootie for medicine. A plague threatens our very existence and the leaves of the Tambootie provide the only cure."

"Why should we give this valuable drug to your people? We might need it later ourselves. Plagues travel wide and unpredictably. Your very presence could infect us all," Nimbulan said.

"This plague will not attack you. I guarantee that." Maarie Kaathliin stood straight and defiant. Her small face suddenly looked much older and jaded than Nimbulan first thought. "As long as we keep the machines out of Kardia Hodos, the plague has nothing to feed on."

Quinnault draped an arm about her shoulders and pulled her close. His gesture clearly signified that they belonged together. The top of her head barely reached his armpit. Granted the king was tall compared to the majority of his people. But a woman's average height was closer to that of the average male. Maarie Kaathliin's head should reach the king's chin, at least.

"How can you guarantee that a plague will not come to us in a trade ship, or on the back of a steed wandering in from SeLenicca, or on the khamsin wind from Rossemeyer? How can we trust you when you say you come from a land that no longer exists?"

"She didn't say she came from Terrania. I did," Quinnault said. Then he turned to face his wife, hands on her shoulders "Why did you confirm the idea I pulled out of the air?"

"There has been a misunderstanding of my origins. I hail from Terra, not Terrania."

"Terra is not a land I have heard of. Why would you claim she hailed from a barren land that has not been inhabited for many hundreds of years?" Nimbulan searched Quinnault's face for signs of the lie he knew must come.

"Because she is a Varn. Her father is a Varn. Her grandfather is emperor of the Varns. Try telling my Council that and make them believe it."

"No one living has ever seen a Varn. Legends. They always appear a hundred years ago. Never now. And they never reveal their true form."

"Because we cannot allow you to learn our secrets. You would destroy yourselves and create the same environment that breeds our plague before you realized the dangers of our technologies," the queen insisted.

"Machines? You do everything with machines?" Yaala tugged at the queen's sleeve. Her passion for her machines was written all over her face. "Can you help me repair my machines? Can you make Old Bertha live again?"

"Old Bertha?" Both Quinnault and his bride stared at Yaala.

"The largest of my machines, the key to a network of littler generators and transformers that powered the lights and gadgets that imitate magic."

"Bertha was the name of one of my ancestors. A strong-willed woman who never married, took numerous inappropriate lovers—they got younger as she aged—and voiced her volatile opinions quite loudly," the queen chuckled.

"That sounds like our Old Bertha," Powwell said from

the doorway. "A cranky and willful old lady who worked at her own convenience and no one else's." For the first time since leaving Kalen behind, he showed some levity.

"How old are your machines?" Maarie Kaathliin turned to Yaala with a new animation.

"Very old. Older than any records. Legends claim the machines go back to the time of the Stargods," Yaala replied.

"Impossible. The three O'Hara brothers established the covenant that protected Kardia Hodos from intrusion by any but a few carefully selected representatives of the family. They forbade technology powered by anything but water, air, or fire. They didn't let you have the wheel and isolated reading skills to a very few."

"But that doesn't answer our questions, Your Grace," Nimbulan tried to bring the subject back to his present concerns. "We have to stop this invasion and the conspiracies you have uncovered in my absence."

"You must destroy the machines!" Maarie Kaathliin urged Yaala. "They contain the seeds of the plague. I pray that no other machines powered by fossil fuels exist. The tainted air that comes from them will lie dormant for centuries waiting for the right mix of pollution and sunlight variance to grow and breed."

"The machines are already dead," Powwell volunteered. "I killed them to give us time to escape." He turned away and muttered under his breath, "Unless the wraith fixes them."

The queen breathed easier. Obviously she hadn't heard the last comment. "Then the generators must stay dead, and isolated. We can never allow technology to taint your air as it has my home's."

"That still doesn't tell me what we can do about the invasion. We haven't time to gather an army and march it to meet King Lorriin." Nimbulan clenched his hand, longing for his staff to help him think. But Powwell had used it to kill the machine. He needed another.

"We need a wall to keep them out. Just like the Kaalipha used the walls of the crater to keep out strangers," Scarface said, his face brightened with ideas. "Powwell had the right idea when he blocked Moncriith's attack with a wall. We need a wall. A magic wall."

Chapter 38

"**D**o you know how much magic would be needed for such a feat?" Nimbulan stared at Scarface, gapemouthed. It could work. They'd need a very large focus to concentrate the minds and talents of every member of the Commune—masters, journeymen, and apprentices combined. Something like a magician's staff.

His old staff had been shaped by his magic, finely tuned over many years to work with him. A staff was too individual. For the combined might of the Commune they needed something else, something common to them all.

"A temporary wall at the passes . . ." Scarface shrugged.

"That will only work at the passes we know Lorriin's using *this time,*" Quinnault said. He didn't pace as he usually did when he thought. The new queen seemed to quiet his restless energy. "King Lorriin will just find different entries and port cities. He's desperate for arable farm land and men to work it. A lot of Kardia Hodos is. A drought rages into its third year across the northern continents. Lorriin can't buy food there, and he has some strange belief that SeLenicca can't be worked."

"You're saying we need a magical wall all around Coronnan?" Scarface whistled his amazement at the audacity of the proposal.

"Except for the Bay," Nimbulan corrected. "The mudflats and your new port city will give us protection there. A massive chain across the port of Baria and towers with armaments on either side of the entrance will protect that harbor by mundane means. Most of the north coast is crumbling clay cliffs, impossible for heavily armed men to climb. So that will reduce the size of the spell by one coastline."

He began to pace, his mind working furiously—as Quinnault used to do. He needed a focus. A big focus.

(A focus made of glass.)

Yes! He paused, looking up at the ceiling as if the idea had come from there. *Why glass?* What properties did glass have that existed in no other compound?

Clarity. Glass magnified and enhanced the vision. Made from all four elements, glass gave the magician access to the power of any one or all of Kardia, Air, Fire, and Water to wrap around his spell without being warped or changed by the spell. Wooden staffs shaped themselves to an individual magician. Glass would remain impervious and accessible to many not just the one.

Yes. The focus must be made of glass. The most precious and rarest substance in all of Kardia Hodos.

"Droughts follow nine-year cycles on this planet," Maarie Kaathliin offered. She moved forward, too, back under Quinnault's arm, as if she needed contact with him to maintain life itself. "The wall must last at least another six or seven years to prevent war until the climate shifts again."

"Could your father build us a physical wall to block the passes?" Quinnault asked Maarie Kaathliin.

"Not in time. The jetties, bridges, and docks at the islands will use up most of our resources. I've just signaled him that he may depart as soon as he is finished. Your part of the bargain is complete, love." She held up the little black box.

Yaala tried to grab it from her for examination. The queen pointedly tossed the box into the hearth fire. Flames engulfed it, glowing hot red and yellow around the black. A strange smell permeated the smoke.

Nimbulan wrinkled his nose. No one else seemed to notice the smell. But Yaala stared at the hearth as if she could will the device back into her own hands, intact and working.

"The islands?" Nimbulan returned to the subject at hand. "You've made all four of the islands into a port? Already?" Nimbulan's heart sank. Now he couldn't appropriate one of the islands as a home for himself and Myri. "Do you really need all four islands?"

"Yes," Maarie Kaathliin said. She continued speaking, dismissing the question. "Kinnsell needs to get back home with the Tambootie as soon as possible. He can't spare any more time than it takes to complete the port. Besides, a physical wall would hamper peaceful trade. I presume you plan on establishing this 'wall' or force field or whatever to have gates and such?"

"We'll have to post magicians at each known road and trade route to do that." Nimbulan forced his disappointment to the back of his mind. He had to tackle one problem at a time. "We don't have enough magicians at the moment to cover every known road into Coronnan, even if you count all the apprentices and journeymen. Presuming we can get the wall up." Nimbulan held his hands up, palm outward, fingers slightly curled. The habitual gesture for weaving magic wasn't enough anymore. As he paced, he looped one arm through Myri's and drew her to his side. Together, they paced. Together, they discussed and defined the necessary elements of the massive spell. Together, their minds worked and built upon each new idea.

He couldn't exile her again. He needed her close by. All of the time.

"We have to use the years of the drought cycle to grow as much surplus as we can to help feed Kardia Hodos," Quinnault mused as he joined them in their pacing, bringing his bride with him.

"Don't forget a way to store reserves for our own drought which will probably follow," the queen added.

"We should sell food at minimum tariff and profit to keep our neighbors from becoming desperate," Nimbulan said.

"Hopefully when they recover from drought and we fall prey to the weather, they will be willing to help us in turn," Quinnault finished the thought. "I'll need strong trade treaties. We'll all meet with the ambassadors first thing in the morning."

"Overseeing the production of all those extra acres will also give your lords an occupation so they don't have time or inclination to plot another civil war, or assassination." Scarface chuckled.

"Aaddler," Nimbulan addressed his new friend. "This is a matter for the Commune, using communal magic. Solitary magicians must be excluded. It is more than the law. It is the only way we can enforce the peaceful use of magic for the benefit of all. You have proved yourself a valuable ally.

But I must have your oath to the Commune, Coronnan, and King Quinnault before you involve yourself any further." He couldn't look at Myri. His statement effectively sent her in exile once more. She dropped his arm as if his touch burned her.

Slowly he turned to face her, one hand resting on her shoulder, the other caressing the baby in her arms. "And when the spell is complete, I will resign my place in the Commune and join you in your clearing. We won't be separated again, Myri. Ever."

"Not even in death, beloved," she vowed, kissing him softly.

"What if I can't spare you, Nimbulan?" Quinnault asked under his breath. "Will you break your oath of loyalty to me?"

Powwell watched Scarface solemnly approach King Quinnault in the little reception room. Soon it would be Powwell's turn to face his king and the Commune. Quick tests, moments before, had proven Scarface's ability to gather dragon magic.

"I, Aadler, do solemnly swear to abide by the laws of the Commune, and to defend the Commune against solitary magicians. I promise to use my magic, gathered only from dragons, for the benefit of all Coronnan as directed by the lawful king, anointed by the people and blessed by the dragons. And if I should stray from this oath, may my staff break, and the dragons desert me," Scarface recited the oath of the Commune, holding his new staff horizontally in front of him with both hands. Beneath the staff rested the softly glowing Coraurlia, the dragon crown. It sat upon its velvet pillow at the king's feet on the dais of the throne room. Its soothing all color/no color light engulfed the staff and the magician in an aura of truth that could not be broken.

As the last words fell from Scarface's lips, the new staff began to twist a little, three strands beginning to braid.

Powwell gulped back his fears and tried to fade into the walls.

"Now it is your turn, Powwell. You left Coronnan before we could determine the necessity of this oath for all those who gather dragon magic," Nimbulan said. He placed a hand on his shoulder, urging him toward the dais.

"I'm only an apprentice, and poorly trained at that. Shouldn't I wait to see if I have the ability to become a full magician?" Powwell protested.

"No, Powwell, we can't wait. We need every magician available for this spell. They must all be confirmed members of the Commune," King Quinnault said from the throne. He and the queen had taken a few moments to dress before presiding over this brief ceremony.

None of the refugees had had a chance to rest or eat since arriving in the capital. Now they would plunge headlong into the defense of Coronnan. Powwell needed time to think.

He looked at the assembly of sleepy-eyed master magicians crowding near the throne. They all stared at him, needing the oath-taking complete so they could get on with the business of creating a massive defense spell. No help there. He had to take the oath.

Once taken, never broken.

Taking a deep breath he stepped forward to face the king and the glass dragon crown. The queen sat beside Quinnault, avidly curious, not missing a single detail that might slip past the weary magicians.

Someone handed him a staff, as newly cut as Nimbulan's and Scarface's. He opened his mouth to recite the words. Nothing came out but a cough, dry as the dust of Hanassa.

He swallowed deeply, thinking hard, and finally croaked out the words.

"I, Powwell, do solemnly swear to abide by the laws of the Commune, and to defend the Commune against solitary magicians. I promise to use my magic gathered only from dragons, *while in Coronnan,* for the benefit of all Coronnan . . ." He continued with the oath as prescribed. Only the queen, with her avid curiosity and attention to detail raised an eyebrow at his insertion. Once he left the borders of Coronnan, he would be free to follow Kalen with whatever magic tools presented themselves.

"Good. Now we must get to work. Is the map table ready?" Nimbulan asked, easily assuming authority over the Commune and Powwell.

* * *

"I don't think we will have enough power," Nimbulan said, resigned to the fact that the border of Coronnan was just too long.

"Can we leave gaps over the impassable parts of the mountains?" Quinnault paced around and around the three-dimensional map built into a sand table. The map of Coronnan measured as long on each side as two tall men—large enough for details of rivers and hills, towns and forests.

Nimbulan rubbed his eyes wearily. The women had gone to bed. Most of the magicians as well. Once the strategy and details of the spell were worked out by Nimbulan the Battlemage, and his king, the others would rise to support them.

He wished Myri could be a part of the spell. Her subtle healing touch just might finish off the rough edges, make it a wall to preserve peace rather than a mere deterrent to war. Life versus death. Love of Coronnan rather than hatred of their enemies.

"Without a focus, we can't do more than push back the enemy for a day, maybe two. *With* a focus we could barricade the border with SeLenicca but not the northern coast or the southern border with Rossemeyer." *And the pass that leads to Hanassa where Moncriith claimed the title of Kaaliph.*

"What if we randomly rotated the wall so that invaders never knew where it would or would not be?" Quinnault offered.

"Too time and energy consuming. All my magicians would be engaged in doing nothing but maintaining the wall. We wouldn't be available for healing, communication, soil fertility—nothing but border patrol. That would defeat the whole purpose of the Commune, to make magic available to all of Coronnan for the benefit of all of Coronnan."

"The dragons are waking. Maybe they have a solution." Quinnault cocked his head, like Myri did, listening.

"I need them to fly over the border and tell us precisely where each of the armies is at the moment we set the spell. Presuming we can."

"Shayla is landing in the courtyard of the school." Myri

wandered in, rubbing sleep from her eyes and yawning. She hadn't slept much either.

Nimbulan welcomed her into his arms. He rested her head against his shoulders as she fought sleep.

"Why is Shayla coming here?" he asked as he kissed her forehead.

"She has a gift," Lyman said as he bounced into the room with a disgusting amount of energy. "She says she found your focus."

"Glass. The dragons have made something of glass." He remembered the whisper across his mind last night as he pondered the problem.

"That would be my guess,' Lyman smiled. Age lines dissolved from his face.

"Are you getting younger, old man?" Nimbulan peered at his friend.

"I wish," he replied and winked at Myri. "I have too many lifetimes to complete for that to happen. Come, come, we mustn't keep Shayla waiting. She's anxious to get on with this business, so she can get to the work of building a nest for her next litter. A new litter of dragons. I remember the last one, over twenty years ago. . . ." He looked sharply around at the others to see if they had noticed his reverie.

"You were there at the birthing," Myri said, eyes alight. She didn't show any surprise that a human had been allowed to view Shayla's babies when man-made magic had injured her and caused her premature labor and subsequent stillbirth of fourteen of the young. Myri and her familiar Amaranth had been two of the six survivors—asexual purple-tipped dragons with a distinct destiny separate from the dragon nimbus.

"Of course, my dear. I gave you and Amaranth your names."

"What is he talking about?" Nimbulan whispered to Myri. "Why was he there?"

Myri smiled obliquely. "Dragons have to have some secrets, Lan."

"Enough reminiscence." Lyman clapped his hands with enthusiasm. "Shayla commands our presence." He ushered them out of the palace and across the bridge to School Isle amid a growing throng of citizens. Wide-eyed and gape-jawed people stumbled over each other as they watched the sky rather than their feet.

Nimbulan realized that dawn had come around again and he hadn't slept more than a few hours in the last four days. Why did dragons always insist on presenting their surprises at this awful hour?

"Because the light makes them appear more spectacular," Myri answered his unvoiced question.

"I must be tired to lose control of my thoughts." Grimly he scrubbed his face with his palm, hiding a yawn behind it. At least he'd eaten his fill every few hours, restoring some of his energy.

"Your thoughts are always close to mine, Lan. You can't hide anything from me." She squeezed his arm affectionately.

"Apparently, your anger toward me for leaving you alone so long has evaporated. I wish my guilt would fade as quickly. I have a lot to make up for." He held her tight against his side, glad to have one complication removed from his life. "As soon as this is over, I will send journeymen on quest to rescue Rollett and Kalen. This time I will stay by your side."

"A good plan, Nimbulan. Keeping my family together is more important than venting my anger."

"I'll remember that you are listening if I should ever be stupid enough to look at another woman."

"You'd better not even think about it." She punched his arm affectionately.

He winced. His nerves were worn thin and everything hurt—her reminder of their problems, her punch on his arm, and the glare of a dozen rainbows streaming from the sky into the courtyard of the school. The courtyard that at one time had contained the well of ley lines.

"What ails you, Lan?" Myri caressed his arm with healing touches.

"I'll be all right when I have eaten again and slept a bit," he said, distracted by the sight of six adult dragons cavorting through the air like dandelion fluff. They soared high, dove with incredible swiftness, turned in a tail length and flew loops around each other. Their play contained an element of deep satisfaction and joy that he'd never seen in them. The males seemed to glow brighter along their colored wing veins and horns, the primary colors pulsed deeper and truer, not fading into obscurity with the rest of their crystal fur.

Shayla was easiest to pick out in the happy antics. Every color in the spectrum rippled along her fur in constantly shifting prisms. Waves of deep satisfaction washed over the dragons, spilling into the crowd of human onlookers.

Nimbulan remembered a day when he, too, had felt like that. The day he first made love to Myri.

His need for sleep vanished, replaced with a deeper need. He wrapped his arm around Myri's shoulders, pulling her closer, tucking her warmth against his side, inhaling her sweet fragrance.

"No time for sleep." Lyman handed him half a round loaf of bread and a hunk of cheese. "We've a spell to work and an invasion to repulse."

"I don't know how we're going to do it," Nimbulan mumbled around a huge bite of bread. Soft and warm from the oven, it nearly melted as he chewed. Energy began to creep back into his veins. "Did the dragons find us a focus?"

"I believe so." Lyman pointed to the center of the courtyard, nearly bouncing in his enthusiasm.

There, atop the mortar that obscured from all senses the ley line well, rested a huge black table. Round, sitting on a single pedestal. Gleaming black, the rising sun glinted off the seamless surface.

"It's made of glass! *Black* glass," Nimbulan shouted, running to examine the treasure more closely. "Black glass forged by dragon fire! We can work the spell."

Chapter 39

"**I** am frightened of this spell, Shayla," Myri confided.

(You have done this before, daughter,) Shayla replied as she rose on a thermal above the courtyard

Myri looked at the large glass table, a wondrous treasure, rather than at the dragon who had given birth to her spirit but not her body. Only one or two sources of sand clean enough to produce usable glass existed in Kardia Hodos. Man-made fires didn't burn hot enough to use the other sands. But dragon breath did.

(You must be the eyes of the magicians. They cannot view the placement of their wall otherwise. You must let your mind fly with us.)

"When I flew before, it was always with Amaranth, my twin, my otherself. I knew his mind better than I knew my own. We blended easily and he always returned me to my own body afterward." She knew this task was essential to the success of Nimulan's spell and the safety of the kingdom. She knew it. And yet she feared the outcome would change everything she held dear.

The outcome or the process? Dread hung around her like an unwelcome ghost.

(Now you are alone in your fragile human body. Blend with me, and we will soar through the clouds. Trust me to know when the time is right to end the joining.)

"How will I feed the images we see to Nimbulan?" She looked to where the Commune placed chairs around the table, crowding them together to accommodate all of the masters, journeymen, and apprentices. An aura of power began to pulse stronger and stronger as the chain of magicians grew. Like heat waves on the desert sands, the power spread. It pushed outsiders away from the table, the joined magicians, and the spell.

Nimbulan sat in the place closest to the center of the school buildings. Lyman sat on his right, Scarface to his left, and a timid Powwell sat close by. Yaala, bathed and clothed in a fine gown of pale green, stood with Quinnault and his foreign queen. She looked like Yaassima's daughter now, a princess in exile rather than the scruffy desert rat who haunted the chambers of the pit. Maarie Kaathliin held Amaranth so that Myri would be free to link communication between the dragons and the magicians. The new queen cooed at the baby and played with her lovingly, absolutely enchanted with the child.

Maia remained inside the school where she couldn't spy on the proceedings. Mundane guards made sure she didn't contact Piedro or any of her clan.

Myri need not concern herself with her companions and family if something should go wrong with the spell. She knew in her heart and her head that something would go wrong that would change the life path of all those involved in the spell.

(The silver cord that connects you to Nimbulan will channel your visions to him. Do not fear, daughter. We will guard you well on this spirit journey.)

Myri knew that. She recognized her questions as a stall. If she released herself to the dragons, she might never come back to her own body.

Yes. She finally recognized the human frame as *her* body. She was Myrilandel, a unique blending of the dragon Amethyst and the human girl. She wanted to remain human, to live with and love Nimbulan, to raise her daughter and bear more children.

Flying with the dragons would jeopardize her anchors to this life.

(There is no other way, Myrilandel. Nimbulan needs you to be his eyes.)

"I know." Myri placed her hand on Nimbulan's shoulder to physically link herself to him. The power building around the table parted slightly, as if a living being with a consciousness, allowed her hand to penetrate only as far as her husband. No magic or love in all of Kardia Hodos could link her to the swelling communal magic.

Unconsciously she shifted her feet until she found a comfortable stance. Awareness of the ley lines beneath the paving tingled through her feet. Nimbulan said he couldn't sense the power within the Kardia any more. She enjoyed the contact with the ground—a solid and firm anchor to the land and her life. He relied on the ephemeral power drifting in the air that she couldn't sense at all.

Their magic centers had shifted. A year ago, she sought flight with the dragons, and he found his magic rooted in the Kardia.

(Now.)

Myri closed her eyes and concentrated on the thoughts of the dragon mother of the nimbus. A continuous patter of gossipy comments about the weather, the taste of last night's meal, and the beauty of the clouds dribbled into her mind. With the words, came pictures, wonderfully vivid pictures. Gradually the words faded, and the pictures came to the front of her vision.

Her focus tilted and spun as her mind gazed down upon the wide stretch of bay glittering in the morning sunshine. Her perspective shifted to an aerial view, and she realized that she looked down upon the string of islands that made up the capital city.

Shayla flew lower. In their shared eyesight, they saw individuals with recognizable features and auras. A circle of lives around the wonderful glass table. Magic inhabited the men and spilled into the table, growing by leaps and bounds like a living thing.

One life stood out, separate from the others and the magic and yet . . . connected.

Suddenly, Myri realized she looked down upon herself, standing beside Nimbulan and the Commune. Beside, not amid.

Acknowledgment of her separation from the men severed her last mental contact with her human body. She and Shayla flew west, upriver, toward the trading city and the mountain pass where an invasion had already begun.

Nimbulan settled into his trance as he focused on the pattern of sunlight on glass. Waves of different colors and textures of black evolved before his eyes. His magic-heightened senses became aware of all the different minerals that made up the glass. He felt the fire that melted them together into a new, cohesive substance. The dragon flames transformed them into something new, bigger and more interesting without damaging his unique individuality.

He recognized that communal magic was like dragon fire on sand. Each magician remained an individual, yet bonded and changed into something more powerful and cohesive than a single man. The dragons had given humans a wonderful gift with this new power.

The first blending of magic always impressed him with this tremendous sense of belonging. All his years as a solitary Battlemage hadn't prepared him for the sensation. Almost better than sex.

At that moment he sensed Myri's hand on his physical shoulder. A different kind of touch than Lyman's, or his own connection to Aadler. His longing to draw her into the wonderful circle of communal magic almost broke his trance and connection to the other magicians.

The safety of Coronnan depended upon completion of this spell. He needed all his concentration, all his experience, all of his power and more to complete the barricade.

He breathed deeply. The essence of Tambootie in the air invaded his nostrils, changed, mutated into power. The energy of dragon magic filled every crevice inside his body and his soul.

(Now.) Now he was ready to create a wall that would protect Coronnan and give the war-ravaged land and people a chance to build a peaceful, cohesive government—as cohesive as the magic that sang through his blood, picking up harmonies from the other men in the circle until they grew into the most beautiful music ever experienced.

"Where?" He heard and felt his question through every sense—born and acquired—within him.

(Here.) Myri's voice whispered across his mind. Myri's voice and yet different. Multiple Myris. As he was a multiple within the circle of magic.

His mind opened to a distant vista. He saw the rolling hills that grew ever taller until they became the old mountains that separated Coronnan from SeLenicca. Streams cut ravines through the hills. The ravines became wide passages through the physical barrier. He imagined a wall, twenty feet tall, immeasurably thick and powerful, yet invisible to the casual eye, along the highest ridges.

(No. Closer. See the armies.)

Hundreds of men crawled along fifteen of those passages, almost to the end. Almost into Coronnan. If he set the wall along the ridge, the armies would be trapped inside Coronnan, free to raid and pillage at will.

He shifted his imagery lower, at the eastern end of the mountains, deep into the foothills.

The men marched closer. Half a mile away.

(Now. You must drop the wall now.)

He dropped the wall across the center passage, where the men were closest to their target. A satisfying *thunk* reverberated through the Kardia, sensed through his whole body. The vibration must have traveled along a ley line to the well beneath his feet.

From Myri's aerial view he surveyed the wall. It looked solid and complete. A deep breath restored his perspective. He began stretching the wall north and south. The magic thinned. The power glowing within the black glass focus dimmed.

His connection with the Kardia, through Myri, told him the wall shrank to knee-height. The first wave of attackers stumbled, then stepped over the invisible barrier.

Myri watched the magnificent wall expand lengthwise, pulling substance from itself to follow the full length of the border. In horror, she watched as it shrank in height with every stretch outward. Nimbulan pushed more and more power into the wall. It continued to shrink. He didn't have enough power at his command to build the new barrier as high and as strong as needed.

Coronnan would fall to invasion and renewed war. Memories of her brief time in the healer's tent after a battle churned inside her physical stomach as well as her soaring mind.

Wounded men had screamed in agony. Their pain became her pain as she tried to heal a few. For every one she helped, three more appeared. There was never an end to the terrible wounds inflicted by other men. The numbers of the dead mounted with each breath.

So many men cut down in their prime that the villages had no more men to plow and hunt and sire new babies.

Nimbulan had helped bring peace to Coronnan. The people had not had enough time to recover from three generations of civil war and consider peace a way of life. A few new lives had been conceived to replace the dead. Not enough. Never enough.

She grieved for the bleak future that stretched thinner than the wall. Tears tracked her physical face as well as her dragon mind. The Kardia trembled beneath her, sobbing for the new assaults on it, rich farmland turned into battlefields, orchards reduced to firewood for massive armies, widows and orphans left to starve. . . .

The Kardia trembled again and the human Myrilandel felt the quake through her feet. Ley lines filled with power trembled beneath her. She knew how to tap the web of lines that crisscrossed Kardia Hodos like the mesh of fine lace and turn them into magic. She could channel the power of the Beginning Place into Nimbulan's spell.

Whatever fate awaited Myri lay in this well of power.

She relaxed her physical body while viewing it from afar, above, and beyond reality. The energy flowed upward, through her receptive muscles and bones. Fire heated the Water in her blood. Air expelled from her lungs. The Kardia in her bones and muscles joined with the other three elements.

The heat of her power continued to build within her body, beyond her ability to contain it. She breathed flame and still the fire grew. So did the magical wall.

Her hand clutched at Nimbulan's shoulder, needing to feel his skin one more time before she gave herself up to the elements. She moved her hand to his, where it rested on the table that organized and focused the spell.

The power burned through her, burned up her fragile humanity. Only a dragon body could withstand the enormous heat she pulled out of the living Kardia.

She couldn't remain human and survive to finish the spell. Coronnan and her family needed the new barrier at the border, desperately.

With love and regret she looked at her husband, felt his love being returned to her through the magical cord that would always connect them, no matter which body she

used. Then she looked toward her baby. Queen Maarie
Kaathliin cuddled her close, protecting her as well as
Myri could.

(*Amaranth!*) she called her love and farewell to her baby.
The only baby she would ever bear.

Then she gave herself up to the tremendous heat and
friction that channeled through her.

Better to live as a dragon and be able to watch and
protect her loved ones than to die and break the chain of
power that built an impenetrable border between Coronnan
and her enemies.

Part of Powwell watched Thorny hunch and relax in
rhythm with the breathing of every magician in the circle
of power. He had one hand on the shoulder of the magician
to his left. His right hand—where Thorny perched—rested
flat against the black glass so he couldn't stroke his familiar's spines. Thorny wiggled and rubbed his nose against
Powwell in mute understanding of the problem.

Only a small piece of Powwell's awareness remained in
the spell. The magicians of Coronnan didn't need his mind,
only his talent. If he could separate his thoughts enough to
touch Thorny, then he could focus on Kalen.

The communal vision of the growing wall between
Coronnan and SeLenicca stood back, looking at the entire
problem. Nimbulan's genius as a Battlemage centered
around his ability to view the entire field, thousands of men
and multitudes of small skirmishes. Powwell needed a
closer look at one particular section.

The magic of the spell offered him the thoughts of every
man sitting at the glass table. These men didn't interest
him. He needed to hone in on the thoughts of Moncriith
and Yaassima. Only they could tell him what happened
to Kalen.

Thorny slid off Powwell's hand onto the table. Only the
tips of the hedgehog's spines brushed his thumb. Was it
enough of a separation? Powwell tapped Thorny's sense of
smell. *Find the Bloodmage,* he ordered himself and the
hedgehog.

Suddenly his awareness jerked away from the courtyard,
beyond Coronnan City. He skimmed along the communal
vision of the border. At a narrow pass far south of the

primary action, Powwell's augmented senses skidded to a halt, backed up and flew into the canyon.

The smell of old blood, of hot rocks, and desert dryness lingered there.

Powwell added sight to smell. Moncriith came into view, his red robe standing out among the dark uniforms of his troops.

"Run forward. Everyone run forward!" Moncriith screamed as the magic barricade threatened to blockade the narrow pass. His men scrambled in all directions to avoid the pulsating energy most of them couldn't see. Discipline dissolved, and the soldiers ignored their leaders. Sergeants and lieutenants abandoned their posts as well as their men.

Steeds screamed and reared. They fought the traces that bound them to sledges and prevented flight.

Yaassima slowed her steps in deliberate defiance of her captor's orders. Strong rope, fortified with magic, encircled her neck in a tight noose and bound her hands before her body. If she moved so that her hands were low enough to secure her balance, she choked. If she raised her hands to ease the pressure on her throat, she stumbled with every step.

The soldier assigned to her tugged sharply on the extension of rope, pulling her forward. She had to take several rapid, short steps to remain upright.

Then she gave in to the Kardia and plunged forward, sideways across the path, careful to land on the unmarred side of her ruined face. The soldier had to stop or choke her to death. Moncriith had ordered her alive until he needed a sacrifice for a battle spell.

Men tripped over her and sprawled across the path beneath the descending wall of magic.

Powwell felt the Kardia tremble, both in the protected courtyard in the city and through the pass where Yaassima and Moncriith kept their thoughts shielded from him. He tried harder to penetrate Yaassima's mind. She had no magic and shouldn't be able to block him.

Suddenly his vision split again. He watched a small shower of rock and dirt slide down the hillside into the pass through eyes that could only be Yaassima's. But her thoughts and memories remained cloudy and indistinct. A blast of heat nearly shattered his partial rapport with her.

The morning air of deep winter heated to the noon temperatures of high summer.

Powwell thought she was remembering her fall into the pit, and he nearly shouted in triumph. At last, he'd see precisely what happened to Kalen.

Then he realized the heat came from the Kardia itself. Heat akin to the molten lava in the pit. Yaassima was lying across a thin ley line that suddenly reversed its flow of energy and with great speed returned . . . returned where? Where did ley lines begin?

No matter. The channel of the retreating magic scorched and collapsed, taking the crust of the Kardia with it. All around them, a spiderweb of cracks opened and spread. The slow spread of the ruptures in the land contrasted sharply with the frantic movements of the men. Movements that accomplished little in getting them out of the path of chaos and death.

Powwell heard a few of their shouts and screams over the crashing of the Kardia.

The soldiers jumped and scrambled away from the fissures that followed them in all directions. Some jumped forward, over the rising magic wall, many backward and up the sides of the hills. The hillsides crumbled beneath the trampling feet, showering more debris down into the pass. If they weren't careful, they'd bury the pass and Moncriith with it.

Yaassima laughed. Her burned and shattered body trembled with pain. Still she laughed. "You're dead, Moncriith. You are dead already and don't realize it!"

"Come!" Moncriith hauled her up, none too gently, by the armpits. "Follow me, all of you." The Bloodmage made a panicky dash for Coronnan, dragging Yaassima with him.

A few soldiers followed them. Most opted for retreat into SeLenicca.

Yaassima continued to laugh at the crumbling of Moncriith's grand invasion.

Powwell tried to retreat. Yaassima wasn't thinking of her fall into the pit. She thought only of watching Moncriith die.

"Stop laughing," Moncriith ordered as he paused for breath and looked back at the wall that separated him from the majority of his troops. He grasped Yaassima's shoulders with clammy hands and shook her. Back and forth. Back and forth until her neck ceased to support her head. Back and forth until her senses whirled and the constant pain of her burns and aching joints intensified beyond endurance.

And still Yaassima laughed. That evil laugh that took delight in watching others in pain. She raised her hands and encircled Moncriith's neck with her preternaturally long fingers. She laughed as she pressed her thumbs into the Bloodmage's vulnerable windpipe.

Her laughter choked and gurgled when Moncriith moved his scarred and sweaty palms to capture her own throat.

The magic wall spurted upward, engulfing Yaassima and Moncriith. They froze, trapped with the magic.

Powwell yanked his mind out of Yaassima's failing body.

Then the wall collapsed again with uneven energy, crushing the Bloodmage and the Kaalipha into a bloody heap.

The wall suddenly grew higher, threatening to capture Powwell's mind. He willed himself back into his own body, back in the safety of Coronnan City.

I failed, Thorny, he moaned. *I didn't learn anything about Kalen. I've failed her again.*

Chapter 40

Myri's vision returned to the body anchored to the Kardia. She didn't need to see the magic, only fuel it. Wings broke free of the tight human skin on her back. Her neck elongated. The vestigial spinal bumps sharpened and shot outward as full horns. Purple-tipped crystal fur erupted from her too smooth skin. Fire rose. Fire glowed. Fire streamed forth as she absorbed more heat, and yet more heat from the Kardia.

Shayla showed her a swelling in the wall at the border. Up and up it rose, separating the army. The power fueling the spell fluctuated up and down. The wall grew and collapsed. She channeled more power into the spell. The wall grew again, up and out. It flowed in a continuous line of energy.

Only a few troops remained east of the wall inside Coronnan. Other men moved to go around the wall and found their passage blocked.

Panicked by the separation, the soldiers in front turned and beat on the barrier, screaming for an opening to return them to the safety of their comrades.

Up and out the barrier grew. It linked and looped across the tops of hills, blocking other passages.

Myri drew more power from the draining well. The boiling lava of Hanassa's living volcano fed the ley lines, draining out of the mountain, collapsing the caves of the pit and the dragonate. The ley lines that snaked across the land ceased flowing outward, reversed and drained back into the well. Scorched channels became burned-out husks in the wake of the reversed flow. And still she pulled power into the spell.

At the border, soldiers hopped and danced to avoid the scorching Kardia beneath their feet.

And still the wall grew.

Myri grew with it.

The wall was nearly complete.

She was nearly transformed into her true dragon-self.

A moment more and she would fly free of the bounds of gravity. Free and empty of love.

Nimbulan watched with horror as his beautiful Myri stretched and expanded, draconic features becoming more and more pronounced. He had to stop her.

How?

This was the person she was born to be.

He loved the woman she had chosen to be.

They couldn't separate now.

The spell demanded his attention. He had to break away from the magic long enough to force Myrilandel back into her own form. The wall was nearly complete. They didn't need so much power now. She could let go. If she would.

"You can't leave the circle," Scarface hissed in his ear. "If any one of us breaks contact, the entire thing will collapse. We'll be right back where we started from and too exhausted to start again."

"I know." His talent was necessary to the completion of the defense of Coronnan.

His talent.

Once before, he had separated from his talent, left it in an inanimate object. He wasn't sure if the glass table was totally inanimate, not the way the magic swirled through the eddies and waves of minerals.

The hand upon his own clutched him with talons that grew by the minute. Myri's bulk increased, threatening to crush his hand.

If you break contact with the table, you'll lose your talent forever.

"I have to take that chance." Quickly, he located the burning blue beacon behind his heart and pushed it into the table. Blue light joined the glittering black and gray. It melded with the combined talents of all the men sitting in the circle.

Nimbulan slid his chair back a little, allowing Scarface to

slide his hand from his shoulder onto Lyman's. The circle remained complete, his talent remained in the combined mass of magic. Scarface's mind took over the completion of the wall.

Keeping his right hand on the table, Nimbulan grasped Myri's still human face with his left. "Beloved. I need you. Our daughter needs you. Return to us, please.

She wrenched herself away from him, tears flowing freely. "I must be a dragon to survive the power I give to this spell and Coronnan."

"The spell is nearly complete. Give back the power you drain from the Kardia."

She shook her head and stepped away from him. Only her talons remained in contact with the table and his talent embedded in it. The power continued to flow through her into the spell.

Then she looked up to the skies where Shayla and the other dragons flew. A heavy film dropped over her eyes, protecting her from the brightness of the sun in the upper atmosphere.

"You forsook dragonkind twenty years ago. Come back to the body and the life you chose. Please. I love you, Myrilandel. My life is incomplete without you." Moisture gathered at the corners of his eyes. His heart threatened to wrench out of his body as she took another step backward.

"I can never give you the sense of completeness and belonging you find in this Commune of magic. You belong here. I belong to the skies."

"No." The words wrenched out of him. His throat nearly closed with unshed tears. "Myrilandel, I love you more than I love my magic." Deliberately he lifted his hand from the table, leaving his talent forever embedded in the rare and perfect black glass.

Myri's concentration shattered with the touch of Nimbulan's hand. Kardia, Air, Fire, and Water fractured and separated within her body and her mind. She shrank in size and awareness. Heat drained out of her, back into the ley lines. Dimly she knew the web of magical power stopped abruptly at the new border wall, unable to restore the empty channels to the west.

The spell, the dragons, her own safety ceased to have importance as Nimbulan collapsed in her arms.

The very touch of the air against her skin sent waves of burning pain throughout her body. She was back in her own body with only vestigial traces of her dragon heritage. Nimbulan's clothing seemed to rub her raw. His weight on her aching muscles and stressed bones sent her to her knees. She couldn't let go. She had to hold him, keep him close. The silver cord connecting them faded to invisibility.

His aura looked different, dimmer, smaller, less dominated by the blue of his magical signature. The blue pulsed within the glass table, adding a different luster to the black minerals and the combined magic of the Commune.

She didn't know how his magic had detached from him and merged with the table, accessible to all in the Commune except him. Desperately she grabbed for the blue. But the glass was impervious to even dragon talons. Her now human fingernails couldn't scratch the glass.

"Nimbulan, beloved, what have you done to yourself?" She held him under the arms, sobbing her fears into him. "Don't you dare die on me. I've just found you again. I can't let you leave me again!"

She fought to keep him from sliding to the ground. If she could hold him long enough, the silver cord would come to life again. It had to. Neither one of them was fully alive without that bond.

Other hands reached out to relieve her of the burden. Familiar hands. Powwell, Scarface, and her brother Quinnault. She stared at the table, blinking away tears as the men settled her husband on the ground. The spell must be complete, for the magicians stood and stretched, talking quietly. They rapidly shifted their gaze from Nimbulan to the table and back again. Amazement touched their expressions.

"How did he separate himself from his talent?" one man asked.

"I've never heard of such a thing," replied another. He shuddered at the concept of life without his magic.

How would Nimbulan survive without the talent that had defined his life for so long?

"Such a waste." Lyman shook his head sadly. "He didn't

have to sacrifice everything. You would have returned to your human body once the spell was complete."

"Are you sure, old man?" Myri knelt at Nimbulan's side, checking his pulse and breathing, loosening his tunic and shirt around his throat and chest.

"Shayla has mated again. The chances are good that she carries purple-tipped twins again. You could not have stayed a dragon once they are born, for there can only be one purple-tipped dragon at a time."

"How do we know that I would be able to come back? You had to find a new body when you left the nimbus. My human body would have been destroyed by the power I channeled and the transformation."

Nimbulan's chest shuddered, and his breath came in ragged gasps.

"You tried to leave me," he whispered through cracked and weary lips. "You tried to join the dragons. I feared you might ever since I learned of your heritage. I dreaded the day you would leave me." He turned his eyes up to hers briefly, before they sagged wearily shut again. The fire had gone out of the green orbs.

"But you never came for me in the clearing. You didn't communicate by magic or by message," she sobbed.

"I can never make up for that lapse. The bad habits of a bachelor interfered with my judgment. I need you, Myrilandel. I need you more than you can ever know." He sagged against her again.

Lacking the silver cord to tell her the state of his heart and pulse, Myri resorted to conventional checks. Nothing blocked his air passages. His heart fluttered and beat irregularly, but not so far off rhythm to endanger him. His skin looked gray but not waxy. Lumbird bumps rose up on his skin and he trembled as if very cold beneath his heavy formal robe and everyday tunic, shirt, and trews.

"I think he needs sleep more than anything," she said, sinking back on her heels. "He'll be in shock for a time."

"As are you, sister." Quinnault rested a heavy hand on her shoulder. She couldn't lean into his warmth, or accept the contact.

"You have called me 'sister?' Are you ready to accept me as family, or must I be exiled again for being a female with magic? Exiled and denied the right to nurse my lawful husband through this terrible trauma?"

"No, we will not deny you the right to nurse your husband, Myrilandel," Katie announced. Her little chin came up in a proud gesture her husband was coming to dread.

"She has to be exiled," Konnaught shouted across the courtyard. A guard stood behind him, carrying a small satchel. "If you are throwing me out of Coronnan, then you must do the same to her!"

Quinnault had forgotten that the boy would sail into exile as soon as the tide changed.

A nasty smile split Konnaught's pudgy face. "She's a witch, and we don't allow witches in Coronnan. The Council will depose you and that foreign hussy you married, if you let your sister stay. Then they'll bring me back as their king."

"Be careful how you address your queen, boy. You no longer have a title or lands. Within the hour you will be a penniless peasant on your way to the Monastic School in Sollthrie. I signed the order last night," Quinnault said slowly and evenly so there could be no mistake in his threat.

Konnaught didn't slink off. He stood straight and defiant, Lord Hanic and two other lords directly behind him. Quinnault met their eyes, girding himself to show no emotion.

Quinnault sighed. Too many of the lords preferred Konnaught's philosophy that titles and land granted privileges and the right of exploitation. Responsibility for the land and people who lived upon the land was a sometime thing with them rather than a way of life. If Quinnault was going to hold sway over those lords, he had to obey his own laws. His entire reign, the benign government he'd fought so hard for, all depended upon law.

He turned back to his wife and sister, hoping to find a compromise. "Katie, Myrilandel, the people of Coronnan have made a law against solitary magicians. For the good of all we have to control magic. Only the Commune can do that. Myri can't gather dragon magic and join the Commune."

"What good is a law without compassion!" Katie stamped

her foot and shouted at him. "There is no justice in exiling her after she saved the kingdom from invasion." Her eyes blazed and bright color tinged her cheeks. Her absurdly short curls bounced about her ears. She had never looked more beautiful.

Quinnault was tempted to kiss her. That would solve nothing but his own need to hold her close and ease his instant passion. He still had a Council of Lords who could override any decision he made with a two-thirds majority vote. That was a law he had requested. The kings of Coronnan couldn't be dictators.

"Compassion and justice are concepts that have been missing from Coronnan for three generations. The people will have a hard time understanding why their king breaks the law for such vague ideas," he said, sighing.

"Then isn't it about time they were exposed to such 'vague' ideas?" A smile tugged at the corners of Katie's mouth. The humor that was never very far from the surface threatened to break through. "All of you recognize the 'vague' idea of diplomatic immunity."

The lords and magicians nodded.

"If SeLenicca sent a magician as ambassador, his diplomatic immunity would exempt him from the law. You'd have to let him stay or risk war."

"Granted, Katie. But Myrilandel isn't the ambassador from one of our neighbors," Quinnault replied. He tried to keep his voice firm. He nearly lost that battle facing the humor that glowed from Katie's face.

"She is the ambassador from the dragons! She is the one they selected to develop the Covenant. Without her, you have no Covenant, no dragons, no communal magic. She is the cornerstone of that *treaty*. That makes her an ambassador and exempt from your laws." She smiled triumphantly.

Quinnault nearly danced her around the courtyard in glee. "Ambassador Myrilandel of Shayla's Nimbus, prepare to present your credentials."

"What credentials?" She cocked her head puzzled.

"Oh, we'll think of something later." He bent down and hugged her tight. "Welcome, sister. Welcome home."

"Someone take this poor man to a comfortable bed and get the healers to look at him," Katie ordered, pointing to Nimbulan who shuddered and trembled on the ground.

"And find a good hot meal for both of them. I can't believe no one thought of this before," she finished, shaking her head.

"Thank you, Your Grace." Myri dipped a slight curtsy toward Katie. She reached for her baby. Katie relinquished the precious burden reluctantly, gazing fondly at Amaranth's innocently sleeping face.

"She is beautiful. I wish you joy of her," Katie whispered. She ran a gentle finger along the baby's cheek. "I look forward to watching her grow."

"Messages are coming in from the border, Your Grace," Lyman said, standing at Quinnault's elbow.

"Did we succeed?" he asked the magician. He studied the man closely, looking for signs of the dragon within him.

"We succeeded admirably. Three of King Lorriin's seven generals and their troops are trapped on this side of the border. They have offered their swords in your service rather than return to SeLenicca as failures. King Lorriin isn't known for his forgiveness."

A happy grin burst from Quinnault. The wars were over. He'd made a peace that could last. He and Nimbulan. And Katie and Myri and dozens of others.

"There is more news from the few magicians on the other side of the border," Lyman continued. "Moncriith and Yaassima killed each other."

"You are free of them, sister. They'll not stalk you again." Quinnault touched Myrilandel's arm reassuringly.

"I must go back to Hanassa," Yaala said. "I have to see what damage Moncriith did before he left. He said the dragongate had collapsed."

"There is no word from Hanassa, child. There never is. It is a city state that remains outside the life of the Three Kingdoms," Lyman said kindly.

"Hanassa is a boil on the backside of the Three Kingdoms," Nimbulan said weakly from the ground at their feet. He didn't rouse enough to sit up or even support himself on an elbow. "Hanassa causes trouble and is a constant pain. The Kaalipha wanted us to think they are separate and aloof, but her assassins and raiders dart in and out, striking where they will. Even without the dragongate they will plague the rest of the world. None of us will be safe until that boil is cauterized."

Quinnault didn't like the magician's color as he closed his eyes once more, too exhausted to say more. Myri knelt beside him, quickly checking his pulse. She placed her long-fingered hand on his brow, brushing her husband's graying hair away from his eyes.

"Take him inside, quickly. He needs more healing than I can give him." She beckoned several young men to fetch a litter. Powwell came forward with a wineskin. He moistened his master's lips with a few drops.

A sense of loss washed over Quinnault. Through this whole adventure of establishing the Commune and the School for Magicians, finding a solution to the civil wars and building a permanent government, Nimbulan had been at his side. Nimbulan, adviser, helper, friend. He had no other friends. Kings didn't have friends, they had courtiers.

"I'll go to Hanassa, Master Nimbulan," Powwell whispered. "I'll go back and make sure the dragongate is closed forever. I'll find Rollett and Kalen, too, and bring them back to you safely."

"That will be your quest, boy. But not until you have more training," Scarface said. "Don't you lords and nobles have a government to run or something? Leave the healing to magicians. We'll keep you informed of any new messages." He dismissed the assembly with a stern look. His ugly scar creased more deeply with his scowl. The implied violence of his wounds sent mundanes scampering for other chores in other places.

Then Scarface turned to the magicians, assuming a leadership role naturally. "We have a conspirator with Rover blood to find. We'll start with the woman under guard and then devise a test for the latent potential. There are communications to monitor. Lambing season and spring planting will be upon us very soon, we need to know which fields will produce the most food and which need to go fallow. Come on, we have work to do." The masters gathered in a knot and spoke in arcane phrases with many wild gestures.

Six young men ran up with a hospital litter. With Myri's guidance they rolled Nimbulan onto it and carried him back inside the school. Myri walked beside her husband, keeping one hand on him at all times.

Nimbulan lifted his own hand and placed it atop hers. "I love you," he whispered.

Quinnault's heart wrenched for the couple, and for his own loss of a trusted adviser and friend.

"I hope I can be your friend as well as your wife, Scarecrow," Katie whispered to him.

"You read my mind again."

"I read your grief. Our grief. He is a great man. We will miss him greatly."

"He left a great legacy for us all. Never again will magicians waste their talents as Battlemages. He ended magic as a weapon of death and destruction and made it an instrument of peace and prosperity." Quinnault returned to the business of continuing the legacy of the last Battlemage.

Epilogue

"**C**ome to Papa, Amaranth," Nimbulan coaxed his giggling daughter.

The little girl, barely a year old, stood on unsteady legs, clutching her mother's skirt. She eyed the distance between her parents skeptically. Then, boldly she let go of the cloth that kept her upright. She swayed, lifted one foot off the ground and sat abruptly on her diapered bottom.

Her lower lip stuck out, and a tear threatened to overflow her wide eyes. Hints of fire-green highlighted the iris—closer to the color of her father's eyes than her mother's. But her light blond hair and pale skin came from Myrilandel's heritage.

"Up!" Amaranth demanded, holding her pudgy arms out to her father. She had learned early that Nimbulan was always willing to hold her in his arms. Her mother wasn't as easy to persuade.

"That's all right, Amaranth. You'll walk when you are ready." Nimbulan plucked his daughter off the ground and hoisted her high in the air.

"Maybe if she walked, she'd slow down for a day or two," Myri chuckled. "She's into everything as it is." She bent to stir the stew that simmered over the central hearth of the hut in the clearing.

Nimbulan and his family retreated to the peace and solitude of this little hut often. As often as their duties in the city allowed. One of Myri's dragon brothers could usually be persuaded to fly them here at short notice.

Directing the School for Magicians—University now—no longer dominated Nimbulan's life. Others could do it better, others who still had magic at their fingertips.

He still sat in Council with the king. But Quinnault had his new wife and a myriad of other advisers to guide him and Coronnan into a new era.

Nimbulan enjoyed the slower pace of life in the clearing more every time they retreated here. Myri certainly flourished in the rural setting. The demands of life at court and her duties as ambassador for the dragons stressed her empathic talent to near exhaustion. She needed the sanctuary of the clearing more than Nimbulan did.

"It's starting to snow," Yaala said, entering the hut with a fresh armload of wood. "Something smells good." She bent her head to draw in the aroma before she dropped the bundle of sticks and logs.

"Then you won't be going back to the capital for several weeks yet," Myri said. "Neither will we." She grinned widely.

"Why do you think I stalled so long." Yaala grinned. Her teeth gleamed in the firelight. "I don't like relying on your brother's hospitality, Myri. Having servants wait on me hand and foot gets boring after about ten minutes. This 'Princess in Exile' nonsense has gone on too long. I need to be doing something, even if it's just chopping firewood."

"There's lots of that to do," Myri replied.

Nimbulan shifted Amaranth to the crook of his right arm, giving her a favorite toy to chew on—a wooden rattle he'd carved himself. He had the scars on his fingers from his first attempts to guide the knife without magic.

Joy simmered in Nimbulan, like Myri's stew. It warmed his heart and grew more savory with time. All of his little regrets about unfinished work and lost magic faded. Only the question of Rollett's and Kalen's fate continued to nag him.

Myri cocked her head as if listening. "Someone is climbing the path from the village. Someone with determination."

"What does Shayla say?" Instinctively he looked toward the south-facing doorway. Shayla had retreated to her lair in the mountains, awaiting the birth of her next litter.

Shayla's voice was something else Nimbulan missed. The dragon hadn't talked to him much, but now that he had no magic, he couldn't hear her even when she directed her mental voice to him.

He wrapped his free arm around Myri's shoulder, almost hoping physical contact with her would open his mind to Shayla's words. "Anyone we know?" he asked.

Nimbulan set Amaranth on the floor where she promptly crawled to the pile of firewood and began investigating the new logs with all of her senses.

"Take that out of your mouth, Ammi," Yaala plucked a piece of bark out of the baby's hands.

Nimbulan reached for his winter cloak. No one would be able to enter the clearing without Myri's permission. He shouldn't worry. But he'd spent too many years as a Battlemage not to worry about unannounced visitors.

"It's Powwell!" Myri cried, reaching for her cloak at the same time.

Together they dashed out the door to meet the boy at the boundary of the clearing.

Nimbulan didn't see the magical boundary swirling bright pastel colors as it parted to admit his former apprentice. One second he saw only trees. The next, Powwell stood in the arching shadow made by two leaning trunks of the Tambootie.

"You've grown! You have a beard. You're taller than I." Myri fussed over the young man.

Fifteen now, Powwell stood broader of shoulder and longer of leg than Nimbulan remembered.

"Are you hungry? Of course you are. Supper is nearly ready." Myri hugged her foster son.

"I'm fine, Myrilandel. Just a little weary." Powwell hugged her back.

Nimbulan watched the boy's hands clench. An air of heavy sadness bent his posture.

"What has happened, son?" he asked joining Myri's embrace of him.

"I figured out how to get into Hanassa, but I need help. I can fetch Rollett back for you, Nimbulan. But you'll have to go with me."

Excitement leaped in Nimbulan's heart. A chance to rescue the journeyman he'd had to leave in Hanassa so many moons ago.

Myri stiffened within Powwell's embrace. She said nothing. Nimbulan didn't need magic to know she waited warily for her husband's response.

"I'm sorry. I can't, Powwell. My place is here." He held Myri tighter. "I promised I'd never leave you again, Myri, and I won't." Disappointment threatened to choke him. "I wouldn't be much use to you anyway, Powwell, not without my magic."

"I'll go," Yaala said from the doorway of the hut.

"The trip will be dangerous, Yaala," Powwell warned.

"That doesn't matter. Hanassa should be mine! The time has come to reclaim my throne."

"We have to leave immediately. The gateway at the city will only be open for short periods this winter." Powwell stood straighter, adjusting his pack.

"It will wait until the snow has stopped and you have packed some provisions," Nimbulan said, ushering them all toward the warmth of the hut.

"Have you also thought of a way to find Kalen in the void?" Myri asked so quietly Nimbulan almost didn't hear her.

"Of course." A big grin creased Powwell's tired face. "That's why I waited so long. I had to find a way to free both my—sister and my fellow journeyman. Finding the right opening into the void is going to be chancy. That's the gateway that will only be open twice this winter and for very short times."

"Then you have accepted Kalen is your sister?" Nimbulan had to ask.

"The dragons say she is. I have to believe them."

"Go with our blessing, Powwell. You, too, Yaala." Nimbulan almost choked. His instincts screamed to keep these vulnerable people close. He'd lost so many good friends and students he couldn't take a chance on letting Powwell and Yaala go into danger alone.

(A journeyman must quest to become a master. A quest by nature must be taken without a mentor,) Shayla reminded him.

"Shayla, I can hear you! Has my magic returned?"

"No, love," Myri said quietly. "The dragon spoke through my voice. You are still mundane. Are you terribly disappointed?"

"Not really. Your love and the life of my daughter is magic enough." Together they ducked into the hut.

Amaranth squealed in delight at sight of them. She let

go of the woodpile that supported her and toddled toward him. She giggled as she wavered and nearly sat down again, but she kept walking until she clutched her father's cloak for balance.

"Up," she demanded.

Nimbulan lifted her high over his head, laughing and rejoicing in his life and his loves.